1980 Song writer's Market

where to sell your songs

Edited By
William Brohaugh

Assistant Editor
Barbara Kuroff

Assisted By
Judith Ann Beraha

Writer's Digest Books

Writer's Digest Books
Cincinnati, Ohio

About this Book

This is the first edition of *Songwriter's Market* produced on a computerized word processing system recently installed in the Writer's Digest Books editorial offices. Developed by the Quadex Corporation, Boston, the system is designed to store all the material in the book on a magnetic disk, which allows for easy and immediate access to information. Thus we have a master file of the most current markets information available. The market listings are read—and updated—on a video display terminal—much like a TV screen.

The text of the book was set in Times Roman, a type face designed by Stanley Morrison at the turn of the century for the *London Times*. It is a practical "work-horse" type which, because of its legibility, allows us to pack a generous amount of type onto the page, thus keeping *Songwriter's Market* to a convenient size.

The book is printed on a blue-white shade of Madison Superset, an uncoated groundwood paper, and is adhesive bound and attached to a hard case.

Barron Krody, a Cincinnati freelance artist, created the interior book design using supergraphic letters and numbers to contrast with the text. He chose a two-column layout for the articles in the front of the book and the market section introductions so as to visually separate this material from the market listings.

The book jacket showcases tools of the songwriting trade and an 1890s brass cash register. The jacket was designed and photographed by Lawrence Zink Inc.

Songwriter's Market. Copyright© 1979. Published by Writer's Digest Books, 9933 Alliance Rd., Cincinnati, Ohio 45242. Publisher/Editorial Director: Richard Rosenthal. Managing Editor: Douglas Sandhage. Assistant to the Managing Editor: Connie Achabal. Printed and bound in the United States of America.

International Standard Serial Number 0161-5971
International Standard Book Number 0-89879-003-4

reface

Songwriter's Market works. We've seen it in action.

At a symposium recently conducted by the Nashville Songwriter's Association International (NSAI), we were able to watch a budding songwriter as he managed to get one of his songs played before a panel comprising some of the top music publishers in Nashville. As the writer's song was played, the publishers maintained the noncommittal expression they'd perfected in years of listening to demonstration tapes. When the song was over, the publishers brightened. Though none were interested in the song, two were interested in the *songwriter* and his talent. The man literally shook with excitement. Later, the songwriter set up appointments with several major publishers to discuss other songs. He placed two tunes with a major publisher the next week. He'd gotten his break.

Why? His answer excited and inspired us.

Without knowing who we were,

he told us that a book called *Songwriter's Market* had convinced him to approach songwriting seriously, and that the book taught him the professional tape preparation method that helped him get his break that day.

When the 1979 edition of *Songwriter's* was published, we were confident it would prove to be a valuable tool and sourcebook. Yet, we weren't totally aware of how valuable the book would be until the incident at the NSAI symposium—coupled with general response from readers and industry professionals—drove the point home to us.

We're thrilled that readers have found our work useful. *Songwriter's Market* is based on the belief that the songwriter is an important person. Serving important people is more than pleasurable; it's exciting.

—**William Brohaugh, Barbara Kuroff, Judith Ann Beraha**

Contents

The Profession

Using Your Songwriter's Market

Like any tool, *Songwriter's Market* can be abused as easily as it can be effectively used. Know how to use this book before you pack up your demo tapes and run to the mailbox or to the nearest music city.

    Songwriter's Market has three sections. "The Profession" is an overview of songwriting opportunities and how to deal with them. Here you'll find information on submitting demonstration tapes, handling auditions, negotiating contracts, etc. These articles discuss the basics of professional songwriting. "The Markets" is a detailed listing of firms using songwriters and musicians, or that seek new songs. Listed are hundreds of music publishers, record companies, record producers, audiovisual firms and advertising agencies. Markets are categorized according to their type.

    Before moving on to the market listings, real all material in "The

Profession," as well as the article introducing each category. This material briefly explains how the industry works, and offers practical hints and tips. More reading is required when you move on to the listings themselves: Read the listing for the firm for which you'd like to work *entirely* before sending material, writing a query letter or visiting them. More than a compendium of names and addresses, *Songwriter's Market* chronicles information a songwriter *must* know in order to sell to a particular market. Listings are designed to provide all information necessary to get your material to the right company in the right form. If you don't read the entire listing, you might overlook something essential to your making a sale. Each listing is stuffed with information, and is a how-to manual in itself. Consider this sample:

MORNING MUSIC (USA), INC., Box 120478, Nashville TN 37212. (416)625-2676. Affiliate: Bathurst Music (BMI). President: Jury Krytiuk. General Manager: Mark Altman. Music publisher and record company. Estab. 1971. ASCAP. Published 100 songs in 1978; plans 100 in 1979. Pays standard royalty.
How to Contact: Submit demo tape and lead sheet. Prefers 7½ ips reel-to-reel or cassette with 1-4 songs on demo. SASE. Reports in 1 month.
Music: Bluegrass; blues; children's; choral; church/religious; classical; C&W; disco; easy listening; folk; gospel; jazz; MOR; progressive; rock; soul; and top 40/pop. Recently published "One More Time," recorded by Crystal Gayle (C&W); "Country Hall of Fame," recorded by Hank Locklin (C&W); and "Flying South," recorded by Chet Atkins and Jerry Reed (instrumental).

Once you've read the listing, pay attention to it. All statements in a listing have been provided and verified by the buyer or a member of his staff prior to our going to press, so they are reported precisely as the buyer wanted them stated. Consider each fact before submitting anything, and follow instructions carefully. If the firm wants to be queried by mail first, *don't* show up at their doorstep with guitar in hand. Ignoring the firm's preferences will only give them cause to reject your material. Some listings will instruct you to query, then will outline the type of demo tape the firms prefer to review. This is *not* an invitation to send your demo tape; this information is included so you'll know what to send *if* the company invites you to submit material based on your query.

Information in listings is as current as possible, but buyers come and go, companies move, and needs change between the publication of *Songwriter's Market* and the time you buy it. Drop us a note if you have any new information about a market, because we research, review and update all listings annually. If you know of a market not listed in this book, write us and give the market's name and address; we'll solicit it for the next edition.

When seeking a specific market, check the index. A market might not be listed for one of these reasons: 1) It's not interested in receiving material. 2) It has gone out of business. 3) It charges for its services. 4) It has failed to verify or update its listing annually. 5) It didn't supply us sufficient information. 6) It has requested that it not be listed.

We don't necessarily endorse the markets in this book. If you have a complaint against any of the firms listed here, or if any of them ask that you pay for services such as publishing your song (considered unethical), and you have made serious attempts to settle the matter with the offending party—including reminder letters sent by certified mail—contact us. Send copies of letters you've sent the firm, and a letter detailing your complaint. Enclose SASE so that we can reply (SASE stands for "self-addressed, stamped envelope," and SASE should be included with any correspondence or submission). The inclusion of this acronym in a listing means that the firm will return you material if you accompany it with SASE. Make certain, however, that the return envelope is large enough to accommodate your material.

Finally, don't limit your marketing attempts to one section of this book. Opportunities for songwriters cover many vocations and industries.

The third section of *Songwriter's Market* is "Opportunities & Services," a guide to organizations, awards, music festivals, and other items and events of interest to songwriters. Here you'll find a wide variety of aid, information and inspiration.

Songwriter's Market finishes up with a series of helpful appendices, including a chart indexing music publishers and record companies by the types of music in which they're interested.

The end result is a valuable tool that, when used properly, will help you become a selling songwriter.

State Abbreviations

Each listing in this book uses the US Postal Service's two letter state abbreviations in the address line. They are as follows:

AK	Alaska	LA	Louisiana	OK	Oklahama
AL	Alabama	MA	Massachusetts	OR	Oregon
AR	Arkansas	MD	Maryland	PA	Pennsylvania
AZ	Arizona	ME	Maine	PR	Puerto Rico
CA	California	MI	Michigan	RI	Rhode Island
CO	Colorado	MN	Minnesota	SC	South Carolina
CT	Connecticut	MO	Missouri	SD	South Dakota
DC	District of Columbia	MS	Mississippi	TN	Tennessee
DE	Delaware	MT	Montana	TX	Texas
FL	Florida	NC	North Carolina	UT	Utah
GA	Georgia	ND	North Dakota	VA	Virginia
HI	Hawaii	NE	Nebraska	VI	Virgin Islands
IA	Iowa	NH	New Hampshire	VT	Vermont
ID	Idaho	NJ	New Jersey	WA	Washington
IL	Illinois	NM	New Mexico	WI	Wisconsin
IN	Indiana	NV	Nevada	WV	West Virginia
KS	Kansas	NY	New York	WY	Wyoming
KY	Kentucky	OH	Ohio		

"Doing it for a Song" Doesn't Mean "Doing it for Peanuts" Anymore

By William Brohaugh

"I'll bet even your husband writes better songs than that," the music publisher said when he finished listening to the demonstration tape.

Surprised, the woman who had written the song said, "My husband doesn't write songs."

"We'll see." The publisher asked for the husband's phone number, called him at his office, and said, "Hey, I've heard about all those great songs you've written."

The husband paused. "How did you know about them?"

This true story illustrates the almost universal dream of creating music, of writing a song. The unlikeliest people have songs in their hearts, if not on the record racks. F. Scott Fitzgerald aspired to songwriting—for musical comedies, to be specific. More recently, successful screenwriter/actor/director Buck Henry (*The Graduate* and *Catch-22* are among his writing credits) once commented, "I'd trade it all if I could write terrific songs. What we do out here in Hollywood is a skill, a craft; but the Elton Johns and the David Bowies—they are the natural geniuses of our lifetime."

"We are *the* glamour business," Del Bryant of Broadcast Music, Inc. (BMI) says of the music industry. "The mansions of the stars in Hollywood are now being bought by people like Linda Ronstadt and Rod Stewart. The song is now king."

The song's ascension to the throne involves not only glamour, but also royal wealth. While Americans spent $2.4 billion in 1977 for evenings out at the movies, they spent $3.5 billion to stay home and listen to recorded music. The music industry is healthy, as are opportunities for songwriters.

"You can make a living writing songs," says Patsy Bruce, president of the Nashville Songwriters Association International (NSAI). "It pays money. Good American money."

How good? "Six or seven good songs will make you more money than you can spend," says Don Gant, senior vice president of Tree International, a major music publisher.

If you have those good songs, the music industry wants them. More important, the industry *needs* them. Arthur Braun of New York's Dick James Music calls songwriters "our main bloodline. . . . We can't cut them off."

Lorraine Rebidas of MCA Music in New York agrees that good songwriters and good songs are staples of the music business—she terms them "our bread and butter." Every music publisher, every record producer, every record company is looking for the next hit. Every ad agency wants the jingle that will play forever in people's minds. Every theater group that produces musicals seeks the show that draws rave reviews. They want the best. They *hunger* for the best.

Keep Your Shirts On

While this hunger opens up opportunities for songwriters, it also intensifies competition. Some good songs, overshadowed by the great songs, go unheard. One music publisher estimates that even the established songwriters produce only three usable (by the industry) songs for every ten songs they write. Yet, competition has by no means closed music industry doors to new songwriters. "Your song doesn't compete with other songs when it comes right down to it," says Tree's Don Gant. "Your song is unique. We're not selling cars here, or shirts."

"A good songwriter will always be able to get in," says Del Bryant. "There is always a need for songs. There are more songwriters, but the industry is absorbing them."

In fact, many industry officials are committed to giving new songwriters a proper shot. For example, "I have an open door policy at MCA because I was on the street once, and I know what it's like," says Ted Barton, staff writer and publishing A&R man of MCA's Nashville office. Like Barton, many industry people empathize with "the struggling songwriter" because they themselves started out that way. Those that didn't, realize that every established songwriter was a beginner at one time, and are willing to listen.

Beginning songwriter and *struggling songwriter* are nearly synonomous, because all beginners must struggle a little to be successful. "If it's art," says songwriter Ron Peterson,

Maggie Cavender, executive director of the Nashville Songwriters Association International, points to the heart of the music industry when she repeats NSAI's motto, "It *all* begins with a song."

former president of NSAI, "it's been paid for." . . . "In blood, sweat and tears, to put it musically," adds Maggie Cavender, NSAI's executive director. The maxim that "overnight successes" usually involve nights years long has been repeated so often that it's likely to become a cliche.

The time you spend reaching for success is the period of "paying dues," another operant cliche you'll hear much about. As songwriter Ed Bruce (who co-wrote "Mamas Don't Let Your Babies Grow Up to be Cowboys" with wife Patsy) points out, paying dues *does not* mean deprivation and starvation. It means getting started, getting direction, getting established.

The first step is to decide on a goal. Consider the various outlets for your talents:

● *The musical theater*. Musical plays are "absolutely vital" to modern theater, says one artistic director. "There is *always* an audience for a good story, song and dance," says ElizaBeth King, literary manager of the prestigious Actors Theater of Louisville.

● *Audiovisual firms*. Though competition is very strong in this field, "There's a real need for fresh material because of the over-reliance on mechanical music," says Jack Gauvitte, producer for Direction Films. Writing background music for filmstrips, educational films, feature films and other audiovisual media is exciting and rewarding.

● *Advertising agencies*. "All producers look for talented jinglewriters, and I see a lot of good ideas and concepts coming from independents," says Marc W. Johnson, production director of Vandecar, DePorte & Johnson. Established writers can earn into five figures for a single jingle for a national ad.

● *Specialized audiences*. Classical, gospel and children's music, as examples, provide rewarding and interesting opportunities.

● *The popular music industry*. This is where most songwriters turn first. *The* glamour industry is *the* most popular draw.

Learn So You Can Earn

After determining your goals, the next step in paying your dues is learning about the industry in which you want to work. "Any man who gets a job as a mechanic should be skilled, trained, or at least mechanically inclined," says Jerry Chestnut, author of "Another Place, Another Time." Norwegian songwriter/artist Njaal Helle realized he needed to learn more about the American music business after his first trip to the US taught him his material was too weak. His second and third trips were spent attending symposiums, visiting music publishers, learning about the music business. Talk to people about the business. Study it. Read about it. Leeds Levy of MCA Music in New York recommends that you not only read about the business, but about the people who are successful in the business. Read biographies of the great songwriters (Levy particularly recommends Sammy Cahn's autobiography).

This is the period in which you can afford to make mistakes—which are, after all, tools of learning. "I made them," says Ron Peterson. "You have to make them."

It's the period in which you develop professionalism. Remember that you're dealing with professionals and competing with professionals. You must match their standards of professionalism. Demonstrate pride and self-confidence at every step. Never say, "I want you to listen to some of my stuff and tell me what's wrong with it," says Jerry Chestnut. "Get a song and charge." Yet, don't allow overconfidence make you obnoxious. Presenting a song should be a simple matter of you saying, "I have this; do you like it?" says Mike Kosser, author of *Bringing It to Nashville*.

Always set up appointments in advance, and arrive on time. Don't show up at *any* firm with your songs in your head, and not on tape; see "Proper Submission Methods" for a detailed discussion of demonstration tapes. Exercise patience—"If you have to wait for an hour or two," says one professional manager of ATV Music.

Be neat and businesslike in person, on the phone and through the mail. Brusque inquiries and demanding writers are turned away hastily. When writing, "Send nice letters; follow up with nicer letters," advises Del Bryant. "Put as much time in on the letter as you do on your best song." Misspellings and disorganized letters are *not* peripheral to the song being accepted. Businessmen like to deal with businessmen, after all.

Paying dues is the period in which you make contacts and get exposure, which are the major problems facing the beginning songwriter, says Lewis Bachman, executive director of American Guild of Authors and Composers (AGAC). "People got to know you, and it takes time to get people to know you," says Peterson. Get exposure by visiting music publishers, ad agencies, and other firms involved in your particular field and demonstrating your material. Attend songwriter showcases (many large cities have bars and clubs that sponsor such showcases; organizations such as the Alternative Chorus Songwriters Showcase in Hollywood also sponsor them). If you are a competent artist yourself, grab your guitar and play some of the night spots.

A discussion of contact with the music industry always balloons into an argument of whether a songwriter can be successful without living in Los Angeles, Nashville, New York or any of the other music centers. Paul Richey of Nashville's First Lady

Music says frankly, "It's hard to pick cotton in the corn patch." It's hard to keep up with trends and to make contacts if you don't live in a music center. MCA Music in New York receives many non-New York submissions that miss the mark because the writer isn't up-to-date with MCA's needs, not to mention the needs of the music industry in general, according to Leeds Levy.

Living close to the music industry also gives you access to workshops, seminars, "rap sessions" and other such songwriter aids. You can develop contacts at such sessions. A beginning songwriter met a publisher at Askapro (a New York seminar held weekly by AGAC), and two weeks later signed an exclusive contract with the publisher, according to Sheila Davis, AGAC's national director of special projects. Beginning songwriter Don Bryant managed to get one of his songs played to a publisher panel at a recent NSAI symposium, and eventually placed two songs with a major publisher.

Visiting a music center can do more than allow you to make valuable contacts; it can also give you a "feel" for the city and the people who work in it. For example, the almost neighborly atmosphere of Nashville's Music Row (left) contrasts sharply with the hectic streets of New York City.

Yet, that latter example goes to show that living in a music center is, by no means, essential to success. Bryant is an Atlanta native who traveled to Nashville for the NSAI seminar. In fact, most music industry people recommend you visit the music center a few times before deciding to move there. "Plan to spend a certain amount of time in one of those places, even if it means taking a vacation from your job and going to Nashville for a couple of weeks," says John Braheny, co-director of the Alternative Chorus. Don't, however, make that trip at traditional vacation times. If *you* have a few days off around Memorial Day, chances are that the people you want to see have those same days off. While you're flying to Los Angeles from Dallas, they may be flying to Dallas for their vacation. By the same token, try not to hit the cities during the spring or the summer, when many of your competitors schedule their visits. "Songwriters this summer will get off the buses in lines, in droves," says Doug Thiele, president of Hollywood's Songwriters Resources and Services (SRS).

After a few visits, you can consider moving, but *don't* move until you have a contract waiting for you. Move only "if you have the right courage, and the right people to encourage you," says Norro Wilson, director of A&R at Warner Bros. in Nashville.

The right people are music industry professionals—*not* your friends or your family. Professionals, aware of the chanciness of such a move, won't whimsically encourage you to move to a music center. Besides, if your family is coaxing you to move on to the big time, consider that "maybe they don't like you at home," says Patsy Bruce.

Maggie Cavender's advice is one that echoes throughout the entire industry: "Don't give up your day job,

and don't move to Nashville." Getting a job in the music industry is ideal, because it allows you to view industry workings from the inside. But even that's a chancy affair, so hold on to your present job. Cavender estimates that Nashville currently supports fewer than 50 fulltime writers. Ron Peterson agrees that the city can be hard on songwriters. "This is no warm, artistic colony like Paris in the '20s," he says. In fact, "The only warmth in this business is the feeling between one songwriter and another," according to Maggie Cavender.

Commercial Announcement

In fact, the camaraderie of songwriters is legend in the music industry. Writers often gather at workshops and late-evening hangouts to comment on each other's work and to exchange ideas. This, unfortunately, can be a trap if you write to please only other songwriters, and not the public—the people who will pay to hear the songs. By the same token, "Don't consider yourself a professional if your neighbors like your song," says Ron Peterson. Songs must be commercial, and "If the man at the Gulf Station doesn't understand it, it isn't commercial," he says. "You must touch someone with your music. You can't touch your neighbors, your mama, your sister. You have to touch the world."

Peterson says commercial songs express basic emotions in new ways. "If you say, 'I love you,' it's been said two thousand times this week. . . . But if you say, 'I honestly love you . . . .'" Peterson lists three constants in popular songs throughout the years: love, pain and relationships. Love remains constant, says Maggie Cavender—"It's just the moon and the June that's changed." We'll always have what Mike Kosser calls the PLS—the Positive Love Song.

Write songs that the audience can identify with, says Ray Stevens, songwriter/artist famous for "Everything is Beautiful," as well as a number of novelty songs. The real test of audience identification, says Stevens, is if the song expresses a thought or emotion that the listener wants to voice, but can't.

That's not to say that you must aim all your work at broad audiences. Do the personal work, too—but, as Ed Bruce points out, no one will understand it (or buy it) if it's *too* personal. Go ahead and write your "shelf songs," says Peterson. "You've got to have some 'soul salvation.'" Realize, however, that "Writing songs and writing songs for money are two different things," as Don Gant points out. "Good and commercial have nothing to do with each other," says Doug Thiele, although "sometimes they occur in the same tune."

The successful commercial songwriter has no choice but to cater to the public's tastes. You can set trends, you can create a new popular sound, but you can't convince the public that it should like something it doesn't like. "You can't change the public's mind," says Peterson. "The President can't do that, and he's got a lot better forum than we do."

Jerry Chestnut points out that no one can tell what's commercial until it's given to the public. "If it sells, it's commercial." Yet, this doesn't mean you can second guess industry professionals, who are in the best position to *predict* what will be commercial. Your guess is *not* as good as theirs. That's why listening to constructive criticism from professionals is important. Don't take one person's opinions too seriously, though. A publisher frowns at your tunes, and you panic. Forget about it. Let your self-confidence win out; you're probably write. But if six

Do you show up in person, or mail your tape first? No definite answer exists for that question, because policies differ with individual companies, and with individuals in the same company. Here Lorraine Rebidas, who occasionally meets with songwriters, and Leeds Levy, who never meets with a songwriter without hearing a demonstration tape first, discuss the value of personal appointments in the New York office of MCA Music, where both work.

publishers frown at it, *they're* probably right. After reviewing one songwriter's material, Peterson told the songwriter that the songs weren't strong enough. "You people in Nashville can't recognize a good song," the songwriter fumed. "I've been to 20 publishers and they've all told me the same thing." Peterson replied, "And we're all wrong and you're right?"

A collaborator is often a good source of constructive criticism. Collaboration often leads to stronger songs because one person's strength sometimes fills in the gap left by his partner's weakness. Twelve of fifteen songs recently awarded NSAI song of the year honors were written collaboratively. Studying sales charts in trade magazines will also demonstrate the strength of co-written songs (reading the trades is almost essential to keeping up with the music industry, by the way). See "The Agonies and Ecstasies of Collaboration" for more information on collaboration.

Attending songwriter workshops is another way to have your material evaluated objectively. One workshop director says workshops "make it harder to fool yourself. They make it harder to be egotistical." On the other hand, Arthur Braun of Dick James Music believes that songwriting can't be taught, and says that "a workshop is a very good encounter group" and little else.

The songwriter's eventual goal—whether through workshops or collaborators or anything else—is to develop objectivity. The objective songwriter can look over his past work and decide where it needs improvement: "The hardest thing to do is recognize your own strengths and weaknesses—your abilities and the areas in which they lie," says Ray Stevens. The objective songwriter has self-confidence: "You've got to *know* it's good; you can't *think* it's good," says Ron Peterson. The objective

songwriter can determine if his faith in a song is justified: Norro Wilson recommends that a songwriter ask himself, "If I worked for a record company, would I spend $7,000 of the company's money to record this song?"

Good Morning to Minnesota

Most of all, the objective songwriter can make improvements in a song without hesitation. Songwriter Randy Goodrum was once booked to play for a Knights of Columbus meeting, but showed up at the wrong meeting hall. The mistake inspired a song idea, but he realized that "It's bad to be in the wrong place at the right time" wasn't a strong enough idea for a commercial song. A quick twist, however, turned the idea into "It's sad to belong to someone else when the right one comes along," the basis for the hit song. What's more, how many people would have heard of "Good Morning to You" if the writers' objectivity hadn't persuaded them to change it to "Happy Birthday to You"? Another song, "On Minnesota," lost the University of Minnesota fight song contest for which it was written. The writers changed it to "On Wisconsin," however, and the song has since become an instantly recognizable college fight song.

Objectivity also allows you to see the song's versatility, and that you needn't pigeonhole your material. "A songwriter is a songwriter—not a country songwriter or a pop songwriter or a rock songwriter, but a songwriter," says Maggie Cavender. "Don't say, 'I'm going to write a pop, country or soul song.' If it's good enough and contemporary enough, it can go in any direction. Let the artist 'put it in the bag.' " Cavender cites songs like "Gentle on My Mind" and "Me and Bobby McGee" as unclassifiable songs that have been hits in a variety of markets.

Such broad-based songs are the

songwriter's true money-makers. They're called "catalog songs" because they stay in a music publisher's catalog for years. "They're the ones that will make you money down the road," says Ron Peterson.

In order to market those songs, you must know what's selling and where to take your material. Your primary outlet will be the music publisher, but other places to take songs include record producers and record companies (the relative merits of each are discussed in the introductions to the above-mentioned categories). The publisher has contacts with producers and record companies, but bypassing the publisher sometimes has advantages. If you aspire to becoming a recording artist, you'll probably approach producers and record companies first. But artists are not always the stars. "You can pick up good artists on any corner in this town," says Gene Kennedy, president of Gene Kennedy Enterprises, an independent production firm. "But good songs are hard to find. . . . I turn down an average of five fine artists a week, but I've never turned down a good song."

If you are eyeing a publisher, find out the sort of music that company handles. Don't waste time trying to sell classical compositions to an R&B and disco publisher. To find publishers that deal in the type of music you write, use this book. Monitor the trade magazines as well; their charts explain which firms published each song.

If an advertising agency is your target, find out what clients the agency serves and study the use of music in commercials produced for those clients (the *Standard Directory of Advertising Agencies*, available in most libraries, lists the clients of most agencies).

If you'd like to work with a particular audiovisual firm, write for a copy of its promotional catalog, which will give a brief rundown of the firm's focus and direction. Go to the library to see if any materials produced by that firm can be checked out for viewing.

If writing for a musical theater is your goal, request to be placed on the theater's mailing list. You'll receive announcements of the theater's projects, giving you a clear impression of the tastes of the producer or director.

In other words, *study your market*. Know what's needed, and supply it. One of the easiest ways to study your market is to listen to the radio, a superb showcase of commercial material. "Listen to anything and everything," says Bob McDill, a songwriter with more than 140 recordings. Get "sensory input," he says, and listen to all styles of music.

"Listen to the top 10, then listen to the ones that hit 75 and fall out the next week, and try to fall in the middle, at least," says Jerry Chestnut.

Don't, however, try to duplicate what you hear. "The biggest mistake amateur songwriters make is listening to the radio a lot and writing material for a particular artist," says Don Gant. He notes that the songs on the radio are three months behind what the artist—and the industry—are doing *now*. "When I get ready to produce a record, I don't listen to the radio to see what's happening."

One professional manager says that listening to the radio can prove detrimental. "Some writers can't hear things without copying them," he says. "These writers shouldn't listen to the radio." On the other hand, Bob McDill says you shouldn't worry about unconsciously duplicating what you've heard. Randy Bachman, formerly of the Guess Who and Bachman-Turner Overdrive and currently with Iron Horse, freely admits that some of his guitar riffs have roots in other riffs he's heard. Such duplication is impossible to avoid, he says, especially considering that certain chords, riffs and musical phrases seem to be "common"—that is, more than one songwriter can come up with certain music.

This may sound like a lot of work. It is. "Songwriting is work, just like everything else," says Tom Collins of Pi-Gem and Chess Music, publisher of "It's a Heartache." It's a job, a business—and should be approached as such. What's more, "Most writers think it's easy money," says Meredith Stewart, general manager of Coal Miner's Music. "It's not easy money." Even if you manage to score a hit, you may not see cash for six months to a year after the song is recorded. "The first time I heard a song of mine on the radio," says writer Wayland Holyfield, "I said, 'I must be rich.'" He soon realized, however, that he wasn't.

After your first success, your next problem is coming up with new material. Songwriters must "keep the momentum going," says AGAC's Lewis Bachman.

"One hit won't do," says songwriter/producer Ray Pennington, a former in-house producer at RCA Records. "You've got to write a lot of songs." Writing a lot of good material is another facet of paying dues, because it gives you a backlog of material you can draw on after that first success. Peterson calls these "bank songs"—that is, money-in-the-bank songs. A good song will always be good, no matter when you wrote it in relation to your first successful song.

Yet, simply having these songs isn't enough. Songwriters must "sell their wares; they've got to push

Workshops, seminars and conferences are becoming increasingly popular across the country. In this New York workshop, conducted by *Songwriter's Market* correspondent Ted Lehrman, songwriters analyze each other's work and offer constructive criticism.

harder," says AGAC's Sheila Davis. "Writing the song is just the first stage."

Success comes of talent, professionalism, drive, ambition, and a day-to-day dedication. Don't ever allow yourself to be discouraged if you have these qualities. *Everyone* started out as an unknown. "At one time I was really unknown," says Randy Goodrum. "They didn't even know me at my own house." The Goodrum household, not to mention the whole of the music industry, however, took notice of Randy when Anne Murray took his "You Needed Me" to the top of the charts. "If you're persistent, and you truly try to learn your craft, you won't get discouraged," says Combine's Bob Beckham.

Still, many songwriters need never worry about being discouraged. Their natures won't allow such pessimism. These are the ones who write songs purely for the joy of it. They're like Jerry Chestnut, who says, "We should write songs because we love them; it's creative." They're like Maggie Cavender, who believes that "the songwriter makes the music for the world, but first he must make it for himself."

They're like Patsy Bruce, who communicates the pride and honor of songwriting when she says, "If they blow up all the radio stations tomorrow and they never play another record, we'll still be writing songs."

Proper Submission Methods

By Harvey Rachlin

Marketing your compositions should be approached like marketing any other commodity: professionally.

People in the music industry will listen sooner and more attentively to the writer who presents his work like a pro. The best way to audition your material is to put in on a *demo*—an industry term for a demonstration record or tape. Your demo is the recording you present to music publishers, record companies, producers, agents, artists, ad agencies, audiovisual firms, theatrical directors and people involved with other markets.

Demos vary widely in type and quality of recording. When making your demo, remember that accurate representation—not the arrangement—of your song is most important. Successful demos have been made on home tape recorders, with the writer singing to piano or guitar accompaniment. The person listening to your demo wants to hear your song in its simplest form so he can evaluate the melody and lyrics without being distracted by embellishment.

A demo can take the form of a reel-to-reel tape, a cassette tape or an acetate dub (a thick disc played like a record). Many companies are equipped to accomodate all three, but check each market's preference in the following pages before submitting anything.

Certain standards have been established for preparing demos, and you'll be expected to meet them. Follow these guidelines when preparing your demo:

- The song need not be done by a professional, but the singer must render the melody accurately and tunefully.
- Always submit songs with musical accompaniment; use at least one musical instrument.
- Keep musical introductions short—i.e., no more than four bars.
- Record your best song first, then the next best, etc. Of course, all should be worthy of presentation.
- Don't submit more than four songs per demo unless the company specifies in its listing that it will listen to more.
- Listen and inspect each demo before mailing it. Something might have been distorted in the recording process; an acetate dub might be scratched; or, worst of all, you could be sending out the wrong demo.
- Never send out your last demo. Always keep one in stock—preferably your master (the original). Keep the master in a safe place at room temperature, away from excessive heat. If possible, file a copy with a local recording studio or duplicating firm as insurance against fire or theft.

Present reel-to-reel tapes in standard tape size (quarter-inch), reel size (5 or 7½ inches) and speed (7½ inches per second—ips). Reel-to-reel tapes should be leadered; that is, splice plastic leader tape between songs. This provides easy access to specific selections. Record songs on one side only.

Whether you're mailing reel-to-reel or cassette tapes, affix a label to the tape box with the following information typed in: your name, address and telephone number; and the names of the songs listed in proper sequence. If your demo is a reel-to-reel tape, indicate near the top of the label the speed at which the tape is to be played and how it was recorded: mono or stereo. Finally, attach a small label listing your name, address and telephone number to the reel or the cassette cartridge. This is simply a safety measure to identify the tape should its box get lost or misplaced.

Acetate dubs should be in one of the standard disc sizes—7, 10 or 12 inches—and playable at standard speeds; 33⅓ or 45 rpm. The dub's label—placed in the center, of course—should list the song's title; speed of the record; and your name, address and phone number. Acetates can be single- or double-faced, thereby containing selections on both sides of the record. One caution: acetate dubs wear out more quickly than regular records.

Lead Sheets and Lyric Sheets

Most markets require that your demo be accompanied by a lead sheet, which contains written lyrics, notated melody, chord symbols, writer's name(s), and copyright notice (see "Lay Down the (Copyright) Law" for details of copyright law). Enclose a lead sheet for each submitted song, and include your name, address and phone number on each sheet.

If you can't write your own lead sheet, you may substitute a lyric sheet—a typed copy of the lyrics. In fact, some markets prefer receiving a lyric sheet instead of a lead sheet.

Never send only a lead or lyric sheet. These are intended to aid in reviewing your material, and can never replace actually hearing the song, hence the importance of the demo.

The actual content of the demo depends on the market to which you're submitting it. For example, a demo sent to an advertising agency, a jingle music house or a production firm will consist of about six 30- to 60-second jingles, linked by "cross-fades"—as one tune fades out, a new one fades in. Don't separate jingles with leader tape.

The selections on a jingle tape should be samples of previous jingle work or examples of commercials you've written for a hypothetical product. Remember, you're competing with the lavishly produced work of jingle houses, and ad agency clients are less able to gauge a tune's potential from a piano voice demo. Therefore, a strictly professional musical approach is recommended here.

Jingle demos should always be

The cost of demonstration tapes can vary widely, depending on the tapes' complexity and production. If you record a demo in your basement on a home reel-to-reel, your cost is only that of the tape itself. If you seek a more professional sound, however, the cost hitches up to a skyrocket and takes off.

Recording studios rent their facilities for recording demos. Small studios charge about $25 an hour, and the cost can go to $75 an hour and higher for better-equipped studios.

If you don't have access to musicians and vocalists, the studio can usually supply them. Cost usually falls into the range of $25 to $75 *per person* for use of musicians and vocalists.

The studio usually charges you for the master tape of a recording session (from which you can make copies). Rates here vary, as do costs of making a demonstration disc, if you want one.

For more information on demo costs and what you should consider when preparing demos, see the "Demonstration Records" chapter in *This Business of Music* (Billboard Books). The May 1979 issue of *Songwriter* magazine is a special demo recording issue. In particular, consult Doug Thiele's article, "Demo-Making: Dollars and Sense."

recorded in mono (full-track) and presented on a quarter-inch, 7½ ips reel-to-reel tape. The 5-inch reel is standard. Don't submit cassettes or acetate dubs, because most agencies and jingle houses have only open-reel playback equipment.

Again, both tape and tape box should be labeled as described previously, but you should also type the word "composer" prominently on the labels, since agencies receive tapes from singers and musicians seeking jingle work. Print your name clearly in magic marker on the spine of your tape box. This will facilitate handling if the agency decides to keep your material on file.

You might submit a resume with the demo, but such information is less important than the quality of the material. Composers with strong track records often submit resumes when seeking staff positions.

Audiovisual Demos

Audiovisual firms and/or motion picture producers usually present a script or a copy of the film or filmstrip to the composer, who then writes the music. To demonstrate your ability in this medium, submit a demo tape of about five different samples of specialized background music, or music that you think would be appropriate for synchronization. For more commercial enterprises such as feature-length films, submit samples of theme songs suitable for motion pictures. Include a variety of themes such as comedy, love and drama in your sampling.

If you have extensive AV credits or a degree in music, include a resume. Composing for film is quite technical, and the more credentials you have, the more favorable are your chances of being selected for a particular project.

Musical Theater Demos

When submitting material to a producer of musical plays, present a neat manuscript of the original play and a demo of about five songs. These selections should be the ones that best set the mood of the play. Submitting lead sheets or lyric sheets shouldn't be necessary, because lyrics should be embodied in the script proper. Most producers appreciate an accompanying score, however.

Most play producers and theatrical agents prefer cassette demos. If your play has been produced locally and you seek production on a larger level, enclose copies of local reviews with the script and demo.

When dealing with most markets, simultaneous submissions of the same material to a number of places are acceptable. The more people that hear the songs, the better the chances of the songs getting picked up.

For more details about standard submission methods in various markets, check the introductions leading off each category in the Markets section.

Queries

Not all markets will audition new material. Some prefer to work only with the material in their catalog; some take new tunes only from writers they know, some simply don't have the personnel to listen to unsolicited demos. Others won't accept unsolicited material for fear of plagiarism suits (if a company rejects a song and later produces a similar one by another writer, the company risks a copyright infringement suit instigated by the first writer).

If you discover a market not listed in *Songwriter's Market* and you're unsure as to whether it accepts outside material, send a query letter to the market and inquire about its needs. Briefly describe the material you wish to send, and ask if you may submit it. Also inquire about the preferred submission procedure. The letter should be typewritten, and should be bright and pleasant without losing a

Sample Reply Form

I would like to hear:
( ) "Name of Song"   ( ) "Name of Song"   ( ) "Name of Song"

I prefer listening to the demo on:
( ) reel-to-reel tape   ( ) cassette tape   ( ) acetate dub
( ) each is acceptable

I require a
( ) lead sheet   ( ) lyric sheet   ( ) either
( ) neither at this
time

I will, will not accept material by registered or certified mail.
(Circle one).
( ) I am not looking for material at this time, try me later.
( ) I am not interested.

---

businesslike attitude. Don't try to be chummy.

You might want to include with the letter self-addressed, stamped post card which can be used as a convenient reply form. Type in potential replies to your query on the card (see sample reply form) so that the buyer need only check off his answer and drop the card in the mail. This saves the buyer time, thus increasing the chances of your receiving a reply.

Once you've decided on a market (assuming you've gotten a go-ahead to submit material, if one is needed), assemble all of your materials for mailing: demo, lead sheet or lyric sheet, resume (when appropriate), and a self-addressed, stamped envelope (SASE) large enough to contain everything you submitted should it be returned, and containing sufficient postage to ensure its return. Introduce your submissions with a brief typewritten cover letter indicating the types of songs you're submitting. You may want to "cast" your songs for the listener, indicating for which recording artists your material might be suitable.

Place your materials in a small box or a sturdy envelope which will withstand the rigors of the postal system.

Neatness is important. It will invite the listener to pay attention to your material. A neat package, of course, won't guarantee a contract; the bottom line is the quality of the song. Carelessness, however, will only diminish your material's chances even before it's played.

You can send your package in a variety of ways: first class, special fourth class rate, registered, certified, insured, special delivery or express mail. First class is your best bet. It will get the material to its destination reasonably soon, and, except for the fourth class rate, is the least expensive rate.

Sending material by registered or certified mail means the addressee must sign for the package, and you can request a receipt for proof of delivery. Some companies refuse to accept delivery of certified or registered mail, however, so you're safest when mailing first class.

Stamp or write "first class mail" on both the outer envelope and the SASE when using this rate. When mailing acetate dubs, mark "phonograph record—keep away from excessive heat—do not drop or crush" on the envelope as well.

You can insure your material against loss or damage, and special delivery or express mail can be used if you need something delivered fast.

These types of mailings are expensive for everyday purposes, however. Consult the post office for details should you need to use these rates.

When mailing to Canada or other foreign countries, don't affix US postage to the SASE; it is useless. Enclose International Reply Coupons with your self-addressed envelope. These coupons can be exchanged by the person returning your material for local postage. International Reply Coupons are available in 42¢ denominations from the post office.

Keep an index card file of everything you send out. On each card, jot in the name of the company and the person to whom the material was sent, when it was sent, the name of the songs included and the type of demo, whether or not lead or lyric sheets were sent, and action taken on the demo. You might also want to jot in a date when you'd like to follow up on your submission if no action is taken. The average length of time a firm takes in reporting back is listed in individual *Songwriter's Market* listings. Two to four weeks is normal. When no time is specified, wait at least four weeks before following up. Your follow-up letter should supply full details about your submission: your name, address and phone number; the names of the submitted songs; the type of demo you submitted; and the date of submission. Gentle prodding is sometimes necessary in getting action taken on your submission, so be persistent; but be courteous, lest you prod the potential buyer into rejecting your material.

And above all, remember this: Professionalism makes the difference.

Harvey Rachlin, author of The Songwriter's Handbook, *is currently writing his second book for Harper and Row/Thomas Y. Crowell.*

The Songshark Bites With His Teeth, Dear

With apologies to Bobby Darin, we ask you to beware of Mack the Nice.

"Mack the Nice" is the song shark, bane of the music publishing industry. The song shark is very nice to you, because he wants to do business with you. He wants to take your money.

The shark compliments your work and assures you that he can make your song a hit. That seems nice enough. However, *you* must pay for these compliments and assurances, and believe us, t'...

One ... ...sic
indust... ...e
a ...
re

A Valentine Greeting

...f
...ey
...A
...the
...pany
... Even
...r signs
...songs do
...ome small
...rk has *paid* to

play your song. *Once.* The shark has fulfilled the terms of the contract, but certainly not with your interests in mind. He's done nothing illegal, but has overstepped ethical guidelines.

Another gambit is promising that your song—again, for a fee—will be recorded by a nationally known star. With those exciting promises buzzing about in your ear, you sign the contract. But a promise made in your ear is not necessarily duplicated on paper. "These 'frauds' don't follow through," says Betty Holt, owner of Chevis Publishing Corporation. "They promise national promotion, etc. It's a matter of interpretation. You're buying a great concept, which turns into nothing. . . . Their contracts are legitimate. People just don't read them. They believe only the lies and this 'great concept' that's being presented to them."

Another practice considered unethical is the "poems set to music" routine. For as "little" as $20, some firms will set your poem or lyrics set to music. They don't necessarily point out that the music they use might have been used on another poem—or on another hundred poems. These "music mills," as they've been termed, often have stock music that almost any poem will fit. Besides, they aren't very discriminating, and are more taken with the power of the dollar than the power of the lyric. "They will, even when presented with a hopelessly inept and unworkable lyric, assure the writer that the work shows talent," says Edward M. Cramer, president of BMI, a performance rights organization.

Cramer goes on to describe another gambit: the club that will—for a membership fee—pair you with a suitable collaborator and offer other services.

The list goes on, but a songwriter doesn't have to know every scheme specifically in order to avoid them. He need only follow a few simple rules:

Never pay to have a song published. "If anyone asks you for a nickle of your own money, forget it," says Felice Bryant, longtime songwriter and cowriter of such hits as "Wake Up Little Susie" and "Love Hurts." "No righteous, professional publisher asks for money," says John Braheny, co-director of the Alternative Chorus Songwriters Showcase in Hollywood. By the same reasoning, never pay to have lyrics set to music (or vice versa), and be wary of anyone who reviews material for a fee.

Be wary of wild promises. Industry people are more realistic than to bury you in accolades and promise you instant stardom no matter how good your material *really* is. Music people are business people, and no matter how much faith they have in a song or a songwriter, they'll temper their enthusiasm with a realization that instant success is a rare happening. By the same token, beware excessive praise, especially praise that leads to any phrase resembling, ". . . and for a fee. . . ." "Song sharks depend heavily on the pride of authorship of beginners in songwriting," says Edward M. Cramer.

Read all contracts carefully. Compare the contract with what was promised you verbally. Show the contract to a lawyer. Don't sign any contract you're unsure about or that you don't understand.

Don't be afraid to ask questions, not only of anyone you deal with directly, but also of people who might know something about the person you're going to deal with. Be wary of any publisher that sidesteps tough questions. Check the company's reputation by going to the performance rights organization with which it's associated (and if it's not associated with BMI, SESAC or ASCAP—or the foreign equivalents of these organizations, be especially wary). Check with any organizations that might have had dealings with the company.

And remember that *Songwriter's Market* doesn't necessarily endorse the companies listed here. Though we try very hard to screen all listings, a rare unethical company might sneak in. If you run across a company that publishes for a fee or charges for reviewing material, do more than shy away from that company. Write us. Write to the performance rights organization to which the company belongs. Also inform applicable songwriters' organizations such as the Nashville Songwriters Association International (NSAI), Songwriters Resources and Services (SRS), the American Guild of Authors and Composers (AGAC) and the National Music Publishers' Association. Include photocopies of your correspondence with the company when contacting us or anyone else. Addresses for these organizations can be found in our "Organizations and Clubs" section.

The song sharks comprise only a small segment of the music industry, but they're often more visible to you than the rest of the industry because they work very hard to find you. If you're wary of come-ons and exercise common sense, you can avoid the song shark and align yourself with one of the many upstanding firms that populate the music industry.

Lay Down the (Copyright) Law

By Doug Thiele
and William Brohaugh

Copyright law is a powerful ally for the songwriter. It guarantees your rights to your material, gives you an element of creative control over your material, and offers far-reaching legal recourse against those who infringe on your song.

Because copyright law is basic to dealings with the music industry, here are answers to commonly asked questions about the law:

To what rights am I entitled under copyright law? You have the right to make and sell copies of your song throughout the world in the form of sheet music, records and tapes; to perform or display the song publicly; to lease the song; and to will the song to heirs. You also have the right to determine who can record the song first. After the first recording of your tune, anyone can record the song as long as they conform to licensing and other requirements.

If, however, you create a song as a "work-for-hire" (which usually occurs when working with audiovisual firms and advertising agencies), you *do not* own any of these rights. The person that commissioned the work-for-hire owns the copyright. The work-for-hire agreement will be discussed in more detail later.

When does copyright law take effect? Your song is protected from the moment of its creation, and you can register the song with the copyright office immediately as an unpublished work. Because the song is copyrighted automatically, you need not register it in order to protect it. For your safety, however, you may want to register the song as an unpublished work for two reasons: First, you can't sue a person who has infringed on an unregistered song for statutory damages (damage

penalties established by law), and you can't recover lawyer's fees or court costs unless you registered the song with the copyright office *before* the infringement took place.

You can't take an infringer to court unless the song has been registered, though you can register it *after* the infringement and *then* take the case to court. If you register the song after the infringement, you can sue for actual damages (the amount of money you lost because of an infringement), but you might have trouble establishing a specific date when you claimed ownership of the tune. Registering your song establishes that date without question.

How does copyright law stop someone from stealing my song? The copyright office can't prevent anyone from using your song illegally. No one can. The office does provide proof that your song was registered at a certain time and establishes your rights to the song. If you think one of your songs has been stolen, see an attorney immediately.

Song infringements are rare, and usually involve the work of established writers. Many music industry people believe new songwriters worry too much about someone stealing their material and about protecting it. Again, song piracy is rare.

What constitutes an infringement? If an unbiased third party can listen to two songs and state that one was copied from the other, an infringement has occurred.

What's the procedure for registering my songs? If registering a song as an unpublished work, request form PA (other forms might apply in special cases) from the copyright office and complete it according to instructions printed on it. Return the application, a $10 registration fee and one copy of your song to Register of Copyrights, Library of Congress, Washington, D.C. 20559. "Copy" can mean a lead sheet, tape or record, which the copyright office will file. Notification of copyright—which consists of the word "Copyright," the abbreviation "Copr.," or the symbol c; the name of the copyright owner(s); and the year date of publication or original registration—must appear on the lead sheets of registered songs.

If you publish your own material (which many songwriters do in order to retain the publishing royalties), submit *two* copies of the song when registering; otherwise, the procedure is the same. Be certain when publishing material that the copyright notice is affixed; you have little recourse against a person who infringes on a published song that lacks notification of copyright.

When an unregistered song is published, the publisher will handle the registration procedure.

What are the alternatives to registering each song? Many songwriters use "song registration" services, most notably the "Songbank" services of Songwriters Resources and Services (SRS). A song registration service involves a disinterested third party establishing a date when you claimed ownership to your song, a date you can use as evidence in court should an infringement take place. This registration is much cheaper than registering with the copyright office. Remember, however, that you can't sue for statutory damages or recover court costs unless the song was specifically registered with the copyright office *before* the infringement occurred.

You needn't register each song individually when registering material with the copyright office. You can register a group of songs simultaneously, with a single application and a single fee submission. To be eligible

for group registration, songs must be grouped in an orderly fashion (which can be as simple as binding all lead sheets together), they must all be written by the same person or collaborators, and they must be registered under a group title (which can be as simple as "Songs by Jon Dough, 1980"). No limit is placed on the number of songs you can register in a group (theoretically, hundreds can be registered under a single application), so this is the most economical way of fully protecting your tunes.

How long are my songs protected? Copyright protection for songs created after Jan. 1, 1978 (when a revised copyright law took effect) is the life of the writer plus 50 years. If the song was written by two or more people, protection lasts for 50 years after the death of the last survivor. Protection under the old law was 28 years with the option to renew the copyright for an additional 28 years. Works copyrighted before 1978 that are in their first 28-year term still must be renewed, but the second term has been extended 19 years for a total of 75 years of protection. Works in their second term will automatically receive the 19-year extension. Unpublished works created before, but registered after, Jan. 1, 1978 will receive the life-plus-50 coverage. Work-for-hire receives protection for 75 years from the time of publication or 100 years from the time of creation, whichever is shorter.

What happens when someone accepts my song? Standard procedure when dealing with a publisher or anyone else interested in your song is to assign rights to the tune to him for the duration of the copyright or for a shorter time period. This doesn't mean you're selling the song outright, but that you have given the publisher the right to handle the song to your mutual benefit. (You can sell songs outright, but that's a foolish and ill-advised move.) The publisher will assign your copyright number (if you have registered the song with the copyright office) to himself, which requires your permission. (Such matters should be clearly outlined in your contract. See "Negotiating Your Contract" for details.)

Can I get my copyright back if I assign my songs to someone else? You can regain rights to your song 35 years after publication or 40 years after creation of the tune. After that time, all you need do is request in writing that the copyright be returned to you—consult the copyright office for procedural details. Don't believe 35 years is in the distant future; a good song will collect royalties for someone—preferably you—for much longer than 35 years.

Again, you should never sell your copyright. If you do, you lose control over the use of the song, and forfeit income from its future use. Also, avoid work-for-hire agreements.

What exactly is a work-for-hire? This is a work another party commissions you to do. Two types of for-hire works exist: work done as a regular employee of a company, and commissioned work that is specifically called a "work-for-hire" in writing at the time of the assignment. The phrase "work-for-hire" or something close must be used in the written agreement, though you should watch for similar phrasings. The work-for-hire provision was included in the new copyright law so that no writer could unwittingly sign away his copyright.

Writing songs under salary from a music publisher isn't usually considered work-for-hire, though you should discuss the matter before taking a salaried position with any publisher or record company.

Does copyright law determine my royalty payments? The law establishes a "mechanical rate" (what a record company pays you and your publisher every time a record or tape of your song is sold; payment of mechanical royalties is administered through the Harry Fox Agency, a licensing organization). The mechanical rate established by law is 2¾¢ per song, or ½¢ per minute of playing time, whichever is more.

Does a songwriter have any power of changes in the law? Definitely. Under the law, a Copyright Tribunal reviews the law and instigates needed change. This five-member tribunal meets every ten years and is primarily interested in areas such as royalty rates. Your input is taken into consideration by the tribunal when it reviews royalty rates (to make certain they are fair in relation to inflation, etc.), so contact the tribunal if you think the present mechanical rates aren't sufficient.

The American Guild of Authors and Composers (AGAC) has banded with the Nashville Songwriters Association International (NSAI) to lobby for changes before the Copyright Tribunal. You can demonstrate your support for changes through these organizations (check the Organizations & Clubs section for addresses). Songwriters have an obligation to effect changes in this area, especially since it will upgrade the quality of your career and the careers of your colleagues.

Where can I get more information? Write to the Library of Congress for free, detailed information about copyright. If you have a number of general questions, request the free Copyright Kit. Copyright information officers can be called at 703/557-8700 (don't call collect). The copyright office will answer questions, but it does place limitations on the help it can provide. As the office itself explains, "The copyright office cannot do any of the following: comment upon the merits, copyright status or ownership of particular works, or upon the extent of protection afforded to particular works by the copyright law; compare for similarities copies of works deposited for registration or give opinions on the validity of claims; advise on questions of possible copyright infringement or prosecution of copyright violations; draft or interpret contract terms; enforce contracts or recover manuscripts; recommend particular publishers, agents, lawyers, 'song services' and the like; help in getting a work published, recorded or performed." The office can't provide legal advice, so consult an attorney should an infringement on your work occur. Many organizations provide legal assistance; consult the "Lawyers Referral Service" of the local bar association in the Yellow Pages as a possible source. Another potential source is Volunteer Lawyers for the Arts (VLA), 36 W. 44th St., Suite 1110, New York City 10036.

The Agonies and Ecstasies of Collaboration

By Jill Williams

"Collaboration is the agony and the ecstasy: When it's bad, it's horrible. And when you've written something great together, it's a wonderful feeling."
—Cynthia Weil, lyricist.

Often called "a kind of marriage" songwriting partnerships have produced some of the biggest hits in music history. "Yesterday" (Lennon/McCartney), "Canadian Sunset" (Gimbel/Heywood) and "More" (Glazer/Alstone) are three such team-written ditties that have, according to BMI vice president Stan Catron, logged more than three million performances.

Who hasn't whistled the happy tunes—and sung the memorable lyrics—of such talented theatrical duos as Rodgers and Hart, Rodgers and Hammerstein, and Lerner and Lowe. Another example is the team of Burt Bacharach and Hal David, whose hits were as common in the '60s as the raindrops they wrote about.

Check the charts in *Billboard*, *Cashbox* and *Record World* and you'll discover that communal creativity is still in vogue. Whether written by a family like the BeeGees or by a producing/writing team like Fekaris and Perren, over 50% of those hit-bound singles result from two people (sometimes four or five) working out a musical hook, a catchy phrase, an offbeat story line.

"Collaborating is easier," admits Adrienne Anderson, who co-wrote "Could It Be Magic" with Barry Manilow. "You get to let somebody else do half the work!"

Easier? Perhaps. "But you really have to get on with the person," warns Richard Kerr, who has also supplied Manilow with hit melodies, including "Mandy" (with Scott English) and "Somewhere in the Night" (with Will Jennings). "You have to be able to say whatever you feel like. If you don't like a line of lyric, for example, you can't hold back your feelings. You have to say so."

Yet, as Carole Bayer Sager recalls, it isn't always that easy: "The first time I met Marvin [Hamlisch], I was very much in awe of him and his accomplishments. After all, those three Oscars were there staring me in the face, right? And I remember thinking to myself after he'd played me a tune he needed words for, 'Gee, I don't know if this is the best thing I've ever heard. But on the other hand, *look who I'm criticizing.*'"

Like a blind date, the initial meeting between composer and lyric writer can be creative. Or boring. Either way, songwriters should meet and collaborate with as many people as possible.

How? With a persistent and professional approach (i.e., legible lyric sheets; unmuddled demo tapes; and a friendly, "up" attitude), you'll begin to establish yourself with various people in the music industry. An enthusiastic record producer, perhaps? A rock band that decides to cut several of your tunes? "One of the best ways to find collaborators is by contacting music publishers and asking them if they have any people that they recommend to co-write with," says Stan Catron. If you're signed with a music publisher, pairing you with "artistically compatible" partners is a part of the publisher's job.

"I put together Barry Mann and Dan Hill," boasts Sam Trust, president of ATV Music. Both writers were signed with ATV at the time. "I sat down with Dan and I told him, 'Look, I love your lyrics. I think you're a poet. But I don't think you've acquired the knack of writing a commercial hook. . . . So they got together in the studio and walked out a couple of hours later with 'Sometimes When We Touch'!"

"If one of our writers needs help—if we feel he's getting stale or in a rut—we will also go outside our own offices to different publishers and try to find collaborators," says Lester Sill of Screen Gems/Col-Gems/EMI. "It's the product, after all, that counts. Right?" Sill knows how to get a good product from a good collaboration; he introduced Michael Masser to Gerry Goffin, who co-wrote "Theme From Mahogany (Do you Know Where You're Going To)."

But what if you aren't quite a Dan Hill or a Michael Masser? What if the only thing you're signed to is a bank loan for the acoustic guitar you just bought? Take the advice of Tad Danz, president of the American Song Festival: "Go to your local musician's union. Most have some sort of bulletin board or house organ wherein they can contact the local musician who's looking for a collaborator." For melodists looking for lyricists, Danz recommends advertising in *Songwriter Magazine* or *Writer's Digest*. (The April 1979 issue of *Songwriter* discusses finding collaborators through classified ads in "Collaborating by Mail: A Crash Course in Etiquette.")

Danz also advises that you attend talent nights, "hoot nights" or songwriters' nights where new artists and writers showcase their work. "There isn't a city in this country with a population of more than 25,000 that doesn't have some sort of club where they hold a weekly talent night," he says. "You go there, you listen, you hang out until you find somebody whose lyrics and/or music feels right to *you*. Maybe you buy 'em a beer,

and then you say you'd like to try writing a few songs together. . . ."

Some organizations systematically match potential collaborators. One such organization is Songwriters Resources and Services (SRS). A membership organization that makes many services available to nonmembers, SRS maintains a *Collaborator's Directory*. "SRS members fill out a very lengthy, very detailed questionnaire about their particular areas and interests in songwriting, their experience, their knowledge, etc.," says SRS staff member Lois Arkin. Questionnaires are filed geographically, and anyone seeking a local collaborator can contact SRS (6386 Hollywood Blvd., Suite 503, Hollywood 90028).

Use as many of these methods as possible in your quest for a musical soulmate, and *don't overlook anybody*. What about that kid in your history class, for example, who's always scribbling lyrics in his notebook? He just might come up with the perfect title and story idea for the melody you're writing. Who knows who the next superstar will be—perhaps it will be the fellow playing piano at your latest audition.

What happens once you've found a potential collaborator? First, you must discuss the arrangement. John Braheny, co-founder of the Alternative Chorus Songwriters Showcase, recommends that you clarify things *on paper* before any actual songwriting is done. "It's good to have an understanding in writing about several things, like how the royalties are going to be split up, whether each partner will retain part of the publishing rights, whose name comes first on the leadsheets," Braheny says. "It's also good to talk out the details of how you plan to work together. Exclusively, for example? Or with a lot of different writing partners?"

According to Braheny, writers with good melodies seeking lyric writers "should be able to say to a potential collaborator, 'Listen, I'd like to give you a week to work on this lyric. After that week, I'll come and see what you have. If it doesn't knock me out, I'll go see another lyric writer. Agreed?' It works the same way for somebody with a great lyric. Just as long as everybody is 'up front,' nobody gets hurt."

If one trial collaboration fizzles, don't get discouraged. *Many* writers search for partners, and one of them is bound to "click" for you sooner or later.

"Each collaboration is like its own little marriage, with its own set of rules and its own good points and bad points," says Cynthia Weil, whose marriage to writing partner Barry Mann has been both creative and legal for more than 15 years. Weil calls the elements of a good collaboration "intangible," and notes that she's worked with some incredibly talented people with no results. "I'd always go home and say to myself, 'My god, there must be something wrong with *me*!' But I've come to understand that there is a certain magic that either is there, or it *isn't* there. It has nothing to do with how good some other writer is, either . . . It either happens or it doesn't. And you just have to keep on trying."

Jill Williams, herself a songwriter, is a contributing editor of Songwriter Magazine.

Negotiating Your Contract

By Doug Thiele

Thousands of fine tunes never reach the public's ears because the writer can't find the right market for material, or because the writer's ignorance about contracts rids the material of commercial life once the right market has been found. Other writers find to their horror that the deal they negotiated in the publisher's office doesn't match the deal outlined in the resultant contract. Bad contracts have cost some songwriters thousands of dollars in lost royalties; in a few severe cases, a poor contract has made otherwise valuable songs worthless.

Some songwriters have done well initially without contracts, though they're in the minority; if you seek a guarantee of another's accountability, you must rely on a contract. Verbal deals aren't acceptable because they're unreliable. If an agreement isn't in writing, it isn't official. In fact, many contracts have a clause to the effect that the contract "represents the entire understanding between the parties."

Contracts in General

A contract is a means toward an end, and a good contract ensures that everyone concerned will profit in some way. Most companies have "standard" contracts prepared, though these contracts won't apply to every situation. Chances are you will want to negotiate and change the contract to apply to your specific situation.

Have a detailed idea of what you want from a deal. Be prepared to relinquish as little as is necessary to meet your goals. For instance, you might be asked to relinquish all publishing royalties on your song when you need only to issue a mechanical license to the recording artist, thereby retaining all your royalties. On the other hand, you should be prepared to give up

something to get something; this is the whole basis of negotiation. If you refuse to compromise, you may lose the deal, and as the saying goes, 100% of nothing is nothing.

Never sign a contract on the spot. Even if you do sign hastily, the law gives you a grace period of a couple of days to, in effect, rescind your signature. Yet, the best cure for a hasty decision is not making a hasty decision.

Don't be frightened to suggest changes in a contract. You won't blow a deal by asking for a fair change. If you do lose the deal, you've been negotiating with an unreasonable party; the deal probably wouldn't have worked, anyway.

Use the contract to gauge the company you're dealing with. A contract is a reflection of the firm's business dealings, and can offer clues to the firm's business practices. Has the firm written a fair contract? Or is the contract weighted on the company's side? You'll want to deal with a firm that's fair from the outset, and has your interests in mind.

Before you sign a contract, take it to an entertainment attorney, or at least to one who specializes in contract law. Your tax lawyer might be great in April, and the bill from a lawyer-relative might be low, but in the long run you might be giving up much more than the money you save by not consulting an attorney who specializes in entertainment or contractual dealings. Despite the cost, seeing an attorney is a wise investment.

Negotiating Your Deal

Publishers and other industry people with whom you'll deal are serious about their business. They want to handle your song because they believe they'll profit from it. A few publishers will take a "name" writer's song for the sake of having a song by that writer. More than a few publishers will charge you to take your song, but these aren't legitimate outlets for your material. The legitimate firms will gamble that their ears are good, and that you've got profit-making material.

That puts you in a position of strength in negotiations. Publishers won't waste their time taking a song to be nice to you; they want your material. The entire industry rises and falls not on artists or record companies or publishers, but on the song itself. Of course, the publisher's strength in negotiating lies in his ability to get the song recorded, and to collect resulting royalties for both of you from throughout the world.

Unless you're foolish enough to sell your song outright (which means loss of all royalties), negotiate the royalty percentage you will earn, and when and how you will receive royalties. Other issues you should discuss are the amount of creative control (if any) you will retain, the publisher's financial accountability to you, and how long the contract will last. These are only a few of the major negotiable issues; others will be discussed later.

The Basic Issues

A song is a piece of property in every sense of the word. It can be willed to heirs, rented out and sold. The only difference between owning a song and owning, say, a table, is that a time limitation is placed on ownership of the song. Fifty years after your death, your songs will revert to the "public domain," meaning they can be used freely by anyone, and no one will collect royalties on the exploitation of the material. This is true unless you're hired to create a "work-for-hire," in which case the person or company who commissioned the work is considered its owner. This situation

arises in jingle writing, composing film music and dealing with special projects where you receive a flat fee for your work. See "Lay Down the (Copyright) Law" for more information.

In all other circumstances, however, you own the copyright to your song and all rights entailed in the copyright, including the right to sell, assign or rent your song, and to say who first records it (after that, anyone may record it if they pay the royalties due you.)

Any person you negotiate with will want as many of these rights as you are willing to part with. In some cases, you will retain almost all your rights, but most publishers require that you assign your rights to him or her. You might receive advance money from the publisher, but that money will be deducted from future royalties. Royalty amounts vary from medium to medium (for instance, theater and film royalties won't cover record sales unless a cast or soundtrack album is recorded, yet are a major source of revenue).

The length of time a person can use your song, the assignability of those rights to an unknown third party, and the publisher's right to amend your words or music are among the other crucial issues covered in your negotiations.

The Publisher Contract

Contrary to the title on most of these contracts, no "standard, uniform popular songwriter contract" exists. Many variations on a theme can be found, and the differences between individual contracts can be very important. Publisher contracts vary from being fair to writers to being patently unfair. The head of one major publishing company is said to have collected the worst clauses from his colleagues' contracts and incorporated them into his. A contract can range from one to twelve or more pages, and can contain some unusual clauses. Never assume your contract is standard in any way.

The American Guild of Authors and Composers (AGAC), a private agency, offers a writer-oriented contract to its members. Most publishers and record companies have agreed to work with this contract if a writer requests it. Some writers complain that companies "lose interest" in their material when they request AGAC contracts; some publishers claim the AGAC contract requires amendments in their bookkeeping practices; others claim to give better contracts than AGAC's. In any case, carefully reviewing the form and intent of the AGAC contract can teach you much about contracts. AGAC has offices in New York and Los Angeles; see the Organizations & Clubs section in this book for details.

Though contracts differ, they usually follow the same general format:

Part One: Defining the Issues. The contract's introduction names the parties in question and the name of the song. The contract then states that you—the writer(s)—will sell, assign, transfer all rights to the song to the publisher. The contract requires you to state that you have made no other agreements that apply to the song, that you have the right to enter into this agreement, and that you did, indeed, writer the material.

Part Two: Your Share of the Profit. This section, which outlines the publishers obligations to you, is usually divided into specific categories:

The Advance. Writers lacking industry credentials or a "track record" probably won't get an advance unless the publisher uses your demo to "shop" (that is, try to get a record of) your song, in which case you might be reimbursed for demo costs. Advances in both these cases range from $50 to $200; $100 is standard. The publisher

recoups the advance from your royalties when the song is recorded, but you don't have to repay the advance if the publisher doesn't get a record.

Sheet Music. Though you share the publisher's profit, the publisher makes about 35¢ for each sheet of piano music sold, while you earn 5¢. You also earn about 10% of the wholesale price of orchestrations or folios. Unless your song is a chart hit or has special application for schools or churches, the publisher today won't bother with sheet music.

Mechanical and Synchronization Royalties. These are the major income sources for most song writers. In this case, and in the cases that follow, your contract will stipulate that you will receive 50% of mechanical royalties, which result from sales of records and tapes of your song. This is termed the "writer's share," and the publisher's 50% is called "the publishing." In a standard contract, you will split the mechanical royalties 50-50. As your reputation grows, you will probably be able to "split the publishing"—that is, dip into "the publishing" in addition to your "writer's share" (for example, the publisher might give you half his share for the right to handle your song, in which case you will earn 75% of all royalties). *In no case (except when you split the writer's share with a co-writer) will you take less than 50%.*

The publisher will issue any artist interested in recording your song a mechanical license (usually through the Harry Fox Agency in New York), which sets the royalties paid to the publisher. Copyright law sets the minimum royalty at 2¾¢ per song or ½¢ per minute, whichever is greater. Every time a recorded copy of your song is sold, you and the publisher split that 2¾¢ in the proportion set forth in your contract (after the publisher deducts expenses on the song). A publisher might license a song to a record company for less than

2¾¢ to "sweeten the deal" for the record company, which pays less for the song. This is incentive for the record company to record the song, but is detrimental to writers because it cuts into writer royalties.

Performance Royalties. Every time your song is performed on radio or television, in a club or on a juke box, you are entitled to a royalty payment. These stations and clubs must pay a fee to the performance rights societies (ASCAP, BMI and SESAC in the US), which, in turn, pay royalties to writers and publishers based on how much an individual song was played. The societies survey and log performances of your song. The more a song is played, the more you earn. For example, if your song is released as the "B" side of a single, you will earn as much in mechanical royalties as the "A" side because as many copies are made. The "A" side will be played more than the flip side, however, so will earn considerably more in performance royalties.

Your contract will probably state that you have no right to share in publisher's performance royalties, and the publisher has no right to yours; royalties are treated separately by the societies.

Performance royalties are important in theater where composer, lyricist and playwright usually split 6% of the weekly box office receipts, and where mechanical royalties are often non-existent.

Foreign Royalties. This clause will also read 50%, but foreign royalties come from foreign publishers who exploit your material and keep part of the profits. You and your publisher, therefore, split the remaining portion.

Other Revenue. Your contract should stipulate that you receive 50% of all other sums received by your publisher. All vehicles for presenting your song haven't been invented yet, and your contract should cover all future uses of your material.

Part Three: The Publisher's Responsibilities. The contract should obligate the publisher to account to you for all monies collected (two or four times a year) with a statement and a check. You should have the right to audit the company (a common practice) at your expense through a certified public accountant if you encounter a financial "misunderstanding." Many contracts allow you to present grievances to a publisher by certified letter if done within a specified period of time. Insist on prompt payment of royalties.

Most contracts include at least two clauses you shouldn't like; only in some cases will you be able to do anything about them. Many publishers demand the option to change the song to make it more salable, including adding new writers (which cuts into your royalties). Try to include a clause stating that you be given first try to amend the song, at least. If the publisher liked the original song, it should remain reasonably intact. Contracts also give the publisher the right to assign the song to anybody else at the publisher's discretion. You might wake up one day to find the publisher sold your song to another publisher—and the unkindest cut of all is that you can't share in that sale. Ask for a voice in any reassignment of your material.

Part Four: Future Problems. Publishers know that legal entanglements can seriously hurt a song, so most contracts cover potential problems. Publishers reserve the right to sue or not to sue, or to conduct cases brought against them. Most disputes are infringement-related; the publisher usually reserves the right to withhold your royalties if such a dispute arises. You should have the right to post a bond to get your royalties, and the amount of royalties withheld should never exceed the amount of the suit plus reasonable attorney's fees and court costs.

One crucial clause often absent from publisher's contracts is the "option" or reversion clause that states that all rights to the song revert to the writer(s) if the publisher doesn't get your song recorded within a certain time period (usually one year, but two is also common). If a reversion clause isn't included in the contract, the publisher owns your song for your lifetime plus 50 years. Copyright law allows you to reclaim your rights eventually, but only after 35 years at the earliest. See "Lay Down the (Copyright) Law" for more information.

One last caution: *No legitimate publisher will charge you for publishing your song.* The company that asks you for money is more interested in the strength of your checking account than the strength of your material.

The Record Company Contract

Record company publishers are essentially the same as independent publishers. Because record company publishers have better access to recording situations, however, your chances of getting a record may be better, though placing a song with a record company publisher is generally more difficult. Also, because publishing is often a subsidiary activity of a record company, you might be able to make a better deal or keep more of the publishing royalties in these situations. If you're fortunate enough to deal directly with an artist or producer who wants to record your song, you may escape the publishing company altogether and simply issue a mechanical license to the company, thereby retaining not only all publishing royalties, but also ownership of the song itself.

When dealing with a record company publisher only as a songwriter (with no ambitions as an artist), you'll find that the contract is similar to that of the independent publisher. You must exercise the same cautions and negotiate in the same

way as with the independent. If, however, you deal with a record company as a writer/artist and hope to get your songs recorded on their label, the company will want more of you than your copyrights.

The main thrust of an artist deal is *exclusivity*. The record company contract will grant the company exclusive right to all your material brought to them, as well as any songs you write during the duration of the contract. You can expect to work only for that company during that period, with the possible exception of doing guest work on another artist's album. In short, you and your songs belong to the record company for the term of the contract, which is usually one year with four yearly options to renew (the option is the record company's).

Publishing and artist contracts are separate issues. They might be covered in the same package, yet should always be exclusive of one another. For example, a record company shouldn't be allowed to recoup money advanced to you for the right to publish your songs by dipping into your artist royalties (a practice called *cross-collateralization*).

A songwriter/artist can expect a contract requiring you to record anything from one side of a single to an album during the initial contract period, for which you'll receive 3-5% of retail sales as royalties. The number of records you can record and the royalty percentage you'll receive should escalate every time the contract is renewed.

The record company might give you an advance, which, as in publishing, is recoupable from your royalties. Artists usually pay for virtually everything they do if their records sell. Artists pay for recording masters (the tape from which records are made), and for room and board for everyone accompanying the artist on tour. The sums can be considerable: from $2,000 for recording a single to $50,000 and up for an album. (These costs are recouped from your royalties.)

Other things to consider are that an artist under contract can be assigned to another company, and that you should ask that ownership of masters revert back to you after a specified time period. In other words, many of the issues concerning your song in a publishing deal will come up about *you* in a recording deal.

Writer/artists must struggle with the question of which material to pitch to other artists and which to save for themselves. Obviously, giving your strongest tunes to a publisher won't leave enough material for you. Of course, bands have no choice in this matter in most cases; they usually save their material and go for the artist deal.

Consider letting go of at least some of your material for other artists. If the songs become hits, your reputation might land you a recording deal as an artist. Prove you can write songs *and* sing, and an artist deal will be a natural. In fact, many artists followed this exact path to success.

Other Contracts

Songwriters should be familiar with other contracts they might encounter, including:

Collaborator Agreements. The new copyright law says that if you simply *intend* to create a joint work (to co-write), the result lives forever. This is fine if you're satisfied with the finished product, but not terrific if you're not. You can remedy the situation by agreeing before doing any co-writing that the song can be separated if either party is dissatisfied (for example, you can use your lyrics with another composition if you're collaborator's melody is unsatisfactory). Work out all details of the partnership in writing before doing any actual work together. Such an agreement can eliminate disputes about who receives what percentage of

the writers' profit, and other such issues. Because no standard collaboration agreements exist, you should see an attorney before the agreement is signed. Songwriters Resources and Services (SRS), a service organization (6381 Hollywood Blvd., Suite 503, Hollywood 90028), will give you a list of issues that must be considered when drawing up a collaborator's agreement.

Administration Deals. If you're fortunate enough to own your song after someone records it, you will be responsible for collecting the publishing royalties from the record company. This presents no problem in the US and Canada, but gets sticky in foreign countries, where you have not control. Most writers in this situation contract with an administration company or a major publisher to exploit the material outside the US for 10-15% of the proceeds. These companies are set up to collect song revenues worldwide, and will gladly handle a valuable song for your.

Exclusive Songwriter Contracts. Successful songwriters are sometimes offered an exlusive deal under which they are paid a regular wage ($75-200 a week), *which is an advance against future royalties.* All songs written under an exclusive contract, which lasts from six months to three years, will be handled by the publisher with which you're signed.

This is not a frivolous deal; you are required to give the publisher the rights to *all* your material. You aren't allowed to write for anybody else during the contract period, and your access to co-writers is eliminated or seriously restricted. What's more, most exclusive contracts will be extended if you don't write the required number of commercially acceptable songs during the contract period.

You benefit from an exclusive deal only if the publisher gets your songs recorded, and most companies won't guarantee records. If you sign with a small company that couldn't get arrested with your songs and they don't get you records, you've effectively postponed your career because you will remain unknown until the contract period is up. If you sign with a large company that doesn't promote you, the same will happen.

There's More . . .

You will encounter other contracts, of course. You might make a co-publishing agreement with another writer or company, a licensing agreement with the Harry Fox Agency or another agency, a publisher/performing rights society agreement, etc. In every case, know the terms of the deal and negotiate your side of the issues, or have your attorney do so. If you run the contract past your attorney, you've taken giant strides toward protecting that special creation: your song.

But it doesn't stop there. As with any business, you must know as much about your profession as possible, and you must do your homework. Here's a brief list of some important reading material:

● *Legal and Practical Aspects of the Music Business* (Part One—Songwriter Agreements), by Alfred W. Schlessinger, SRS, 6381 Hollywood Blvd., Suite 503, Hollywood 90028.

● *Music/Record Copyright Contracts and Other Business and Law*, by Walter E. Hurst and William Storm Hale, 7 Arts Press, 6605 Hollywood Blvd., Suite 215, Hollywood 90028.

● *This Business of Music*, by Sidney Sheemel and William Krasilovsky, Billboard Publications, 1 Astor Plaza, New York City 10019.

Doug Thiele, who recently co-wrote a song recorded by Dolly Parton, is a frequent contributor to Songwriter *Magazine. He recently became president of Songwriters Resources and Services (SRS) in Hollywood.*

Markets

Music Publishers

The music publisher is the songwriter's agent. "In most cases, he is our link between the songs and the artist," says songwriter Laynge Martine Jr., who has had songs recorded by Elvis Presley and Billy "Crash" Craddock. Yet, he's "more than just an agent, a conduit for your songs." A publisher is an advisor, a partner, a counselor, a psychologist who helps the songwriter develop and gives direction to his career. Publishers are "in the business of building writers, and writers' reputations," in addition to developing songs, says writer/producer/publisher Bob Montgomery. Working with a publisher is "a family situation, and one that grows in time," says Norro Wilson, A&R director of Warner Bros. Records in Nashville.

What's more, publishers are plankton.

Plankton?

"We're the plankton, so to speak, of the musical ocean," says Leeds Levy of MCA Music's New York office. Publishers are the base of the "musical food chain"—that is, they supply all the material that the rest of the music industry feeds on. When artists, producers or record companies need material, they turn to publishers. That's why your first contact with the music industry will probably be a publisher, and why Del Bryant of Broadcast Music, Inc. (BMI) says, "This is the writer's first and most natural socket to plug into the music industry."

Lower (or, shall we say, more important) than the plankton are the songwriters, without whom music publishers (or music in general, for that matter) couldn't exist. Publishers need new songwriters. To Arthur Braun of Dick James Music, songwriters "are the main bloodline. It's been my philosophy that we couldn't cut them off. They need us, but we need them." Talented songwriters help publishers respond to any trend, to any request. "If we are asked for a pop R&B disco polka," says Leeds Levy, "we should be able to supply it or have one of our writers write it."

Publishers seek songs with wide

appeal—ones that will be recorded not once, but a number of times. Each recording means more money for writer and publisher alike. "A good song fits more than one artist," says Don Gant, senior vice president of Tree International, a major Nashville publisher. That's why publishers prefer powerful material that can be adapted to a variety of formats—formats that will be invented in years to come as well as present-day formats. Songwriter Jimmy Webb couldn't have known about the disco craze when he wrote "MacArthur's Park," a song that Donna Summers sang with a disco beat and made almost as popular as the original version by Richard Harris. Between the Harris and the Summers versions, artist Waylon Jennings gave the song a country flavor, a further tribute to the song's versatility.

It's this shot at multiple recordings that makes dealing with a publisher so profitable. A songwriter who pushes the song himself without the help of a publisher might get one record if he's lucky, but probably won't get multiple recordings. The other advantage of dealing with a publisher is that he handles the business end of publishing: copyrighting the song, making a demo and a lead sheet of it, and showing it to various artists, producers and record companies that might record it. (This is called "pitching," "shopping" or "working" the song.) For this service, publishers take half the royalties a song accrues. (For details on this and other duties of the publisher, see "Negotiating Your Contract.")

Songwriters have two basic options when submitting material to publishers: They can arrange a personal interview to demonstrate the song, or you can submit songs through the mail. The following listings explain the best method of contacting individual publishers.

Whether you're submitting songs in person or through the mail, you must put them on a demonstration tape. Don't put more than four songs on the tape (unless a particular company asks for more in its listing). "If someone's sending me 12 songs, he's basically

shotgunning," says Don Gant. "The song business is a one-at-a-time business. I can't pitch 12 songs at one time."

Most publishers will review "rough" demos—that is, tapes recorded only with a vocal and a guitar or piano. "A good publisher is not going to miss a great song simply because it's not in finished form." But others disagree. Linda and Gene Kennedy of Gene Kennedy Enterprises believe that a songwriter should put as much good production into a song as possible, because they find that persuading some artists to record a song is difficult if the artists can't hear it in an arranged, well-produced form. Leeds Levy falls somewhere in the middle, asking songwriters to keep the demo simple while at the same time giving it a definite "feel." A good demo "sounds like more than it is," he says.

Get the names straight when approaching publishers. "If you don't, they spot you as being a newcomer, an outsider, someone who doesn't know anything," says John Braheny, co-director of the Alternative Chorus Songwriters Showcase in Hollywood. *Don't* show up at anyone's office without first setting up an appointment—at the *publisher's* convenience; don't demand an appointment at *your* convenience. Be polite during the interview. "I look for a person who treats me the way I'd like to treat him," says Tom Collins of Pi-Gem and Chess Music. "Just be a basic human being, and I don't think you'll have any problems."

Some publishers refuse to see songwriters in person. "I would never see a songwriter until I've heard the tape," says Leeds Levy. Personal interviews are "a routine, and I don't like being hyped." This is often a matter of personal taste and not company policy, as demonstrated by the fact that Lorraine Rebidas, Levy's associate at MCA Music, often meets with songwriters. Again, check the following listings for individual policies.

When submitting through the mail, make certain your tape is neat and professionally presented. Meredith Stew-

In the following listings, you'll find references to ASCAP, BMI and SESAC (as well as CAPAC and PROCAN in Canadian listings). These are "performance rights societies," which collect performance fees from radio stations, TV stations and other sources, and distribute the fees to songwriters. Broadcasters pay an annual fee (based on the size of the broadcasters' audiences) to each performance rights organization for the right to play the songs affiliated with that particular organization. For example, a radio station pays ASCAP a set annual fee for the right to play all ASCAP-affiliated songs. The performance rights society then distributes the fees among its member songwriters—the amount earned by each songwriter depends on how many times a song is performed. The more a song is performed, the more a songwriter earns through his performance rights organization.

Performance fees differ from "mechanical fees," which are fees paid for the right to *record* a song, and these fees don't vary according to the amound of airplay a song receives. If your song is recorded on the A side of a single, for example, you will receive the same mechanical fee as the songwriter who wrote the song on the B side, because an equal number of copies were made of each song. However, you'll probably earn more in performance fees, because A sides of singles almost always receive more airplay than B sides.

Every published songwriter must belong to one of the performance rights organizations, and you must deal with a publisher that belongs to the same organization that you do. For example, if you've joined BMI, the publisher you work with must have a BMI affiliation. This sounds restrictive, but most publishers establish affiliate companies so they can deal with writers affiliated with any of the performance rights societies.

Carefully look into the policies, procedures, benefits and requirements of each organization before deciding which to join. The primary difference between the three societies is in how they "log" performances (that is, how they determine which songs are being played most, and therefore which songwriters should be paid most). ASCAP and BMI monitor individual radio and television stations—and other places where music is performed—as the primary method of logging, while SESAC depends greatly of the airplay and popularity charts in trade magazines. Only one organization, ASCAP, charges a membership fee.

This, of course, is a vast oversimplification of the performance rights organizations, and of the differences between them. Write to each of the organizations (addresses are in the Organizations & Clubs section) for further details. Also, consult the chapter on these organizations in *This Business of Music* (Billboard Publications), an invaluable book written by Sidney Shemel and M. William Krasilovski.

art, general manager of Coal Miner's Music, says it's difficult to take someone seriously if their submissions are not properly presented, and points to cases of receiving lyrics scribbled on bar napkins as evidence. Enclose postage for the return of your tape. Arthur Braun says that many songwriters who submit tapes without return postage turn around and call him, long distance, several times to find out the tapes' fate. "For the amount of money they spend on long distance calls, they might as well throw in the postage," he says.

Some writers forget something even more important, says Patsy Bruce, president of the National Songwriters Association International (NSAI) and herself a publisher: "You'd be amazed at the number of tapes I receive that have no name, address and phone number."

On the other hand, songwriters sometimes include unnecessary material—pictures and long letters explaining the songs (people in the industry agree that any song a writer must explain isn't worth anything).

By the same token, don't go into long explanations when playing your tape in person. Publishers are busy people; don't impose on them.

At any gathering of songwriters or industry people, you'll hear a discussion about whether a songwriter can really break in through the mail. The consensus is that it's difficult, but not impossible. If the song is good, it will get a hearing. For example, Harlan Howard's "Heartaches by the Number," was accepted through the mail. Bob Beckham of the Combine Music Group once accepted a song submitted through the mail and signed the songwriter. Three of the writer's tunes were recorded almost right away. Two went on to win BMI awards, the songwriter eventually wrote "Burning Love," recorded by Elvis Presley, "and then he married my daughter," says Beckham.

Whatever method you use, be certain you're presenting your best. Some songwriters try to pitch material they know is mediocre, hoping that someone will be "stupid enough" to take it, says Jerry Chestnut, writer of "Another Place, Another Time." Chestnut tells of the songwriter who approached a major publisher with some obviously sub-par material. When asked what he thought of it, the publisher said, "I think it's a piece of crap." The songwriter replied, "I think so, too, and I wanted to see if you agree with me."

The songwriter's first thought probably will be to approach only large publishers, but that's a decision that should be given some consideration. Del Bryant notes that a writer who is not part of the "cream" may get buried in the large publisher's catalog. If you're not a "push writer" (a writer that the company will actively promote and "push" to producers and record companies, you might be better off at a small publisher with fewer songs in its catalog. Ed Bruce (who co-wrote Grammy winner "Mamas Don't Let Your Babies Grow Up to Be Cowboys" with wife Patsy Bruce) recommends going to the publisher that can get your song to the right person. If a small company can get your song to the right person, it has put itself on the same level as a large publisher; it has

achieved its goal.

Also consider that you deal with individuals, not the company as a whole. "It isn't so much signing with a company as it is signing with an individual who is excited about your songs," says John Braheny. Try to deal with an individual you like, one that likes you and is excited about your material, because excitement is important in publishing. If a publisher doesn't have a recording contract for your song in 60 to 90 days after its acceptance, the chances of it being recorded diminish sharply, according to Don Gant. That 60- to 90-day period is the time in which the publisher is excited about the tune and works hardest to place it. After the excitement wears off, the song becomes just another item in the catalog, and, though it may eventually see vinyl, it may be lost forever.

Combat this in one of two ways. First, ask for a reversion clause in your contract, which will return rights to the song to you if it isn't recorded in a set period of time, usually a year. You can then place the tune with another publisher, or, if you believe the first publisher can still get the song recorded, you can extend the contract with the first (see "Negotiating Your Contract"). Second, you can keep your song alive by pitching it yourself. "One of the best pitchmen in the world is the writer," says Randy Goodrum, who wrote "You Needed Me." Some publishers make a point of introducing songwriters to producers and A&R men so the writer can help sell his tunes.

Other publishers frown on the practice, however. "I don't believe in that unless the songwriter says, 'I'm best friends with Olivia Newton-John,' " says Arthur Braun. "Any publisher that expects the songwriter to help plug is insecure in his own job." In many cases you'll have to trust the publisher to do his job of selling the song. "No one in our position makes money sitting on your song," says publisher Bob Montgomery.

Giving your publisher an occasional gentle push doesn't hurt. Don Gant of Tree International was once on his way to pitch material to producer Billy Sherrill for Johnny Paycheck when he ran into Sonny Throckmorton, one of Tree's writers. Throckmorton asked that a particular song be pitched to Sherrill, and though Gant thought the song wouldn't fit Paycheck, he took Throckmorton's advice. That song was the only one Sherrill selected that day. Input from the songwriter helped get a recording.

Yet, remember the word "gentle" in the above advice. Publisher/producer Mike Kosser (author of *Bringing it to Nashville*) says he will turn down a song if he knows the writer will pester him about it. "I'd rather not enlarge a catalog with something that would have a writer calling and calling," he says.

When you land your publishing contract, fill the publisher in on your goals. Let the publisher know, for example, if you want to become a recording artist. The publisher can possibly use contacts in helping you achieve that goal; after all, if you become a star, the publisher stands to profit from increased exposure of your songs. Ask if you can sing or play on the publisher's demos, whether they're your songs or someone else's. Many publishers maintain their own recording studios, and hire musicians and vocalists to record demos. Tree, for instance, relies in part on its "family" of songwriters in getting demo session musicians and vocalists. Leeds Levy notes that Glen Campbell and Tony Bennett got started as demo singers.

Arthur Braun allows his writers to sing on demos if possible, because "It helps them develop," he says. "It gives them studio experience." This practice, he adds, is becoming more commonplace. To prove his point, he shows off a telegram that happens to be on his desk: "RE MY LETTER DATED 16 MARCH KINDLY TELX SONG TITLE PUBLISHER COMPOSER AS WE WOULD LIKE TO RECORD IT YR HELP GREATLY APPRECIATED ALSO WHO IS THE SINGER ON TAPE WE LIKE HER VOICE."

"The publishers, we have to remember, are also dealing with producers and record companies continually," notes John Braheny. "So if you're singing on your own demos, they—as a side effect to bringing your songs to the producer—are also exposing you as an artist."

The following is a list of publishers that are eager to provide that service, and all the others mentioned above, to you if your material matches their needs. Additional publishers can be found in the *International Buyer's Guide*, published by *Billboard* magazine, though the *Buyer's Guide* lists names and addresses only.

A DISH-A-TUNES, LTD., 1650 Broadway, Suite 1107, New York NY 10019. (212)245-9612. Affiliate: Mighty Mo Music (ASCAP). President: Ken Williams. Music publisher. Estab. 1970. BMI. Pays standard royalties.
How to Contact: Submit demo tape and lead sheet. Prefers 7½ ips reel-to-reel or cassette with 4 songs maximum on demo. SASE. Reports in 1 month.
Music: Disco; R&B; and soul.

A.Q.E.M. LTEE, 450 E. Beaumont Ave., St. Bruno, Quebec, Canada J3V 2R3. (514)563-7838. President: Christian Lefort. Music publisher and record company. Estab. 1967. CAPAC. See S.M.C.L. Productions for details.

ABLE MUSIC, INC., Box 306, Vansant VA 24631. (703)498-4556. Affiliates: Modoc Music (ASCAP) and Penny Pinchers (SESAC). President: Roy John Fuller. Music publisher. Estab. 1974. BMI. Published 100 songs in 1977; plans 300 in 1979. Pays standard royalty. Sometimes secures songwriters on salary basis: pays $150/week plus royalties to develop new material.
How to Contact: Submit demo tape and lead sheet. Prefers 7½ ips reel-to-reel or 8-track cartridge with 1-3 songs on demo. "Do not expect tape to be returned. If it's good, we'll contact

you. Material will be returned only if prior arrangements are made by phone." Reports in 1 week.
Music: Church/religious; C&W; disco; folk; gospel; MOR; progressive; rock (hard); soul; and top 40/pop. Recently published "Angel in Disguise" and "Your Song," recorded by Roy John Fuller (C&W); and "The Biggest Lie," recorded by Ken Jordan (C&W).

ABOVE MUSIC PUBLICATIONS, Box 111291, Nashville TN 37211. (615)242-0414. Affiliates: High Bluff Music (ASCAP), Beyond Music (BMI) and Lively Music (BMI). Owner/President: Tom McConnell. Music publisher and record producer. Estab. 1970. ASCAP. Pays standard royalty. Sometimes secures songwriters on salary basis.
How to Contact: Submit demo tape and lead sheet. Prefers 7½ ips mono reel-to-reel with 1-5 songs on demo. SASE. Reports in 3 weeks.
Music: Blues; C&W; disco; easy listening; gospel; MOR; progressive; rock; soul; and top 40/pop. Recently published "Easy Touch," recorded by Sammi Smith; "If I Never Had Met You, Baby," recorded by Narvel Felts; "Loser, Keeps, Finders, Weepers," recorded by John Wesly Ryles; and "Loving You," recorded by Ray Sanders.

ACCABONAC MUSIC, 50 Holly Hill Lane, Greenwich CT 06830. (203)661-0707. Music publisher. ASCAP. See Cherry Lane Music for details. "We do not accept unsolicited material."

ACCRETIVE COPYRIGHT, Doug Moody Productions, 6277 Selma Ave., Hollywood CA 90028. (213)464-9667. Affiliate: Accumulated Copyrights (BMI). President: Doug Moody. Coordinator: Nancy Faith. Music publisher, record company and production company. Estab. 1968. ASCAP. Published 100 songs in 1978; plans 100 in 1979. Pays standard royalty. Charges for some services: "We charge only if they wish to produce masters or demos not to be published by us in our own studios."
How to Contact: Submit demo tape or submit demo tape and lead sheet. Prefers 7½ ips quarter-track, 15 ips half-track, or 15 ips 16-track reel-to-reel or cassette. SASE. Reports in 1 month.
Music: Blues; C&W; easy listening; gospel (modern rock/pop); MOR; rockabilly; soul; top 40/pop; and spoken word plays (up to 1 hour in length).

ACCUMULATED COPYRIGHTS, Doug Moody Productions, 6277 Selma Ave., Hollywood CA 90028. (213)464-9667. President: Doug Moody. Coordinator: Nancy Faith. Music publisher, record company and production company. Estab. 1968. BMI. "We produce and originate TV and film themes. We need instrumental music: country and pop."
Music: Blues; church/religious; C&W; easy listening; gospel; jazz instrumental; MOR; R&B; soul; top 40/pop; and rockabilly. Recently published "Hang Gliding," recorded by Gary Joe Wade/Mystic Records (rockabilly); "Van Nuys Boulevard," recorded by Dennis and the Angels/Mystic Records (pop); and "Send It On Down," recorded by the Long Beach Southernairs/Hooks Records (gospel). See Accretive Copyright for submission details.

ACE DEUCE TREY MUSIC, 39 W. 55th St., New York NY 10019. (212)586-3350. A&R Director: Nate Adams Jr. Music publisher.
Music: Disco; R&B; and soul. See Lorijoy Music for submission details.

ACKEE MUSIC, 7720 Sunset Blvd., Los Angeles CA 90046. (213)851-1466. President: Lionel Conway. General Manager: Allan McDougall. Music publisher. ASCAP. See Island Music for details.

ACOUSTIC MUSIC, INC., Box 1546, Nashville TN 37202. (615)244-3450. Affiliates: Lawday Music Corp. (BMI), Daydan Music Corp. (ASCAP), and Allmusic Inc. (ASCAP). Professional manager: Lamar Morris. Music publisher. Estab. 1970. BMI. Published 50 songs in 1978. Pays standard royalties.
How to Contact: Query, arrange personal interview, or submit demo tape and lead sheet. Prefers 7½ ips reel-to-reel with 2-5 songs on demo. SASE. Reports in 1 month.
Music: C&W; folk; MOR and gospel. Recently published "Woman" (by Gary S. Paxton) recorded by Don Gibson/Hickory (country); "Honeymoon Feelin'" (by Gary S. Paxton) recorded by Roy Clark/ABC Records (pop, country); "Sweet Susannah" (by Floyd Guilbeau) recorded by Kris and Rita/Monument Records (Cajun, country); and "The Best is Yet to Come" (by Lamar Morris and Lathan Hudson), recorded on CBS Records (pop, country).

ACUFF ROSE, INC., 2510 Franklin Rd., Nashville TN 37204. Affiliate: Milene Music

(ASCAP). (615)385-3031. Vice President: John R. Brown. Music publisher. Estab. 1942. BMI. Published 200 songs in 1978. Pays standard royalties.
How to Contact: Query. Prefers 7½ ips reel-to-reel with 2-4 songs on demo. "Must be addressed to a person previously contacted." SASE. Reports in 1 month.
Music: C&W.

ADDIX MUSIC CO., INC., 6430 Sunset Blvd., Suite 921, Los Angeles CA 90028. (213)461-3091. Director of Creative Affairs: B. Ficks, 2 Music Circle S., Nashville TN 37203. Music publisher. ASCAP. See Famous Music Corp. for details.

ADVENTURE MUSIC CO., 1201 16th Ave. S., Nashville TN 37212. (615)320-7287. Affiliates: Touchdown Music (BMI) Purple Cow Music (ASCAP), Turkey Creek Music (BMI) and Andiron Music (BMI). President/Owner: Chuck Chellman. Music publisher and record producer. Estab. 1967. ASCAP. Published 75 songs in 1977. Pays negotiable royalty.
How to Contact: Submit demo tape and lead sheet. Prefers 7½ ips reel-to-reel with 1-4 songs on demo. SASE. Reports in 3 weeks.
Music: Bluegrass; blues; C&W; easy listening; rock; and soul. Recently published "Hangin' on by a Heartstring," recorded by Freddie Hart (C&W); "Charley Hustle," recorded by Pamela Neal/RCA Records (disco); "2,000 Years Ahead of His Time," recorded by Billy Don Burns/Four Star Records (religious pop/disco); and "Baby When It Comes to Loving You," recorded by Bobby Vinton/ABC Records (country/pop).

AFTER DARK MUSIC, Playboy Music Publishing, 8560 Sunset Blvd., Los Angeles CA 90069. Assistant to the President: Jonne-Marie Switzler. BMI. "Our companies are not currently active. We are only working our catalogs."

ALGEE MUSIC, 6255 Sunset Blvd., Suite 603, Hollywood CA 90028. (213)462-2251. Air Assistant: Kevin Magowan. Music publisher. Estab. 1963. BMI. See Al Gallico Music for details.

ALICIA MUSIC, 82 St. Joseph Blvd. W., Montreal, Quebec, Canada H2T 2P4. (514)849-3776. President: Christopher J. Reed. Music publisher. Estab. 1974. CAPAC. See Intermede Musique for details.

ALL OF A SUDDEN MUSIC, INC., 750 Kappock St., Riverdale NY 10463. (212)884-6014. President: Alan Korwin. Creative Director: Michael Berman. A&R Director: Steve Michaels. Music publisher. Estab. 1975. ASCAP.
Music: Top 40/pop; disco; R&B; rock; and MOR. Recently published "Who's Gonna Love Me" (by Alfie Davison), recorded by the Imperials/Omni Records (pop/disco). See Sudden Rush Music for submission details.

ALLEGHENY MOUNTAIN MUSIC, Box 50, Goodlettsville TN 37072. Professional Manager: Dick Shuey. Music publisher. SESAC. See Lufaye Publishing for details.

ALLIES DU NORD, 82 St. Joseph Blvd. W., Montreal, Quebec, Canada H2T 2P4. (514)849-3776. President: Christopher J. Reed. Music publisher. Estab. 1974. PROCAN. See Intermede Musique for details.

ALLMUSIC, INC., Box 1546, Nashville TN 37202. (615) 244-3450. Professional Manager: Lamar Morris. Music publisher. ASCAP. See Acoustic Music for details.

ALMO MUSIC, 1416 N. La Brea, Hollywood CA 90028. (213)469-2411. Contact: Brenda Andrews. Music publisher and record company. See Irving Music for details.

AL'S WRITTEN MUSIC PUBLISHERS, 1313 Washington, Parsons KS 67357. (316)421-1666. Manager: Albert H. Monday. Music publisher and record company. Estab. 1970. BMI. Published 5 songs in 1977. Pays 3% royalty.
How to Contact: Submit demo tape and lead sheet or submit master tape. Prefers 7½ ips reel-to-reel with 2-20 songs on demo. SASE. Reports in 1 month. "We're not responsible for misplaced or lost songs. No songs will be returned that do not include SASE."
Music: Bluegrass; blues; C&W; disco; easy listening; jazz; MOR; progressive; R&B; rock; and top 40/pop. Recently published "Reading My Heart" (by Al Monday), recorded by Debbie Sue/Queen City Records and "Big Time Joe" (by Verge Brown), recorded by Debbie Sue/Queen City Records.

ALTAM, 6255 Sunset Blvd., Suite 603, Hollywood CA 90028. (213)462-2251. Air Assistant: Kevin Magowan. Music publisher. Estab. 1963. BMI. See Al Gallico Music for details.

ALVA MUSIC, E.J. Gurren Music Group, 3929 Kentucky Dr., Los Angeles CA 90068. (213)980-7501. Owner: Eddie Gurren. Music publisher. Estab. 1972. BMI. See E.J. Gurren Music for details.

AMALGAMATED TULIP CORP., 117 W. Rockland Rd., Libertyville IL 60048. (312)362-4060. Affiliate: Much More Music (BMI). Director of Publishing and Administration: Mary Chris. Music publisher and record company. Estab. 1969. BMI. Published 59 songs in 1977. Pays standard royalties.
How to Contact: Submit demo tape. Prefers reel-to-reel or cassette with 2-5 songs on demo. SASE. Reports in 1-3 months.
Music: Progressive country; easy listening; and MOR.

ANACRUSIS MUSIC, 1650 Broadway, New York NY 10019. (212)765-4495. Affiliate: Bandora Music (BMI). A&R Directors: Ezra Cook, Steve Loeb. Music publisher, record company and record producer. Estab. 1972. ASCAP. Payment negotiable.
How to Contact: Submit demo tape and lead sheet. Prefers 7½ ips reel-to-reel with 1-3 songs on demo. "If lyrics aren't clear, send a copy of them." Does not return unsolicited material. Reports in 1 month.
Music: C&W; easy listening; MOR; rock; soul; and top 40/pop. Recently published "One Step Away," recorded by the Spinners (soul); "Birthday Boy," recorded by Buzz Cason (rock); and "Foxy Bitch," recorded by Cherry Vanilla (punk rock).

ANDIRON MUSIC CO., 1201 16th Ave. S., Nashville TN 37212. (615)320-7287. President/Owner: Chuck Chellman. Music publisher and record producer. Estab. 1967. BMI. See Adventure Music for details.

ANDROMEDA MUSIC, 9034 Sunset Blvd., Los Angeles CA 90069. (213)275-5002. Director of Publishing: Lori Leis. Music publisher. ASCAP. See Heavy Music for details.

ANGELA DAWN MUSIC, Box U, Hendersonville TN 37075. (615)824-9577. Affiliate: Textor Music (BMI). Owner: Bill Textor. Music publisher. Estab. 1977. ASCAP. Published 50 songs in 1978; plans 100 in 1979. Pays 5-10% royalty.
How to Contact: Submit demo tape and lead sheet. Prefers cassette with 1-5 songs on demo. SASE. Reports in 1 month.
Music: Church/religious and gospel.

ANNIE OVER MUSIC, 3422 Hopkins St., Nashville TN 37215. Affiliates: Tessies Tunes (BMI) and Bobby's Beat Music (SESAC). General Manager: Bobby Fischer. Music publisher. ASCAP. Pays standard royalties.
How to Contact: Submit demo tape and lyric sheet. Prefers 7½ ips reel-to-reel or cassette. Will return material "if time permits." SASE. Reports as soon as possible.
Music: C&W (modern) and MOR. Recently published "What in Her World Did I Do" (by Bobby Fischer and Don Wayne), recorded by Eddy Arnold/RCA Records (modern C&W); and "The Great Chicago Fire" (by Bobby Fischer and Dave Kirby), recorded by Faron Young/MCA Records (modern C&W).

ANTONE MUSIC PUBLISHERS, Box 113, Woburn MA 01801. (617)933-1474. Manager: Frank Paul. Music publisher, record company and theatrical booking agency. Estab. 1950. ASCAP. See Donna Music for details.

AOUT, 82 St. Joseph Blvd. W., Montreal, Quebec, Canada H2T 2P4. (514)849-3776. President: Christopher J. Reed. Music publisher. Estab. 1974. PROCAN. See Intermede Musique for details.

APPLE BUTTER MUSIC, Box 6507, 2181 Victory Pkwy., Cincinnati OH 45206. (513)861-1500. Owner: Dan Morgan. Estab. 1968. ASCAP. See Hal Bernard Enterprises for details.

APPLEBERRY MUSIC, 11 Riverside Dr. #13C-W, New York NY 10023. (212)724-6120. Managing Director: Laurie Goldstein. Music publisher. Estab. 1960. BMI. See Gopam Enterprises for details.

APRIL/BLACKWOOD MUSIC, 1801 Century Park W., Los Angeles CA 90067. (213)556-4700. Contact: Terry Powell. Music publisher and record company.
How to Contact: Submit demo tape and lead sheet. Prefers cassette with 1-3 songs on demo. SASE. Reports in 1 month.
Music: Blues; C&W; disco; easy listening; folk; jazz; MOR; progressive; R&B; rock; soul; and top 40/pop.

APRIL/BLACKWOOD MUSIC, 1350 Avenue of the Americas, New York NY 10019. (212)975-4889. Professional Manager: Bert Haber. Music publisher. BMI. ASCAP. Pays negotiable royalties.
How to Contact: Query. Does not return unsolicited material.
Music: All types.

ARCHER MUSIC, Box 201, Tecumseh OK 74873. Affiliate: Rapture Music (SESAC). President: Darrell Archer. Music publisher and record company. Estab. 1970. SESAC. Published 8 songs in 1977; plans 60 in 1979. Pays 10% royalty. Buys some material outright; pays $20-85. Charges for some services: "Most of the time, we do not. Occasionally, we will ask the writer to pay for printing. All typesetting, cover design, arranging costs, promotion and other costs are part of our expense."
How to Contact: Submit demo tape and lead sheet. Prefers 7½ ips reel-to-reel or cassette with 3-6 songs on demo. "Lyric sheets will suffice if the writer does not have lead sheets. We do like to see complete choral arrangements, too." SASE. Reports in 1 month.
Music: Children's (choruses for young age groups for Sunday school); choral (sacred); church/religious; and gospel. Recently published "The Sounds of a Gospel Song," recorded by Pilgrim's Quartet (gospel); "God Still Lives," recorded by Brosher Family (gospel); and "Then the Light Shone In," recorded by Darrel Archer (gospel).

ARIAN PUBLICATIONS, O.A.S. Music Group, 805 18th Ave. S., Nashville TN 37203. Co-Directors: Dane Bryant, Steve Singleton. Music publisher. Estab. 1975. ASCAP. See O.A.S. Music Group for details.

ARZEE MUSIC, Arzee Recording Co., 3010 N. Front St., Philadelphia PA 19133. (215)739-7501. Affiliates: Valleybrook (ASCAP), Rex Zario Music (BMI) and Seabreeze Music (BMI). President: Rex Zario. General Manager: Dave Wilson. Music publisher, booking agency and record company. Estab. 1950. ASCAP. Plans 100 in 1979. Pays standard royalties.
How to Contact: Submit demo tape and lead sheet. Prefers 7½ or 15 ips reel-to-reel or cassette with 5-10 songs on demo. SASE. Reports in 1 month.
Music: Bluegrass; C&W; easy listening; folk; and top 40/pop. Recently published "Go Man, Go Get Gone," recorded by Rex Zario; and "I Was the One," recorded by Bob Saven (pop/rock).

ASH VALLEY MUSIC, 25 Music Square E., Nashville TN 37203. Contact: Bobby Bradley. Music publisher. ASCAP. See Forrest Hills Music for details.

ASSORTED MUSIC, 2212 4th Ave., Seattle WA 98121. (206)682-5278. Director, West Coast Operations: JoDee Omer. Music publisher. Estab. 1973. BMI. See Mighty Three Music, Seattle WA office, for details.

ATLANTIC MUSIC, 6124 Selma Ave., Hollywood CA 90028. Contact: Professional Manager. Music publisher. BMI. See Criterion Music for details.

ATV MUSIC, ATV Music Corp., 1370 Avenue of the Americas, New York NY 10019. Contact: Professional Manager. Music publisher. BMI. See ATV Music, Nashville TN office, for details.

ATV MUSIC, ATV Music Corp., 1217 16th Ave. S., Nashville TN 37212. (615)327-2753. Affiliate: Welbeck (ASCAP). Professional Manager: Jim Rushing. Music Publisher. BMI. Pays standard royalties.
How to Contact: Submit demo tape and lyric sheet. Prefers 7½ ips reel-to-reel with 1-3 songs on demo. SASE. Reports as soon as possible.
Music: Bluegrass; C&W; disco; easy listening; gospel; MOR; R&B; rock; soul; and top 40/pop. Recently published "Dig a Little Deeper" (by Roger Bowling and Jody Emerson), recorded by Oak Ridge Boys/ABC Records (country); "The Diplomat (by Roger Bowling), recorded by Cal Smith/MCA Records (country); and "Yesterday" (by Lennon and

McCartney), recorded by Billie Jo Spears/UA Records (country/pop).

AUGUST THIRD MUSIC, System Four Artists, Ltd., 145 E. 82nd St., New York NY 10028. President: Stephen F. Johnson. Music publisher and management firm. Estab. 1976. ASCAP. See Mistral Music for details.

AVIATION MUSIC/JEF RECORDS, LTD., 102-104 Gloucester Place, London, England W1H 3PH. Director of Publicity: Peter Felstead. Music publisher and record company. Estab. 1976.
How to Contact: Submit cassette with 3 maximum songs on demo. "Put name and address on cassette as well as box or envelope." SASE. Reports in 10 weeks.
Music: C&W; disco; easy listening; progressive; rock; and top 40/pop.

AXENT, LTD., 700 W. Jackson St., Biloxi MS 39533. (601)374-1900. Producers: Doug Mays, Rusty Russum. Music publisher, booking agency and record company. Estab. 1970. BMI. Pays 2-5% royalty.
How to Contact: Submit demo tape. Prefers 7½ ips reel-to-reel with 4-7 songs on demo. SASE. Reports in 1 month.
Music: Bluegrass; blues; children's; choral; church/religious; classical; C&W; disco; easy listening; folk; gospel; jazz; MOR; progressive; rock; soul; and top 40/pop. Recently published "I Can Feel the Rain," recorded by Storm (pop); "Tonight I'll Be Sleeping Alone," recorded by Patsy Mitchell (C&W); and "Strawberry Man," recorded by Heater (rock).

AXENT PUBLISHING CO., Biloxi MS 39530. (601)436-3927. President: Marion Carpenter. Music publisher, record company and record producer. ASCAP. See Singing River Publishing for details.

BABY POWDER MUSIC, 132 Merrimac Dr., Trumbull CT 06611. (203)261-9610. President: Paul Leka. Music publisher and record producer. Estab. 1968. ASCAP.
Music: Disco; easy listening; MOR; progressive; R&B; rock; soul; and top 40/pop. See Paul Leka Music for submission details.

BAG ENRG., 450 E. Beaumont Ave., St. Bruno, Quebec, Canada J3V 2R3. (514)653-7838. President: Christian Lefort. Music publisher and record company. Estab. 1967. CAPAC. See S.M.C.L. Productions for submission details.

BAINBRIDGE MUSIC, First American Records, Box 3925, Bellevue WA 98009. (206)625-9992. Affiliates: Burdette Music (BMI) and Marinwood Music (ASCAP). President: Jerry Dennon. Music publisher and record company. Estab. 1965. BMI. Published 50 songs in 1977; plans 500 in 1979. Pays standard royalties.
How to Contact: Submit demo tape or submit demo tape and lead sheet. Prefers 7½ ips reel-to-reel or cassette with 2-6 songs on demo. SASE. Reports in 2 months.
Music: Blues; easy listening; folk; jazz; MOR; progressive; rock; soul; and top 40/pop.

BAKER'S MULE, Box 3233, Berkeley CA 94703. Contact: Stefan Grossman. Music publisher. BMI. See Kicking Mule Publishing for details.

BAL AND BAL MUSIC PUBLISHING CO., Box 369, LaCanada CA 91011. (213)790-1242. President: Adrian Bal. Music publisher. Estab. 1965. ASCAP. Published 5 songs in 1978. Pays 10% royalty.
How to Contact: Submit demo tape and lead sheet. Prefers 7½ ips reel-to-reel or cassette with 3-5 songs on demo. SASE. Reports in 3 weeks.
Music: Children's; choral; church/religious; C&W; easy listening; MOR; rock (medium); and top 40/pop. Recently published "Christmas is Coming" (choral arrangement) and "Bach and Forth," recorded by Adrian L. Bal, Lee Ritenour and Dave Crotwell (classical rock).

BAMBOO MUSIC, 1670 Inkster Blvd., Winnipeg, Manitoba, Canada R2X 2W8. Copyright Coordinator: Rick Kives. Music publisher and record company. Estab. 1964. BMI. See K-Tel Music for details.

BANDOLERO MUSIC, Box 1005, Englewood Cliffs NJ 07632. President/A&R Director: Clancy Morales. Music publisher. Estab. 1972. BMI. See Maranta Music for details.

BANDORA MUSIC, 1650 Broadway, New York NY 10019. (212)765-4495. A&R Directors:

Ezra Cook, Steve Loeb. Music publisher, record company and record producer. Estab. 1972. BMI. See Anacrusis Music for details.

BARADAT MUSIC, 1310 E. Kern St., Tulare CA 93274. (209)686-2533. President: Raymond A. Baradat. A&R Director: Art Stewart. Music publisher and record company. Estab. 1975. BMI. Published 4 songs in 1978. Pays 25-50% royalty.
How to Contact: Submit demo tape. Prefers 7½ ips reel-to-reel with 2-6 songs on demo. SASE. Reports in 3 weeks.
Music: C&W; disco; jazz; rock (soft); soul; and top 40/pop. Recently published "Sierra Breeze" (by Gene Short), recorded by Gene Short/Tadarab Records (jazz); "Set Her Free" (by Joe Luiz and Rod Gibson), recorded by Joe Luiz/Charade Records (country); and "If I Get Through To You" (by Frank Spina), recorded by Arvada/Charade Records (soft rock).

BARLENMIR HOUSE MUSIC, INC., 413 City Island Ave., New York NY 10064. President: Barry L. Mirenburg. Creative Director: Leonard Steffan. Music publisher, record company and book publisher. Estab. 1972. Published 10 songs in 1978; plans 10 in 1979. BMI. Pays negotiable royalties.
How to Contact: SASE. Reports in 1 month.
Music: Creative.

BARREN RIVER MUSIC, 602 Inverness Ave., Nashville TN 37204. Affiliate: Japonicis Music (ASCAP). Vice President: Don Vinson. Music publisher. BMI. Pays standard royalties.
How to Contact: Submit demo tape. Prefers reel-to-reel. SASE. Reports in 3 weeks.
Music: C&W; country gospel; MOR; progressive; and top 40/pop. Recently published "All I Want for Christmas is My Daddy" (by Richard Koehn), recorded by Michelle Cody/Safari Records (Christmas country); "Merry Christmas, Elvis" (by Jack Toombe), recorded by Michelle Cody/Safari Records (Christmas country); and "Aderian McCarthy" (by Glenn Ashworth), recorded by Don Vinson/Safari Records (country religious).

bARTISTIC MUSIC, 1921 Walnut St., Philadelphia PA 19103. (215)561-1283. Music Director/A&R: Bart Arntz. Music publisher, record company and management firm. Estab. 1975. BMI. Published 50 songs in 1977. Offers $25 advance on royalties.
How to Contact: Submit demo tape. Prefers 7½ ips reel-to-reel or cassette with 1-4 songs on demo. SASE. Reports in 3 weeks.
Music: Disco; soul; top 40/pop; and "strong instrumentals of all types."

BARUTH MUSIC, 12501 Madison Ave., Cleveland OH 44107. (216)521-1222. Professional Manager: Debbie Wolfe. Music publisher, record company, record producer, management firm and promoter. Estab. 1972. ASCAP. Published 4 songs in 1978; plans 24 in 1979, 75 in 1980. Pays standard royalties.
How to Contact: Submit demo tape and lead sheet. Prefers 7½ ips reel-to-reel tape with 2-4 songs on demo. SASE. Reports in 3 weeks.
Music: Folk; progressive; R&B; rock; and top 40/pop. Recently published "Soothe Me," (by David Baruth) recorded by Quartz/Music Adventures (rock); "Jack the Ripper," (by Joe Uherc) recorded by Strychnine/Music Adventures (rock); and "This Time to the End," (by Eddie Pecchio) recorded by Great Lakes Band/Music Adventures (pop).

BAS MUSIC PUBLISHING, 5925 Kirby Dr., Suite 226, Houston TX 77005. (713)522-2713. Owner: Shelton Bissell. Music publisher and record producer. Estab. 1964. ASCAP. See Tuff Enuff Music Publishing for details.

BASSE VILLE, 82 St. Joseph Blvd. W., Montreal, Quebec, Canada H2T 2P4. (514)849-3776. President: Christopher J. Reed. Music publisher. Estab. 1974. CAPAC. See Intermede Musique for details.

BATHURST MUSIC, Box 12647, Nashville TN 37212. (416)625-2676. President: Jury Krytiuk. General Manager: Mark Altman. Music publisher and record company. Estab. 1971. BMI. See Morning Music (USA) for details.

JOHN BAVA MUSIC, Box 187, Davis WV 26260. Affiliate: Panhandle Music (BMI). Owner: John Bava. SESAC. Pays standard royalty.
How to Contact: Submit demo tape and lead sheet or submit lead sheet. Accepts any kind of tape. SASE. Reports in 3 weeks.
Music: C&W and hillbilly gospel. Recently published "Pain in My Heart," recorded by Roy

Clark (C&W); "The Darker the Night," recorded by Alan McGill (sacred); and "To See My Saviour's Face," recorded by Blue Ridge Quartet.

BEACON HILL MUSIC, Box 527, Kansas City MO 64141. (816)931-1900. Music Editor: Lyndell Leatherman. Music publisher. Estab. 1926. SESAC.
Music: Church/religious and gospel. Recently published *Spirit of '76* (album by Paul Johnson), recorded by Tempo Singers/Tempo Records (patriotic rock musical); *Songs of Praise* (arranged by Robert Berglund, recorded by Robert Berglund Chorale/Tempo Records (collection of hymn arrangements); and *America Depends on You* (album by Otis Skillings), recorded by Renaissance/Tempo Records (patriotic rock musical). See Lillenas Publishing for submission details.

THE BEAU-JIM AGENCY, INC., Box 758, Lake Jackson TX 77566. (713)393-1703. President: James E. "Buddy" Hooper. Music publisher, record company, booking agency and management firm. Estab. 1972. ASCAP. Published 2 songs in 1978. Pays standard minimum royalty.
How to Contact: Arrange personal interview or submit demo tape and lead sheet. Prefers cassette with 1-5 songs on demo. SASE. Reports in 3 weeks.
Music: Blues; C&W; easy listening; MOR; rock (no hard rock); and top 40/pop. Recently published "Life," recorded by Barry Kayle; and "She's My Lover," recorded by Jimmy Hooper (C&W).

BEKSON, Gene Kennedy Enterprises, Inc., 2125 8th Ave. S., Nashville TN 37204. (615)383-6002. Vice President: Linda Kennedy. Music publisher. Estab. 1975. BMI. See Gene Kennedy Enterprises for details.

BELINDA MUSIC, 21 Music Circle E., Nashville TN 37203.BMI. See Chappell Music for details.

BELL BOY MUSIC, 2212 4th Ave., Seattle WA 98J21. (206)682-5278. Director, West Coast Operations: JoDee Omer. Music publisher. Estab. 1973. BMI. See Mighty Three Music, Seattle office, for details.

BELL HOLDING MUSIC, 1260 E. Main, Meriden CT 06450. (203)728-5639. President: Bruce Lloyd. Music publisher. Estab. 1970. ASCAP. Pays 2-5% royalty. Buys some material outright; pays $500 minimum.
How to Contact: Submit demo tape. Prefers chromium dioxide cassette with 3-10 songs on demo. SASE. Reports in 1 week.
Music: Bluegrass; blues; C&W; easy listening; folk; jazz; and MOR. Recently published "Starting All Over Again," recorded by David Liska (Bluegrass); and "Fonzie for President," recorded by Bob Davey (rock).

JOHN T. BENSON PUBLISHING CO., 365 Great Circle Rd., Nashville TN 37228. Affiliates: Heartwarming Music (BMI) and Dimension Music (SESAC). Contact: Unsolicited Music Review Committee. Music publisher. ASCAP. Pays standard royalty on quarterly basis.
How to Contact: Query about needs and submission policy. Prefers cassette. SASE. Reports as soon as possible.
Music: Gospel (all-Southern gospel, MOR, contemporary, traditional, etc.). Recently published "Rise Again," recorded by Dallas Holm (gospel ballad); "Learning to Lean," recorded by Blackwood Brothers (Southern gospel); and "Love Lifted Me," recorded by Kenny Rogers (gospel).

BEOLF MUSIC, Box 169, Bridgeport MI 48722. (517)777-8638. President: J.S. Leach. Music publisher and record company. Estab. 1973. BMI. See James S. Enterprises for details.

HAL BERNARD ENTERPRISES, INC., Box 6507, 2181 Victory Pkwy., Cincinnati OH 45206. (513)861-1500. Affiliates: Sunnyslope Music (ASCAP), Baker's Lane (ASCAP), Bumpershoot Music (BMI), Apple Butter Music (ASCAP), Bluestocking (ASCAP), OPI Music (ASCAP), Rong (ASCAP), Teakbird (ASCAP) and Smorgaschord Music (ASCAP). President: Stan Hertzman. Music publisher, record company and management firm. Estab. 1968. Pays negotiable royalty.
How to Contact: Submit demo tape and lead sheet. Prefers 7½ ips reel-to-reel or cassette with 1-6 songs on demo. Wants leadered tapes with an index. SASE. Reports in 1 month.
Music: Disco; progressive; rock; soul; and top 40/pop. Recently published "Jaime," recorded

Songwriter's Market Close-Up

Ray Stevens' advice to songwriters is simple: "If you're going to be a songwriter, be a songwriter." To Stevens, writer of a variety of songs from "Guitarzan" to "Everything Is Beautiful," being a songwriter means working at it every day. Stevens recalls talking to an aspiring songwriter:

"What did you write today?" Stevens asked.

"Well, nothing today."

"Yesterday?"

"Well, nothing yesterday either. I haven't written anything in a long time."

"Why, then," Stevens asked, "do you call yourself a songwriter?"

by Blaze (top 40/pop); "Face the Music," recorded by Meg Christian (pop); "Eastern Avenue River Railway Blues," recorded by Jerry Jeff Walker/Elektra Records (pop/country); and "Like a Falling Star," recorded by Blaze (top 40/rock).

JOHN BERTHELOT & ASSOCIATESS, Box 13977, New Orleans LA 70185. Affiliate: Storyville Publishing (BMI). President: John Berthelot. Music publisher. Estab. 1970. ASCAP. Published 4 songs in 1977; plans 20 in 1979. Pays standard royalty.
How to Contact: Submit demo tape and lyric or lead sheet. Prefers 7½ ip reel-to-reel or cassette with 1-4 songs on demo. SASE. Reports in 1 month.
Music: C&W; jazz; MOR; soul; and top 40/pop. Recently published "Lookin' for Love," recorded by Scooter Lee (C&W); "The Roach," recorded by Alvin Thomas (jazz/R&B); and "Lovin' Memories," recorded by Cynthia Sheeler (R&B/pop/MOR).

BETH-ANN MUSIC CO., 615 Baldwin Lane, Carrcroft, Wilmington DE 19803. (302)762-2410. President: Albert G. Teoli. Music publisher. Estab. 1963. ASCAP. Published 4 songs in 1978. Pays 10% royalty.
How to Contact: Submit demo tape and lead sheet. Prefers 7½ ips reel-to-reel or cassette with 3 songs on demo. SASE. Reports in 3 weeks.
Music: C&W; easy listening; folk; gospel; rock (country); and top 40/pop. Recently published "Time" and "It's So Nice to Dream," recorded by Mary Mulligan (gospel/easy listening); and "Paesano Mio," recorded by Clem West (novelty).

BEVERLY HILLS MUSIC PUBLISHING, c/o Lawrence Herbst Investment Trust Fund, Box 1659, Beverly Hills CA 90213. (213)248-1084. President/Administrator: Lawrence Herbst. Music publisher and record company. Estab. 1966. BMI. Pays standard royalties.
How to Contact: Submit demo tape and lead sheet, arrange personal interview, submit demo tape or submit lead sheet. Prefers reel-to-reel, cassette or 8-track cartridge. SASE. Reports in 3 weeks.
Music: Bluegrass; blues; children's; choral; church/religious; classical; C&W; disco; easy listening; folk; gospel; jazz; MOR; progressive; rock; soul; and top 40/pop.

BEYOND MUSIC CO., Box i11291, Nashville TN 37211. (615)242-0414. Owner/President: Tom McConnell. Music publisher and record producer. Estab. 1970. BMI. See Above Music Publications for details.

BI-CIRCLE MUSIC, 11 Riverside Dr., #13C-W, New York NY 10023. (212)724-6120. Managing Director: Laurie Goldstein. Music publisher. Estab. 1960. BMI. See Gopam Enterprises for details.

JOHNNY BIENSTOCK MUSIC, 1619 Broadway, New York NY 10019. Professional Manager: Robert Bienstock. Currently overstocked with material.

BIG BAZAAR MUSIC, 450 E. Beaumont Ave., St. Bruno, Quebec, Canada J3V 2R3. (514)653-7838. President: Christian Lefort. Music publisher and record company. Estab. 1967. CAPAC. See S.M.C.L. Productions for submission details.

BIG CIGAR MUSIC CO., 8033 Highland Trail, Los Angeles CA 90046. Affiliates: Evie Sands Music (ASCAP) and Hot Banana Music (ASCAP). Contact: General Manager. Music publisher and record producer. Estab. 1974. BMI. Published 17 songs in 1977; plans 34 in 1978, 40 in 1979. Pays 33&-50% royalty.
How to Contact: Submit demo tape and lead sheet. Prefers 7½ or 15 ips quarter- or half-track reel-to-reel or cassette with 2-4 songs on demo. "Any other information that would be of interest can accompany the tape in letter form." SASE. Reports "as soon as possible."
Music: Disco; easy listening; MOR; progressive; rock (hard, soft, country or progressive); soul; and top 40/pop. Recently published "Love in the Afternoon," recorded by Barbra Streisand and Dionne Warwicke (top 40); "Lady of the Night," recorded by Helen Reddy (top 40); and "I Love Makin' Love to You," recorded by Cher and Gregg Allman (disco/rock/soul).

BIG FUSS MUSIC, 901 Kenilworth Rd., Montreal, Quebec, Canada H3R 2R5. (514)341-6721. President: Leon Aronson. Music publisher, record company and record producer. PROCAN. See Think Big Music for details.

BIG HEART MUSIC, 9454 Wilshire Blvd., Suite 305, Beverly Hills CA 90212. (213)273-7020. Affiliate: Wooden Bear Music (ASCAP). Managing Director: Randy Bash. Randy Bash. Music publisher. Estab. 1976. BMI. Payment negotiable.
How to Contact: Submit demo tape or submit demo tape and lead sheet. Prefers 7½ ips reel-to-reel or cassette with 3-5 songs on demo. SASE. Reports in 2 weeks.
Music: C&W; MOR; rock; soul; and top 40/pop.

BIG MIKE MUSIC, Big Mike Productions, 408 W. 115th St., Suite 2-W, New York NY 10025. (212)222-8715. Manager: Bill Downs. Music publisher. Estab. 1957. BMI. Published 32 songs in 1977. Pays 2½-3% royalty.
How to Contact: Submit demo tape and lead sheet. Prefers cassette with 2-3 songs on demo. "Must have clean lead sheet and good demo with instrumental background. We will not accept tapes with vocal only." SASE. Reports in 1 month.
Music: Disco and soul. Recently published "Mandingo," recorded by P.J.&P. (disco) and "Dance With Me Children," recorded by Chris Bartley and the Ad Libs (disco).

BIG MUSIC, 10 George St., Wallingford CT 06492. (203)269-4465. President: Thomas Cavalier. Vice President: Rudolf Szlaui. Music publisher, record company and management firm. Estab. 1967. ASCAP.
Music: Rock. Recently published "Stupid Enough," "Chemical Fire" and "Waiting" (by Van Duren), recorded by Van Duren/Big Sound Records (rock). See Rohm Music for submission details.

BIG SEVEN MUSIC CORP., 1790 Broadway, New York NY 10019. Affiliate: Planetary (ASCAP). Professional Manager: Phil Kahl. Music publisher and record company. Estab. 1950. BMI.
How to Contact: Submit demo tape and lyric sheets. Prefers 7½ ips reel-to-reel with 1-3 songs on demo. SASE. Reports in 1 month.
Music: Blues; choral; C&W; disco; easy listening; folk; gospel; jazz; MOR; progressive; R&B; rock; soul; and top 40/pop. Recently published the material in *American Graffiti*.

BIG STATE MUSIC, Texas Sound, Inc., 1311 Candlelight Ave., Dallas TX 75116. Affiliate: Pineapple Music (ASCAP). President: Paul Ketter. Music publisher and record company. Estab. 1973. BMI. Published 20 songs in 1978; plans 25 in 1979. Pays standard royalties.
How to Contact: Submit demo tape and lead sheet. Prefers 7½ ips reel-to-reel with 3-6 songs on demo. SASE. Reports in 3 weeks.
Music: C&W; and MOR (country). Recently published "Theodore," recorded by Dave Gregory (Christmas); "Games Grown-Ups Play," recorded by Bunnie Mills (C&W); "Adam's Rib," recorded by Debbie Dierks (C&W); and "Honky Tonkin Woman" (Buddy Howard), recorded by Buddy Howard/Sagittar Records (C&W).

BIL-ETTA MUSIC, 7507 Sunset Blvd., Suite 1, Hollywood CA 90046. (213)935-5786. President: Billy Foster. Vice President: Etta James. Vice President/A&R: Horace Coleman Jr. Music publisher. Estab. 1968. BMI. See Coleman, Kestin & Smith for details.

BILLY BOB PUBLISHING, 2251 Casey Ave., Las Vegas NV 89119. (702)739-6622. Professional Manager: Jay Ramsey. Music publisher. Estab. 1974. BMI. Published 14 songs in 1977. Pays standard royalty.
How to Contact: Submit demo tape and lead sheet. Prefers 7½ ips reel-to-reel or cassette with 1-3 songs on demo. SASE. Reports in 1 month.
Music: C&W; MOR; and top 40/pop. Recently published "Smokey Mountain Cowboy," recorded by Larry Mahan (country); "Wonder Woman," recorded by Jerry Inman (pop); and "People Are Alive and Well," by Expression (MOR).

BIRTHRIGHT MUSIC, 3101 S. Western, Los Angeles CA 90018. (213)731-2460. ASCAP. See Emandell Tunes for details.

BLACK COFFEE MUSIC, INC., Box 4945, Austin TX 78765. (512)452-9411. Vice President: T. White. Music publisher. Estab. 1972. BMI. See Prophecy Publishing for details.

BLACK EAGLE PUBLISHING CO., Box 50, Goodlettsville TN 37072. Professional Manager: Dick Shuey. Music publisher. ASCAP. See Lufaye Publishing for details.

BLEECKER STREET MUSIC, 3929 New Seneca Turnpike, Marcellus NY 13108. (315)673-1117. President/A&R Manager: Vincent Taft. Music publisher, record company and production company. Estab. 1971. BMI. See Katch Nazar for details.

BLEGMAN, VOCCO & CONN, INC., 8544 Sunset Blvd., Los Angeles CA 90069. (213)657-8210. Director of Creative Activities: Ron Vance. Music publisher and record company. ASCAP. See 20th Century Fox Music Publishing for details.

BLUE BOOK MUSIC, 1225 N. Chester Ave., Bakersfield CA 93308. Director: Jim Shaw. Music publisher. Currently overstocked with material.

BLUE BRANCH PUBLISHING, Austin Recording Studio, 4606 Clawson Rd., Austin TX 78745. President: W. Tyler. Vice President: Tommy Byrd. Music publisher, record company and recording studio. BMI. See Erection Publishing for details.

BLUE CUP MUSIC, Little Gem Music, Inc., 38 Music Square E., Nashville TN 37203. (615)254-0892. President: Jack Stillwell. Music publisher, record company and record producer. Estab. 1972. BMI.
Music: C&W and MOR. See Little Gem Music for submission details.

BLUE MACE MUSIC, Box 62263, Virginia Beach VA 23462. (804)340-3366. President: Alex Spencer. Music publisher and record company. Estab. 1969. BMI. Pays standard minimum royalty.
How to Contact: Submit demo tape and lyric sheet or arrange personal interview. Prefers 7½

ips reel-to-reel or cassette with 1-3 songs on demo. SASE. Reports in 2 weeks.
Music: Disco; top 40/pop; rock; and MOR.

BLUE MOUNTAIN MUSIC, 7720 Sunset Blvd., Los Angeles CA 90046. (213)851-1466.
General Manager: Alan McDougall. Music publisher. ASCAP. See Island Music for details

BLUEFORD MUSIC, Box 2271, Palm Springs CA 92262. (714)327-3271. Owner: Kent Fox.
Music publisher and record producer. ASCAP. See Mercantile Music for details.

BLUEMARK MUSIC, 2832 Spring Grove Ave., Cincinnati OH 45225. (513)681-8400.
Contact: A&R Dept. Music publisher and record company. Estab. 1976. ASCAP. See QCA
Music for details.

BLUESTOCKING, Box 6507, 2181 Victory Pkwy., Cincinnati OH 45206. (513)861-1500.
Owner: Annie Dinerman. Music publisher. Estab. 1976. ASCAP. See Hal Bernard Enterprises
for details.

BLUFF CITY CORP., Rt. 1, Vandalia IL 62471. President: Neil F. Clark. Music publisher,
record company, record producer and management firm. Estab. 1978. BMI. Published 26 songs
in 1978. Pays standard royalties.
How to Contact: Query or submit demo tape. Prefers 7½ ips reel-to-reel with 2-6 songs on
demo. SASE. Reports in 1 month.
Music: C&W; disco; rock; and top 40/pop.

BO GAL MUSIC,Box 6687, Wheeling WV 26003. (614)758-5812. Affiliate: Green Up Music
(BMI). President: Bob Gallion. Music publisher and record company. BMI. Published 6 songs
in 1978. Pays standard royalties.
How to Contact: Submit demo tape. Prefers reel-to-reel tape. SASE. Reports in 1 month.
Music: Bluegrass; blues; church/religious; C&W; folk; gospel; MOR; and top 40/pop.
Recently published "The Next Time," (by Don Sniffin) recorded by Patti Powell/Arby
(MOR); and "Looks Like You're Going Anyway" (by Sniffin) recorded by Powell/Arby
(MOR).

BOBBY'S BEAT MUSIC, 3422 Hopkins St., Nashville TN 37215. General Manager: Bobby
Fischer. Music publisher. SESAC.
Music: C&W and MOR. See Annie Over Music for submission details.

BONDI MUSIC, 145 Marlee Ave., Suite 1606, Toronto, Ontario, Canada. US Address: Box
431, Hollywood CA 90028. Affiliate: Palmerston Publishing (CAPAC). President: Peter Foldy.
Music publisher. Estab. 1974. PROCAN. Pays standard royalties.
How to Contact: Submit demo tape or submit acetate disc. Prefers 7½ ips reel-to-reel or
cassette with 1-4 songs on demo. SASE. Reports in 1 month.
Music: Disco; easy listening; MOR; rock; and top 40/pop. Recently published "Face the
Music" and "Roxanne" (Foldy), recorded by P. Foldy/Capitol Records (pop).

BOOMERANG MUSIC, 39 Belmont, Rancho Mirage CA 92270. (714)-346-0075. President:
Scott Seely. Music publisher. See S&R for details.

BORDER STAR MUSIC, Box 0107, Los Angeles CA 90048. Affiliates: Saturday Night Music
(ASCAP); Goodnight Kiss Music (BMI) and Fine Colorado Music (BMI). President: Roger B.
Perry. Music publisher and management firm. Estab. 1976. BMI. Published 50 songs in 1978;
plans 100 in 1979. Pays standard royalties.
How to Contact: Submit demo tape and lyric sheet. Prefers 7½ ips reel-to-reel or cassette with
1-4 songs on demo. Reel-to-reel tapes must be leadered. SASE. Reports in 2 weeks.
Music: Blues; C&W; disco; easy listening; MOR; progressive; R&B; rock; soul; and top
40/pop. Recently published "All the Way" (by Perry, Loe and Reilly), recorded by Pure
Prairie League/RCA Records (country rock); "Murder in the First Degree" (by Pruet),
recorded by Mike Pruet Band/Columbia Records (R&R); and "Gentlemen" (by Fisher),
recorded by Janet Fisher/Kiss Records (top 40/pop).
Tips: "I prefer songs with storylines and strong book choruses. Songs with commerical appeal
only."

BOSKEN MUSIC, 2832 Spring Grove Ave., Cincinnati OH 45225. (513)681-8400. Contact:
A&R Dept. Music publisher and record company. Estab. 1976. BMI. See QCA Music for
details.

BOTTOM LINE MUSIC, INC., 15 W. 4th St., New York NY 10012. (212)228-6300. Contact: Peter Westerbelt. Music publisher. Estab. 1977. ASCAP. Pays standard royalty. Sometimes secures songwriters on salary basis.
How to Contact: Submit demo tape and lead sheet. Prefers reel-to-reel or cassette with 3-4 songs on demo. SASE. Reports in 1 month.
Music: Disco; easy listening; MOR; rock (hard or country); soul; and top 40/pop. Recently published "This Could Be the Night" and " 'Cause You're Mine Now," recorded by R.B. Hudmon (R&B).

BOXCAR MUSIC, 13615 Pinerock, Houston TX 77079. (713) 465-6199. Manager: Peter Breaz. Assistant Manager: Paul Eakin. Music publisher, record company and record producer. Estab. 1978. BMI. Published 15 songs in 1978; plans 50 in 1979, 50 in 1980. Pays standard royalties.
How to Contact: Query, arrange personal interview, submit demo tape, or submit demo tape and lead sheet. Prefers 7½ ips reel-to-reel or cassette with 4-8 songs on demo. "Will also accept 45s and LPs or EPs." Also include biography and photo. SASE. Reports in 1 month.
Music: Bluegrass; C&W; easy listening; folk; MOR; progressive; rock; and top 40/pop. Recently published "Cajun Melody," (by P. Breaz) recorded by Hickory/Country Kitchen (country); "Tell Me You Love Me," (by Breaz) recorded by Hickory/Country Kitchen (country); and "Arkansas," (by Damon Black) recorded by Marcia Breaz (ballad/bluegrass).

BOXER MUSIC, Box 120501, Nashville TN 37212. Affiliates: Fruit Music (BMI), and KoKo Music (ASCAP). President: Curtis Allen. Music publisher. BMI. Estab. 1954. "We do not accept or review unsolicited material in any form."
How to Contact: Query. Prefers 7½ ips reel-to-reel with 2-4 songs on demo. SASE. Reports in 1 month.
Music: C&W; easy listening; rock (country); and top 40/pop. Recently published "Can You Hear Those Pioneers?" and "Don't Say Goodby," recorded by Rex Allen Jr. (C&W); and "I'll Be Your Lover (I'll Be Your Friend)," recorded by Sherry Brice (C&W).
Tips: "To date, we haven't accepted any outside material, but we are still looking."

TOMMY BOYCE & MELVIN POWERS MUSIC ENTERPRISES, 2015 Sherman Rd., North Hollywood CA 91605. (213)875-1711. President: Melvin Powers. Music publisher and record company. Estab. 1974. ASCAP. Published 24 songs in 1978; plans 24 in 1979. Pays 10% royalty.
How to Contact: Submit demo tape and lyric sheet. Prefers cassette with 3 songs on demo, or disc. SASE. Reports in 1 month.
Music: C&W and MOR. Recently published "Willie Burgundy," recorded by Teresa Brewer (MOR); "Mr. Songwriter," recorded by Sunday Sharpe (C&W); and "Who Wants a Slightly Used Woman?", recorded by Connie Cato (C&W).

BRANDY MUSIC, Oak Manor, Box 1000, Oak Ridges, Ontario, Canada L0G 1P0. (416)773-4371. BMI. See Core Music for details.

BRETON-CYR, 82 St. Joseph Blvd. W., Montreal, Quebec, Canada H2T 2P4. (514)849-3776. President: Christopher J. Reed. Music publisher. Estab. 1974. CAPAC. See Intermede Musique for details.

BRIAN-JAMES MUSIC, Box 169, Bridgeport MI 48722. President: J.S. Leach. Music publisher and record company. Estab. 1973. BMI. See James S. Enterprises for details.

BRIARPATCH MUSIC/DEB DAVE MUSIC, INC., 700 18th Ave. S., Nashville TN 37203. (615)320-7227. Manager: Keni Wehrman. Music publisher. Estab. 1972. BMI. Pays standard royalties.
How to Contact: "Before submitting material, please inquire by mail." Prefers 7½ ips reel-to-reel with 2 songs on demo. SASE. Reports in 1 month.
Music: C&W; MOR; and progressive. Recently published "You Don't Love Me Anymore" (by Alan Ray and Jeff Raymont), recorded by Eddie Rabbitt/Electra Records (country/MOR); "When You're in Love with a Beautiful Woman" (by Even Stevens), recorded by Dr. Hook/Capitol Records (MOR/rock); and "Room at the Top of the Stairs" (by Stevens and Dan Tyler), recorded by Stella Parton/Elektra Records (country).

BRIDGE MUSIC, The Herald Association, Inc., Box 218, Wellman Heights, Johnsonville SC 29555. (803)386-2600. Director: Erv Lewis. Music publisher and record company. Estab. 1975. BMI. See Silhouette Music for details.

BRIM MUSIC, 38 Music Square E., Nashville TN 37203. (615)256-3373. Affiliates: Herford Music (ASCAP) and Slim-Bull Music (BMI). President: Marty Williamson. Music publisher. SESAC. Pays standard royalty.
How to Contact: Arrange personal interview or submit demo tape and lead sheet. Prefers 7½ ips reel-to-reel with 2 songs on demo. SASE. Reports in 2 weeks.
Music: Church/religious; C&W; easy listening; gospel; and MOR. Recently published "The King is Gone" and "I Love You," recorded by Ronnie McDowell (country/MOR).

BRITISH ROCKET MUSIC PUBLISHING CO., 489 5th Ave., New York NY 10017. (212)986-9361. Director of Professional Activities: Al Altman. Music Publisher. ASCAP. See Rocket Publishing for details.

BROAD RIVER PUBLISHING CO., Rt. 1, Box 304, Blacksburg SC 29702. Music Editor: Tena Shull. Estab. 1973. BMI. "We write our own material."

BROADLAND MUSIC, 380 Birchmont Rd., Scarborough, Ontario, Canada M1K 1M2. (416)691-2757. General Manager: W.B. Kearns. Music publisher and record company. Estab. 1974. BMI. See Quality Music Publishing for details.

BROADMAN PRESS, 127 9th Ave. N., Nashville TN 37234. (615)251-2500. Music Editor: Mark Blankenship. Music publisher. Estab. 1937. SESAC. Published 400 songs in 1978; plans 400 in 1979. Pays 5-10% royalty.
How to Contact: Submit demo tape and lead sheet. Prefers reel-to-reel or cassette with 1-10 songs on demo. SASE. Reports in 6 weeks.
Music: Choral; church/religious; and gospel. "We publish all forms of sacred music. Included are solo/choral for all ages, and instrumental for handbell, organ, recorder and orchestra."

BROTHER BILL'S MUSIC, Box 6987, Atlanta GA 30319. Producer: Sonny Limbo. Music publisher and record producer. Estab. 1956. ASCAP. See Lowery Music for details.

BROTHER KARL'S MUSIC, Box 6987, Atlanta GA 30319. Producer: Sonny Limbo. Music publisher and record producer. Estab. 1956. BMI. See Lowery Music for details.

BRUBOON PUBLISHING, Box 3388, 319 Highland Ave., Albany GA 31701. (912)436-6508. Owner: Jesse Boone. Manager: Keith Boone. Music publisher, booking agency and record company. Estab. 1971. BMI. Published 3 songs in 1977; plans 30 in 1979. Pays 1½% royalty.
How to Contact: Arrange personal interview, submit demo tape, or submit demo tape and lead sheet. Prefers 7½ ips reel-to-reel or cassette. SASE. Reports in 2 weeks.
Music: Blues; choral; church/religious; disco; easy listening; folk; gospel; soul; and top 40/pop. Recently published "You Gonna Miss Me," recorded by Chuck Robinson (soul); and "The Grapevine Will Lie" and "Know What You're Doing," recorded by Roshell Anderson (soul).

BRUIN MUSIC CO., 6430 Sunset Blvd., Suite 921, Los Angeles CA 90028. (213)461-3091. Director of Creative Affairs: B. Ficks, 2 Music Circle S., Nashville TN 37203. Music publisher. BMI. See Famous Music Corp. for details.

BRUJO MUSIC, Box 19, Bulverde TX 78163. (512)438-2465. President: Angie Meyers. Manager: Carol Meyers. Director: Lucky Tomlin. Music publisher, record company, record producer and booking agency. BMI.
Music: C&W; easy listening; MOR; progressive; R&B; rock; and top 40/pop. See Western Head Music for submission details.

ALBERT E. BRUMLEY & SONS, Powell MO 65730. (417)435-2225. Affiliate: Hartford Music (SESAC). Contact: Bob Brumley. Music publisher and booking agency. Estab. 1946. SESAC. Published 30 songs in 1978. Pays standard royalties.
How to Contact: Submit demo tape and lead sheet. Prefers cassette with 3-4 songs on demo. SASE. Reports in 3 weeks.
Music: Choral; church/religious; C&W; and gospel.

BRUSHAPE MUSIC CO., 809 18th Ave. S., Nashville TN 37203. (615)327-3211. Owners: Pete Drake, Gary S. Paxton. Office Manager: Rose Trimble. Music publisher. Estab. 1961. BMI. See Window Music Publishing for details.

BRUTO MUSIC, Box 19, Bulverde TX 78163. (512)438-2465. Vice President: Carol Meyer.

Music publisher, record company, record producer and booking agency. BMI. See Western Head Music for details.

BUG EYES MUSIC, Bug Music Group, 6777 Hollywood Blvd., 9th Floor, Los Angeles CA 90028. Professional Manager: Fred Bourgoise. BMI. See Bug Music for details.

BUG MUSIC, Bug Music Group, 6777 Hollywood Blvd., 9th Floor, Los Angeles CA 90028. Affiliates: Bug Eyes Music (BMI) and Bug Juice Music (ASCAP). Professional Manager: Fred Bourgoise. BMI. Pays negotiable royalty. Charges for some services: "depends on terms, sometimes for particular expenses."
How to Contact: Submit demo tape and lyric sheet. Prefers cassette. SASE. Reports "as soon as possible".
Music: R&B and top 40/pop. Recently published "Runaway" and "I Go to Pieces."

JAM BULL MUSIC, 10220 Glade Ave., Chatsworth CA 91311. (213)341-2264. President: James Bullard. Music Publisher. BMI. See Emandell Tunes for details.

BUMPERSHOOT MUSIC, INC., Box 6507, 2181 Victory Pkwy., Cincinnati OH 45206. (513)861-1500. President: Stan Hertzman. Estab. 1968. BMI. See Hal Bernard Enterprises for details.

BURDETTE MUSIC, First American Records, Box 3925, Bellevue WA 98009. (206)625-9992. President: Jerry Dennon. Music publisher and record company. Estab. 1960. See Bainbridge Music for details.

BURIED TREASURE MUSIC, INC., 524 Doral Country Dr., Nashville TN 37221. Executive Producer: Scott Turner. Music publisher and record producer. Estab. 1977. ASCAP. See Captain Kidd Music for details.

BUSH/LEHRMAN PRODUCTIONS, 119 W. 57th St., New York NY 10019. Professional Managers: Ted Lehrman, Libby Bush. Music publisher and record producer. Estab. 1975. ASCAP.
How to Contact: Submit demo tape and lyric sheet. Prefers 7½ ips reel-to-reel or cassette with 2-4 songs on demo. SASE. Reports in 6 weeks.
Music: C&W; disco; adult contemporary; MOR; R&B; rock; and top 40/pop.

BUTTERMILK SKY ASSOCIATES, 515 Madison Ave., New York NY 10022. (212)759-2275. President: Murray Deutch. Music publisher. Estab. 1974. Works with songwriters on salary.
How to Contact: Arrange personal interview or submit demo tape and lead sheet. Prefers cassette with 5 songs minimum on demo. Does not return unsolicited material. Reports in 2 weeks.
Music: Blues; disco; easy listening; gospel; jazz; MOR; R&B; rock; soul; and top 40/pop.

B-W MUSIC, The WelDee Music Co., Box 561, Wooster OH 44691. Affiliates: LaShaRuDa Music (BMI) and Spangle Music (BMI). General Manager: Quentin W. Welty. Music publisher. Estab. 1959. BMI. Published 12 songs in 1978. Pays standard royalty.
How to Contact: Submit demo tape. Prefers 7½ ips reel-to-reel with 1-5 songs on demo. "Mono or full-track only." SASE. Reports in 2 weeks.
Music: Bluegrass; C&W; folk; and gospel. Recently published "Take Your Shoes Off Moses," recorded by the Lewis Family (C&W); "Multiply the Heartaches," recorded by G. Jones and M. Montgomery (C&W); and "Unkind Words," recorded by Kathy Dee (pop/C&W).

BY-NASH OF NASHVILLE, Box 22701, Nashville TN 37202. Owner: Murray Nash. Doesn't consider outside material.

C.F. MUSIC, 450 E. Beaumont Ave., St. Bruno, Quebec, Canada J3V 2R3. (514)653-7838. President: Christian Lefort. Music publisher and record company. Estab. 1967. CAPAC. See S.M.C.L. Productions for details.

CABRIOLET MUSIC, Box 7422, Shreveport LA 71107. Contact: Don Logan. Music publisher. Estab. 1970. BMI. Published 5 songs in 1978. Pays standard royalty.
How to Contact: Submit demo tape. Prefers 7½ ips reel-to-reel with 2-4 songs on demo. SASE. Reports as soon as possible.
Music: C&W; disco; gospel; soul; and spiritual. Recently published "That's Alright," recorded

by Zion Jubilees (spiritual); "Do You Believe in Disco?", recorded by Sam Benson (disco); and "Hide Behind the Mountain," recorded by Mt. Pleasant Choir (gospel).

CACTUS MUSIC CO., 157 W. 57th St., New York NY 10019. (212)582-6135. Affiliate: Gudi Music. (ASCAP). Vice President: Rhodes Spedale. Music publisher, record company, record producer and management firm. BMI. Published 12 songs in 1978; plans 15 in 1979, 25 in 1980. Pays standard royalties.
How to Contact: Submit demo tape and lead sheet. Prefers 7½ ips reel-to-reel with 2-4 songs on demo. SASE. Reports in 3 months.
Music: C&W; jazz; MOR; and top 40/pop. Recently published "Royal Street" (by Tom Talbert), recorded by Modern Jazz (jazz); "Whiskey in the Jar" (by Roger James), recorded by Cobblers (folk); and "I Don't Need You Anymore" (by Glenn Ash), recorded by Ash (C&W).

CADIGRA PUBLISHING CO., 2819 NW 7th Ave., Miami FL 33127. (305)635-4890, 635-7925. President: Carlos D. Granados. Music publisher and record company.
How to Contact: Query.

CAFE AMERICANA, 8255 Sunset Blvd., Los Angeles CA 90046. (213)650-8300. Vice President of Publishing: Stephen L. Bedell. Music publisher and record company. ASCAP. Estab. 1974.
How to Contact: Submit demo tape and lead sheet. Prefers cassette with 3-6 songs on demo. SASE. Reports as soon as possible.
Music: Blues; disco; easy listening; MOR; progressive; rock (country, pop or soft); soul; and top 40/pop.

CAJUN MUSIC, 39 Music Square E., Nashville TN 37203. (615)255-6535. President: J. William Denny. Music publisher. See Cedarwood Publishing for details.

CALIGULA, INC., 1 Hudson St., New York NY 10013. Vice President: Charles Baxter. Music publisher. Estab. 1975. ASCAP. Published 15 songs in 1978; plans 15 in 1979. Pays standard royalties.
How to Contact: Submit demo tape or submit demo tape and lead sheet. Prefers 7½ ips reel-to-reel with 2-4 songs on demo. SASE. Reports in 1 month.
Music: Folk; rock; and top 40/pop. Recently published "If It Takes All Night," recorded by Eddie Kendricks (pop); "A-Train Lady," recorded by Mink DeVille (rock); and "Dream of a Child," recorded by David Forman (pop).

THE CAMERON ORGANISATION, INC., 320 S. Waiola Ave., LaGrange IL 60525. (312)352-2026. Affiliates: Monona Music (BMI), Watertoons Music (BMI), Hoochie Coochie Music (BMI) and Rathsino Publishing (BMI). Vice President/General Manager: Jean M. Cameron. Music publisher. Estab. 1973. BMI. Pays standard royalty.
How to Contact: Submit demo tape and lead sheet. Prefers 7½ ips reel-to-reel or cassette with 1-3 songs on demo. SASE. Reports in 1 month.
Music: Blues; progressive; rock; soul; and top 40/pop. Recently published "The Blues Had a Baby and They Called It Rock and Roll," recorded by Muddy Waters; "What Happened to My Blues?," recorded by Willie Dixon; and "Green Light," recorded by Mighty Joe Young.

GLEN CAMPBELL MUSIC, 10920 Wilshire Blvd., Los Angeles CA 90024. President: Glen Campbell. Doesn't consider outside material.

CAM-U.S.A., INC., 489 5th Ave., New York NY 10017. General Professional Manager: Faye Rosen.
How to Contact: Submit demo tape and lyric sheet. Prefers reel to reel or cassette with 3-6 songs on demo. Reports as soon as possible.
Music: C&W; disco; easy listening; MOR; progressive; R&B; rock; soul; and top 40/pop. Recently published "Boats Against the Current" (by Eric Carmen), recorded by Olivia Newton-John (AOR); "This is Love" (by Tepper/Sunshine), recorded by Paul Anka (AOR); and "Never Gonna Fall In Love Again" (by Eric Carmen), recorded by John Travolta (AOR).

CANDLESTICK PUBLISHING CO., 582 Armour Circle NE, Atlanta GA 30324. (404)875-2555. Affiliate: Dream Merchant Music (BMI). Partners: Larry King, R.B. Hudmon, Gwen Kesler. Music publisher. Estab. 1975. BMI. Published 4 songs in 1977. Pays standard royalty.
How to Contact: Submit demo tape and lead sheet. Prefers 7½ ips reel-to-reel with 1-6 songs on demo. SASE. Reports in 1 month.

Music: Rock; soul; and top 40/pop. Recently published "How Can I Be a Witness?", "If You Don't Cheat on Me" and "Holdin' On," recorded by R.B. Hudmon (soul).

CAN'T STOP MUSIC, Can't Stop Productions, Inc., 65 E. 55th St., Suite 302, New York NY 10022. (212)751-6177. Affiliate: Green Light Music (ASCAP). President: Henri Belolo. National/International Relations Manager: Marsha Stern. Music publisher and production company. Estab. 1975. BMI. Published 75 songs in 1977; plans 200 in 1979. Pays 30-50% royalty.
How to Contact: Submit demo tape. Prefers cassette. Does not return unsolicited material. Reports in 1 week.
Music: Disco; easy listening; rock; soul; and top 40/pop. Recently published "Best Disco in Town," recorded by the Ritchie Family (disco); and "San Francisco/Hollywood" and "Macho Man," recorded by the Village People (disco/pop).

CANTUS PUBLISHING CO., 66 Sherwood Ave., Toronto, Ontario, Canada. Affiliate: Firmus Publishing (PROCAN). President: Milan Kymlicka. Music publisher and record producer. Estab. 1973. CAPAC. Pays standard royalties.
How to Contact: Submit demo tape, submit demo tape and lead sheet, submit acetate disc, or submit acetate disc and lead sheet. Prefers 7½ ips reel-to-reel or cassette with 4 songs maximum on demo. SASE. Reports in 1 month.
Music: Classical; disco; easy listening; MOR; rock; and top 40/pop. Recently published "Funny," (by Marc Cashman), recorded by Peter Foldy/Capitol Records (pop); and "Big Ship" (by N. Doman), recorded on CBS Records (pop).

CAPAQUARIUS PUBLISHING & ARTIST MGT, INC., 750 Kappock St.,, Riverdale NY 10463. (212)796-2490. Affiliate: Yanita Music (BMI). President: P.J. Watts. Music publisher and management firm. Estab. 1975. ASCAP. Published 20 songs in 1978; plans 50 in 1979. Pays 10-50% royalty.
How to Contact: Submit demo tape and lead sheet. Prefers 7½ ips reel-to-reel with 3-5 songs on demo. Prefers leader between selections. SASE. Reports in 3 weeks.
Music: C&W; disco; gospel (rock); and soul. Recently published "Ain't it Time?", recorded by Queen Yahna.

CAPPY MUSIC CO., 50 Holly Hill Lane, Greenwich CT 06830. (203)661-0707. Music publisher. ASCAP. See Cherry Lane Music for details. "We do not accept unsolicited material."

CAPTAIN KIDD MUSIC, 524 Doral Country Dr., Nashville TN 37221. Affiliate: Buried Treasure Music (ASCAP). Executive Producer: Scott Turner. Music publisher and record producer. Estab. 1977. BMI. Published 30 songs in 1978; plans 50 in 1979. Pays standard royalties.
How to Contact: Submit demo tape and lead sheet. Prefers cassette with 1-4 songs on demo. SASE. Reports in 2 weeks.
Music: C&W; easy listening; folk; MOR; progressive (country); rock; and top 40/pop. Recently published "Early Tymes," recorded by Nilsson.

CARLWOOD MUSIC, 125 Main St., Reading MA 01867. (617)944-0423. Contact: Professional Manager. Music publisher, record producer and promotion firm. SESAC. See Critique Music Publishing for details.

CARRICATUM, 82 St. Joseph Blvd. W., Montreal, Quebec, Canada H2T 2P4. (514)849-3776. President: Christopher J. Reed. Music publisher. Estab. 1974. CAPAC. See Intermede Musique for details.

CARWIN PUBLISHING CO., C/C International Records, 13357 Lorain Ave., Cleveland OH 44111. (216)476-2695. Affiliate: Carl French Music (ASCAP). President: Carl French. Music publisher and record company. Estab. 1965. BMI. Published 10 songs in 1977; plans 30 in 1979. Pays 1½% royalty.
How to Contact: Arrange personal interview or submit demo tape and lead sheet. Prefers 7½ ips reel-to-reel with 2-10 songs on demo. SASE. Reports in 2 weeks.
Music: Bluegrass; C&W; and gospel. Recently published "Mighty Band of Gold," "When I Climb Back Up to Living" and "Cowboy from Texas," recorded by Rodger Wilhoit (C&W).

CASABLANCA PUBLISHING, 8255 Sunset Blvd., Los Angeles CA 90046. (213)650-8300.

Vice President of Publishing: Stephen L. Bedell. Music publisher and record company. Estab. 1974. ASCAP.
How to Contact: Submit demo tape and lead sheet. Prefers cassette with 3-6 songs on demo. SASE. Reports as soon as possible.
Music: Blues; disco; easy listening; MOR; progressive; rock (country, pop or soft); soul; and top 40/pop.

DON CASALE MUSIC, 377 Plainfield St., Westbury NY 11590. (516)333-7898. President: Don Casale. Music publisher and record company. Estab. 1977. BMI. Pays standard royalties.
How to Contact: Arrange personal interview or submit demo tape and lead sheet. Reel-to-reel or cassette OK. "Tape quality should be reasonably good." SASE. Reports in 2 weeks.
Music: C&W (catchy stories); disco; MOR (must have mass appeal); rock (soft rock); R&B; soul (ballads or uptempo); top 40/pop (strong melodies only); and "gimmick songs." Recently published "Losing You," recorded by Rhys O'Brien (MOR ballad); and "Gonna Boogie Right Behind Ya," recorded by Gary Murway (uptempo R&B).

CATCH FIRE MUSIC ENTERPRISES, 115 Shaketree Lane, Scotts Valley CA 95066. President: John Greenbach. Music publisher, record producer and management firm. Estab. 1975. BMI. Published 14 songs in 1978. Pays standard royalties.
How to Contact: Query, submit demo tape, or submit demo tape and lead sheet. Prefers reel-to-reel or cassette. SASE. Reports in 2 weeks.
Music: C&W; disco; easy listening; R&B; rock; soul; and top 40/pop. Recently published "Lock up my Body" (by Vic Phillips) recorded by Sweathog/Columbia Records (top 40/pop).

CEDARWOOD PUBLISHING CO., INC., 39 Music Square E., Nashville TN 37203. (615)255-6535. Affiliates: Denny Music (ASCAP), Cajun Music (BMI), Driftwood Music (BMI) and Stonewall Music (BMI). President: J. William Denny. Music publisher. Estab. 1953. BMI. Published over 400 songs in 1978; plans over 500 in 1979. Pays standard royalties.
How to Contact: Submit demo tape and lead sheet. Prefers 7½ ips reel-to-reel with 1-3 songs on demo. SASE. Reports in 1 month.
Music: C&W; gospel; MOR; progressive; and top 40/pop. Recently published "Ruby Don't Take Your Love to Town," recorded by Kenny Rogers (pop, country); "Teddy Bear," recorded by Red Sovine (country); and "I'll Find it Where I Can," recorded by Jerry Lee Lewis (country/rock).

CETRA MUSIC, 5828 S. University Ave., Chicago IL 60637. (312)493-9781. President: Morton A. Kaplan. Music publisher. Estab. 1961. BMI. Published 4 songs in 1978. Pays standard royalties.
How to Contact: Submit lead sheet. Does not return unsolicited material. Reports in 2 weeks.
Music: Blues; church/religious; C&W; disco; folk; gospel; jazz; MOR; R&B; soul; and top 40/pop.

CHAMPION MUSIC, 9100 Wilshire Blvd., Suite 530, Beverly Hills CA 90212. (213)550-3913. Contact: Dude McLean. Music publisher. Estab. 1964. BMI. See MCA Music for details.

CHAPIE MUSIC, Chapman Recording Studios, 228 W. 5th St., Kansas City MO 64105. (816)842-6854. Owner: Chuck Chapman. Music publisher and record company. Estab. 1973. BMI. Published 15 songs in 1977. Pays standard royalty.
How to Contact: Submit demo tape. Prefers cassette with 3 songs minimum on tape. SASE. Reports in 1 month.
Music: Bluegrass; choral; church/religious; classical; C&W; disco; easy listening; folk; gospel; jazz; MOR; progressive; rock; soul; and top 40/pop. Recently published "He Lives," recorded by Tarry Westley (C&W); and "Somewhere Down in Texas," recorded by Norton Canfield (country rock).

CHAPPELL MUSIC, 6255 Sunset Blvd., Los Angeles CA (213)469-5141. Affiliate: Unichappell. Music publisher. Estab. 1811. Contact: Professional Manager. ASCAP. Pays negotiable royalties.
How to Contact: Query or submit demo tape and lead sheet. Prefers 7½ ips reel-to-reel or cassette with 2-3 songs on demo. SASE. Reports in 1 month.
Music: C&W; disco; easy listening; MOR; R&B; rock; soul; and top 40/pop. Recently published "Stayin' Alive," by the Bee Gees.

CHAPPELL MUSIC CO., 21 Music Circle E., Nashville TN 37203. Affiliates: Unichappell

(BMI), Trichappell (SESAC), Intersong Music (ASCAP) and Rightsong Music (BMI). Estab. 1811. ASCAP. "We only review material recommended to us by music industry personnel."

CHAPPELL MUSIC, 810 7th Ave., New York NY 10019. Professional Managers: Bob Cutarella, Richie Cordell. Music publisher. Estab. 1811. ASCAP.
How to Contact: Submit demo tape and lyric sheets. Prefers 7½ ips reel-to-reel or cassette with 1-3 songs on demo. SASE. Reports in 1 month.
Music: Disco; MOR; progressive; R&B; rock; and top 40/pop. Recently published "You Needed Me" (by Randy Goodrum), recorded by Anne Murray (country/pop).

CHAR-BELLE MUSIC, Box 10612, Birmingham AL 35202. (205)252-8271. President: Ann Scott. Talent Coordinator: Arabella Labarber. Music publisher. Estab. 1967. BMI. Published 10 songs in 1978; plans 25 in 1979. Pays standard royalties.
How to Contact: Query, then submit demo tape or arrange personal interview. Prefers 7½ ips reel-to-reel or cassette with 3-8 songs on demo. SASE. Reports in 3 weeks.
Music: C&W; gospel; rock (country or hard); soul; and top 40/pop. Recently published "I Got the Place," recorded by Allison and South Funk Boulevard (soul).

CHARLOT, 82 St. Joseph Blvd. W., Montreal, Quebec, Canada H2T 2P4. (514)849-3776. President: Christopher J. Reed. Music publisher. Estab. 1974. CAPAC. See Intermede Musique for details.

CHARSY MUSIC, 8 Music Square W., Nashville TN 37202. BMI. See Tree Publishing for details.

CHASCOT MUSIC PUBLISHING, Box 3161, Atlanta GA 30302. President: Charles E. Scott. Music publisher, record company and record producer. Estab. 1967. BMI. Plans 17 songs in 1979, 42 in 1980. Pays standard royalties.
How to Contact: Submit demo tape and lead sheet. Prefers cassette. SASE. Reports in 3 weeks.
Music: Blues; disco; gospel; R&B; soul; and top 40/pop.

CHAT, 82 St. Joseph Blvd. W., Montreal, Quebec, Canada H2T 2P4. (514)849-3776. President: Christopher J. Reed. Music publisher. Estab. 1974. CAPAC. See Intermede Musique for details.

CHATHAM MUSIC CORP., 8544 Sunset Blvd., Los Angeles CA 90069. (213)657-8210. Director of Creative Activities: Ron Vance. Music publisher and record company. ASCAP. See 20th Century Fox for details.

CHEAVORIA MUSIC CO., 1219 Kerlin Ave., Brewton AL 36426. (205)867-2228. Songwriter: Roy Edwards. Producer: Mike Tracy. Music publisher, record producer and management firm. Estab. 1972. BMI. Published 6 songs in 1978; plans 18 in 1979, 30 in 1980. Pays standard royalties.
How to Contact: Query or submit demo tape and lead sheet. Prefers cassette with 2-5 songs on demo. SASE. Reports in 3 weeks.
Music: C&W; disco; easy lisening; MOR; progressive; R&B; soul; and top 40/pop. Recently published "I'm Just Not Your Kind" (by C. Edwards), recorded by Bobbie Roberson/Bolivia Records (C&W/MOR); "You Were The One" (by E. Cornell), recorded by Bobbie Roberson/Boliva Records (C&W)/MOR; and "Empty Promises" (by W. B. Mitchell and C. Edwards), recorded by Bobbie Roberson/Bolivia Records (C&W/MOR).

CHERRY LANE MUSIC CO., 50 Holly Hill Lane, Greenwich CT 06830. (203)661-0707; (212)824-7711. (New York Tie-line). Affiliated and/or administered companies: Windstar Music (ASCAP), Accabonac Music (ASCAP), Jolly Rogers Publishing (ASCAP), M-3 Music (ASCAP), Cappy Music (ASCAP), Cherry Wood Music (ASCAP), Hemlane Music (ASCAP), Cherry River Music (BMI), Windsea Music (BMI), Milton Okum Publishing (BMI), Mar-Ken Music (BMI), Chicken Key Music (BMI) and Third Song Music (ASCAP). Music publisher. Estab. 1960. ASCAP. Pays standard royalties.
How to Contact: Query. SASE.
Music: Easy listening; folk; MOR; and top 40/pop. Publishers of John Denver, Kenny Rogers, Steve Glassmeyer, Bill & Taffy Danoff, Tom Paxton, Mentor Williams and Jeffrey Comanor."

CHERRY RIVER MUSIC CO., 50 Holly Hill Lane, Greenwich CT 06830. (203)661-0707. Music publisher. BMI. See Cherry Lane Music for details. " We do not accept unsolicited material."

CHERRY WOOD MUSIC CO., 50 Holly Hill Lane, Greenwich CT 06830. (203)661-0707. Music publisher. ASCAP. See Cherry Lane Music for details. "We do not accept unsolicited material."

CHESS MUSIC, INC., Box 40984, Nashville TN 37204. (615)320-7800. Professional Manager: Dave Conrad. Music publisher. ASCAP. See Pi Gem Music for details.

CHEST OF DRAWERS, INC., Box 8011, Mobile AL 36608. President: Milton L. Brown. Vice President: Travis Turk. See Top Drawer Music for details.

CHEST OF DRAWERS, INC., Box 17464, Nashville TN 37217. (615)367-0144. See Top Drawer Music for details.

CHEVIS PUBLISHING CORP., 1206 17th Ave. S., Nashville TN 37212. (615)320-7947. Affiliate: Shada Music, Inc. (ASCAP). Manager: Betty Holt. Music publisher. Estab. 1960. BMI. Pays standard royalties.
How to Contact: Submit demo tape and lyric sheet. Prefers 7½ ips reel-to-reel with 3 songs maximum on demo. SASE. Reports in 1 month.
Music: Easy listening; MOR; progressive; soul; and top/40 pop. Recently published "Your Love Has Lifted Me Higher" recorded by Rita Coolidge; "Rescue Me" recorded by Cher; and "Don't Mess Up a Good Thing" recorded by Greg Allman.

CHICKEN KEY MUSIC, 50 Holly Hill Lane, Greenwich CT 06830. (203)661-0707. Music publisher. BMI. See Cherry Lane Music for details. Does not accept unsolicited material.

CHICORY MUSIC CO., 6381 Hollywood Blvd., Suite 318, Los Angeles CA 90028. (213)469-8149. Contact: Frank Slay. Music publisher. BMI. See Claridge Music for details.

CHIEN NOIR, 82 St. Joseph Blvd. W., Montreal, Quebec, Canada H2T 2P4. (514)849-3776. President: Christopher J. Reed. Music publisher. Estab. 1974. CAPAC. See Intermede Musique for details.

CHINGUACOUSEY MUSIC, Fivetake Group Productions, Ltd., 484 Waterloo Ct., Oshawa, Ontario, Canada L1H 3X1. Contact: Bob Stone. Music publisher. PROCAN. See Fivetake Music for details.

CHINWAH SONGS, 10220 Glade Ave., Chatsworth CA 91311.President: B.R. Spears. Music publisher. SESAC. See Emandell Tunes for details.

CHIP 'N DALE, Gene Kennedy Enterprises, 2125 8th Ave. S., Nashville TN 37204. (615)383-6002. Vice President: Linda Kennedy. Music publisher. Estab. 1975. ASCAP. See Gene Kennedy Enterprises for details.

CHORAL PRESS, Delaware Water Gap PA 18327. (717)476-0550. Director of Publications: Lewis M. Kirby Jr. Music publisher and record company. SESAC.
Music: Children's; choral; church/religious; and gospel. See Shawnee Press for submission details.

CHRIS MUSIC PUBLISHING, Box 268, Manistique MI 49854. Affiliate: Saralee Music (BMI). President: Reg B. Christensen. Music publisher and record company. Estab. 1956. BMI. Published 10 songs in 1978; plans 20 in 1979. Pays standard royalty.
How to Contact: Query, then submit demo tape and lead sheet. Prefers 7½ ips reel-to-reel or cassette with 2-5 songs on demo. "No fancy, big band demo is necessary; just one instrument with a clean, clear voice is adequate." SASE. Reports in 1 month.
Music: Bluegrass; C&W; gospel; MOR; and soul. Recently published "Diamonds and Pearls," recorded by the Paradons (R&B); "Heart, You Fool," recorded by Louie Moore (C&W); and "Ask Me No Questions," recorded by Bill Woods (C&W).

CIANO PUBLISHING, Box 263, Hasbrouck Heights NJ 07604. (201)288-8935. President: Ron Luciano. Music publisher, record company and record producer. Estab. 1968. BMI. Published 6 songs in 1978; plans 12 in 1979, 24 in 1980. Pays standard royalties (copartnership on each song published).
How to Contact: Query, submit demo tape and lead sheet or submit acetate disc and lead sheet. Prefers 7½ ips reel-to-reel, cassette or acetate with 2-6 songs on demo. SASE. Reports in 1 month.

Music: Disco; easy listening; MOR; R&B; rock; soul; top 40/pop. Recently published "Lucky" (by T. Galloway), recorded by Lucifer 302/Legz Records (rock n roll); "Fly Away" (by Philip Mitchell and Barron and Susan Sillars), recorded by Lucifer 301/Tiara (folk); and "Love's a Crazy Game" (by Joseph M. Leo and Paul Cannarella), recorded by Lucifer 303/Pending (top 40/disco).

CIN-KAY MUSIC, 56 Music Square W., Nashville TN 37203. (615)244-3570. Owner: Hal Freeman. Music publisher, record company and management firm. Estab. 1975. BMI. See Hal Freeman Music for details.

CLAB MUSIC, Box 267, Perry Point MD 21902. Producer: Clifton Lewis. Music publisher, record company and record producer. Estab. 1969. BMI. Published 6 songs in 1978; plans 6 in 1979. Pays standard royalties.
How to Contact: Query or submit demo tape. Prefers 7½ ips reel-to-reel or cassette with 2-4 songs on demo. SASE. Reports in 1 month.
Music: C&W. Recently published "Losing Man" (by Buddy Taylor), recorded by Chavis Brothers (country); "Our Love Is" (by Ronald Simons), recorded by Ronald Simons (country); and "Star Light Lady," (by Ronald Simons) recorded by Simons/Bay (country).

CLARIDGE MUSIC, INC., 6381 Hollywood Blvd., Suite 318, Los Angeles CA 90028. (213)469-8149. Affiliates: Conley Music, Inc. (ASCAP) and Chicory Music Co. (BMI). Contact: Frank Slay. Music publisher. Estab. 1953. ASCAP. Plans 25 songs in 1979.
How to Contact: Arrange personal interview. Prefers 7½ ips reel-to-reel or cassette.
Music: Disco; rock; soul; and top 40/pop. Recently published "Green Eyed Lady," recorded by Sugarloaf; "Big Girls Don't Cry," recorded by Four Seasons; "Incense and Peppermints," recorded by Strawberry Alarm Clock; and "Don't Call Us, We'll Call You," recorded by Sugarloaf.
Tips: "Demo can be rough if it accompanied by a typewritten lyric sheet."

CLARK MUSIC PUBLISHING, Clark Musical Productions, Box 299, Watseka IL 60970. President: Dr. Paul E. Clark. Music publisher, booking agency and record company. Estab. 1970. BMI. Published 30 songs in 1978; plans 50 in 1979. Pays standard royalties. Sometimes secures songwriters on salary basis: Duties include writing songs and jingles.
How to Contact: Submit demo tape and lead sheet. Prefers cassette with 3-8 songs on demo. SASE. Reports in 1 month.
Music: Choral; church/religious; C&W; easy listening; folk; gospel; MOR; rock (soft); soul; and top 40/pop. Recently published "Spring Was But a Child," recorded by Mike Peterson (C&W); "Country Livin'," recorded by Cindy Lee (C&W); and "Jesus, Dear Jesus," recorded by the Gospelaires (religious).

THE NORMAN CLAYTON PUBLISHING CO., Box 1790, Waco TX 76703. Music Editor: John Purifoy. Music publisher and record company. SESAC. See Word Music for details.

CLEVETOWN MUSIC, 10220 Glade Ave., Chatsworth CA 91311. (213)341-2264. President: James Bullard. Music Publisher. SESAC. See Emandell Tunes for details.

CLOUD BURST MUSIC PUBLISHING, Box 2066, Oshawa, Ontario, Canada L1H 7N2. (705)793-2737. Affiliate: Startrack Music Publishing (CAPAC). President: George Petralia. Music publisher, record company, record producer and management firm. Estab. 1975. PROCAN. Published 4 songs in 1978. Pays standard royalties.
How to Contact: Query, submit demo tape or submit demo tape and lead sheet. Prefers 7½ ips reel-to-reel with 1-10 songs on demo. "Please also submit a typewritten copy of lyrics." SAE and International Reply Coupons. Reports in 1 month.
Music: C&W; easy listening; MOR; and top 40/pop. Recently published "Honestly I Love You," (by Jerry Palmer and Don Grashey) recorded by Heather Haig/Cloudburst Records (country/MOR); "Come On Country," (by Lance Younger) recorded by Younger/Cloud Burst Records (contemporary country); and "I Can't Get Your Lovin," (by Bill Barnhart) recorded by Haig/Cloud Burst Records (country).
Tips: "Any songs submitted to this company for consideration must be free of publishing with any other company; Cloud Burst Music Publishing wants sole publishing so that in the future if they want to work out a deal with another company, they have the rights to split the publishing."

COAT OF ARMS PUBLISHING, Box 217, Oak Hill OH 45656. (614)682-7771. Producer: D.

Howell. Record company, music publisher, record producer and management firm. Estab. 1970. BMI. Published 1 song in 1978. Pays standard royalties.
How to Contact: Query, submit demo tape, or submit demo tape and lead sheet. Prefers 7½ ips reel-to-reel or cassette with 1-3 songs on demo. Does not return unsolicited material. Reports in 2 weeks.
Music: Bluegrass; C&W; easy listening; MOR; and top 40/pop. Recently published "Old Joe" (by Randall Boring) recorded by Whetstone Run (instrumental).

BRUCE COHN MUSIC, Box 878, Sonoma CA 95476. (707)938-4060. Affiliates: Flat Lizard Music (ASCAP), Maybe Music (ASCAP), Quark Music (BMI), Skunkster Publishing (ASCAP), Snug Music (BMI), Noodle Tunes (BMI), Pants Down Music (BMI), Spikes Music (BMI), Soquel Songs (ASCAP), Tauripin Tunes (ASCAP), Windecor Music (BMI) and R.P. Winkelman Tunes (ASCAP). Manager/Owner: Bruce Cohn. Music publisher and management firm. Estab. 1975. Published 10 songs in 1977; plans 20 in 1978. Pays negotiable royalty.
How to Contact: Query. SASE. Reports in 3 weeks.
Music: C&W; disco; MOR; rock; soul; and top 40/pop. Recently published "It Keeps You Running" and "Taking it to the Streets," recorded by the Doobie Brothers (pop).

COLEMAN, KESTIN & SMITH, LTD., 7507 Sunset Blvd., Suite 1, Hollywood CA 90046. (213)935-5786. Affiliates: Keristene Music (BMI) and Bil-Etta Music (BMI). Vice President, A&R: Horace Coleman Jr. Music publisher, record company and production company. Estab. 1976. BMI. Published 12 songs in 1977; plans 33 in 1979. Pays 25-100% royalty.
How to Contact: Submit demo tape and lyric or lead sheet. Prefers 7½ ips reel-to-reel or cassette with 1-3 songs on demo. Certified return receipt requested. SASE. Reports in 1 month.
Music: Blues; C&W; disco; folk; gospel; jazz; MOR; progressive; rock; soul; and top 40/pop. Recently published "Learn to Ride," recorded by Nancy Smith (country rock); "Squeeze Me, Tease Me," recorded by the L.A. Sharks (progressive rock); and "Learned My Lesson Now," recorded by Total Force (disco rock).

COLGEMS MUSIC, 7033 Sunset Blvd., Hollywood CA 90028. (213)461-9141. Talent Manager: Ronnie Glakal. Music publisher. ASCAP. See Screen Gems/EMI Music for details.

COLGEMS/EMI MUSIC, INC., 1370 Avenue of the Americas, New York NY 10019. Professional Manager: Bob Currie. Music publisher. ASCAP.
Music: Disco; progressive; R&B; rock; soul; and top 40/pop. See Screen Gems/EMI for submission details.

COLUMN ONE MUSIC (formerly Hotei Publishing), Box 4086, Springfield MO 65804. President: James M. Martin. Estab. 1973. ASCAP. Published 30 songs in 1978; plans 50 in 1959. Pays standard royalties.
How to Contact: Submit cassette or 7½ reel-to-reel. SASE.
Music: C&W; pop; rock; and MOR. Recently published "Hank You Tried To Tell Me," recorded by Johnny Paycheck (C&W) "From Cotton To Satin," recorded by Johnny Paycheck (C&W); "Six-String Tennessee Flat Top," recorded by Hank Snow(C&W); "Your Sweet Lies," recorded by Tammy Wynett (C&W); "I'm Not Easy," recorded by Billie Jo Spears (C&W) and "Number One Lovin Man," recorded by Jerry Lee Lewis (rock).

COLUMN TWO MUSIC (formerly Kuan Yin Publishing), Box 4086, Springfield MO 65804. President: James M. Martin. Music publisher. Estab. 1973. BMI. See Column One Music for details.

COMMERCIAL STUDIOS, INC., 412 Holly Dr. SE, Atlanta GA 30354. (404)361-7931. Affiliate: Seasun Experience (ASCAP). President: Howard Wright. Music publisher and production consultants. Estab. 1971. BMI. Published 10 in 1978. Pays 5% royalty.
How to Contact: Submit demo tape and lead sheet. Prefers 7½ ips reel-to-reel or cassette with 2-3 songs on demo. SASE. Reports in 1 month.
Music: Children's; disco; easy listening; jazz; rock; soul; top 40/pop.

COMPO MUSIC PUBLISHING, 105 Burk Dr., Oklahoma City OK 73115. (405)677-6448. General Manager: Sonny Lane. Music publisher, record company and record producer. BMI. See Country Classics Music for details.
Music: Church/religious, C&W, easy listening, gospel, MOR and top 40/pop.

CON BRIO MUSIC, Suite 405, 49 Music Square W., Nashville TN 37203. (615)329-1944. Affiliates: Wiljex Publishing (ASCAP) and Concorde Publishing (SESAC). Publishing Directors: Rex Peer, Esther Witt. Vice President, Operations: Jeff Walker. Music publisher, record company and production company. Estab. 1976. BMI. Published 150 songs in 1977; plans 250 in 1979. Pays standard royalty.
How to Contact: Submit demo tape and lead or lyric sheet. Prefers 7½ ips reel-to-reel or cassette with 1-3 songs on demo. SASE. Reports in 1 month.
Music: C&W; easy listening; MOR; and top 40/pop. Recently published "She's the Girl of My Dreams" and "Music Is My Woman," recorded by Don King (C&W/MOR); and "Sweet Love Song," recorded by Dale McBride (C&W).

CONCEPTION, 82 St. Joseph Blvd. W., Montreal, Quebec, Canada H2T 2P4. (514)849-3776. President: Christopher J. Reed. Music publisher. Estab. 1974. CAPAC. See Intermede Musique for details.

CONCORDE PUBLISHING, Suite 405, 49 Music Square W., Nashville TN 37203. (615)329-1944. Publishing Directors: Rex Peer, Esther Witt. Music publisher, record company and production company. Estab. 1976. SESAC. See Con Brio Music for details.

CONLEY MUSIC, INC., 6381 Hollywood Blvd., Suite 318, Los Angeles CA 90028. (213)469-8149. Contact: Frank Slay. Music publisher. ASCAP. See Claridge Music for details.

JERRY CONNELL PUBLISHING, 130 Pilgrim Dr., San Antonio TX 78213. (512)344-5033. Affiliate: J.C.E. Publishing Company (ASCAP). Owner: Jerry Connell. Record company, music publisher, record producer and booking agency. Estab. 1965. BMI. Published 50 songs in 1978; plans 75 songs in 1979, 100 in 1980. Pays standard royalties.
How to Contact: Query, submit demo tape, submit acetate disc, or submit lead sheet. Prefers 7½ or 15 ips reel-to-reel or cassette with 1 song on demo. Does not return unsolicited material. Reports in 2 weeks.
Music: Bluegrass; church/religious; C&W; disco; easy listening; folk; gospel; jazz; MOR; R&B; rock; and top 40/pop. Recently published "Every Breath You Take" (by Ed Smith) and "Sing a Song to Cry By" (by Wynn Stewart), recorded by Ed Smith/Cherokee (country); "Lonely Hearts Club" (by Ronnie Mason) recorded by Ronnie Mason/Cherokee (C&W); and "The Crab Song" (by Vito Talerico) recorded by Vito Talerico/Cherokee (rock).

COOKAWAY MUSIC, 119 W. 57th St., New York NY 10019. (212)581-3420. General Manager: Arthur Braun. Music publisher. ASCAP. Recently published "Doctor's Orders," recorded by Carol Douglas (pop/soul). See Dick James Music for submission details.

CORAL BLOSSOM MUSIC, 50 Music Square W., Suite 902, United Artists Tower, Nashville TN 37203. (615)329-0714. Professional Manager: Bobby Fischer. Music publisher, record company and record producer. BMI. See Iron Blossom Music for details.

CORE MUSIC PUBLISHING, c/o Oak Manor, Box 1000, Oak Ridges, Ontario, Canada L0G 1P0. (416)773-4371. Affiliates: Mark-Cain Music (CAPAC) and Brandy Music (BMI). President: Vic Wilson. Chairman: Ray Danniels. A&R Director: Michael Tilka. Music publisher with affiliated management, record and production companies. CAPAC. Published 60 songs in 1978; plans 70 in 1979, 80 in 1980.
How to Contact: Submit demo tape with bio material. Prefers 7½ ips reel-to-reel or cassette with 3-6 songs on demo. SAE and International Reply Coupons. Reports in 6 weeks.
Music: Progressive; rock; and top 40/pop. Recently published "Circumstances" and "Hemispheres," recorded by Rush (rock).

CORINTH MUSIC, GRT of Canada, Ltd., 3816 Victoria Park Ave., Toronto, Ontario, Canada. (416)497-2340. Director, Publishing Division: F. Davies. Music publisher and record company. Estab. 1969. BMI. See GRT of Canada for details.

COTILLION MUSIC, INC., 75 Rockefeller Plaza, New York NY 10019. (212)484-8406. Affiliate: Walden (ASCAP). Manager, Business Affairs: Joanne Davidson. Music publisher. Works with artists and writers from Atlantic records only.
How to contact: Query. Does not return unsolicited material.
Music: Blues; disco; and rock.

COUNTRY CLASSICS MUSIC PUBLISHING CO., 105 Burk Dr., Oklahoma City OK

73115. (405)677-6448. Affiliates: Sunny Lane Music. (ASCAP), Compo Music Publishing (BMI), and Devaney Music Publishing (BMI). General Manager: Sonny Lane. Music publisher, record company and record producer. Estab. 1972. BMI. Published 2 songs in 1978; plans 12 in 1979. Pays standard royalties.
How to Contact: Submit demo tape. Prefers 7½ ips reel-to-reel with 2-6 songs on demo. SASE. Reports in 3 weeks.
Music: Church/religious; C&W; easy listening; gospel; MOR; and top 40/pop. Recently published "Forever and One Day" (by Yvonne Devaney), recorded by Hank Snow/RCA Records (country); "Teardrop Number One" (by Yvonne Devaney), recorded by Wanda Jackson/Myrrh Records (country); and "Some Call Him Jesus" (by Devaney), recorded by Wanda Jackson/Myrrh Records (gospel).

COUNTRY SONG FACTORY, Box 9639, North Hollywood CA 91609. (213)461-4804. Vice President: Jim Mize. Music publisher and record company. Estab. 1978. BMI. Pays standard royalty.
How to Contact: Arrange personal interview. Prefers 7½ ips reel-to-reel or cassette with 1-5 songs on demo. "Enclose all vital information—lyrics, ownership of song, writers." Does not return unsolicited material.
Music: Bluegrass; blues; children's; church/religious; C&W; easy listening; folk; gospel; and MOR.

COUNTRY STAR MUSIC, 439 Wiley Ave., Franklin PA 16323. (814)432-4633. Affiliates: Kelly Music Publications (BMI) and Process Music Publications (BMI). President: Norman Kelly. Music publisher, record company and booking agency. Estab. 1943. ASCAP. Published 100 songs in 1978. Pays standard royalties.
How to Contact: Submit demo tape and lead sheet or arrange personal interview. Prefers 3¾, 7½ or 15 ips reel-to-reel, cassette or 8-track cartridge with 1-4 songs on demo. SASE. Reports in 2 weeks.
Music: Bluegrass; C&W; easy listening; gospel; MOR; rock ("good soft/easy rock, like the Beatles"); and top 40/pop. Recently published "Hand Him Down to Me," recorded by Junie Lou/Starship Records; "Drinkin' Beer'll Make It Right," to be recorded by a polka band/Process Records; and "I Want To Be With You," recorded by Link James/Country Star Records.

CREEMORE MUSIC, Fivetake Group Productions, Ltd., 484 Waterloo Ct., Oshawa, Ontario, Canada L1H 3X1. Contact: Bob Stone. Music publisher. CAPAC. See Fivetake Music for details.

CRIMSON DYNASTY, Crimson Dynasty Record Corp., Box 271, Jenkintown PA 19046. President: Stan Peahota. Music publisher, record company and recording studio. ASCAP. Published 12 songs in 1977; plans 24 in 1978, 36 in 1979. Pays 1-10% royalty. Offers cash advance against royalty. Sometimes secures songwriters on salary basis. Charges for some services: "We charge if the songwriter wishes to have an album produced."
How to Contact: Submit demo tape and lead sheet. Include photo and resume. Prefers 7½ ips reel-to-reel, cassette, 8-track cartridge or disc. SASE. Reports in 1 week.
Music: Blues; C&W; easy listening; and novelty. Recently released "I'm the Greatest," recorded by Muhammad Ali (disco/novelty/rock).
Tips: "All submissions will be reviewed. We are looking for songs that Muhammad Ali, Frank Sinatra or the Beatles would sing if they were to listen to them. That is the style we want."

CRITERION MUSIC CORP., 6124 Selma Ave., Hollywood CA 90028. Affiliates: Granite Music (ASCAP) and Atlantic Music (BMI). Contact: Professional Manager. Music publisher. ASCAP. Pays standard minimum royalty.
How to Contact: Submit demo tape and lead sheet. Prefers cassette with 1-2 songs on demo. SASE. Reports in 3 weeks.
Music: MOR; progressive; rock; soul; and top 40/pop. Recently published "Let the Good Times Roll," recorded by various artists (rock); and "Doctor My Eyes," recorded by Jackson Browne and the Jackson 5.

CRITIQUE MUSIC PUBLISHING CO., 125 Main St., Reading MA 01867. Affiliates: Carlwood Music (SESAC) and Skys the Limit Music (SESAC). Contact: Professional Manager. Music publisher, record producer and promotion firm. Estab. 1965. BMI. Published 20 songs in 1978; plans 30 in 1979. Pays standard royalties.

How to Contact: Submit demo tape and lead sheet. Prefers cassette with 3-5 songs on demo. SASE. Reports in 3 weeks.
Music: C&W; disco; easy listening; MOR; rock; and top 40/pop.

CROOKED CREEK MUSIC, 19 Music Square W., Nashville TN 37203. (615)256-1886. President: Jean S. Zimmerman. Professional Manager: Mary Louise Smith. Music publisher. Estab. 1972. BMI.
Music: Bluegrass; blues; C&W; disco; easy listening; MOR; and top 40/pop. Recently published "In My World of Fantasy" (by Joyce Brookshire), recorded by Sylvia Lowry/Sing Me Records (pop); "Cinderella" (by Kelly Bach), recorded by Dale Houston/Country International (C&W); and "I Done Cleaned My House" (by Bobby Martin), recorded by Ramona Duvall/Sing Me Records (disco). See Sing Me Music for submission details.

CROSS KEYS PUBLISHING CO., INC., 8 Music Square W., Nashville TN 37203. ASCAP. See Tree Publishing for details.

CROW-SMITH PRODUCTIONS, 6004 Bull Creek Rd., Austin TX 78757. (512)451-6764. Affiliate: Lone Grove Music (BMI). President: Bobby Earl Smith. Vice President/A&R: Herb Steiner. BMI.
How to Contact: Submit demo tape or submit demo tape and lead sheet. Prefers cassette. Does not return unsolicited material. Reports in 4 weeks.
Music: C&W; rock; and R&B. Recently published "Nyquil Blues" (rockabilly novelty) and "Fiddler's Lady," recorded by Alvin Crow (swing).

CUTA RUG MUSIC, Box 174, Seeley CA 92273. A&R Director: Jimmie Doyle. Music publisher. BMI. Pays standard royalty.
How to Contact: Submit demo tape, arrange personal interview or submit demo tape and lead sheet. "Please submit demo tape and lead sheet, if possible. Personal interview will be requested if material is accepted." Prefers reel-to-reel or cassette. SASE. Reports in 2 weeks.
Music: C&W and rock (country). Recently published "One More Night With You," recorded by Jimmie Doyle.

CUZZ PUBLISHING CO., INC., 2061 Edgewood Dr., Charlestown IN 47111. (812)256-2310. A&R: Kenny Sowder. President: Brenda Sowder. Music publisher and record company. Estab. 1967. BMI. Published 12 songs in 1978. Pays 2¢/copy for sheet music.
How to Contact: Submit demo tape and lead sheet or arrange personal interview. Prefers reel-to-reel. SASE. Reports in 1 month.
Music: Bluegrass; C&W; and gospel. Recently published "Loved All Over" (by Becky Stack), "Elegant Lady" and "Smoother Ground" (by Ange Humphrey), all recorded by Ange Humphrey/Derbytown Records (country).

DANBORO PUBLISHING CO., Box 2199, Vancouver, British Columbia, Canada V6B 3V7. (604)688-1820. Affiliate: Synchron Publishing (CAPAC). President: John Rodney. Music publisher and record company. Estab. 1970. BMI. Published 24 songs in 1977; plans 36 in 1979. Pays standard royalties.
How to Contact: Submit demo tape. Prefers 7½ ips reel-to-reel with 2-6 songs on demo. "Be selective. Send only the best songs. Identify tapes fully." SAE and International Reply Coupons. Reports in 1 month.
Music: C&W; easy listening; MOR; rock; and top 40/pop. Recently published "Do It," recorded by Jud Paynter (top 40); "I'm a Yo-Yo," recorded by K Country (C&W); and "Confronto," recorded by Frederico.

DARAMUS MUSIC, 119 W. 57th St., New York NY 10019. (212)581-3420. General Manager: Arthur Braun. Music publisher. ASCAP. See Dick James Music for details.

DAVIDA RECORD & PUBLISHING CO., Finnal Connections Productions, Box 77611, Los Angeles CA 90007. (213)235-2835. Chairman: Dana V. Andrews. Music publisher, booking agency and record company. Estab. 1975. BMI. Published 50 songs in 1978; plans 100 in 1979. Pays 5-10% royalty.
How to Contact: Submit demo tape and lead sheet. Prefers 7½ ips reel-to-reel or cassette with 3-6 songs on demo. SASE. Reports in 3 weeks.
Music: C&W; easy listening; jazz; MOR; R&B; soul; and top 40/pop.

DAVIDA RECORD & PUBLISHING CO., Finnal Connections Productions, Box 24A, Detroit

MI 48232. (313)491-7409, 834-2798. President: David Futch. Music Editors: Joseph Futch, Augustus O. Hill. Music publisher, booking agency and record company. Estab. 1975. BMI. Published 50 songs in 1978; plans 100 in 1979. Pays 5-10% royalty.
How to Contact: Submit demo tape and lead sheet. Prefers 7½ ips reel-to-reel or cassette with 3-6 songs on demo. SASE. Reports in 3 weeks.
Music: Church/religious and gospel. Recently published "You Can't be Saved Without the Blood," "Stand" and "Clean Me Up, Lord," recorded by the Highland Park Community Choir.

DAWNBREAKER MUSIC CO., 216 Chatsworth Dr., San Fernando CA 91340. (213)873-3724. Affiliate: Jasmine (ASCAP). Professional Director: Judy Barron. BMI. Published 30 songs in 1978. Pays standard royalties.
How to Contact: Query, submit demo tape or submit demo tape and lead sheet. Prefers cassette with 1-3 songs on demo. SASE. Reports in 1 month.
Music: All except hard country. "We want commercial radio-oriented songs—anything that can be played on the radio. No album songs." Recently published "We'll Never Have to Say Goodbye Again" (by Jeffrey Comanor), recorded by England Dan and John Ford Coley.
Tips: "Most songs are from our staff writers, but we listen to everything and occasionally accept outside material."

DAWN OF CREATION PUBLISHING CO., Box 452, Cambridge, Ontario, Canada N1R 5V5. (416)924-8121. President: Robert Liddell. Music publisher and record company. Estab. 1970. BMI and ASCAP. Pays 10-20% royalty.
How to Contact: Submit demo tape or submit demo tape and lead sheet. Prefers cassette with 10 songs on demo. SAE and International Reply Coupons. Reports in 2 weeks.
Music: Children's; choral; church/religious; classical; easy listening; gospel; MOR; and top 40/pop. Recently published "Swan Song" and "We Travel Together," recorded by Rob Liddell (pop).

DAYDAN MUSIC CORP., Box 1546, Nashville TN 37202. (615) 244-3450. Professional Manager: Lamar Morris. Music publisher. ASCAP. See Acoustic Music for details.

DAYSPRING, Box 1790, Waco TX 76703. Music Editor: John Purifoy. Music publisher and record company. BMI. See Word Music for details.

JASON DEE MUSIC, 44 Music Square E., Nashville TN 37203. (615)255-2175. President: Charles Fields. Music publisher, record company and record producer. BMI. See Mr. Mort Music for details.

DE LEON PUBLISHING, Box 3818, 704 S. 7th, Temple TX 76501. (817)773-1775. Contact: Alberto Lopez, Top Hernandez. Music publisher, record company, record producer and booking agency. Estab. 1968. BMI. Published 16 songs in 1978; plans 25 in 1979, 25 in 1980. Pays standard royalties.
How to Contact: Query or submit demo tape. Prefers 7½ ips reel-to-reel or cassette with 5-20 songs on demo. SASE. Reports in 1 month.
Music: Latin/Spanish. Recently published "Apoco No," (by Joe D. Hernandez) recorded by Big Lu/BSR Records (polka); "California," (by Johnny D. Hernandez) recorded by Hernandez/Cherry Records (pop); and "Alma Rienaba," (by Big Lu) recorded by Big Lu/LRC Records (polka).

DEB MI MUSIC, Box 3892, North Providence RI 02911. (401)331-5354. Contact: Jimmie Crane. Music publisher, record producer and management firm. ASCAP. See Waste Away Music for details.

DEEP NOTE MUSIC, MCH Productions, 6801 Jericho Turnpike, Syosset, Long Island NY 11791. (516)364-8666. Contact: Bill Civitella, Andy Matranga and Nancy Sirianni. Music publisher, record company and production company. Estab. 1976. ASCAP. Publishes 50 songs/year.
How to Contact: Arrange personal interview or submit demo tape and lead sheet. Prefers 7½ ips reel-to-reel or cassette. SASE.
Music: C&W; disco; rock; soul; and top 40/pop.

DEER CREEK PUBLISHING, 300 N. Broad, Bremen OH 43107. Owner/President: Clay Eager. Music publisher, record producer and booking agency. Estab. 1961. BMI. Pays standard royalties.

How to Contact: Query or submit demo tape. Prefers reel-to-reel with 1-12 songs on demo. SASE. Reports in 1 month.
Music: Bluegrass; church/religious; C&W; folk; and gospel.

DEJAMUS MUSIC, 119 W. 57th St., New York NY 10019. (212)581-3420. General Manager: Arthur Braun. Music publisher. ASCAP. See Dick James Music for details.

DELIGHTFUL MUSIC, LTD., 200 W. 57th St., New York NY 10019. Affiliate: Vignette Music (BMI). Vice President: Ted Eddy. Music publisher. Estab. 1969. BMI. Published 30 songs in 1977; plans 30 in 1978, 30 in 1979. Pays 10-50% royalty.
How to Contact: Submit demo tape and lead sheet. Prefers cassette with 1-3 songs on demo. SASE. Reports in 1 month.
Music: Disco; easy listening; rock; and soul. Recently published "Summer Madness" and "Hollywood Swinging," recorded by Kool and the Gang (easy listening/rock); "Never Get Enough of Your Love," recorded by L.T.D. (rock); and "Open Sesame," recorded by the Bee Gees (rock).

DEMAND MUSIC, Box 57291, Dallas TX 75207. (214)526-8936. President: Don Schafer. Music publisher. Estab. 1966. BMI. Published 42 songs in 1977; plans 42 in 1978, 42 in 1979. Pays negotiable royalty.
How to Contact: Submit demo tape. Prefers reel-to-reel with 5 songs minimum on tape. SASE. Reports in 2 months.
Music: Church/religious; C&W; gospel; progressive; and top 40/pop. Recently published "Hear That Whistle Blow," recorded by the Side of the Road Gang (C&W); and "Stuntman," recorded by Larry Mahan (country).

DENNY MUSIC, 39 Music Square E., Nashville TN 37203. (615)255-6535. President: J. William Denny. Music publisher. ASCAP. See Cedarwood Publishing for details.

DERBY MUSIC, Las Vegas Recording Studio, 3977 Vegas Valley Dr., Las Vegas NV 89121. (702)457-4365. President: Hank Castro. Affiliates: Ru-Dot-To Music (BMI) and Hankeychip Music (ASCAP). Music publisher and recording studio. Estab. 1970. SESAC. Payment negotiable.
Music: Bluegrass; blues; C&W; easy listening; gospel; jazz; MOR; progressive; R&B; rock; soul; and top 40/pop. Recently published "Take Me" (by Leland Scott), recorded by Leland Scott/Marquee Records (top 40/pop).

DESERT MOON SONGS, Roadshow Music Group, 850 7th Ave., New York NY 10019. Vice President: Julie Lipsius. International Manager: Susan Reed. BMI. See Roadshow Music Group for details.

DESERT RAIN MUSIC, LTD., Roadshow Music Group, 850 7th Ave., New York NY 10019. Vice President: Julie Lipsius. ASCAP. See Roadshow Music Group for details.

DEVANEY MUSIC PUBLISHING, 105 Burk Dr., Oklahoma City OK 73115. (405)677-6448. Affiliate: Country Classics Music Publishing Co. (BMI). General Manager: Sonny Lane. Music publisher, record company and record producer. BMI.
Music: Church/religious; country and western; easy listening; gospel; MOR and top 40/pop. Recently published "We'll Make It This Time" (by Yvonne DeVaney), recorded by Yvonne DeVaney/AGA Records (country); and "Everytime I'm Near You" (by Rudy Moody & Marvin Thompson), recorded by Kathy Nunn/Silver Star Records (country). See Country Classics Music for submission details.

DIAMOND IN THE ROUGH MUSIC, 1440 Kearny St. NE, Washington DC 20017. (202)635-0464. Vice President A&R: Rodney Brown. Music publisher, record company and record producer. Estab. 1974. BMI. Published 17 songs in 1978; plans 20 in 1979, 28 in 1980. Pays standard royalties.
How to Contact: Submit demo tape. Prefers 7½ ips reel-to-reel or cassette with 2-4 songs on demo. SASE. Reports in 1 month.
Music: Disco; R&B; and soul. Recently published "Flash," "I Want Your Body," and "We've Got So Much to Stay Together For" (by Willie Lester and Rodney Brown) recorded by Bobby Thurston/Mainline Records (soul).

DIAMONDBACK MUSIC, 10 Waterville St., San Francisco CA 94124. Administrator: Joseph Buchwald. Music publisher. Estab. 1973. BMI.

How to Contact: Submit demo tape and lead sheet. Prefers cassette with 3-6 songs on demo. SASE. Reports "as soon as possible."
Music: Rock.

DICAP MUSIC PUBLISHING CO., Hugh Dixon Music Organization, 292 Lorraine Dr., Baie D'Urfe, Quebec, Canada H9X 2R1. (514)457-5959. President: Hugh D. Dixon. Executive Assistant: C.M.A. van Ogtrop. Music publisher and record company. Estab. 1972. CAPAC. See Dipro Music for details.

DIDDEM DADDUM MUSIC, 13615 Victory Blvd., Suite 216, Van Nuys CA 91401. (213)997-9100. Manager: Mary McNeil. Music publisher, record company and record producer. BMI.
Music: C&W; disco; easy listening; MOR; R&B; rock; soul; and top 40/pop. Recently published "Great White Procelain Seat" (by J.C. Martin), recorded by Martin/Magnum Records (country rock); and "Jewish Country Singer" and "Your Dog" (by Arnold Rosenthal and Jolly), recorded by Rosenthal/Pedigree Records (country).See Goldentree Music for submission details.

DIMENSION MUSIC, 365 Great Circle Rd., Nashville TN 37228. Contact: Unsolicited Music Review Committee. Music publisher. SESAC. See John T. Benson Publishing for details.

DIPRO MUSIC PUBLISHING CO., Hugh Dixon Music Organization, 292 Lorraine Dr., Baie D'Urfe, Quebec, Canada H9X 2R1. (514)457-5959. Affiliates: Dicap Music (CAPAC) and Hugh Dixon Music (PROCAN). President: Hugh D. Dixon. Executive Assistant: C.M.A. van Ogtrop. Music publisher and record company. Estab. 1972. PROCAN. Published 25 songs in 1977. Pays standard royalty.
How to Contact: Submit demo tape and lead or lyric sheet. Prefers 7½ ips reel-to-reel with 2-5 songs on demo. SAE and International Reply Coupons. Reports in 1 month.
Music: Rock (country with strong message); top 40/pop; and church/religious (positive, realistic, inspirational approach). Recently published "You Don't Really Love Me," recorded by Ian Cooney (pop); "No Black Clouds," recorded by Frank Waytor (MOR/inspirational); and "Little Venus," recorded by MPH Band (space disco).
Tips: "Put best song first and put leader between cuts. Don't forget to include copyright notices, name, address and phone number."

B.L. DIXON PUBLISHING, 7212 S. Wabash Ave., Chicago IL 60619. (312)783-3186. A&R Director: B.L. Dixon. Music publisher and record company. Estab. 1974. BMI. Pays standard royalty.
How to Contact: Submit demo tape or submit demo tape and lead or lyric sheet. Prefers 7½ ips reel-to-reel with 2-3 songs on demo. SASE. Reports in 2 weeks.
Music: Blues; disco; easy listening; MOR; rock; soul; and top 40/pop.

HUGH DIXON MUSIC PUBLISHING CO., Hugh Dixon Music Organization, 292 Lorraine Dr., Baie D'Urfe, Quebec, Canada H9X 2R1. (514)457-5959. President: Hugh D. Dixon. Executive Assistant: C.M.A. van Ogtrop. Music publisher and record company. Estab. 1972. PROCAN. See Dipro Music for details.

DOC DICK ENTERPRISES, 16 E. Broad St., Mt. Vernon NY 10552. (914)668-4488. President: Richard Rashbaum. Music publisher and management firm. Estab. 1975. BMI. Published 6 songs in 1978; plans 8 in 1979, 16 in 1980. Pays standard royalties.
How to Contact: Query, submit demo tape, submit demo tape and lead sheet, submit acetate disc, or submit acetate disc and lead sheet. Prefers cassette with 1-4 songs on demo. SASE. Reports in 2 weeks.
Music: Disco; R&B; soul; and top 40/pop. Recently published "Music Moves Me" and "I Need Love" (by Ken Simmons), recorded by Daybreak/RCA Records (disco); "Everything Man" and "What Does It Take," (by Patrick Adams), recorded by Daybreak (disco); and "Romance at a Disco" and "Johnny" (by Lance Waleck), recorded by Sweet Tooth/Beaulahland Records (disco).

DOG RIVER MUSIC, 8872 Hwy. 166, Winston GA 30187. (404)489-2909. Owner: Danny Mote. Music publisher, record company and record producer. Estab. 1975. BMI. Published 10 songs in 1978; plans 50 in 1979, 75 in 1980. Pays standard royalties.
How to Contact: Arrange personal interview, submit demo tape, or submit acetate disc. Prefers 7½ or 15 ips reel-to-reel tape with 1-10 songs on demo. Does not return unsolicited material. Reports in 1 month.

Music: Children's; church/religious; C&W; gospel; R&B; rock; and top 40/pop. Recently published "Full Time Christian" (by Tommy Godwin), recorded by Godwin/Rivera Records (gospel); "Who is Santa Claus" (by Floyd and Troy Crumpton Jr.), recorded by Crumpton/Opal Records (Christmas); and "Crying Eyes" (by Danny Mote), recorded by Mote/ARP Records (country).

DONNA MUSIC PUBLISHING CO., Box 113, Woburn MA 01801. (617)933-1474. General Manager: Frank Paul. Music publisher, record company, record producer, management firm and booking agency. Estab. 1952. BMI. Published 45 songs in 1978; plans 50 in 1979, 75 in 1980. Pays standard royalties.
How to Contact: Submit demo tape and lead sheet. Prefers cassette with 3-6 songs on demo. SASE for returns. Reports in 1 month.
Music: C&W; easy listening; gospel; MOR; R&B; rock; soul; and top 40/pop. Recently published "Happy Happy Birthday Baby," recorded by Mango Sylvia and Gilbert Lopez/Casa Grande Records (R&B).

DOOMS MUSIC PUBLISHING CO., Box 2072, Waynesboro VA 22980. (703)942-0106. Owners: John Major, Margie Major. Music publisher and record company. Estab. 1966. BMI. Published 150 songs in 1977. Pays on royalty basis.
How to Contact: Submit demo tape. Prefers cassette. SASE. Reports in 2 weeks.
Music: Bluegrass; C&W; easy listening; gospel; and MOR. Recently published "Somebody Socked it to Mine," recorded by the McPeak Brothers (bluegrass); "Leavin'," recorded by Kenny Price (C&W); and "Gypsy Lady," recorded by Joey Davis (country rock).

DOOR KNOB MUSIC, Gene Kennedy Enterprises, Inc., 2125 8th Ave. S., Nashville TN 37204. (615)383-6002. Vice President: Linda Kennedy. Music publisher. Estab. 1975. See Gene Kennedy Enterprises for details.

DOUBLE BOURBON MUSIC, 6001 Old Hickory Blvd., Hermitage TN 37076. General Manager: Tony DiRizziano. Music publisher and record producer. SESAC. See King of Music Publishing.

DOUBLE DIAMOND MUSIC, 3146 Arrowhead Dr., Hollywood CA 90068. (213)461-4756. Affiliate: Young Ideas Music (ASCAP). Vice President: John J. Madara. Music publisher and record producer. Estab. 1975. BMI. Payment negotiable. Sometimes secures songwriters on salary basis: "Duties would be to write many songs a year, with a $100-150 a week salary."
How to Contact: Submit demo tape and lead sheet. Prefers 7½ or 15 ips reel-to-reel or cassette with 2-5 songs on demo. "Please list how long you've been writing and how old you are." SASE. Reports in 3 weeks.
Music: Disco; jazz; MOR; progressive; rock; soul; and top 40/pop.Recently published "My Everlasting Love" (by Rick Sandler), recorded by Dionne Warwick/Arista Records (ballad); "Enemy Line" (by Rick Sandler), recorded by Jermaine Jackson/Motown Records (disco); and "A Good Love" (by Chris Bond), recorded by Jim Capaldi/RSO (rock).

DOUBLE R MUSIC CORP., 8 Music Square W., Nashville TN 37203. ASCAP. See Tree Publishing for details.

DOUBLEPLAY MUSIC, 380 Birchmount Rd., Scarborough, Ontario, Canada M1K 1M7. (416)691-2757. General Manager: W.B. Kearns. Music publisher and record company. Estab. 1974. PROCAN. See Quality Music Publishing for details.

DOVETAIL PUBLISHING CO., Box 2802, Corpus Christi TX 78403. (512)992-5126. Contact: Bruce Taylor or John Davis. Record company, music publisher, record producer, management firm and booking agency. Estab. 1972. BMI. Published 4 songs in 1978; plans 12 in 1979, 40 in 1980. Pays standard royalties.
How To Contact: Submit demo tape. Prefers 7½ ips reel-to-reel or cassette with 2-5 songs on demo. Does not return unsolicited material. Reports in 2 weeks.
Music: Recently published "If I Don't Drink Myself to Death," "El Capitan," and "Ask Me No Questions," recorded by the Gary Davis Band (country/progressive/country).

DOWNSTAIRS MUSIC, 2212 4th Ave., Seattle WA 98121. (206)682-5278. Director, West Coast Operations: JoDee Omer. Music publisher. Estab. 1973. BMI. See Mighty Three Music, Seattle WA office, for details.

DRAGON FLY MUSIC, 219 Meriden Rd., Waterbury CT 06705. (203)754-3674. Owner:

Ralph Calabrese. Music publisher and record producer. Estab. 1969. BMI. Published 10 songs in 1978. Pays standard royalties.
How to Contact: Submit demo tape or demo tape and lead sheet. Prefers 7½ ips reel-to-reel with 3-6 songs on demo. SASE. Reports in 1 month.
Music: Disco; rock; soul; and top 40/pop. Recently published "Don't Want to Live Without You," "My Baby's Gone" and "Bad, Bad Girl" (by R. Calabrese), recorded on ABC Records; and "Going Nowhere Fast" (by R. Calabrese), recorded on London Records (top 40/pop).

DREAM MERCHANT MUSIC CO., 582 Armour Circle NE, Atlanta GA 30324. (404)875-2555. Partners: Larry King, Gwen Kesler. Music publisher. Estab. 1975. BMI. See Candlestick Publishing for details.

DRIFTWOOD MUSIC, 39 Music Square E., Nashville TN 37203. (615)255-6535. President: J. William Denny. Music publisher. See Cedarwood Publishing Co. for details.

DUANE MUSIC, INC., 382 Clarence Ave., Sunnydale CA 94086. (408)739-6133. Affiliate: Morhits Publishing (BMI). President: Garrie Thompson. Music publisher. Estab. 1966. BMI. Pays standard royalty.
How to Contact: Submit demo tape and lead sheet. Prefers 7½ ips reel-to-reel or cassette with 1-4 songs on demo. SASE. Reports in 1 month.
Music: Blues; C&W; disco; easy listening; rock; soul; and top 40/pop. Recently published "Little Girl," recorded by Ban (rock); "Warm Tender Love," recorded by Percy Sledge (soul); and "My Adorable One," recorded by Joe Simon (blues).

DUCHESS MUSIC, 9100 Wilshire Blvd., Suite 530, Beverly Hills CA 90212. (213)550-3913. Contact: Dude McLean. Music publisher. Estab. 1964. BMI. See MCA Music listing for details.

DYNAMITE MUSIC, 450 E. Beaumont Ave., St. Bruno, Quebec, Canada J3V 2R3. (514)653-7838. President: Christian Lefort. Music publisher and record company. Estab. 1967. CAPAC. See S.M.C.L. Productions for details.

E.L.J. RECORD CO., 1344 Waldron, St. Louis MO 63130. (314)803-3605. President: Eddie Johnson. Vice President: William Johnson. Music publisher and record company. Estab. 1950. BMI. Published 8 songs in 1977; plans 15 in 1979. Pays 5-10% royalty.
How to Contact: Submit demo tape or submit demo tape and lead sheet. Prefers 7½ ips reel-to-reel or cassette with 4 songs on demo. SASE. Reports in 2 weeks.
Music: Blues; easy listening; soul; and top 40/pop. Recently published "Take Me Back Baby," recorded by Joe Buckner (blues); and "Who Am I?" and "You Got Me," recorded by Tab Smith (top 40/pop).

E&M PUBLISHING CO., 2674 Steele, Memphis TN 38127. (901)357-0064. Music Director: Patti Frith. Music publisher, record company and record producer. Estab. 1957. BMI. Published 10 songs in 1978; plans 10 in 1979, 10 in 1980. Pays standard royalties.
How to Contact: Submit demo tape. Prefers 7½ ips reel-to-reel or cassette with 4 songs on demo. "Be sure the words are clear. Don't try to make a master, just a good clean tape." Reports in 2 weeks.
Music: Blues; church/religious; C&W; easy listening; progressive; and R&B. Recently published "It's a Little More Like Heaven" (by Hoyt Johnson and Jim Atkins), recorded by Hank Lockin/Sun Records (country); "Queen of New Orleans" (by Danny Williams), recorded by Williams/Zone Records (country); and "Baby You Don't Know Me Anymore" (by J. Pullman), recorded by Pullman/Zone Records (country).

EARLY BIRD MUSIC, Waltner Enterprises, 14702 Canterbury, Tustin CA 92680. (714)731-2981. Owner/President: Steve Waltner. Music publisher and record company. Estab. 1971. BMI. Published 14 songs in 1977. Pays standard royalty.
How to Contact: Submit demo tape and lead sheet. Prefers 7½ ips reel-to-reel or cassette with 2-4 songs on demo. SASE. Reports in 3 weeks.
Music: C&W; easy listening; MOR; and top 40/pop.

EARTHSCREAM MUSIC PUBLISHING CO., 2036 Pasket, Houston TX 77092. (713)688-8067. Contact: Jeff Johnson. Music publisher, record company and record producer. Estab. 1974. BMI. Published 16 songs in 1978; plans 24 in 1979. Pays standard royalties.
How to Contact: Submit demo tape and lyric sheet. Prefers cassette with 2-5 songs on demo. SASE. Reports in 1 month.

┌─ Songwriter's Market Close-Up ─────────────

The question most frequently asked by beginning songwriters is, "How do I protect my songs?," says Ron Peterson, former president of the Nashville Songwriters Association International and himself a songwriter. Peterson, shown here talking with *Songwriter's Market* assistant editor Barbara Kuroff, finds this ironic, because songs are rarely stolen, he says.

Music: Blues; rock; and top 40/pop. Recently published "Texas Morning" (by Pete Reed), recorded by Reed (country/pop); "This Shouldn't Happen to Me" (by Pennington and Wells), recorded by Tempest (top 40/pop); and "There's a Way" (by Craig Bransfield), recorded by Lionhart (rock).

EASTEX MUSIC, 8537 Sunset Blvd., #2, Los Angeles CA 90069. (213)657-8852. Owner: Travis Lehman. Music publisher and record producer. Estab. 1977. Published 3 songs in 1977. Pays standard royalty.
How to Contact: Submit demo tape. Prefers 7½ ips reel-to-reel or cassette. SASE. Reports in 3 weeks.
Music: C&W and top 40/pop. Recently published "Tear in Your Eye," "Bar of Broken Hearts" and "When You Loved Me," recorded by Rick Ellis (C&W/pop).

EASY LISTENING MUSIC, 6255 Sunset Blvd., Suite 603, Hollywood CA 90028. (213)462-2251. Air Assistant: Kevin Magowan. Music publisher. Estab. 1963. ASCAP. See Al Gallico Music for details.

EAT YOUR HEART OUT MUSIC, 250 W. 57th St., New York NY 10019. Affiliates: Gospel Birds (BMI) and Augmented Music (BMI). General Manager: Vicki Wickham. Music publisher. Estab. 1977. BMI. Published 8 songs in 1977; plans 16 in 1978, 32 in 1979. Pays standard minimum royalty.
How to Contact: Submit demo tape and lead sheet. Prefers cassette with 3 songs on demo. SASE. Reports in 3 weeks.
Music: Progressive; rock; and top 40/pop. Recently published "Everybody Wants to Be Somebody," "Tout de Suite Mamselle" and "Tax Exiles," recorded by Nona Hendryx (pop/rock).

EDANMOOR SONGS, Box 222, Groveport OH 43125. General Manager: Ed Graham. Music publisher. Estab. 1978. ASCAP. "If the songwriter has self-published sheet music of his songs on which he owns the copyright, and which is in salable, printed form, Edanmoor Songs will act as 'sole selling agent' for the songs on a contract basis. Write to us and submit copies of the songs." See Grenoble Songs for submission details.

EDEN MUSIC CORP., Box 325, Englewood NJ 07631. Contact: Clyde Otis. Music publisher, record company and record producer. Estab. 1956. BMI and ASCAP. Pays standard royalties.
How to Contact: Submit demo tape and lead sheet. Wants 7½ ips reel-to-reel with 1-3 songs on demo. SASE. Reports in 1 month.
Music: Blues; C&W; disco; R&B; rock; soul; and top 40/pop.

EL CHICANO MUSIC, 20531 Plummer St., Chatsworth CA 91311. (213)998-0443. A&R Director: A. Sullivan. Music publisher, booking agency and record company. Estab. 1969. ASCAP. Published 2 songs in 1977. Pays 25% royalty.

How to Contact: Submit demo tape and lead sheet. Prefers 7½ ips reel-to-reel. SASE. Reports in 3 weeks.
Music: Bluegrass; blues; C&W; disco; easy listening; jazz; MOR; progressive; rock; soul; and top 40/pop. Recently published "Dancing Mama" (disco); "Just Cruisin' " (MOR); and "Ron Con-Con" (Latin rock).

ELATION MUSIC, 2141 Pemberton Rd. SW, Atlanta GA 30331. (404)349-1459. A&R Director: Gordon Boykin. Music publisher and record producer. Estab. 1968. BMI. Pays standard royalty.
How to Contact: Submit lead sheet. Prefers 7½ ips reel-to-reel with 4-8 songs on demo. SASE. Reports in 3 weeks.
Music: Blues; church/religious; disco; easy listening; gospel; jazz; rock; soul; and top 40/pop.

ELBEJAY ENTERPRISES, Box 40544, Nashville TN 37204. (615)297-3767. General Manager: H. Raymond Ligon. Music publisher and record company. Estab. 1969. BMI. Published 11 songs in 1977. Pays 49-60% royalty.
How to Contact: Submit demo tape and lead sheet. Prefers cassette with 1-4 songs on demo. SASE. Reports in 1 month.
Music: C&W; soul; and top 40/pop. Recently published "What Can I Do About Loving You?", and "Drinking Brown Eyes Out of My Mind," recorded by Carleton Raines (C&W); and "Is It True?", recorded by Johnny Bragg (soul).

ELVITRUE RECORDING MUSIC PUBLISHING CO., Music Makers Network of America Productions, Box 3022, W St., 1603 Forbes Ct., Wilmington NC 28401. (919)762-4706. Publicity: Joseph R. Franks. Music publisher and record company. Estab. 1952. BMI. Published 6 songs in 1977; plans 4 in 1978. Pays standard royalty.
How to Contact: Submit lead sheet. Prefers 7½ ips reel-to-reel or cassette with 2 songs on demo. SASE. Reports in 1 month.
Music: Blues; children's; church/religious; easy listening; gospel; MOR; and soul.

EMANDELL TUNES, 10220 Glade Ave., Chatsworth CA 91311. (213)341-2264. Affiliates: Chinwah Songs (SESAC), Birthright Music (ASCAP), Ben Lee Music (BMI), Jepacla Music (SESAC), House of Solomon (SESAC), Kenco (BMI), Together We Stand (BMI), Clevetown Music (SESAC) and Jam Bull Music. (BMI) President & Administrator: Leroy C. Levett Jr. Music Publisher andrecord Producer. Published 80 songs in 1978; plans 150 in 1979. Pays standard royalties.
How to Contact: Submit demo cassette and lead sheet (lyric sheet OK). Prefers cassette with 4-7 songs. Submit information about the group and the songwriter. SASE. Reports in 3 weeks.
Music: Religious; easy listening; and gospel. Recently published "The Comforter" and "Wonderful" (by Edwin Hawkins), recorded by the Edwin Hawkins Singers/Birthright Records (top 40/pop, gospel); "Taylor Made" (by Steve Hunt), recorded by Bobby Humphreys/Columbia Records (jazz); and "Tomorrow" (by George Bryant), recorded by James Cleveland/Savoy Records (pop/gospel). "Songbooks and sheet music available through Big Three/United Artist Music, New York."

ENGLISH MOUNTAIN PUBLISHING CO., 332 N. Brinker Ave., Columbus OH 43204. (614)279-5251. Script Manager: Jetta Brown. Music publisher, record company, record producer, management firm and booking agency. Estab. 1958. BMI. Published 50 songs in 1978; plans 500 in 1979, 1,000 in 1980. Pays standard royalties. Also works with songwriters on salary to write or rewrite lyrics for parts of music.
How to Contact: Query, arrange personal interview, submit demo, submit demo tape and lead sheet, submit lead sheet, or arrange in-person audition. Prefers 7½ or 15 ips reel-to-reel or cassette. Does not return unsolicited material.
Music: Bluegrass; blues; church/religious; C&W; folk; gospel; MOR; and top 40/pop. Recently published "Way Back in West Virginia" (by Kae and Walt Cochran), recorded by Walt Cochran/Holly Records (C&W); "Each Side of the River" (by K. and W. Cochran), recorded by W. Cochran/Holly (C&W); and "I Already Know" (by M. Cordle and W. Cochran), recorded by W. Cochran/Holly (C&W).

ENSIGN MUSIC CORP., 2 Music Circle S., Nashville TN 37203. Director of Nashville Operations: Judi Gottier. Director of Creative Affairs: Bill Ficks. Music publisher. BMI. See Famous Music Publishing Companies, Nashville TN office, for details.

ENTEKA, 82 St. Joseph Blvd. W., Montreal, Quebec, Canada H2T 2P4. (514)849-3776.

President: Christopher J. Reed. Music publisher. Estab. 1974. CAPAC. See Intermede Musique for details.

ENVOLVE MUSIC GROUP, Box 767, New York NY 10019. Affiliates: Envolve Publishing (ASCAP) and Tri-Envolve (SESAC). Vice President: R. O'Brien. President: Eugene Frank. Music publisher, record producer and management firm. Estab. 1970. BMI. Published 102 songs in 1978. Pays standard royalties.
How to Contact: Submit demo tape and lead sheet. Prefers cassette with 3-6 songs on demo. Does not return unsolicited material. Reports in 1 month.
Music: Bluegrass; choral; church/religious; classical; C&W; easy listening; folk; gospel; jazz; MOR; R&B; and rock.

ENVOLVE PUBLISHING CO., Box 767, New York NY 10019. President: Eugene Frank. Vice President: R. O'Brien. Music publisher, record producer and management firm. Estab. 1970. ASCAP. See Envolve Music Group listing for details.

EPP'S MUSIC CO., Box 28123, San Antonio TX 78228. Affiliate: Senisa Music (ASCAP). Owner: A. Epstein. Music Director/Manager: Joe L. Scates. Music publisher and record company. Estab. 1962. BMI. Pays standard royalty.
How to Contact: Submit demo tape and lead sheet. Prefers 7½ ips reel-to-reel or cassette with 1-4 songs on demo. SASE. Reports in 3-4 weeks; "time varies depending on the consideration given material."
Music: Children's; church/religious; C&W; disco; easy listening; gospel; MOR; rock; soul; and top 40/pop. "Always interested in receiving new material."

EPTEMBER ENTERPRISES, 231 W. 58th St., New York NY 10019. Executive Director: Jerry Silverhardt. Estab. 1979. ASCAP.
How to Contact: Submit demo tape and lyric sheet. Prefers cassette with 1-4 songs on demo. SASE. Reports in 3 weeks.
Music: Disco; jazz; MOR; R&B; top 40/pop.

ERECTION PUBLISHING, Austin Recording Studio, 4606 Clawson Rd., Austin TX 78745. (512)444-5489. Affiliate: Blue Branch Publishing (BMI). President: W. Tyler. Vice President: Tommy Byrd. Music publisher, record company and recording studio. BMI. Published 10 songs in 1977. Pays on royalty basis. "Sometimes songwriters rent our studios and we help get arrangements, musicians, etc. Under this situation, we don't own any interest in the song."
How to Contact: Submit demo tape and lyric sheet. Prefers 7½ ips reel-to-reel or cassette with 3 songs on demo. SASE. Reports "right away if it is a hit—we're only interested in hits!"
Music: Blues; church/religious; C&W; easy listening; gospel; MOR; progressive; rock; and top 40/pop. Recently published "Ordinary Man," recorded by Dale McBride (C&W); "One White Rose," recorded by Ted Hardin (pop/C&W); and "Touch Your Mind," recorded by Jackie Holland (rock/C&W).

ESKIMO/NUNA MUSIC, 380 Birchmount Rd., Scarborough, Ontario, Canada M1K 1M7. (416)691-2757. General Manager: W.B. Kearns. Music publisher and record company. Estab. 1974. PROCAN/CAPAC. See Quality Music Publishing for details.

ETNOS, 82 St. Joseph Blvd. W., Montreal, Quebec, Canada H2T 2P4. (514)849-3776. President: Christopher J. Reed. Music publisher. Estab. 1974. CAPAC. See Intermede Musique for details.

FAITH MUSIC, Box 527, Kansas City MO 64141. (816)931-1900. Music Editor: Lyndell Leatherman. Music publisher. Estab. 1926. SESAC. See Lillenas Publishing for details.

FAME PUBLISHING CO., INC., Box 2527, Muscle Shoals AL 35630. (205)381-0801. Affiliate: Rick Hall Music (ASCAP). Publishing Manager: Walt Aldridge. Music publisher, record company and record producer. BMI. Published 50 songs in 1978. Pays standard royalties.
How to Contact: Submit demo tape. Prefers 7½ ips reel-to-reel or cassette with 1-3 songs on demo. "Please include legible lyrics." SASE. Reports in 3 weeks.
Music: Disco; R&B; and top 40/pop. Recently published "Try a Piece of My Love," (by Barrett and Cunningham) recorded by Wild Cherry/Sweet City (rock); "Let This Man Take Hold of Your Life," (by Grimm and Norman) recorded by Dobie Gray/Infinity (MOR); and "Funky Situation," (by Wilkins) recorded by Wilson Pickett/Big Tree (R&B).

FAMEVILLE MUSIC CORP., 6430 Sunset Blvd., Suite 921, Los Angeles CA 90028. (213)461-3091. Director of Creative Affairs: B. Ficks, 2 Music Circle S., Nashville TN 37203. Music publisher. BMI. See Famous Music for details.

FAMOUS MUSIC PUBLISHING COMPANIES, 6430 Sunset Blvd., Suite 921, Los Angeles CA 90028. (213)461-3091. Affiliates: Addix Music Co., Inc. (ASCAP), Ensign Music (BMI), Bruin Music (BMI), Pala Sac Music (SESAC), Vinsun Music (ASCAP), Fameville Music (BMI), Infinite Music (ASCAP), Parabut Music(BMI), Paramount Music (ASCAP), and Sun Vine Music (BMI). Director of Creative Affairs: B. Ficks, 2 Music Circle S., Nashville TN 37203. Music publisher. Estab. 1929.
How to Contact: Submit demo tape and lead sheet. Prefers cassette with 3-4 songs on demo. "Don't send by registered or certified mail." SASE. Reports in 6 weeks.
Music: Disco; easy listening; MOR; progressive; R&B; rock; and top 40/pop. Recently published "The Closer I Get to You," recorded by Donny Hathaway and Roberta Flack; "Ready to Take a Chance Again," recorded by Barry Manilow; and "Angela, recorded by Boh James.

FAMOUS MUSIC PUBLISHING COMPANIES, 2 Music Circle S., Nashville TN 37203. Affiliates: Ensign Music (BMI), Famous Music (ASCAP) and Para Sac Music (SESAC). Director of Nashville Operations: Judi Gottier. Director of Creative Affairs: Bill Ficks. Music publisher.
How to Contact: Arrange personal interview or submit demo tape and lead sheet. Prefers 7½ ips reel-to-reel with 4 songs on demo. "Don't send by registered or certified mail." SASE. Reports in 2 weeks.
Music: "All types, although primarily country in Nashville." Recently published "That's the Way Love Should Be," recorded by Dave and Sugar (C&W); "It's Sad to Belong," recorded by England Dan and John Ford Coley (MOR); and "Painting This Old Town Blue" by Crystal Gayle.

FARJAY MUSIC, Box 600516, North Miami Beach FL 33160. (305)945-3738. Publisher: J. Gilday. Music publisher, record company and record producer. BMI. See "Gil" Gilday Publishing for details.

FAROUT MUSIC INC., 7417 Sunset Blvd., Los Angeles CA 90046. (213)874-1300. Contact: Steve Gold. Music publisher, record producer and management firm. ASCAP.
How to Contact: Submit demo tape. Prefers cassette. Does not return unsolicited material. Reports back "if interested."
Music: Disco; R&B; rock and top 40/pop.

FARR MUSIC, INC., Box 1098, 350 Grove St., Somerville NJ 08876. (201)526-6310. Affiliate: Grove Music (ASCAP). Controller/Manager: Candice Campbell. Music publisher and record company. Estab. 1974. BMI. Published 25 songs in 1977; plans 50 in 1979. Pays standard royalty. "We plan on establishing our in-house publishing very extensively the next two years. We are interested in hiring in-house writers as well as people to work publishing."
How to Contact: Arrange personal interview or submit demo tape and lead sheet. Prefers 7½ or 15 ips reel-to-reel or cassette, or disc. SASE.
Music: C&W; disco; easy listening; MOR; soul; and top 40/pop. Recently published "We'll Show Them All," recorded by R. Dean Taylor (pop); "Vulcan Voyage," recorded by the Tribe (disco/instrumental); and "Baby Give Some Love Back," recorded by Terry Webster (pop).

FAST FINGERS MUSIC, 39 W. 55th St., New York NY 10019. (212)586-3350. A&R Director: Nate Adams Jr. Music publisher.
Music: Disco; R&B; rock and soul. See Lorijoy Music for submission details.

FAVOR MUSIC, 1254 S. Holt, Los Angeles CA 90035. (213)655-5745. Affiliate: Off Hollywood Music (ASCAP). President: Howard Rosen. Music publisher and management firm. Estab. 1969. BMI. Published 50 songs in 1978; plans 50 in 1979.
How to Contact: Query or arrange personal interview. Prefers 7½ or 15 ips reel-to-reel or cassette. Tape should be leadered. SASE. Reports in 3 weeks.
Music: C&W; disco; easy listening; gospel; jazz; MOR; progressive; R&B; rock; and top 40/pop. Recently published "Taking My Love for Granted," recorded by Hot/Big Tree Records (pop); and "The Valentino Tango," recorded by Helen Schneider (disco).
Tips: "Piano, guitar and vocal demos will suffice. Be prepared to make changes in the song if necessary."

FENDER BENDER MUSIC, 2030 N. Oakland St., Arlington VA 22207. (703)527-2692. President: John Van Horn. Music publisher. Estab. 1970. BMI. Published 35 songs in 1977; plans 50-60 in 1979. Pays standard royalty.
How to Contact: Submit demo tape and lead sheet. Prefers 7½ ips reel-to-reel with 3-6 songs on demo. SASE. Reports in 3 weeks.
Music: C&W; disco; easy listening; rock (hard or 50s-60s types); and top 40/pop. Recently published "Get Off My Hog," "Knuckle Head" and "Cadillac Joe," recorded by the Pack (rock).

FILMWAYS MUSIC PUBLISHING, INC., 1800 Century Park E., Suite 300, Los Angeles CA 90067. (213)552-1133. Vice President: Terri Fricon. Professional Manager: Cathy Schleussner. Music publisher. Estab. 1975. ASCAP. See Musicways for details.

FINE COLORADO MUSIC, Box 0107, Los Angeles CA 90048. President: Richard M. Perry. Music publisher. BMI. See Border Star Music for details.

FIRMUS PUBLISHING, 66 Sherwood Ave., Toronto, Ontario, Canada. President: Milan Kymlicka. Music publisher and record producer. PROCAN.
Music: Disco; easy listening; MOR; and top 40/pop. Recently published "Hollywood" (P. Foldy), recorded by P. Foldy/Capitol Records (pop). See Cantus Publishing for submission details.

FIRST ARTISTS MUSIC CO., 4000 Warner Blvd., Burbank CA 91522. (213)843-6000, ext. 3634. Affiliate: Primus Artists Music (BMI). Vice President of Music Operations: Gary LaMel. Music publisher. Estab. 1969. ASCAP. Published 75 songs in 1978.
How to Contact: Query or submit demo tape and lead sheet. Prefers 7½ ips reel-to-reel or cassette with maximum 6 songs on demo. SASE. Reports in 8 weeks.
Music: Blues; C&W; disco; easy listening; folk; MOR; progressive; R&B; rock; soul; and top 40/pop. Recently published "Last Dance," recorded by Donna Summer; and "Evergreen," recorded by Barbra Streisand.

FIST-O-FUNK, LTD., The Sophisticated Funk Co., 293 Richard Ct., Pomona NY 10970. (914)354-7157. President: Kevin Misevis. Music publisher, record company and management firm. Estab. 1976. BMI. Published 7 songs in 1977. Pays 10-50% royalty. Sometimes secures songwriters on salary basis.
How to Contact: Submit demo tape and lead sheet. Prefers 7½ ips reel-to-reel cassette with 1-10 songs on demo. Does not return unsolicited material. Reports in 1 month.
Music: Blues; classical; disco; jazz; soul; and top 40/pop. Recently published "Dance All Over the World" (pop) and "It's So Nice" (ballad), recorded by T.C. James; and "Keep on Dancin'," recorded by Joe Davis (pop/jazz/disco).

FIVETAKE MUSIC, Fivetake Group Productions, Ltd., 484 Waterloo Ct., Oshawa, Ontario, Canada L1H 3X1. Affiliates: Creemore Music (CAPAC), Chinguacousey Music (PROCAN), Kashago Music (PROCAN) and Muffinman Music (CAPAC). Contact: Bob Stone. Music publisher. PROCAN.
How to Contact: Submit demo tape and lead sheet. Prefers reel-to-reel or cassette.
Music: MOR and top 40/pop (crossover).

HAROLD FLAMMER, INC., Delaware Water Gap PA 18327. (717)476-0550. Director of Publications: Lewis M. Kirby Jr. Music publisher and record company. ASCAP.
Music: Children's; choral; church/religious; and gospel. See Shawnee Press for submission details.

FLAT LIZARD MUSIC, Box 878, Sonoma CA 95476. (707)938-4060. Manager/Owner: Bruce Cohn. Music publisher and management firm. Estab. 1975. ASCAP. See Bruce Cohn Music for details.

FLIN-FLON MUSIC, Box 103, Main St., Mullen NE 69152. (308)546-2293. General Manager: L.E. Walker. Music publisher. Estab. 1966. BMI. Published 4 songs in 1977. Pays "by regular songwriter's contract."
How to Contact: Submit demo tape and lead sheet. Prefers 7½ ips reel-to-reel with 4 songs on demo. SASE. Reports in 3 weeks.
Music: C&W; contemporary; gospel; jazz; MOR; and rock (country). Recently published "Music Street," recorded by the Enterprize (R&B); "Goodbye—So Long—Goodbye," recorded

by the Nova-Kanes; and "Coal Miner's Blues," recorded by WDLJ So-Calif (MOR).

FLORENTINE MUSIC, Dawn Productions, Cloud 40, Paradise PA 17562. President: Vernon Wray. A&R Director: Joey Welz. Music publisher. Estab. 1965. BMI. See Ursula Music listing for details.

FOCAL POINT MUSIC PUBLISHERS, 922 McArthur Blvd., Warner Robins GA 31093. (912)923-6533. Affiliate: House of Melton (ASCAP). Owner/Manager: Ray Melton. Music publisher and record company. Estab. 1966. BMI. Published 25 songs in 1977; plans 50 in 1979. Pays standard royalty.
How to Contact: Submit demo tape and lead sheet. Prefers 7½ ips reel-to-reel or cassette with 2-4 songs on demo. SASE. Reports in 1 week.
Music: Bluegrass; children's; church/religious; C&W; easy listening; folk; gospel; and top 40/pop. Recently published "My Woman's Love," recorded by Hal and Charlie (C&W/top 40/pop); "Say the Word," recorded by the Green Family (gospel); and "Sweet, Sweet Love," recorded by Bud Criswell (C&W).

FOLKSTONE MUSIC PUBLISHING CO., South Branch Charge, Rt. 42, Arthur WV 26816. (304)749-7688. President: I. Lynn Beckman. Music publisher and record company. Estab. 1972. BMI. Published 10 songs in 1978. Pays standard royalty.
How to Contact: Submit demo tape and lead sheet. Prefers 7½ ips reel-to-reel or cassette with 1-12 songs on demo. SASE. Reports in 2 weeks.
Music: Bluegrass; church/religious; C&W; easy listening; folk; gospel; and MOR. "We are mostly interested in good gospel and/or good country music. Our main thrust right now is gospel: only music with a good flowing melody, no radical material." Recently published "He's My Son" (C&W), "I've Found My Strength in Thee" (gospel) and "Wasting Time" (C&W/MOR), recorded by Lynn Beckman.

FOR MY LADY MUSIC, Drawer 887, Truro, Nova Scotia, Canada B2N 5G6. (902)895-9317. Music publisher, record company, record producer, management firm and public relations firm. Estab. 1976. BMI. Published 4 songs in 1978.
How To Contact: Query or submit demo tape and lead sheet. Prefers 7½ or 15 ips reel-to-reel or cassette with "whatever the tape will hold with leader and separation." Would also like to "have the songs clearly titled and related to the lead sheets." SASE. Reports in 2 weeks.
Music: Easy listening; gospel; MOR; rock; and top 40/pop. Recently published "No More Reruns" (by Peter D'Amico), recorded by Tribe/Big Harold's (rock); "Rock and Roll Queen" (by Peter D'Amico), recorded by Tribe/Big Harold's (rock); and "A Sweet Dream" (by D'Amico), recorded by Tribe/Big Harold's (rock).

FORREST HILLS MUSIC, INC., 25 Music Square E., Nashville TN 37203. Affiliates: Ash Valley Music (ASCAP) and Roadrunner Music (BMI). Music publisher. BMI. Pays standard minimum royalty.
How to Contact: Submit demo tape and lyric sheet. Prefers reel-to-reel. SASE. Reports in 4 weeks.
Music: Bluegrass; blues; children's; choral; classical; C&W; disco; easy listening; folk; jazz; MOR; progressive; rock; soul; and top 40/pop. Recently published "Dream on Little Dreamer," recorded by Perry Como (MOR); and "I'm Living in Two Worlds," recorded by Bonnie Guitar (C&W).

FORT KNOX MUSIC CO., 1619 Broadway, New York NY 10019. Professional Manager: Robert Bienstock. BMI. Currently overstocked with material.

FORUM PUBLISHING, Drew Studios, 1420 N. Beachwood, Hollywood CA 90028. Owners: Tom Gunn, Mark Traversino. Music publisher and production company. Estab. 1974. ASCAP. See Good Changes Music for details.

FOUR GRAND MUSIC PUBLISHERS, Box 680460, Miami FL 33168. (305)891-0633. General Manager: Marlene Novak. Music publisher. Estab. 1971. BMI. Published 12 songs in 1977; plans 30 in 1979. Pays standard royalty.
How to Contact: Submit demo tape and lead sheet. Prefers 7½ ips reel-to-reel with 1-4 songs on demo. SASE. Reports in 3 weeks.
Music: Children's; C&W; disco; folk; gospel; MOR; rock (hard); soul; and top 40/pop. Recently published "Angel Disguised as a Barmaid," recorded by Cal Devlin (C&W); "He's a Better Liar Than Me," recorded by Tony Lampkin (soul); and "Miracle of Love," recorded by John Collins (gospel).

FOURTH HOUSE MUSIC PUBLISHING CO., 1217 S. Ogden Dr., ., Los Angeles CA 90019. (213)936-9149. Affiliates: Otis Music (BMI), Joel Webster Music (BMI), Mavid Music (ASCAP) and Golden Taylim Music (BMI). Chief of Production: Lim Taylor. Director: Deloras Anderson. Music publisher and production company. BMI. Published 10 songs in 1977; plans 30 in 1978, 25 in 1979. Pays 25% royalty. Sometimes secures songwriters on salary basis.
How to Contact: Submit demo tape and lead sheet. Prefers 7½ ips reel-to-reel or cassette with 3-6 songs on demo. SASE. Reports in 1 month.
Music: Blues; disco; soul; and top 40/pop. Recently published "Heavenly Music" (C&W/gospel) and "Anonymous Love" (pop), recorded by Ray Charles; and "I Gave My Love to Mary," recorded by Joel Webster (MOR).

FOX FANFARE MUSIC, INC., 8544 Sunset Blvd., Los Angeles CA 90069. (213)657-8210. Director of Creative Activities: Ron Vance. President: Herbert N. Eisemp. Music publisher and record company. BMI. See 20th Century Music for details.

FOXY LADY MUSIC, Multi-Media Enterprises, 1180 Forestwood Dr., Suite 304, Mississauga, Ontario, Canada L5C 1H9. Affiliate: Foxy Mama Music (PROCAN). Director: William Moran. Music publisher, record company and management firm. Estab. 1970. CAPAC. Pays 25-50% royalty. Buys some material outright; pays $300-1,000/song. Sometimes secures songwriters on salary basis: "preferably a singer or musician useful for making demos."
How to Contact: Submit demo tape and lead sheet. Include bio. Prefers 7½ ips reel-to-reel or cassette with 1-12 songs on demo. "Put titles in order. Include names of collaborators, if any, and tell whether or not you want the song published or sold outright." SAE and International Reply Coupons. Reports in 2 weeks.
Music: Blues; disco; easy listening; jazz; rock (country); soul; and top 40/pop. Recently published "Where Did the Good Times Go?", recorded by Jeff Adams (easy listening); "I Love to Sing," recorded by Terry Logan (jazz); and "It Happened One Night," recorded by Jeff and Jackie (top 40).

FOXY MAMA MUSIC, Multi-Media Enterprises, 1180 Forestwood Dr., Suite 304, Mississauga, Ontario, Canada L5C 1H9. Director: William Moran. Music publisher, record company and management firm. Estab. 1970. PROCAN. See Foxy Lady Music for details.

FRIENDLY FINLEY MUSIC, 103 Westview Ave., Valparaiso FL 32580. (904)678-7211. Affiliate: Shelly Singleton Music (BMI). Owner: Finley Duncan. President: Bruce Duncan. Music publisher, record company and record producer. Estab. 1958. BMI. Published 52 songs in 1978; plans 80 in 1979. Pays standard royalties.
How to Contact: Query, arrange personal interview, or submit demo tape and lead sheet. Prefers 7½ ips reel-to-reel tape with 5-10 songs on demo. "Send what you consider your best, and at least one of what you consider your worst." SASE. Reports in 1 week.
Music: C&W; disco; easy listening; MOR; R&B; rock; soul; and top 40/pop. Recently published "Alabama" and "Feel Like a Steel" (by Colwell),recorded by Bert Colwell/Country Artists Records (C&W).

FRIENDSHIP STORE MUSIC, Box M 777, Gary IN 46401. (312)OR4-6655. Artists Director: Joseph Cohen. Record company, music publisher and record producer. Estab. 1974. BMI. Plans to publish 12 songs in 1979 and 12 in 1980. Pays standard royalties.
How to Contact: Query or submit demo tape. Prefers 7½ ips reel with 1-3 songs on demo. "All songs must be copyrighted before being submitted to us." SASE. Reports in 3 weeks.
Music: Folk; and top 40/pop. Recently published "Rainbow," "Please Stay Forever," "Lonesome Song" and "Tired of Searching" (by Joe Cohen), recorded on Friendship Store Music Records (folk/pop).

FRONT POLAIRE, 82 St. Joseph Blvd. W., Montreal, Quebec, Canada H2T 2P4. (514)849-3776. President: Christopher J. Reed. Music publisher. Estab. 1974. CAPAC. See Intermede Musique for details.

FUNK BOX MUSIC, 880 NE 7th St., Miami FL 33138. President: Carlos Oliva. Music publisher, booking agency and record company. Estab. 1978.
Music: Disco; easy listening; MOR; rock and top 40/pop. Recently published "Note Conte" (by Frank Victory), recorded by Rammiro/Miami Records (disco); "Tus Ojos" (by C. Oliun and F. Marcos), recorded by Clouds/Miami Records (ballad) and "Tu Yo" (by C. Oliun and C. Dlanas), recorded by Clouds/Miami Records (disco-samba).

FYDAQ MUSIC, 240 E. Radcliffe Dr., Claremont CA 91711. (714)624-0677. Affiliate: Jubilation Music (BMI). President: Gary Buckley. Music publisher and record company. Estab. 1970. BMI. Published 35 songs in 1978.
How to Contact: Submit demo tape or submit demo tape and lead sheet. Prefers 7½ ips reel-to-reel or cassette with 1-4 songs on demo. SASE. Reports in 3 weeks.
Music: Children's; C&W; easy listening; gospel; MOR; progressive; rock (country); soul; and top 40/pop. Recently published "Leading Home," recorded by Jerry Roark and Rick Buche (C&W); "We're Working Together," recorded by Rick Buche (pop); "Singing Cowboy" (by Jody Barry), recorded by Jerry Roark/Majega Records (C&W); "Pie in the Sky" (by Ed Dato and Carolyn Harris), recorded by Jerry Roark/Majega Records (top 40/pop); and "Me and My Boy (by Ed Dato and Carolyn Harris), recorded by Jody Barry/Majega Records (MOR).

G.J. MUSIC CO., Box 4171, Princeton FL 33032. Owner: Morton Glosser. Music publisher. BMI. Pays standard royalty.
How to Contact: Submit demo tape and lead sheet. "Include lyric sheet with chords." Prefers 7½ ips reel-to-reel or mono cassette. SASE. Reports "depending on placement possibilities."
Music: C&W; easy listening; MOR; pop; and contemporary adult. "No teeny bopper rock."

GALLANT ROBERTSON, INC., 1115 Sherbrooke St. W., Suite 2504, Montreal, Quebec, Canada H3A 1H3. (514)288-8880. Affiliate: Robgal Music (PROCAN). Vice President: Ian Robertson. Music publisher and record producer. Estab. 1972. CAPAC. Published 20 songs in 1978; plans 20 in 1979. Pays 12½-50% royalty.
How to Contact: Submit demo tape or submit demo tape and lead sheet. Prefers 7½ ips reel-to-reel or cassette with 1-3 songs on demo. SAE and International Reply Coupons. Reports in 1 month.
Music: Disco; rock (not heavy); R&B and top 40/pop. Recently published "Will You Give Me Your Love" (by Patsy Gallant), "Te Calente" (by Jimmy Tanaka) and "Party Baby" (by Jack Lenz), all recorded by Patsy Gallant/Attic Records.

AL GALLICO MUSIC CORP., 9255 Sunset Blvd., Suite 507, Los Angeles CA 90069. (213)274-0165. Affiliates: Algee (BMI), Altam (BMI) and Easy Listening (ASCAP). Air Assistant: Kevin Magowan. Music publisher. Estab. 1963. BMI. Pays standard royalty. Buys some material outright; pays $100 minimum. Sometimes secures songwriters on salary basis.
How to Contact: Submit demo tape and lead sheet. Prefers 7½ ips reel-to-reel with 1-3 songs on demo. SASE. Reports in 2 weeks.
Music: C&W; easy listening; and top 40/pop. "We're very strong in contemporary country and crossover material." Recently published "The Fool Strikes Again," recorded by Charlie Rich/United Artists Records; "Beautiful Woman," recorded by Charlie Rich/Epic Records; "Still a Woman," recorded by Margo Smith/Warner Brothers Records; "Too Far Gone," recorded by Emmylou Harris/Warner Brothers Records; "Friend Lover Wife," recorded by Johnny Paycheck/Epic Records; "Please Don't Play a Love Song," recorded by Marty Robbins/Columbia Records; "If You've Got Ten Minutes," recorded by Joe Stampley/Epec Records; and "Rivers of Babylon" recorded by Boney M/Sire Records.

GAMMON AND GURREN MUSIC, E.J. Gurren Music Group, 3929 Kentucky Dr., Los Angeles CA 90068. (213)980-7501. Owner: Eddie Gurren. Music publisher. Estab. 1972. ASCAP. See E.J. Gurren Music for details.

GASTO RECORDING STUDIO, 220 Bascobel St., Nashville TN 37207. Producer: Tommy Hill. Needs vary; query about needs and submission policy.

GAVIOTA MUSIC, 2111 Kenmere Ave., Burbank CA 91504. President: Hal Spencer. Music publisher and record company. Estab. 1954. BMI. See Manna Music for details.

GEAR PUBLISHING CO., 567 Purdy, Birmingham MI 48009. (313)642-0910. Music publisher and record company.

GEMWAY MUSIC PUBLISHING, Little Gem Music, Inc., 19 Music Square W., Nashville TN 37203. (615)255-6606. President: A. W. Hodge. Music publisher, record company and record producer. Estab. 1972. SESAC. See Little Gem Music for details.

GIGUE ETERNELLE, 82 St. Joseph Blvd. W., Montreal, Quebec, Canada H2T 2P4. (514)849-3776. President: Christopher J. Reed. Music publisher. Estab. 1974. CAPAC. See Intermede Musique for details.

GIGUENT, 82 St. Joseph Blvd. W., Montreal, Quebec, Canada H2T 2P4. (514)849-3776. President: Christopher J. Reed. Music publisher. Estab. 1974. CAPAC. See Intermede Musique for details.

GIL GILDAY PUBLISHING CO., Box 600516, North Miami Beach FL 33160. (305)945-3738. Affiliates: Farjay (BMI) and Sancti (SESAC). Executive Director: J. "Gil" Gilday. A&R Director: Rufus Smith. Music publisher, record company and record producer. Estab. 1947. ASCAP. Published 126 songs in 1978; plans 200 in 1979, 200-250 in 1980. Pays standard royalties.
How to Contact: Submit demo tape and lead sheet. Prefers 7½ ips reel-to-reel or cassette with 1-3 songs on demo. "Make sure name and address are listed." SASE. Reports in 1 month, "sooner if possible."
Music: Church/religious; C&W; easy listening; gospel; MOR; and top 40/pop. Recently published "Father's Prayer," recorded by the Blackwood Brothers (MOR/gospel); "Pussy Cat Song," recorded by Connie Vannet (C&W); and "So All Alone," recorded by Don C. Davis (MOR).

GIPE, 82 St. Joseph Blvd. W., Montreal, Quebec, Canada H2T 2P4. (514)849-3776. President: Christopher J. Reed. Music publisher. Estab. 1974. CAPAC. See Intermede Musique for details.

GOG & MAGOG, 82 St. Joseph Blvd. W., Montreal, Quebec, Canada H2T 2P4. (514)849-3776. President: Christopher J. Reed. Music publisher. Estab. 1974. PROCAN. See Intermede Musique for details.

GOLD CHEF MUSIC PUBLISHING CO., Box 43, Chester PA 19016. President/Owner: Alexander Czarenko. Music publisher and record company. Estab. 1958. BMI.
How to Contact: Submit acetate disc and lead sheet. SASE. Reports in 1 month.
Music: Blues; C&W; disco; easy listening; MOR; R&B; and top 40/pop.

GOLDCREST PUBLISHING, INC., 10th and Parker, Berkeley CA 94710. (415)549-2500. Associate Director A&R: Hank Cosby. Music publisher and record company.
How to Contact: Submit demo tape. Prefers 7½ ips reel-to-reel or cassette. SASE. Reports in 3 weeks.
Music: Disco; easy listening; jazz; MOR; progressive; R&B; soul; and top 40/pop.

GOLDEN TAYLIM MUSIC, 1217 S. Ogden Dr., #1, Los Angeles CA 90019. (213)277-1197. Chief of Production: Lim Taylor. Director: Deloras Anderson. Music publisher and production company. Estab. 1972. BMI. See Fourth House Music Publishing for submission details.

GOLDENTREE MUSIC, 13615 Victory Blvd., Suite 216, Van Nuys CA 91401. (213)997-9100. Affiliate: Diddem Daddum Music (BMI). Manager: Mary McNeil. Music publisher, record company and record producer. Estab. 1975. BMI. Published 8 songs in 1978; plans 25 in 1979, 50 in 1980. Pays standard royalties.
How to Contact: Submit demo tape and lead sheet. Prefers 7½ ips reel-to-reel with 3-6 songs on demo. Also include lyric sheet. SASE. Reports in 3 weeks.
Music: C&W; disco; easy listening; MOR; R&B; soul; rock; and top 40/pop. Recently published "I Love Makin' Love" (by D. Whitney), recorded by Dean Whitney/Pedigree Records (country); "Feet Back on the Ground" (by D. Whitney), recorded by Eddie Howard/Pedigree (country); and "Back to the Beer and Country Dear" (by J.C. Martin), recorded by J.C. Martin/Magnum Records (country/rock).

GOLDLINE MUSIC, 329 Rockland Rd., Hendersonville TN 37075. General Manager: Noel Fox. Music publisher. ASCAP. See Silverline Music for details.

GOLDMONT PUBLISHING CO., 24 Music Square E., Nashville TN 37203. (615)254-3725. General Manager: Bettye McInturff. Music publisher and record company. Estab. 1966. BMI. Published 28 songs in 1977; plans 60 in 1979. Pays standard royalty.
How to Contact: Submit demo tape and lead sheet. Prefers 7½ ips reel-to-reel or cassette with 1-6 songs on demo. "We prefer 7½ ips, but we can review any speed. We prefer that the singer be accompanied by at least one musical instrument." SASE. Reports in 1 month.
Music: Bluegrass; blues; children's; church/religious; C&W; easy listening; folk (all); gospel (all); MOR; rock (country); soul; and top 40/pop. Recently published "It Ain't Gonna Rain

on Me," recorded by Stream (rock); "I Can't Help Myself," recorded by Steve Krug (C&W/folk); and "Sunshine," recorded by Eddie McConnell (C&W).

GOOD CHANGES MUSIC, Drew Studios, 1420 N. Beachwood, Hollywood CA 90028. Affiliates: Forum Publications (ASCAP) and TNT Publications (BMI). Owners: Tom Gunn, Mark Traversino. Music publisher and production company. Estab. 1974. ASCAP. Published 4 songs in 1977. Pays 5-7% royalty. Charges for some services: "independent producer for recording artists."
How to Contact: Arrange personal interview or submit demo tape. Prefers 7½ ips reel-to-reel or cassette with 1-3 songs on demo. SASE. Reports in 1 month.
Music: Disco; easy listening; MOR; rock; soul; and top 40/pop. Recently published "Pours When it Rains," recorded by Eric Mercury (pop); "Forever," recorded by John Simeone (pop); and "Country Kissin'," recorded by Marylou Sobel (C&W).

GOOD LUVIN' PUBLISHING, Box 66, Manhattan Beach CA 90266. (213)371-9578. Vice President, Publishing: Larry Thatt. Music publisher and record company. Estab. 1971. BMI. See Sundaze Music for details.

GOODNIGHT KISS MUSIC, Box 0107, Los Angeles CA 90048. President: Janet Fisher. Music publisher. BMI. See Border Star Music for details.

GOOGLES MUSIC, INC., 7800 Woodman Ave., #19A, Panorama City CA 91402. (213)786-3324. President: Jeff Wheat. Music publisher and record company. Estab. 1973. ASCAP. Published 20 songs in 1978. Pays negotiable royalty.
How to Contact: Submit demo tape. Prefers 7½ or 15 ips reel-to-reel or cassette with 4-6 songs on demo. SASE. Reports in 3 weeks.
Music: Folk; rock (hard, country or soft); and top 40/pop. Recently published "Bad Luck," recorded by October Young (hard rock); "Captain," recorded by Dee Carstenan (pop); and "Fort Wayne," recorded by Pearl Alley (rock).

GOPAM ENTERPRISES, INC., Box 24A53, Los Angeles CA 90024. (213)559-3139. Affiliates: Upam Music (BMI), Zawinul Music (BMI), Taggie Music (BMI), Jodax Music Co. (BMI), Semenya Music (BMI), Margenia Music (BMI), Turbine Music (BMI), Appleberry Music (BMI), Kae-Lyn Music (BMI), Jillean Music (BMI), Jowat Music (BMI), John Oscar Music, Inc. (ASCAP), Norahs Music, Dillard Music, Prill Music (BMI) and Jam-Lear Music. Managing Director: Laurie Goldstein. Music publisher. Estab. 1960. BMI. Pays standard royalties.
How to Contact: Query or submit demo tape and lead sheet. Prefers cassette with 1-3 songs. "Primarily interested in jazz and jazz related compositions." SASE. Reports as soon as possible.
Music: Blues; easy listening; jazz; R&B; soul; and pop.

GOSPEL BIRDS, INC., 250 W. 57th St., New York NY 10079. General Manager: Vicki Wickham. Music publisher. Estab. 1977. BMI. See Eat Your Heart Out Music for details.

GOSPEL PUBLISHING HOUSE, 1445 Boonville, Springfield MO 65802. Secretary, National Music Department: Lawrence B. Larsen. Doesn't consider outside material.

GOSPEL SENDERS MUSIC PUBLISHING CO., Box 55943, Houston TX 77055. (713)686-1749. Affiliate: Redeemer Music Publishing (SESAC). President: Gary R. Smith. Music publisher, record company, record producer, management firm and booking agency. Estab. 1972. BMI. Published 5 songs in 1978; plans 30 in 1979, 40 in 1980. Pays standard royalties.
How to Contact: Arrange personal interview. Prefers reel-to-reel or cassette with 3-10 songs on demo. SASE. Reports in 1 month.
Music: Church/religious; and gospel. Recently published "Comin' Home" (by Clay Howell), recorded on Redeemer Records (contemporary gospel); "Let Him Shine" (by Gary Smith and Tom Brewer), recorded on Redeemer Records (contemporary gospel); and "Come Lord, Right Now" (by Smith), recorded on Redeemer Records (contemporary gospel).

GOTTABE MUSIC, Box 9073, Chattanooga TN 37412. President: W. Stanley Hall Jr. Estab. 1968. BMI. Pays negotiable royalties.
How to Contact: Query or submit demo tape and lead sheet. Prefers 7½ or 15 ips reel-to-reel or cassette with 1-5 songs on demo. SASE. Reports in 1 month.

Music: Recently published "Train 69" (by S. Hall), recorded by S. Hall Jr./United Artists Records (rock); *Theme from Gentle People & Quiet Land* (by D. Parker and D. Johnston), recorded by E. Fambrough et al/BJW Records (feature motion picture score); "Home Country" (by Johnston/Hall/Bell), recorded by the Glaser Brothers/MGM Records (C&W). **Tips:** "We are always interested in novel ideas for concepts (jingles) as well as commercial material. We do, however, operate on a contract basis as regards specific projects in which we are engaged."

GRAND LEO, 82 St. Joseph Blvd. W., Montreal, Quebec, Canada H2T 2P4. (514)849-3776. President: Christopher J. Reed. Music publisher. Estab. 1974. CAPAC. See Intermede Musique for details.

GRAVENHURST MUSIC, 105 Park Lane, Beaver Falls PA 15010. (412)843-2431. Promotion Director: Roz Miller. President: Jerry Reed. Music publisher and record company. Estab. 1965. BMI. Published 75 songs in 1978; plans 30-50 in 1979. Pays standard royalty.
How to Contact: Submit demo tape and lead and lyric sheets. Prefers 7½ ips reel-to-reel or cassette with 1-3 songs on demo. SASE. Reports in 3 weeks.
Music: Blues; C&W; disco; easy listening; MOR; rock; and soul. Recently published "Dancin' Man," recorded by Q (pop); and "Alone," recorded by the JBC Band (soul).

GRAVENHURST MUSIC, 1469 3rd Ave., New Brighton PA 15066. (412)847-0111. President: Jerry Reed. Music publisher and record company. Estab. 1962. BMI. Published 30 songs on 1978; plans 40 in 1979, and 50 in 1980. Pays standard royalties.
How to Contact: Query or submit demo tape and lead sheet. Prefers 7½ reel-to-reel or cassette with 1-3 songs on demo. SASE. Reports in 2 weeks.
Music: C&W; disco; easy listening; MOR; R&B; soul; and top 40/pop. Recently published "Dancin' Man" (by R. Peckman), recorded by Q/Epic Records (top 40).

GREAT LEAWOOD MUSIC, INC., Box A 20, Lebanon TN 37087. (615)444-3753. Affiliate: Twinsong Music. (BMI). Secretary/Treasurer: Orlene Johnson. Music publisher and record company. Estab. 1974. ASCAP. Pays standard royalties.
How to Contact: Submit demo tape and lead sheet. Prefers 7½ ips reel-to-reel or cassette with 1-3 songs on demo. SASE. Reports in 1 month.
Music: C&W; MOR; rock; and top 40/pop. Recently published "A Little Something on the Side" and "Coldest Toes in Town" (by Pat Garrett), recorded by Garrett/Kansa Records (country rock).
Tips: "Make sure that the material mailed was done on a tape with at least one musical instrument and easily understood. Also that the material was in the right category. The artists we have now are country and country rock with a little MOR."

GREAT POWER MUSIC CO., 7033 Sunset Blvd., Suite 322, Los Angeles CA 90028. General Manager: Maritta Boyle. Music publisher. BMI. See Valgroup Music (USA) for details.

GREEN LIGHT MUSIC, 65 E. 55th St., Suite 302, New York NY 10022. (212)751-6177. President: Henri Belolo. National/International Relations Manager: Marsha Stern. Music publisher and production company. Estab. 1975. ASCAP. See Can't Stop Music for details.

GREEN UP MUSIC, Box 6687, Wheeling WV 26003. (614)758-5812. President: Bob Gallion. Music publisher, record company and booking agency. BMI. See Bo Gal Music for details.

GRENOBLE SONGS, Box 222, Groveport OH 43125. Affiliate: Edanmoor Songs (ASCAP). General Manager: Ed Graham. Music publisher and record company. Estab. 1951. BMI. Published 25 songs in 1978; plans 25 in 1979. Pays standard royalty.
How to Contact: Submit demo tape and lyric sheet. Prefers 7½ ips reel-to-reel or cassette with 1-3 songs on demo. "Tape should be titled and have leader tape on each song." SASE. Reports in 2-8 weeks.
Music: C&W; gospel (including choral); and pop. Recently published "Bless Them All," "For the Truth and the Right" and "Johnny Marchin'," recorded by Barry Sadler (patriotic).
Tips: "If the songwriter has self-published sheet music of his songs on which he owns the copyright, and which are in salable, printed form, Grenoble Songs will act as 'sole selling agent' for these songs, on a contract basis. Write to us and submit copies of the songs."

GROOVESVILLE MUSIC, 15855 Wyoming, Detroit MI 48238. Affiliates: Conquistador (ASCAP) and Double Sharp (ASCAP). Director: Brian Spiers. Operations Manager: Jerry

Allaere. Music publisher, record company and record producer. Estab. 1968. BMI. Published 50 songs in 1978; plans 75 in 1979, 100 in 1980. Pays standard royalties.
How to Contact: Query, submit demo tape, submit demo tape and lyric sheet, submit acetate disc or submit acetate disc and lyric sheet. Prefers 7½ ips reel-to-reel or cassette with 1-5 songs on demo. SASE. Reports in 3 weeks.
Music: Blues; disco; easy listening; MOR; progressive; R&B; rock; soul; and top 40/pop. Recently published "Disco Lady" (by Don Davis, Al Vance and Harvey Scales), recorded by Johnny Taylor (pop); "You Don't Have to be a Star" (by James Dean and John Glover), recorded by Marilyn McCoo and Billie Davis (pop); and "I Just Want to Dance With You" (by Don Davis and Cecil Womack), recorded by the Dramatics (pop).

GROSVENOR HOUSE MUSIC, Box 1563, Hollywood CA 90028. Affiliate: Star Tunes Music (BMI). President: Art Benson. Music publisher and record company. Estab. 1954. ASCAP. Published 200 songs in 1977; plans 100 in 1978, 100 in 1979. Pays standard royalty.
How to Contact: Submit demo tape and lead sheet. Prefers reel-to-reel or cassette with 1-3 songs on demo. SASE. Reports in 1 month.
Music: Bluegrass; blues; church/religious; C&W; easy listening; folk; jazz; MOR; soul; top 40/pop; and big band. Recently published "The Thrill Is Gone," recorded by B.B. King (R&B); and "I'll Sing the Blues" and "Another Leaf Falls," recorded by Tommy Cooper (pop/C&W).

GROVE MUSIC, INC., Box 1098, 350 Grove St., Somerville NJ 08876. (201)526-6310. Controller/Manager: Candice Campbell. Music publisher and record company. Estab. 1974. ASCAP. See Farr Music for details.

GRT OF CANADA, LTD., 3816 Victoria Park Ave., Toronto, Ontario, Canada. (416)497-2340. Affiliates: Corinth Music (BMI) and Tarana Music (CAPAC). Manager, Publishing Division: Jeanne Easton. Music publisher and record company. Estab. 1969. Published 50 songs in 1978; plans 75 in 1979, 100 in 1980. Pays standard royalty, less administration charge of 10-20% on mechanicals.
How to Contact: Submit demo tape. Prefers cassette. SASE. Reports in 1 month.
Music: Folk; MOR; progressive; rock; and top 40/pop. Recently published "I'm Comin' Home," recorded by Ian Thomas (top 40/pop); "Spaceship Superstar," recorded by Prism (rock); and "What You're Doin' To Me," recorded by David McCluskey (folk/rock).

FRANK GUBALA MUSIC, Hillside Rd., Cumberland RI 02864. (401)333-6097. Contact: Frank Gubala. Music publisher and booking agency. Estab. 1967.
How to Contact: Submit demo tape or submit demo tape and lead sheet. Prefers 7½ ips reel-to-reel or cassette. Does not return unsolicited material. Reports in 1 month.
Music: Blues; disco; easy listening; MOR; and top 40/pop.

GULE RECORD, 7046 Hollywood Blvd., Hollywood CA 90028. (213)462-0502. Vice President: Harry Gordon. Music publisher, record company and record producedr.
How to Contact: Submit demo tape or submit acetate disc. Prefers 7½ ips reel-to-reel tape with 2 songs on demo. SASE.
Music C&W; gospel; R&B; rock; soul; and top 40/pop.

E.J. GURREN MUSIC, E.J. Gurren Music Group, 3929 Kentucky Dr., Los Angeles CA 90068. (213)980-7501. Affiliates: Alva Music (BMI) and Gammon and Gurren Music (ASCAP). Owner: Eddie Gurren. Music publisher. Estab. 1972. ASCAP. Published 35 songs in 1977; plans 60 in 1979. Pays standard royalty. Sometimes secures songwriters on salary basis.
How to Contact: Arrange personal interview or submit demo tape and lead sheet. Prefers 7½ ips reel-to-reel with 1-3 songs on demo. SASE. Reports in 1 month.
Music: C&W; disco; MOR; soul; and top 40/pop. Recently published "It Feels Like Love," recorded by Larry Curtis (MOR); "Sweet September Morning," recorded by Back Home (C&W); and "Really Got Me Going," recorded by Brothers-By-Choice (disco).

HHH MUSIC, 11746 Goshen Ave., Suite 7, Los Angeles CA 90049. (213)479-6091. President: Hank Haldeman. Music publisher and record producer. ASCAP. See Triple H Music for details.

RICK HALL, Box 2527, Muscle Shoals AL 35630. (205)381-0801. Publishing Manager: Walt Aldridge. Music publisher, record company and record producer. ASCAP. See Fame Publishing for details.

HALLNOTE MUSIC CO., Box 40209, Nashville TN 37204. General Operations Manager: Ms. Lyn Phillips. BMI. Currently overstocked with material.

HAL-NAT PUBLISHING, 18550 Hatteras, #28, Tarzana CA 91356. (213)342-2985. President: Saul Halper. Music publisher. Estab. 1969. BMI. See Saul Avenue Publishing for details.

HALWILL MUSIC, 355 Harlem Rd., Buffalo NY 14224. (716)826-9560. Contact: Barbara Chinsky or Lynn Boehringer. Music publisher. ASCAP.
Music: Blues; disco; easy listening; folk; jazz; MOR; progressive; R&B; rock; soul and top 40/pop. Recently published "Don't Let The Flame Burn Out," "Just To Teel This Love From You" and "You're The Only Dancer" (by Jackie DeShannon), all recorded by Jackie DeShannon. See Harlem Music for submission details.

HANKBEE MUSIC CO., 1619 Broadway, Room 1009, New York NY 10019. (212)757-2695. Production Director: Henry Boye. General Manager: Gil Miller. Music publisher. Estab. 1960. BMI. See Joli Music for details.

HANKEYCHIP MUSIC, Las Vegas Recording Studio, 3977 Vegas Valley Dr., Las Vegas NV 89121. (702)457-4365. President: Hank Castro. Music publisher and recording studio. Estab. 1970. ASCAP. See Derby Music for details.

HAPPY DAY MUSIC CO., Box 602, Kennett MO 63857. Affiliate: Lincoln Road Music (BMI). President: Joe Keene. BMI. Pays standard royalty.
How to Contact: Submit demo tape and lead sheet. Prefers reel-to-reel. SASE. Reports in 2 weeks.
Music: Gospel and religious. Recently published "I'm Going Up," recorded by the Inspirations (gospel); and "Glory Bound," recorded by the Lewis Family (gospel).

HARLEM MUSIC, 355 Harlem Rd., Buffalo NY 14224. (716)826-9560. Affiliates: Halwill Music (ASCAP). Contact: Barbara Chinsky, Lynn Boehringer. Music publisher. Estab. 1975. BMI.
How To Contact: Submit demo tape and lead sheet. Prefers 7½ ips or cassette with 2-5 songs on demo. SASE. Reports in 1 month.
Music: Blues; disco; easy listening; folk; jazz (any type, preferably commercial); MOR (vocalists); progressive; R&B; rock (any type); soul; and top 40/pop. Recently published "Shaker Song," recorded by Spyro Gyra; "Don't Let The Flame Burn Out," recorded by Jackie DeShannon; and "Just To Feel This Love From You," recorded by Anne Murray.

HARRICK MUSIC, INC., Box 1780, Hialeah FL 33011. Manager: Sherry Smith. Music publisher and record company. Estab. 1976. BMI. Published 15 songs in 1977; plans 150 in 1979. Pays standard royalty.
How to Contact: Submit demo tape or submit demo tape and lead sheet. Prefers 7½ ips reel-to-reel or cassette with 1-3 songs on demo. SASE. Reports in 2 months.
Music: Disco; progressive; rock; soul; and top 40/pop. Recently published "Shake Your Booty," "I'm Your Boogie Man" and "Keep It Comin' Love," recorded by K.C. and the Sunshine Band (top 40/pop/soul); and "Dance Across the Floor," recorded by Jimmy "Bo" Horne (top 40/pop/soul).
Tips: Tapes should be addressed to "Attn: Preliminary Screening Committee." Lyrics unaccompanied by music are not accepted for review.

THE HARRIS MACHINE, 126 E. Mayland St., Philadelphia PA 19144. Executive Vice-President: Caryle Blackwell. President: Norman Harris. Music publisher, record company and production company. Estab. 1976. BMI.
Music: Disco; easy listening; jazz; MOR; R&B; rock; soul and top 40/pop. See Six Strings Music for submission details.

CHARLES K. HARRIS MUSIC PUBLISHING, 6922 Hollywood Blvd., Hollywood CA 90028. (213)469-1667. Professional Manager: Roy Kohn. Music publisher and record company. Estab. 1928. ASCAP. See Peer-Southern, Hollywood office, for details.

HARTFORD MUSIC CO., Powell MO 65730. (417)435-2225. Contact: Bob Brumley. Music publisher and booking agency. SESAC.
Music: Choral; church/religious; C&W; and gospel. See Albert E. Brumley & Sons for submission details.

JOHN HARVEY PUBLISHING CO., Box 245, Encinal TX 78019. President: John Harvey. Music publisher and record producer. Estab. 1969. BMI. Pays on royalty basis.
How to Contact: Submit demo tape and lead sheet. Prefers cassette with 2-6 songs on demo. Include brief resume. Does not return unsolicited material. Reports in 1 month.
Music: Children's; C&W; easy listening; folk; and Latin. Recently published "Sincere Love" (easy listening); "Love Without Ending" (C&W); "Nunca Entendi" (Latin); and "Mundos Mejores" (Latin).

HAT-N-BOOTS MUSIC PUBLISHING, Little Gem Music, Inc., 19 Music Square W., Nashville TN 37203. (615)255-6606. President: A.W. Hodge. Music publisher, record company and record producer. Estab. 1972. ASCAP. See Little Gem Music for details.

HATTRESS MUSIC PUBLISHING, 17544 Sorrento, Detroit MI 48235. (313)863-3839. President: Will Hatcher. Music publisher and record company. Estab. 1975. BMI. Published 20 songs in 1977. Pays negotiable royalty.
How to Contact: Submit demo tape and lead sheet. Prefers 7½ ips reel-to-reel with 2-4 songs on demo. SASE. Reports in 2 weeks.
Music: Disco; gospel; soul; and top 40/pop. Recently published "Who Am I?", recorded by William Hatcher (R&B); "Lets Stick Together," recorded by Beverly and Duane (pop); and "Caught Making Love," recorded by Clarence Carter (R&B).

HAVANA MOON MUSIC, Box 5853, Pasadena CA 91107. (213)355-8759. Owner: John Delgatto. Music publisher and record company. Estab. 1971. BMI. See Kentucky Colonel Music for details.

HAVE A HEART MUSIC, Northern Productions, Ltd., Box 3713, Station B, Calgary, Alberta, Canada T2M 4M4. (403)274-8638. Affiliate: Lovin' Heart Songs (CAPAC). President: Ron Mahonin. Music publisher, record producer, record company, and management firm. Estab. 1975. BMI. Published 15 songs in 1977; plans 20 in 1979. Pays standard royalty.
How to Contact: Submit demo tape and lead sheet. Prefers 7½ ips reel-to-reel or cassette with 1-4 songs on demo. "Be selective, songs submitted must be commercial. They should tell a story the public can relate to. Make sure the vocals are up front." SASE. Reports in 1 month.
Music: C&W; easy listening; MOR; progressive; rock; and top 40/pop. Recently published "A Hit Song," recorded by Ron Mahonin (AOR); "That Lady of Mine," recorded by Rick Morgenstern (C&W); and "Waiting for Me," recorded by Brian Bickerton (MOR).

HEARTSTONE MUSIC PUBLISHING CO., Love/Peace/Service Records, Inc., 2140 St. Clair St., Bellingham WA 98225. (206)733-3807. President: Renie Peterson. Music publisher, record company and tape supplier. Estab. 1970. BMI. Published 20 songs in 1978; plans 10 in 1979. Pays standard royalty.
How to Contact: Submit demo tape and lyric sheet. Prefers 7½ ips reel-to-reel or cassette with 1-4 songs on demo. "We require return envelope and postage." Reports in 2 weeks.
Music: Gospel (inspirational top/40). Recently published "How About You?" (by Ann Vernon), recorded by Claudette Dykstra/LPS Records (contemporary C&W); "He Is All to Me" (by Neil Vosburgh), recorded by Claudette Dykstra/LPS Records (Contemporary C&W); and "Thank You Lord For Watching Over Me" (by Vern Carlson), recorded by Claudette Dykstra/LPS (contemporary C&W).
Tips: "We want inspirational/MOR top 40 only—similar styles to Evie Tornquist and Stefanie Booshada. Writers should study what's on the radio to write for the market. We receive so much archaic material and it is not only time-consuming to return it but difficult to give encouragement to the writer, which we like to do regardless if a song is not for us."

HEARTWARMING MUSIC, 365 Great Circle Rd., Nashville TN 37228. Contact: Unsolicited Music Review Committee. Music publisher. BMI. See John T. Benson Publishing for details.

HEAVY JAMIN' MUSIC, Box 4740, Nashville TN 37216. (615)361-5356. Assistant Manager: Susan Neal. Music publisher, record company and record producer. Estab. 1971. ASCAP. Published 5 songs in 1978; plans 15 in 1979, 25 in 1980. Pays standard royalties.
How to Contact: Submit demo tape and lead sheet. Prefers 7½ ips reel-to-reel with 2-6 songs on demo. SASE. Reports in 3 weeks.
Music: Bluegrass; blues; C&W; disco; easy listening; folk; gospel; jazz; MOR; R&B; rock; soul; and top 40/pop. Recently published "Up And Down" (by Allan Mann), recorded by Allan Mann/Curtiss Records (rock); "Running Back" (by Allan Mann), recorded by Allan

┌ Songwriter's Market Close-Up ─────────────

"Writers should never sell their songs," songwriter Sheila Davis says emphatically. Never give up your rights to your material by selling it outright, says Davis, national director of special projects for the American Guild of Authors and Composers (AGAC) and writer of "Who Will Answer?", recorded by Ed Ames. If you sell a song outright, you give up all income the song earns in the future. What's more, Davis dislikes loosely using the word "selling" to mean pitching or marketing your songs. "That word offends me as a writer," she says. "You *place* your songs."

Mann/Curtiss Records (ballad); and "Punxsy" (by T. Russell), recorded by Rhythm Rockers/Tenock Records (instrumental).

HEAVY MUSIC, 9034 Sunset Blvd., Los Angeles CA 90069. (213)275-5002. Affiliate: Andromeda Music (ASCA). Director of Publishing: Lori Leis. Music publisher, record company and record producer. Estab. 1967. BMI. Pays standard royalties.
How to Contact: Submit copywritten material, lyric or lead sheet, and brief resume. SASE. Reports in 1 week.
Music: Choral; church/religious; C&W; disco; easy listening; gospel; MOR; progressive; R&B; rock; and top 40/pop. "No ethnic music."

HELPING HAND MUSIC, 9229 58th Ave., Edmonton, Alberta, Canada T6E 0B7. (403)436-0665. Director A&R: R. Harlan Smith. Music publisher, record company, record producer and management firm. Estab. 1966. PROCAN. Published 40 songs in 1978; plans 50 in 1979, 70 in 1980. Pays standard royalties.
How to Contact: Arrange personal interview, submit demo tape, or submit demo tape and lead sheet. Prefers 7½ ips reel-to-reel or cassette with 5-8 songs on demo. Would also like "a written statement verifying that publishing is available internationally on the material submitted". Does not return unsolicited material. Reports in 1 month.
Music: C&W; easy listening; MOR; rock; and top 40/pop. Recently published "Hold on the My Heart" (by C. Fjelligard), recorded by Nielson and Smith/Royalty Records of Canada (pop/country); "Half of What You've Been to Me" (by R. Thornberry), recorded by Smith (pop,country); and "Country Dreams" (by B. Allen), recorded by Nielsen (pop/country).

HEMLANE MUSIC CO., 50 Holly Hill Lane, Greenwich CT 06830. (203)661-0707. Music publisher. ASCAP. See Cherry Lane Music for details. "We do not accept unsolicited material."

THE HERALD SQUARE MUSIC CO., 1619 Broadway, New York NY 10019. Professional Manager: Robert Bienstock. Currently overstocked with material.

HERALDIC MUSIC, The Herald Association, Inc., Box 218, Wellman Heights, Johnsonville SC 29555. (803)386-2600. Director: Erv Lewis. Music publisher and record company. Estab. 1975. ASCAP. See Silhouette Music for details.

HERFORD, 38 Music Square E., Nashville TN 37203. (615)256-3373. President: Marty Williamson. Music publisher. ASCAP. See Brim Music for submission details.

HERO MUSIC PUBLISHING, 8927 Nevada Ave., Canoga Park CA 91304. President: Con Merten. Music publisher and record producer. Estab. 1971.
How to Contact: Submit demo tape and lead sheet, or submit acetate disc and lead sheet. Prefers cassette with 4 songs on demo. SASE. Reports in 1 month.
Music: Disco; rock; and top 40/pop.

HIP HILL MUSIC PUBLISHING, 4307 Saundersville Rd., Old Hickory TN 37138. (615)847-4419. Affiliate: Ragged Island Music (BMI). Contact: Professional Manager. President: Mira Ann Smith. Music publisher and record company. Estab. 1955. BMI. Published 80 songs in 1977; plans 200-500 in 1979. Pays standard royalty. "Advance accounts to proven songwriters."
How to Contact: Submit demo tape and lead or lyric sheet. Prefers 7½ ips 5-inch mono reel-to-reel with 1-5 songs on demo. "We would like leader between selections. Send material on regular fourth class mail on the special sound recording rate. Send only duplicate tapes, never the master." SASE. Reports in 1 month.
Music: Bluegrass; blues; C&W; disco; easy listening; folk; gospel; jazz; MOR; progressive; rock; soul; top 40/pop; and spoken word with original music. Recently published "Buffalo Soldier," recorded by the Persuasions (pop); "Flat Foot Sam," recorded by T.V. Slim (rock); and "I Almost Called Your Name," recorded by Freddy Fender (pop/C&W).

HIPOLIT MUSIC CO., Box 84, Glen Cove NY 11542. President: Krzysztof Z. Purzycki. Music publisher. Estab. 1974. ASCAP. See Memnon, Ltd. for details.

HITKIT MUSIC, Box 22325, Nashville TN 37202. Manager: Jerry Duncan. Music publisher. BMI. See Music Craftshop for details.

THE HIT MACHINE MUSIC CO., subsidiary of Diversified Management Group, Box 20692, San Diego CA 92120. (714)277-3141. President: Marty Kuritz. Music publisher and record company. Estab. 1971. BMI. Published 10 songs in 1978; plans 20 in 1979. Pays standard royalty.
How to Contact: Submit demo tape and lead sheet. Prefers cassette with 3 songs on demo. SASE. Reports in 1 month.
Music: MOR; rock (soft); soul; and top 40/pop. Recently published "Your Kind of Love," recorded by Quiet Fire (soul ballad); "This Time It's for Love," recorded by David Compton (top 40 ballad); and "I Hardly Know You," recorded by Romona Brooks (soul ballad).

HITSBURGH MUSIC CO., Box 195, 157 Ford Ave., Gallatin TN 37066. (615)452-1479. Affiliate: 7th Day Music (BMI). President/General Manager: Harold Gilbert. Music publisher. Estab. 1964. BMI. Published 30 songs in 1978. Pays standard royalties.
How to Contact: Submit demo tape and lead sheet. Prefers cassette with 2-4 songs on demo. Does not return unsolicited material. Reports in 3 weeks.
Music: C&W and MOR. Recently published "Blue Tears," recorded by Hal Gilbert (MOR); "(You Know) I Really Love You," recorded by the Fox Sex (MOR); and "I've Made Up My Mind," recorded by the Paramount Four (MOR).

HOLLYVILLE MUSIC, 2111 Kenmere Ave., Burbank CA 91504. President: Hal Spencer. Music publisher and record company. Estab. 1954. SESAC. See Manna Music for details.

HOOCHIE COOCHIE MUSIC, The Cameron Organisation, Inc., 320 S. Waiola Ave., LaGrange IL 60525. (312)352-2026. Vice President/General Manager: Jean M. Cameron. Music Publisher. Estab. 1978. BMI. See The Cameron Organisation for details.

HOOLIE MUSIC, 10341 San Pablo Ave., El Cerrito CA 94530. Music publisher. ASCAP. See Tradition Music for details.

HORNSBY MUSIC CO., Box 13661, Houston TX 77019. Producer: J.D. Horn. Music publisher. Estab. 1965. BMI. Published 12 songs in 1978. Pays standard royalty.
How to Contact: Submit demo tape. Prefers 7½ ips reel-to-reel or cassette with 2-3 songs on demo. Does not return unsolicited material.
Music: Blues and gospel. Recently published "Hattie Green" and "The Ma Grinder," recorded by Robert Shaw; and "In the Whole World," recorded by Jesse Thomas.

HOT BANANA MUSIC, 8033 Highland Trail, Los Angeles CA 90046. Contact: General Manager. Music publisher. Estab. 1977. ASCAP. See Big Cigar Music for details.

HOT GOLD MUSIC PUBLISHING CO., Box 25654, Richmond VA 23260. (804)282-6690. President: Joseph J. Carter Jr. Music publisher, booking agency and record company. Estab. 1976. BMI. Published 20 songs in 1977; plans 100 in 1979. Pays standard royalty.
How to Contact: Submit demo tape. Prefers 7½ ips reel-to-reel with 1-8 songs on demo. SASE. Reports in 2 weeks.
Music: Disco; rock; soul; and top 40/pop. Recently published "I Believe in You," recorded by the Waller Family (rock); "Do What You Wanna Do," recorded by Poison (soul); and "I Want to Sing This Song for You," recorded by Starfire (top 40/pop).

HOT POT MUSIC, Box 58, Glendora NJ 08029. (609)939-0034. General Manager: Eddie Jay Harris. Office Manager: Patricia Davis. Music publisher and record company. Estab. 1970. BMI. See Never Ending Music for details.

HOUSE OF DAVID, Songs of David, Inc., Suite 116, Music Park Bldg., Box 22653, Nashville TN 37202. (615)885-0713. Affiliates: Lit'l David Music (ASCAP) and Star of David (SESAC). President: Dave Mathes. Estab. 1975. BMI. Published 40 songs in 1977; plans 100 in 1979. Pays standard royalty.
How to Contact: Submit demo tape and lyric sheet. Prefers 7½ ips reel-to-reel with 3-5 songs on demo. "Enclose $1 to help defray postage and handling.
Music: Bluegrass; blues; C&W; disco; easy listening; gospel; MOR; progressive rock (country); soul; top 40/pop and instrumental. Recently published "Baby You Know How I Love You," recorded by Jim Ed Brown and Helen Cornelius (C&W); "My Sweet Melinda," recorded by Johnny C. Newman/Stone Company (C&W); and "The Last Goodbye," recorded by Faron Young (C&W).

HOUSE OF HI HO, Box 8135, Chicago IL 60680. (312)787-8220. President: Frank Howard Jr. Executive Vice President: R.C. Hillsman. Music publisher. Estab. 1972. BMI. Published 10 songs in 1977; plans 50 in 1979. Pays 3-5% royalty.
How to Contact: Submit demo tape and lead sheet. Prefers 7½ or 15 ips quarter-track reel-to-reel or cassette with 4-6 songs on demo. SASE. Reports in 3 weeks.
Music: Blues; choral; church/religious; C&W; disco; easy listening; gospel; jazz; MOR; progressive; rock; soul; and top 40/pop. Recently published "Up There" and "Since I Found Jesus," recorded by Allen Duo (gospel).

HOUSE OF SOLOMON, 10220 Glade Ave., Chatsworth CA 91311. (213)341-2264. SESAC. See Emandell Tunes for details.

HOUSE OF MELTON, 922 McArthur Blvd., Warner Robins GA 31093. (912)923-6533. Owner/Manager: Ray Melton. Music publisher and record company. Estab. 1966. ASCAP. See Focal Point Music Publishers for details.

THE HUDSON BAY MUSIC CO., 1619 Broadway, New York NY 10019. Professional Manager: Robert Bienstock. BMI. Currently overstocked with material.

RUBEN HUGHES MUSIC CO., 711 St. Stephens Rd., Prichard AL 366610. (205)457-9431. Professional Manager: Ruben Hughes. Music publisher, record company, record producer and booking agency. Estab. 1967. Published 1 song in 1978; plans 5 in 1979, 7 in 1980. Pays standard royalties.
How to Contact: Arrange personal interview, submit demo tape and lead sheet, submit acetate disc, submit acetate disc and lead sheet or submit lead sheet. Prefers 7½ ips reel-to-reel or cassette with 2-4 songs on demo. Does not return unsolicited material. Reports in 3 weeks.
Music: Blues; church/religious; C&W; gospel; R&B; and soul. Recently published "Lord Tell Me" (by Roy L. King), recorded by Trumptaires/Red Ball Records (gospel); "Soldiers Sad Story" (by E. Watkins), recorded by Tiny Watkins/Excello Records (R&B); and "Some People Believe in Hou Dou" (by S. Pendelton), recorded by the Trumptaires/Red Ball Records (gospel).

HUSTLERS, INC., 602 Southern Trust Bldg., Macon GA 31201. (912)745-5391. President: Alan Walden. Music publisher. Estab. 1970. BMI. Published 20 songs in 1977; plans 40 in 1979. Pays standard royalty.
How to Contact: Submit demo tape and lead or lyric sheet. Prefers cassette with 3-8 songs on demo. SASE. Reports in 2 weeks.

Music: Rock and country rock. Recently published "Sweet Home Alabama" and "Free Bird," recorded by Lynyrd Skynyrd (rock); and "There Goes Another Love Song," recorded by the Outlaws (country rock).

IQUANA MUSIC, INC. c/o Toby Byron Management, 225 Central Park W., New York NY 10024. (212)580-7210. Music publisher and management firm.
How to Contact: Query or send demo tape only. Prefers cassette with 4 songs minimum on demo. Reports in 1 month.
Music: Rock; jazz; top 40/pop; soul; MOR; disco; and R&B.

ILOT, 82 St. Joseph Blvd. W., Montreal, Quebec, Canada H2T 2P4. (514)849-3776. President: Christopher J. Reed. Music publisher. Estab. 1974. PROCAN. See Intermede Musique for details.

IMPULSIONS, 82 St. Joseph Blvd. W., Montreal, Quebec, Canada H2T 2P4. (514)849-3776. President: Christopher J. Reed. Music publisher. Estab. 1974. CAPAC. See Intermede Musique for details.

INFINITE MUSIC CORP., 6430 Sunset Blvd., Suite 921, Los Angeles CA 90028. (213)461-3091. Director of Creative Affairs: B. Ficks, 2 Music Circle S., Nashville TN 37203. Music publisher. ASCAP. See Famous Music Corporation for details.

INSANITY'S MUSIC, 24548 Pierce, Southfield MI 48075. (313)559-7630. President: Bruce Lorfel. Music publisher and booking agency. Estab. 1971. BMI.
How to Contact: Submit demo tape. Prefers cassette with 1-4 songs on demo. SASE. Reports in 1 month.
Music: C&W; easy listening; MOR; rock; and top/40 pop.

INSTANT REPLAY MUSIC CO., Box 353, Marina CA 93933. General Manager of Publishing: Robert Waldrup II. Music publisher. Estab. 1973. ASCAP. Published 35 songs in 1978; plans 50 in 1979. Pays standard royalty.
How to Contact: Submit demo tape and lead sheet. Prefers reel-to-reel with 2-4 songs on demo. "Use piano and vocal; or bass drums, piano and vocal. Guitar can also be used." SASE. Reports in 3 weeks.
Music: Disco; jazz; and soul. Recently published "Together," recorded by Elements of Peace (soul); "Walk Down My Street," recorded by Johnny Jackson (soul); and "Reach Out for Love," recorded by Bobbye (disco).

INTERMEDE MUSIQUE, 82 St. Joseph Blvd. W., Montreal, Quebec, Canada H2T 2P4. (514)849-3776. Affiliates: Ailes Du Nord (PROCAN); Alicia Music (CAPAC); Aout (PROCAN); Basse Ville (CAPAC); Breton-Cyr (CAPAC); Carricatum (CAPAC); Charlot (CAPAC); Chat (CAPAC); Chien Noir (CAPAC); Conception (CAPAC); Etnos (CAPAC); Enteka (CAPAC); Front Polaire (CAPAC); Gigue Eternelle (CAPAC); Giguent (CAPAC); Gipe (CAPAC); Gog & Magog (CAPAC); Grand Leo (CAPAC); Ilot (PROCAN); Impulsions (CAPAC); Intermede Quebec (CAPAC); Jean Chevrier (CAPAC); Jerome (CAPAC); Jour De L'An (CAPAC); Just Her Music (CAPAC); Kapocire (CAPAC); Lirana (CAPAC); Marais Bouleur (PROCAN); Michel Lefrancois (CAPAC); Mozusse (CAPAC); Musique Frisee (CAPAC); Musiquette (CAPAC); O.K. (CAPAC); P.L. (CAPAC); Rang Double (PROCAN); Sarah Porte (PROCAN); Surprise (CAPAC); Triangle (CAPAC); 1, 2, 3, 4 (CAPAC); Universol (CAPAC); Val D'Espoir (PROCAN); Vent Qui Vire (CAPAC); Vert Pays (CAPAC); Vibrations (CAPAC); 22/22 Music (CAPAC); and Y.D. (CAPAC). President: Christopher J. Reed. Music publisher. Estab. 1974. CAPAC and PROCAN. Published 45 songs in 1978; plans 45 in 1979. Pays 10-50% royalty.
How to Contact: Arrange personal interview. Prefers 7½ ips reel-to-reel with 1-6 songs on demo. "A copy of lyrics should be submitted with tape." Does not return unsolicited material. Reports in 2 months.
Music: MOR and rock (hard). Recently published "Frog Song," recorded by Robert Charlebois (rock); "Welcome Soleil," recorded by Jim and Bertrand (folk); and "Ragtime," recorded by Gaston Brisson (MOR instrumental).

INTERMEDE QUEBEC, 82 St. Joseph Blvd. W., Montreal, Quebec, Canada H2T 2P4. (514)849-3776. President: Christopher J. Reed. Music publisher. Estab. 1974. CAPAC. See Intermede Musique for details.

INTERPLANETARY MUSIC, 7901 S. La Salle St., Chicago IL 60620. (312)846-0099. President: James R. Hall III. Vice President: Joe Martin. Music publisher, booking agency and record company. Estab. 1972. BMI. Published 18 songs in 1977; plans 25 in 1979. Pays standard maximum royalty.
How to Contact: Submit demo tape or arrange personal interview. Prefers cassette. SASE. Reports in 3 weeks.
Music: Disco; soul; and top 40/pop. Recently published "Girl, Why Do You Want to Take My Heart?", recorded by Magical Connection (pop); and "You Blew My Mind This Time," recorded by Joe Martin (soul/pop/easy listening).

INTERSONG MUSIC, 21 Music Circle E., Nashville TN 37203. ASCAP. See Chappell Music for details.

INTERWORLD MUSIC GROUP, 6255 Sunset Blvd., Suite 709, Los Angeles CA 90028. (213)467-5108. Contact: Barry Oslander. Music publisher. ASCAP.
How to Contact: Submit demo tape and lyric sheet. Prefers cassette with 3-5 songs on demo. SASE. Reports in 2 weeks.
Music: Children's; choral; church/religious; C&W; disco; easy listening; folk; gospel; R&B; rock; soul and top 40/pop.
Tips: "Don't make it too busy. Simple rhythm tracks with vocals are fine. Include lyric sheets for full songs. No half-songs wanted."

IRON BLOSSOM MUSIC GROUP, 50 Music Square W., Suite 902, United Artist Tower, Nashville TN 37203. (615)329-0714. Affiliates: Coral Blossom Music (BMI) and Orange Blossom Music (SESAC). Professional Manager: Bobby Fischer. Music publisher, record company and record producer. Estab. 1978. ASCAP. Pays standard royalties.
How to Contact: Query or arrange personal interview. Prefers cassette with 3-4 songs on demo. SASE. Will return material "if time allows." Reports as soon as possible.
Music: "Mainly modern country, but we're capable of any type if we hear what we think is a hit. We just think music."

IRONSIDE PUBLISHING, 2712 Larmon Dr., Nashville TN 37204. (615)297-7521. Secretary: Terri Mullins. Music publisher and record producer. Estab. 1973. ASCAP. Published 30 songs in 1978; plans 50 in 1979.
How to Contact: Arrange personal interview or submit demo tape and lead sheet. Prefers 7½ ips reel-to-reel or cassette with 3-5 songs on demo. SASE. Reports in 3 weeks.
Music: Children's; choral; church/religious; C&W; disco; easy listening; gospel; MOR; country rock; and top 40/pop.

IRVING/ALMO MUSIC OF CANADA, LTD., 939 Warden Ave., Toronto, Ontario, Canada. (416)752-7191. Administrator: Brian Chater. Music publisher. Estab. 1973. BMI. Published 50 songs in 1978; plans 50 in 1979. Pays standard royalty.
How to Contact: Submit demo tape or submit demo tape and lead sheet. Prefers cassette with 3-6 songs on demo. SAE and International Reply Coupons. Reports in 3 weeks.
Music: Easy listening; folk; MOR; progressive; rock; and top 40/pop. Recently published "Long, Long Road," recorded by David Bradstreet (pop/folk); and "I'm Ready" and "Hometown Band," recorded by Hometown Band (pop/folk).

ISLAND MUSIC, INC., 7720 Sunset Blvd., Los Angeles CA 90046. (213)851-1466. Affiliates: UFO Music (ASCAP), Ackee Music (ASCAP) and Blue Mountain Music (ASCAP). President: Lionel Conway. General Manager: Allan McDougall. Music publisher. Estab. 1964. BMI. Pays standard royalties. Also works with songwriters on salary.
How to Contact: Submit demo tape and lead sheet or lyric sheet. Prefers 7½ ips reel-to-reel or cassette with 3-4 songs on demo. SASE. Reports in 2 months.
Music: Disco; easy listening; MOR; progressive; R&B; rock; soul; and top 40/pop. Recently published "Miss You Nights," recorded by Art Garfunkel; "Feeling All Right" (by Dave Mason), recorded by over 100 artists; and "Gimme Some Lovin'," recorded by Olivia Newton-John.

ISONODE PUBLISHING, Rainbow Recording Studios, 2322 S. 64th Ave., Omaha NE 68106. (402)554-0123. Manager: Lars P. Erickson. Music publisher and record company. Estab. 1976. BMI. Pays standard royalty. Sometimes secures songwriters on salary basis; "e.g., commercial writers who produce jingles, soundtracks and audiovisual shows."
How to Contact: Arrange personal interview or submit demo tape and lead sheet. Prefers

cassette with 1-6 songs on demo. "Please, only professionally done demos." SASE. Reports in 1 month.
Music: Church/religious; C&W; easy listening; rock (soft or country); top 40/pop; and jingles/commercials.
Tips: "We are primarily a small, independent recording studio; however, we find other clients needing a source of good, original music. As of 1978, we are starting to publish."

ITT MUSIC, 450 E. Beaumont Ave., St. Bruno, Quebec, Canada J3V 2R3. (514)653-7838. President: Christian Lefort. Music publisher and record company. Estab. 1967. CAPAC. See S.M.C.L. Productions for submission details.

I'VE GOT THE MUSIC, Box 2631, Muscle Shoals AL 35660. (205)381-1455. Professional Manager: Kevin Lamb. Music publisher and record company. Estab. 1978. ASCAP. See Song Tailors Music for details.

J.C.E. PUBLISHING, 130 Pilgrim Dr., San Antonio TX 78213. Owner: Jerry Connell. Music publisher, record company, record producer and booking agency. ASCAP. See Jerry Connell Publishing for details.

DICK JAMES MUSIC, INC., 119 W. 57th St., Suite 400, New York NY 10019. (212)581-3420. Affiliates: Cookaway Music (ASCAP), Dejamus Music (ASCAP), Maribus Music (BMI), Daramus Music (ASCAP) and Yamaha. General Manager: Arthur Braun. Professional Manager: Gary D'Anato. Music publisher. Estab. 1961. BMI.
How to Contact: Submit demo tape and lead sheet. Prefers cassette with 1-3 songs on demo. SASE. Reports "as soon as possible."
Music: C&W; disco; easy listening; MOR; rock (country and hard); soul; R&B; and top 40/pop. Recently published "Can't Smile Without You," recorded by Barry Manilow/Arista Records (MOR); "Tell Me to My Face," recorded Dan Fogelberg and Tom Weisberg/Full Moon Records (rock); "Love Stealer," recorded by Brownsville/Epic Records (rock); and "Time Passages" recorded by Al Stewart.

JAMES S. ENTERPRISES, 3190 Hallmark Court, Saginaw MI 48603. (517)792-7889. Affiliates: Brian-James Music (BMI) and Beowulf Music (BMI). President: J.S. Leach. Music publisher and record company. Estab. 1973. BMI. Pays 2-5% royalty.
How to Contact: Submit demo tape and lead sheet. Prefers 7½ ips reel-to-reel or cassette with 3-5 songs on demo. Label song order on the tape. SASE. Reports in 2 weeks.
Music: C&W; disco; easy listening; MOR; rock (country); and top 40/pop. Recently published "Walkin' in the Country," recorded by the Zoo (top 40/pop); and "If You Can't Be Good" and "May We Both Get What We Want," recorded by Magic (top 40/pop).

JAMIE JAZ MUSIC, System Four Artists, Ltd., 145 E. 82nd St., New York NY 10028. President: Stephen F. Johnson. Music publisher and management firm. Estab. 1976. BMI. See Mistral Music for details.

JANELL MUSIC PUBLISHING, Tiki Enterprises, Inc., 792 E. Julian St., San Jose CA 95112. (408)286-9840. Vice President: Gradie O'Neal. Secretary: Barbara Tallmadge. Music publisher and record company. Estab. 1965. BMI. Published 100 songs in 1978; plans 100 1979. Pays standard minimum royalty.
How to Contact: Submit demo tape or submit demo tape and lead sheet. Prefers 7½ ips reel-to-reel or cassette with 4 songs on demo. SASE. Reports in 2 weeks.
Music: C&W; easy listening; gospel; MOR; rock (soft or hard); soul; and top 40/pop. Recently published "I Feel the Country Callin' Me," recorded by Mac Davis and Charlie Pride (MOR); "Bad Talk," recorded by Cookie Wong (disco); and "Justice," recorded by Steppenwolf (rock).

JANVIER MUSIC, INC., 23 Av. Parc, Ste. Jolie, Quebec, Canada J01 250. (514)649-6853. Director: Rancourt Rehsan. Music publisher, record company, record producer and management firm. Estab. 1972. BMI. Published 50 songs in 1978; plans 50 in 1979, 100 in 1980. Pays standard royalties.
How to Contact: Query, arrange personal interview, submit demo tape, submit demo tape and lead sheet, submit acetate disc, submit acetate disc and lead sheet, or submit videocassette. Prefers 7½ ips reel-to-reel or cassette with 2-10 songs on demo. Does not return unsolicited material. Reports in 1 month.
Music: Disco; easy listening; folk; MOR; rock; soul; and top 40/pop. Recently published

"The Strip Samba" (by Simille), recorded by Osmose/Cinq Records (top 40); "Never Get to Sing Blues" (by D. Lavoie), recorded by Lovoie/London Records (rock/blues); "Hoo Ga Hoo" (by Lady Love), recorded by Lady Love/Traffic Records (disco); "Chissa Cosa Cerchi" (by Davoli and Fortmann), recorded by Lucifer 303/Pending (top 40isco).

JAPONICIA MUSIC, 602 Inverness Ave., Nashville TN 37204. Vice President: Don Vinson. Music publisher. ASCAP. See Barren River Music for details.

JASMINE MUSIC CO., 216 Chatsworth Dr., San fernando CA 91340. (213)873-3724. Professional Director: Judy Barron. ASCAP. See Dawnbreaker Music for details.

JASON DEE MUSIC, 44 Music Square E., Nashville TN 37203. (615)242-3249. President: Charlie Fields. Music publisher, record company and booking agency. Estab. 1977. BMI. **Music:** Blues; C&W; easy listening; MOR; and top 40/pop. Recently published "Doing the Best I Can" (by Lincoln Bodine), recorded by Barbara Tackett/Charta Records (country) and "Look at Me Now" (by Gibson and Higdon/Forrester), recorded by Jessey Higdon/Charta Records (country). See Mr. Mort Music for submission details.

JEAN CHEVRIER, 82 St. Joseph Blvd. W., Montreal, Quebec, Canada H2T 2P4. (514)849-3776. President: Christopher J. Reed. Music publisher. Estab. 1974. CAPAC. See Intermede Musique for details.

JELD MUSIC, N12067 Freya, Rt. 2, Box 45B, Mead WA 99021. Manager: Ed Raney. Music publisher and record producer. Estab. 1967. BMI. Published 14 songs in 1978; plans 12 in 1979. Pays standard royalties.
How to Contact: Query, submit demo tape, or submit acetate disc. Prefers 7½ ips reel-to-reel tape with 2-4 songs on demo. SASE. Reports in 6 weeks.
Music: C&W; folk; and top 40/pop. Recently published "Ol' Lead Bottom," "Brother Oh Dear Brother" and "Johnson's Gone to Hell" (by Ed Raney), recorded by Ed Raney/Storm Records (western/folk)

JEPACLA MUSIC, 10220 Glade Ave., Chatsworth CA 91311. (213)341-2264. President: Leroy C. Lovett Jr. Music publisher and record producer. BMI. See Emandell Tunes for details.

JEROME, 82 St. Joseph Blvd. W., Montreal, Quebec, Canada H2T 2P4. (514)849-3776. President: Christopher J. Reed. Music publisher. Estab. 1974. CAPAC. See Intermede Musique for details.

JIBARO MUSIC CO., INC., Box 424, Mount Clemens MI 48043. (313)791-2678. President/Professional Manager: Jim Roach. General Manager: Ann Roach. Music publisher and production company. Estab. 1964. BMI. Published 24 songs in 1977; plans 70 in 1979. Pays standard royalty.
How to Contact: Submit demo tape and lead sheet. Prefers cassette with 1-4 songs on demo. SASE. Reports in 2 weeks.
Music: Disco; jazz; MOR; and soul. Recently published "Casanova Brown," recorded by Gloria Gaynor (disco/soul); "Thank God You're My Lady," recorded by the Dells (ballad); and "I Dig Your Music," recorded by the Dramatics (disco/soul).

JILLEAN MUSIC, INC., c/o Gopam Enterprises, Inc., 11 Riverside Dr., #13C-W, New York NY 10023. (212)724-6120. Managing Director: Laurie Goldstein. Music publisher. Estab. 1960. BMI. See Gopam Enterprises for details.

JLT CHRISTIAN AGAPE MUSIC CO., 104 8th St., Salem NJ 08079. (609)935-1908. Owner: John L. Tussey Jr. Music publisher. Estab. 1978. ASCAP. Published 4 songs in 1978; plans 2 in 1979. Pays standard royalties: 10% on sheet music and 50% for recordings.
How to Contact: Query. Prefers cassette with 1-3 songs on demo. "Submission of tape must include lead sheet." SASE. Reports in 1 month.
Music: Church/religious and gospel.

JO CHER MUSIC CO., Box 102C, Chubbic Rd., Rt. 1, Canonsburg PA 15317. (412)746-2540. General Manager: Jerry Walker. Music publisher. Estab. 1973. BMI. Published 20 songs in 1978; plans 30 in 1979. Pays standard maximum royalty.
How to Contact: Submit demo tape. Prefers 7½ ips reel-to-reel with 1-4 songs on demo. SASE. Reports in 2 weeks.

Music: Church/religious; C&W; gospel; MOR; rock (country); and top 40/pop. Recently published "Still Waters" and "Ladder of Love," recorded by Al Homburg (C&W); and "Who Is This Man?", recorded by Shirley Hawilland (gospel).

JOBETE MUSIC CO., INC., 6255 Sunset Blvd., Hollywood CA 90028. (213)468-3400. Affiliate: Stone Diamond Music. (BMI). Executive Vice President: Robert Gordy. Vice President/General Manager: Jay Lowy. Music publisher. Estab. 1958. ASCAP. Published 1,500 songs in 1978. Also works with songwriters on salary.
How to Contact: Submit demo tape and lead or lyric sheet. Prefers 7½ or 15 ips reel-to-reel or cassette with 1-3 songs on demo. SASE. Reports in 1 month.
Music: Blues; C&W; disco; easy listening; gospel; jazz; MOR; progressive; R&B; rock; soul; and top 40/pop. Recently published "Three Times a Lady," recorded by The Commodores; "Ooh, Baby, Baby," recorded by Linda Ronstadt; and "You Are The Sunshine of My Life," recorded by Stevie Wonder.

JODAX MUSIC CO., c/o Gopam Enterprises, Inc., 11 Riverside Dr., #13C-W, New York NY 10023. (212)724-6120. Managing Director: Laurie Goldstein. Music publisher. Estab. 1960. BMI. See Gopam Enterprises for details.

JOLI MUSIC, INC., 1619 Broadway, New York NY 10019. (212)757-2695. Affiliate: Hankbee Music (BMI). Production Director: Henry Boye. General Manager: Gil Miller. Music publisher. Estab. 1960. BMI. Pays standard royalty, AGAC-approved.
How to Contact: Submit lead sheet; "we'll request demo tape, if we're interested." SASE. Reports in 1 month.
Music: Blues; C&W; disco; easy listening; jazz; MOR; rock; soul; and top 40/pop. Recently published "Deep in My Heart," recorded by the Shells (ballad); "If I Only Had Magic," recorded by the Dubs (ballad); and "Rough and Bold," recorded by Andy Dio (rock).

JOLLY ROGERS PUBLISHING CO., 50 Holly Hill Lane, Greenwich CT 06830. (203)661-0707. Music publisher. ASCAP. See Cherry Lane Music for details. "We do not accept unsolicited material."

JOMEWA MUSIC, 135 E. 65th St., New York NY 10021. (212)289-8805. Contact: Mel Small. Music publisher. Estab. 1975. Uses AGAC-approved contract.
How to Contact: Submit demo tape and lead sheet. Prefers reel-to-reel or cassette with 1-4 songs on demo. SASE. Reports in 2 weeks.
Music: Easy listening; folk; MOR; and top 40/pop.

JON MUSIC, Box 233, 329 N. Main St., Church Point LA 70525. (318)684-2176. Owner: Lee Lavergne. Music publisher and record company. Estab. 1960. BMI. Pubished 10 in 1978. Pays standard royalty.
How to Contact: Submit demo tape. Prefers 7½ ips reel-to-reel or cassette with 2-6 songs on demo. SASE. Reports in 2 weeks.
Music: C&W; rock; and soul. Recently published "No More and No Less," recorded by Hugh Boynton (R&B); "Mama's Gown," recorded by Becky Richard (country rock); and "Play It Fair," recorded by Johnny and Joyce (C&W).

JONAN MUSIC, 342 Westminster Ave., Elizabeth NJ 07208. Office Manager: Helen Gottesmann. Music publisher. BMI. Only publishes material of artists recording on Savoy Records.

JOP MUSIC CO., 50 Music Square W., Suite 800, Nashville TN 37203. Affiliate: Pointed Star (BMI). President: Bob Witte. Music publisher. Estab. 1976. ASCAP. Pays "standard songwriter contract fees."
How to Contact: Submit demo tape and lead sheet. Prefers 7½ ips reel-to-reel with 2-3 songs on demo. SASE. Reports in 3 weeks.
Music: Church/religious; C&W; easy listening; MOR; rock (general); and top 40/pop. Recently published "Mr. DJ," recorded by T.G. Sheppard (country rock); "It's About Time," recorded by Mel McDaniels (MOR); and "A Cowboy Is," recorded by Chris LeDoux (C&W).

JOUR DE L'AN, 82 St. Joseph Blvd. W., Montreal, Quebec, Canada H2T 2P4. (514)849-3776. President: Christopher J. Reed. Music publisher. Estab. 1974. CAPAC. See Intermede Musique for details.

JOWAT MUSIC, c/o Gopam Enterprises, Inc., 11 Riverside Dr., #13C-W, New York NY 10023. (212)724-6120. Managing Director: Laurie Goldstein. Music publisher. Estab. 1960. BMI. See Gopam Enterprises for details.

JUBILATION MUSIC, 240 E. Radcliffe Dr., Claremont CA 91711. (714)624-0677. President: Gary Buckley. Music publisher. Estab. 1970. BMI.
Music: Recently published "To Hear My Daddy Pray" and "Our America," recorded by the Country Congregation (gospel). See FYDAQ Music for submission details.

JUST HER MUSIC, 82 St. Joseph Blvd. W., Montreal, Quebec, Canada H2T 2P4. (514)849-3776. President: Christopher J. Reed. Music publisher. Estab. 1974. CAPAC. See Intermede Musique for details.

K-TEL MUSIC, LTD., 1670 Inkster Blvd., Winnipeg, Manitoba, Canada R2X 2W8. (204)633-1076. Affiliates: Pattern Music (ASCAP) and Bamboo Music (BMI). Copyright Coordinator: Rick Kives. Music publisher and record company. Estab. 1964. Payment negotiable.
How to Contact: Submit demo tape. Prefers 7½ or 15 ips reel-to-reel with 5 songs on demo. SAE and International Reply Coupons. Reports in 1 month.
Music: Bluegrass; blues; children's; choral; church/religious; C&W; disco; easy listening; folk; gospel; MOR; progressive; rock; soul; and top 40/pop. Recently published "Mission Bell," recorded by Donnie Brooks (ballad); "Birds and the Bees," recorded by Jewel Akens (pop); and "Tall Oak Tree," recorded by Dorsey Burnette (ballad).

KACK KLICK, INC., Mirror Records, Inc., 645 Titus Ave., Rochester NY 14617. (716)544-3500. Vice President: Armand Schaubroeck. Manager: Greg Prevost. Music publisher and record company. Estab. 1967. BMI. Published 5 songs in 1977; plans 10 in 1979. Pays negotiable royalty.
How to Contact: Submit demo tape. Prefers 7½ ips reel-to-reel. Include photo. SASE. Reports in 2 months.
Music: MOR; progressive; rock; top 40/pop; and new wave.

KAE-LYN MUSIC CO., c/o Gopam Enterprises, 11 Riverside Dr., #13C-W, New York NY 10023. (212)724-6120. Managing Director: Laurie Goldstein. Music publisher. Estab. 1960. BMI. See Gopam Enterprises for submission details.

KAPOCIRE, 82 St. Joseph Blvd. W., Montreal, Quebec, Canada H2T 2P4. (514)849-3776. President: Christopher J. Reed. Music publisher. Estab. 1974. CAPAC. See Intermede Musique for details.

BOB KARCY MUSIC, 437 W. 16th St., New York NY 10011. (212)989-1989. President: Bob Karcy. Vice President: Jack Arel. Music publisher, record producer and management firm. Estab. 1971. ASCAP and BMI. Published 35 songs in 1978. Payment negotiable.
How to Contact: Query or submit demo tape and lead sheet. "No interviews without prior appointment." Prefers cassette with 1-6 songs on demo. SASE. Reports in 3 weeks.
Music: Disco; easy listening; MOR; rock ("all types except hard, acid or punk rock"); and top 40/pop. Recently published "Melody Lady," recorded by Sunshine (top 40); "Rockola-Rockola," recorded by Anne Murphy (top 40); and "More Than Happy," recorded by Sellout (top 40).

KARLA MUSIC CO., 11042 Aqua Vista St., North Hollywood CA 91602. President: James Argiro. Music publisher. Estab. 1971. ASCAP. Published 4 songs in 1977; plans 24 in 1979. Pays standard minimum royalty.
How to Contact: Submit demo tape and lead sheet or submit lead sheet. Prefers cassette with 1-6 songs on demo. SASE. Reports in 1 month.
Music: Easy listening; jazz; MOR; progressive; soul; and top 40/pop.

KASHAGO MUSIC, Fivetake Group Productions, Ltd., 484 Waterloo Ct., Oshawa, Ontario, Canada L1H 3X1. Contact: Bob Stone. Music publisher. PROCAN. See Fivetake Music for details.

KATCH NAZAR MUSIC, 3929 New Seneca Turnpike, Marcellus NY 13108. (315)673-1117. Affiliate: Bleecker Street Music (BMI). President/A&R Manager: Vincent Taft. Music publisher, record company and production company. Estab. 1971. ASCAP. Published 12 songs

in 1978. Pays standard royalty. Buys some material outright; pays $100 maximum.
How to Contact: Submit demo tape and lyric sheet. Accepts cassette with 1-4 songs on tape. SASE. Reports in 2 weeks.
Music: C&W; disco; jazz; rock; soul; and top 40/pop. Recently published "Keep Me Warm Forever," recorded by Bajj (rock/pop); "A Wave of Your Hand," recorded by Steak Nite (rock/pop); and "Too Much in Love With You," recorded by Foxy Jay (top 40/MOR).

JOE KEENE MUSIC CO., Box 602, Kennett MO 63857. Affiliate: Lincoln Road Music (BMI). President: Joe Keene. Music publisher. BMI. Pays standard royalty.
How to Contact: Submit demo tape and lead sheet. Prefers reel-to-reel. SASE. Reports in 2 weeks.
Music: C&W; rock; and easy listening. Recently published "Big Chested Woman," recorded by Chuck Ramey (country rock); and "Back to You," recorded by Joe Keene (rock).

KELLY MUSIC PUBLICATIONS, 439 Wiley Ave., Franklin PA 16323. (814)432-4633. President: Norman Kelly. Music publisher, record company and booking agency. Estab. 1943. BMI. See Country Star Music for details.

KENCO, 10020 Glade Ave., Chatsworth CA 91311. (213)341-2264. BMI. See Emandell Tunes for submission details.

GENE KENNEDY ENTERPRISES, INC., 2125 8th Ave. S., Nashville TN 37204. (615)383-6002. Affiliates: Bekson (BMI), Chip 'n Dale (ASCAP), Door Knob Music (BMI) and Kenwall (ASCAP). Vice President: Linda Kennedy. Music publisher. Estab. 1975.
How to Contact: Query or arrange personal interview. Prefers 7½ ips reel-to-reel with 1-5 songs on demo. "We do not accept cassettes. We prefer that you make contact by phone or mail prior to submitting material. Tape should be accompanied by lyrics." SASE. Reports in 5 weeks.
Music: Bluegrass; C&W; gospel; MOR; and top 40/pop.

KENTREE MUSIC, 8 Music Square W., Nashville TN 37203. See Tree Publishing for details.

KENTUCKY COLONEL MUSIC, Box 5853, Pasadena CA 91107. (213)355-8759. Affiliate: Havana Moon Music (BMI). Owner: John Delgatto. Music publisher and record company. Estab. 1971. BMI. Pays standard royalty.
How to Contact: Submit demo tape. Prefers 7½ ips reel-to-reel with 3-6 songs on demo. SASE. Reports in 2 weeks.
Music: Bluegrass; C&W; and folk. Recently published "Living in the Past," recorded by the Stone Mountain Boys (bluegrass); "Julius Finkbine's Rag," recorded by Clarence White (bluegrass); and "Fire in O'Doodle's Popcorn Factory," recorded by Toulouse Engelhardt (folk).

KENWALL, Gene Kennedy Enterprises, Inc., 2125 8th Ave. S., Nashville TN 37204. (615)383-6002. Vice President: Linda Kennedy. Music publisher. Estab. 1975. See Gene Kennedy Enterprises for details.

KERISTENE MUSIC, LTD., 7507 Sunset Blvd., Suite 1, Hollywood CA 90046. (213)935-5786. Vice President, A&R: Horace Coleman Jr. Music publisher, record company and production company. Estab. 1972. BMI. See Coleman, Kestin & Smith for details.

KICKING MULE PUBLISHING, INC., Kicking Mule Records, Box 3233, Berkeley CA 94703. Manager: Ed Denson. Music publisher and record company. Estab. 1973. BMI. Published 200 songs in 1978; plans 200 in 1979. Pays standard royalties.
How to Contact: Submit demo tape. Prefers 7½ ips reel-to-reel with 3 songs on demo. Does not return unsolicited material. Reports "as soon as possible."
Music: Bluegrass (flatpicking); blues (flatpicking); and folk (guitar/banjo only). Recently published "The Raven," recorded by Bob Hadley (guitar instrumental); and "Flatpicking Guitar Festival," recorded by various artists (bluegrass)
Tips: "We specialize in guitar and banjo instrumentals; lyrics are secondary to us. A good guitar arrangement can stand alone, but we can't use a great song with poor playing. We publish only material that we record."

KING OF MUSIC PUBLISHING, 6001 Hickory Blvd., Hermitage TN 37076. Affiliates: To Jo (ASCAP) and Double Bourbon (SESAC). General Manager: Tony DiRizziano. Music

publisher and record producer. Estab. 1975. BMI. Published 60 songs in 1978; plans 75 in 1979, 100 in 1980. Pays standard royalties.
How to Contact: Submit demo tape or submit demo tape and lead sheet. Prefers 7½ ips reel-to-reel or cassette with 1-4 songs on demo. SASE. Report in 3 weeks.
Music: Contemporary gospel; MOR; R&B; rock; and top 40/pop. Recently published "Best Side of Me" (by Pete Sumner), recorded by Randy Parton/Meteor Records (pop); "Other Women" (by Randy Parton), recorded by Parton/Meteor Records; and "Maggie, the Baby is Crying" (by Benny Williams), recorded by Vernon Oxford/Rounder Records (country).

KINGHOUSE MUSIC PUBLICATIONS, Rt. 1, Navan, Ontario, Canada K0A 2S0. (613)833-2236. Affiliate: San-Lyn Music (ASCAP). Contact: Bob King. Music publisher and record company. Estab. 1972. BMI. Pays 10-50% royalty.
How to Contact: Submit demo tape or submit demo tape and lead sheet. Prefers 15 ips reel-to-reel or cassette with 6-12 songs on demo. "Good quality only." SAE and International Reply Coupons. Reports in 2 weeks.
Music: Bluegrass; C&W (modern); folk; and rock (country). Recently published "Louisiana Swampman," recorded by Bob King (C&W); "Tappin' the Maples," recorded by Jimmy Allen (C&W instrumental); and "Let's Make a Fair Trade," recorded by Marie and Bob King (C&W).

DON KIRSHNER MUSIC, 1370 Avenue of the Americas, New York NY 10019. (212)489-0440. Music publisher and TV and theater producer. Estab. 1972. BMI. Secures some songwriters on salary basis.
How to Contact: Query or submit demo tape. Prefers 7½ ips reel-to-reel or cassette with 2-3 songs on demo. "Please enclose lyric sheet. Nothing fancy. No big production. Everything is listened to." SASE. Reports in 2 weeks.
Music: All types. Recently published "Dust in the Wind," recorded by Kansas; "Sinner Man," recorded by Sarah Dash; and "You Never Done it Like That," recorded by the Captain and Tennille.
Tips: "We deal mainly with writers as opposed to songs and we're always looking for new writers with hit songs."

JIMMY KISH MUSIC PUBLISHING, Box 2316, Nashville TN 37214. (615)889-6675. Music publisher and record company. Estab. 1954. BMI. Pays negotiable royalties.
How to Contact: Submit demo tape and lead sheet. Prefers 7½ ips reel-to-reel or cassette. SASE. Reports in 2 weeks.
Music: C&W and gospel. Recently released "I Dare to Dream" (by Jimmy Kish and Les Peterson); That's What Makes a Heartache" (by Kish and Peterson); and "Nite Plane to Nashville" (by Kish and Red River Dave), all recorded by Jimmy Kish/Kess Records (C&W).

KISS ME MUSIC, 19 Music Square W., Nashville TN 37203. (615)256-1886. President: Jean S. Zimmerman. Music publisher. Estab. 1972. SESAC.
Music: Bluegrass; blues; C&W; disco; easy listening; MOR; progressive; and top 40/pop. Recently published "West Virginia Ann" (by Ed Felts), recorded by Benny Williams/Autumn Records (bluegrass); and "K.C. the KooCoo" (by Arno Pace), recorded by Arno Pace/Sing Me Records (C&W). See Sing Me Music for submission details.

KLEANZA MUSIC, Box 631, Hendersonville TN 37075. Owner: Ray Emmett. Music publisher. Estab. 1974. BMI. Published 2 songs in 1978. Pays standard royalties.
Music: C&W and MOR.

KOLORMARK MUSIC, 2832 Spring Grove Ave., Cincinnati OH 45225. (513)681-8400. Contact: A&R Dept. Music publisher and record company. Estab. 1976. BMI. See QCA Music for details.

KOKO MUSIC, Box 12501, Nashville TN 37211. Vice President: Rex Allen Jr. Manager: Curtis L. Allen. Music publisher and record company. Estab. 1954. ASCAP. See Boxer Music for details.

L.M.S. LTEE, 450 E. Beaumont Ave., St. Bruno, Quebec, Canada J3V 2R3. (514)653-7838. President: Christian Lefort. Music publisher and record company. Estab. 1967. CAPAC. See S.M.C.L. Productions for details.

LA-DE-DA MUSIC, Box 12513, Nashville TN 37212. (615)373-1225. Owner/President: Chips

Moman. Music publisher. ASCAP. See Baby Chick Music listing for details.

LA SALLE MUSIC, 6922 Hollywood Blvd., Hollywood CA 90028. (213)469-1667. Professional Manager: Roy Kohn. Music publisher and record company. Estab. 1928. ASCAP. See Peer-Southern Organization, Hollywood CA office, for details.

LACKEY PUBLISHING CO., Box 269, Caddo OK 74729. (405)367-2798. President: Robert F. Lackey. Music publisher and record producer. Estab. 1968. BMI. Published 8 songs in 1978; plans 14 in 1979, 40 in 1980. Pays standard royalties.
How to Contact: Submit demo tape. Prefers 7½ ips reel-to-reel tape with 1-10 songs on demo. SASE. Reports in 2 weeks.
Music: Bluegrass; blues; church/religious; C&W; easy listening; folk; gospel; MOR; progressive; R&B; and top 40/pop; easy Recently published "Bury My Heart at Wounded Knee" (by R.F. Lackey), recorded by Lackey/Major Records (country); "Living in Luxury" (by Lackey), recorded by Lackey/Major Records (country); and "Living on the Bayou" (by Lackey), Major Records (country).

LADD MUSIC CO., 401 Wintermantle Ave., Scranton PA 18505. (717)343-6718. President: Phil Ladd. Music publisher, record company and record producer. Estab. 1960. BMI. Published 2 songs in 1978; plans 8 in 1979, 16 in 1980. Pays standard royalties.
How to Contact: Query or submit demo tape and lead sheet. Prefers cassette with minimum 2 songs on demo. SASE. Reports in 3 weeks.
Music: Children's; C&W; easy listening; R&B; rock; and top 40/pop. Recently published "Piano Nelly," (by Bobby Poe), recorded by Bobby Brant/Whiterock (rock); "Miss Lucy" (by Poe), recorded by Big Al Downing/Whiterock (rock); and "I Loved and Lost" (by Tom Genova), recorded by Genova/Whiterock (ballad).

LAMBERT & POTTER MUSIC CO., 9220 Sunset Blvd., Los Angeles CA 90069. (213)278-8970. Affiliates: Touch of Gold Music (BMI) and Natural Songs (ASCAP). President: Dennis Lambert. Director of Publishing: Marsha Ingraham. Music publisher, record company and production company. Estab. 1968. BMI. Published 30 songs in 1977; 30 in 1979. Pays standard royalty. Sometimes secures songwriters on salary basis: "Depending on the quality of songs initially presented, we pay anywhere from $5,000-25,000 per year usually as advances against earned royalties."
How to Contact: Submit demo tape and lead sheet or "live presentation after tape review." Prefers cassette with 1-4 songs on demo. SASE. Reports in 1 month.
Music: Disco; easy listening; MOR; rock; soul; and top 40/pop. Recently published "Baby Come Back," recorded by Player (rock/soul); "Country Boy," recorded by Glen Campbell (pop/country); and "It Only Takes a Minute," recorded by Tavares (soul/disco).

LAND O' ROSES PUBLISHERS, Box 45, Thomasville GA 31792. (912)226-7911. Vice President: Emery T. Evans. Music publisher, record company, record producer and recording studio. BMI. See Millevan Music Publishers for details.

LANDERS ROBERTS MUSIC, 9255 Sunset Blvd., Los Angeles CA 90069. (213)550-8819. Affiliate: Landers/Roberts Songs (BMI). President: Bobby Roberts. Vice-President: Jay Landers. General Manager: Barry Jay Josephson. Music publisher, record producer and management firm. Estab. 1972. ASCAP. Published 200 songs in 1978; plans 200 in 1979. Pays standard royalties.
How to Contact: Query, arrange personal interview, or submit demo tape and lead sheet. Prefers cassette with 1-5 songs on demo. SASE. Reports in 2 weeks.
Music: Blues; C&W; disco; jazz; MOR; progressive; R&B; rock; and top 40/pop. Recently published "When I Need You," (by Albert Hammond and Carol Bayer Sager) recorded by Leo Sayer (MOR/pop); "It Never Rains in Southern California," (by Hammond and Mike Hazelwood) recorded by Hammond (MOR/pop); and "The Air That I Breathe," (by Hammond) recorded by Hollies (MOR/pop) and "99 Miles From LA" (by Albert Hammond/Dal David) recorded by Johny Mathis.

CRISTY LANE MUSIC, L S Record Co., 120 Hickory St., Madison TN 37115. (615)868-7171. Affiliate: Cindy Lee Music (SESAC). Publishing Director: Michael Radford. Music publisher and record company. Estab. 1975. ASCAP. Published 50 songs in 1977; 150 in 1979. Pays standard royalty. "We would consider placing a writer on a draw against future royalties, based on his/her writing potential."
How to Contact: Submit demo tape and lyric sheet or arrange personal interview. Prefers 7½

┌─Songwriter's Market Close-Up─

To songwriter/artist Janis Ian, songwriting is a matter of maturity and experience. "The most you can do for your writing is to write," says Ian, who has been writing since she was 12. "Write a lot. Make mistakes." In other words, learn your craft by practicing it.

For example, the question most frequently asked of Ian by young (in terms of experience) songwriters is, "Where do you get inspiration?" Ian says, "The more you write, the less you depend on inspiration and the more you depend on craft." The songwriter who has been matured by experience doesn't worry about getting ideas—they're the easiest part. "There's so many things to say, and your ability to say them is limited by your talent and expertise."

That's why Ian has begun collaborating with songwriters like Carol Bayer Sager and Albert Hammond in the past year. Though Ian thinks of herself primarily as a solo songwriter, she enjoys collaboration as an "expanding" experience. Collaboration has given her insights into craft and objectivity, for example. "It's making me a little more open to change." She's found that sometimes "you become attached to what you're writing to the point of letting the song never see the light of day because you can't find the right bridge." She can now look at the song more objectively and decide that perhaps that particular song doesn't need a bridge.

Ian believes that a songwriter who takes writing seriously helps not only himself, but songwriting as a whole. If more songwriters take the profession seriously, the public will take it more seriously. In that regard, she says, songwriting is maturing. "I'm finding lately that young songwriters are taking it more seriously than they did ten or fifteen years ago. And that's nice."

ips reel-to-reel or cassette with 2-10 songs on demo. SASE. Reports in 1 month.
Music: C&W (modern); easy listening; MOR; rock (soft); and top 40/pop. Recently published "By the Way" and "I Can't Tell You," recorded by Cristy Lane (MOR/C&W); and "Pretend," recorded by T.G. Sheppard (MOR/C&W).

LANGLEY MUSIC CO., 65 W. 55th St., New York NY 10019. President: Eddie White. Music publisher and record producer. Estab. 1948. BMI. See White Way Music for details.

LAPELLE MUSIC PUBLISHING, Box 2248, Calgary, Alberta, Canada T2P 2M7.

(403)269-7270. Contact: Bruce Thompson. Music publisher. PROCAN.
How to Contact: Submit demo tape and lead sheet. Prefers reel-to-reel or cassette. SASE.
Music: C&W and gospel (contemporary and "Jesus" music). Recently published "Gently
Through" (by Lamar Boschman), recorded by Lamar Boschman/Praise Records (gospel); "It's
Up To You" (by Paul Wylie), recorded by Stan Swindbn/Circa Records (gospel); and "I Have
Seen The Rain" (by B. Thompson), recorded by B. Thompson/London Records (C&W).

LARBALL PUBLISHING, 1650 Broadway, New York NY 10019. (212)581-6162. Affiliates:
Peach Cobbler Music (ASCAP), Rapp/Matz Music (ASCAP) and Snow/Matz Music
(ASCAP). Vice President: Paul Brown. Music publisher and record producer. Estab. 1976.
BMI. Published 33 songs in 1978; plans 40 in 1979, 50 in 1980. Pays standard royalties.
How to Contact: Arrange personal interview, submit demo tape, or submit demo tape and lead
sheet. Prefers 7½ ips reel-to-reel or cassette with maximum 3 songs on demo. SASE. Reports in
1 month.
Music: C&W; disco; easy listening; MOR; rock; and top 40/pop. Recently published "Fancy
Dancer," (by Bob Crew and C. Brown) recorded by Frank Valli (top 40/pop); "Gone Gone
Gone," (by Brown and Hayworth) recorded by Johnny Mathis (top 40/pop); and "Spend the
Night With Me," (by Brown and Levine) recorded by Johnny Mathis (top 40/pop).

LARDON MUSIC, Box 200, River Grove IL 60171. General Manager: Larry Nestor. Music
publisher. Estab. 1970. BMI. Published 10 songs in 1978; plans 10 in 1979 and 10 in 1980. Pays
standard royalties.
How to Contact: Submit demo tape and lead sheet. Prefers 7½ ips reel-to-reel or cassette with
a maximum of 3 songs on demo. SASE. Reports in 2 weeks.
Music: Children's (educational material as used on *Sesame Street* and *Captain Kangaroo*).
Recently published "Whiz Me a Frisbee" (by Nestor), recorded by Joe Cantafio and the Kids
in the Park/Solar Records (children's pop); "Meet Me Halfway" (by Nestor), recorded by Jade
50's/Aspen Records (MOR); "My One and Only Dream" recorded on Toddlin' Town Records
(pop); and "Here Comes Santa in his Snowmobile," recorded by the Muffins (pop/children's).

LASHARUDA MUSIC, WelDee Music Co., Box 561, Wooster OH 44691. General Manager:
Quentin W. Welty. Music publisher. Estab. 1959. BMI. See B-W Music for details.

LATE MUSIC, 223 Broadway, Rensselaer NY 12144. (518)434-2014. Co-Owner: Vincent
Meyer II. Music publisher and record producer. Estab. 1975. Plans to publish 40 songs in 1979.
Pays standard royalties.
How to Contact: Query, submit demo tape, submit demo tape and lead sheet, submit acetate
disc, submit acetate disc and lead sheet or submit lead sheet only. Prefers 7½ ips reel-to-reel or
cassette with minimum 2 songs on demo. SASE. Reports in 3 weeks.
Music: Children's; disco; folk; jazz; progressive; rock; and top 40/pop.

LAWDAY MUSIC CORP., Box 1546, Nashville TN 37202. (615) 244-3450. Professional
Manager: Lamar Morris. Music publisher. BMI. See Acoustic Music for details.

LAYBACK MUSIC, 5220 Essen Lane, Baton Rouge LA 70808. (504)766-3233. General
Manager: John Fred. Music publisher, record company and record producer. BMI. See RCS
Publishing for details.

BEN LEE MUSIC, 10220 Glade Ave., Chatsworth CA 91311. (213)341-2264. President: Leroy
C. Lovett Jr. Music publisher. BMI. See Emandell Tunes for details.

CINDY LEE MUSIC, L S Record Co., 120 Hickory St., Madison TN 37115. (615)868-7171.
Publicity Director: Michael Radford. Music publisher and record company. Estab. 1975.
SESAC. See Cristy Lane Music for details.

DON LEE MUSIC, 6036 Mayflower St., Maywood CA 90270. (213)581-7713. President: Don
Sessions. Music publisher. Estab. 1960. ASCAP. Published 30 songs in 1978. Pays standard
royalties.
How to Contact: Submit reel-to-reel. Prefers 4-8 songs on demo. SASE. Reports in 2 weeks.
Music: Bluegrass; C&W; easy listening; folk; gospel; and top 40/pop. Recently published "We
Get Love" (by Gene Davis) recorded by David Houston/Columbia (C&W); "Book in the
Basement" recorded by Ernie Ford/Capitol (MOR); and "Our Love is Our Castle" recorded
by Freddie Hart/Capitol Records (C&W).

ROB LEE MUSIC, Box 1385, Merchantville NJ 08109. (609)663-4540. Affiliates: Pyramid Music (BMI) and Rock Island Music (ASCAP). Vice President: Bob Francis. Music publisher, record company, record producer, management firm and booking agency. Estab. 1966. BMI. Published 18 songs in 1978; plans 20 in 1979, 30 in 1980. Pays standard royalties.
How to Contact: Query or submit demo tape and lead sheet. Prefers 7½ ips reel-to-reel or cassette with 2-12 songs on demo. SASE. Reports in 1 month.
Music: C&W; disco; easy listening; jazz; MOR; rock; soul; and top 40/pop. Recently published "(I'm Not) Destined to Become a Loser," (by Rob Russen) recorded by the Ellingtons/Castle Records (disco); "A Good Love is Worth Waiting For," (by Russen) recorded by Millionaires/Castle (R&B/disco); and "Alabama Girl," (by Pal Rakes) recorded by Big El/Quadra Records (C&W/rock).

LEEDS MUSIC CORP., 9100 Wilshire Blvd., Suite 530, Beverly Hills CA 90212. (213)550-3913. Contact: Dude McLean. Music publisher. Estab. 1964. ASCAP. See MCA Music listing for details.

PAUL LEKA MUSIC, 132 Merrimac Dr., Trumbull CT 06611. (203)261-9610. Affiliate: Baby Powder Music (ASCAP). President: Paul Leka. Music publisher and record producer. Estab. 1968. BMI. Published 150 songs in 1977. Pays standard royalty.
How To Contact: Submit demo tape and lead sheet. Prefers 7½ ips reel-to-reel or cassette with 1-6 songs on demo. SASE. Reports in 3 weeks.
Music: C&W ("Eagles type only"); MOR ("Carpenters/Paul Williams type material"); rock ("Fleetwood Mac/Rolling Stones calibre"); and top 40/pop. Recently published "Na, Na, Hey, Hey (Kiss Him Goodbye)," recorded by Steam (top 40); and "Honey Bee," recorded by Gloria Gaynor (R&B).

LEMHI MUSIC PUBLISHING, 717 West H St., Elizabethton TN 37643. Owners: LaNita and Windle Stout. Music publisher. BMI.
How to Contact: Submit demo tape. Prefers 7½ ips reel-to-reel. SASE. Reports in 2 weeks.
Music: C&W and easy listening. Recently published "Desperation Waltz" (by John McGuire); "Leaves Look So Pretty" (by Frank Marcum); and "Ain't Love Wonderful" (by Windle Stout and Frank Marcum).
Tips: "We're willing to work with any writers who contact us."

LILLENAS PUBLISHING CO., Box 527, Kansas City MO 64141. (816)931-1900. Affiliates: Beacon Hill Music (SESAC) and Faith Music (SESAC). Music Editor: Lyndell Leatherman. Music publisher. Estab. 1926. SESAC. Published 550 songs in 1978; plans 600 in 1979. Pays 10% royalty.
How to Contact: Submit lead sheet. "A demo tape is helpful, but is not necessary." Prefers reel-to-reel or cassette with 1-5 songs on demo. SASE. Reports in 2 weeks.
Music: Church/religious and gospel. Recently published "The Body of the Lord" (by Jon Stemkoski), recorded by the Celebrant Singers/Tempo Records (contemporary religious); "Too Precious" (by Dab Whittemore), recorded by the Haven of Rest Quartet/Tempo Records (contemporary religious); and "Restore My Soul" (by Mosie Lister), recorded by the Couriers/Tempo Records (gospel).

SONNY LIMBO INTERNATIONAL, Box 9869, Atlanta GA 30319. Music publisher and record producer. Estab. March, 1979. BMI.
Music: Blues; C&W; disco; easy listening; MOR; progressive; R&B; rock; soul; and top 40/pop.

LINCOLN ROAD MUSIC CO., Box 602, Kennett MO 63857. President: Joe Keene. Music publisher. BMI.
Music: C&W; disco; easy listening; MOR; rock; and top 40/pop. Recently published "(I Can) Wrap My Arms Around the World," recorded by Narvel Felts (C&W); and "I'll Be Willing to Try," recorded by Terry Ray Bradley (rock). See Joe Keene Music and Happy Day Music for submission details.

LINDSEYANNE MUSIC, 65 E. 55th St., Penthouse, New York NY 10022. (212)752-0160. Professional Manager: Amy Bolton. Music publisher and record company. BMI. See Sherlyn Publishing for details.

LINESIDER PRODUCTIONS, 10 George St., Wallingford CT 06492. (203)269-4465.

President: Thomas Cavalier. Vice President: Rudolf Szlaui. Music publisher, record company and management firm. Estab. 1967. BMI.
Music: Rock. See Rohm Music for submission details.

LIRANA, 82 St. Joseph Blvd. W., Montreal, Quebec, Canada H2T 2P4. (514)849-3776. President: Christopher J. Reed. Music publisher. Estab. 1974. CAPAC. See Intermede Musique for details.

LIT'L DAVID MUSIC, Songs of David, Inc., Suite 116, Music Park Bldg., Box 22653, Nashville TN 37202. (615)885-0713. President: Dave Mathes. Estab. 1975. ASCAP. See House of David for details.

LITTLE DEBBIE MUSIC, Box 52, Perkasie PA 18944. (215)257-9616. President: John Wolf. Production Manager: Tom Fausto. Music publisher, record company and recording studio. Estab. 1963. ASCAP.
Music: Disco; folk; rock; soul; and top 40/pop. See Masterview Music Publishing for submission details.

LITTLE FUGITIVE MUSIC, Box 15764, Sarasota FL 33579. (813)922-5849. Owner: Nancy Josie. Music publisher. Estab. 1967. BMI. Published 15 songs in 1978; plans 25 in 1979. Pays standard royalties.
How to Contact: Submit demo tape and lead sheet. Prefers reel-to-reel or cassette with 2-4 songs on demo. SASE. Reports in 3 weeks.
Music: C&W; disco; and top 40/pop. Recently recorded "Watchin the River Run," (by Lou T. Josie) recorded by Pat Boone/Warner Bros. Records and Kenny Star/MCA Records (country/pop); "Disco Train," (by Josie) recorded by Donny Osmond/Polydor Records (disco/top 40); and "Midnight Confessions," (by Josie) recorded by the Grassroots/ABC Records (top 40).

LITTLE GEM MUSIC, INC., 38 Music Square E., Suite 114, Nashville TN 37203. (615)254-0892. Affiliates: Blue Cup Music (BMI), Gemway Music Publishing (SESAC) and Hat-n-Boots Music Publishing (ASCAP). President: Jack Stillwell. Vice President/General Manager: Bill Wence. Music publisher, record company and record producer. Estab. 1972. Published 100 songs in 1978. Pays standard royalty.
How to Contact: Submit demo tape and lyric or lead sheet. Prefers 7½ ips reel-to-reel with 2-4 songs on demo. "We will also accept cassettes. Use new tape." SASE. Reports in 3 weeks.
Music: C&W; gospel; MOR; and spiritual/inspirational. Recently published "Goodbye Bing, Elvis & Guy," recorded by Diana Williams (tribute); "Avon Calling," recorded by Lee Lewis (C&W); and "Gerldine," recorded by Little Jimmy Dickens (novelty).

LITTLE JOE MUSIC CO., 604 Broad St., Johnstown PA 15906. (814)539-8117. Owner: Al Page. Music publisher. Estab. 1950. BMI. Published 5 songs in 1978; plans 5 in 1979. Payment negotiable.
How to Contact: Submit demo tape and lead sheet. Prefers 3¾ ips reel-to-reel with 2-4 songs on demo. SASE. Reports in 2 weeks.
Music: Bluegrass; church/religious; C&W; disco; folk; and polka's. Recently published "Kane Polka," recorded by the Trontel-Zagger Orchestra; "Why Don't You Be Mine Polka," recorded by the Peppermint Stix Polka Band; and "I Won't Return Polka," recorded by the Ultratones.

LITTLE OTIS MUSIC, 101 Westchester Ave., Port Chester NY 10573. (914)939-1066. General manager: Judy Novy. Music publisher and record producer. Estab. 1973. BMI. Published 10 songs in 1978; plans 25 in 1979 and 50 in 1980. Pays standard royalties.
How to Contact: Submit demo tape. Prefers 7½ ips reel-to-reel or cassette with 1-5 songs on demo. SASE. Reports in 1 month.
Music: Disco; jazz (with vocals only); MOR; R&B; rock; soul; and top 40/pop. Recently published "Stone Freak" (by Carlton McWilliams) recorded by Frog/Mainstream (disco); "The Fair Way" (by A. Masi) recorded by Johnny Sundance/Little Otis Records (R&B); and "Let The Music Stone You" (by G. Siano) recorded by Johnny Sundance/Little Otis Records (rock).

LIVELY MUSIC, Box 111291, Nashville TN 37211. (615)242-0414. Owner/President: Tom McConnell. Music publisher and record producer. Estab. 1970. BMI. See Above Music Publications for submission details.

LIVE-WIRE MUSIC PUBLISHERS, Rt. 2, Box 13-B, Marion SC 29571. (803)423-6666. A&R Director: A.R. Perkins. Manager: D.L. Perkins. Music publisher, booking agency and record company. Estab. 1962. BMI. Published 15 songs in 1978; plans 20 in 1979. Pays standard royalties.
How to Contact: Submit demo tape and lead sheet. Prefers 7½ ips reel-to-reel or cassette with 1-6 songs on demo. SASE. Reports in 1 month.
Music: Bluegrass; C&W; easy listening; folk; and MOR. Recently published "Big Wheels Rolling" and "Mister Bluegrass," recorded by B. Atkins (C&W/bluegrass); and "Silver Tears," recorded by Ray Josey (MOR).

LOCHWOOD PUBLISHING CO., 2651 Globe Ave., Dallas TX 75228. (214)321-6576. Owner: John E. Price. Music publisher. Estab. 1965. BMI. Published 100 songs in 1978; plans 200 in 1979. Pays standard royalties.
How to Contact: Submit demo tape and lead sheet. Prefers 7½ or 15 ips reel-to-reel or cassette with 4-6 songs on demo. SASE. Reports in 2 weeks.
Music: C&W; easy listening; and R&B.

LOMBARDO MUSIC, INC., 8544 Sunset Blvd., Los Angeles CA 90069. (213)657-8210. Director of Creative Activities: Ron Vance. Music publisher and record company. ASCAP. See 20th Century Fox Music Publishing for details.

LONE GROVE MUSIC, INC., 6004 Bull Creek Rd., Austin TX 78757. (512)451-6764. President: Bobby Earl Smith. Vice President/A&R: Herb Steiner. BMI. See Crow-Smith Productions for details.
How to Contact: Submit 7½ ips reel-to-reel or cassette. Lead sheet optional. Does not return unsolicited material.
Music: Blues; children's; C&W; easy listening; gospel; MOR; progressive; rock; soul; and top 40/pop.

LONE LAKE SONGS, INC., Box 126, 93 N. Central Ave., Elmsford NY 10523. President: Ron Carpenter. Music publisher. Estab. 1968. ASCAP. Published 136 songs in 1978; plans 136 in 1979. Pays 33⅓-100% royalty. Sometimes secures songwriters on salary basis; "must be established musicians and be able to arrange and to write material for certain occasions, such as commercials."
How to Contact: Submit demo tape, submit demo tape and lead sheet, or submit lead sheet. Prefers 7½ ips reel-to-reel or cassette with 1-10 songs on demo. "Do not send original copies." SASE. Reports in 1 month.
Music: Bluegrass; C&W; disco; easy listening; folk; gospel; MOR; rock (mellow); soul; and top 40/pop. Recently published "Please Don't Ever Let Me Go," recorded by Ray Sanders and Bobby Baker (C&W); "Now That You're Back in My Heart," recorded by the Final Touch (disco); and "Behind Every Great Man," recorded by Buddy Hall (disco).

LORIJOY MUSIC, INC., 39 W. 55th St., New York NY 10019. (212)586-3350. Affiliates: Ace Deuce Trey Music, Fast Fingers Music and Lucky Star Music. A&R Director: Nate Adams Jr. Music publisher. Estab. 1970. BMI. Published 30 songs in 1978; plans 50 in 1979, 100 in 1980. Pays standard royalties.
How to Contact: Submit demo tape or submit demo tape and lead sheet. Prefers 7½ or 15 reel-to-reel or cassette with minimum 2 songs on demo. SASE. Reports in 2 weeks.
Music: R&B; soul; and top 40/pop. Recently published "Peaceful" (by A.O. Johnson), recorded by Al Johnson/Marina Records (pop); and "Shake What You Got" (by J. Johnson), recorded by Pulse/Olde World Records (soul).

LOVE STREET PUBLISHING, Box 2501, Des Moines IA 50315. (515)285-6564. President/Owner: Art Smart Stenstrom. Music publisher, booking agency and record company (Fanfare Records). Estab. 1975. BMI. Pays standard royalties.
How to Contact: Submit demo tape and lead sheet "with any promotional material on the songwriter." Prefers cassette tape with 1-4 songs on demo. Does not return unsolicited material. Reports in 2 weeks.
Music: Wants "very top 40, radio-ish rock only." Recently published "Lover," "Sing Me Your Love Songs" and "Don't Feel Bad" (by Ludtke-Orton), recorded by Silver Laughter/Fanfare Records (top 40/pop).

LOVIN' HEART SONGS, Northern Productions, Ltd., Box 3713, Station B, Calgary, Alberta, Canada T2M 4M4. (403)274-8638. President: Ron Mahonin. Music publisher, record producer, record company and management firm. CAPAC. See Have A Heart Music for details.

LOW-BAM MUSIC, Box 6987, Atlanta GA 30319. Producer: Sonny Limbo. Music publisher and record producer. Estab. 1956. BMI. See Lowery Music for details.

LOWERY MUSIC CO., INC., Box 6987, Atlanta GA 30319. Affiliates: Brother Bill's Music (ASCAP), Brother Karl's Music (BMI), Low-Bam Music (BMI), Low-Sal Music (BMI) and Low-Twi Music (BMI). Producer: Sonny Limbo. Music publisher and record producer. Estab. 1956. BMI.
How to Contact: Submit demo tape and lead sheet. Prefers 7½ ips reel-to-reel or cassette with 1-4 songs on demo. SASE. Reports in 2 weeks.
Music: C&W; disco; easy listening; MOR; progressive; rock; soul; and top 40/pop.

LOW-SAL MUSIC, Sonny Limbo International, Box 9869, Atlanta GA 30319. (404)346-0700. President/Publisher/Producer: Sonny Limbo. Music publisher and record producer. Estab. 1956. BMI. See Lowery Music for details.

LOW-TWI MUSIC, Box 6987, Atlanta GA 30319. Producer: Sonny Limbo. Music publisher and record producer. Estab. 1956. BMI. See Lowery Music for details.

LUCKY MAN MUSIC, (formerly American Cowboy Songs, Inc.), The Homeplace, Mount Juliet TN 37122. Owner: Alfred H. LeDoux. Music publisher, record company and record producer. Estab. 1972. ASCAP. Published 20 songs in 1978; plans 20 in 1979, 20 in 1980. Pays standard royalties.
How to Contact: Submit demo tape and lead sheet. Prefers cassette with 1-3 songs on demo. SASE. Reports in 2 weeks.
Music: C&W; and folk. Recently published "Lean, Mean and Hungry," (by Chris LeDoux) recorded by LeDoux/Lucky Man Music (rodeo ballad); "Silence on the Line," (by Sterling Whipple) recorded by LeDoux/Lucky Man Music (rodeo ballad); and "Raised by the Railroad Line," (by Paul Craft) recorded by LeDoux/Lucky Man Music (railroad ballad).

LUCKY PENNY MUSIC, 110 21st Ave. S., Nashville TN 37203. General Manager: Ed Penney. Music publisher. ASCAP.
Music: C&W; easy listening and top 40/pop. See Show Biz Music Group for submission details.

LUCKY STAR MUSIC, 39 W. 55th St., New York NY 10019. (212)586-3350. A&R Director: Nate Adams Jr. Music publisher.
Music: Disco; R&B and soul. See Lorijoy Music for submission details.

LUFAYE PUBLISHING CO., Box 50, Goodlettsville TN 37072. Affiliates: Black Eagle Publishing (ASCAP), Brian Scott's Music Factory (ASCAP) and Allegheny Mountain Music (SESAC). Professional Manager: Dick Shuey. Music publisher. BMI. Pays negotiable royalty.
How to Contact: Submit demo tape and lead sheet. Prefers reel-to-reel or cassette with 1-3 songs on demo. SASE. Reports in 1 month.
Music: C&W. Recently published "I'm Not Living," recorded by Jeff Knight (C&W); "Down in the Mine," recorded by Sonny Swift (C&W); and "Bush Tavern Inn," recorded by Dick Shuey (C&W).

LYRESONG MUSIC, 1228 Spring St. NW, Atlanta GA 30309. (404)873-6425. Professional Manager: Tom Long. Music publisher and recording studio. BMI. See Seyah Music for submission details.

M-3 MUSIC CO., 50 Holly Hill Lane, Greenwich CT 06830. (203)661-0707. Music publisher. ASCAP. See Cherry Lane Music for details. "We do not accept unsolicited material."

JIM McCOY MUSIC/ALEAR MUSIC, Box 574, Sounds of Winchester, Winchester VA 22601. (703)667-9379. Owner: Jim McCoy. Music publisher, record company, record producer and management firm. Estab. 1971. BMI. Published 8 songs in 1978; plans 10 in 1979, 20 in 1980. Pays standard royalties.
How to Contact: Submit demo tape and lead sheet. Prefers 7½ ips reel-to-reel or cassette with 5-10 songs on demo. SASE. Reports in 1 month.
Music: Bluegrass; church/religious; C&W; folk; gospel; progressive; and rock. Recently published "This Woman" (by Gloria Jean Megee), recorded by Megee (country); "Interstate

95" (by Jean Alford), recorded by David Alliott (country); "Beertops and Teardrops" (by Alford and Jim McCoy), recorded by Larry Sutphin (country); and "May the Force Be With You Always" (by Kenny Johnson), recorded by Johnson (gospel).

McCULLY MUSIC, 226 Waysons Court., Lothian MD 20820. (301)627-5830. President: Robert M. Johnson. Music publisher, record company and record producer. Estab. 1975. BMI. Pays standard royalties.
How to Contact: Submit demo tape or submit acetate disc. Prefers 7½ or 15 ips reel-to-reel or cassette with 1-25 songs on demo. SASE. Reports in 1 month.
Music: Bluegrass; C&W; and rock. Recently published "A House Called Earth" and "Rainy Days" (by A. Sonny Gordon), recorded by Ray Clauson (MOR/country).

MACHINE MUSIC, 450 E. Beaumont Ave., St. Bruno, Quebec, Canada J3V 2R3. (514)653-7838. President: Christian Lefort. Music publisher and record company. Estab. 1967. CAPAC. See S.M.C.L. Productions for submission details.

MADRID MUSIC CO., Box 504, Bonita CA 92002. Affiliate: Sweet 'n Low Music (BMI). President: Virginia Anderson. Music publisher, record company and record producer. Estab. 1975. ASCAP. Published 4 songs in 1978. Pays standard royalties.
How to Contact: Query or submit demo tape and lead sheet. Prefers 7½ ips reel-to-reel or cassette with 1-3 songs on demo. SASE. Reports in 1 month.
Music: C&W; easy listening; MOR; top 40/pop.

MAKAMILLION MUSIC, 8 Music Square W., Nashville TN 37203. See Tree Publishing for details.

MAKAMINT MUSIC, 8 Music Square W., Nashville TN 37203. See Tree Publishing for details.

MALCOLM MUSIC, Delaware Water Gap PA 18327. (717)476-0550. Director of Publications: Lewis M. Kirby Jr. Music publisher and record company. BMI. See Shawnee Press for details.

MANFIELD MUSIC, Holy Spirit Records, 27335 Penn St., Inkster MI 48141. (313)274-5905. President: Elder Otis G. Johnson. Music publisher and record company. Estab. 1970. BMI. Pays standard royalty.
How to Contact: Submit demo tape and lead sheet. Prefers cassette with 2 songs minimum on tape. SASE. Reports in 2 weeks.
Music: Church/religious and gospel. Recently published "We Need Love," recorded by Holy Spirit (gospel); "Evil and Good," recorded by Otis G. Johnson (gospel); and "Beautiful Savior," recorded by Joyce Freud (religious).

MANNA MUSIC, INC., 2111 Kenmere Ave., Burbank CA 91504. Affiliates: Gaviota Music (BMI), Hollyville Music (SESAC) and Nashwood Music (ASCAP). President: Hal Spencer. Music publisher and record company. Estab. 1954. ASCAP. Pays 5-10% royalty. Sometimes secures songwriters on salary basis.
How to Contact: Submit demo tape or submit demo tape and lead sheet. Prefers cassette with 1-5 songs on demo. Does not return unsolicited material. Reports in 2 weeks.
Music: Choral; church/religious; and gospel. Recently published "How Great Thou Art," recorded by Elvis Presley (religious); "Sweet, Sweet Spirit," recorded by Pat Boone (religious); and "His Name Is Wonderful," recorded by Norma Zimmer (religious).

MAR-KEN MUSIC CO., 50 Holly Hill Lane, Greenwich CT 06830. (203)661-0707. Music publisher. BMI. See Cherry Lane Music for details.

MAPLE CREEK MUSIC, 1659 Bayview Ave., Suite 102, Toronto, Ontario, Canada M4G 3C1. (416)485-1157. Vice President: John D. Watt. Music publisher. Estab. 1972. CAPAC. See Snowberry Music for details.

MARAIS BOULEUR, 82 St. Joseph Blvd. W., Montreal, Quebec, Canada H2T 2P4. (514)849-3776. President: Christopher J. Reed. Music publisher. Estab. 1974. PROCAN. See Intermede Musique for details.

MARANTA MUSIC PUBLISHING CO., Box 1005, Englewood Cliffs NJ 07632. Affiliates:

Bandolero Music (BMI) and Aguirre Music (SESAC). President/A&R Director: Clancy Morales. Music publisher. Estab. 1972. BMI. Published 10 songs in 1978; plans 20 in 1979. Pays standard royalties. Buys some material outright; pays $50-500.
How to Contact: Submit demo tape and lead sheet. Prefers 7½ ips reel-to-reel with 2-4 songs on demo. "All material should have the person's name, address and phone number on all tape boxes, lead sheets and lyric sheets. The envelope must be big enough for material to be returned." SASE. Reports in 1 month.
Music: Blues; disco; jazz; R&B; rock; soul; top 40/pop; and Latin (salsa). Recently published "Enter Paradise" (by Clancy Morales), recorded by Clancy Morales (jazz/disco); "C Zone" (by Woody Sparrow), recorded by Morales (soul/rock); and "Latin Dreams" (by Randy Hanas), recorded by Morales (jazz/disco).
Tips: "Well-recorded demos are listened to more than those not professionally done. A 4-track recording of guitar, vocals, bass and drums (or piano) instead of only guitar is better. The better the demo, the better its chances of being listened to."

MARGENIA MUSIC, c/o Gopam Enterprises, Inc., 11 Riverside Dr., #13C-W New York NY 10023. (212)724-6120. Managing Director: Laurie Goldstein. Music publisher. Estab. 1960. BMI. See Gopam Enterprises for details.

MARIBUS MUSIC, 119 W. 57th St., New York NY 10019. (212)581-3420. General Manager: Arthur Braun. Music publisher. BMI.
Music: Recently published "Carolina's Comin' Home," recorded by Shaun Cassidy (pop). See Dick James Music for submission details.

MARIELLE MUSIC CORP., Box 842, Radio City, New York NY 10019. Affiliates: Moo Moo Music (BMI) and Moorpark Music (ASCAP). President: Don Seat. Vice President: Darlene Gorzela. Music publisher. Estab. 1952. BMI. Pays standard royalties.
How to Contact: Submit demo tape. Prefers cassette. "Be sure melody and lyrics are clear." SASE. Reports in 3 months.
Music: Bluegrass; blues; church/religious; classical; C&W; disco; easy listening; folk; gospel; jazz; MOR; progressive; rock; soul; and top 40/pop. Recently published "It's Only Make Believe," recorded by Glen Campbell (C&W); and "Half Way to Heaven" (pop).

MARINWOOD MUSIC, First American Records, Box 3925, Bellevue WA 98009. (206)762-5793. President: Gil Bateman. Music publisher and record company. Estab. 1965. ASCAP. See Bainbridge Music for details.

MAR KEN MUSIC CO., 50 Holly Hill Lane, Greenwich CT 06830. (203)661-0707. Music publisher. BMI. See M-3/Cherry Lane Music for details. "We do not accept unsolicited material."

MARK-CAIN MUSIC, Oak Manor, Box 1000, Oak Ridges, Ontario, Canada L0G 1P0. (416)773-4371. CAPAC.
Music: Recently published "A Million Vacations" by Max Webster (rock group); and "In the Middle of the Night" by Aerial (rock group). See Core Music for details.

MARMIK MUSIC, INC., 135 E. Muller Rd., East Peoria IL 61611. (309)699-7204. President: Martin Mitchell. Music publisher and record company. Estab. 1972. BMI. Published 47 songs in 1978. Pays standard royalties.
How to Contact: Query, submit demo tape, or submit demo tape and lead sheet. Prefers reel-to-reel tape or cassette with 2-10 songs on demo. "With first submission include an affidavit of ownership of the material." SASE. Reports in 2 weeks.
Music: Blues; children's; choral; church/religious; C&W; easy listening; gospel; and MOR.

MARSAINT MUSIC, 5220 Essen Lane, Baton Rouge LA 70808. (504)766-3233. General Manager: John Fred. Music publisher, record company and record producer. BMI. See RCS Publishing for details.

MASTERSHIP MUSIC, INC., 1017 N. LaCienega, Los Angeles CA 90069. (213)657-8730. President: Juggy Murray. Music publisher, record company, record producer and management firm. Estab. 1975. BMI. Published 20 songs in 1978. Pays standard royalties.
How to Contact: Submit demo tape and lead sheet, or submit acetate disc and lead sheet. Prefers reel-to-reel tape or cassette. SASE. Reports in 1 week.
Music: Blues; disco; gospel; jazz; progressive; R&B; and soul. Recently published "Inside

America" (by J. Murray and K. Wayman), recorded by Juggy Murray Jones/Jupiter Records (disco); and "Disco Extraordinaire" and "Come On Do It Some More" (by Murray and Wayman), recorded by Murray/Jupiter Records (disco).

MASTERVIEW MUSIC PUBLISHING CORP., Box 52, Perkasie PA 18944. (215)257-9616. Affiliate: Little Debbie Music (ASCAP). President: John Wolf. Production Manager: Tom Fausto. Music publisher, record company and recording studio. Estab. 1963. BMI. Published 50 songs in 1978; plans 75 in 1979. Pays negotiable royalty.
How to Contact: Submit demo tape or arrange personal interview. Prefers 7½ or 15 ips reel-to-reel or cassette with 2-6 songs on demo. SASE. Reports in 1 week.
Music: Disco; folk; gospel; rock (hard or country); and soul. Recently published "Hollywood Girl" and "One Hundred Years Old," recorded by Sugarcaine (rock).

MAVID MUSIC ENTERPRISES, 1217 S. Ogden Dr., #1, Los Angeles CA 90019. (213)277-1197. Chief of Production: Lim Taylor. Director: Brenda Hasty. Music publisher and production company. Estab. 1972. ASCAP. See Fourth House Music Publishing for details.

MAYBE MUSIC, Box 878, Sonoma CA 95476. (707)938-4060. Manager/Owner: Bruce Cohn. Music publisher and management firm. Estab. 1975. ASCAP. See Bruce Cohn Music for details.

MCA MUSIC, MCA, Inc., 9100 Wilshire Blvd., Suite 530, Beverly Hills CA 90212. (213)550-3913. Affiliates: Leeds Music (ASCAP), Duchess Music (BMI) and Champion Music (BMI). Director of Writer and Artist Development: Dude McLean. Music publisher. ASCAP. Pays standard royalties. Secures some songwriters on contract or salary basis.
How to Contact: Submit demo tape and lead sheet or demo tape and lyric sheet. Prefers 7½ ips reel-to-reel or cassette with 1-3 songs on demo. SASE. Reports in 1 month.
Music: Blues; easy listening; jazz; MOR; R&B; rock; soul; and top 40/pop. Recently published "Long, Long Time," by Linda Ronstadt; *Jesus Christ Superstar*; and *Evita* scores, by Webber/Rice; and "Please Come to Boston," recorded by Dave Loggins.

MCA MUSIC, MCA, Inc., 1106 17th Ave. S., Nashville TN. Affiliates: Leeds Music (ASCAP), Duchess Music (BMI) and Champion Music (BMI). Contact: Professional Department. Estab. 1964. ASCAP and BMI. Pays standard royalties.
How to Contact: Submit demo tape and lead sheet or demo tape and lyric sheet. Prefers 7½ ips reel-to-reel or cassette with 1-3 songs on demo. SASE. Reports in 1 month.
Music: "All forms of commercial contemporary music."

MCA MUSIC, MCA, Inc., 445 Park Ave., New York NY 10022. Affiliates: Leeds Music (ASCAP), Duchess Music (BMI) and Champion Music (BMI). Contact: Mark Koren. Music publisher. Estab. 1964. ASCAP. Pays standard royalties.
How to Contact: Submit demo tape and lead sheet or demo tape and lyric sheet. Prefers 7½ ips reel-to-reel or cassette with 1-3 songs on demo. SASE. Reports in 1 month.
Music: Blues; disco; easy listening; jazz; MOR; R&B; rock; soul; and top 40/pop.

MDK MUSIC, LTD, c/o Paul Kigar, Amcongen, Sao Paulo, APO Miami FL 34030. (011)203-6692 (San Paulo, Brazil). Owner: Malcolm Forest. Music publisher and record producer. Estab. 1973. ASCAP/BMI. Published 12 songs in 1978; plans 20 in 1979, 40 in 1980. Pays standard royalties.
How to Contact: Submit demo tape and lead or lyric sheet. Prefers cassette with 1-4 songs on demo. SASE. Reports in 1 month.
Music: Disco; easy listening; MOR; progressive; R&B; rock; soul; top 40/pop; and AOR. Recently published "Ecstasy" (by Anthony), and "Good-Bye Baby" (by Malcolm Forest), recorded by Malcolm Forest.

MEDIA INTERSTELLAR MUSIC, Box 20346, Chicago IL 60620. (312)476-2553. Professional Manager: V. Beleska. Music publisher. Estab. 1975. BMI. Published 20 songs in 1978; 35 in 1979, plans 40 in 1980. Pays 25% minimum royalty. Also "joint ownership plans, where a songwriter becomes co-publisher. Expenses and profits are shared. We *don't* charge the songwriter for our services as publisher. We cannot consider any material without a written query first describing yourself and your songs."
How to Contact: "Inquire first, describing yourself and songs available." Prefers 7½ ips reel-to-reel, cassette or disc with 1-5 songs on demo. SASE. Reports in 2-8 weeks.
Music: Avant-garde; C&W; disco; easy listening; MOR; progressive; rock; soul; and top

40/pop. Recently published "All for You," and "The Show Never Ends," recorded by Christopher (MOR/rock); and "Tricentennial 2076," recorded by Vyto B (avant-garde).

MELLYRIC MUSIC CO., 2325 Oakland Dr., Cleveland TN 37311. (615)479-1415. Publisher: Donald B. Gibson. Music publisher. Estab. 1976. ASCAP. Published 3 songs in 1977; plans 25 in 1979. Pays standard royalty.
How to Contact: Submit demo tape and lead sheet. Prefers 7½ ips reel-to-reel with 2 songs on demo. "Tape should be low noise, dynamic range, with leader at beginning and between songs. We are not responsible for tapes damaged by postal handling." SASE. Reports in 1 month.
Music: Children's; C&W; easy listening; gospel; MOR: progressive; top 40/pop; and commercials. Recently published "Please Lord, One More Time" and "There Is a World of Sugar" (sheet music); and "I Am America" recorded by Don Revere (educational/historical narration set to music).
Tips: "Send a signed and notarized affidavit with all lyrics and lead sheets stating name(s) and address(es) of authors, and that the material is original and unpublished. This is for your protection, as well as ours."

MELODY LANE, 6922 Hollywood Blvd., Hollywood CA 90028. (213)469-1667. Professional Manager: Roy Kohn. Music publisher and record company. Estab. 1928. BMI. See Peer-Southern Organization, Hollywood office, for details.

MELSTER MUSIC, Rt. 1, Box 213, Rogersville AL 35652. (205)247-3983. Affiliates: Mernee Music (ASCAP). President: Syble C. Richardson. Music publisher and recording studio. BMI. Plans 4 songs in 1979, 8 in 1980. Pays standard royalties.
How to Contact: Submit demo tape. Prefers 7½ or 3¾ ips reel-to-reel or cassette with 1-4 songs on demo. SASE. Reports in 1 month.
Music: Bluegrass; blues; C&W; gospel; MOR; R&B; rock; soul; and top 40/pop.

MEMNON, LTD., 1619 Broadway, New York NY 10019. Affiliates: Tithonus Music, Ltd. (BMI) and Hipolit Music (ASCAP). President: Krzysztof Z. Purzycki. Music publisher. Estab. 1969. ASCAP. Published 47 songs in 1978, 67 in 1979. Pays 10% royalty.
How to Contact: Submit demo tape and lead sheet. Prefers 7½ ips reel-to-reel with 3-7 songs on demo. "All songs submitted on reel-to-reel must have leader at the beginning and between musical compositions." Reports in 1 month.
Music: Choral; classical; easy listening; MOR; top 40/pop; and ethnic/foreign language songs. Recently published "Don't Give Your Love to Anyone," recorded by Wazoo (top 40/pop); "Squattin' Little Squillit," recorded by Donna Sands (novelty/pop); and "Jak Sie Masz," recorded by Happy End/Muza (top 40/pop).
Tips: "Write songs adaptable for both male and female artists."

MEMORY LANE MUSIC CORP., 240 Madison Ave., New York NY 10016. (212)686-1777. President: Larry Spier. Music publisher. Estab. 1921. BMI. See Larry Spier, Inc. for details.

MERCANTILE MUSIC, Box 2271, Palm Springs CA 92262. (714)327-3271. Affiliate: Blueford Music (ASCAP). President: Kent Fox. Music publisher and record producer. Estab. 1972. Published 10 songs in 1978. Pays standard royalties.
How to Contact: Submit demo tape and lead sheet. Prefers 7½ ips reel-to-reel with 3-10 songs on demo. SASE. Reports in 1 month.
Music: Church/religious; C&W; disco; easy listening; gospel; progressive; rock; and top 40/pop. Recently published "Midnight in the Morning," "Garage Sale" and "Married to the Girl I Love."

MERNEE MUSIC, Box 38, Lexington AL 35648. (205)247-3983. President: Woody Richardson. Music publisher and record company. Estab. 1959. ASCAP. See Woodrich Publishing for details.

METRONOME MUSIC PUBLISHING CO. OF PENNSYLVANIA, INC., 400 W. Glenwood Ave., Philadelphia PA 19140. President: Albert Schwab. Music publisher. Estab. 1977. ASCAP. Published 3 songs in 1977; plans 6 in 1979. Pays negotiable royalty.
How to Contact: Submit demo tape and lead sheet. Prefers 7½ ips reel-to-reel with 3-6 songs on demo. SASE. Reports in 1 month.
Music: Easy listening and jazz.

METROPOLITAN MUSIC CO., 4225 University Blvd., Houston TX 77005. (713)668-3279.

Manager: J.R. Lee. Music publisher. Estab. 1941. BMI. Pays 6-8% royalty.
How to Contact: Submit lead sheet. Prefers cassette with 1-3 songs on demo. SASE. Reports in 3 weeks.
Music: Choral and church/religious. Recently published "The Via Dolorosa," recorded by the Royals (religious).

MICHAVIN MUSIC, Box 2061, Daytona Beach FL 32015. Owner/Manager: Vincent L. Smith III. Music publisher, record producer and music arranging service. Estab. 1975.
How to Contact: Query. Prefers cassette.
Music: Disco; jazz; R&B; soul; and top 40/pop.

MICHEL LEFRANCOIS, 82 St. Joseph Blvd. W., Montreal, Quebec, Canada H2T 2P4. (514)849-3776. President: Christopher J. Reed. Music publisher. Estab. 1974. CAPAC. See Intermede Musique for details.

MID AMERICA MUSIC PUBLISHING CO., Box 242, Osage Beach MO 65065. (314)348-2270. General Manager: Harold L. Luick. Music publisher, record company and record producer. ASCAP. See Lee Maces Ozark Opry Music Publishing for details.

MID AMERICA MUSIC, (a division of Ozark Opry Records, Inc.), Box 242, Osage Beach MO 65065. (515)989-0876. Affiliate: Tall Corn Publishing (BMI). General Manager: Harold L. Luick. Music publisher. Estab. 1971. ASCAP. Pays standard royalty.
How to Contact: Arrange personal interview or submit demo tape and lead sheet. Prefers 7½ ips reel-to-reel or cassette with 1-3 songs on demo. "Tape should be of good quality, and the voice should be louder than the music." SASE. Reports in 3 weeks.
Music: Bluegrass; children's; church/religious; C&W; disco; easy listening; gospel; MOR; and rock. Recently published "I Don't Care About Tomorrow," recorded by Marvin Rainwater (C&W); and "It Sets Me Free," recorded by Jack Pavis (C&W).

MIGHTY MO MUSIC, 1650 Broadway, Suite 1107, New York NY 10019. (212)245-9612. President: Ken Williams. Music publisher. ASCAP. See A Dish A Tunes for details.

MIGHTY MUSIC, 2901 W. Maryland, Phoenix AZ 85017. (602)276-8520. President: Mike Lenaburg. Music publisher, record company and record producer. Estab. 1969. BMI. Published 28 songs in 1978. Pays standard royalties.
How to Contact: Query, submit demo tape, submit demo tape and lead sheet, submit acetate disc, submit acetate disc and lead sheet. Prefers cassette or 8-track tape. SASE. Reports in 1 month.
Music: Blues; disco; gospel; and R&B. Recently published "Lord Woke Me Up This Morning" (by Lee Kingdon), recorded by Willie Parker and the Sensational Souls/B&B Records (gospel); "Function Underground" (by M. Jennell and S. James), recorded by We the People/Darlene Records (disco); and "Don't Take My Money If You Won't Give Me Your Honey" (by M. Lenaburg), recorded by Oklahoma Zeke/Bluestown Records (blues).

MIGHTY THREE MUSIC, 309 S. Board St., Phildelphia PA 19107. (215)546-3510. President: Earl Shelton. Director, Publishing Administration:Constance Heigler. Music publisher. Estab. 1968. BMI.

MIGHTY THREE MUSIC, 117 S. Main St., Suite 200, Seattle WA 98121. (206)682-5278. Affiliates: Assorted Music (BMI), Bell Boy Music (BMI), Downstairs Music (BMI), Razor Sharp Music (BMI), Rose Tree Music (ASCAP) and World War Three Music (BMI). Director, West Coast Operations: JoDee Omer. Managing Partner: Thom Bell. Professional Manager: Ed Martinez. Music publisher. BMI. Estab. 1973. Published 300 songs in 1978, 350 in 1979. Pays standard royalty, less 15% administration fee. Sometimes secures songwriters on salary basis: "If a writer is signed to us exclusively, we offer him writer advances recoupable against writer royalties."
How to Contact: Submit demo tape or arrange personal interview. Prefers 7½ ips reel-to-reel or cassette with 1-5 songs on demo. "Must provide large envelope for return." SASE. Reports "as soon as possible."
Music: C&W; disco; easy listening; folk; gospel; jazz; MOR; progressive; rock (hard, country, etc.); soul; and top 40/pop. Recently published "You'll Never Find Another Love Like Mine" and "Lady Love," recorded by Lou Rawls (R&B/pop/MOR); and "Don't Leave Me This Way," recorded by Thelma Houston.

MILENE MUSIC, 2510 Franklin Rd., Nashville TN 37204. (615)385-3031. Vice President: John R. Brown. Music publisher. ASCAP.
Music: C&W. See Acuff-Rose for submission details.

MILL RUN PUBLISHING CO., Kingsmill Recording Studio, 1033 Kingsmill Pkwy., Columbus OH 43229. President: Don Spangler. BMI. Pays standard royalty.
How to Contact: Submit demo tape and lead sheet. Prefers cassette with 1-3 songs on demo. SASE. Reports in 3 weeks.
Music: Bluegrass; blues; children's; choral; church/religious; classical; C&W; disco; easy listening; folk; gospel; jazz; MOR; progressive; rock; soul; and top 40/pop. Recently published "I Think of You," recorded by Gary Sullivan (pop); and "Pure Jam," recorded by Pure Jam (rock).

BRIAN MILLAN MUSIC CORP., Box 1322, Station B, Montreal, Quebec, Canada H3B 3K9. (514)288-8191. President: Brian Millan. Music publisher and record producer. Estab. 1963. ASCAP. Published 6 songs in 1977; plans 30 in 1979. Pays 1-50% royalty.
How to Contact: Submit demo tape and lead sheet. Prefers reel-to-reel, cassette or 8-track cartridge with 1-4 songs on demo. SAE and International Reply Coupons. Reports in 2 weeks.
Music: C&W; disco; easy listening; MOR; rock; and soul. Recently published "Maria Helaine," recorded by Steve Dray (MOR); "Gloria," recorded by Johnny White (Christmas carol); and "Sempre Cossi," recorded by Tony Gamo (MOR).

MILLER SOUL-KRAFT MUSIC, 347 Litchfield Ave., Babylon NY 11702. (516)661-9842. Publisher: William H. Miller. Music publisher and record producer. Estab. 1955. BMI. Pays 5-10% royalty.
How to Contact: Submit demo tape and lead sheet. Prefers cassette with 4 songs minimum on tape. SASE. Reports in 1 month.
Music: Blues; C&W; disco; rock; soul; and top 40/pop. Recently published "I'm Going to Get You," recorded by Allan Turner (pop); and "I Still Love You, Uh! Huh!", recorded by Maxine Miller (disco).

MILLEVAN MUSIC PUBLISHERS, Box 45, Thomasville GA 31792. (912)226-7911. Affiliate: Land o' Roses Publishers (BMI). Vice President: Emery T. Evans. Music publisher, record company, record producer and recording studio. Estab. 1974. SESAC. Published 25 songs in 1978; plans 30 in 1979, 40 in 1980. Pays standard royalties.
How to Contact: Query, arrange personal interview, submit demo tape, or submit demo tape and lead sheet. Prefers 7½ ips reel-to-reel or cassette with 1-3 songs on demo. SASE. Reports in 2 weeks.
Music: Bluegrass; church/religious; C&W; folk; and gospel. Recently published "Be Proud of America" (by Dawson Mathis), recorded by Crownsmen Quartet (country); "Days of Glory" (by Emery Evans), recorded by Tonemasters Quartet (gospel); "Satisfied with Jesus" (by Isaah Revells), recorded by Holy Mighty Crusaders (spiritual); and "Jesus is Real" (by Evans), recorded by Crownsmen Quartet (gospel).

MINTA MUSIC, 7033 Sunset Blvd., Suite 303, Los Angeles CA 90028. (213)469-2213. President: Philip R. Jones. Music publisher, record company and production company. Estab. 1975. BMI. Published 33 songs in 1977; plans 70 in 1979. Pays standard royalty.
How to Contact: Submit demo tape. Prefers 7½ ips quarter-track reel-to-reel or cassette with 2-5 songs on demo. SASE. Reports in 1 month.
Music: MOR; rock; soul; and top 40/pop. Recently published "Anything You Want," recorded by John Valente (R&B/top 40/pop); "Machines," recorded by Bad Boy (top 40/pop/rock); and "Weak in the Knees," recorded by Caren Armstrong (top 40/pop).

MIRACLE-JOY PUBLICATIONS, 425 Park St., Suite 9, Hackensack NJ 07601. (201)488-5211. President: Johnny Miracle. Vice President: Aileen Joy. Music publisher and record company. Estab. 1970. BMI. Pays 2-5% royalty.
How to Contact: Submit demo tape or submit demo tape and lead sheet. Prefers 7½ ips reel-to-reel or cassette with 2-6 songs on demo. SASE. Reports in 2 weeks.
Music: Children's; church/religious; C&W; easy listening; folk; and gospel. Recently published "Pizzaman," recorded by Tiny (novelty); "Memories I Hold of You," recorded by Sam Starr (C&W); and "The Ashes Are Still Warm," recorded by Al and Carrol (C&W).

MR. MORT MUSIC, 44 Music Square E., Nashville TN 37203. (615)255-2175. Affiliate: Jason Dee Music (BMI). President: Charles Fields. Music publisher, record company and record

producer. Estab. 1977. ASCAP. Published 30 songs in 1978; plans 50 in 1979, 50 in 1980. Pays standard royalties.
How to Contact: Submit demo tape and lead sheet. Prefers 7½ ips reel-to-reel or cassette with 1-4 songs on demo. SASE. Reports in 2 weeks.
Music: Blues; C&W; easy listening; MOR; and top 40/pop. Recently published "Can't Shake You Off My Mind" (by C. Fields), recorded by Bobby W. Loftis (country); "Fool with a Big Heartache" (by Fields), recorded by Lor Ray Luke/Charta Records (country); and "Baby That's All" (by Eric Daniels), recorded by Eric Daniels/Charta Records (country).

MISTRAL MUSIC, System Four Artists, Ltd., 145 E. 82nd St., New York NY 10028. Affiliates: Jamie Jaz Music (BMI), August Third Music (ASCAP) and System for Barclay (ASCAP). President: Stephen F. Johnson. Music publisher and management firm. Estab. 1976. BMI. Pays 25-40% royalty. Buys some material outright; pays $50-200.
How to Contact: Submit demo tape and lead sheet. Prefers 7½ ips reel-to-reel or cassette with 2-6 songs on demo. SASE. Reports in 2 weeks.
Music: Disco; easy listening; jazz; MOR; and top 40/pop. Recently published "I Found Love," recorded by Love and Kisses (disco); "Parisian Lady," recorded by Manhattan Transfer (pop/jazz); and "Rainin'," recorded by Jolis and Simone (MOR).

MODOC MUSIC, INC., Box 306, Vansant VA 24631. (703)498-4556. President: Roy John Fuller. Music publisher. Estab. 1974. ASCAP. See Able Music for details.

MONKHOUSE MUSIC, Rt. 6, 906 Ashby Dr., Brentwood TN 37027. (615)244-9412. Manager: Ann M. Stuckey. Music publisher. Estab. 1967. BMI. See Stuckey Publishing for details.

MONONA MUSIC CO., The Cameron Organisation Inc., 320 S. Waiola Ave., LaGrange IL 60525. (312)352-2026. Vice President/General Manager: Jean M. Cameron. Music Publisher. Estab. 1959. BMI. See The Cameron Organisation for details.

MONSTER MUSIC, 110 21st Ave. S., Nashville TN 37203. General Manager: Ed Penney. Music publisher. ASCAP.
Music: C&W; easy listening; MOR; rock and top 40/pop. See Show Biz Music Group for submission details.

MOO MOO MUSIC, Box 842, Radio City, New York NY 10019. President: Don Seat. Vice President: Darlene Gorzela. Music publisher. Estab. 1952. BMI.
Music: Bluegrass; blues; church/religious; classical; C&W; disco; easy listening; folk; gospel; jazz; MOR; progressive; R&B; rock; soul; and top 40/pop. See Marielle Music for submission details.

MOON JUNE MUSIC, 5821 SE Powell Blvd., Portland OR 97206. President: Bob Stoutenburg. Music publisher. Estab. 1972. Pays standard royalty.
How to Contact: Submit demo tape or submit demo tape and lead sheet. Prefers 7½ ips reel-to-reel or cassette with 2-10 songs on demo. SASE. Reports in 1 month.
Music: C&W; disco; easy listening; MOR; progressive; rock; soul; and top 40/pop. Recently published "My Future Comes and Goes" and "Hard Times," recorded by Jerry Bulick (C&W); and "It Will Take a Miracle," recorded by Ron Fogarty (C&W).

MOORPARK MUSIC, Box 842, Radio City, New York NY 10019. President: Don Seat. Vice President: Darlent Gorzela. Music publisher. Estab. 1952. ASCAP.
Music: Bluegrass; blues; church/religious; classical; C&W; disco; easy listening; folk; gospel; jazz; MOR; progressive; R&B; rock; soul; top 40/pop. See Marielle Music for submission details.

MORHITS PUBLISHING CO., 382 Clarence Ave., Sunnyvale CA 94086. (408)739-6133. President: Garrie Thompson. Music publisher. Estab. 1966. BMI. See Duane Music for details.

MORNING MUSIC, LTD., 1343 Matheson Blvd. W., Mississauga, Ontario, Canada L4W 1R1. Affiliate: Skinners Pond Music (BMI). General Manager: Mark Altman. Music publisher. CAPAC. Pays standard royalty.
How to Contact: Submit demo tape and lead sheet. Prefers reel-to-reel or cassette. SAE and International Reply Coupons. Reports in 2 weeks.
Music: "We seek all formats." Recently published "Good Morning World," recorded by Julie

Lynn (C&W); and "Bud the Spud," recorded by Stompin' Tom Connors (C&W).

MORNING MUSIC (USA), INC., Box 120478, Nashville TN 37212. (416)625-2676. Affiliate: Bathurst Music (BMI). President: Jury Krytiuk. General Manager: Mark Altman. Music publisher and record company. Estab. 1971. ASCAP. Published 100 songs in 1978; plans 100 in 1979. Pays standard royalty.
How to Contact: Submit demo tape and lead sheet. Prefers 7½ ips reel-to-reel or cassette with 1-4 songs on demo. SASE. Reports in 1 month.
Music: Bluegrass; blues; children's; choral; church/religious; classical; C&W; disco; easy listening; folk; gospel; jazz; MOR; progressive; rock; soul; and top 40/pop. Recently published "One More Time," recorded by Crystal Gayle (C&W); "Country Hall of Fame," recorded by Hank Locklin (C&W); and "Flying South," recorded by Chet Atkins and Jerry Reed (instrumental).

EDWIN H. MORRIS & CO., of MPL Communications, Inc., 39 W. 54th St., New York NY 10019. Music publisher. Not presently accepting new material.

MORRIS MUSIC, INC., 6255 Sunset Blvd., Suite 1904, Hollywood CA 90028. (213)463-5102. Affiliate: Sashay Music (ASCAP). President: Steve Morris. Music publisher. Estab. 1976. BMI. Published 40 songs in 1978. Pays standard royalty.
How to Contact: Arrange personal interview, submit demo tape or submit demo tape and lead sheet. Prefers 7½ ips reel-to-reel or cassette with 1-6 songs on demo. SASE. Reports in 2 weeks.
Music: MOR; progressive; rock; soul; and top 40/pop. Recently published "Rock & Roll Slave," recorded by Stephen Bishop (rock); and "Mandy," recorded by Barry Manilow (top 40).

MOZUSSE, 82 St. Joseph Blvd. W., Montreal, Quebec, Canada H2T 2P4. (514)849-3776. President: Christopher J. Reed. Music publisher. Estab. 1974. CAPAC. See Intermede Musique for details.

MUCH MORE MUSIC, 117 W. Rockland Rd., Libertyville IL 60048. (312)362-4060. Director of Publishing and Administration: Mary Chris. Music publisher and record company. Estab. 1969. BMI. See Amalgamated Tulip for details.

MUFFINMAN MUSIC, Fivetake Group Productions, Ltd., 484 Waterloo Ct., Oshawa, Ontario, Canada L1H 3X1. Contact: Bob Stone. Music publisher. CAPAC. See Fivetake Music for details.

MUSEDCO, Box 5916, Richardson TX 75080. Owner: Dick A. Shuff. Music publisher. Estab. 1979. Plans 2 songs in 1979, 8 in 1980. Pays standard royalties.
How to Contact: Query or submit demo tape and lead sheet. Prefers cassette with 2-4 songs on demo. SASE. Reports in 1 month.
Music: Blues; children's; C&W; easy listening; folk; gospel; MOR; top 40/pop; and children's piano.
Tips: "We want songs that have been worked, checked, rewritten, edited and improved until they are good. We will listen to everything. Send tapes of the highest quality and the finest recording possible accompanied by a legible lead sheet and a letter saying something about the writer's background. Submit the best demo you can afford so that you will give your songs proper credit."

MUSIC CRAFTSHOP, Box 22325, Nashville TN 37202. Affiliates: Hit Kit Music (BMI) and Phono Music (SESAC). Manager: Jerry Duncan. Music publisher. ASCAP. Published 158 songs in 1978; plans 150 in 1979, 150 in 1980. Pays standard royalties.
How to Contact: Query, submit demo tape or submit demo tape and lead sheet. Prefers 7½ ips reel-to-reel with 1-5 songs on demo. SASE. Reports in 1 week.
Music: C&W; and MOR. Recently published "I Hate Hate" (by Razzy Bailey), recorded by Razzy/MGM Records (pop); "Mirror Mirror" (by Ben Reece), recorded by Ben Reece/20th Century Records (country); and "He Loves Me All to Pieces" (by Fields-Riis), recorded by Ruby Falls/50 States Records (country).

MUSIC DESIGNERS, 1126 Boylston St., Boston MA 02123. (617)262-3546. Affiliates: Mutiny Music and EMI Music. President: Fred Berk. Music publisher, record company and production company. Estab. 1977. BMI. Published 23 songs in 1978; plans 30 in 1979. Pays standard royalties.

How to Contact: Submit demo tape and lead sheet. Prefers 7½ ips reel-to-reel or cassette with 1-6 songs on demo. SASE. Reports in 3 weeks.
Music: Children's; C&W; disco; folk; MOR; progressive; rock; soul; and top 40/pop. Recently released "Man Enough," recorded by No Slack (pop/R&B); "Why Don't We Love Each Other?", recorded by the Ellis Hall Group (pop/R&B); and "Breaker 1-9," recorded by the Back Bay Rhythm Section (disco).

MUSIC FOR PERCUSSION, INC., 170 NE 33rd St., Fort Lauderdale FL 33334. (305)563-1844. Affiliate: Plymouth Music (ASCAP). Contact: Bernard Fisher, Fran Taber. Music publisher. BMI. Published 10 songs in 1978.
How to Contact: Submit demo tape and lead sheet. Prefers 7½ ips reel-to-reel. "Be sure that the tapes submitted are carefully labeled with title, name and address of composer." SASE. Reports in 1 month.
Music: Classical; progressive; and rock.

MUSIC OF CALVARY, 142 8th Ave. N., Nashville TN 37203. A&R Director: Ronnie Drake. Music publisher. SESAC. See Songs of Calvary for details.

MUSICWAYS, INC., 2049 Century Park E., 35th Floor, Los Angeles CA 90067. (213)557-8815. Affiliate: Filmways Music (ASCAP). President: Terri Fricon. Professional Manager: Jonathon Stone. Music publisher. Estab. 1975. BMI. Published 168 songs in 1978; plans 200 in 1979. Pays standard royalty "for most uses"; pays 6¢/copy for sheet music and 10% royalty on folios. Sometimes secures songwriters on salary basis: duties "vary with each writer."
How to Contact: Submit demo tape and lead sheet. Prefers 7½ ips reel-to-reel with 1-3 songs on demo. "Use leader tape. Be sure tape and box are marked with the name and address of writer." SASE. Reports in 1 month.
Music: C&W; MOR; rock; soul; and top 40/pop. Recently published "I Believe You" recorded by the Carpenters (top 40/pop); "Two Different People" recorded by Susie Allanson (C&W); and "Let Me Be Your Woman" recorded by Linda Clifford (top 40/pop/R&B/disco).

MUSIQUE FRISEE, 82 St. Joseph Blvd. W., Montreal, Quebec, Canada H2T 2P4. (514)849-3776. President: Christopher J. Reed. Music publisher. Estab. 1974. CAPAC. See Intermede Musique for details.

MUSIQUETTE, 82 St. Joseph Blvd. W., Montreal, Quebec, Canada H2T 2P4. (514)849-3776. President: Christopher J. Reed. Music publisher. Estab. 1974. CAPAC. See Intermede Musique for details.

MUSTAFF MUSIC PUBLISHERS, 726 Carlson Dr., Orlando FL 32804. (305)644-3853. President: Will Campbell. Music publisher and record company. Estab. 1970. BMI. See Palamar Music Publishers for details.

MUTINY MUSIC, 1126 Boylston St., Boston MA 02123. (617)262-3546. Music publisher and production company. See Music Designer for details.

MUZACAN PUBLISHING CO., 44844 Michigan Ave., Canton MI 48188. President: Bruce Young. Music publisher and booking agency. Estab. 1977. BMI. Pays 50-75% royalty.
How to Contact: Submit demo tape and lead sheet. Prefers cassette with 4 songs minimum on tape. SASE. Reports in 2 weeks.
Music: Rock (hard, acid or middle—"no country") and top 40/pop.

MY SON'S PUBLISHING, Box 2194, Memphis TN 38101. (901)948-7455. President: B.J. Cole. Vice President: Michal M. Cole. Music publisher, booking agency and record company. Estab. 1962. BMI. Published 6 songs in 1977. Pays 3% royalty.
How to Contact: Submit demo tape. Prefers 7½ ips reel-to-reel or cassette. SASE. Reports in 1 month.
Music: Blues; church/religious; gospel; and soul. Recently published "Yesterday," recorded by Lula Collins (gospel); "Here Larry," recorded by Larry Davis (blues); and "Days," recorded by the Gospel Song Birds (gospel).

NASHWOOD MUSIC, 2111 Kenmere Ave., Burbank CA 91504. President: Hal Spencer. Music publisher and record company. Estab. 1954. ASCAP. See Manna Music for details.

NATURAL GROOVE MUSIC, INC., 3588 Big Tree Ave., Memphis TN 38128. (901)525-2042. Affiliate: Ron Townsend Music (BMI). President: Ronald Townsend. Music publisher. Estab. 1972. BMI. Published 50 songs in 1978; plans 100 in 1979. Pays 2-5% royalty. Sometimes secures songwriters on salary basis: "Songwriters must arrange demo sessions, make lyric and lead sheets, have musical background and have sound knowledge of what the writer's concept is and how to sell his lyrics." Pays $150/week.
How to Contact: Submit demo tape and lead sheet. Prefers 7½ ips reel-to-reel or cassette with 3-8 songs on demo. "List songs titles in order, and list time and what artist the song is slanted to." SASE. Reports in 3 weeks.
Music: Blues; C&W; disco; gospel; jazz; progressive; rock (hard or country); soul; and top 40/pop. Recently published "Don't Walk Away," recorded by Chained Reactions (soul); "It Makes No Sense," recorded by Betty Wilson (soul); and "You Are the Girl for Me," recorded by Jerry Weaver (soul).

NATURAL SONGS, INC., 9220 Sunset Blvd., Los Angeles CA 90069. (213)278-8970. President: Dennis Lambert. Director of Publishing: Marsha Ingraham. Music publisher, record company and production company. Estab. 1968. ASCAP. See Lambert & Potter Music for details.

NAUTICAL MUSIC CO., 100 Harvard Ave., Gadsden AL 35901. (205)546-6906. President/Music Editor: Ray McGinnis. Music publisher. Estab. 1967. BMI. Published 15 songs in 1979; plans 25 in 1980. Pays 5-8% royalty.
How to Contact: Submit demo tape and lead sheet. Prefers 7½ ips reel-to-reel with 4-8 songs on demo. SASE. Reports in 6 weeks.
Music: C&W; MOR; rock (country or hard); and soul. Recently published "Summer," recorded by Lemon Fog (rock); and "Alabama Home Grown Wine," recorded by Malibus (country rock).

NEVER ENDING MUSIC, Box 58, Glendora NJ 08029. (609)939-0034. Affiliates: Hot Pot Music (BMI) and Record Room Music (ASCAP). General Manager: Eddie Jay Harris. Music publisher and record company. Estab. 1970. BMI. Payment negotiable.
How to Contact: Submit demo tape and lead sheet. SASE.

JOSEPH NICOLETTI MUSIC, Box 2818, Newport Beach CA 92663. (714)497-3758. President: Joseph Nicoletti. Vice President: Cheryl Lee Gammon. Music publisher, record company and record producer. Estab. 1976. ASCAP. Published 18 songs in 1978; plans 25 in 1979. Payment negotiable.
How to Contact: Submit demo tape and lead sheet. Prefers "good quality" cassette with 1-3 songs on demo. SASE. Reports in 1 month.
Music: Disco; easy listening; MOR; rock; soul; and top 40/pop. Recently published "Love Has Come to Stay" (by Joseph Nicoletti), recorded by Joseph Nicoletti/Starline Records (easy listening); "I Am Free" (by Cheryl Gammon and Nicoletti), recorded by Joseph Nicoletti/Starline Records (disco/rock); and "Gypsy" (by Nicoletti), recorded by David Oliver/Mercury Records (disco).

NEWWRITERS MUSIC PUBLISHING/STARGEM RECORDS (formerly Gemway Music Publishing), 19 Music Square W., Nashville TN 37203. (615)255-6606. President: A. W. Hodge. Music publisher, record company and record producer. Estab. 1972. BMI. See Stargem Records.

NILKAM MUSIC/KIMSHA MUSIC, 5305 Church Ave., Brooklyn NY 11203. (212)498-7111. Owner: William R. Kamorra. Music publisher, record company and record producer. Estab. 1976. BMI. Published 10 songs in 1978. Pays standard royalties.
How to Contact: Query, submit demo tape and lead sheet, or submit acetate disc and lead sheet. Prefers 7½ ips reel-to-reel or cassette with 3-6 songs on demo. SASE. Reports in 2 weeks.
Music: Disco; MOR; R&B; rock; soul; and top 40/pop. Recently published "Making Love," recorded by Sammy Gordon (disco); "Love Bug," recorded by U. Robert (disco); and "Unity," recorded by Future 2,000 (disco).

NISE PRODUCTIONS, INC., Box 5132, Philadelphia PA 19141. (215)276-0100. Recording studio: 413 Cooper St., Suite 101, Camden NJ 08102. President: Michael Nise. Music publisher, record company and recording studio. Estab. 1969. BMI. Published 80 songs in 1978; plans 150 in 1979. Pays standard royalty.

How to Contact: Submit demo tape. Prefers 7½ ips reel-to-reel or cassette with 3-4 songs on demo. SASE. Reports in 1 month.
Music: Children's; church/religious; disco; folk; gospel; soul; and top 40/pop. Recently published "Bruce Lee's Return of Dragon," recorded by Ninchucks (disco); "100 South of Broadway," recorded by Philadelphia Society (disco); and "Just Want to Be Your Joy," recorded by Joy Stanford (ballad).

NO. 11 MUSIC, 5112 Hollywood Blvd., Los Angeles CA 90027. Professional Managers: Gary Heaton, Eric Troff. BMI. See Skyhill Publishing for details.

KENNY NOLAN PUBLISHING CO., c/o Peter C. Bennett, 211 S. Beverly Dr., Suite 108, Beverly Hills CA 90212. General Manager: Peter C. Bennett. Music publisher. Estab. 1969. ASCAP. Recently published "My Eyes Adored You," recorded by Frankie Valli (top 40/pop); "Lady Marmalade," recorded by Labelle (disco/soul); and "Get Dancin'," recorded by Disco Tex and the Sexolettes (disco). See Sound of Nolan Music for details.

NOODLE TUNES, Box 878, Sonoma CA 95476. (707)938-4060. Manager: Bruce Cohn. Music publisher and management firm. Estab. 1975. BMI. See Bruce Cohn Music for details.

NU-GEN PUBLISHING CO., Box 2199, Vancouver, British Columbia, Canada V6B 3V7. (604)688-1820. Affiliate: Pyros Publishing (CAPAC). President: John Rodney. Music publisher and record company. Estab. 1970. PROCAN. Published 20 songs in 1978; plans 30 in 1979. Pays standard royalties.
How to Contact: Submit demo tape. Prefers 7½ ips reel-to-reel with 2-6 songs on demo. SAE and International Reply Coupons. Reports in 1 month.
Music: Classical; C&W; jazz; MOR; and top 40/pop. Recently published "Mister, Go Softly," recorded by Linda Marlene (C&W); and "Maranatha," recorded by Marek Norman (top 40).

NYAMM NEOWD MUSIC, INC., 38 N. Pennsylvania St., Indianapolis IN 46204. (317)634-3954. Counsel: Clarence Bolden Jr. Music publisher. Estab. 1977. BMI. Published 6 songs in 1978; plans 8 in 1980. Pays standard royalties.
Music: Blues; disco; easy listening; gospel; jazz; MOR; progressive; R&B; soul; and top 40/pop. Recently published "Don't Get Me Rowdy" (by Griffin and Ferrill); "Especially for You" (by C. Bush) ; and "Maybe My Baby" (by Bush), all recorded by Chi/Sound Records (R&B).

O.A.S. MUSIC GROUP, 805 18th Ave. S., Nashville TN 37203. Affiliates: Arian Publications (ASCAP), On His Own Music (BMI) and Shadowfax Music (BMI). Co-Directors: Dane Bryant, Steve Singleton. Music publisher. Estab. 1975. Pays standard royalty.
How to Contact: Arrange personal interview for any Monday, or submit demo tape and lyric sheet. Prefers 7½ ips reel-to-reel with 3-4 songs on demo. SASE. Reports in 3 months.
Music: Bluegrass; blues; C&W; disco; easy listening; MOR; progressive; rock; soul; and top 40/pop. Recently published "Don't Believe My Heart Can Stand Another You," recorded by Tanya Tucker (C&W); "I Cheated on a Good Woman's Love," recorded by Billy "Crash" Craddock (C&W); and "Atlanta's Burning Down," recorded by Dickie Betts (Southern rock).

O.K., 82 St. Joseph Blvd. W., Montreal, Quebec, Canada H2T 2P4. (514)849-3776. President: Christopher J. Reed. Music publisher. Estab. 1974. CAPAC. See Intermede Musique for details.

OAK SPRINGS MUSIC, Rt. 5, Box 382, Yakima WA 98903. (509)966-1193. President: Hiram White. Music publisher. Estab. 1977. Published 15 songs in 1978. Pays standard royalty.
How to Contact: Submit demo tape and lead sheet. Prefers cassette with 1-4 songs on demo. "Keep it simple (voice and guitar), with no promo material." SASE. Reports in 1 month.
Music: Bluegrass; blues; C&W; disco; folk; MOR; progressive; and rock. Recently published "I Can't Get the You out of Me" and "Georgia Wine," recorded by Barbara Jean Taylor (C&W); and "I'm Too Shy," recorded by Penny Stadler (C&W).

OAKRIDGE MUSIC RECORDING SERVICE, 2001 Elton Rd., Haltom City TX 76117. (817)838-8001. President: Homer Lee Sewell. Music publisher and record company. Estab. 1961. BMI. Pays 4-20% royalty. Charges for some services: "If the writer is under contract to me, I don't charge. Otherwise, I do charge."
How to Contact: Submit demo tape. Prefers 7½ ips stereo or mono reel-to-reel with 2-4 songs

on demo. "Send parcel post and mark the box 'Don't X-ray'." SASE. Reports in 6 weeks.
Music: Bluegrass; church/religious; C&W; disco; and gospel. Recently published "Whisper/Mad" (by Homer Lee Sewell), recorded by Lee Sawyer/Oakridge Records (C&W); "Sandra Kay/Walk and Talk" (by D.R. Hudson), recorded by Don Hudson/Crossfire Records (country/pop); and "The Tennis Shoe Cowboy/The Black Texas Cowboy" (by J. Rollins and J.E. Hamilton), recorded by James and Willie/Crossfire records (disco/country).

OCEANS BLUE MUSIC, LTD., 220 Central Park S., New York NY 10019. Affiliate: Silver Blue Music (ASCAP). Professional Manager: Fara Feinerman. Music publisher and record producer. BMI. Estab. 1971.
How to Contact: Submit demo tape. Prefers cassette with 1-3 songs on demo. SASE. Reports in 3 weeks.
Music: Disco; MOR; and top 40/pop.

MARY FRANCES ODLE RECORDING & PUBLISHING CO., 8431 Howard Dr., Houston TX 77017. (713)649-5579. President: Mary Frances Odle. Music publisher, booking agency and record company. Estab. 1963. BMI. Published 8 songs in 1978; plans 10 in 1979. Pays standard royalties.
How to Contact: Submit demo tape or submit demo tape and lead sheet. Prefers 7½ ips reel-to-reel or cassette with 5 songs minimum on tape. SASE. Reports in 2 weeks.
Music: Blues; church/religious; C&W; easy listening; gospel; MOR; rock; and soul. Recently published "Women, Clothes, Cars and Whiskey" and "Hello Lonely, Lonely World" (by John Butterworth), recorded by John Butterworth (C&W); and Looking Back Over Life," "Big, Big Mama," and "Cry, Cry on My Shoulder," written by Jerry Deyo (C&W).

OFF HOLLYWOOD MUSIC, 1254 S. Holt, Los Angeles CA 90035. (213)655-5745. President: Howard Rosen. Music publisher and management firm. ASCAP. See Favor Music for details.

MILTON OKUN PUBLISHING CO., 50 Holly Hill Lane, Greenwich CT 06830. (203)661-0707. Music publisher. BMI. See Cherry Lane Music for details. "We do not accept unsolicited material.

OLD SPARTA MUSIC, Box 638, Main St., Bailey NC 27807. President: Richard H. Royall. Vice President: Michael R. Birzon. Music publisher. Estab. 1976. BMI. Published 75 songs in 1977; plans 300-500 in 1979. Pays standard royalty.
How to Contact: Submit demo tape, arrange personal interview, or submit demo tape and lead sheet. Prefers 7½ ips reel-to-reel with 1-12 songs on demo. SASE. Reports in 1 week. "Because we receive a number of submissions, it's to the writer's advantage to produce as professional a demo as possible."
Music: Disco; easy listening; rock; soul; and top 40/pop. Recently published "Party Life," "Prisoner" and "I Thought You Wanted to Dance," recorded by Symbol 8 (soul).

OMNIBUS, 6255 Sunset Blvd., Suite 1911, Hollywood CA 90028. Professional Manager: Michael O'Connor. Music publisher. Estab. 1978. BMI. ASCAP. Published 50 songs in 1978; plans 50 in 1979. Secures some songwriters on salary basis.
How to Contact: Submit demo tape and lead sheet. Prefers cassette with 1-3 songs on demo. SASE. Reports in 1 month.
Music: Disco; easy listening; MOR; rock; and top 40/pop. Recently published "Can You Fool," recorded by Glen Campbell (MOR); "Baby Me Baby" (by Roger Miller), recorded by Barbra Streisand (MOR); and "This Is Getting Funny," recorded by Waylon Jennings (country-rock).

ON HIS OWN MUSIC, O.A.S. Music Group, 805 18th Ave. S., Nashville TN 37203. Co-Directors: Dane Bryant, Steve Singleton. Music publisher. Estab. 1975. BMI. See O.A.S. Music Group for details.

ONE FOR THE ROAD MUSIC CO., 3317 Ledgewood Dr., Los Angeles CA 90068. Contact: Alan Brackett. Music publisher and record producer. Estab. 1977. BMI. Plans 30 songs in 1979. Pays standard royalties.
How to Contact: Submit demo tape. Prefers cassette with 1-4 songs on demo. "The words must be clear; if not, include a lyric sheet." SASE. Reports in 1 month.
Music: C&W; MOR; rock; soul; and top 40/pop. Recently published "I Really Want You Here Tonight" (by A. Brackett), recorded by Randy Meisner/E-A Records (R&B/MOR/ballad); and "Lonesome Cowgirl," (by A. Brackett and J. Merrill), recorded by Randy Meisner/E-A Records (C&W/jazz).

Songwriter's Market Close-Up

"You can't let yourself be discouraged," says songwriter Randy Goodrum. If you have talent, can take constructive criticism, and can stick it out, you'll get your chance. Goodrum stuck it out, and several of his songs eventually became hits, including Anne Murray's version of "You Needed Me." Like most songwriters, he started out on the ground floor—or perhaps it was the basement for Goodrum. "At one time I was really unknown," he says. "They didn't even know me at my own house."

1, 2, 3, 4 MUSIC, 82 St. Joseph Blvd. W., Montreal, Quebec, Canada H2T 2P4. (514)849-3776. President: Christopher J. Reed. Music publisher. Estab. 1974. CAPAC. See Intermede Musique for details.

ORANGE BEAR MUSIC CO., The Sunshine Group, 800 S. 4th St., Philadelphia PA 19147. (215)755-7000. Contact: Cathi Leveille. Music publisher, record producer, recording studio and management firm. BMI. See Scully Music for details.

ORANGE BLOSSOM MUSIC, 50 Music Square W., Suite 902, United Artists Tower, Nashville TN 37203. Music publisher, record company and record producer. SESAC. See Iron Blossom Music for details.

ORCHID PUBLISHING, Bouquet-Orchid Enterprises, Box 4220, 'Shreveport LA 71104. (318)686-7362. President: Bill Bohannon. Music publisher and record company. Estab. 1977. BMI. Published 2 songs in 1977; plans 25 in 1979. Pays 5-10% royalty.
How to Contact: Submit demo tape and lead sheet. Prefers 7½ ips reel-to-reel or cassette with 3-5 songs on demo. SASE. Reports in 1 month.
Music: Church/religious (country gospel); C&W ("Dolly Parton/Linda Ronstadt type material"); and top 40/pop ("John Denver/Bee Gees type material"). Recently published "Gonna Be a Brighter Day Tomorrow" and "I Need You Today," recorded by Shan Wilson (C&W).

JOHN OSCAR MUSIC CORP., c/o Gopam Enterprises, Inc., 11 Riverside Dr., #13C-W, New York NY 10023. (212)724-6120. Managing Director: Laurie Goldstein. Music publisher. Estab. 1960. ASCAP. See Gopam Enterprises for details.

OSV MUSIC PUBLISHING, Noll Plaza, Huntington IN 46750. (219)356-8400. Director: Ray Repp. Music publisher and record company. Estab. 1977. Plans 150 songs in 1979. Pays 10% royalty.
How to Contact: Submit demo tape. Prefers 7½ ips reel-to-reel or cassette with 4-6 songs on demo. SASE. Reports in 1 month.
Music: "General Christian listening: all styles from pop to classical." Recently published "Peaceable Kingdom," recorded by Mary Lu Walker (children's); "Harvest Rain," recorded by Pat Cullen II (pop Christian); and "Benedicamus," recorded by Ray Repp (liturgical).

OTHER MUSIC, The Barn, North Ferrisburg VT 05473. (802)425-2111. Affiliate: Pleiades Music (BMI). Vice President: Bill Schubart. Music publisher and record company. Estab. 1975. ASCAP. Pays standard royalties. Secures some songwriters on salary basis.
How to Contact: Submit demo tape. Prefers 7½ ips reel-to-reel or cassette with 1-3 songs on demo. SASE. Reports in 1 month.
Music: Blues; children's; classical; C&W; folk; jazz; progressive; rock; soul; and top 40/pop. Recently published "Young Westley" (progressive C&W) and "Mrs. De Lion's Lament" (pop/folk), recorded by David Bromberg; "Green Rolling Hills of West Virginia," recorded by Emmy Lou Harris (pop/folk); and "Up Is a Nice Place to Be," recorded by Bonnie Koloc (pop/jazz).

OTIS MUSIC, 1217 S. Ogden Dr., Los Angeles CA 90019. (213)277-1197, 473-5639. Chief of Production: Lim Taylor. Director: Brenda Hasty. Music publisher and production company. Estab. 1972. BMI. See Fourth House Music Publishing for details.

RAY OVERHOLT MUSIC, 112 S. 26th St., Battle Creek MI 49015. (616)963-0554. A&R Director: Mildred Overholt. Manager: Ray Overholt. Music publisher. Estab. 1959. BMI. Published 5 songs in 1978; plans 20 in 1979. Pays 10-25% royalty. "We also use the standard songwriter's contract at the going rate."
How to Contact: Submit demo tape and lead sheet. Prefers cassette with 1-3 songs on demo. SASE. Reports in 3 weeks.
Music: Church/religious and gospel. Recently published "Hallelujah Square," recorded by the Blackwood Brothers (gospel); "Ten Thousand Angels," recorded by Kate Smith (gospel); and "God's Choir," recorded by London Symphonic Orchestra (gospel).

LEE MACES OZARK OPRY MUSIC PUBLISHING, Box 242, Osage Beach MO 65065. (314)348-2702. Affiliates: Tall Corn Publishing (BMI) and Mid America Music Publishing (ASCAP). General Manager: Harold L. Luick. Music publisher, record company and record producer. Estab. 1953. Published 35 songs in 1978; plans 40 in 1979, 250 in 1980. Pays standard royalties.
How to Contact: Arrange personal interview or submit demo tape and lead sheet. Prefers 7½ ips reel-to-reel or cassette with 2-4 songs on demo. SASE. Reports in 2 weeks.
Music: Bluegrass; blues; church/religious; C&W; gospel; and R&B. Recently published "From a Home to a Tavern" (by W.L. Maynard), recorded by Robbie Witkowski/KKR Records (country); "In Walked a Tear Drop" (by R.L. Rooker), recorded by Witkowski/KKR Records (country); "I Don't Care About Tomorrow" (by Marvin Rainwater), recorded by Rainwater/Kajac Records (country); "It Sets Me Free" (by Jack Paris), recorded by Paris/2J Records (country); and "Waylon, Sing To Mama" (by Darrell C. Thomas), recorded by Darrell C. Thomas/Ozark Opry Records.

P.F.S. MUSIC CO., Box 680460, Miami FL 33168. (305)891-0633. Publisher: Emil Petitte. Music publisher. Estab. 1971. ASCAP. Published 6 songs in 1977; plans 20 in 1979. Pays standard royalty.
How to Contact: Submit demo tape and lead sheet. Prefers 7½ ips reel-to-reel with 1-4 songs on demo. SASE. Reports in 3 weeks.
Music: Children's; C&W; disco; folk; gospel; MOR; rock (hard); soul; and top 40/pop. Recently published "I'm Foot Loose and Fancy Free," recorded by Cal Devlin (C&W); "Born to Love," recorded by Kiela Cunningham (MOR); and "Disco Fever," recorded by Leroy Morrison (disco).

P.L. MUSIC, 82 St. Joseph Blvd. W., Montreal, Quebec, Canada H2T 2P4. (514)849-3776. President: Christopher J. Reed. Music publisher. Estab. 1974. CAPAC. See Intermede Musique for details.

PACIFIC VIEW MUSIC, 5112 Hollywood Blvd., Los Angeles CA 90027. Professional Managers: Gary Heaton, Eric Troff. ASCAP. See Skyhill Publishing for details.

PACKAGE GOOD MUSIC, 1145 Green St., Manville NJ 08835. (201)725-4366. Vice President/A&R Director: Mary Ellen Clark. Music publisher. Estab. 1977. BMI. Pays negotiable royalty.
How to Contact: Submit demo tape. Prefers 7½ ips reel-to-reel or cassete with 3 songs minimum on tape. SASE. Reports in 1 month.
Music: Easy listening; folk (progressive); MOR; progressive; rock; and top 40/pop. Recently published "There's No Place Like You" (country rock); "Frosty the Dopeman" (progressive

folk); "Nymphomaniac Blues," recorded by Marc Zydiak; and "Let's Start a Punk Rock Band," recorded by Professor Marx (punk rock).

PACKY MUSIC, 3114 Radford Rd., Memphis TN 38111. (901)327-8187. Director of Publishing: Steve Gatlin. Music publisher, record company, record producer and management firm. ASCAP. See Stafree Publishing for details.

PALA SAC MUSIC CORP., 6430 Sunset Blvd., Suite 921, Los Angeles CA 90028. (213)461-3091. Director of Creative Affairs: B. Ficks, 2 Music Circle S., Nashville TN 37203. Music publisher. SESAC. See Famous Music Corporation for details.

PALAMAR MUSIC PUBLISHERS, 726 Carlson Dr., Orlando FL 32804. (305)644-3853. Affiliate: MuStaff Music Publishers (BMI). President: Will Campbell. Music publisher and record company. Estab. 1970. BMI. Published 25 songs in 1978; plans 25 in 1979. Pays 25-50% royalty.
How to Contact: Submit demo tape and lead sheet. Prefers 7½ ips reel-to-reel with 3-6 songs on demo. SASE. Reports in 1 week.
Music: Bluegrass; church/religious; C&W; gospel; and MOR. Recently published "Homespun Memories," recorded by Nelson Young (bluegrass); and "I Get Lonely," recorded by Larada Collins (C&W).

PALMERSTON PUBLISHING, 145 Marlee Ave., Suite 1606, Toronto, Ontario, Canada. President: Peter Foldy. Music publisher. CAPAC. See Bondi Music for details.

PANHANDLE MUSIC, Box 187, Davis WV 26260. Owner: John Bava. BMI. See John Bava Music for details.

PANTHER MUSIC, 6922 Hollywood Blvd., Hollywood CA 90028. (213)469-1667. Professional Manager: Roy Kohn. Music publisher and record company. Estab. 1928. ASCAP.
Music: C&W; disco; jazz; MOR; R&B; rock; and top 40/pop. See Peer-Southern Music for submission details.

PANTS DOWN MUSIC, Box 878, Sonoma CA 95476. (707)938-4060. Manager: Bruce Cohn. Music publisher and management firm. Estab. 1975. BMI. See Bruce Cohn Music for details.

PARA SAC MUSIC CORP., 2 Music Circle S., Nashville TN 37203. Director of Nashville Operations: Judi Gottier. Director of Creative Affairs: Bill Ficks. Music publisher. SESAC. See Famous Music Publishing Companies for details.

PARABUT MUSIC CORP., 6430 Sunset Blvd., Suite 921, Los Angeles CA 90028. (213)461-3091. Director of Creative Affairs: B. Ficks, 2 Music Circle S., Nashville TN 37203. Music publisher. BMI. See Famous Music Corporation for details.

PARAMOUNT MUSIC, 6430 Sunset Blvd., Suite 921, Los Angeles CA 90028. (213)461-3091. Director of Creative Affairs: B. Ficks, 2 Music Circle S., Nashville TN 37203. Music publisher. ASCAP. See Famous Music Corporation for details.

DON PARK MUSIC, INC., 190 Don Park Rd., Markham, Ontario, Canada L3R 2V8. (416)495-1710. Affiliates: Rereco (PROCAN) and Super Music (CAPAC). President: John C. Irvine. Music publisher, booking agency, management firm and record company. Payment negotiable.
How to Contact: Submit demo tape, submit demo tape and lead sheet, or arrange personal interview. Prefers 7½ or 15 ips reel-to-reel or cassette with 2 songs minimum on tape. SAE and International Reply Coupons. Reports in 2 weeks.
Music: Bluegrass; blues; children's; C&W; folk; gospel; jazz; and "esoteric." Recently published "Sweet Forget Me Not," recorded by Eddie Coffey (C&W); "Sunny Afternoon," recorded by Short Turn (C&W/folk); and "Country Lovers," recorded by Easy Lovin' (C&W).

PASA ALTA MUSIC, 54 E. Colorado Blvd., Pasadena CA 91105. President: Irvin Hunt. Music publisher, record company and record producer. Estab. 1969. BMI. Published 15 songs in 1978; plans 20 in 1979, 40 in 1980. Pays standard royalties.
How to Contact: Query or submit demo tape. Prefers cassette. SASE. Reports in 1 month.
Music: Folk; gospel; jazz; MOR; R&B; rock; soul; and top 40/pop.

PATTERN MUSIC, 1670 Inkster Blvd., Winnipeg, Manitoba, Canada R2X 2W8.

(204)633-1076. Copyright Coordinator: Rick Kives. Music publisher and record company. Estab. 1964. ASCAP. See K-Tel Music for details.

PAYDIRT MUSIC, 1228 Spring St. NW, Atlanta GA 30309. (404)873-6425. Professional Manager: Tom Long. Music publisher and recording studio. ASCAP.
Music: C&W; gospel; and top 40/pop. See Seyah Music for submission details.

PBR MUSIC CO., 7033 Sunset Blvd., Suite 322, Los Angeles CA 90029. General Manager: Maritta Boyle. Music publisher. ASCAP. See Valgroup Music (USA) for details.

PEACH COBBLER MUSIC, 1650 Broadway, New York NY 10019. (212)581-6162. Vice President: Paul Brown. Music publisher and record producer. ASCAP. See Larball Publishing for details.

PEAK PUBLISHING CO., 12 E. 39th St., Kansas City MO 64111. (816)531-1375. President: Don Warnock. Manager: Claire Warnock. Music publisher and record company. Estab. 1968. BMI. Royalty paid "depends on our agreement."
How to Contact: Submit demo tape. Prefers cassette. SASE. Reports "as soon as possible."
Music: Bluegrass; blues; children's; choral; church/religious; classical; C&W; disco; easy listening; folk; gospel; jazz; MOR; progressive; rock; soul; and top 40/pop.

PEER-INTERNATIONAL CORP., 6922 Hollywood Blvd., Hollywood CA 90028. (213)469-1667. Professional Manager: Roy Kohn. Music publisher and record company. Estab. 1928. BMI. See Peer-Southern Organization, Hollywood CA office, for details.

PEER-SOUTHERN ORGANIZATION, 6922 Hollywood Blvd., Hollywood CA 90028. (213)469-1667. Affiliates: Charles K. Harris Music Publishing (ASCAP), La Salle Music (ASCAP), Melody Lane (BMI), Panther Music (ASCAP), Peer International (BMI), Pera Music (BMI), RFD Music (ASCAP) and Southern Music (ASCAP). Professional Manager: Roy Kohn. Music publisher and record company. Estab. 1928. Pays standard royalty; 5¢/sheet on sheet music.
How to Contact: Arrange personal interview or submit demo tape and lead sheet. Prefers 7½ or 15 ips reel-to-reel or cassette with 2-5 songs on demo. SASE. Reports in 1 month.
Music: C&W; disco; easy listening; MOR; rock; and top 40/pop. Recently published "Superman," recorded by Celi Bee (disco); "Return to Me," recorded by Marty Robbins (C&W); and "Lay Love on You," recorded by Luisa Fernandez (top 40/pop).

PEER-SOUTHERN ORGANIZATION, 7 Music Circle N., Nashville TN 37203. (615)244-6200. Affiliates: Charles K. Harris Music (ASCAP), La Salle Music (ASCAP), Melody Lane (BMI), Panther Music (ASCAP), Peer International (BMI), Pera Music (BMI), RFD Music (ASCAP) and Southern Music (ASCAP). General Manager: Debbie Cobb. Estab. 1928. Pays standard royalties.
How to Contact: Arrange personal interview or submit demo tape and lead sheet. Prefers 7½ ips reel-to-reel or cassette with 2-5 songs on demo. SASE. Reports in 1 month.
Music: C&W; rock; and top 40/pop.

PEER-SOUTHERN ORGANIZATION, 1740 Broadway, New York NY 10019. (212)265-3910. President: Monique I. Peer. Vice President: Ralph Peer II. Vice President: Mario Conti. Main office. See Peer-Southern Organization, Hollywood and Nashville offices, for details.

PEER-SOUTHERN ORGANIZATION, 4 New St., Suite 107, Toronto, Ontario, Canada M5R 1P6. Managing Director: Matthew Heft. Music publisher. PROCAN and CAPAC.
How to Contact: Submit demo tape. Prefers cassette with 1-3 songs on demo. SAE and International Reply Coupons. Reports in 1 month.
Music: Bluegrass; blues; children's; choral; church/religious; classical; C&W; disco; easy listening; folk; gospel; jazz; MOR; progressive; rock; soul; and top 40/pop.

PELLEGRINO MUSIC CO., INC., 311 Brook Ave., Bay Shore, Long Island NY 11706. President: Joseph U. Pellegrino Jr. Music publisher, record company and production company. Estab. 1971. ASCAP. Published 40 songs in 1975-1977. Pays standard royalty.
How to Contact: Submit copyrighted demo tape and lead sheet. Prefers 7½ ips reel-to-reel or cassette with 3-6 songs on demo. SASE. Reports in 1 week.
Music: Church/religious and gospel. Recently published "Bottle of Wine," recorded by Calhoon (rock); "Skyline of Manhattan," recorded by Jade Four (oldie); and "On My Way to Colorado," recorded by Sounds Unlimited (instrumental).

PENNY PINCHERS, INC., Box 306, Vansant VA 24631. (703)498-4556. President: Roy John Fuller. Music publisher. Estab. 1974. SESAC. See Able Music for details.

PERA MUSIC, 6922 Hollywood Blvd., Hollywood CA 90028. (213)469-1667. Professional Manager: Roy Kohn. Music publisher and record company. Estab. 1928. BMI. See Peer-Southern Organization, Hollywood office, for details.

PEREGRIN SONGS, Woodshed Records, Ltd., Box 6312, Station F, Hamilton, Ontario, Canada L9C 6L9. (416)527-8721. Affiliate: Teoc Music (PROCAN). President: David Essig. Music publisher and record company. Estab. 1972. CAPAC. Published 30 songs in 1978; plans 30 in 1979. Pays 10% royalty.
How to Contact: Submit demo tape. Prefers 7½ ips reel-to-reel with 3-5 songs on demo. SAE and International Reply Coupons. Reports in 1 month.
Music: Bluegrass; blues; C&W; folk; and rock (country). Recently published "Music in Your Eyes," "Startin' Out Clean" and "Stealin' Away," recorded by Colleen Peterson and Willie P. Bennett (C&W/folk).

PERRYAL MUSIC CO., Solar Sound Records, Box 1162, Buffalo NY 14240. President: Barney Perry. Music publisher and record company. Estab. 1975. BMI. Published 7 songs in 1977; plans 21 in 1979. Uses AGAC-approved contract.
How to Contact: Submit demo tape and lead sheet. Prefers 7½ ips reel-to-reel or cassette. "Please be sure to outline songs, writers and any other information on all containers." SASE. Reports in 2 months.
Music: Blues; choral; church/religious; classical; disco; easy listening; gospel; jazz; MOR; progressive; rock; soul; and top 40/pop. Recently published "Walking in Rhythm," recorded by the Blackbyrds (MOR); and "Nightlife" and "Hey Sexy Mama," recorded by Blair (R&B/MOR).

PET-MAC PUBLISHING, Damon Productions, Ltd., 6844 76th Ave., Edmonton, Alberta, Canada T6B 0A8. Affiliate: 3PM Music (CAPAC). President: Garry McDonall. Music publisher and record company. Estab. 1969. BMI. Published 50 songs in 1978; plans 50 in 1979. Pays standard royalty.
How to Contact: Submit demo tape. Prefers 7½ ips reel-to-reel with 3-10 songs on demo. SAE and International Reply Coupons. Reports in 1 month.
Music: C&W; disco; jazz; MOR; rock (country or commercial); and top 40/pop. Recently published "Georgia Eyes," recorded by Mary Saxton (Georgia funk); "Beer and Country Music," recorded by Tim Jeffery (C&W); and "Who Put the Love in Your Eyes?", recorded by Donna Adams (MOR/C&W).

PHILIPPOPOLIS MUSIC, 12027 Califa St., North Hollywood CA 91607. President: Milcho Leviev. Music publisher. Estab. 1975. BMI. Published 12 songs in 1978; plans 10 songs in 1979, 20 songs in 1980. Pays standard royalties.
How to Contact: Query. Prefers cassette with 1-3 songs on demo. SASE. Reports in 1 month.
Music: Jazz and classical. Recently published "Moody Modes" (by Milcho Leviev), recorded by Billy Cobham/Atlantic Records (jazz); "Two," "A Child's Day" and "Toccatina" (by Leviev) recorded by Milcho Leviev/Dobre Records (jazz/classical).

PHONO MUSIC, Box 22325, Nashville TN 37202. Manager: Jerry Duncan. Music publisher. SESAC. See Music Craftshop for details.

PI GEM MUSIC, INC./CHESS MUSIC, INC., Box 40204, Nashville TN 37204. (615)320-7800. Professional manager: Dave Conrad. Music publisher. Estab. 1968. BMI. Published 200 songs in 1978. Pays standard royalties.
How to Contact: Submit demo tape and lead and typed lyric sheet. Prefers 7½ ips reel-to-reel or cassette with 1-2 songs on demo. SASE. Reports in 1 month.
Music: C&W; disco; easy listening; MOR; progressive; R&B; rock; soul; and top 40/pop. Recently published "It Was Almost Like a Song" (by Archie P. Jordan and Hal David), recorded by Ronnie Milsap (country/MOR); "It's a Heartache" (by R. Scott and S. Wolfe), recorded by Bonnie Tyler (top 40/pop); and "Sleeping Single in a Double Bed" (by K. Fleming and D. Morgan), recorded by Barbara Mandrell (country).

PICK-A-HIT MUSIC, 816 19th Ave. S., Nashville TN 37209. (615)327-3553. Contact: Clark Williams. Music publisher and booking agency. Estab. 1974. BMI. Pays standard royalties.
How to Contact: Submit demo tape and lead sheet. Prefers 7½ ips reel-to-reel with 3-5 songs on demo. SASE. Reports in 2 weeks.

Music: C&W. Recently published "Broken Down in Tiny Pieces" (by John Adrian), recorded by Billy "Crash" Craddock (C&W ballad).

PINATO MUSIC, 22 Roxborough St. W., Toronto, Ontario, Canada M5R 1T8. (416)921-0660. President: Peter Donato. Music publisher. Estab. 1975. CAPAC. Published 12 songs in 1978; plans 20 in 1979. Pays standard royalties.
How to Contact: Submit demo tape and lead sheet. Prefers cassette with 2-6 songs on demo. Does not return unsolicited material. Reports in 1 month.
Music: C&W; disco; easy listening; jazz; MOR; R&B; rock; and top 40/pop. Recently published "Blue Melody" (by Peter Donato), recorded by Peter Donato/Capitol (pop).

PINEAPPLE MUSIC, Texas Sound, Inc., 1311 Candlelight Ave., Dallas TX 75116. President: Paul Ketter. Music publisher and record company. Estab. 1973. ASCAP. See Big State Music for details.

PINELLAS MUSIC, 21315 Ibanez Ave., Woodland Hills CA 91364. (213)992-4922. Owner: Ron Hitchcock. Music publisher and record producer. Estab. 1973. BMI. Pays standard royalties.
How to Contact: Submit demo tape. Prefers cassette with 3-5 songs on demo. SASE. Reports in 1 month.
Music: Rock and top 40/pop. Recently published "Easy Street," recorded by Dave Munyon (MOR); "Butterfly Tear," recorded by Yvonne Ballard (MOR); and "Hollywood Square," recorded by the Hollywood Squares (pop).

PLANETARY MUSIC, 1790 Broadway, New York NY 10019. Professional Manager: Phil Kahl. Music publisher and record company. ASCAP. See Big Seven Music for details.

PLAYBOY MUSIC PUBLISHING, 8560 Sunset Blvd., Los Angeles CA 90069. Affiliate: After Dark Music (BMI). ASCAP. "Our companies are not currently active. We are only working our catalogs."

PLEIADES MUSIC, The Barn, North Ferrisburg VT 05473. (802)425-2111. Vice President: Bill Schubart. Music publisher and record company. Estab. 1975. BMI. See Other Music for details.

PLYMOUTH MUSIC CO., INC., 170 NE 33rd St., Fort Lauderdale FL 33334. (305)563-1844. Contact: Bernard Fisher, Fran Taber. Music publisher. ASCAP. See Music for Percussion for details.

POINTED STAR MUSIC, 50 Music Square W., Suite 800, Nashville TN 37203. President: Bob Witte. Music publisher. Estab. 1976. BMI. See Jop Music for details.

POLKA TOWNE MUSIC, 211 Post Ave., Westbury NY 1590. President: Teresa Zapolska. Music publisher, record company, record producer and booking agency. Estab. 1963. BMI.
How to Contact: Submit demo tape and lead sheet. Prefers cassette with 1-3 songs on demo. SASE. Reports in 1 month.
Music: Polkas and waltzes.

SARAH PORTE, 82 St. Joseph Blvd. W., Montreal, Quebec, Canada H2T 2P4. (514)849-3776. President: Christopher J. Reed. Music publisher. Estab. 1974. PROCAN. See Intermede Musique for details.

POSITIVE PRODUCTIONS, Box 1405, Highland Park NJ 08904. (201)463-8845. President: J. Vincenzo. Music publisher and record producer. Estab. 1976. BMI. Payment negotiable.
How to Contact: Submit demo tape and lead sheet. Prefers 7½ ips reel-to-reel with 4-5 songs on demo. Does not return unsolicited material. Reports in 3 weeks.
Music: MOR and rock. Recently published "Carrie's Airplane" and "Rainin' in the Morning," recorded by Chaves and James (MOR).

POWER-PLAY PUBLISHING, Box 8188, Nashville TN 37207. (615)226-6080. Vice President: Tommy Hill. Music publisher and record company. Estab. 1973. BMI. Pays standard royalties.
How to Contact: Arrange personal interview. Prefers 7½ ips reel-to-reel with 2 songs on demo. SASE. Reports in 1 month.
Music: Bluegrass; blues; C&W; disco; easy listening; folk; gospel; R&B; rock; soul; and top 40/pop. Recently published "Honey Hungry" (by Charlie Craig), recorded by Mike

Lunsford/Gusto Records (country); "Days of Me and You" (by Craig), recorded by Red Sovine/Gusto Records (country); and "Stealin' Feelin' " (by James Coleman), recorded by Red Sovine/Gusto Records (country).

JOHNNY POWERS MUSIC PRODUCTIONS, INC., 3384 W. 12 Mile Rd., Berkley MI 48072. (313)543-0588. President: Johnny Powers. Music publisher and production company. Estab. 1976. BMI. Pays 10-50% royalty.
How to Contact: Submit demo tape and lead sheet. Prefers 7½ ips reel-to-reel with 3-5 songs on demo. SASE. Reports in 3 weeks.
Music: C&W; disco; easy listening; MOR; progressive; soul; and top 40/pop. Recently published "Got to Find a Way to Get Back Home" and "I Just Want to Love You," recorded by Innervision (R&B/pop/top 40); and "All I Want to Do Is to Love You," recorded by Jack Rainwater (C&W/MOR).

THEODORE PRESSER CO., Bryn Mawr PA 19010. President: Arnold Broido. Doesn't consider outside material.

JANIE PRICE MUSIC, Box 34886, Dallas TX 75234. (214)387-1101. Administrative Assistant: Joy Adams. Music publisher and booking agency. Estab. 1972. ASCAP. See Ray Price Music for details.

JIMMY PRICE MUSIC, 1662 Wyatt Pkwy., Lexington KY 40505. (606)254-7474. Contact: Allen Vanderpool. President/Owner: James T. Price. Music publisher and record company. Estab. 1950. BMI. Pays standard royalty.
How to Contact: Submit demo tape and lead sheet. Prefers 7½ ips reel-to-reel with 2-6 songs on demo. SASE. Reports in 3 weeks.
Music: Bluegrass (sacred or C&W); church/religious; C&W; and gospel. Recently published "I Alone Will Answer Lord," recorded by Ray Jones/Sun-Ray Records (sacred); "All Them Wives," recorded by Harold Montgomery/Sun-Ray Records (C&W); and "I Wish I Was There Loving You," recorded by Charles Hall/Sun-Ray Records (C&W).
Tips: "We are in the process of printing music courses for Spanish lead guitar; dobro, Hawaiian and bass guitars; and the five-string and tenor banjos. There are three books with each course and a record club with the new songs the student will learn. For this I need good songs."

RAY PRICE MUSIC, Box 34886, Dallas TX 75234. (214)387-1101. Affiliate: Janie Price Music (ASCAP). Administrative Assistant: Joy Adams. Music publisher and booking agency. Estab. 1952. BMI. Pays negotiable royalty.
How to Contact: Submit demo tape with lead or lyric sheet. Prefers reel-to-reel or cassette with 2 songs on demo. SASE. Reports in 1 month. "All material submitted by mail is listened to by Janie Price, personal manager. We prefer material from established publishers but do accept unpublished material from individual writers. Every bit of material that's submitted is answered by post card or personal letter."
Music: Church/religious; C&W; easy listening; folk; gospel; MOR; and rock (country). Recently published "I Don't Feel Nothin' " (C&W); "What Kind of Love Is This?" (easy listening) and "Don't Wait for Sunday to Pray" (religious), all recorded by Ray Price.

PRIL MUSIC CO., c/o Gopam Enterprises, Inc., 11 Riverside Dr., #13C-W, New York NY 10023. (212)724-6120. Managing Director: Laurie Goldstein. Music publisher. Estab. 1960. BMI. See Gopam Enterprises for details.

PRIMUS ARTISTS MUSIC, 4000 Warner Blvd., Burbank CA 91522. (213)843-6000. Vice President of Music Operations: Gary La Mel. Music publisher. BMI. See First Artists for details.

PRINGLE MUSIC, 7021 Hatillo Ave., Canoga Park CA 91306. (213)347-3902. Owner: Norm Pringle. Music publisher. Estab. 1960. BMI. Pays standard royalties.
How to Contact: Submit demo tape. Prefers 7½ ips reel-to-reel with 2 songs on demo. SASE.
Music: C&W. Recently published "The Man Who Started It All" and "The Legend of Turtle Mountain," recorded by Evan Kemp and the Trailriders (folk/country).

PRITCHETT PUBLICATONS, 38603 Sage Tree St., Palmdale CA 93550. Manager: L.R. Pritchett. Music publisher and record company. Estab. 1950. BMI. Published 4 songs in 1978.
How to Contact: Submit lead sheet. "If we're interested, then a demo tape will be requested."

Prefers 3¾ or 7½ ips reel-to-reel with 1-5 songs on demo. SASE. Reports in 1 month.
Music: Gospel; MOR; soul; and top 40/pop. Recently published "Another Dawn," recorded by Charles Vickers (MOR); "Johnny Blue," recorded by Niki Stevens (folk/ballad); and "If I Can Help Somebody," recorded by Charles Vickers (gospel).

PROCESS MUSIC PUBLICATIONS, 439 Wiley Ave., Franklin PA 16323. (814)432-4633. President: Norman Kelly. Music publisher. Estab. 1943. BMI. See Country Star Music for details.

PROPHECY PUBLISHING, INC., Box 4945, Austin TX 78765. (512)452-9411. Affiliate: Black Coffee Music (BMI). Vice President: T. White. Music publisher. Estab. 1972. ASCAP. Published 100 songs in 1978; plans 200 in 1979. Pays standard royalties, less expenses; "expenses such as tape duplicating, photocopying and long distance phone calls are recouped from the writer's earnings."
How to Contact: Submit demo tape and lyric sheet. Prefers 7½ ips reel-to-reel with 1-4 songs on demo. Does not return unsolicited material. "No reply can be expected, unless we're interested in the material."
Music: Bluegrass; blues; classical; C&W; disco; easy listening; folk; gospel; jazz; MOR; progressive; rock; soul; and top 40/pop. Recently published "Lost in the Late, Late Show," recorded by Traveler (rock); "She's Everybody's Baby But Mine," recorded by Steve Fromholz (C&W); and "Deep in the West," recorded by Shake Russell (folk).

PROVO MUSIC, Box 66, Manhattan Beach CA 90266. (213)371-9578. Vice President, Publishing: Larry Thatt. Music publisher and record company. Estab. 1971. BMI. See Sundaze Music for details.

PUBIT MUSIC, 2510 Tarrytown Mall, Houston TX 77051. (713)780-4506. Producer Liaison: David McCumber. Owner: Jim D. Johnson. Music publisher, record company and production company. Estab. 1969. BMI. See Publicare Music for details.

PUBLICARE MUSIC, LTD., 2510 Tarrytown Mall, Houston TX 77051. (713)780-4506. Affiliate: Pubit Music (BMI). Producer Liaison: David McCumber. Owner: Jim D. Johnson. Music publisher, record company and production company. Estab. 1969. ASCAP. Pays 50-75% royalty. Sometimes secures songwriters on salary basis: determined by individual situation.
How to Contact: Submit demo tape and lead sheet. Prefers cassette with 2-4 songs on demo. SASE. Reports in 3 weeks.
Music: C&W; disco; MOR; progressive; rock; and top 40/pop. Prefers songs that have market crossover potential. Recently published "Heart Don't Fail Me Now," recorded by Randy Cornor (C&W/pop); "Bluest Heartache" and "Shame, Shame on Me," recorded by Kenny Dale (C&W).

PURPLE COW MUSIC CO., 1201 16th Ave. S., Nashville TN 37212. (615)320-7287. President/Owner: Chuck Chellman. Music publisher and record producer. Estab. 1967. ASCAP. See Adventure Music for details.

PURPLE HAZE MUSIC, Box 1243, Beckley WV 25801. (304)252-4836. Executive Professional Manager: Richard L. Petry. General Manager: Doug Gent. Music publisher. Estab. 1968. BMI. Published 25 songs in 1978; plans 25 in 1979. Pays standard royalties. "If songwriter pays for copyright, we reimburse him when song is recorded and royalties come in."
How to Contact: Submit demo tape or submit demo tape and lead sheet. Prefers 7½ ips reel-to-reel with 1-5 songs on demo. SASE. Reports in 1 month.
Music: C&W; disco; easy listening; MOR; rock; and top 40/pop. Recently published "Gonna Find My Dream" and "Linda," recorded by Bob McCormick (MOR); and "Women and Music" and "City of Love," by Stone Mountain (soft rock).

PYRAMID MUSIC, Box 1385, Merchantville NJ 08109. (609)663-4540. Vice President: Bob Francis. Music publisher, record company, record producer, management firm and booking agency. BMI. See Rob Lee Music for details.

PYROS PUBLISHING CO., Box 2199, Vancouver, British Columbia, Canada V6B 3V7. (604)688-1820. President: John Rodney. Music publisher and record company. Estab. 1970. CAPAC. See Nu-Gen Publishing for details.

QCA MUSIC, INC., 2832 Spring Grove Ave., Cincinnati OH 45225. (513)681-8400. Affiliates:

Kolormark Music (BMI), Bluemark Music (ASCAP) and Redmark Music (SESAC). Contact: A&R Dept. Music publisher, record company and record manufacturer. Estab. 1976.
How to Contact: Submit demo tape and lead sheet. Prefers 7½ ips reel-to-reel or cassette with 1-6 songs on demo.
Music: C&W; gospel; jazz; R&B; rock; and soul.

QUALITY MUSIC PUBLISHING, LTD., 380 Birchmount Rd., Scarborough, Ontario, Canada M1W 1M7. (416)691-2757. Affiliates: Shediac Music (CAPAC), Broadland Music (PROCAN), Doubleplay Music (PROCAN), Grandslam Music (CAPAC), Eskimo/Nuna Music (CAPAC), Rycha Music (PROCAN), Old Shanty Music (CAPAC) and Sons Celeste (CAPAC). General Manager: W.B. Kearns. Music publisher and record company. Estab. 1974. BMI. Published 150 songs in 1978. Pays standard royalty.
How to Contact: Submit demo tape and lead sheet. Prefers 7½ ips reel-to-reel or cassette with 2-5 songs on demo. SAE and International Reply Coupons. Reports in 1 month.
Music: C&W; disco; gospel; MOR; progressive; rock (country or hard); and top 40/pop. Recently published "Paper Rosie" and "Old Man and His Horn," recorded by Gene Watson (C&W); "Harmonium," recorded by Harmonium (top 40/pop); and "Dancer" by Gino Soccio.

QUARK MUSIC, Box 878, Sonoma CA 95476. (707)938-4060. Manager/Owner: Bruce Cohn. Music publisher and management firm. Estab. 1975. BMI. See Bruce Cohn Music for details.

R.R. MUSIC, 663 5th Ave., New York NY 10022. (212)757-3638. President: Rena L. Feeney. Music publisher and record company. Estab. 1968. ASCAP. See Ren Maur Music for details.

RAE-COX & COOKE MUSIC CORP., 1697 Broadway, New York NY 10019. President: Theodore McRae. Music publisher, record company and record producer. Estab. 1959. Published 5 songs in 1978; plans 2 in 1979, 8 in 1980. Pays standard royalties.
How to Contact: Query. Prefers reel-to-reel or cassette. SASE. Reports in 2 weeks.
Music: Blues; choral; church/religious; disco; gospel; R&B; rock; and soul.

RAGGED ISLAND MUSIC, 4307 Saundersville Rd., Old Hickory TN 37138. (615)847-4419. Contact: Professional Manager. President: Mira Ann Smith. Music publisher and record company. Estab. 1955. BMI. See Hip Hill Music for details.

H&G RANDALL PUBLISHING CO., 29 Elaine Rd., Milford CT 06460. (203)878-7383. President: Gerald Randall. Music publisher, record company and record producer. Estab. 1972. ASCAP. Published 63 songs in 1978. Pays standard royalties.
How to Contact: Submit demo tape and lead sheet. Prefers 3¾ or 7½ ips cassette or 8-track cartridge. SASE. Reports in 1 month.
Music: Easy listening; MOR; rock; and top 40/pop. Recently published "Why Is Your Love Haunting Me?", (by Maceo Jefferson, Gerald Randall and Samuel Turiano), recorded by Turiano/Randall Records (easy listening); "Zodiac Zoo" (by Tobias C. Frey and Randall), recorded by Satyrs/Randall Records (rock); and "Sahib Sam" (by Jefferson, Randall and Turiano), recorded by Satyrs/Randall Records (rock).

RANG DOUBLE, 82 St. Joseph Blvd. W., Montreal, Quebec, Canada H2T 2P4. (514)849-3776. President: Christopher J. Reed. Music publisher. Estab. 1974. PROCAN. See Intermede Musique for details.

JIM RANNE MUSIC CO., 3216 Mapleleaf Cir., Dallas TX 75233. (214)331-8683. Owner: Jim Ranne. Music director: Cliff Chancey. Record company, music publisher and record producer. Estab. 1964. BMI. Published 28 songs in 1978; plans 50 songs in 1979, 75 songs in 1980. Pays standard royalties.
How to Contact: Submit demo tape and lead sheet. Prefers 7½ ips reel-to-reel with 1-4 songs on demo. Also include writer's name, address and Social Security number. Submit songs by no more than 2 writers. SASE. Reports in 3 weeks.
Music: Bluegrass; blues; C&W; disco; gospel; and rock.

RAPP/MATZ MUSIC, 1650 Broadway, New York NY 10019. (212)581-6162. Vice President: Paul Brown. Music publisher and record producer. ASCAP. See Larball Publishing for details.

RATHSINO PUBLISHING CO., The Cameron Organization, Inc., 320 S. Waiola Ave., LaGrange IL 60525. (312)352-2026. Vice President/General Manager: Jean M. Cameron.

Music publisher. Estab. 1973. BMI. See The Cameron Organisation for details.

RAY'S, Box 103, E., New York Station, Brooklyn NY 11207. (212)827-2582. Producer: Ray Smith. Music publisher and record producer. BMI. Published 3 songs in 1978. Payment determined by royalty or outright purchase.
How to Contact: Query, arrange personal interview, submit demo tape, or submit demo tape and lead sheet. Prefers cassette with 2-4 songs on demo. SASE. Reports in 2 weeks.
Music: Disco; easy listening; and reggae. Recently published "Nine O'Clock" and "Christmas" (by A.J. Smith), recorded by A.J. Smith/Ray's Records (reggae/disco); and "I'm in Love With You" (by V. Johnson), recorded by Johnson/Ray's Records (disco).

RAZOR SHARP MUSIC, 2212 4th Ave., Seattle WA 98121. (206)682-5278. Director, West Coast Operations: JoDee Omer. Music publisher. Estab. 1973. BMI. See Mighty Three Music, Seattle WA office, for details.

RCS PUBLISHING CO., 5220 Essen Lane, Baton Rouge LA 70808. (504)766-3233. Affiliates: Layback Music (BMI) and Marsaint Music (BMI). General Manager: John Fred. Music publisher, record company and record producer. Estab. 1977. ASCAP. Published 14 songs in 1978; plans 30 in 1979, 50 in 1980. Pays standard royalties.
How to Contact: Submit demo tape and lead sheet. Prefers 7½ ips reel-to-reel or cassette with 2-10 songs on demo. SASE. Reports in 1 month.
Music: C&W; R&B; rock; soul; and top 40/pop. Recently published "So Hot" (by Gregg Wright), recorded by Wright/RCS Records (rock); "What's Your Name" (by Wright), recorded by Wright/RCS Records (rock); "Suddenly Single" (by Butch Hornsby), recorded by Hornsby (country/rock); and "Hey, Hey Bunny" (by John Fred and Playboys), recorded by Paula and John Fred (top 40).

RECORD ROOM MUSIC, Box 58, Glendora NJ 08029. (609)939-0034. General Manager: Eddie Jay Harris. Music publisher and record company. Estab. 1970. ASCAP. See Never Ending Music for details.

REDEEMER MUSIC PUBLISHING CO., Box 55943, Houston TX 77055. (713)686-1749. President: Gary R. Smith. Music publisher, record company, record producer, management firm and booking agency. SESAC. See Gospel Senders Music Publishing for details.

REDMARK, 2832 Spring Grove Ave., Cincinnati OH 45225. (513)681-8400. Contact: A&R Dept. Music publisher and record company. Estab. 1976. SESAC. See QCA Music for details.

REN MAUR MUSIC CORP., 663 5th Ave., New York NY 10022. (212)757-3638. Affiliate: R.R. Music (ASCAP). President: Rena L. Feeney. Music publisher and record company. Estab. 1968. BMI. Pays 4-8% royalty.
How to Contact: Submit demo tape and lead sheet. Prefers cassette with 4-8 songs on demo. SASE. Reports in 1 month.
Music: Disco; MOR; rock; soul; and top 40/pop.

RENBOURN'S MULE, Box 3233, Berkeley CA 94703. Contact: Stefan Grossman. Music publisher. BMI. See Kicking Mule Publishing for details.

RERECO, Box 32, Willowdale, Ontario, Canada M2N 5S7. (416)495-1710. President: John C. Irvine. Music publisher, booking agency, management firm and record company. Estab. 1967. PROCAN. See Don Park Music for details.

WILLIAM REZEY MUSIC CO., 11 N. Pearl St., Home Savings Bank Bldg., Albany NY 12207. (518)462-4462. President: Bill Rezey. Professional Manager: John Conlin. Music publisher and booking agency. Estab. 1969. BMI. Pays standard royalty. Buys lyric ideas outright for $25 minimum; complete lyrics for negotiable fee.
How to Contact: Submit demo tape, submit demo tape and lead sheet or submit lead sheet. Prefers 7½ ips reel-to-reel or cassette with 3-10 songs on demo. SASE. Reports in 2 weeks.
Music: Rock (country); soul; and top 40/pop. Recently published "Been Down So Long," recorded by Nick Brignola (rock).

RFD MUSIC, 6922 Hollywood Blvd., Hollywood CA 90028. (213)469-1667. Professional Manager: Roy Kohn. Music publisher and record company. Estab. 1928. ASCAP. See Peer-Southern Organization, Hollywood office, for details.

RHYTHM VALLEY MUSIC, 1304 Blewett St., Graham TX 76046. President: Orville Clarida. Music publisher. Estab. 1949. ASCAP. Pays standard royalty.
How to Contact: Submit demo tape and lead sheet. Prefers reel-to-reel with 1-3 songs on demo. SASE. Reports in 3 weeks.
Music: C&W and gospel. Recently published "The Smile on Your Face," recorded by Billy Wilson (C&W); and "Our Love Fell Victim," recorded by Orville Clarida (C&W).

RHYTHMS PRODUCTIONS, Whitney Bldg., Box 34485, Los Angeles CA 90034. Affiliate: Tom Thumb Music (ASCAP). President: Ruth White. Music publisher and record company. Estab. 1955. ASCAP. Published 22 songs in 1978. Pays negotiable royalty.
How to Contact: Submit lead sheet with letter outlining background in educational children's music. Prefers cassette. SASE. Reports in 1 month.
Music: "We're only interested in children's songs for the education market. Our materials are sold primarily in schools, so artists/writers with a teaching background would be most likely to understand our requirements." Recently published "It's a Happy Feeling" and "Spare Parts," recorded by Terry Gris (educational); and "Everybody's Different," recorded by Michael Lembeck (educational).

RICK'S MUSIC, INC., 8255 Sunset Blvd., Los Angeles CA 90046. (213)650-8300. Vice President: Stephen Bedell. Music publisher. Estab. 1974. BMI. Published 200 songs in 1978; plans 300 in 1979.
How to Contact: Submit demo tape and lead sheet. Prefers reel-to-reel or cassette with 3-5 songs on demo. Does not return unsolicited material. Reports in 3 weeks.
Music: Disco; easy listening; MOR; rock; soul; and top 40/pop. Recently published "Flashlight," recorded by Parliament (R&B); "I Feel Love," recorded by Donna Summer (disco); "T.G.I.F.," recorded by Love and Kisses (disco); and "Take Me Home," recorded by Cher.

RIGHTSONG MUSIC, 21 Music Circle E., Nashville TN 37203. BMI. See Chappell Music for details.

CHARLIE ROACH MUSIC, 125 Taylor St., Jackson TN 38301. (901)427-7714. Owner: Charlie Roach. Music publisher and record company. Estab. 1959. BMI. Published 25 songs in 1978. Pays standard royalties.
How to Contact: Query or submit demo tape. Prefers 7½ ips reel-to-reel or cassette with 4-10 songs on demo. "We only want to hear work that is copyrighted." SASE. Reports in 1 month.
Music: Bluegrass; blues; church/religious; C&W; gospel; R&B; rock; soul; and Hawaiian. Recently published "Move Over Rover" and "Tornado Twist" (by Larry Brinkley), recorded on Westwood Records (rock).
Tips: "We also want to lease for overseas rock and R&B that was recorded between 1950 and 1979. This includes the master tapes—the finished product. Tapes should be 7½ or 15 ips."

ROADRUNNER MUSIC, 25 Music Square E., Nashville TN 37203. Music publisher. Contact: Bobby Bradley. BMI. See Forrest Hills Music for details.

ROADSHOW MUSIC GROUP, 850 7th Ave., New York NY 10019. Affiliates: Desert Moon Songs (BMI), Desert Rain Music (ASCAP) and Triple O Songs (BMI). Vice President: Julie Lipsius. International Manager: Susan Reed. Music publisher and record company. Pays standard royalty.
How to Contact: Submit demo tape and lead or lyric sheet. Prefers 7½ ips reel-to-reel or cassette. SASE. Reporting time "varies according to what we're looking for."
Music: Church/religious; disco; gospel (contemporary); soul; and top 40/pop. Recently published "It's You That I Need," recorded by Enchantment (rock).

FREDDIE ROBERTS MUSIC, Box 99, Rougemont NC 27572. (919)477-4077. Manager: Freddie Roberts. Music publisher, record producer and booking agency. Estab. 1967. BMI. Published 14 songs in 1978; plans 18-22 in 1979. Pays standard royalties.
How to Contact: Query, submit demo tape, submit demo tape and lead sheet, submit acetate disc, or submit acetate disc and lead sheet. Prefers 7½ ips reel-to-reel or cassette with 1-8 songs on demo. SASE. Reports in 2 weeks.
Music: Bluegrass; blues; C&W; disco; folk; gospel; MOR; R&B; rock; soul; and top 40/pop. Recently published "Beach Towels" (by Freddie Roberts), recorded by the Roberts and the Ravens/MilMar Records (Southern rock/country rock); and "Just One Time" (by Billy McKellar), recorded by Billy McKellar/Bull City Records (C&W).

ROCKET PUBLISHING, 489 5th Ave., New York NY 10017. (212)986-9361. Affiliates: British Rocket Music Publishing (ASCAP) and Rocket Songs (BMI). Director of Professional Activities: Al Altman. Music publisher. Estab. 1976.
How to Contact: Submit demo tape and lead sheet or submit acetate disc and lead sheet. Prefers 7½ ips reel-to-reel or cassette with 1-5 songs on demo. "Please include lyric or lead sheets and your name and address and phone number and SASE." Does not return unsolicited material. Reports in 1 month.
Music: Disco; R&B; and rock. Recently published "Philadelphia Freedom," (by Elton John and Bernie Taupin), recorded by Elton John; "Slow Down," (by John Miles), recorded by John Miles (top 40/disco); "How You Gonna See Me Now," (by Bernie Taupin and Alice Cooper), recorded by Alice Cooper (top 40/MOR); and "Part Time Love" (by E. John and Gary Osborne), recorded by Elton John..

ROCKET SONGS, INC., 489 5th Ave., New York NY 10017. (212)986-9361. Director of Professional Activities: Al Altman. Music publisher. BMI. See Rocket Publishing for details.

ROCKFORD MUSIC CO., 150 West End Ave., Suite 6-D, New York NY 10023. (212)873-5968. Affiliate: Stateside Music (BMI). Manager: Phillip Ross Zinn. Music publisher and record company. Estab. 1959. BMI. Pays negotiable royalty.
How to Contact: Submit finished master tape and lead sheet. Prefers cassette or disc with 2 songs on demo. SASE. Reports in 2 weeks.
Music: Disco and top 40/pop. Recently published "Baby Let Your Love Run Free" and "The Woman of Love" (by Phillip Ross Zinn and Robert Lee Lowery), and "Impulse" (by Phillip Ross Zinn), recorded by Danny Darrow/Mighty Records (disco).

ROCK ISLAND MUSIC, Box 1385, Merchantville NJ 08109. (609)663-4540. Vice President: Bob Francis. Music publisher, record company, record producer, management firm and booking agency. ASCAP. See Rob Lee Music for details.

ROCKY BELL MUSIC, Box 3357, Shawnee KS 66203. (913)631-6060. Affiliate: White Cat Music (ASCAP). Professional Manager: Frank Fara. Music publisher, record company, record producer and management firm. Estab. 1976. BMI. Published 14 songs in 1978; plans ·20 in 1979, 30 in 1980. Pays standard royalties.
How to Contact: Arrange personal interview or submit demo tape. Cassette only with 1-5 songs on demo. SASE. Reports in 2 weeks.
Music: C&W. Recently published "Faith" (by Jon Steel and J. Sandusky), recorded by the Steeles/Comstock Records (mod/country); "Help You Find a Way" (by F. FaFara), recorded by Patty Parker/Comstock (MOR/country); and "Four States to Go" (by FaFara), recorded by Alex Fraser/Comstock and Boot Records (mod/country).

THE RODEHEAVER CO., Box 1790, Waco TX 76703. Music Editor: John Purifoy. Music publisher and record company. ASCAP. See Word Music for details.

ROGAN PUBLISHING CO., Box 9287, Jackson MS 39206. (601)982-4522. Affiliate: Sound City Music (ASCAP). President: Stewart Madison. Music publisher and record company. Estab. 1968. BMI. Published 50 songs in 1978; plans 50 in 1979. Pays standard royalty, "less actual costs." Charges for some services: "for actual costs only." Sometimes secures songwriters on salary basis; "strictly to write songs—pays $75-100/week."
How to Contact: Submit demo tape and lead sheet or arrange personal interview. Prefers 7½ ips reel-to-reel or cassette with 4-6 songs on demo. SASE. Reports in 2 weeks.
Music: C&W; disco; soul; and top 40/pop. Recently published "I'll Play the Blues for You," recorded by Albert King (R&B); "This Man and Woman Thing," recorded by Johnny Russell (C&W); and "Black Water Gold," recorded by the Sunshine Band (disco/soul).

ROHM MUSIC, 10 George St., Box 57, Wallingford CT 06492. (203)269-4465. Affiliates: Linesider Productions (BMI) and Big Music (BMI). Vice President: Rudolf Szlaui. Music publisher, record company and management firm. Estab. 1967. BMI. Payment negotiable.
How to Contact: Submit demo tape. Prefers cassette with 1-4 songs on demo. SASE. Reports "as soon as possible."
Music: Rock and top 40/pop. Recently published "Stop and Go" (by Roger C. Reale), recorded by Roger C. Reale/Big Sound Records (rock 'n roll); and "Prisoner of Romance" (by G.E. Smith) and "Wonder" (by Karen Gronback and Bob Ors), recorded by the Scratch Band/Big Sound Records.

RONG MUSIC, Box 6507, 2181 Victory Pkwy., Cincinnati OH 45206. (513)861-1500. Owner: Adrian Belew. Estab. 1977. ASCAP. See Hal Bernard Enterprises for details.

ROSE TREE MUSIC, 117 S. Main St., Suite 200, Seattle WA 98121. (206)682-5278. Contact: JoDee Omer. Music publisher. Estab. 1973. ASCAP. See Mighty Three Music Organization for details.

ROTIGA MUSIC CO., 7141 Rutland St., Philadelphia PA 19149. (215)728-1699. Manager: Phil Gaber. Record company, music publisher, record producer and management firm. Estab. 1963. BMI. Pays standard royalties.
How to Contact: Arrange personal interview or submit demo tape and lead sheet. Prefers 7½ ips cassette with 2 songs minimum on demo. Does not return unsolicited material. Reports in 3 weeks.
Music: Blues; disco; easy listening; jazz; MOR; R&B; rock; soul; and top 40/pop. Recently published "Guess I'll Never Understand" (by R. Walker and V. Montana), recorded by Fletcher Walker III/Paramount Records (R&B/pop); "Precious" (by R. Walker), recorded by Ronnie Walker/ABC Records (R&B/pop); and "By the Hair of My Chinny Chin" (by F. Smith) recorded by Music Machine/Red Coach Delite Records (R&B/disco).

ROWILCO, Box 8135, Chicago IL 60680. (312)224-5612. Professional Manager: R.C. Hillsman. Music publisher. Estab. 1961. BMI. Published 8 songs in 1977; plans 20 in 1979. Pays 3-5% royalty.
How to Contact: Arrange personal interview or submit demo tape and lead sheet. Prefers 7½ or 15 ips quarter-inch reel-to-reel with 4-6 songs on demo. Submissions should be sent via registered mail. SASE. Reports in 3 weeks.
Music: Blues; church/religious; C&W; disco; easy listening; gospel; jazz; MOR; rock; and top 40/pop.

ROYAL FLAIR PUBLISHING, 106 Navajo, Council Bluffs IA 51501. (712)366-1136. Music publisher and record producer. Estab. 1964. BMI. Published 6 songs in 1978; plans 12 songs in 1979, 12 in 1980. Pays standard royalties.
How to Contact: Query. Prefers cassette with 2-6 songs on demo. SASE. Reports in 1 month.
Music: Old time country. Recently published "Renegade," "Brownville" and "The Last Train" (by Bob Everhart), recorded by Bob Everhart/Folkways (country).

ROYAL STAR PUBLISHING CO., Box 1037, Des Plaines IL 60018. (312)824-8205. Affiliate: Star Bound Publishing (ASCAP). President: Joseph Starr. Vice President: Mary Starr. Record company, music publisher and management firm. Estab. 1972. BMI. Published 175 songs in 1978. Pays standard royalties.
How to Contact: Query, submit demo tape, or submit demo tape and lead sheet. Prefers 7½ ips reel-to-reel or cassette with 1-3 songs on demo. SASE. Reports in 1 month.
Music: Bluegrass; church/religious; C&W; easy listening; gospel; MOR; R&B; rock; and top 40/pop. Recently published "Engraved on My Mind" (by Mary L. Star and Bill Jones), recorded by Boyce Hill/Starr Records (country); and "Reasons" (by Robert and Jack Frasure), recorded by Jack Cotton/Starr Records (country).

RSO MUSIC PUBLISHING GROUP, 8335 Sunset Blvd., Los Angeles 90069. A&R: Richard Fitzgerald. Music publisher. Estab. 1968. BMI.
How to Contact: Submit demo tape. Prefers cassette. SASE.
Music: Blues; disco; easy listening; folk; progressive; R&B; rock; soul; and top 40/pop.

RSO MUSIC PUBLISHING GROUP, 1775 Broadway, New York NY 10019. Vice President: Eileen Rothschild. Music publisher. Estab. 1968. BMI.
How to Contact: Submit demo tape. Prefers cassette. SASE.
Music: Blues; disco; easy listening; folk; progressive; R&B; rock; soul; and top 40/pop.

RU-DOT-TO MUSIC, Las Vegas Recording Studio, 3977 Vegas Valley Dr., Las Vegas NV 89121. (702)457-4365. President: Hank Castro. Music publisher and recording studio. Estab. 1970. BMI. See Derby Music for details.

RUN IT MUSIC, INC., 250 W. 57th St., Number 632, New York NY 10019. (212)541-7283. President: Dick Fraser. Music publisher, record producer and management firm. Estab. 1977. BMI. Royalties vary.
How to Contact: Query or submit demo tape. Prefers cassette with 3-6 songs on demo. SASE. Reporting time varies.

Music: Jazz and rock. Recently published "Follow You Follow Me" (by Genesis), recorded by Genesis (progressive rock); and "D.I.Y." and "Solsbury Hill" (by Peter Gabriel), recorded by Peter Gabriel (progressive rock).

RUSTIC RECORDS, 38 Music Square, Nashville TN 37203. (615)254-0892. President: Jack Stillwell. Vice President/General Manager: Bill Wence.
How to Contact: Submit demo tape and lyric or lead sheet. Prefers 7½ ips reel-to-reel with 2-4 songs on demo. "We will also accept cassettes. Use new tape." SASE. Reports in 3 weeks.
Music: C&W and MOR. Recently published "Hug Your Shadow," recorded by Bambi; "Quicksand," recorded by Bill Wence; and "(Ain't It Amazing) What One Little Screw Will Do," recorded by Jack Stillwell.

RUSTRON MUSIC PUBLISHERS, 35 S. Broadway, Suite B-3, Irvington NY 10533. (914)591-6151. Contact: Ron Caruso. See Rustron Music Publishers, White Plains NY office, for details.

RUSTRON MUSIC PUBLISHERS, 200 Westmoreland Ave., White Plains NY 10606. (914)946-1689. Director: Rusty Gordon. Professional Manager: Ron Caruso. Music publisher. Estab. 1974. BMI. Published 30 songs in 1978; plans 50 in 1979. Pays standard royalties; uses AGAC contract.
How to Contact: Arrange personal interview or submit demo tape and lead or lyric sheet. Prefers cassette or 7½ ips reel-to-reel. "Put leader between all songs and at the beginning and end of the tape. Use a tape box. Label it." SASE. Reports in 1 month.
Music: C&W (contemporary or story songs); disco; easy listening; folk (folk-rock); MOR; rock (pop or soft); and top 40/pop (originals only). Recently published "My Very Best Friend," recorded by Lois Britten (pop/disco); "Sign Painter" and "Everything She Touches" (by Christian Camilo), recorded by Veda and the Tingalayo Rhythm Bank (salsa/disco/pop); and "Sunrise in the Mountains," recorded by Dianne Mower (C&W/pop).

S & R MUSIC PUBLISHING CO., 39 Belmont, Racho Mirage CA 92270. (714)346-0075. President: Scott Seely. Affiliate: Boomerang Music (BMI). Music publisher. Estab. 1961. ASCAP. Published 50 songs in 1978; plans 50 in 1979. Pays 20-50% royalty.
How to Contact: Submit demo tape and lead sheet.

S.M.C.L. PRODUCTIONS, INC., 450 E. Beaumont Ave., St. Bruno, Quebec, Canada J3V 2R3. (514)653-7838. Affiliates: A.Q.E.M. Ltee (CAPAC), Bag Enrg. (CAPAC), C.F. Music (CAPAC), Big Bazaar Music (CAPAC), Sunrise Music (CAPAC), Stage One Music (CAPAC), L.M.S. Ltee (CAPAC), ITT Music (CAPAC), Machine Music (CAPAC), and Dynamite Music (CAPAC). President: Christian Lefort. Music publisher and record company. Estab. 1967. CAPAC. Published 750 songs in 1978; plans 1,000 in 1979. Pays 25-50% royalty.
How to Contact: Submit demo tape and lead sheet. Prefers 7½ ips reel-to-reel with 4-12 songs on demo. SAE and International Reply Coupons. Reports in 1 month.
Music: Disco; easy listening; MOR; and top 40/pop. Recently published "My Way," recorded by Elvis Presley (top 40); and "Best Disco in Town," recorded by the Ritchie Family (disco).

SABAL MUSIC, INC., 1722 West End Ave., Nashville TN 37203. Professional Manager: Jimmy Darrell. Music publisher. ASCAP. See Sawgrass Music Publishing for details.

SADDLE SONG MUSIC, INC., TWC Entertainment Corp., Box 2021, New York NY 10001. (212)691-4565. Manager: Walter Balderson. Music publisher and record company. Estab. 1974. SESAC. See TWC Music for details.

SAKA MUSIC CO., 3800 S. Ocean Dr., Hollywood FL 33019. (305)456-0847. Affiliate: Sing 'n Dance Music (ASCAP). General Manager: Stu Chernoff. Music publisher, record company and record producer. BMI. Pays standard royalties.
How to Contact: Submit demo tape. Prefers 7½ ips reel-to-reel tape. SASE. Reports in 2 weeks.
Music: All types.

SALLY MUSIC CO., 65 W. 55th St., New York NY 10019. President: Eddie White. Music publisher and record producer. Estab. 1948. BMI. See White Way Music for details.

SALT LAKE PUBLISHING, Box 11901, Salt Lake City UT 84147. (801)967-5040. Owner:

James B. Angelos. Music publisher and record company. Estab. 1971. BMI. Published 7 songs in 1978; plans 10 in 1979. Pays standard royalties.
How to Contact: Query or submit demo tape and lead sheet. Prefers 7½ reel-to-reel or cassette with 1-4 songs on demo. SASE. Reports in 3 weeks.
Music: Children's; church/religious; C&W; and gospel. Recently published "Gear Jammer's Wife" (by John Smith), recorded by John Horse/Jimbo Records (country); "Hello Santa" (by Gail Angelos and Carol Christenson), recorded by Angelos and Christenson (country); and "It's All Because of You" (by K. Shields), recorded by Joyce Atkinson/Jimbo Records (country).

SANCTI MUSIC, Box 600516, North Miami Beach FL 33160. (305)945-3738. Publisher: J. Gilday. Music publisher, record company and record producer. SESAC. See "Gil" Gilday Publishing for details.

SATURDAY NIGHT MUSIC, Box 0107, Los Angeles CA 90048. President: James Barton. Music publisher. ASCAP. See Border Star Music for details.

EVIE SANDS MUSIC, 8033 Highland Trial, Los Angeles CA 90046. Contact: General Manager. Music publisher and record producer. Estab. 1976. ASCAP. See Big Cigar Music for details.

SAN-LYN MUSIC PUBLICATIONS, 414 Cortland Ave., Syracuse NY 12180. General Manager: Jack Swanson. Music publisher and record company. Estab. 1972. ASCAP. See Kinghouse Music for details.

SARALEE MUSIC, Box 207, Manistique MI 49854. President: Reg B. Christensen. Music publisher and record company. Estab. 1956. BMI. See Chris Music Publishing for details.

SASHAY MUSIC, INC., 6255 Sunset Blvd., Suite 1904, Hollywood CA 90028. (213)463-5102. President: Steve Morris. Music publisher. Estab. 1976. ASCAP. See Morris Music for details.

SAUL AVENUE PUBLISHING CO., Box 37156. Cincinnati OH 45222. (513)793-6075. Affiliate: Hal-Nat Publishing (BMI). President: Saul Halper. Music publisher. Estab. 1969. BMI. Published 6 songs in 1977; plans 28 in 1979. Pays 25-50% royalty.
How to Contact: Submit demo tape and lead sheet. Prefers cassette with 3-6 songs on demo. SASE. Reports in 2 weeks.
Music: Bluegrass; blues; C&W; folk; gospel; and soul. Recently published "Kansas City," recorded by the Beatles (rock); and "Ain't Never Seen So Much Rain Before," recorded by Christine Kittrell (soul).

SAVGOS MUSIC, INC., 342 Westminster Ave., Elizabeth NJ 07208. Affiliate: Jonan Music (ASCAP). Office Manager: Helen Gottesmann. Music publisher. ASCAP. Publishes only material of artists recording on Savoy Records.

SAWGRASS MUSIC PUBLISHING, INC., 1722 West End Ave., Nashville TN 37203. Affiliate: Sabal Music (ASCAP). Professional Manager: Jimmy Darrell. Music publisher. Estab. 1966. BMI. Pays standard royalties.
How to Contact: Submit demo tape and lead sheet. Prefers reel-to-reel tape with 1-3 songs on demo. SASE. Reports in 2 weeks.
Music: C&W and MOR. Recently published "I Believe in You" (by Gene Dunlap and Buddy Cannon), recorded by Mel Tillis/MCA Records (ballad); and "What Did I Promise Her Last Night?" (by Ronald McCown and Wayne Walker), recorded by Tillis/MCA Records (country).

SCONE MUSIC, Scott Music Publications, Box 148, Hollywood CA 90028. President: Scott Fredrickson. Music publisher and record company. Estab. 1977. ASCAP. Published 25 songs in 1977; plans 25 in 1979. Pays 10-20% royalty.
How to Contact: Submit demo tape and lead sheet. Prefers cassette with 3-5 songs on demo. SASE. Reports in 1 month.
Music: Choral; church/religious; easy listening; gospel; jazz; MOR; and Latin (bossa nova, etc.). "We primarily publish sheet music for high school and college choirs, gospel and church groups. We produce recordings of all the music we publish, and offer them commercially. We are interested in all types of music, and have staff arrangers to adapt the lead sheet to our particular needs and markets." Recently published "Where Do We Go?", (Latin); and "Great Feelin'" (jazz) and "Da Lovely" (bossa nova), recorded by Great Feelin'.

BRYAN SCOTT'S MUSIC FACTORY, Box 50, Goodlettsville TN 37072. Professional Manager: Dick Shuey. Music publisher. ASCAP. See Lufaye Publishing for details.

SCREEN GEMS/EMI MUSIC, INC., 7033 Sunset Blvd., Hollywood CA 90028. (213)461-9141. Affiliate: Colgems Music (ASCAP). Talent Manager: Ronnie Glakal. Music publisher. BMI. Pays negotiable royalties. Secures some songwriters on a salary basis.
How to Contact: Query, arrange personal interview, or submit demo tape. Prefers 7½ ips reel-to-reel or cassette with 1-5 songs on demo. SASE. Reports in 1 month.
Music: Bluegrass; blues; children's; choral; church/religious; C&W; disco; easy listening; folk; gospel; jazz; MOR; progressive; R&B; rock; soul; and top 40/pop. Recently published "Here You Come Again," recorded by Dolly Parton; and "On Broadway," recorded by George Benson.

SCREEN GEMS/EMI, INC., 1370 Avenue of the Americas, New York NY 10019. Affiliate: Colgems/EMI Music (ASCAP). Vice President and Director of Professional Activities: Paul Tannen. Professional Manager: Bob Carrie. Pays negotiable royalty.
How to Contact: Submit demo tape and lead sheet. Prefers reel-to-reel or cassette. SASE. "Registered or insured mail will not be accepted."
Music: "We're interested in all styles of music." Recently published "Here You Come Again" (by Dolly Parton), recorded by Dolly Parton; "Close Encounters" (by John Williams and Meco Menardo), recorded by Meco; "Reminiscing" and "Old Lady" (by Little River Band); and "Surrender," recorded by Cheap Trick.

SCULLY MUSIC CO., The Sunshine Group, 800 South 4th St., Philadelphia PA 19147. (215)755-7000. Affiliate: Orange Bear Music (BMI). Contact: Cathi Leveille. Music publisher, record producer, recording studio and management firm. Estab. 1971. ASCAP. Published 8 songs in 1978; plans 24 in 1979, 36 in 1980. Pays standard royalties.
How to Contact: Submit demo tape and lead sheet or disc and lead sheet. Prefers 7½ ips or cassette with 1-4 songs on demo. "Please submit clearly understandable lyrics with accompaniment." SASE. Reports in 1 month.
Music: Disco; R&B; rock (disco); soul; and top 40/pop. Recently published "Hot Shot," "Bring on the Boys" and "Baby You Ain't Nothin' Without Me," all recorded by Karen Young/West End Records.

SEABREEZE MUSIC, Arzee Recording Co., 3010 N. Front St., Philadelphia PA 19133. (215)739-7501. President: Bill Haley. General Managers: Rex Zario, Dave Wilson. Music publisher, booking agency and record company. Estab. 1950. BMI. See Arzee Music for details.

ROBIN SEAN MUSIC PUBLISHING, 5635 Verona Rd., Verona PA 15147. (412)793-9503. President: James F. O'Leary Jr. Professional Manager: P.C. O'Leary. Music publisher and record company. Estab. 1974. BMI. Published 25 songs in 1978; plans 30 in 1979. Pays standard royalty.
How to Contact: Arrange personal interview or submit demo tape and lead sheet. Prefers 7½ ips reel-to-reel with 1-4 songs on demo. "Put leader between selections." SASE. Reports in 1 month.
Music: Blues; C&W; easy listening; MOR; rock; and top 40/pop. Recently published "Who Did It?" and "Gift of Love," recorded by Fauns Bell (R&B); "Lay That Rhythm Down," recorded by the Night Owl Band (rock/disco); and "(Year of) 69," recorded by Denny Marek (country rock).

SEASUN EXPERIENCE, 412 Holly Dr. SE, Atlanta GA 30354. (404)361-7931. President: Howard Wright. Music publisher and production consultants. Estab. 1971. ASCAP. See Commercial Studios for details.

SELLERS MUSIC, INC., 1350 Avenue of the Americas, 12th Floor, New York NY 10019. (212)687-4800. Administrator: Mimi Ryder. Music publisher. Estab. 1973. BMI. Published 10 songs in 1978; plans 50-60 in 1979. Payment negotiable.
How to Contact: Submit demo tape and lead sheet. Prefers cassette with 1-4 songs on demo. Reports "when the A&R staff likes something; otherwise no report will be given."
Music: Top 40/pop; R&B; and disco. Recently published "Young and in Love," recorded by Millington (pop); "Broken Down DJ," recorded by Lee Garrett (R&B ballad); and "Oo-Ah," recorded by Fleming Williams (pop/R&B crossover).

┌─Songwriter's Market Close-Up─

Songwriter Bob McDill compares songwriting with an Oriental art form in which the artist is allowed only one brush stroke for each line that will appear in the completed painting. "I think you can treat songs that way," he says. "No wasted lines, no wasted thoughts." McDill has been wasting neither his lines, his thoughts nor his time in songwriting: More than 140 of his songs have been recorded.

SEMENYA MUSIC, c/o Gopam Enterprises, Inc., 11 Lakeshore Dr., #13C-W, New York NY 10023. (212)724-6120. Managing Director: Laurie Goldstein. Music publisher. Estab. 1960. BMI. See Gopam Enterprises for details.

SENISA MUSIC CO., Box 28123, San Antonio TX 78228. Owner: A. Epstein. Music Director/Manager: Joe L. Scates. Music publisher and record company. Estab. 1962. ASCAP. See Epp's Music for details.

SESAME STREET MUSIC, 1 Lincoln Plaza, New York NY 10023. Contact: Geri Van Rees. Music publisher and record producer. Estab. 1974.
How to Contact: Submit demo tape and lyric sheet. Prefers reel-to-reel or cassette with 1-3 songs on demo. SASE.
Music: Children's.

7th DAY MUSIC, Box 195, 157 Ford Ave., Gallatin TN 37066. (615)452-1479. President/General Manager: Harold Gilbert. Music publisher. Estab. 1964. BMI. See Hitsburgh Music for details.

SEVENTH NOTE MUSIC, Box 400843, Dallas TX 75240. (214)690-8165. Labels include Thanks Records. President: Michael Stanglin. Music publisher and record company. Estab. 1968. Pays standard royalty.
How to Contact: Submit demo tape. Prefers 7½ ips reel-to-reel or cassette. With 1-3 songs on demo. SASE. Reports in 3 weeks.
Music: C&W; disco; easy listening; and top 40/pop.

SEYAH MUSIC, Master Audio, Inc., 1228 Spring St. NW, Atlanta GA 30309. (404)873-6425. Affiliates: Paydirt Music (ASCAP) and Lyresong Music (BMI). Professional Manager: Tom Long. President: Babs Richardson. Music publisher and recording studio. Estab. 1966. BMI. Published 10 songs in 1978. Pays standard royalties.
How to Contact: Submit demo tape. Prefers 7½ ips reel-to-reel or cassette with 14 songs. SASE. Reports in 1 month.
Music: C&W; disco; gospel; R&B; soul; and top 40/pop. Recently published "Great Change," (by Troy Ramey), recorded by Troy Ramey and the Soul Searchers/Nashboro Records (black gospel); and "Tea Cups and Doilies," (by Mac Frampton), recorded by Mac Frampton/Triumvirate Records (Broadway show type).

SHADA MUSIC, INC., 1206 17th Ave. S., Nashville TN 37212. (615)320-7947. Affiliate: Chevis Publishing (BMI). Manager: Betty Holt. Music publisher. Estab. 1960. ASCAP. Pays standard royalties.

How to Contact: Submit demo tape and lyric sheet. Prefers 7½ ips reel-to-reel with 1-3 on demo. SASE. Reports in 1 month.
Music: Easy listening; MOR; progressive; soul; and top 40/pop. Recently published "I'd Like to Teach the World to Sing in Perfect Harmony," recorded by the New Seekers; and "I Was Raised on Country Sunshine," recorded by Dottie West.

SHADOWFAX MUSIC, O.A.S. Music Group, 805 18th Ave. S., Nashville TN 37203. Co-Directors: Dane Bryant, Steve Singleton. Music publisher. Estab. 1975. BMI. See O.A.S. Music Group for details.

SHAWNEE PRESS, INC., Delaware Water Gap PA 18327. (717)476-0550. Affiliates: Harold Flammer Music (ASCAP), Templeton Music (ASCAP), Malcolm Music (BMI) and Choral Press (SESAC). Director of Publications: Lewis M. Kirby Jr. Music publisher and record company. ASCAP. Published 150 songs in 1978; plans 150 in 1979, 150 in 1980.
How to Contact: Submit demo tape and lead sheet or submit lead sheet. Prefers cassette. SASE. Reports in 2 weeks.
Music: Children's; choral; church/religious; classical; easy listening; folk; gospel; MOR; and top 40/pop. Recently published "Black and White" (by Robinson and Arkin), recorded by Three Dog Night/ABC-Dunhill Records (top 40); "This is My Country" (by Raye and Jacobs), recorded by Anita Bryant/Columbia Records (patriotic); "Let Me Call You Sweetheart" (by Whitson and Friedman), recorded by Mitch Miller/Columbia Records (easy listening/pop); and "If I Had My Way" (by Kendis and Klein), recorded by the Mills Brothers/Brunswick Records (pop).
Tips: "Send material for review suitable for use in schools or churches or for publication/recording for gospel market. Shawnee Press is primarily a publisher of choral music for educational or religious use."

SHEDIAC MUSIC, 380 Birchmont Rd., Scarborough, Ontario, Canada M1K 1M2. (416)691-2757. General Manager: W.B. Kearns. Music publisher and record company. Estab. 1974. CAPAC. See Quality Music Publishing for details.

SHELTON ASSOCIATES, 2250 Bryn Mawr Ave., Philadelphia PA 19131. (215)477-7122. A&R Director: Leo Gayton. Adminstrator: Richard Jackson. Music publisher. Estab. 1967. BMI. Published 12 songs in 1978; plans 12 in 1979. Pays standard royalty.
How to Contact: Submit demo tape. Prefers 7½ ips reel-to-reel or cassette with 3-5 songs on demo. SASE. Reports in 2 weeks.
Music: Disco; easy listening; MOR; progressive; R&B; rock; soul; and top 40/pop. Recently published "Got Cha" (by Ernest Evans), recorded by Day One/Pear Harbor Records (R&B); "Yes I Can" (by Larry Briggs), recorded by Showmen's Orchestra/A&M Records (top 40); and "Dark Shadows" (by Guess and Knox), recorded by George Guess/Voyage Records (R&B).

SHERLYN PUBLISHING CO., 65 E. 55th St., Penthouse, New York NY 10022. (212)752-0160. Affiliates: Kimlyn Music (ASCAP) and Lindseyanne Music (BMI). Professional Manager: Amy Bolton. Music publisher and record company. Estab. 1968. BMI. Published 200 songs in 1978; plans 200 in 1979, 300 in 1980. Pays standard royalties. Secures some songwriters on salary basis.
How to Contact: Query or submit demo tape and lyric sheet. Prefers cassette with 1-3 songs on demo. SASE. Reports in 2 weeks.
Music: C&W; disco; R&B; rock; soul; and top 40/pop. Recently published "Get Off" (by Ish Ledisma), recorded by Foxy/Dash TK Records (R&B/disco); "What You Won't Do for Love" (by Bobby Caldwell), recorded by Bobby Caldwell/Cloud TK Records (R&B/pop); and "Dance With Me" (by Peter Brown and Robert Rans), recorded by Peter Brown/TK Records (disco).

SHIRLEY'S MUSIC, Box 15110, New Orleans LA 70175. (504)949-8386. President: Jo Ann Johnson. Vice President/General Manager: Earl K. Johnson. Music publisher. BMI. See Sound of America for details.

SHORT PUMP PUBLISHING, Short Pump Associates, Box 11292, Richmond VA 23230. (804)355-4117. President: Ken Brown. Vice President: Dennis Huber. Music publisher and record company. Estab. 1976. BMI. Published 15 songs in 1978; plans 30 in 1979. Pays on royalty basis.
How to Contact: Submit demo tape and lead sheet. Prefers 7½ ips reel-to-reel with 3-6 songs on demo. SASE. Reports in 2 weeks.

Music: Jazz; rock (light); soul; and top 40/pop. Recently published "Holdin' On," "Love and Lies" and "New Day," recorded by Andrew Lewis Band (rock).

SHOW BIZ MUSIC GROUP, 110 21st Ave. S., Nashville TN 37203. Affiliates: Showbiz Music (BMI), Song Biz Music (BMI), Monster Music (ASCAP) and Lucky Penny Music (ASCAP). General manager: Ed Penney. Music publisher. Estab. 1968. Pays standard royalties.
How to Contact: Query or submit demo tape and lead sheet. Prefers 7½ ips reel-to-reel or cassette with 1-2 songs on demo. SASE. Reports "as soon as possible."
Music: C&W; disco; easy listening; folk; gospel; MOR; and top 40/pop. Recently published "Morning" and "That Time of the Night" (by Bill Graham), recorded by Jim Ed Brown/RCA Records (pop/C&W); and "Word Games" (by Graham) recorded by Billy Walker/RCA Records (country).

SILHOUETTE MUSIC, The Herald Association, Inc., Box 218, Wellman Heights, Johnsonville SC 29555. (803)386-2600. Affiliates: Bridge Music (BMI) and Heraldic Music (ASCAP). Director: Erv Lewis. Music publisher and record company. Estab. 1975. SESAC. Published 60 songs in 1978; plans 100 in 1979. Pays 5-10% royalty.
How to Contact: Submit demo tape and lead sheet. Prefers 7½ ips reel-to-reel with 3-6 songs on demo. "Record the tape on one side only, as we use mono equipment on playback." SASE. Reports in 1 month.
Music: Church/religious and gospel. Recently published "Breaker, Breaker, Sweet Jesus," recorded by Jerry Arhelger (country/gospel); "Things that Matter Now," recorded by Rick Eldridge (MOR/gospel); and "Today I Followed Jesus," recorded by Erv Lewis (gospel).

SILICON MUSIC PUBLISHING CO., 222 Tulane St., Garland TX 75043. Vice President: Deanna Lane. Music publisher. Estab. 1965. BMI. Plans 4-6 songs in 1979. Pays standard royalties.
How to Contact: Submit demo tape. Prefers cassette with 1-2 songs on demo. Does not return unsolicited material.
Music: C&W; MOR; and rock. Recently published "A Place Called Friendlyville" and "Dungeon of Jealously" (by Bill Kelly and Bill Ashley), recorded by Bill Kelly/Domino Records; "Tomorrow Will Never Be" (by Al Struble), recorded by the Struble Brothers Band/Domino Records (rock); and "Cloudy Day," recorded by Gene Summers (MOR).
Tip: "We are very interested in '50s rock and rockabilly *original masters* for release through overseas affiliates. If you are the owner of any '50s masters, contact us first! We have releases in Holland, Switzerland and England at the present time."

SILVER BLUE MUSIC, LTD., 220 Central Park S., New York NY 10019. Affiliate: Oceans Blue Music (BMI). President: Joel Diamond. Professional Manager: Fara Feinerman. Music publisher and record producer. ASCAP.
How to Contact: Submit demo tape and lead sheet. Prefers cassette with 3-4 songs on demo. SASE.
Music: Disco; easy listening; MOR; rock; and top 40/pop. Recently published and produced "After the Lovin' " (by Bernstein and Adams), recorded by Engelbert Humperdinck.

SILVERLINE MUSIC, INC., 329 Rockland Rd., Hendersonville TN 37075. Affiliate: Goldline Music (ASCAP). General Manager: Noel Fox. Music publisher. BMI. Payment negotiable.
How to Contact: Arrange personal interview. Prefers reel-to-reel or cassette. SASE. Reports "as soon as possible."
Music: C&W (crossover) and top 40/pop. Recently published "Bringing It Back," recorded by Elvis Presley (pop/C&W); and "Let Me Be the One," recorded by the Oak Ridge Boys (C&W).

SING ME MUSIC, INC., 19 Music Square W., Nashville TN 37203. (615)256-1886. Affiliates: Crooked Creek (BMI) and Kiss Me Music (SESAC). President: Jean S. Zimmerman. Professional Manager: Mary Louise Smith. Music publisher. Estab. 1972. ASCAP. Published 120 songs in 1978; plans 120 in 1979. Pays standard royalties.
How to Contact: Submit demo tape, arrange personal interview, or submit demo tape and lead sheet. Prefers 7½ ips reel-to-reel with 1-4 songs on demo. SASE. Reports in 3 weeks.
Music: Bluegrass; blues; church/religious; C&W; disco; easy listening; folk; gospel; MOR; rock (hard or C&W); soul; and top 40/pop. Recently published "Tupelo Joe" (by Jack Brouse), recorded by Doyle Holly/Sing Me Records (country ballad); and "Only Yesterday" (by Arthur Kent and Jim Burns), recorded by Don Buckley (MOR/pop).

SINGING RIVER PUBLISHING CO., INC., Biloxi MS 39530. (601)436-3927. Affiliate: Axent Publishing (ASCAP). President: Marion Carpenter. Music publisher, record company and record producer. Estab. 1955. BMI. Published 12 songs in 1978. Pays standard royalties. **How to Contact:** Query or submit demo tape. Prefers 7½ ips reel-to-reel or cassette with 1-4 songs on demo. SASE. Reports in 1 month.
Music: Bluegrass; blues; C&W; easy listening; folk; MOR; and top 40/pop. Recently published "World of Make Believe" (by Carpenter, Maddox and Smith), recorded by Bill Anderson/MCA Records and Johnny Bragg/Decca Records (country); "Searching" (by Maddox), recorded by Kitty Wells/Decca Records and Melba Montgomery (country); and "Rocking Little Angel" (by J. Rodgers), recorded by Ray Smith/Capitol Records (country).

SHELBY SINGLETON MUSIC INC., 3106 Belmont Blvd., Nashville TN 37212. (615)385-1960. Office Manager: Vivian Keith. Music publisher and record company. Estab. 1967. BMI. Pays standard royalties.
How to Contact: Submit demo tape. Prefers cassette. SASE. Reports "as soon as possible."
Music: Bluegrass; blues; C&W; disco; easy listening; folk; gospel; jazz; MOR; progressive; R&B; rock; soul; and top 40/pop. Recently published "Before the Next Teardrop Falls" (by Vivian Keith and Ben Peters), recorded by Freddy Fender/ABC Records (country/MOR); "We Try" (by Rita Remington), recorded by Rita Remington/Plantation Records (country); and "Got You on My Mind" (by Joe Thomas and Howard Biggs), recorded by Bobby Hood/Plantation Records (country/MOR).

SHELLY SINGLETON MUSIC, INC., 103 Westview Ave., Valparaiso FL 32580. (904)678-7211. Owner: Finley Duncan. President: Bruce Duncan. Music publisher, record company and record producer. BMI. See Friendly Finley Music for details.

SIVATT MUSIC PUBLISHING CO., Box 7172, Greenville SC 29610. (803)269-5529. President: Jesse B. Evatte. Music publisher and record company. Estab. 1974. BMI.
How to Contact: Submit demo tape and lead sheet. Prefers cassette with 2-6 songs on demo. SASE. Reports in 1 month.
Music: Bluegrass; church/religious; C&W; easy listening; folk; and gospel. Recently published "Weary Traveler" and "Hear the Bells" (by Martha Miranda), recorded by Martha and the Singing Angels/Pioneer Records (gospel); and "I've Got a Hand" (by Sherri Ensley), recorded by the Laymen Quartet/Pioneer Records (gospel).

SIX STRINGS MUSIC, 2201 N. 54th St., Philadelphia PA 19131. Affiliate: The Harris Machine (BMI). Professional Manager: Caryle Blackwell. President: Norman Harris. Music publisher, record company and production company. Estab. 1976. BMI. Published 175 songs in 1977; plans 300 in 1979. Pays 25% minimum royalty.
How to Contact: Submit demo tape and lead sheet. Prefers 7½ ips reel-to-reel or cassette with 1-4 songs on demo. SASE. Reports in 1 month.
Music: Blues; disco; easy listening; MOR; rock; soul; and top 40/pop. Recently published "Disco Inferno," recorded by the Trammps (disco); "Private Property," recorded by the Dells (ballad); and "Think for Yourself," recorded by the Temptations (R&B).

SKINNERS POND MUSIC, 1343 Matheson Blvd. W., Mississauga, Ontario, Canada L4W 1R1. General Manager: Mark Altman. Music publisher. PROCAN. See Morning Music for details.

SKUNKSTER PUBLISHING, Box 878, Sonoma CA 95476. (707)938-4060. Manager/Owner: Bruce Cohn. Music publisher and management firm. Estab. 1975. ASCAP. See Bruce Cohn Music for details.

SKYS THE LIMIT MUSIC, 125 Main St., Reading MA 01867. (617)944-0423. Contact: Professional Manager. Music publisher, record producer and promotion firm. SESAC. See Critique Music Publishing for details.

SLIM-BULL, 38 Music Square E., Nashville TN 37203. (615)256-3373. President: Marty Williamson. Music publisher. BMI. See Brim Music for details.

MACK SMITH MUSIC, 814 W. Claiborne St., Box 672, Greenwood MS 38930. (601)453-3302. Owner: Mack Allen Smith. Music publisher and record company. Estab. 1962. BMI. Published 10 songs in 1978; plans 25 in 1979, 35 in 1980. Pays standard royalties.
How to Contact: Submit demo tape and lead or lyric sheet. Prefers 7½ ips reel-to-reel or

cassette with 1-5 songs on demo. "On reel-to-reel, put leaders between songs." SASE. Reports in 1 month.
Music: C&W; rock; and top 40/pop. Recently published "If I Could Get One More Hit" (by Mack Allen Smith), recorded by James O'Gwynn/Plantation Records (country); and "Angel Face Body Full of Sin" and "Who the Heck is Bob Wills?" (by Smith), recorded by Mack Allen Smith/Ace Records (country).

EARLE SMITH MUSIC, Box 2101, Salinas CA 93902. (408)449-1706 Affiliate: Centra-Cal Music (ASCAP). President: Earle F. Smith. Music publisher. Estab. 1975. BMI. Published 1 song in 1978; plans 4 in 1979, 6 in 1980. Pays standard royalties.
How to Contact: Submit demo tape and lead sheet. Prefers 7½ reel-to-reel or cassette with 1-4 on demo. SASE. Reports in 3 weeks.
Music: C&W; MOR; soul; and top 40/pop. Recently published "All Alone" (by Layton and Foster), recorded by Layton and Foster/Bre-Wa-Ma Records (MOR); "Beautiful Sunshine" (by Allen Greene), recorded by Donna Stumpf/Bre-Wa-Ma Records (MOR); and "Pretty Sales Lady" (by Harold Kolthoff), recorded by Jimmie Ray/Solo Records (country).

SMORGASCHORD, Box 6507, 2181 Victory Pkwy., Cincinnati OH 45206. (513)861-1500. Owner: Rob Fetters. Estab. 1968. ASCAP. See Hal Bernard Enterprises for details.

SNAPFINGER MUSIC, Box 35158, Decatur GA 30035. Owner: Don Bryant. Music publisher. Estab. 1978. BMI. Plans 5 songs in 1979, 10 in 1980. Pays standard royalties.
How to Contact: Submit demo tape and typed lyric sheet. Prefers 7½ ips reel-to-reel with 1-4 songs on demo. "Please use leader tape before first song and between each song." SASE. Reports in 1 month.
Music: C&W; disco; easy listening; gospel; MOR; rock; and top 40/pop.

SNOOPY MUSIC, Graveline Enterprises, Inc., 1975 NE 249 St., North Miami FL 33181. (305)940-6999. President: Dave Graveline. Executive Vice President: Jim Rudd. Music publisher, record company, record producer and recording studio. Estab. 1968. BMI. Plans 12 songs in 1979. Pays standard royalties.
How to Contact: Submit demo tape and lead sheet. Prefers 7½ or 15 ips reel-to-reel. SASE. Reports in 2 weeks.
Music: Blues; C&W; disco; easy listening; Latin (with English translation); MOR; progressive; rock; soul; and top 40/pop. Recently published "Are You Ready?" and "SOS," recorded by Sky Mitchell (MOR/disco); and "I'm Gonna Make It," recorded by Paul Richards (MOR).
Tips: "We're *really* looking for disco material."

SNOW/MATZ MUSIC, 1650 Broadway, New York NY 10019. (212)581-6162. Vice President: Paul Brown. Music publisher and record producer. ASCAP. See Larball Publishing for details.

SNOWBERRY MUSIC, 1659 Bayview Ave., Suite 102, Toronto, Ontario, Canada M4G 3C1. (416)485-1157. Affiliate: Maple Creek Music (PROCAN). Vice President: John D. Watt. Music publisher. Estab. 1972. CAPAC. Published 10 songs in 1978; plans 12 in 1979. Pays standard royalty.
How to Contact: Submit demo tape or arrange personal interview. Prefers 7½ ips reel-to-reel with 2-6 songs on demo. SAE and International Reply Coupons. Reports in 3 weeks.
Music: C&W; disco; easy listening; MOR; rock; and top 40/pop. Recently published "Set the Night on Fire," recorded by Johnny Lovesin (rock); "Rainbows, Pots of Gold and Moonbeams," recorded by Studebaker Hawk (pop); "Lazy Love," recorded by New City Jam Band (pop); and "Talk to Me," recorded by Tony Orlando and Dawn.

SNUG MUSIC, Box 878, Sonoma CA 95476. (707)938-4060. Manager/Owner: Bruce Cohn. Music publisher and management firm. Estab. 1975. BMI. See Bruce Cohn Music for details.

SOFT MUSIC, INC., 7033 Sunset Blvd., Suite 322, Los Angeles CA 90028. General Manager: Maritta Boyle. Music publisher. BMI. See Valgroup Music (USA) for details.

SOLAR WIND MUSIC, Box 110, Howard Beach NY 11414. (212)738-4806. President: Rocco Giamundo. Music publisher and record company. Estab. 1977. BMI.
How to Contact: Submit demo. Prefers 7½ or 15 ips reel-to-reel or disc. "Do not send cassettes or 8-track cartridges. Send copyrighted material only. Enclose a self-addressed postage paid envelope if you wish us to return your product after review. We will not necessarily comment on unsolicited material."

Music: Classical; disco; easy listening; folk; jazz; MOR; progressive; rock; soul; top 40/pop; and "authentic Jamaican reggae."

SONG CYCLE, Wild Productions, 12135 Valley Spring Lane, Studio City CA 91604. President: Christian Wilde. Music publisher and record producer. Estab. 1970. BMI. See Wild Music for details.

SONG TAILORS MUSIC CO., Box 2631, Muscle Shoals AL 35660. (205)381-1455. Affiliate: I've Got the Music (ASCAP). Professional Manager: Kevin Lamb. Music publisher. Estab. 1971. BMI. Pays standard royalty.
How to Contact: Submit demo tape and lead sheet. Prefers 7½ or 15 ips reel-to-reel or cassette with 1-10 songs on demo. "Put leader between songs on reel-to-reel." SASE. Reports "as soon as possible."
Music: Blues; C&W; disco; easy listening; folk; jazz; MOR; progressive; rock; soul; and top 40/pop. Recently published "The Angel in Your Arms" and "The Right Feeling at the Wrong Time," recorded by Hot (top 40); and "It's a Crazy World," recorded by Mac McAnally (top 40).

SONGS OF CALVARY, Calvary Records, Inc., 142 8th Ave. N., Nashville TN 37203. Affiliate: Music of Calvary (SESAC). A&R Director: Ronnie Drake. Music publisher. BMI. Pays 10% maximum royalty.
How to Contact: Submit demo tape and lead sheet. Prefers 7½ ips reel-to-reel or cassette. Does not return unsolicited material. Reports in 2 weeks.
Music: Gospel (C&W, traditional or contemporary). Recently published "The Lighthouse," and "Touch of Master's Strong Hand," recorded by Hinson (gospel).

SONHEATH PUBLISHING, 3300 Warner Blvd., Burbank CA 91510. (213)846-9090. Contact: Ruth Latshaw. Music publisher and record company. ASCAP. See 3300 Publishing for details.

SOQUEL SONGS, Box 878, Sonoma CA 95476. (707)938-4060. Manager: Bruce Cohn. Music publisher and management firm. Estab. 1975. ASCAP. See Bruce Cohn Music for details.

SOUND CITY MUSIC, Box 9287, Jackson MS 39206. (601)982-4522. President: Stewart Madison. Music publisher and record company. Estab. 1968. ASCAP. See Rogan Publishing for details.

SOUND OF AMERICA PUBLISHING CO., Box 15110, New Orleans LA 70179. (504)949-8386. Affiliate: Shirley's Music (BMI). President: Jo Ann Johnson. Vice President/General Manager: Earl K. Johnson. Music publisher. BMI. Published 18 songs in 1977; plans 45 in 1979.
How to Contact: Submit demo tape and lead or lyric sheet. Prefers 7½ ips reel-to-reel or cassette. SASE. Reports in 1 month.
Music: Blues; C&W; disco; folk; gospel; jazz instrumental; MOR; rock (no hard); soul; and top 40/pop. Recently published "Let's Make a Better World," recorded by Levon Helm and the RCO All Stars (MOR); "Big Chief," recorded by Dr. John (R&B); and "Time for the Sun to Rise," recorded by Earl King (R&B).

SOUND OF NOLAN MUSIC, c/o Peter C. Bennett, 211 S. Beverly Dr., Suite 108B, Beverly Hills CA 90212. Affiliate: Kenny Nolan Publishing (ASCAP). General Manager: Peter C. Bennett. Music publisher. Estab. 1974. BMI. Published 10 songs in 1977; plans 30 in 1979. Pays standard royalty.
How to Contact: Submit demo tape. Prefers cassette. SASE. Reports in 2 weeks.
Music: Disco; easy listening; MOR; progressive; R&B; rock; soul; and top 40/pop. Recently published "I Like Dreamin'" (by Kenny Nolan), recorded by Kenny Nolan/20th Century Records (top 40/pop); "My Eyes Adored You" (by Kenny Nolan and Bob Crewe), recorded by Frank Valli/Private Stock Records (top 40/pop); and "Lady Marmalade" (by Kenny Nolan and Bob Crewe), recorded by Labelle/CBS Records (top 40/pop).

SOUTHERN MUSIC, 6922 Hollywood Blvd., Hollywood CA 90028. (213)469-1667. Professional Manager: Roy Kohn. Music publisher and record company. Estab. 1928. ASCAP. See Peer-Southern Organization, Hollywood office, for details.

SOUTHERN WRITERS GROUP USA, Box 40764, Nashville TN 37204. Office Manager: Bill

Martin. Music publisher. Estab. 1977. BMI. Published 50 songs in 1978. Pays standard royalties.
How to Contact: "We are not soliciting outside material at this time, and we ask that songwriters not contact us until further notice." Does not return unsolicited material.
Music: Blues; C&W; disco; easy listening; folk; jazz; MOR; progressive; R&B; rock; soul; and top 40/pop. Recently published "Bluer than Blue" (by Randy Goodrum), recorded by Michael Johnson/EMI (MOR); and "She Believes in Me" (by Steve Gibb), recorded by Kenny Rogers/UA Records (country).

SOUTHWEST WORDS AND MUSIC, 14 E. 2nd St., Tucson AZ 85705. (602)792-3194. President: Fred Knipe. "Send demos to Steve Chandler, Vice President." Music publisher, record company and record producer. Estab. 1975. BMI. See Suncountry Song for details.

SPANGLE MUSIC, WelDee Music Co., Box 561, Wooster OH 44691. General Manager: Quentin W. Welty. Music publisher. Estab. 1959. BMI. See B-W Music for details.

SPEAK MUSIC CO., 809 18th Ave. S., Nashville TN 37203. (615)327-3211. Owners: Pete Drake, Buddy Spicher. Officer Manager: Rose Trimble. Music publisher. Estab. 1961. BMI. See Window Music Publishing for details.

BEN SPEER MUSIC, Box 40201, Nashville TN 37204. Doesn't consider outside material.

LARRY SPIER, INC., 240 Madison Ave., New York NY 10016. (212)686-1777. Affiliate: Memory Lane Music (BMI). President: Larry Spier. Music publisher. Estab. 1921. ASCAP. Pays standard royalty.
How to Contact: Arrange personal interview or submit demo tape and lead sheet. Prefers cassette. SASE. Reports in 3 weeks.
Music: C&W; disco; easy listening; folk; jazz; MOR; progressive; soul; and top 40/pop. Recently published "The Greatest Performance of My Life" and "It's Peaceful Out There" (MOR).

SPIKES MUSIC, Box 878, Sonoma CA 95476. (707)938-4060. Manager: Bruce Cohn. Music publisher and management firm. Estab. 1975. BMI. See Bruce Cohn Music for details.

SQUILLIT PRODUCTIONS, INC., 1619 Broadway, New York NY 10019. (212)265-1292. Music publisher.
How to Contact: "We are open to review new artists; you must include a demo tape, photo and bio."

SRI RECORDS & TAPES, Box 720, Palo Alto CA 94302. President: Steven Halpern. Not accepting unsolicited material at this time.

TERRY STAFFORD MUSIC, Box 6546, Burbank CA 91510. President: Terry Stafford. Music publisher. Estab. 1968. BMI. Published 25 songs in 1978; plans 25 in 1979. Pays standard royalties.
How to Contact: Submit demo tape or submit demo tape and lead sheet. Prefers cassette with 3-5 songs on demo. SASE. Reports in 1 month.
Music: C&W and top 40/pop. Recently published "Amarillo by Morning," "Bad to Love Her" and "Darlin' Think it Over," recorded by Terry Stafford (C&W).

STAFREE PUBLISHING CO., 3114 Radford Rd., Memphis TN 38111. (901)327-8187. Affiliate: Packy Music (ASCAP). Director of Publishing: Steve Gatlin. Music publisher, record company, record producer and management firm. Estab. 1972. BMI. Published 15 songs in 1978; plans 25 in 1979, 35 in 1980. Pays standard royalties less any collection or licensing fees.
How to Contact: Submit demo tape, submit demo tape and lead sheet, or submit demo tape and lyric sheet. Prefers 7½ reel-to-reel tape with 1-4 songs on demo. SASE. Reports in 1 month.
Music: Disco; top 40/pop. Recently published "Disco Duck" (by R. Dees), recorded by Rick Dees/RSO Records and Fretone Records (disco novelty); "Fold Out Girl" (by R. Orange, L. Snell and B. Manuel), recorded by Pat Taylor/Mercury Records and Fretone Records (top 40/pop); and "Wookie" (by S. Samudio), recorded by Sam the Sham/Fretone Records (top 40/pop).
Tips: "Submit only tunes that are of caliber to be 'A' side on 45 rpm record for AM radio play on top 40-type stations. We use very few ballads and no album cuts."

STAGE ONE MUSIC, LTD., 450 E. Beaumont Ave., St. Bruno, Quebec, Canada J3V 2R3. (514)653-7838. President: Christian Lefort. Music publisher and record company. Estab. 1967. CAPAC. See S.M.C.L. Productions for details.

STAIRWAY MUSIC, 8 Music Square W., Nashville TN 37203. BMI. See Tree Publishing for details.

STALLION MUSIC, 8 Music Square W., Nashville TN 37203. BMI. See Tree Publishing for details.

STARR BOUND PUBLISHING CO., Box 1037, Des Plaines IL 60018. (312)824-8205. President: Mary Starr. Vice President: Joseph Starr. Music publisher, record company and management firm. See Royal Star Publishing for details.

STAR OF DAVID, Songs of David, Inc., Suite 116, Music Park Bldg., Box 22653, Nashville TN 37202. (615)885-0713. President: Dave Mathes. Estab. 1975. SESAC. See House of David for details.

STAR TUNES MUSIC, Box 1563, Hollywood CA 90028. President: Art Benson. Music publisher and record company. Estab. 1954. BMI. See Grosvenor House Music for details.

STARR BOUND PUBLISHING CO., Box 1037, Des Plaines IL 60018. (312)824-8205. President: Joseph Starr. Vice President: Mary Starr. Music publisher, record company and management firm. ASCAP. See Royal Star Publishing for details.

STARTIME MUSIC, Box 643, LaQuinta CA 92253. (714)564-4823. Affiliate: Yo Yo Music (BMI). President: Fred Rice. Music publisher, record company. Pays standard royalties.
How to Contact: Submit demo tape and lead sheet. Prefers cassette with 1-2 songs on demo. Does not return unsolicited material. Reports in 6 weeks.
Music: Country; rock; top 40/pop; and novelty. Recently published "Bad Boy" (by Bill Bogert), recorded by Nico Princely and His Blue Diamond Band/Startime Records (rock).

STARTRACK MUSIC PUBLISHING, Box 2066, Oshawa, Ontario, Canada L1H 7N2. (705)793-2737. President: George Petralia. Music publisher, record company, record producer and management firm. CAPAC. See Cloud Burst Music Publishing for details.

STARFOX PUBLISHING, Box 13584, Atlanta GA 30324. (404)872-0266. President: Alexander Janoulis. Vice President, Creative: Oliver Cooper. General Manager: Hamilton Underwood. Music publisher. Estab. 1973. BMI. Published 30 songs in 1978; plans 40 in 1979. Pays 25-50% royalty. Buys some material outright; pays $25-250. Does not charge for services; however, "if requested by letter, will critique a song for $25, payable in advance."
How to Contact: Submit demo tape and lyric sheet. Prefers reel-to-reel or cassette with 2-3 songs on demo. Does not return unsolicited material. Reports "as soon as possible."
Music: Blues; C&W; disco; MOR; progressive; rock; and top 40/pop. Recently published "So Much" (by P. Jackson and A. Janoulis), recorded by Little Phil and the Night Shadows/ABC-Dot Records (top 40/pop); "Rock & Roll Radio" (by Oliver Cooper), recorded by Starfoxx/Hottrax Records (rock); and "Love Generator" (by Chuck Diamond), recorded by Diamond Lil/Glamour & Grease Records (disco).

STATESIDE MUSIC CO., 150 West End Ave., Suite 6-D, New York NY 10023. (212)873-5968. Manager: Phillip Ross Zinn. Music publisher and record company. Estab. 1959. BMI.
Music: Disco. Recently released "Telephone" and "Dooms Day" (by Phillip Ross Zinn and Robert Lee Lowery), recorded by Danny Darrow (disco); and *Wonderland of Dreams* (by Zinn), album recorded on Mighty Records (disco). See Rockford Music for submission details.

STEADY ARM MUSIC, Box 12239, Gainesville FL 32604. (904)372-5233. General Manager: Charles V. Steadham Jr. A&R Director: Allen R. McCollum. Music publisher. Estab. 1977.
How to Contact: Query or submit demo tape. Prefers cassette with 2-5 songs on demo. Does not return unsolicited material. Reports "as soon as possible."
Music: Bluegrass; C&W; disco; folk; MOR; rock (country); soul; top 40/pop; R&B; and comedy. Recently released "Micah" and "Enoch Ludford" (by Don Dunaway), recorded by Dunaway/Milltop Records (folk); and "Kennesaw Line" (by Dunaway) recorded by Dunaway/Mountain Railroad Records (folk).

STEEL RIVER MUSIC, Box 256, Dalhousie, New Brunswick, Canada. Owner: Gerald C. Shaw. Music publisher. Estab. 1977. BMI. Published 9 songs in 1978. Pays standard royalties. **How to Contact:** Query or submit demo tape. Prefers cassette with 1-4 songs on demo. SASE. Reports in 2 weeks.
Music: Bluegrass; C&W; gospel; and MOR.

STONE DIAMOND MUSIC CORP., 6255 Sunset Blvd., Hollywood CA 90028. (213)468-3400. Executive Vice President: Robert Gordy. Vice President and General Manager: Jay Lowy. Music publisher. BMI.
Music: Blues; disco; easy listening; jazz; MOR; R&B; rock; soul; and top/40 pop. See Jobete Music for submission details.

STONE POST MUSIC, Box 1213, Emporia KS 66801. (316)343-2727. President: Richard Bisterfeldt. Vice President/Manager: Jackie Bestufeldt. Disco Coordinator: Jann Joy. Music publisher and record company. Estab. 1975. BMI. Published 9 songs in 1979. Pays negotable royalty.
How to Contact: Submit demo tape. Prefers 7½ ips reel-to-reel or 8-track cartridge with 3-5 songs on demo. SASE. Reports in 2 weeks.
Music: Progressive (country); rock (progressive or hard); and top 40/pop. Recently published "Georgia Girl, She's So Warm" recorded by Fyre (rock)

STONE ROW MUSIC CO., 2022 Vardon, Flossmour IL 60422. President: Joanne Swanson. Music publisher. Estab. 1975. BMI. Published 2 songs in 1978; plans 4 in 1979, 6 in 1980. Pays standard royalties.
How to Contact: Query or submit lead sheet. "Must be copyrighted." SASE. Reports in 3 weeks.
Music: Classical (new music scores); jazz; rock (soft); and top 40/pop.

STONEWALL MUSIC, 39 Music Square E., Nashville TN 37203. (615)255-6535. President: J. William Denny. Music publisher. See Cedarwood Publishing for details.

STORYVILLE PUBLISHING CO., Box 13977, New Orleans LA 70185. President: John Berthelot. Music publisher. Estab. 1970. BMI. See John Berthelot and Associates for details.

JEB STUART MUSIC CO., Box 6032, Station B, Miami FL 33123. (305)547-1424. President: Jeb Stuart. Music publisher, record producer and management firm. Estab. 1973. BMI. Published 5 songs in 1978. Pays 1-2% royalty.
How to Contact: Query, submit demo tape and lead sheet or contact by telephone. Prefers cassette or disc with 2-4 songs on demo. SASE. Reports in 1 month.
Music: Blues; church/religious; C&W; disco; gospel; jazz; rock; soul; and top 40/pop. Recently published "Can't Count the Days" and "Hung Up on Your Love," recorded by Jeb Stuart (pop/R&B).

STUCKEY PUBLISHING CO., Rt. 6, 906 Ashby Dr., Brentwood TN 37027. (615)244-9412. Affiliates: Monkhouse Music (BMI), Green Pastures Music and 2 Plus 2 Music (ASCAP). Manager: Ann M. Stuckey. Music publisher. Estab. 1967. BMI. Pays standard royalties.
How to Contact: Submit demo tape and lead sheet.
Music: C&W. Recently published "Sun Comin' Up" (by Nat Stuckey), recorded by Nat Stuckey/MCA Records (C&W); "Sweet Thang" (by Stuckey), recorded by Stuckey and Paula (C&W); and "Pop a Top" (by Stuckey), recorded by Jim Ed Brown/RCA Records (C&W).

SUDDEN RUSH MUSIC, INC., 750 Kappock St., Riverdale NY 10463. (212)884-6014. Affiliate: All of a Sudden Music (ASCAP). President: Alan Korwin. Creative Director: Micahel Berman. A&R Director: Steve Michaels. Music publisher. Estab. 1975. BMI. Published 50 songs in 1977; plans 100 in 1979. Pays standard minimum royalty. Sometimes secures songwriters on salary basis: "Only when a writer has demonstrated truly outstanding talent and a prolific nature will a salaried, exclusive writer deal be considered. Salary and terms are completely negotiable, depending on individual circumstance."
How to Contact: Submit demo tape and lyric sheet. Prefers 7½ ips reel-to-reel or cassette with 1-3 songs on demo. SASE. Reports "as soon as possible."
Music: Blues; disco; MOR; progressive; rock; and top 40/pop. Recently published "Who's Gonna Love Me?", recorded by the Imperials (disco); "Christine," recorded by Sunrise (ballad); and "Too Late to Put it Down," recorded by Gary Glitter (rock).

SUFI PIPKIN MUSIC, Box 3991, Hollywood CA 90028. (213)276-2063. Owner/President: Linda Moxley. Repertory Manager: John Cursone. Music publisher. Estab. 1969. BMI. Pays standard royalty.
How to Contact: Query: "Send letter describing type of music." Prefers cassette. SASE. Reports in 3 months.
Music: C&W; disco; easy listening; MOR; rock; and top 40/pop.

SUGAR BEAR MUSIC, 1044 Lilly Ave. NE, Canton OH 44730. (216)488-0065. President: Robert L. Lenzy. Music publisher, record company and production company. Estab. 1973. BMI. Published 20 songs in 1978. Pays 7-10% royalty.
How to Contact: Submit demo tape and lead sheet. Prefers 7½ ips reel-to-reel with 2-4 songs on demo. SASE. Reports in 1 month.
Music: Disco; soul; and top 40/pop.

SUGAR FREE MUSIC, 3929 Carpenter Ave., Bronx NY 10466. (212)655-8217. Professional Manager: Mark Sameth. Music publisher. Estab. 1975. BMI. See Sugar n' Soul Music for details.

SUGAR N' SOUL MUSIC, INC., 3929 Carpenter Ave., Bronx NY 10466. (212)655-8217. Affiliate: Sugar Free Music (BMI). Professional Manager: Mark Sameth. Music publisher. Estab. 1975. ASCAP. Pays standard royalties.
How to Contact: Submit demo tape and lyric or lead sheet. Prefers 7½ ips reel-to-reel or cassette with 1-5 songs on demo. Prefers leader between selections. SASE. Reports in 2 weeks.
Music: C&W; disco; easy listening; folk; MOR; rock (country/pop); soul (R&B/funk); and top 40/pop (ballads). "Write for a listing of recent and current recordings."

SULZER MUSIC, Dave Wilson Productions, Box 19518, Philadelphia PA 19124. (215)743-8549. Affiliates: Arzee Music (ASCAP), Valley Brook (ASCAP), Rex Zario Music (BMI), Seabreeze Music (BMI), Wilson/Zario Publishers (BMI), Jack Howard Pubishers (BMI), Arcade Music (ASCAP) and Mike Bennett Music (BMI). President: Dave Wilson. Vice President: Claire Mac. General Manager: Rex Zario. Published 100 songs in 1979; plans 150 in 1980. BMI. Pays standard royalties.
How to Contact: Submit demo tape or submit demo tape and lead sheet. Prefers 7½ or 15 ips reel-to-reel cassette with 6-10 songs on demo. SASE. Reports in 1 month.
Music: C&W; easy listening; folk; top 40/pop; and pop country. Recently published "I Will Make Some Room in My Heart," recorded by Nicky Dee (pop country) and "Missin' You Baby Lately," recorded by Mike Bennett (top/40).

SU-MA PUBLISHING CO., INC., Box 1125, Shreveport LA 71163. (318)222-0195. Publishing Manager: Peggy Mims. Music publisher. Estab. 1964. BMI. Published 75 songs in 1978; plans 75 in 1979. Pays standard maximum royalties.
How to Contact: Submit demo tape or submit demo tape and lead sheet. Prefers 7½ ips reel-to-reel, cassette or 8-track cartridge. SASE. Reports in 1 month.
Music: C&W; gospel; and soul. Recently published "I'm Just Another Soldier," recorded by Five Blind Boys from Mississippi (gospel); and "Seattle in the Rain," recorded by Susanne Phillips (C&W).
Tips: "All songs must contain both lyrics and melody."

SUN VINE MUSIC, 6430 Sunset Blvd., Suite 921, Los Angeles CA 90028. (213)461-3091. Director of Creative Affairs: B. Ficks, 2 Music Circle S., Nashville TN 37203. Music publisher. BMI. See Famous Music Corporation for details.

SUNCOUNTRY SONG CO., 14 E. 2nd St., Tucson AZ 85705. (602)792-3194. Affiliate: Southwest Words and Music (BMI). President: Fred Knipe. Music publisher, record company and record producer. Estab. 1975. ASCAP. Published 40 songs in 1978. Pays standard royalty.
How to Contact: Submit demo tape and lyric sheet. Prefers cassette with 1-4 songs on demo. "Leaders are appreciated." SASE. Reports in 1 month.
Music: C&W (modern); disco; rock (rhythm ballads, not heavy metal or blues); R&B; soul; and top 40/pop. Recently published "Honky Tonk Music," recorded by Jerry Jeff Walker, Hoyt Axton and Commander Cody (C&W); "Get Up & Get Out," recorded by Force (disco); and "You Can't Stop Her," recorded by Zo-Zo (rock).

SUNDAZE MUSIC, Box 66, Manhattan Beach CA 90266. (213)371-9578. Affiliates: Good Luvin' Publishing (BMI) and Provo Music (BMI). Vice President, Publishing: Larry Thatt.

Music publisher and record company. Estab. 1971. BMI. Published 150 songs in 1978; plans 200 in 1979. Pays standard royalty.
How to Contact: Submit demo tape or arrange personal interview. Prefers 7½ ips reel-to-reel or cassette with 1-5 songs on demo. Include resume with tape submissions. SASE. Reports in 1 month.
Music: Top 40/pop; R&B; C&W (progressive); disco; easy listening; and rock. Recently published "California Bly," recorded by California (rock); "Suite America," recorded by SAS (pop); and "No Blues Bay," recorded by Cardinali and Young (country rock).

SUNNY LANE MUSIC, INC., 105 Burk Dr., Oklahoma City OK 73115. (405)677-6448. General Manager: Sonny Lane. Music publisher, record company and record producer. ASCAP. See Country Classics Music for details.

SUNNYSLOPE MUSIC, INC., Box 6507, 2181 Victory Pkwy., Cincinnati OH 45206. (513)861-1500. President: Stan Hertzman. Music publisher. Estab. 1968. ASCAP. See Hal Bernard Enterprises for details.

SUNRISE MUSIC, 450 E. Beaumont Ave., St. Bruno, Quebec, Canada J3V 2R3. (514)653-7838. President: Christian Lefort. Music publisher and record company. Estab. 1967. CAPAC. See S.M.C.L. Productions for details.

SUNSHINE COUNTRY ENTERPRISES, INC., Box 31351, Dallas TX 75231. (214)690-8875. Producer: "The General." A&R: Mike Anthony. Music publisher and record company. Estab. 1970. BMI. Pays negotiable royalty.
How to Contact: Submit demo tape and lead sheet. Prefers 7½ ips reel-to-reel with 1-4 songs on demo. SASE. Reports in 1 month.
Music: C&W and gospel. Recently published "Baby, Baby, Why Do You Always?", recorded by Janet Sue (C&W); "Let a Fool Take a Bow," recorded by Billy Parker (C&W); and "Too Many Rainbows," recorded by Dick Hammonds (C&W).

SUPER MUSIC, Box 32, Willowdale, Ontario, Canada M2N 5S7. (416)495-1710. President: John C. Irvine. Music publisher, booking agency, management firm and record company. Estab. 1967. CAPAC. See Don Park Music for details.

SURE-FIRE MUSIC CO., INC., 60 Music Square W., Nashville TN 37203. (615)327-4635. Contact: Leslie Wilburn. Music publisher. BMI. Pays standard royalties.
How to Contact: Submit demo tape and lyric sheet. Accepts 7½ ips reel-to-reel only. SASE. Reports "as soon as possible."
Music: Bluegrass; C&W; MOR; and folk. Recently published "Statue of a Fool" (by Jan Crutchfield), recorded by Jack Greene/MCA Records; "Coal Miner's Daughter" (by Loretta Lynn), recorded by Loretta Lynn/MCA Records; and "Someone Before Me" (by Bob Hicks), recorded by the Wilburn Brothers/MCA Records.

SURPRISE, 82 St. Joseph Blvd. W., Montreal, Quebec, Canada H2T 2P4. (514)849-3776. President: Christopher J. Reed. Music publisher. Estab. 1974. CAPAC. See Intermede Musique for details.

SWEET POLLY MUSIC, Box 521, Newberry SC 29108. (803)276-0639. Studio Manager: Polly Davis. Producer: Hayne Davis. Music publisher and record producer. Estab. 1970. BMI. Published 30 songs in 1978; plans 40 in 1979. Pays 10-50% royalty.
How to Contact: Submit demo tape. Prefers 7½ ips reel-to-reel or cassette with 4-8 songs on demo. SASE. Reports in 2 weeks.
Music: C&W (contemporary); easy listening; MOR; rock; top 40/pop. Recently published "Thank You Lord" (by Ronnie Hayes), recorded by Sledgehammer/Mother Cleo Records; "She's Hell" (by Hayne Davis), recorded by Davis/Mother Cleo Records (pop/country); and "Goodbye Cry" (by Davis), recorded by Sugar and Spice/Mother Cleo Records (disco).

SUNNY LANE MUSIC, INC., 105 Burk Dr., Oklahoma City OK 73115. (405)677-6448. Affiliate: Country Classics Music Publishing (BMI). General Manager: Sonny Lane. Music publisher, record company and record producer. ASCAP.
Music: Church/religious; C&W; easy listening; gospel; MOR; and top 40/pop. Recently

published "One Teardrop Too Long" (by Yvonne DeVaney), recorded by Gary McCray/Compo Records (country); and "Ten Million and Two" and "I'm Just Fool Enough" (by DeVaney), recorded by Yvonne DeVaney/Compo Records (country). See Country Classics Music for submission details.

SWEET 'N LOW MUSIC, Box 504, Bonita CA 92002. President: Virginia Anderson. Music publisher, record company and record producer. BMI. See Madrid Music for details.

SWEET SWAMP MUSIC, The Gables, Halcott Rd., Fleischmanns NY 12430. (914)254-4565. President/General Manager: Barry Drake. Music publisher, booking agency, record company and management firm. Estab. 1970. BMI. Published 25 songs in 1978; plans 50 in 1979. Pays standard royalties.
How to Contact: Submit demo tape and lead sheet. Prefers cassette with 3-5 songs on demo. SASE. Reports in 1 month.
Music: Bluegrass; blues; C&W; easy listening; folk; MOR; progressive; rock (hard or country) and top 40/pop. Recently published "I Won't Be Reconstructed," "Troubadors" and "She's My Woman," recorded by Barry Drake (folk/rock/MOR).

SYNCHRON PUBLISHING CO., Box 2199, Vancouver, British Columbia, Canada V6B 3V7. (604)688-1820. President: John Rodney. Music publisher and record company. Estab. 1970. CAPAC. See Danboro Publishing for details.

SYSTEM FOR BARCLAY, System Four Artists, Ltd., 145 E. 82nd St., New York NY 10028. President: Stephen F. Johnson. Music publisher and management firm. Estab. 1976. See Mistral Music for details.

T.P. MUSIC PUBLISHING, North Country Faire Recording Co., 314 Clemow Ave., Ottawa, Ontario, Canada K1S 2B8. (613)234-6992. President: T. Peter Hern. Music publisher and record company. Estab. 1976. CAPAC. Published 10 songs in 1977; plans 30 in 1979. Pays 25-50% royalty.
How to Contact: Submit demo tape, arrange personal interview, or submit demo tape and lead sheet. Prefers 7½ ips quarter-track stereo reel-to-reel or cassette with 3-6 songs on demo. SAE and International Reply Coupons. Reports in 2 weeks.
Music: Disco; easy listening; and top 40/pop (progressive pop). Recently published "Happy Song," "I Can Smile," "Headed Home" and "Everyday I Wonder," recorded by Peter Hern (pop/MOR).
Tips: "We will act as a Canadian representative for an artist/singer/songwriter, and test and develop a market cooperatively."

TAGGIE MUSIC CO., c/o Gopam Enterprises, Inc., 11 Lakeside Dr., #13C-W, New York NY 10023. (212)724-6120. Managing Director: Laurie Goldstein. Music publisher. Estab. 1960. BMI. See Gopam Enterprises for details.

TAL MUSIC, INC., 16147 Littlefield, Detroit MI 48238. (313)863-9510. President: Edith Talley. Vice President A&R: Harold McKinney. Music publisher and record company. Estab. 1968. BMI. Pays 50-100% royalty.
How to Contact: Submit demo tape, arrange personal interview, submit demo tape and lead sheet or submit lead sheet. Prefers 7½ ips reel-to-reel or cassette. SASE. Reports "as soon as possible."
Music: Choral; church/religious; C&W; disco; easy listening; gospel; jazz; rock; soul; and top 40/pop. Recently published "Someone," recorded by Contrail (pop); "Since I Lost You," recorded by Little Maxine (soul); and "I Feel My Love Growing," recorded by Bobby U. Brown (soul).

TALL CORN PUBLISHING CO., Ozark Records, Inc., Box 242, Osage Beach MO 65065. (314)348-2270. General Manager: Harold L. Luick. Music publisher. Estab. 1971. BMI.
Music: Bluegrass; church/religious; C&W; easy listening; gospel; jazz; MOR; rock; and top 40/pop. Recently published "From a Home to a Tavern" (by William Maynard), recorded by Robbie Wittkowski (country); and "If We Have Faith" (by Judith Harden/K. Cooper), recorded by Linda Riley/Century Records (gospel). See Mid America Music for submission details.

TARANA MUSIC, GRT of Canada, Ltd., 3816 Victoria Park Ave., Toronto, Ontario, Canada. (416)497-2340. Director, Publishing Division: F. Davies. Music publisher and record company. Estab. 1969. CAPAC. See GRT of Canada for details.

TARKA MUSIC, 5112 Hollywood Blvd., Los Angeles CA 90027. Professional Managers: Gary Heaton, Eric Troff. BMI. See Skyhill Publishing for details.

TAURIPIN TUNES, Box 878, Sonoma CA 95476. (707)938-4060. Manager/Owner: Bruce Cohn. Music publisher and management firm. Estab. 1975. ASCAP. See Bruce Cohn Music for details.

TEAKBIRD, Box 6507, 2181 Victory Pkwy., Cincinnati OH 45206. (513)861-1500. President: Chris Jolly. Estab. 1968. ASCAP. See Hal Bernard Enterprises for details.

TELESPIN MUSIC, INC., Box 55, McLeon VA 22101. Vice President: Richard S. Mason. Music publisher. Estab. 1972. ASCAP. Published 2 songs in 1977. Pays standard royalty.
How to Contact: Submit demo tape and lead sheet. Prefers cassette, but 7½ ips reel-to-reel or 8-track cartridge acceptable. SASE. Reports in 1 month.
Music: Easy listening and MOR. "We prefer medium and uptempo songs that can be used for dancing." Recently published "Tramonte," recorded by the Phil Tate Orchestra (instrumental waltz); and "Telemark Tango," recorded by the Charles Barlow Orchestra (tango).

TELL DELL MUSIC, 14926 Ward, Detroit MI 48227. (313)863-9510. President: Edith Talley. Music publisher and record company. Estab. 1968. See Tal Music for details.

TEMPLETON MUSIC, Delaware Water Gap PA 18327. (717)476-0550. Director of Publications: Lewis M. Kirby Jr. Music publisher and record company. ASCAP. See Shawnee Press for details.

TEOC MUSIC, Woodshed Records, Ltd., Box 6312, Station F, Hamilton, Ontario, Canada L9C 6L9. (416)527-8721. President: David Essig. Music publisher and record company. Estab. 1972. PROCAN.
Music: Bluegrass; blues; C&W; folk; and jazz. See Peregrin Songs for submission details.

TERRACE MUSIC GROUP, Nashville TN 37203. (615)327-4871. Music publishing branch of Ovation Records. Director: Michael Kosser. Vice President, A&R: Brien Fisher.
How to Contact: Submit demo tape and lyric sheet to Kosser or Robert John Jones. Prefers 7½ ips reel-to-reel or cassette with 1-3 songs on demo.
Music: Country and pop. Recently published "Heaven's Just a Sin Away," recorded by the Kendalls; and "Old Flames Can't Hold a Candle To You," recorded by Joe Sun. Ovation country artists include the Kendalls, Joe Sun, the Cates and Sheila Andrews. Pop artists include Tantrum and Mark Gaddis, and disco artist, Cleveland Eaton.

TESSIES TUNES, 3422 Hopkins St., Nashville TN 37215. General Manager: Bobby Fischer. Music publisher. BMI.
Music: C&W and MOR. See Annie Over Music for submission details.

TEXTOR MUSIC, Box U, Hendersonville TN 37075. Owner: Bill Textor. Music publisher. Estab. 1977. BMI.
Music: Church/religious and gospel. See Angela Dawn Music for submission details.

THINK BIG MUSIC, 901 Kenilworth Rd., Montreal, Quebec, Canada H3R 2R5 (514)341-6721. Affiliate: Big Fuss Music (PROCAN). President: Leon Aronson. Music publisher, record company and record producer. Estab. 1975. CAPAC. Published 60 songs in 1978. Pays standard royalties.
How to Contact: Query or submit demo tape and lead sheet. Prefers 7½ ips reel-to-reel tape with 1-4 songs on demo. SAE and International Reply Coupons. Reports in 3 weeks.
Music: Disco; MOR; rock; and top 40/pop. Recently published "Sugar Daddy" (by Carlyle Miller), recorded by Patsy Gallant/Attic Records (top 40); "Lie to Myself" (by Marty Butler and Bob Bilyk), recorded by Butler/Wam Records (MOR/top 40); and "Nighty Night" (by Miller), recorded by the Insiders/Mercury Records (R&B).

THIRD SON MUSIC, 50 Holly Hill Lane, Greenwich CT 06830. (203)661-0707. Music publisher. See Cherry Lane Music for details. Does not accept unsolicited material.

THIRD STORY MUSIC, INC., 6430 Sunset Blvd., Suite 1500, Los Angeles CA 90028. (213)463-1151. President: Herb Cohen. Music publisher. BMI.
How to Contact: Submit demo tape and lyric sheet. Prefers cassette with 1-3 songs on demo. Does not return unsolicited material. Report in 2 weeks.

Music: Disco; R&B; rock; and top 40/pop. Recently published "Everybody's Talking," recorded by Fred Neale/Elektra Records; and "Hey Joe" and "Old 55," recorded by Tom Waits/Elektra Records.
Tips: "Send simple demos; nothing elaborate."

THREE KINGS MUSIC, Box 22088, Nashville TN 37202. President: Robby Roberson. Vice President: Jean Roberson. Music publisher. BMI. Pays standard royalties.
How to Contact: Submit demo tape or "call for interview. We accept interviews when we have time available." Prefers reel-to-reel. SASE. Reports in 1 month.
Music: Church/religious; C&W; easy listening; gospel; and MOR. Recently published "To Love Him" (by R. Roberson/Sandra Kelly), recorded by Jane Denim/Bluegrass Opra Records (country); and "Come Follow Me" and "I Am the Way" (by Tony Monaco), recorded by Vineyard Singers/3 Kings Records (Christian).

3 PM MUSIC CO., Damon Productions, Ltd., 6844 76th Ave., Edmonton, Alberta, Canada T6B 0A8. President: Garry McDonall. Music publisher and record company. Estab. 1969. CAPAC. See Pet-Mac Music for details.

3300 PUBLISHING, 3300 Warner Blvd., Burbank CA 91510. (213)846-9090. Affiliate: Sonheath Publishing (ASCAP). Contact: Ruth Latshaw. Music publisher and record company. Estab. 1958. BMI.
How to Contact: Submit demo tape. Prefers 7½ ips reel-to-reel or cassette. "Please include any information you feel is beneficial to the presentation of the material." SASE. Reports in 8 weeks.
Music: Bluegrass; blues; children's; choral; church/religious; C&W; disco; easy listening; folk; gospel; jazz; MOR; progressive; R&B; rock; soul; and top 40/pop.

TIDEWATER MUSIC CO., Box 4192, Huntsville AL 35803. (205)881-7976. Owner: George Wells. Music publisher and record company. Estab. 1971. BMI. Pays 2-10% royalty.
How to Contact: Submit demo tape and lyric sheet or arrange personal interview. Prefers 7½ ips reel-to-reel with 1-3 songs on demo. SASE. Reports in 1 month; "we report back on accepted material only."
Music: C&W; gospel; and MOR. Recently published "Greenie the Christmas Tree," recorded by the Regents (novelty song); "That Jesus Loves Me Feeling," recorded by the Kingsmen (gospel); and "Puppy Dogs," recorded by Barbara Leigh (MOR).

TIMELESS ENTERTAINMENT CORP., 160 E. 56th St., 11th Floor, New York NY 10022. (212)233-5949. President: Fred Bailin. Music publisher and record company. Estab. 1977. BMI and ASCAP. Published 25 songs in 1978. Pays standard royalties.
How to Contact: Submit demo tape and lead sheet.
Music: Disco; jazz; R&B; rock; soul; and top 40/pop.

THE TIMES SQUARE MUSIC PUBLICATIONS CO., 1619 Broadway, New York NY 10019. BMI. Currently overstocked with material.

TIMESPANN MUSIC, Box 23088, Nashville TN 37202. Music Editor: Morgan Lowry. Vice President/General Manager: Elwyn Raymer. Music publisher and record company. Estab. 1975. BMI. See Triune Music for details.

TITHONUS MUSIC, LTD., 1619 Broadway, New York NY 10019. President: Krzysztof Z. Purzycki. Music publisher. Estab. 1969. BMI. See Memnon, Ltd. for details.

TNEXA MUSIC, 700 W. Jackson St., Biloxi MS 39533. (601)374-1900. Producers: Doug Mays, Rusty Russum. Music publisher, booking agency and record company. Estab. 1970. BMI. See Axent, Ltd. for details.

TOGETHER WE STAND, 10220 Glade Ave., Chatsworth CA 91311. (213)341-2264. BMI. See Emandell Tunes for details.

TOM THUMB MUSIC CO., Whitney Bldg., Box 34485, Los Angeles CA 90034. President: Ruth White. Music publisher and record company. Estab. 1955. ASCAP. See Rhythms Productions for details.

TOM TOM PUBLISHING CO., Box 566, Massena NY 13662. (315)769-2448. Vice President: Thomas Gramuglia. Music publisher and record company. Estab. 1970. Pays standard royalty.

How to Contact: Submit demo tape. Prefers 7½ ips reel-to-reel with 1-12 songs on demo. SASE. Reports in 1 month.
Music: Bluegrass; children's; and rock (easy).

TOMAKE MUSIC CO., INC., 809 18th Ave. S., Nashville TN 37203. (615)327-3211. Owner: Pete Drake. Office Manager: Rose Trimble. Music publisher. Estab. 1961. ASCAP. See Window Music Publishing for details.

TOMCAT MUSIC PUBLISHING CO., 8 Music Square W., Nashville TN 37202. BMI. See Tree Publishing for details.

TOMPAUL MUSIC CO., 628 South St., Mount Airy NC 27030. (919)786-2865. Owner: Paul E. Johnson. Music publisher and record company. Estab. 1960. BMI. Published 50 songs in 1978; plans 70 in 1979. Pays standard royalities.
How to Contact: Submit demo tape and lead sheet. Prefers 7½ ips reel-to-reel with 3-5 songs on demo. SASE. Reports in 1 month.
Music: Bluegrass; church/religious; C&W; easy listening; folk; gospel; MOR; rock (country); soul; and top 40/pop. Recently published "Love Is a Lot to Understand" and "Bob Special" (by Bobby Lee Atkins), recorded by Bobby Lee Atkins/Stark Records (bluegrass); "How Many Times" (by Evans and Deatherage), recorded by the Nomads/Stark Records (top 40/pop); and "Not for Me" (by Evans and Deatherage), recorded by the Nomads/Hello Records (top 40/pop).

TOP DRAWER MUSIC, Box 8011, Mobile AL 36606. (205)343-3124. Owner: Milton L. Brown. Music publisher. BMI. Pays standard royalty.
How to Contact: Submit demo tape or submit demo tape and lead sheet. Prefers 7½ ips reel-to-reel or cassette with 3 songs on demo. "Tapes should be accompanied by either lead sheet or lyric sheet." SASE. Reports in 3 weeks.
Music: C&W; easy listening; MOR; and top 40/pop. Recently published "Empty Saddles," recorded by Marty Martin (C&W); "Jelly Belly," recorded by Tony Keen (pop); and "The Magic Word," recorded by Fraeda Wallace (pop).

TOPSAIL MUSIC (formerly Music Designers, Inc.), 1126 Boylston St., Boston MA 02123. (617)262-3546. Affiliate: Mutiny Music. International subpublisher: EMI Music. President: Fred Berk. Music publisher, recording company and production company. Estab. 1977. BMI. Published 12 songs in 1978; plans 30 in 1979. Pays standard royalties.
How to Contact: Submit demo tape or lead sheet. Prefers reel-to-reel or cassette with 1-6 songs on demo. SASE. Reports in 3 weeks.
Music: Children's; C&W; disco; folk; MOR; progressive; rock; soul; and top 40/pop. Recently published "Man Enough," recorded by No Slack (pop/R&B); "Why Don't We Love Each Other?", recorded by the Ellis Hall Group (pop/R&B); and "Breaker 1-9," recorded by the Back Bay Rhythm Section (disco).

TOUCH OF GOLD MUSIC, INC., 9220 Sunset Blvd., Los Angeles CA 90069. (213)278-8970. President: Dennis Lambert. Director of Publishing: Marsha Ingraham. Music publisher, record company and production company. Estab. 1968. BMI. See Lambert & Potter Music for details.

TOUCHDOWN MUSIC CO., 1201 16th Ave. S., Nashville TN 37212. (651)320-7287. President/Owner: Chuck Chellman. Music publisher and record producer. Estab. 1967. BMI. See Adventure Music for details.

RON TOWNSEND MUSIC, INC., 3588 Big Tree Ave., Memphis TN 38128. (901)525-2042. President: Ronald Townsend. Music publisher. Estab. 1972. BMI. See Natural Groove Music for details.

TRADITION MUSIC CO., 10341 San Pablo Ave., El Cerrito CA 94530. Affiliate: Hoolie Music (ASCAP). Contact: C. Strachwitz. Music publisher. BMI. Pays standard royalty.
How to Contact: Submit demo tape. "We only publish songs by writers who have material recorded on their own label or Arhoolie Records." Prefers 7½ ips reel-to-reel or cassette. Does not return unsolicited material.
Music: Folk. Recently published "I Feel Like I'm Fixin' to Die Rag," recorded by Joe McDonald (folk).

TRAITORS MUSIC, Box 966, La Mirada CA 90637. President: Ray Arnold. Music publisher. BMI. Pays on royalty basis.

How to Contact: Submit demo tape or submit lead sheet. Prefers reel-to-reel or cassette. Reports in 1 month.
Music: C&W and rock. Recently published "Meet Me on the Other Side of Town," recorded by Joe Gibson (C&W).

TRANSATLANTIC MUSIC, Box 64, Davis CA 95616. (916)758-2567. President: Fred de Rafols. Music publisher. Estab. 1975. BMI. Published 30 songs in 1977; plans 40-50 in 1979. Payment negotiable.
How to Contact: Submit demo tape and lead sheet. Prefers 7½ or 15 ips quarter- or half-track reel-to-reel or cassette with 2 songs on demo. SASE. Reports in 3 weeks.
Music: Top 40/pop; Latin; easy listening; international; rock; C&W; MOR; and soul. Recently published "Rain or Shine" and "Kick up a Storm," recorded by Squid (pop/rock); and "Cafe Cinema," recorded by Tennis (pop/Broadway).

TREE PUBLISHING CO., INC., 8 Music Square W., Nashville TN 37203. (615)327-3162. Affiliates: Cross Keys Publishing (ASCAP), Twittybird Music Publishing (BMI), Stallion Music (BMI), Uncanny Music (ASCAP), Warhawk Music (BMI), Tree/Harlan Howard Songs (BMI), Makamint Music (ASCAP), Makamillion Music (BMI), Double R Music (ASCAP), Charsy Music (BMI), Tomcat Music Publishing (BMI), Kentree Music (BMI) and Stairway Music (BMI). Chairman of the Board: Jack Stapp. President: Buddy Killen. Senior Vice President: Don Gant. Music publisher. Estab. 1951. Published 750-1,000 songs in 1978; plans 750-1,000 in 1979. Pays negotiable royalty.
How to Contact: Submit demo tape. Prefers 7½ ips reel-to-reel with 1-5 songs on demo. "Voice and guitar or piano accompaniment is sufficient. There is no need to have full orchestra or band on track. We just need to hear the words and melody clearly." SASE. Reports in 3 weeks.
Music: C&W; MOR; rock (hard or country); soul; and top 40/pop. Recently published "Mammas Don't Let Your Babies Grow up to Be Cowboys" (by Ed and Patsy Bruce), recorded by Willie Nelson and Waylon Jennings (country/pop); "Ain't Gonna Bump No More With No Big Fat Woman," recorded by Joe Tex (R&B); and "Sure As I'm Sittin' Here," recorded by Three Dog Night (pop).

TREE/HARLAN HOWARD SONGS, 8 Music Square W., Nashville TN 37203. See Tree Publishing for details.

TRICHAPPELL, 21 Music Circle E., Nashville TN 37203. SESAC. See Chappell Music for details.

TRIANGLE, 82 St. Joseph Blvd. W., Montreal, Quebec, Canada H2T 2P4. (514)849-3776. President: Christopher J. Reed. Music publisher. Estab. 1974. CAPAC. See Intermede Musique for details.

TRI-CIRCLE MUSIC, c/o Gopam Enterprises, Inc., 11 Riverside Dr., #13C-W, New York NY 10023. (212)724-6120. Managing Director: Laurie Goldstein. Music publisher. Estab. 1960. ASCAP. See Gopam Enterprises for details.

TRI-ENVOLVE MUSIC CO., Box 767, New York NY 10019. President: Eugene Frank. Vice President: R. O'Brien. Music publisher, record producer and management firm. Estab. 1970. SESAC. See Envolve Music Group for details.

TRIGON MUSIC, Box 23088, Nashville TN 37202. Music Editor: Morgan Lowry. Vice President/General Manager: Elwyn Raymer. Music publisher and record company. Estab. 1975. ASCAP. See Triune Music for details.

TRIO MUSIC, INC., 1619 Broadway, New York NY 10019. BMI. Currently overstocked with material.

TRIPLE H MUSIC, 11746 Goshen Ave., Suite 7, Los Angeles CA 90049. (213)479-6091. Affiliate: HHH Music (ASCAP). President: Hank Haldeman. Music publisher and record producer. Estab. 1977. BMI. Published 300 songs in 1978; plans 60 in 1979. Pays standard royalties.
How to Contact: Query. Prefers 7½ ips reel-to-reel tape with 1-4 songs on demo. SASE. Reports in 1 month.
Music: C&W; easy listening; MOR; rock; and top 40/pop. Recently published "Watchin' the River Run," recorded by Pat Boone.

TRIPLE O SONGS, INC., Roadshow Music Group, 850 7th Ave., New York NY 10019. Vice President: Julie Lipsius. International Manager: Susan Reed. BMI. See Roadshow Music Group for details.

TRIUNE MUSIC, INC., Box 23088, Nashville TN 37202. Affiliates: Trigon Music (ASCAP) and Timespann Music (BMI). Music Editor: Morgan Lowry. Vice President/General Manager: Elwyn Raymer. Music publisher and record company. Estab. 1975. ASCAP. Published 70 songs in 1977; plans 100 in 1979. Pays 10% maximum royalty.
How to Contact: Submit demo tape and lead sheet. Prefers 7½ ips reel-to-reel or cassette with 1-3 songs on demo. SASE. Reports in 2 months.
Music: Children's; choral; church/religious; classical; and gospel. Recently published "Softly and Tenderly" and "The Journey," recorded by Cynthia Clawson; and "Holy Spirit, Breath of God," recorded by David Ford (all gospel/MOR).

TRUCKER MAN MUSIC, Centerline Rd., Cruz Bay, St. John, Virgin Islands 00830. (809)776-6814. Manager: Elroy Tatem. Music publisher, record company, record producer, management firm and booking agency. Estab. 1977. BMI. Published 16 songs in 1978; plans 20 in 1979, 50 in 1980. Pays standard royalties.
How to Contact: Submit demo tape and lead sheet, or submit lead sheet. Prefers cassette with 2-4 songs on demo. SASE. Reports in 3 weeks.
Music: Church/religious; disco; R&B; soul; and top 40/pop. Recently published "Winey Eva Mae," recorded by Kenrick Augustus/Trucker Man Records (calypso); "Time is Running Out," recorded by Glen Mason/Trucker Man Records (reggae); and "Dread High," recorded by Robert Francis/Trucker Man Records (calypso).

TRUE BLUE MUSIC PUBLISHING CO., 16027 Sunburst St., Sepulveda CA 91343. Owner: Larry Fotine. "We don't accept outside songs. Don't submit anything. Nothing will be returned if sent."

TRUE MUSIC, INC., 9902 Adams Ave., Cleveland OH 44108. (216)851-6087. President: William Spivery. General Manager: Michael Spivery. Music publisher. Estab. 1977. "For 1978 we have 20 split publishing deals going with affiliated companies." BMI. Pays 50-100% net royalty received.
How to Contact: Submit demo tape, submit demo tape and lead sheet or arrange personal interview. Prefers cassette with 3-6 songs on demo. SASE. Reports in 1 month.
Music: Blues; church/religious; C&W; disco; easy listening; folk; gospel; rock (hard or country); soul; and top 40/pop.

TRUSTY PUBLICATIONS, Rt. 1, Box 100, Nebo KY 42441. (502)249-3194. President: Elsie Childers. Music publisher and record company. BMI. Published 15 songs in 1978; plans 15 in 1979. Pays standard royalties.
How to Contact: Submit demo tape and lead sheet. Prefers 7½ ips reel-to-reel or cassette with 2-4 songs on demo. SASE. Reports in 1 month.
Music: Blues; church/religious; C&W; disco; easy listening; folk; gospel; MOR; soul; and top 40/pop. Recently published "Spring in Kentucky" (by Elsie Childers), recorded by Jamie Bowles/Master Records (MOR); "Look Whatcha Gone & Done" (by Childers), recorded by Tracy White/Master Records (disco); and "I'll Be Home Soon" (by Jamie Bowles), recorded by Bowles/Master Records (easy listening).

TUFF ENUFF MUSIC PUBLISHING, 5925 Kirby Dr., Suite 226, Houston TX 77005. (713)522-2713. Affiliate: BAS Music Publishing (ASCAP). Owner: Shelton Bissell. Music publisher, recording studio, arranger and record producer. Estab. 1964. BMI. Published 12 songs in 1978; plans 12 in 1979. Pays standard maximum royalty.
How to Contact: Arrange personal interview or submit demo tape and lead or lyric sheet. Prefers 7½ ips reel-to-reel with 1-4 songs on demo. "We prefer a rhythm section and vocal, but will listen to piano-vocal or guitar-vocal." SASE. Reports in 1 week.
Music: C&W; disco; soul; rock (country); and top 40/pop. Interested only in professionals (ASCAP or BMI members). "We are especially looking for hard country honkytonk, beer drinking songs. We need uptempo material." Recently published "Black Snow," recorded by Kool and Together (disco); "I Saw His Memory Cross Your Mind" and "I Ain't Playing With a Full Deck," recorded by Jo Dunn (C&W); and "Proud to Be a Kicker" and "Women's Lib," recorded by J.C. and the Moonshine Band (C&W).

TUMAC MUSIC & SHANDY GAFF MUSIC, 2097 Vistadale Ct., Trucker GA 30084.

(404)938-1210. Professional Manager: Phil McDaniel. General Manager: Joe McTamney. Music publisher and record company. Estab. 1974. ASCAP and BMI. Published 6 songs in 1978; plans 8-12 in 1979. Pays standard royalties.
How to Contact: Submit demo tape and lead or lyric sheet. Prefers cassette with 1-3 songs on demo. SASE. Reports in 3 weeks.
Music: Bluegrass; blues; C&W; disco; easy listening; MOR; R&B; rock (adult/country); top 40/pop; and R&B. Recently published "Shandy" and "Why Must I Be Lonely?", recorded by Peggy Stuart (easy listening/R&B); and "She Was a Fallen Angel" and "Share the Dream," recorded by Dan Buckley (C&W/easy listening).

TURBINE MUSIC, c/o Gopam Enterprises, Inc., 11 Lakeside Dr., #13C-W, New York NY 10023. (212)724-6120. Managing Director: Laurie Goldstein. Music publisher. Estab. 1960. BMI. See Gopam Enterprises for details.

TURKEY CREEK MUSIC CO., 1201 16th Ave. S., Nashville TN 37212. (615)320-7287. President/Owner: Chuck Chellman. Music publisher and record producer. Estab. 1967. BMI. See Adventure Music for details.

TWC MUSIC, TWC Entertainment Corp., Box 2021, New York NY 10001. (212)691-4565. Affiliate: Saddle Song Music (BMI). Manager: Walter Balderson. Music publisher and record company. Estab. 1974. SESAC. Published 12 songs in 1978. Pays standard royalties.
How to Contact: Submit demo tape and lead sheet. Prefers 7½ ips reel-to-reel with 1-5 songs on demo. Does not return unsolicited material. Reports in 2 weeks.
Music: C&W; folk; and gospel. Recently published "Mother and Dog," "You're Right" and "Nature of a Man," recorded by Tommy Blue (C&W).

20TH CENTURY FOX MUSIC PUBLISHING, 8544 Sunset Blvd. Los Angeles CA 90069. (213)657-8210. Affiliates: Fox Fanfare Music (BMI); Bregman, Vocco and Conn (ASCAP); Chatham Music (ASCAP); Lombardo Music (ASCAP); Supreme Music (ASCAP); and Vernan Music (ASCAP). President: Herb Eiseman. Director of Creative Activities: Ron Vance. Music publisher and record company. Estab. 1967. ASCAP. Published 100 songs in 1978. Secures some songwriters on salary basis. Payment negotiable.
How to Contact: Submit demo tape and lead sheet or lyric sheet. Prefers 7½ ips reel-to-reel or cassette with 1-2 songs on demo. SASE. Reports in 8 weeks.
Music: C&W; disco; easy listening; MOR; progressive; R&B; rock; soul; and top 40/pop. Recently published "The Wiz," recorded by Diana Ross; and "Star Wars," recorded by John Williams and the London Symphony.

22/22 MUSIC, 82 St. Joseph Blvd. W., Montreal, Quebec, Canada H2T 2P4. (514)849-3776. President: Christopher J. Reed. Music publisher. Estab. 1974. CAPAC. See Intermede Musique for details.

TWIN LIONS MUSIC PUBLISHING, 2024 S. Cooper St., Arlington TX 76010. Manager: Bill Stansell. Music publisher and record company. Estab. 1973. BMI. Published 2 songs in 1978; plans 10 in 1979, 20 in 1980. Pays standard royalties.
How to Contact: Query. Prefers cassette with 1 song on demo. SASE. Reports in 1 month.
Music: Children's; C&W; gospel; and novelty. Recently published "Broken Hearted Lovers," "Little Sunny Meeting Place" and "Words on Paper" (by Bill Stansell), recorded by Stansell/Stan Records (C&W).

TWINSONG MUSIC, INC., Box A-20, Lebanon TN 37087. (615)444-3753. ASCAP. Secretary/Treasurer: Orlene Johnson. Music publisher and record company. BMI. See Great Leawood Music for details.

TWINSONG MUSIC, INC., 3012 W. 84th St., Leawood KA 66206. (913)381-8165. Secretary/Treasurer: Orlene Johnson. Music publisher and record company. BMI. See Great Leawood Music for details.

TWITTYBIRD MUSIC PUBLISHING CO., 8 Music Square W., Nashville TN 37203. See Tree Publishing for details.

2 PLUS 2 MUSIC, Rt. 6, 906 Ashby Dr., Brentwood TN 37027. (615)244-9412. Manager: Ann M. Stuckey. Music publisher. Estab. 1967. ASCAP. See Stuckey Publishing for details.

TYMER MUSIC, Box 1669, Carlsbad CA 92008. (714)729-8406. Owner: Denny Tymer. Music

publisher. Estab. 1976. BMI. Plans 10-12 songs in 1978. Pays standard royalties. "We honor the AGAC contract."
How to Contact: Submit demo tape and lead sheet. Prefers 7½ ips reel-to-reel or cassette with 1-3 songs on demo. "Use leader between songs." SASE. Reports in 3 weeks.
Music: C&W; easy listening; MOR; and top 40/pop. Recently published "Blanket of Love," "We're Living in Harmony" and "Alone" (by Denny Tymer), recorded by Tymer/Wilwin Records (easy listening/country).

TYRENIC MUSIC CO., 903 Penn Circle Dr., #503A, King of Prussia PA 19406. (215)265-7569. Vice President: Tyrone Broxton. Music publisher and record company. Estab. 1973. BMI. Published 3 songs in 1978; plans 10 in 1979, 20 in 1980. Pays standard royalties.
How to Contact: Query, arrange personal interview, submit demo tape, or submit demo tape and lead sheet. Prefers cassette with 4-6 songs on demo. SASE. Reports in 1 month.
Music: Blues; children's; choral; classical; disco; easy listening; gospel; jazz; MOR; R&B; soul; and top 40/pop.

UFO MUSIC, 7720 Sunset Blvd., Los Angeles CA 90046. (213)851-1466. President: Lionel Conway. General Manager: Allan McDougall. Music publisher. ASCAP. See Island Music for details.

UNART MUSIC CORP., 6920 Sunset Blvd., Los Angeles CA 90028. (213)461-9141. Music publisher. BMI. See United Artists for details.

UNCLE JACK MUSIC CO., Box 128, Bono AR 72416. Owner: Larry D. Gillihan. Record company, music publisher and record producer. Estab. 1972. BMI. Pays standard royalties.
How to Contact: Query or submit demo tape and lyric sheet. Prefers reel-to-reel or cassette. SASE. Reports in 1 month.
Music: C&W; disco; gospel; MOR; and top 40/pop. Recently published "Poor Crazy Sally" (by Larry Donn), recorded by Jess Mobley/Americountry Records (country); "I Can't Get Her Face Out of My Mind" (by Donn), recorded by Larry Donn/Shelby Records (country); "The Sun Rose Over the Mountain" (by Bill Crook), recorded by Larry Donn/Shelby Records (country); and "Sittin' in the Bathroom" (by Donn), recorded by Gene Barnett/Wheel Records (country).

UNDER MT. PUBLISHING, R.D. 1, Box 161, Sheffield MA 01257. (413)229-2043. Manager: William Perry. Music publisher. Estab. 1974. BMI. Pays standard royalties.
How to Contact: Query. Prefers 7½ ips reel-to-reel with 2-4 songs on demo. SASE. Reports in 1 month.
Music: C&W and country gospel.

UNCANNY MUSIC, 8 Music Square W., Nashville TN 37203. See Tree Publishing for details.

UNICHAPPELL, 21 Music Circle E., Nashville TN 37203. BMI. See Chappell Music for details.

UNICHAPPELL MUSIC, 6255 Sunset Blvd., Los Angeles CA 90028. (213)469-5141. Music publisher. BMI. See Chappell Music for details.

UNITED ARTISTS MUSIC PUBLISHING GROUP, INC., 6920 Sunset Blvd., Los Angeles CA 90028. (213)461-9141. Affiliate: Unart Music (BMI). Professional Managers: Suzanne Logan, Danny Stric, Peter Pasternak. ASCAP.
How to Contact: Submit demo tape and lyric sheet. Prefers 7½ ips reel-to-reel. SASE. Reports in 1 month.
Music: C&W; disco; easy listening; folk; jazz; MOR; R&B; rock; soul; and top 40/pop.
Tips: "We will listen to simple vocal/instrumental demos, as long as they are clear and the lyric can be heard. Do not submit just sheet music."

UNITED ARTISTS MUSIC PUBLISHING, 729 7th Ave., New York NY 10019. Professional Manager: Stu Greenberg. Music publisher. ASCAP.
How to Contact: Submit demo tape and lyric sheets. Prefers 7½ ips reel-to-reel or cassette with 1-3 songs on demo. SASE. Reports in 6 weeks.
Music: Disco; MOR; R&B; rock; and top 40/pop.

UNIVERSOL, 82 St. Joseph Blvd. W., Montreal, Quebec, Canada H2T 2P4. (514)849-3776.

President: Christopher J. Reed. Music publisher. Estab. 1974. CAPAC. See Intermede Musique for details.

UPAM MUSIC CO., c/o Gopam Enterprises, Inc., 11 Lakeshore Dr., #13C-W, New York NY 10023. (212)724-6120. Managing Director: Laurie Goldstein. Music publisher. Estab. 1960. BMI. See Gopam Enterprises for details.

URSULA MUSIC, Dawn Productions, Cloud 40, Paradise PA 17562. Affiliates: Welz Music (ASCAP), Florentine Music (BMI) and Wynwood Music (BMI). President/A&R Director: Joey Welz. Music publisher, record company and booking agency. Estab. 1965. BMI. Published 12 songs in 1978; plans 12 in 1979. Pays standard royalitites.
How to Contact: Submit demo tape and lead sheet. Prefers 7½ ips reel-to-reel or cassette with 6-12 songs on demo. Does not return unsolicited material. "We hold until we need material for a session, then we search our files."
Music: C&W; disco; easy listening; folk; MOR; rock; and top 40/pop. Recently published "It's a Long Way From Country" and "We Should Be in Love," by Joey Welz/Music City Records; and "New Wave Blues" and "Rippenem off in the Name of Love," by the New Wave Comets/Disco Records.

UTOPIA MUSIC, INC., Box 5314, Macon GA 31208. President: Randy Howard. Music publisher and record company. Estab. 1972. ASCAP. Pays 25-75% royalty.
How to Contact: Submit demo tape. Prefers 7½ ips reel-to-reel with 1-4 songs on demo. SASE. Reports in 1 month.
Music: C&W (progressive); gospel (traditional); and rock (country). Recently published "God Don't Live in Nashville, Tennessee," recorded by Randy Howard; and "Leavin'," recorded by Stillriver (progressive C&W).

VAL D'ESPOIR, 82 St. Joseph Blvd. W., Montreal, Quebec, Canada H2T 2P4. (514)849-3776. President: Christopher J. Reed. Music publisher. Estab. 1974. CAPAC. See Intermede Musique for details.

VALGROUP MUSIC (USA) CO., 7033 Sunset Blvd., Suite 322, Los Angeles CA 90028. Affiliates: PBR Music (ASCAP), Valswift Music (BMI), Soft Music (BMI), Woodmont Music (BMI) and Great Power Music (BMI). General Manager: Maritta Boyle. Music publisher. BMI. Pays standard royalty.
How to Contact: Submit demo tape and lead sheet. Prefers cassette. SASE. Reports in 1 month.
Music: Pop; rock; MOR; and easy listening. Recently published "Come Hell or Waters High," recorded by Omaha Sheriff (pop); and "Fingers and Thumbs," recorded by Charlie Brown (pop).

VALLEYBROOK MUSIC, Arzee Recording Co., 3010 N. Front St., Philadelphia PA 19133. (215)739-7501. President: Bill Haley. General Managers: Rex Zario, Dave Wilson. Music publisher, booking agency and record company. Estab. 1950. ASCAP.
Music: Bluegrass; C&W; easy listening; folk; rock; and top 40/pop. See Arzee Music for submission details.

VALSWIFT MUSIC, 7033 Sunset Blvd., Suite 322, Los Angeles CA 90028. General Manager: Maritta Boyle. Music publisher. BMI. See Valgroup Music (USA) for details.

VECTOR MUSIC, 1107 18th Ave. S., Nashville TN 37212. (615)327-3818. Affiliate: Belton Music (ASCAP). Manager: Harry M. Warner. Music publisher. Estab. 1966. BMI. Pays standard royalties.
How to Contact: Submit demo tape and lead sheet. Prefers reel-to-reel tape or cassette with 6 songs maximum on demo. SASE. Reports in 1 month.
Music: C&W; easy listening; MOR; and country rock. Recently published "East Bound and Down" (by Dick Feller and Jerry Reed), recorded by Jerry Reed (country/pop); and "Ragamuffin Man" (by Stewart Harris), recorded by Donna Fargo (country).

VENT QUI VIRE, 82 St. Joseph Blvd. W., Montreal, Quebec, Canada H2T 2P4. (514)849-3776. President: Christopher J. Reed. Music publisher. Estab. 1974. CAPAC. See Intermede Musique for details.

VERNAN MUSIC CORP., 8544 Sunset Blvd., Los Angeles CA 90069. (213)657-8210. Director

─Songwriter's Market Close-Up─

"There's still room for more songwriters at the top, a lot of room for
songwriters at the bottom and good
money in the middle," says Don
Schlitz, writer of Grammy-winning,
"The Gambler." "I know people who
have never written a 'hit' song, only
mid-chart singles and album cuts.
None of their songs hit America in the
face like 'Blue Eyes Cryin' in the
Rain,' but they still make 20 to 30
thousand dollars a year." Yet, these
prospects for success shouldn't entice
you to quit your job in order to pursue
"the room at the top and the money
within." Even Schlitz didn't give up
the security of a job as a computer
operator until "just six months to the
day before I won the Grammy."

of Creative Activities: Ron Vance. Music publisher and record company. ASCAP. See 20th
Century Fox Music Publishing for details.

VERT PAYS, 82 St. Joseph Blvd. W., Montreal, Quebec, Canada H2T 2P4. (513)849-3776.
President: Christopher J. Reed. Music publisher. Estab. 1974. CAPAC. See Intermede
Musique for details.

VIBRATION MUSIC CO., Box 9726, West Gate Station, San Jose CA 95117. President: Dr.
John E. Morlan. Music publisher and record company. Estab. 1973. BMI. Pays negotiable
royalty.
How to Contact: Submit demo tape and lead sheet.

VIBRATIONS, 82 St. Joseph Blvd. W., Montreal, Quebec, Canada H2T 2P4. (514)849-3776.
President: Christopher J. Reed. Music publisher. Estab. 1974. CAPAC. See Intermede
Musique for details.

VICKSBURG MUSIC, 1700 Openwood St., Vicksburg MS 39180. (601)638-6647. President:
John Ferguson. Music publisher. Estab. 1975. BMI. Published 14 songs in 1978. Pays standard
royalties.
How to Contact: Submit demo tape and lead sheet. Prefers 7½ ips reel-to-reel or cassette with
1-3 songs on demo. SASE. Reports in 3 weeks.
Music: Blues; disco; gospel; R&B; rock; soul; and top 40/pop. Recently published "Dance for
Me" (by James Taylor), recorded by James Pane/GSP Records (soul); and "I'll Take Care of
You" (by Wynd Chymes), recorded by Wynd Chymes/GSP Records (soul).

VIGNETTE MUSIC, 200 W. 57th St., New York NY 10019. Vice President: Ted Eddy. Music
publisher. Estab. 1969. BMI. See Delightful Music for details.

VINSUN MUSIC CORP., 6430 Sunset Blvd., Suite 921, Los Angeles CA 90028. (213)461-3091.
Director of Creative Affairs: B. Ficks, 2 Music Circle S., Nashville TN 37203. Music publisher.
ASCAP. See Famous Music Corporation for details.

VOKES MUSIC PUBLISHING, Box 12, New Kensington PA 15068. (412)335-2775. President: Howard Vokes. Music publisher, record company, booking agency and promotion company. Estab. 1954. BMI. Published 15 songs in 1978. Pays 2½-4¢ royalty/song.
How to Contact: Submit demo tape and lead sheet. Prefers reel-to-reel, cassette or 8-track cartridge. SASE. Reports "a few days after receiving."
Music: Bluegrass; C&W; and gospel. Recently published "Your Kisses and Lies," "Keep Cool But Don't Freeze," "Judge of Hearts," "Born Without a Name," "I Was a Fool" and "Tomorrow Is My Last Day."

WALDEN MUSIC, 75 Rockefeller Plaza, New York NY 10019. (212)484-8406. Music publisher. BMI. See Cotillion Music for details.

WARHAWK MUSIC, 8 Music Square W., Nashville TN 37203. See Tree Publishing for details.

WARNER BROS., INC., 9200 Sunset Blvd., Suite 222, Los Angeles CA 90069. (213)273-3323. General Manager: Bob Stabile. Music publisher. ASCAP.
How to Contact: Submit demo tape, lead sheet and lyric sheet. Prefers 7½ ips reel-to-reel or cassette with 1-3 songs on demo. SASE. Reports in 2 months.
Music: Blues; C&W; disco; easy listening; jazz; MOR; progressive; R&B; rock; soul; and top 40/pop.
Tips: "Don't spend a lot of money or overproduce your demos."

WARNER BROS. MUSIC, 44 Music Square W., Nashville TN 37203. Doesn't consider outside material.

WASTE AWAY MUSIC, Box 3892, North Providence RI 02911. (401)331-5354. Affiliate: Deb Mi Music (ASCAP). Contact: Bill Goodman. Music publisher, record producer and management firm. Estab. 1978. BMI. Published 4 songs in 1978.
How to Contact: Query or submit demo tape and lead sheet. Prefers cassette with 2-4 songs on demo. SASE. Reports in 3 weeks.
Music: C&W; disco; easy listening; folk; jazz; progressive; R&B; rock; soul; and top 40/pop. Recently published "Make up Your Mind," recorded by Chariot and the Lady (R&B); "Somewhere Elvis Is Smiling" (by Jimmie Crane), recorded by Keith Bradford (C&W); and "Falling for You" (by Bill Goodman), recorded by Art Caraman (ballad).

WASU MUSIC, Box 1206, Plano TX 75074. President: Fred Watkins. Vice President: Frank Sutton. Music publisher and record company. Estab. 1976. BMI. Published 10 songs in 1978; plans 30 in 1979. Pays standard maximum royalty. Charges for some services: "If lead sheet has to be redone or revised, we charge whatever that costs."
How to Contact: Submit demo tape and lead sheet. Prefers 7½ ips reel-to-reel or cassette with 2-5 songs on demo. "No speeches. Be sure to send a list of the order of the songs and include name on tape. Submit as clear a tape as possible so the lyrics and melody can be understood." SASE. Reports in 2 month.
Music: Folk; rock (hard, soft or country—no acid); and musicals. Recently published "Echoes" (folk); and "Visions of Molly" (soft rock).

WATERTOONS MUSIC, The Cameron Organisation, Inc., 320 S. Waiola Ave., LaGrange IL 60525. (312)352-2026. Vice President/General Manager: Jean M. Cameron. Music publisher. Estab. 1977. BMI. See The Cameron Organisation for details.

WEATHERLY MUSIC, 1415 N. Hudson Ave., Hollywood CA 90028. Owner: Sam Weatherly. Music publisher, record company and production company. Estab. 1969. BMI. Published 60 songs in 1978; plans 100 in 1979. Pays 25-50% royalty. "Advance on some songs: $1-100." Sometimes secures songwriters on salary basis: Duties include "tailoring songs for particular artists. Staff writers receive $7,000-10,000 annually, or right of first refusal. All writers receive writers royalty and some receive advances on particular songs."
How to Contact: Submit demo tape or submit demo tape and lead sheet. Prefers 7½ ips quarter-track reel-to-reel copy with 1-3 songs on demo. SASE. Reports "as soon as possible."
Music: Blues (torch-type); C&W (soft or crossover); disco (vocal-oriented); easy listening; MOR; rock (pop); top 40/pop; and jazz (rock). "Singles-oriented material preferred." Recently published "Here's to a Very Nice Christmas" and "Christmas in L.A.," recorded by Jonathan Arthur (seasonal); and "Come the Dawn," recorded by Willie Weatherly (country-rock).

JOEL WEBSTER MUSIC, 1217 S. Ogden Dr., #1, Los Angeles CA 90019. (213)277-1197, 473-5639. Chief of Production: Lim Taylor. Director: Brenda Hasty. Music publisher and production company. Estab. 1972. BMI. See Fourth House Music Publishing for details.

WELBECK, ATV Music Corp., 1217 16th Ave. S., Nashville TN 37212. (615)327-2753. Professional Manager: Byron Hill. Music publisher. ASCAP.
Music: Bluegrass; C&W; disco; easy listening; folk; gospel; MOR; R&B; rock; soul; and top 40/pop. Recently published "Dance With Me Molly" (by Roger Bowling and Steve Tutsie), recorded by Hank Thompson/ABC Records (country). See ATV Music, Nashville TN office for submission details.

WELZ MUSIC, Dawn Productions, Cloud 40, Paradise PA 17562. President/A&R Director: Joey Welz. Music publisher. Estab. 1965. ASCAP. See Ursula Music listing for details.

WES MUSIC CO., Box 28609, Dallas TX 75228. (214)681-1548. President: Bobe Wes. Music publisher. Estab. 1977. ASCAP. See Bobe Wes Music for details.

BOBE WES MUSIC, Box 28609, Dallas TX 75228. (214)681-1548. Affiliate: Wes Music (ASCAP). President: Bobe Wes. Music publisher. Estab. 1956. BMI. Pays standard royalty.
How to Contact: Submit demo tape. Prefers 7½ ips reel-to-reel or cassette. "State if songs have been copyrighted and if you have previously assigned songs to someone else. Include titles, readable lyrics and your full name and address. Give the same information for your cowriter(s) if you have one. State if you are a member of BMI, ASCAP or SESAC. Lead sheets are not required." SASE. Reports in 2 weeks.
Music: Blues; C&W; disco; gospel; MOR; progressive; rock (hard or soft); soul; top 40/pop; polka; and Latin dance. Recently published "It Won't Seem Like Christmas (Without You)," recorded by Elvis Presley (pop/C&W); "You're Slipping Away From Me," recorded by Jim Reeves (C&W); and "Blue Memories" and "I Don't Know What I'm Doing," recorded by Dean Martin (pop/C&W).

WESJAC MUSIC, Box 743, 317 S. Church St., Lake City SC 29560. General Manager: W.R. Bragdton Jr. Music publisher and record company. Estab. 1972. BMI. Published 3 songs in 1977; plans 10 in 1979. Pays 5% royalty.
How to Contact: Submit demo tape and lead sheet or submit lead sheet. Prefers 7½ or 15 ips reel-to-reel with 2 songs minimum on tape. SASE. Reports in 1 month.
Music: Church/religious and gospel. Recently published "I'm Glad I Wasn't Made By Man" and "Every Now and Then," recorded by the Gospel Songbirds (gospel); and "I Can't Stop Loving God," recorded by the Traveling Four (gospel).

WESTERN HEAD MUSIC, Box 19, Bulverde TX 78163. 43(512)438-2465. Affiliate: Bruto Music (BMI). Vice President: Carol Meyer. Music publisher, record company, record producer and booking agency. Estab. 1971. ASCAP. Published 71 songs in 1978. Pays standard royalties.
How to Contact: Submit demo tape, submit demo tape and lead sheet, or submit acetate disc. Prefers 7½ ips reel-to-reel or cassette with 3-5 songs on demo. SASE. Reports in 2 weeks.
Music: Blues; C&W; jazz; progressive; and rock. Recently published "Meet Me in Seguin" (by Carol Meyer), recorded by Carol Meyer/Texas Record Co. (country); "Skylight" (by Jackie King), recorded by Jackie King/Texas Record Co. (jazz); and "Summertime" (by Steve Long), recorded by Steve Long Group/Texas Record Co. (rock).

WHEEZER MUSIC, 1701 Nichols Canyon Rd., Los Angeles CA 90046. President: Howard Bloch. Music publisher. Estab. 1974. ASCAP. Published 20 songs in 1978; plans 25 in 1979. Pays standary royalities.
How to Contact: Submit demo tape and lead or lyric sheet. Prefers 7½ ips reel-to-reel or cassette with 1-3 songs on demo. SASE. "I hold interesting material and then contact the writer. All others with envelopes are returned."
Music: C&W; MOR; rock (country); and top 40/pop. Recently published "Come Fill Your Cup Again," recorded by Barry Richards (MOR); "Here Comes Love," recorded by New Top Notes (MOR); and "Rainbow City," recorded by Tightrope (MOR).

WHITE CAT MUSIC, Box 3357, Shawnee KS 66203. (913)631-6060. Professional Manager: Frank Fara. Music publisher, record company, record producer and management firm. ASCAP. See Rocky Bell Music for details.

WHITE WAY MUSIC CO., 65 W. 55th St., New York NY 10019. Affiliates: Sally Music

(BMI) and Langley Music (BMI). President: Eddie White. Music publisher and record producer. Estab. 1948. ASCAP. Published 65 in 1978; 65 in 1979. Pays standard royalties.
How to Contact: Submit demo tape and lead sheet. Prefers cassette with 1-5 songs on demo. SASE. Reports in 2 weeks.
Music: Bluegrass; blues; church/religious; C&W; easy listening; folk; gospel; MOR; rock; soul; and top 40/pop. Recently published "Don't Take Pretty to the City," by Howdy Glenn (C&W).

WILD MUSIC, Wild Productions, 12135 Valley Spring Lane, Studio City CA 91604. Affiliate: Song Cycle (BMI). President: Christian Wilde. Music publisher and record producer. Estab. 1970. ASCAP. Published 12 songs in 1977; plans 25-30 in 1979. Pays standard royalty.
How to Contact: Submit demo tape or submit demo tape and lead sheet. Prefers 7½ ips quarter-track reel-to-reel or cassette with 1-4 songs on demo. SASE. Reports in 3 weeks.
Music: Church/religious (commercial); C&W (pop); disco; easy listening; folk; gospel; MOR; rock (light); soul; and top 40/pop. Recently published "Grover Henson," recorded by Bill Cosby (narrative/orchestra); "Soul Breeze," recorded by Ventures (instrumental); and "Which Way Home?", recorded by Tom Jones (top 40/pop).

WILHOS MUSIC PUBLISHING, Box 3443, Hollywood CA 90028. (213)291-0539. President: Willie E. Hoskins Jr. Music publisher and production company. Estab. 1966. BMI. Published 28 songs in 1978; plans 56 in 1979. Pays 33⅓-50% royalty.
How to Contact: Submit demo tape or submit demo tape and lead sheet. Prefers 7½ ips reel-to-reel or cassette with 2-5 songs on demo. SASE. Reports in 3 weeks.
Music: Soul and top 40/pop. Recently published "The Worm," "Dedicated" and "All About Me," recorded by La Tefu (soul).

WILJEX PUBLISHING, Suite 405, 49 Music Square W., Nashville TN 37203. (615)329-1944. Publishing Directors: Rex Peer, Esther Witt. Music publisher, record company and production company. Estab. 1976. ASCAP. See Con Brio Music for details.

WINDECOR MUSIC, Box 878, Sonoma CA 95476. (707)938-4060. Manager/Owner: Bruce Cohn. Music publisher and management firm. Estab. 1975. BMI. See Bruce Cohn Music for details.

WINDOW MUSIC PUBLISHING CO., INC., 809 18th Ave. S., Nashville TN 37203. (615)327-3211. Affiliates: Tomake Music (ASCAP), Speak Music (BMI) and Brushape Music (BMI). Office Manager: Rose Trimble. Music publisher. Estab. 1961. BMI. Pays standard royalities.
How to Contact: Submit demo tape and lead sheet. Prefers 7½ ips reel-to-reel with 3 songs minimum on tape. SASE. Reports in 1 month.
Music: C&W; easy listening; gospel; rock; and top 40/pop. Recently published "Just Get up and Close the Door," recorded by Johnny Rodriquez (C&W); "Let It Shine," recorded by Olivia Newton-John (pop); and "Everytime Two Fools Collide," recorded by Kenny Rogers and Dottie West (C&W/pop).

WINDSEA MUSIC, 50 Holly Hill Lane, Greenwich CT 06830. (203)661-0707. Music publisher. BMI. See Cherry Lane Music for details. "We do not accept unsolicited material."

WINDSTAR MUSIC, 50 Holly Hill Lane, Greenwich CT 06830. (203)661-0707. Music publisher. ASCAP. See Cherry Lane for details. "We do not accept unsolicited material."

R.P. WINKELMAN, Box 878, Sonoma CA 95476. (707)938-4060. Manager/Owner: Bruce Cohn. Music publisher and management firm. Estab. 1975. ASCAP. See Bruce Cohn Music for details.

WISHBONE MUSIC, 5112 Hollywood Blvd., Los Angeles CA 90027. Professional Managers: Gary Heaton, Eric Troff. ASCAP. See Skyhill Publishing for details.

WOODEN BEAR MUSIC, 9454 Wilshire Blvd., Suite 305, Beverly Hills CA 90212. (213)273-7020. Managing Editor: Randy Bash. Music publisher. Estab. 1976. ASCAP. See Big Heart Music for details.

WOODMONT MUSIC, 7033 Sunset Blvd., Suite 322, Los Angeles CA 90028. General Manager: Maritta Boyle. Music publisher. BMI. See Valgroup Music (USA) for details.

WOODRICH PUBLISHING CO., Rt. 1, Box 213, Rogersville AL 35652. (205)247-3983. President: Syble C. Richardson. Music publisher and recording studio. BMI. See Melster Music for details.

WOODRICH PUBLISHING CO., Box 38, Lexington AL 35648. (205)247-3983. Affiliate: Mernee Music (ASCAP). President: Woody Richardson. Music publisher and record company. Estab. 1959. BMI. Published 40 songs in 1977; plans 60 in 1979. Pays 10% royalty.
How to Contact: Submit demo tape. Prefers 7½ ips reel-to-reel or cassette with 2-4 songs on demo. SASE. Reports in 1 month.
Music: Bluegrass; blues; children's; choral; church/religious; C&W; easy listening; folk; gospel; jazz; MOR; progressive; rock; soul; and top 40/pop. Recently published "Daddy Come on In," recorded by Happy Goodman Family (gospel); "Sundown in Nashville," recorded by Carl and Pearl Butler (C&W); and "High on Bluegrass Music," recorded by Madison County Ramblers (bluegrass).

WORD MUSIC, INC., Box 1790, Waco TX 76703. Affiliates: The Rodeheaver (ASCAP), Dayspring (BMI) and The Norman Clayton Publishing Co. (SESAC). Music Editor: John Purifoy. Music publisher and record company. Estab. 1952. ASCAP.
How to Contact: Submit demo tape and lead sheet or submit acetate disc and lead sheet. Prefers 7½ ips reel-to-reel or cassette with 1-5 songs on demo. "Songs of a choral nature should be submitted to our publishing company." SASE. Reports in 1 month.
Music: Children's; choral; church/religious; and gospel. "All songs submitted to our publishing company should be a choral setting. Songs of a solo nature should be submitted to the A&R department of our record company."

WORLD WAR THREE MUSIC, 2212 4th Ave., Seattle WA 98121. (206)682-5278. Director, West Coast Operations: JoDee Omer. Music publisher. Estab. 1973. BMI. See Mighty Three Music, Seattle WA office, for details.

WYNWOOD MUSIC, Dawn Productions, Cloud 40, Paradise PA 17562. President: Dave Smith. A&R Director: Joey Welz. Music publisher. Estab. 1965. BMI. See Ursula Music for details.

Y.D., 82 St. Joseph Blvd. W., Montreal, Quebec, Canada H2T 2P4. (514)849-3776. President: Christopher J. Reed. Music publisher. Estab. 1974. CAPAC. See Intermede Musique for details.

YANITA MUSIC, 750 Kappock St., Riverdale NY 10463. (212)796-2490. President: P.J. Watts. Music publisher and management firm. Estab. 1975. BMI. See Capaquarius Publishing and Management for details.

YATAHEY MUSIC, Box 31819, Dallas TX 75231. (214)690-8875. Owner: Pat McKool. A&R Director: Mike Anthony. Music publisher and record company. Estab. 1974. BMI. Published 10 songs in 1977; plans 75 in 1979. Pays standard maximum royalty.
How to Contact: Submit demo tape and lead or lyric sheet. Prefers 7½ ips reel-to-reel with 1-4 songs on demo. SASE. Reports in 1 month.
Music: C&W and gospel. Recently published "If I Don't Love You (Why Do I Miss You Now?)" and "Hurt Me One More Time," recorded by Dugg Collins (C&W); and "Wild Life," recorded by Dale Noe (C&W).

YBARRA MUSIC, Box 665, Lemon Grove CA 92045. (714)462-6538. Owner: Dick Braun. Music publisher, booking agency and record company. Estab. 1959. ASCAP. Pays standard royalities.
How to Contact: Submit demo tape or submit lead sheet. Prefers cassette. "We're unable to return tapes that are not solicited." Reports in 1 month on solicited material.
Music: Easy listening; jazz; and big band. Recently published "San Diego," recorded by the D.B. Big Band (big band); "Shiftless Shuffle" and "Get Smart," recorded by the Bassoon Bugs (easy listening).

YELLOW DOG MUSIC, INC., 1619 Broadway, New York NY 10019. Professional Manager: Robert Bienstock. Currently overstocked with material.

YO YO MUSIC, Box 643, LaQuinta CA 92253. (714)564-4823. Affiliate: Startime Music (ASCAP). President: Fred Rice. Music publisher, record company and record producer. BMI.

Music: C&W; MOR; rock; and top 40/pop. Recently published "Monster Twist" (by Ross/Rice), recorded by Stan Ross/Warner Bros. Records (novelty); and "Shrimpenstein" (by Dormer/Teacher), recorded by Gene Moss/Startime Records (novelty). See Startime Music for submission details.

YOUNG IDEAS MUSIC, 3146 Arrowhead Dr., Hollywood CA 90068. (213)461-4756. Vice President: John J. Madara. Estab. 1975. Music publisher. ASCAP. See Double Diamond Music for details.

YOUNGWOOD MUSIC PUBLISHING, Porter-Soper Enterprises, 970 O'Brian Dr., Menlo Park CA 94025. (408)249-1143. President: Jeff Young. Music publisher and record company. Estab. 1974. BMI. Published 20 songs in 1978; plans 30 in 1979. Pays standard royalties. **How to Contact:** Arrange personal interview or submit demo tape and lead sheet. Prefers 7½ ips reel-to-reel or cassette with 1-5 songs on demo. Does not return unsolicited material. Reports in 1 month.
Music: Bluegrass; C&W; easy listening; MOR; rock (country); and top 40/pop.

REX ZARIO MUSIC, Arzee Recording Co., 3010 N. Front St., Philadelphia PA 19133. (215)739-7501. President: Rex Zario. General Manager: Dave Wilson. Music publisher, booking agency and record company. Estab. 1950. BMI. See Arzee Music for details.

ZAWINUL MUSIC, Gopam Enterprises, Inc., 11 Lakeside Dr., #13C-W, New York NY 10023. (212)724-6120. Managing Director: Laurie Goldstein. Music publisher. Estab. 1960. BMI. See Gopam Enterprises for details.

Throughout 1979, the editors and correspondents of *Songwriter's Market* contacted all important American and Canadian music publishers at least once—and in some cases, two or three times. Most major publishers responded to our information requests. Some, however, chose not to give us information. Publishers in the following list declined to give us information for one of the following reasons:
- They are not actively seeking material from songwriters.
- They *will* listen to material, but believe that they receive sufficient material without listing in *Songwriter's Market*.
- They are a branch office that concentrates on marketing or other business endeavors, and leaves song selection to branches in other cities.
- They work only with songwriters recommended to them from other sources.
- They are staffed with in-house songwriters.
- They don't have a staff large enough to handle the increased number of submissions a listing would create.
- They are concerned with copyright problems that might result if they publish a song similar to one they've reviewed and rejected.
- They have once listed with another songwriter directory and were deluged with inappropriate submissions.

Though many of the following firms will review material, we suggest that you not send demo tapes. Write a brief query letter describing your material and asking about the company's current submission policies. Always use a self-addressed, stamped envelope or post card for such queries (see "Proper Submission Methods" for details).

ABKO Music, Inc., 1700 Broadway, New York NY 10019.

April/Blackwood Music, Inc., 31 Music Square W., Nashville TN 37203.

ARC Music Corp., 110 E. 59th St., New York NY 10022.

Ariola America, Inc., (Interworld), 8671 Wilshire Blvd., Beverly Hills CA 90211.

ATV Music Corp., 115 E. 57th St., New York NY 10022.

Aunt Polly's Publishing Co., Box 12647, Nashville TN 37212.

Baby Chick, 1111 17th Ave. S., Nashville TN 37212.

Beechwood Music Corp., 1750 N. Vine St., Hollywood CA 90028

Bertram Music Publishing, 1358 N. La Brea Ave., Hollywood CA 90028.

Bicycle Music Co., (Stonebridge), 8756 Holloway Dr., Los Angeles CA 90069.

Buckhorn, 1007 17th Ave. S., Nashville TN 37212.

Burlington Music Corp., 539 W. 25th St., New York NY 10001.

Bushka Music, 1888 Century Park E., Los Angeles CA 90067.

Chrysalis, 9255 Sunset Blvd., Los Angeles CA 90069.

Clita Music Inc., 527 Madison Ave., Suite 317, New York NY 10022.

Martin Cohen, 6430 Sunset Blvd., Los Angeles CA 90028.

Combine Music Group, 35 Music Square E., Nashville TN 37203.

Crowbreck, 9200 Sunset Blvd., Suite 1000, Los Angeles CA 90069.

Deb Dave, Box 2154, Nashville TN 37214.

Delightful Music Co., 527 Madison Ave., Suite 317, New York NY 10022.

First Generation Music Co., 35 Music Square E., Nashville TN 37203.

Galleon Music Inc., 120 E. 56th St., New York NY 10022.

Al Gallico Music Corp., 120 E. 56th St., New York NY 10022.

Hello Darlin', 8 Music Square W., Nashville TN 37203.

House of Gold Music, Inc., Box 50338, Belle Meade Station, Nashville TN 37205.

Joelsongs, 1350 Avenue of the Americas, 23rd Floor, New York NY 10019.

Kamakazi Music Corp., 314 W. 71st St., New York NY 10023.

Don Kirshner Music, 9000 Sunset Blvd., Los Angeles CA 90069.

Klondike Enterprises, Ltd., 888 7th Avenue, New York NY 10019.

Maclen Music Inc., 6255 Sunset Blvd., Hollywood CA 90028.

Edward B. Marks Music Corp., 1790 Broadway, New York NY 10019.

Midsong Music International, Ltd., 1650 Broadway, New York NY 10019.

Ivan Mogul Music Corp., 40 E. 49th St., New York NY 10017.

Edwin H. Morris & Co., 39 W. 54th St., New York NY 10019.

MPL Communications, Inc., 40 John Eastman, Eastman & Eastman, 39 W. 54th St., New York NY 10019.

Music Mill Publishing, Inc., 1111-17 Ave. S., Nashville TN 37212.

Nick-O-Val Music, 332 W. 71st St., New York NY 10023.

Owepar Publishing Co., 811 18th Ave., S., Nashville TN 37203.

Peer-Southern Organization, 1740 Broadway, New York NY 10019.

Rondor, 1358 N. La Brea Ave., Hollywood CA 90028.

Sa-Vette, 25 W. 56th St., New York NY 10019.

Neil Sedaka Music Publishing, 1370

Avenue of the Americas, New York
NY 10019.

Segel & Goldman, Inc., Sunset Towers,
Suite 525, 9200 Sunset Blvd., Los
Angeles CA 90069.

Shade Tree Music Inc., 50 Music
Square W., Suite 300, Nashville TN
37203.

Paul Simon Music, 36 E. 61st St., New
York NY 10021.

Singletree Music Co., 815 18th Ave.
S., Nashville TN 37203.

P. Smith & S. Frank, 1610 N. Argyle,
Suite 112, Hollywood CA 90058.

Stygian Songs, 1358 N. La Brea Ave.,
Hollywood CA 90028.

United Artists Music, 729 7th Ave.,
New York NY 10019.

Velvet Apple Music, 4321 Esteswood
Dr., Nashville TN 37215.

Record Companies

"The songwriter is the heart to a record company," says Eugene Gold, president of N-M-I Productions. "Without him: no song."

Though record companies first turn to music publishers for new material, they often accept material from songwriters. Record companies want the best songs possible, and the source usually doesn't matter to them. Submitting your material to a record company is just one avenue into the recording business. A combination of submissions to publishers, independent producers *and* record companies is your best route. Musicians and groups should send material to producers and managers, in addition to record companies.

You'll encounter a different set of rules for each company with which you deal. Some like personal interviews, while others will refuse to see you even if you married the vice president's daughter.

In either case, your demonstration tape will do your talking for you. "Present your material in the most professional way possible," says Gary K. Buckley, president of Majega Records. "Send no more than three songs and provide a leadered 7½ ips reel-to-reel or cassette copy of the material. . . . Understand that record companies receive many such tapes and be patient in waiting for a reply. Be sure to enclose a self-addressed, stamped envelope if you want your material returned. Most important, don't be discouraged by rejection or criticism." Study the following listings for details of each company's submission policies.

In an accompanying letter, explain whether the songs are being submitted for consideration as material for another artist, or if you're seeking a recording contract. Many companies also like to know something about you or your group, so include a resume of your successes, reviews of your act and a synopsis of your background. If you're

promoting yourself as an act, "submit the best promotional package to sell the act," advises a representative of El Chicano Music. That's why Marla Banks of Janus Records recommends that groups get a manager—he will help you make a solid, professional presentation to a record company, and will also help in contractual matters.

"Your manager should now exactly what he wants so negotiations can begin," says Chrysalis Records' Thom Trumbo. "He should plan a marketing strategy. A company not only signs the artist, it signs the management, too."

When submitting your demo, include a legible lead sheet or a lyric sheet. A typed list of the song order is also helpful. The box containing your demo should be labeled with your name and address; including such a label on your tape is also advisable.

For the songwriter trying to place material, many record company people recommend that you keep your demos simple. Your song should have a definite "feel," but don't overproduce the demo because you should give the company's producer room to work with the song. A completed demo will tend to pigeonhole your songs. Vocal and piano or guitar accompaniment is basic to a demo.

Artists' demos should be more complex; A&R (artist and repertoire) people want to know how the group will sound on record.

Landing an artist's contract will be difficult. Record companies tend to concentrate on promoting already signed artists before signing new ones. "We have 24 acts," an MCA representative says. "We can't have 50." Recent cutbacks in the number of albums released also puts a damper on new artist signings.

Many record company people recommend using your talents as a songwriter first. Get your songs recorded by someone else (you'll get royalties) and use this to further your contacts in record company circles. "If one establishes oneself as a hit writer, it will be easy to become a hit artist with the right producer," says Stu Fine, manager of East Coast A&R for Polydor Records. Record company officials point to Mac Davis, Kris Kristofferson, Warren Zevon and various other artists as examples of artists who first established themselves as hit writers.

Independent producers note that songwriter/artists are in demand. The demand is definitely not for artists, says producer Walt Gollender. "The biggest need is for artist/writers, then *writers*. Everything begins with the song." Yet, serving both roles can be draining. "It is beneficial to be a writer/artist," says Gary Buckley, "but both areas demand expertise if you are to be successful. There are many writer/artists that would be more successful if they gave up one part or the other and devoted 100% of their efforts to the area they've chosen."

Before submitting anything, review your market. Seek a company that handles your type of act or song, says Thom Trumbo. If you have a disco act or song, don't waste your time with a progressive rock label. Go to a label that handles disco without overlapping any of its established acts. "Familiarize yourself with the company's product in order to tailor your writing to the specific needs of the company's artists and to the styles the company caters to," says one record company official. Yet, don't try too hard to tailor your material. For instance, "Don't worry about matching your songs with other artists," says Stu Fine. "Let the A&R people do that."

If you plan a personal visit to a music center like Los Angeles or New York, submit your demo tape and publicity material according to the instructions in the following lestings. Inform the company when you'll be in town and ask for an appointment. You will then have had some contact before arriving. The appointment should be made at the company's convenience. Some A&R people will refuse to see you if *you* try to dictate when they will set up the appointment.

Additional names and addresses can be found in *Billboard* magazine's *International Buyer's Guide*, though the guide contains no submission information.

A&M RECORDS, INC., 1416 N. La Brea, Hollywood CA 90028. (213)469-2411. Labels include Horizon Records. Record company. Estab. 1963. Released 100 singles and 72 albums in 1978; plans 100 singles and 72 albums in 1979. Works with musicians and songwriters on contract.
How to Contact: "Direct all material through a publisher." SASE.
Music: C&W; disco; easy listening; folk; jazz; MOR; progressive; R&B; rock; soul; and top 40/pop. Recently released *Pieces of Eight*, by Styx (LP); *Worlds Away*, by Pablo Cruse (LP); and *Brother to Brother*, by Gino Vanelli (LP).

A&M RECORDS, 595 Madison Ave., New York NY 10022. Labels include Horizon. National Director of A&R: Mark Spector. Record company.
How to Contact: Submit demo tape. Prefers reel-to-reel or cassette with 1-5 songs on demo. SASE. Reports in 1 month.
Music: Disco; jazz (crossover); progressive; R&B; rock; and top 40/pop. Recently released *Breakfast in America*, by Supertramp.

ALARM RECORDS, 3316 Line Ave., Shreveport LA 71104. (318)861-0569. President: Stewart Madison. Record company and music publisher. Estab. 1968. Released 12 singles and 1 album in 1977. Works with musicians and songwriters on contract. Pays negotiable royalty.
How to Contact: Arrange personal interview or submit demo tape and lead sheet. Prefers 7½ ips reel-to-reel or cassette with 4-6 songs on demo. SASE. Reports in 2 weeks.
Music: C&W; disco; soul; and top 40/pop. Recently released "Steal Away" and "Gonna Hate Myself," by Ted Taylor (R&B singles); and "I Still Have to Say Goodbye," by Reuben Bell (R&B single).

ℭ **ALEAR RECORDS**, Box 574, Sounds of Winchester, Winchester VA 22601. (703)667-9379.
Labels include Winchester Records and Real McCoy Records. Secretary: Bertha McCoy.
Record company, music publisher, record producer and recording studio. Estab. 1971.
Released 5 singles and 3 albums in 1978; plans 8 singles in 1979, 10 singles and 6 albums in
1980. Works with musicians and songwriters on contract; musicians on salary. Pays 2%
minimum royalty to artists.
How to Contact: Submit demo tape and lead sheet. Prefers 7½ ips reel-to-reel or cassette with
5-10 songs on demo. SASE. Reports in 1 month.
Music: Bluegrass; church/religious; C&W; folk; gospel; progressive; and rock. Recently
released "This Woman," by Gloria Jean Megee (country single); "Interstate 95," by David
Elliott (country single); and "Beertops and Teardrops," by Larry Sutphin (country single).

ALEGRE RECORDS, INC., 888 7th Ave., New York NY 10019. Labels include Alegre and
Fania. Director: Louis Ramirez. Record company. Estab. 1964. Released 40 singles and 30
albums in 1977. Works with musicians and songwriters on contract. Payment negotiable.
How to Contact: Submit demo tape and lead sheet. Prefers cassette with 4-10 songs on demo.
SASE. Reports in 3 weeks.
Music: Jazz; soul; and Latin. Recently released "Perdido," by the Alegre All Stars; (Latin/jazz
single); "Pa Bailar Na'Ma," by Dioris Valladares (Latin single); and "Ponce," by the
Neo-Rican Orchestra (salsa single).

ALMANAC RECORDS, Box 13661, Houston TX 77019. Labels include Almanac and Depth
Records. A&R Director: Mack McCormick. Record company and music publisher. Estab.
1965. Released 6 albums in 1978; plans 6 albums in 1979. Works with musicians on contract.
Pays 10% royalty to artists on contract; payment varies for songwriters.
How to Contact: Submit demo tape and lead sheet. Prefers cassette with 6 songs minimum on
demo. Does not return unsolicited material. Reports in 1 month.
Music: Blues; traditional songs; toasts; and spoken poems. "We're interested only in material
appropriate to presentation in documentary albums representing cultural traditions." Recently
released *Songs of Death & Tragedy*, by various artists; and *Texas Barrelhouse Piano*, by Robert
Shaw.

ALVA RECORDS, 3929 Kentucky Dr., Los Angeles CA 90068. (213)980-7501. Promotion
Director: Gloria Monroe. Owner: Eddie Gurren. Record company. Estab. 1972. Released 5
singles and 2 albums in 1977. Works with musicians on contract; songwriters on salary or
contract. Pays 6% royalty to artists on contract; 50% royalty to songwriters on contract.
How to Contact: Arrange personal interview or submit demo tape and lead sheet. Prefers 7½
ips reel-to-reel with 1-3 songs on demo. SASE. Reports in 1 month.
Music: C&W; disco; MOR; soul; and top 40/pop. Recently released "Turntable Lady," by
Larry Curtis (MOR single); "Really Got Me Goin'," by Brothers by Choice (soul single); and
"Touch and Go," by Darlene Valentine (C&W).

AMALGAMATED TULIP CORP., 117 W. Rockland Rd., Libertyville IL 60048.
(312)362-4060. Labels include Dharma Records. Director of Publishing and Administration:
Mary Chris. Record company and music publisher. Estab. 1969. Released 3 albums in 1977.
Works with musicians on salary or contract; songwriters on contract. Pays negotiable royalty to
artists and songwriters on contract. Buys some songs outright, "but not as a policy." Charges
for some services.
How to Contact: Submit demo tape. Prefers reel-to-reel or cassette with 2-5 songs on demo.
SASE. Reports in 1-3 months.
Music: Rock (progressive and easy listening) and top 40/pop. Recently released "Another Trip
to Earth," by Gabriel Bondage (progressive rock single); and *Corky Siegel*, by Corky Siegel
(folk LP).

AMERICAN COMMUNICATIONS INDUSTRIES, Box 1036, Milan IL 61264.
(309)793-1889. Labels include ACI, Collage, Rawood, VRA International and GTM Records.
A&R Director: Gary Unger. Record company and music publisher. Estab. 1975. Released 3
singles in 1977; plans 6-9 singles and 3 albums in 1979. Works with musicians on salary or
contract, songwriters on contract. Pays 10% royalty to artists on contract; 2-4% royalty to
songwriters on contract.
How to Contact: Submit demo tape and lead sheet. Prefers 7½ or 15 ips reel-to-reel with 2-4
songs on demo. SASE. Reports in 3 weeks.
Music: C&W (country rock); easy listening; progressive; rock (hard); and top 40/pop.

Recently released "Goodnight Jackie" and "Girl, Where Are you?", by Gary Unger (top 40/country rock singles); and "My Share of Love," by Judy McClary (C&W single).

AMERICAN MUSIC CORP., 123 Water St., Sauk City WI 53583. (604)437-8970. Labels include American, Cuca, Jolly Dutchman, Age of Aquarius, Sound Power and Night Owl Records. President: James Kirchstein. Record company and music publisher. Estab. 1961. Released 6 singles and 18 albums in 1977; plans 36 singles and 36 albums in 1979. Works with musicians and songwriters on contract. Pays 10% royalty to artists on contract; 50% royalty to songwriters on contract.
How to Contact: Submit demo tape. Prefers cassette with 2-20 songs on demo. SASE. Reports in 6 months.
Music: Bluegrass; folk; and ethnic. Recently released "Hupsadyna," by Styczynski (ethnic single); *Polka 76*, by Meisner (ethnic LP); and "Muleskinner Blues," by the Fendermen (rock single).

AMERICAN RECORDING CO., Box 1007, Williamston NC 27892. (919)792-5483. Labels include Joybell Records and American Records. Owner: William D. Lewis. Record company and music publisher. Released 1 single in 1978. Works with songwriters on contract. Pays standard royalties to songwriters on contract.
How to Contact: Submit demo tape and lead sheet. Prefers reel-to-reel with 1-3 songs on demo. SASE. Reports in 1 month.
Music: All types.

AMHERST RECORDS, 355 Harlem Rd., Buffalo NY 14224. (716)826-9560. Contact: Barbara Chinsky. Estab. 1975. Works with musicians/artists on contract.
How to Contact: Submit demo tape and lead sheet. Prefers 7½ ips reel-to-reel or cassette with 2-5 songs on demo. SASE. Reports in 1 month.
Music: Blues; disco; easy listening; folk; jazz (any type, preferably commercial); MOR; progressive; R&B; rock; soul; and top 40/pop. Recently released *Spyro Gyra*, by Spyro Gyra (jazz/rock fusion, LP); "Shaker Song" by Spyro Gyra (fusion single); *You're the Only Dancer*, by Jackie DeShannon (pop LP); and "Please Don't You Say Goodbye to Me," by Solomon Burke. (R&B single).

AMIRON MUSIC/AZTEC PRODUCTIONS, 20531 Plummer St., Chatsworth CA 91311. (213)998-0443. Labels include Dorn Records and Aztec Records. General Manager: A. Sullivan. Record company, booking agency and music publisher. Estab. 1968. Released 2 singles in 1978; plans 4 singles and 1 album in 1979. Works with musicians and songwriters on contract. Pays 10% maximum royalty to musicians on contract; 50% maximum royalty to songwriters on contract. Buys some material outright; payment negotiable.
How to Contact: Submit demo tape and lead sheet. Prefers 7½ ips reel-to-reel or cassette. SASE. Reports in 3 weeks.
Music: Bluegrass; blues; C&W; disco; easy listening; folk; gospel; jazz; MOR; rock ("no heavy metal"); and top 40/pop. Recently released "Blood from My Hand" and "It Feels Good," by Quicksand (R&B/disco singles), and "Act of Mercy" by Abraxas (top 40/pop single).
Tips: "Be sure the material has a hook; it should make people want to make love or fight."

ANSAP RECORDS, INC., 205 N. 20th St., Box 10612, Birmingham AL 35202. (205)252-8271. Labels include Ansap, Faith Gospel, Applause and Miracles. Talent Coordinator: Arabella Labarber. Record company. Estab. 1967. Published 10 singles in 1978; plans 15 singles in 1979. Works with musicians and songwriters on contract. Pays 12% royalty to artists on contract. Buys some material outright; pays $500 minimum/song.
How to Contact: Arrange personal interview or submit demo tape and lead sheet. Prefers 7½ ips reel-to-reel or cassette with 1-8 songs on demo. SASE. Reports in 1 month.
Music: Rock (hard or country); soul; and top 40/pop. Recently released "I Got the Place, If You Got the Time," by Allison (soul single).

ANTHEM RECORDS OF CANADA, Oak Manor, 12261 Yonge St., Box 1000, Oak Ridges, Ontario, Canada. (416)881-3212. Managing Director: Tom Berry. Promotion Director: Linda Emmerson. Record company. Estab. 1977. Released 5 singles and 3 albums in 1978; plans 5 singles and 4 albums in 1979. Works with musicians on contract. Pays 5-16% royalty to artists on contract.
How to Contact: Submit demo tape or arrange personal interview.

CHUCK ANTHONY MUSIC, INC., Box 2000, Holbrook NY 11741. (516)472-0900. Labels include CVR Records. President: Chuck Anthony. Record company, booking agency and music publisher. Estab. 1975. Released 4 singles and 3 albums in 1978; plans 4 singles and 6 albums in 1979. Works with musicians and songwriters on contract. Pays 9% royalty to artists on contract; 2½¢/song royalty to songwriters on contract.
How to Contact: Submit demo tape and lead sheet. Prefers cassette with 1-6 songs on demo. Does not return unsolicited material. Reports in 1 month "if we decide to use it."
Music: Disco and top 40/pop. Recently released "Oh, Baby," by Wayne Miran and Rush Release (top 40 single); "Disco Ranger," by Tangerine (disco single); "Girl From Ipanema," by Zakariah (disco single); and "Helplessly," by Wayne Miranda and Rush Release (disco single).

ANTIQUE-CATFISH RECORDS, Box 192, Pittsburg KS 66762. (316)231-6443. Labels include Antique and Catfish Records. President: Gene Strasser. Record company and music publisher. Estab. 1974. Released 4 singles and 1 album in 1977; plans 20 singles and 10 albums in 1979. Works with songwriters on contract. Payment negotiable.
How to Contact: Submit demo tape and lead sheet. Prefers 7½ ips reel-to-reel or cassette with 2 songs on demo. SASE. Reports "as soon as possible."
Music: Bluegrass; children's; C&W; disco; easy listening; folk; gospel; MOR; rock; soul; top 40/pop; and comedy. Recently released "Man on Page 602," by Zoot Fenster (comedy single); "Rope-a-Dope," by G. Strasser (comedy single); "Alabama Summershine," by Tony Teebo (pop single); and "Hey, Mister Santa," by Shawn Strasser (Christmas single).

AQUILA RECORDS, Box 600516, North Miami Beach FL 33160. (305)945-3738. Labels include Gil's Funny Records, U.K., and Laurel. Executive Director: J. Gilday. Record company, music publisher and record producer. Estab. 1950. Released 17 singles and 5 albums in 1978; plans 10 albums in 1979.
How to Contact: Submit demo tape and lead sheet. Prefers 7½ ips reel-to-reel tape with 2 songs on demo. "Please include simple piano vocal." SASE. Reports in 3 weeks.
Music: Disco; gospel; MOR; and top 40/pop.

ARBY RECORDS, Box 6687, Wheeling WV 26003. (614)758-5812. President: S.P. Tarpley. Record company. Estab. 1972. Released 4 singles and 2 albums in 1978. Works with musicians on contract. Pays 6% royalty to artists and songwriters on contract.
How to Contact: Submit demo tape. Prefers 7½ ips reel-to-reel with 2 songs minimum on tape. Does not return unsolicited material. Reports in 1 month.
Music: Bluegrass; blues; church/religious; C&W; easy listening; folk; gospel; MOR; and progressive. Recently released "Looks Like You're Going Anyway" and "The Next Time," by Patti Powell (country/MOR singles); and "Stranger on the Bridge," by George Elliott (C&W single).

ARGUS RECORD PRODUCTIONS, Box 58, Glendora NJ 08029. (609)939-0034. Labels include Argus and Record Room. General Manager: Eddie Jay Harris. Office Manager: Linda Holland. Record company. Estab. 1970.
How to Contact: Submit demo tape and lead sheet. Prefers 7½ ips reel-to-reel with 1-2 songs on demo. SASE. Does not return unsolicited material. Reports in 1 month.
Music: Children's; church/religious; disco; rock; and top 40/pop.

ARIOLA RECORDS, 8671 Wilshire Blvd., Beverly Hills CA 90211. (213)659-6530. A&R Director: Harvey Bruce. Record company. Estab. 1975. Works with musicians on contract. Payment negotiable to musicians on contract.
How to Contact: Submit demo tape. Prefers cassette with 4 songs on demo. SASE. Reports "as soon as possible."
Music: Disco; easy listening; MOR; progressive; rock; soul; and top 40/pop.

ARISTA RECORDS INC., 1888 Century Park E., Suite 1510, Los Angeles CA 90067. (213)553-1777. Labels include Buddha. A&R Directors: Bud Scoppa, Bob Ferden. Vice President: Larkin Arnold. Record company. Released 72 albums in 1978. Works with musicians on contract.
How to Contact: Submit demo tape. Prefers cassette. SASE. Reports "as soon as possible."
Music: Disco; easy listening; folk; jazz; MOR; progressive; R&B; rock (primarily); soul; and top 40/pop. Recently released *Greatest Hits*, recorded by Barry Manilow (MOR LP); *Disco Nights*, recorded by GQ (disco LP); and *Squeezing Out Sparks*, recorded by Graham Parker (rock LP).

Tip: "Minimum standards should be adhered to. Demos don't have to be fancy—just plainly understood."

ARISTA RECORDS INC., 6 W. 57th St., New York NY 10019. Contact: Bob Feiden. Record company. Works with musicians on contract.
How to Contact: Submit demo tape and lyric sheet. Prefers 7½ ips reel-to-reel or cassette with 1-4 songs on demo. SASE. Reports in 3 weeks.
Music: Blues; C&W; disco; easy listening; jazz; MOR; progressive; R&B; rock; soul; and top 40/pop. Recently released *Don't Cry Out Loud*, by Melissa Manchester (MOR LP); *Live*, by Barry Manilow (MOR LP); and *Disco Nights*, by GQ (disco LP).

ARTEMIS RECORDS, LTD., Box 110, Howard Beach NY 11414. (212)738-4806. President: John Giamundo. Record company and music publisher. Estab. 1976. Works with musicians and songwriters on contract. Payment negotiable.
How to Contact: Submit demo tape. Prefers 7½ or 15 ips reel-to-reel, or disc. SASE.
Music: Classical; disco; easy listening; folk; jazz; MOR; progressive; rock; soul; top 40/pop; and reggae.
Tips: "Send copyrighted material only. Enclose SASE of you wish us to return your product after review. We will not necessarily comment on unsolicited material."

ARZEE MUSIC CO., 3010 N. Front St., Philadelphia PA 19133. (215)739-7501. Labels include Arzee and Cowgirl Records. General Manager: Dave Wilson. President: Rex Zario. Record company, booking agency and music publisher. Estab. 1950. Released 25 singles in 1977; plans 50 singles in 1978, 100 singles in 1979. Works with musicians and songwriters on contract. Pays standard royalty to artists and songwriters on contract.
How to Contact: Submit demo tape and lead sheet. Prefers 7½ ips reel-to-reel or cassette with 5-10 songs on demo. SASE. Reports in 2 weeks.
Music: Bluegrass; blues; C&W; folk; and rock (hard or country). Recently released "Christmas in the Country," by Dick Thomas (C&W single) and "Within This Broken Heart of Mine," by Bill Haley (C&W single).

ASSOCIATED RECORDING COMPANIES, 2250 Bryn Mawr Ave., Philadelphia PA 19131. (215)477-7122. Labels include Pearl Harbor, Jaguar and Jenges Records. A&R Directors: Ted Brown, Leo Gaton. Administrator: Richard Jackson. Record company and music publisher. Estab. 1972. Released 8 singles and 8 albums in 1978; plans 8 singles and 6 albums in 1979, 8 singles and 8 albums in 1980. Works with musicians and songwriters on contract. Pays 6% royalty to artists on contract; 50% royalty to songwriters on contract.
How to Contact: Submit demo tape. Prefers 7½ ips reel-to-reel or cassette with 3-5 songs on demo. SASE. Reports in 2 weeks.
Music: Easy listening; MOR; soul; and top 40/pop. Recently released "It Takes Two," by Day One (R&B single); "Give Up," by Dream Merchants (R&B single); and "Do It to Death," by George Guess (top 40 single).

ATLANTIC RECORDING CORP., 9229 Sunset Blvd., Los Angeles CA 90069. (213)278-9230. Labels include Atco and Custom. Manager, Artists' Relations: Mike Friedman. Director of West Coast A&R: John Kaladner. Works with musicians on contract.
How to Contact: Submit demo tape. Prefers 7½ ips reel-to-reel or cassette with 3-5 songs on demo. SASE. Reports in 2 weeks.
Music: Bluegrass; blues; disco; easy listening; folk; jazz; MOR; progressive; R&B; rock; soul; and top 40/pop.

ATLANTIC RECORDS, 75 Rockefeller Plaza, New York NY 10019. Vice President/A&R Director: Jim Delehant. Needs vary; query about needs and submission policy.

AXENT RECORDS, Biloxi MS 39530. (601)436-3927. Labels include River Records. President: Marion Carpenter. Record company, music publisher and record producer. Estab. 1955. Released 2 singles in 1978; plans 8 singles and 2 albums in 1980. Works with songwriters on contract. Pays 5-8% royalty to artists on contract; statutory royalties to songwriters on contract. Sometimes buys material from songwriters outright; payment negotiable.
How to Contact: Query or submit demo tape. Prefers 7½ ips reel-to-reel or cassette with 1-4 songs on demo. SASE. Reports in 1 month.
Music: Bluegrass; blues; C&W; easy listening; folk; MOR; and top 40/pop. Recently released "Turtle Dove," by Leo Ladiner (country single); "Come Back to Me," by Ernie Chaffin (country single); and "Biloxi," by Marion Carpenter (dixieland jazz single).

AXENT & DOUG MAYS PRODUCTIONS, 700 W. Jackson, Biloxi MS 39533. (601)374-1900. Labels include Gulf Sound and Axent Records. President: Rusty Russum. A&R Director: Doug Mays. Record company, booking agency, music publisher and production company. Estab. 1970. Released 5 singles and 2 albums in 1977; plans 10 singles and 4 albums in 1978, 20 singles and 6 albums in 1979. Works with musicians and songwriters on salary or contract. Pays 3-5% royalty to artists on contract; 2-4% royalty to songwriters on contract. Charges for some services: "if they want to lease studio for independent productions."
How to Contact: Submit demo tape or arrange personal interview. Prefers 7½ ips reel-to-reel or cassette with 4-10 songs on demo. SASE. Reports "as soon as possible."
Music: Blues; choral; C&W; disco; easy listening; gospel; MOR; rock; soul; and top 40/pop. Recently released "I Can Feel the Rain," by Storm (rock single); "If You've Got Leavin' on Your Mind," by Patsy Mitchell (country single); and "Hangover Morning," by C.D. Morgan (country single).

LEN BAILEY PRODUCTIONS, INC., Box 1647, Grand Central Station, New York NY 10017. President: Lenny Bailey. Record company, production company, promotions firm and music publisher. Estab. 1979. Released 1 album and 6 singles in 1979; plans 3 albums and 12 singles in 1980, 5 albums and 20 singles in 1981. Pays standard royalties to artists and songwriters on contract.
How to Contact: Submit demo tape and lead sheet. Prefers cassette. Reports in 1 month.
Music: Disco; rock; soul; MOR; jazz; and top 40/pop. Recently released "Do It With Me," by the Lenny Bailey Orchestra (top 40/disco single); and "Everybody Let's Party," by Joe Rivers and the Lenny Bailey Orchestra (top 40/disco single).

BAL RECORDS, Box 369, La Canada CA 91011. (213)790-1242. President: Adrian Bal. Record company. Estab. 1965. Released 8 singles in 1978; plans 15 singles in 1979. Works with musicians and songwriters on contract. Pays 10% royalty to artists on contract; 50% royalty to songwriters on contract.
How to Contact: Submit demo tape and lead sheet. Prefers 7½ ips reel-to-reel or cassette with 1-3 songs on demo. SASE. Reports in 3 weeks.
Music: Children's; choral; church/religious; C&W; easy listening; gospel; MOR; rock; and top 40/pop. Recently released *Christmas Is Coming*, by Choral (children's LP); and "Bach & Forth—Part I & II" by Adrian Lee Bal with Lee Ritenour and Dave Crotwell (jazz rock single).

BALBOA RECORD CO., 16027 Sunburst St., Sepulveda CA 91343. Owner: Larry Fotine. "We don't accept outside songs. Don't submit anything. Nothing will be returned if sent."

BARLENMIR HOUSE MUSIC, INC., 413 City Island Ave., New York NY 10064. President: Barry L. Mirenburg. Creative Director: Leonard Steffan. Estab. 1972. Record company, music publisher and book publisher.
How to Contact: Query. SASE. Reports in 1 month.
Music: Creative.

BEAU-JIM RECORDS, INC., Box 758, Lake Jackson TX 77566. (713)393-1703. President: James E. "Buddy" Hooper. Record company. Estab. 1972. Released 8 singles in 1978. Works with musicians on salary or contract; songwriters on contract. Payment negotiable.
How to Contact: Submit demo tape and lead sheet or arrange personal interview. Prefers cassette with 1-5 songs on demo. SASE. Reports in 3 weeks.
Music: Blues; C&W; easy listening; MOR; rock (soft); and top 40/pop. Recently released "Feelings," by Berry Kaye (easy listening single).

BEAVERWOOD RECORDING STUDIO, 133 Walton Ferry Rd., Hendersonville TN 37075. (615)824-2820. Labels include Ka$h Records and JCL (Jesus Christ is Lord) Records. Owner/Manager: Clyde Beavers. Record company, music publisher, management firm and booking agency. Estab. 1969. Released 15 singles and 20 albums in 1978. Works with musicians on salary or contract; songwriters on contract.
How to Contact: Query, arrange personal interview, submit demo tape, or submit demo tape and lead sheet. Prefers reel-to-reel or cassette with 1-5 songs on demo. SASE.
Music: Bluegrass; blues; children's; choral; church/religious; classical; C&W; disco; folk; gospel; jazz; MOR; opera; polka; progressive; rock; soul; and top 40/pop. Recently released "Crutches," by Darnell Miller (country); and "My Friend's Friend," by Clyde Beavers (country).

BEMA MUSIC CO., 28001 Chagrin Blvd., Suite 205, Cleveland OH 44122. (216)464-5990.

Labels include Sweet City and Midwest Records. "Sweet City is a custom label on Epic Records." Professional Manager: Gary Doberstyn. Record company, music publisher, concert promoter and management firm. Estab. 1966. Released 8 singles and 3 albums in 1977; plans 15 singles and 7 albums in 1979. Works with musicians and songwriters on contract. Pays negotiable royalty to artists on contract; offers "standard contract" to songwriters.
How to Contact: Submit demo tape and lead sheet. Prefers 7½ or 15 ips reel-to-reel or cassette with 1-5 songs on demo. Does not return unsolicited material. Reports in 3 weeks.
Music: Easy listening; jazz; MOR; progressive; rock; soul (funky); top 40/pop; and novelty. Recently release "Play That Funky Music" and "I Love My Music," by Wild Cherry (funky/top 40 singles); and "Dancin' Man," by Q (top/40 single).

BIG MIKE MUSIC, 408 W. 115th St., New York NY 10025. (212)222-8715. Labels include Right On! and Big Mike Records. Manager: Bill Downs. Record company and music publisher. Estab. 1959. Released 12 singles in 1978. Works with musicians and songwriters on contract. Pays standard royalty to artists and songwriters on contract.
How to Contact: Submit demo tape and lead sheet. Prefers cassette with 2-4 songs on demo. SASE. Reports in 1 month.
Music: Disco and soul. Recently released "Because of You," by A.C. Soulful Symphony (disco single); "Dance with Me," by Chris Bartley (disco single); and "Mandingo," by P.G.&P. (disco single).

BIG SOUND RECORDS, INC., Box 9, 10 George St., Wallingford CT 06492. (203)269-4465. Labels include Big Sound, Simple and Miracle Records. General Manager/Publisher: Theodore Fantazia. Record company, music publisher and recording studio. Estab. 1977. Released 1 single and 3 albums in 1978; plans 10 albums in 1979, 10 albums in 1980. Works with musicians and songwriters on contract. Payment varies for artists on contract; pays standard royalty to songwriters on contract.
How to Contact: Submit demo tape. Prefers cassette with 2-6 songs on demo. "Supply prepaid postage and packet if tape is to be returned. If not, it will eventually be destroyed." SASE. Reports in 1 month or less.
Music: MOR; progressive; rock; and top 40/pop. Recently released *RadioActive*, by Roger C. Reale and Rue Morgue (rock LP); *High 'n Inside*, by the Yankees (rock 'n roll); and "The Scratch Band," by BP and the Prix (single/Miracle Records).
Tips: "Submit a tape of various original tunes; send information and photo of self; and state purpose and main goal."

BLACK BEAR RECORDS, Drawer 887, Truro, Nova Scotia, Canada B2N 5G6. (902)895-9317. Manager: Rhoda Taylor. Record company, record producer and management firm. Estab. 1976. Released 3 albums in 1978; plans 8 singles and 7 albums in 1979. Works with musicians and songwriters on contract. Pays standard royalties to songwriters on contract.
How to Contact: Query or submit demo tape and lead sheet. Prefers 7½ or 15 ips reel-to-reel or cassette with whatever "the tape will hold with leader and separation. Please have the songs clearly titled and related to the lead sheets." SAE and International Reply Coupons. Reports in 2 weeks.
Music: Easy listening; gospel; MOR; rock; and top 40/pop. Recently released *The Pair Extraordinaire*, by the Pair (rock LP); *Solid Rock*, by the Gospel Sounds (gospel LP); and *Together Again*, by the Lincolns (rock LP).
Tips: "Submit material often and geared to the market we are reaching."

BLACKLAND MUSIC CO, Box 7349, Tulsa OK 74105. (918)663-1610. President: James Garland. Record company and music publisher. Estab. 1974. Released 4 singles and 2 albums in 1977; plans 4 singles and 2 albums in 1978, 4 singles and 2 albums in 1979. Works with musicians on salary or contract; songwriters on contract. Pays 5¢/record to artists on contract; 1¢/record to songwriters on contract.
How to Contact: Submit demo tape and lead sheet. Prefers 7½ ips reel-to-reel. SASE. Reports in 1 month.
Music: Gospel; MOR; rock (country); and top 40/pop. Recently released "Blue Skies and Roses," "I Wanna Love You" and *Karon*M*Live* by Karon Blackwell.

EUBIE BLAKE MUSIC, 284-A Stuyvesant Ave., Brooklyn NY 11221. Labels include E.B.M. Records. President: Carl Seltzer. Record company. Estab. 1972. Released 2 albums in 1978. Works with musicians on contract. Pays 5% royalty to artists on contract.
How to Contact: Submit demo tape. Prefers reel-to-reel with 2-4 songs on demo. SASE. Reports in 3 weeks.

Music: Blues; jazz; and ragtime. Recently released *Rags to Classics*, by Eubie Blake (piano solo LP).

BLUE ASH RECORDS, Kingsmill Recording Studio, 1033 Kingsmill Pkwy., Columbus OH 43229. (614)846-4494. President: Don Spangler. Record company and music publisher. Estab. 1974. Released 35 singles and 8 albums in 1978; plans 40 singles and 10 albums in 1979, 45 singles and 12 albums in 1980. Works with musicians on salary or contract; songwriters on contract. Payment negotiable.
How to Contact: Submit demo tape. Prefers 7½ ips reel-to-reel or cassette with 1-3 songs on demo. SASE. Reports in 2 weeks.
Music: Blues; C&W; disco; easy listening; jazz; MOR; progressive; rock; soul; and top 40/pop. Recently released *Continale' Disco*, by the Monacos (disco/jazz LP); "Let's Call it a Day," by Kent Darbyshire (pop single); "Juke Box Band," by W.R. Gas (rock single); and "On the Road," by Randy Clayton (country single).

BOLNIK MUSIC, 2124 Darby Dr. NW, Massillon OH 44646. (216)833-2061. Labels include Bold Records. President: Nick Boldi. Record company and music publisher. Estab. 1973. Released 3 singles in 1978. Works with musicians and songwriters on contract. Pays 4% royalty to artists on contract; 2% royalty to songwriters on contract.
How to Contact: Submit demo tape and lead sheet. "Send copyrighted material only." Prefers cassette with 3-8 songs on demo. Does not return unsolicited material. Reports in 1 month.
Music: C&W; disco; easy listening; MOR; rock (country or medium rock); and top 40/pop. Recently released "God Help You, Girl," by Dan-o-Ford (country/pop single); "Man in the Beaver Van," by Moon (country rock single); and "Magic of the Mind," by J. Holiday (MOR single).

BOOT RECORDS, LTD., 1343 Matheson Blvd. W., Mississauga, Ontario, Canada L4W 1R1. (416)625-2676. Labels include Boot, Cynda, Generation, Boot Master Concert Series and Boot International Records. General Manager: Peter Krytiuk. President: Jury Krytiuk. Record company. Estab. 1971. Released 50 singles and 27 albums in 1977; plans 50 singles and 40 albums in 1979. Works with musicians on contract. Pays negotiable royalty. Charges for some services: "We operate on a lease basis with the artist paying the cost of the session."
How to Contact: Submit demo tape. Prefers 7½ or 15 ips reel-to-reel or cassette with 3-6 songs on demo. "Prefer some originals and some standards." SASE. Reports in 1 week.
Music: Bluegrass; classical; C&W; disco; easy listening; folk; MOR; rock; and top 40/pop. Recently released *The Guitar*, by Liona Boyd (classical LP); *The Emeralds*, by the Emeralds (easy listening LP); and "Bud the Spud," by Stompin' Tom (C&W single).

BOUQUET RECORDS, Bouquet-Orchid Enterprises, Box 4220, Shreveport LA 71104. (318)686-7362. President: Bill Bohannon. Record company and music publisher. Estab. 1977. Released 3 singles in 1978; plans 4 singles and 2 albums in 1979, 4 singles and 2 albums in 1980. Works with musicians and songwriters on contract. Pays 5% royalty to artists on contract.
How to Contact: Submit demo tape and lead sheet. Prefers 7½ ips reel-to-reel or cassette with 3-5 songs on demo. SASE. Reports in 1 month.
Music: Church/religious (prefers country gospel); C&W (the type suitable for Loretta Lynn, Dolly Parton, Linda Ronstadt, etc.); and top 40/pop (the type suitable for John Denver, the Bee Gees, etc.).

BOYCE & POWERS MUSIC, 12015 Sherman Rd., North Hollywood CA 91605. (213)875-1711. President: Melvin Powers. Record company and music publisher. Estab. 1974. Released 12 singles in 1978; plans 12 singles in 1979, 12 singles in 1980. Works with songwriters on contract. Pays 10% royalty to songwriters on contract.
How to Contact: Submit demo tape and lyric sheet. Prefers cassette or disc with 3 songs minimum on demo. SASE. Reports in 1 month.
Music: C&W and MOR. Recently released "Who Wants a Slightly Used Woman?", by Connie Cato (country single); "Mr. Songwriter," by Sunday Sharpe (country single); and "Willie Burgundy," by Teresa Brewer (MOR single).

BOYD RECORDS, 2609 NW 36th St., Oklahoma City OK 73112. (405)942-0462. President: Bobby Boyd. Record company and music publisher. Estab. 1960. Plans 20 singles and 6-10 albums in 1979, 6-10 albums in 1980. Works with musicians and songwriters on contract. Payment negotiable.
How to Contact: Submit demo tape and lead sheet. Prefers 7½ ips reel-to-reel. "Do not send anything that has to be returned." Reports "as soon as I have a chance to listen."

Music: C&W; disco; rock; and soul. Recently released "Say You Love Me (One More Time)," by Dale Ward (C&W single); "There's No Way to Measure Love," by Dale Greear (C&W single); "Snap Your Fingers," by Debbie Smith (top 40 single); "One Teardrop at a Time," by Tina Camarillo (pop/C&W single); "Flip the Switch," by Cherie Greear; and "Legends Never Die," by Jim Whitaker (pop single).

BUCKSKIN RECORDS, 7800 Woodman Ave., 19A, Panorama City CA 91402. (213)786-3324. President: Jeff Wheat, Record company and music publisher. Estab. 1973. Released 2 singles and 1 album in 1978; plans 2 singles and 2 albums in 1979. Works with musicians on contract. Payment negotiable.
How to Contact: Submit demo tape. Prefers 7½ or 15 ips reel-to-reel or cassette with 4-6 songs on demo. SASE. Reports in 3 weeks.
Music: Folk; rock (hard, country or soft); and top 40/pop. Recently released "The Orb," by Bobby O'Brien (single); "Laugh with the Wind," by the Heard (single); and "Gotta Move," by October Young (single).

BUDDAH RECORDS, 1350 Avenue of the Americas, New York NY 10019. A&R Coordinator: Bill Kornreich. Record company. Released 20 singles and 15 albums in 1978; plans 20 singles and 15 albums in 1979. Works with musicians and songwriters on contract. Pays negotiable royalty.
How to Contact: "At this time we're not aggressively seeking new artists." Query and indicate state of material; primarily considers "finished" demos from artists. SASE. Reports in 2 weeks.
Music: Disco; jazz; progressive rock; R&B; rock; and top 40/pop. Recently released *Do it All*, by Michael Henderson (R&B LP); and *Come on Inside*, by Rena Scott (R&B LP).

CANTUS PRODUCTIONS, 66 Sherwood Ave., Toronto, Ontario, Canada. President: Milan Kymlicka. Record producer. Estab. 1973. Works with artists on contract. Pays negotiable royalties.
How to Contact: Submit demo or submit demo and lead sheet. Prefers 7½ ips reel-to-reel, cassette or disc with 1-4 songs on demo. SAE and International Reply Coupons. Reports in 1 month.
Music: Recently released "Roxanne," by Peter Foldy (pop single); "Make Me Your Baby," by Suzanne Stevens (pop single); *Love is the Only Game in Town*, by Stevens (pop LP); and "My Prayer," by Jackie Ritchardson (soul single).

CAPITOL RECORDS, INC., 1750 N. Vine St., Hollywood CA 90028. (213)462-6252. Labels include United Artists and Angel Records. Contact: Bruce Garheld. Record company. Released 170 singles in 1978. Works with musicians on contract.
How to Contact. Submit demo tape. Prefers 7½ ips reel-to-reel with 4-5 songs on demo. SASE. Reports in 3 months.
Music: Classical; C&W; disco; easy listening; jazz; MOR; progressive; R&B; rock; soul; and top 40/pop. Recently released *Fly Like an Eagle*, by Steve Miller (rock LP); *Stranger in Town*, by Bob Seger (rock LP); and *French Kiss*, by Bob Welch (rock LP).
Tips: "Have an agent, manager or publisher submit material for you and submit the best-quality demo you can afford."

CASABLANCA RECORD & FILM WORKS, 8255 Sunset Blvd., Los Angeles CA 90046. (213)650-8300. Labels include Rick's Music, Cafe Americana, Starrin, Grin, Skydiver and Combat Records. Contact: A&R Dept. Record company, music publisher and film company. Estab. 1974. Works with musicians and songwriters on contract. Payment negotiable.
How to Contact: Submit demo tape and lead sheet. Prefers cassette with 3-6 songs on demo. SASE. Reports "as soon as possible."
Music: Blues; disco; easy listening; MOR; progressive; rock (country, pop or soft rock); soul; and top 40/pop. Recently released "Rocket Ride," by Kiss (hard rock single); "Flashlight," by Parliament (R&B disco single); and "Take Me Home," by Cher (disco single).

CASTLE RECORDS, Box 1385, Merchantville NJ 08109. (609)663-4540. Labels include Pyramid Records, Jade Records, Rock Island Records and Camden Soul Records. Executive Vice President: R.F. Russon. Record company, music publisher, record producer, management firm and booking agency. Estab. 1966. Released 6 singles and 2 albums in 1978; plans 10 singles and 4 albums in 1979, 10 singles and 4 albums in 1980. Works with musicians and songwriters on contract. Pays 4-6% royalty to artists on contract; statutory royalties to songwriters on contract.
How to Contact: Query or submit demo tape and lead sheet. Prefers 7½ ips reel-to-reel or

cassette with 2-12 songs on demo. SASE. Reports in 1 month.
Music: C&W; disco; easy listening; jazz; MOR; rock; soul; and top 40/pop. Recently released
"Alabama Girl," by Big El (country rock single); *Big El in Concert*, by Big El and TCB Band
(rock LP); and "I'm Not Destined to Become a Loser," by Ellingtons (disco single).

CBS RECORDS, INC., 1801 Century Park W., Los Angeles CA 90067. (213)556-4700. Labels
include Columbia, EPA, Epic and Portrait. Contact: A&R Department. Record company.
Works with musicians and songwriters on contract.
How to Contact: Submit demo tape and lead sheet. Prefers cassette with 1-3 songs on demo.
SASE. Reports in 1 month.
Music: Blues; C&W; disco; easy listening; folk; jazz; MOR; progressive; R&B; rock; soul;
and top 40/pop. Recently released *52nd Street*, by Billy Joel (LP); *Greatest Hits Vol. II*, by
Barbra Streisand (LP); and *Greatest Hits*, by Earth, Wind and Fire (LP).
Tips: "Piano with vocal is totally sufficient. The simpler the better."

CELESTIAL RECORDS RELEASING CORP., 1560 N. La Brea, Box 1563, Hollywood CA
90028. Labels include Creative Records. President: Art Benson. Record company, music
publisher, record producer and management firm. Estab. 1952. Released 25 singles and 6
albums in 1978; plans 25 singles and 6 albums in 1979, 25 singles and 6 albums in 1980. Works
with musicians and songwriters on contract; musicians on salary. Pays 3-7% royalty to artists
on contract; standard royalties to songwriters on contract.
How to Contact: Query or submit demo tape and lead sheet. "If singer, also submit picture of
self or group." Prefers reel-to-reel or cassette with 1-3 songs on demo. SASE. Reports in 1
month.
Music: Bluegrass; blues; C&W; disco; easy listening; gospel; jazz; and MOR. Recently
released "Love Exchange," by Sonny Craver (R&B single); "I'll Sing the Blues," by Tommy
Cooper (C&W single); *Country Dreaming*, by Cooper (C&W LP); and *20th Century Oz*, (movie
score LP).

CHAPMAN RECORDS, 228 W. 5th St., Kansas City MO 64105. (816)842-6854. Owner:
Chuck Chapman. Record company and music publisher. Estab. 1973. Released 6 singles and 3
albums in 1978; plans 15 singles and 5 albums in 1979. Works with musicians on contract. Pays
negotiable royalty. Charges for some services: "We charge for recording services for music that
we don't publish."
How to Contact: Submit demo tape. Prefers cassette with 3 songs minimum on tape. SASE.
Reports in 1 month.
Music: Bluegrass; choral; church/religious; classical; C&W; disco; easy listening; folk; gospel;
jazz; MOR; progressive; rock; soul; and top 40/pop. Recently released "It's Your Heart
Tonight" by the Secrets (rock single)); and "Shark" and "Brown Eyes" by Gary Charlson (rock
singles).

CHARADE RECORDS, 1310 E. Kern St., Tulare CA 93274. (209)686-2533. Labels include
Charade Records and Tadarab Records. President: Raymond A. Baradat. A&R Director: Art
Stewart. Record company and music publisher. Estab. 1975. Released 4 singles and 2 albums
in 1978; plans 4 singles and 2 albums in 1979, 4 singles and 2 albums in 1980. Works with
musicians on salary or contract; songwriters on contract. Pays 4% royalty to artists on contract;
2% royalty to songwriters on contract. Charges for some services: "We own an 8-track studio
for demo work open to all. If we should be interested in an artist, other arrangements are
made."
How to Contact: Submit demo tape. Prefers 7½ ips reel-to-reel with 2-6 songs on demo. SASE.
Reports in 3 weeks.
Music: C&W; disco; jazz; rock (soft); soul; and top 40/pop. Recently released "I Believe in
Country Music," by Randie Coulter (country single); "Corruption," by the Charades (soul
single); and "I'm Only Me," by Arvada (soft rock single).

CHARTA RECORDS, 44 Music Square E., Nashville TN 37203. (615)255-2175. Labels
include Time Records. President: Charles Fields. Record company, music publisher and record
producer. Estab. 1977. Released 19 singles and 3 albums in 1978; plans 24 singles and 4
albums in 1979, 30 singles and 4 albums in 1980. Works with musicians and songwriters on
contract; musicians on salary. Pays 4-7% royalty to artists on contract; statutory royalties to
songwriters on contract.
How to Contact: Submit demo tape and lead sheet. Prefers 7½ ips reel-to-reel or cassette with
1-4 songs on demo. SASE. Reports in 2 weeks.

Music: Blues; C&W; easy listening; MOR; and top 40/pop. Recently released "Poor Side of Town," "See the Big Man Cry" and "Can't Shake You Off My Mind," by Bobby W. Loftis (country singles).

CHRISTY RECORDS, 726 Carlson Dr., Orlando FL 32804. (305)644-3853. Labels include Decade Records and Green Leaf Records. President: Will Campbell. Record company and music publisher. Estab. 1970. Released 5 singles and 2 albums in 1978; plans 10 singles and 5 albums in 1979. Works with musicians and songwriters on contract. Pays 25% royalty to artists and songwriters on contract.
How to Contact: Submit demo tape or submit demo tape and lead sheet. Prefers 7½ ips reel-to-reel with 3-6 songs on demo. SASE. Reports in 1 week.
Music: Bluegrass; church/religious; C&W; gospel; and MOR. Recently released "Don't I Know You?", by Don Rader (country single); "Homespun Mem'ries," by Nelson Young (bluegrass single); and "I Get Lonely," by Larada Collins (MOR single).

CHRYSALIS RECORDS, INC., 9255 Sunset Blvd., Los Angeles CA 90069. Assistant AR Manager: Thom Trumbo. Record company and music publisher. Released 35 in albums 1978; plans 40 albums in 1979. Works with musicians on contract; songwriters on salary or contract. Payment negotiable. Buys some material outright.
How to Contact: Submit demo tape. Prefers 7½ ips reel-to-reel or cassette with 3-4 songs on demo. Include photo and bio. SASE. Reports in 1 month.
Music: Disco; jazz; MOR; progressive; rock (general); and top 40/pop. Recently released *Bursting Out*, by Jethro Tull (progressive rock LP); *Head First*, by the Babys (rock LP); *Michel Colombier* (jazz LP); *Strangers in the Night*, by U.F.O. (rock LP); and *City Nights*, by Nick Gilder (top 40/pop LP).

CIN/KAY RECORD CO., 56 Music Square W., Nashville TN 37203. (615)244-3570. Labels include Cin/Kay, Music Square, White Dove and Hallelujah Records. Owner: Hal Freeman. Record company, booking agency and music publisher. Estab. 1975. Released 14 singles and 2 albums in 1977. Works with musicians and songwriters on salary or contract. Pays 6-8% royalty to artists on contract; 50% royalty to songwriters on contract.
How to Contact: Submit demo tape and lead sheet. Prefers 7½ ips reel-to-reel or cassette with 2-5 songs on demo. "Name, address and phone number should be on the tape reel." SASE. Reports in 2 weeks.
Music: C&W and gospel. Recently released "Burn Atlanta Down," by Bobby Barnett; "Little Teardrops," by Linda Cassady; and "Empty Whiskey Bottles," by Bobby Spears (C&W singles).

CLARK'S COUNTRY RECORDS, 2039 Cedarville Rd., Goshen OH 45122. (513)625-9469. Owner: Grace Clark. Record company and music publisher. Estab. 1973. Works with musicians and songwriters on contract.
How to Contact: Submit demo tape and lyric sheet. Prefers 7½ ips reel-to-reel, cassette or 8 track cartridge with 1-4 songs on demo. SASE. Reports "as soon as possible."
Music: Bluegrass; C&W; gospel; and country rock. Recently released "Little Teardrops," "I'm Not the Only Woman," "Our Man Elvis" and "Elvis is Still the King," by Linda Sue; "Love Has Died" and "Would She Do the Same to Me," by Danny Angel; and "It's All Over Now" and "What's the Matter Now," by "Pappy" Tipton.

CLAY PIGEON RECORDS, Box 20346, Chicago IL 60620. (312)476-2533. Labels include Clay Pigeon, Clay Pigeon International and Patefonas Records. President: V. Beleska. A&R Director: Rudy Markus. Record company. Estab. 1975. Released 3 singles and 2 albums in 1978; plans 5 singles and 5 albums in 1980. Works with musicians on salary or contract; songwriters on contract. "Royalties on records start at 2% of retail. All acts with us negotiate individually. Four percent is common. Royalties paid to publishers are often at 2¢ per selection, per record sold."
How to Contact: "Inquire by mail first, describing yourself and your material. We cannot consider any material without a written query." Prefers 7½ ips reel-to-reel, cassette or disc with 1-5 songs on demo. SASE. Reports in 2-8 weeks.
Music: Avant-garde; MOR; progressive; rock; and top 40/pop. Recently released "All for You" and "The Show Never Ends," by Christopher (rock singles); and *Tricentennial 2076*, by Vyto B (avant-garde LP).

CLOUD BURST RECORDS, Box 2066, Oshawa, Ontario, Canada L1H 7N2. (416)668-0754. President: George Petralia. Record company, music publisher, record producer and

─Songwriter's Market Close-Up─

The music industry demands higher-quality material than it did years ago, says Jerry Chestnut, who wrote "Another Place, Another Time." The days of album "fill"—that is, bad songs or cover versions of popular songs—are over. Record companies try to fill albums with as much commercial material as possible—therefore, songwriters should concentrate on writing commercial songs. Yet, as Chestnut points out, it isn't quite that simple. "No one knows what's commercial until it's out. If it sells, then it's commercial."

management firm. Estab. 1975. Released 2 singles and 1 album in 1978. Works with musicians and songwriters on contract. Pays 2% minimum royalty to artists on contract; statutory royalties to songwriters on contract.
How to Contact: Query, submit demo tape, or submit demo tape and lead sheet. Prefers 7½ ips reel-to-reel with 1-10 songs on demo. "Please also submit a typewritten copy of lyrics." SAE and International Reply Coupons. Reports in 1 month.
Music: C&W; easy listening; MOR; and top 40/pop. Recently released "Honestly I Love You," by Heather Haig (MOR/country single); "Come On Country," by Lance Younger (contemporary country single); and "I Can't Get Your Lovin," by Haig (country single).
Tips; "Any songs submitted to this company for consideration must be free of publishing with any other company; Cloud Burst Music wants sole publishing so that in the future if they want to work out a deal with another company, they have the rights to split the publishing."

CLUB OF SPADE RECORDS, Box 1771, Studio City CA 91604. (213)656-0574. Owner: Harvey Appell. Record company. Estab. 1976. Released 3 albums in 1978; plans 6 albums in 1979, 12 albums in 1980. Works with musicians on salary or contract; songwriters on contract. Pays 5% minimum royalty to artists and songwriters on contract.
How to Contact: Submit demo tape, arrange personal interview, or submit demo tape and lead sheet. Prefers 15 ips reel-to-reel or cassette with 10-20 songs on demo. SASE. Reports in 3 weeks.
Music: Bluegrass; C&W; and folk. Recently released *Mr. Music Vols. I, II and III*, recorded by Spade Cooley (C&W).
Tips: "We are mostly interested in oldies-but-goodies artists who have not recorded for many years but still have appeal."

COAT OF ARMS, Box 217, Oak Hill OH 45656. (614)682-7771. Labels include Gutbucket Records. President: D. Howell. Record company, music publisher, record producer and management firm. Estab. 1970. Plans 1 album in 1979, 1 album in 1980. Pays standard royalty to artists on contract; statutory royalties to songwriters on contract.
How to Contact: Query, submit demo tape, or submit demo tape and lead sheet. Prefers 7½ ips reel-to-reel or cassette with 1-3 songs on demo. Does not return unsolicited material. Reports in 2 weeks.
Music: Bluegrass; C&W; easy listening; MOR; and top 40/pop. Recently released "I Shall Be Released," by Paul Hanks (MOR/country single); "How You Gonna Stand It?", by Hanks (MOR/country single); and "Walkers Woods," by Mike Morgan (country single).

COMMERCIAL RECORD CORP., Box 40069, Nashville TN 37204. (615)385-3674. Labels include Commercial and CDC Records. Vice President/General Manager: Bob May. Record company. Estab. 1972. Released 3 singles and 1 album in 1977; 30 singles and 8 albums in 1979. Works with musicians and songwriters on salary and contract. Pays negotiable royalty to artists on contract; 1% royalty to songwriters on contract.
How to Contact: Submit demo tape or submit demo tape and lead sheet. Prefers 3¾ or 7½ ips

reel-to-reel with 1-12 songs on demo. SASE. "The composer should contact this office in about 2 weeks."

Music: Blues; C&W; easy listening; MOR; soul; and top 40/pop. Recently released "Let Me Be Your Friend" and "Just Out of Reach" (country/MOR singles), and *Lonely in the Crowd*, (country/MOR LP), by Mack White.

COMMUNICATION RECORDS, 7212 S. Wabash Ave., Chicago IL 60619. (312)783-3186. A&R Director: B.L. Dixon. Record company and music publisher. Estab. 1974. Plans 2 singles and 1 album in 1979, 3 singles and 1 album in 1980. Works with musicians on salary and contract; songwriters on contract. Pays union scale to artists on contract.
How to Contact: Submit demo tape, or submit demo tape and lead or lyric sheet. Prefers 1-4 songs on demo.

COMPO RECORD AND PUBLISHING CO., Box 15222, Oklahoma City OK 73115. (405)677-6448. President: Yvonne De Vaney. General Manager: Sonny Lane. Record company and music publisher. Estab. 1972. Released 4 singles and 1 album 1978; plans 4 singles and 2 albums in 1979. Works with musicians and songwriters on contract. Pays standard royalty to artists and songwriters on contract.
How to Contact: Submit demo tape and lead sheet. Prefers 7½ ips reel-to-reel with 4-8 songs on demo. SASE. Reports in 3 weeks.
Music: C&W; gospel; MOR; and top 40/pop. Recently released "Forever and One Day," by Yvonne De Vaney; and "Anything to Stop the Hurt," by Gary McCray (C&W singles).

COMSTOCK RECORDS, Box 3357, Shawnee KS 66203. (913)631-6060. Canadian distribution on Broadland Records. Production Manager: Frank Fara. Record company, music publisher, record producer and management firm. Estab. 1976. Released 4 singles and 1 album in 1978; plans 6 singles and 2 albums in 1979, 8 singles and 3 albums in 1980. Works with musicians and songwriters on contract; musicians on salary. Pays 2-5% royalty to artists on contract; statutory royalties to songwriters on contract.
How to Contact: Arrange personal interview or submit demo tape. Prefers cassette with 1-5 songs on demo. "Enclose stamped return envelope if cassette is to be returned." Reports in 2 weeks.
Music: C&W. Recently released "Four States to Go," by Alex Fraser (country single); "Help You Find a Way," by Patty Parker (MOR/country single); and "My Happiness," by Jon and Sondra Steele (pop/country single).

CON BRIO RECORDS, Suite 405, 49 Music Square W., Nashville TN 37203. (615)329-1944. Labels include Con Brio Records and Concorde Records. President/A&R Director: Bill Walker. Vice President, Operations: Jeff Walker. Vice President, Publishing: Rex Peer. Record company, music publisher and production company. Estab. 1976. Released 14 singles and 2 albums in 1977; 20 singles and 8 albums in 1979. Works with artists and songwriters on contract. Pays 4-5% royalty to artists on contract.
How to Contact: Submit demo tape and lead or lyric sheet. Prefers 7½ ips reel-to-reel or cassette with 1-3 songs on demo. SASE. Reports in 1 month.
Music: C&W; easy listening; MOR; and top 40/pop. Recently released "Don't Make No Promises (You Can't Keep)," by Don King (country/MOR single); and "Sweet Love Song the World Can Sing," by Dale McBride (C&W single).

CORD RECORDS, Box 7422, Shreveport LA 71107. Labels include Memorial, Faces, 50%, Pose and Summer Records. Owner: Don Logan. Record company. Estab. 1960. Released 6 singles and 3 albums in 1978. Works with musicians and songwriters on contract. Pays negotiable royalty to artists on contract; 1% royalty to songwriters on contract.
How to Contact: Submit demo tape. Prefers 7½ ips reel-to-reel with 2-4 songs on demo. SASE. Reports in 1 month.
Music: C&W; disco; gospel; soul; and spiritual. Recently released *Do You Believe in Disco?*, by Sam Benson (disco LP); *Live 'n Dirty*, by Sister Love (party LP); and *That's Alright*, by the Zion Jubilees (gospel LP).

COUNTERPART CREATIVE STUDIOS, 3744 Applegate Ave., Cincinnati OH 45211. (513)661-8810. President: Shad O'Shea. Record company, music publisher and jingle company. Works with musicians and songwriters on salary or contract. Pays 5% royalty to artists on contract; 2% royalty to songwriters on contract.
How to Contact: Submit demo tape. Prefers 7½ ips reel-to-reel with 1-2 songs on demo. SASE. Reports in 1 week.

Music: Bluegrass; blues; children's; choral; church/religious; classical; C&W; disco; easy listening; folk; gospel; jazz; MOR; progressive; rock; soul; and top 40/pop. Recently released "Jamie," by Blaize (pop/MOR single); "Colorado Call," by Shad O'Shea (novelty/C&W single); and "Easy Lovin' You," by Jerry Don Martin (C&W/pop single).

COUNTRY ARTISTS RECORDS, 103 Westview Ave., Valparaiso FL 32580. (904)678-7211. Labels include Circle Records and Minaret Records. Owner: Finley Duncan. Record company, music publisher and record producer. Estab. 1958. Released 6 singles in 1978; plans 10 singles in 1979. Works with musicians and songwriters on contract; musicians on salary. Pays standard royalty to artists on contract: 1¢/record sold royalty to songwriters.
How to Contact: Query, arrange personal interview, or submit demo tape and lead sheet. Prefers 7½ ips reel-to-reel tape with 5-10 songs on demo. "Send what you consider your best, and at least one of what you consider your worst." SASE. Reports in 1 week.
Music: C&W; disco; easy listening; MOR; R&B; rock; soul; and top 40/pop.

COUNTRY KITCHEN RECORDS, 13615 Pinerock, Houston TX 770979. (713)465-6199. A&R Coordinator: P. Breaz. Record company, music publisher and record producer. Estab. 1978. Released 2 singles and 2 albums in 1978; plans 2 singles and 2 albums in 1979, 4 singles and 6 albums in 1980. Works with musicians and songwriters on contract. Pays 5-10% royalty to artists on freelance contract: statutory royalties to songwriters on contract. Sometimes buys songs outright for $100-1,000/song.
How-To-Contact: Query, arrange personal interview, submit demo tape, or submit demo tape and lead sheet. Prefers 7½ ips reel-to-reel or cassette with 4-8 songs on demo. "Groups should include biography and photo; same for single artists." SASE. Reports in 2 weeks.
Music: Bluegrass; C&W; easy listening; folk; MOR; progressive; rock; and top 40/pop. Recently released *Cajun Melody* and *Tell Me You Love Me* by Hickory (country LPs); and "Arkansas" by Marcia Breaz (ballad bluegrass single).

COUNTRY ROAD, 1108 Gallatin Rd., Nashville TN 37206. Labels include Juliette Records and Cobra Records. Manager: Manford Harper. Record company, record producer, management firm and booking agency. Estab. 1971. Released 6 singles and 5 albums in 1978; plans 5 singles and 8 albums in 1979, 10 singles and 15 albums in 1980. Works with musicians and songwriters on contract. Pays 10% minimum royalty to artists on contract; statutory royalties to songwriters on contract.
How to Contact: Submit demo tape. Prefers 7½ ips reel-to-reel tape with 3 songs minimum on demo. SASE. Reports in 1 month.
Music: Bluegrass; church/religious; C&W; gospel; progressive; and rock. Recently released "I'll Remember," by the Stephenson Sisters (single); *My Kind of Country*, by Steve Honeycutt (LP); and *Loving You*, by Harold McLeod (LP).

COUNTRY SHOWCASE RECORDS AND PUBLISHERS, 11350 Baltimore Ave., Beltsville MD 20705. Labels include Country Showcase America. President: Frank Gosman. Record company and music publisher. Estab. 1970. Released 2 singles in 1977; plans 4 singles in 1978, 4 singles in 1979. Works with musicians and songwriters on contract. Pays 1½% royalty to artists and songwriters on contract.
How to Contact: Submit demo tape. Prefers 7½ or 15 ips reel-to-reel or cassette with 2 songs on demo. SASE. Reports in 2 weeks.
Music: Country (popular) and top 40/pop. Recently released "Mrs. Jones," by Don Drum ("sexy country"); and "I Love You" and "Sweet Yesterdays," by the Country Cavaliers (country duo singles).

COUNTRY STAR, INC., 439 Wiley Ave., Franklin PA 16323. (814)432-4633. Labels include Country Star Records, Process Records and Mersey Records. President: Norman Kelly. Record company, booking agency and music publisher. Estab. 1970. Released 24 singles and 12 albums in 1978. Works with musicians and songwriters on contract. Pays 5% royalty to artists on contract; 50% royalty to songwriters on contract.
How to Contact: Submit demo tape and lead sheet or arrange personal interview. Prefers 7½ ips reel-to-reel with 1-4 songs on demo. "We will accept 3¾ or 15 ips tape. Cassettes or 8-track cartridges are also acceptable." SASE. Reports in 2 weeks.
Music: Bluegrass; C&W; easy listening; gospel; MOR; rock ("soft, easy rock, like the Beatles"); and top 40/pop. Recently released "Prices Keep Going Up," by Gene Huddleston (Country Star Records); "Sweet Sack of Sugar" and "Hello Kate," by Virge Brown (Country Star Records); and "Rah! Pittsburgh Pirates" (Process Records).

CREATIVE SOUND, INC., Box 607, Malibu CA 90265. Labels include Sonrise and Creative Sound Records. President: Bob Cotterell. Record company. Estab. 1966. Released 20 albums in 1978; plans 20 albums in 1979. Works with musicians on contract. Payment varies.
How to Contact: Submit demo tape or submit demo tape and lead sheet. Prefers cassette or 8-track cartridge. SASE.
Music: "Contemporary Christian music. We're looking for good finished masters." Recently released "Evermore," by Love Song Strings; "Angel Food," by Mountain Angel Band; and "Finished Work," by Bob and Cindy Kilpatrick.

CRESCENDO RECORD CO., 3203 36th Ave., Long Island City NY 11106. President: Guido Sgambellone. Record company. Estab. 1950. Works with musicians on contract; songwriters on salary or contract. Pays 4% royalty to artists and songwriters on contract.
How to Contact: Submit demo tape. Prefers cassette with 2-3 songs on demo. SASE. Reports in 3 weeks.
Music: Easy listening and MOR. Recently released "Rose D'Altri Tempi," "Novelli," "Calabria," and *Middle of the Road* (LP), by Ugo Sarri.

CURTISS RECORDS, Box 4740, Nashville TN 37216. (615)361-5356. President: Wade Curtiss. Record company and producer. Estab. 1975. Released 6 singles and 2 albums in 1978; plans 10 singles and 3 albums in 1979, 20 singles and 5 albums in 1980. Works with musicians and songwriters on contract. Pays 8¢/record royalty to artists on contract; 2½¢/record royalty to songwriters on contract.
How to Contact: Submit demo tape and lead sheet. Prefers 7½ ips reel-to-reel with 2-8 songs on demo. SASE. Reports in 3 weeks.
Music: Bluegrass; blues; C&W; disco; folk; gospel; jazz; rock; soul; and top 40/pop. Recently released "Book of Matches," by Gary White; and "Rompin'" and "Punsky," by the Rhythm Rockers.

CURTOM RECORDS, 5915 N. Lincoln Ave., Chicago IL 60659. (312)769-4676. A&R Director: Clarice Polock. Record company, music publisher, record producer and management firm. Estab. 1967.
How to Contact: Query, submit demo tape, submit demo tape and lead sheet or submit lead sheet. Prefers 7½ ips reel-to-reel. SASE. Reports in 6 weeks.
Music: Disco; easy listening; progressive; R&B; rock; soul; and top 40/pop.

DANCE-A-THON RECORDS, Station K, Box 13584, Atlanta GA 30324. (404)872-0266. Labels include Banned, Hotlanta, Hottrax and Spectrum Stereo Records. President: Aleck Janoulis. Vice President/A&R Director: Oliver P. Cooper. Record company and music publisher. Estab. 1973. Released 10 singles and 2 albums in 1978; plans 12 singles and 4 albums in 1979, 12 singles and 4 albums in 1980. Works with musicians and songwriters on contract. Pays "3½-5% on 90% sold" to artists on contract; pays 2¾¢/song to publisher. Buys some material outright; pays $25-250. Publishing arm charges for some services: "If requested by letter, our publishing arm will evaluate a song and send the writer a written critique for a consultant's fee of $25 payable in advance."
How to Contact: Submit tape and lyric sheet. Prefers 7½ ips reel-to-reel or cassette with 1-3 songs on demo. Does not return unsolicited material.
Music: C&W; disco; easy listening; MOR; rock (punk and C&W); and top 40/pop. Recently released "Disco Rock," by Starfoxx (top 40 single); "Downtown Lady," by Schmaltz (MOR single); and "Oh Honey, Do I Look Funny to You?", by Alex James and the Texas Rhythm Rangers (C&W single).
Tips: "Demo tapes should be submitted with voice and either guitar or piano accompaniment only. A master should be sent only after a letter is submitted and replied to."

DAWN OF CREATION RECORDS, Box 452, Cambridge, Ontario, Canada N1R 5V5. (416)924-8121. President: Robert Liddell. Record company and music publisher. Estab. 1970. Works with musicians and songwriters on contract. Pays 5% royalty to artists on contract; 1¢/song royalty to songwriters on contract.
How to Contact: Submit demo tape or submit demo tape and lead sheet. Prefers cassette with 10 songs on demo. SAE and International Reply Coupons. Reports in 2 weeks.
Music: Children's; choral; church/religious; classical; easy listening; gospel; MOR; and top 40/pop.

DAWN PRODUCTIONS, Cloud 40, Paradise PA 17562. Labels include Bat, LeFevre, Canadian American Recordings, Grafitti, Music Machine, Music City, Palmer and Vermillion

Records. President: Joey Welz. Record company, booking agency and music publisher. Estab. 1965. Released 3 singles and 4 albums in 1978; plans 6 singles and 4 albums in 1979. Works with musicians and songwriters on contract. "We lease the record to a major label, who is responsible for paying the royalties."
How to Contact: Submit demo tape and lead sheet. Prefers 7½ ips reel-to-reel or cassette with 6-12 songs on demo. Does not return unsolicited material. "We hold it until we need material for a session, then we search our files."
Music: C&W; disco; easy listening; folk; MOR; rock; and top 40/pop.

DEDDY RECORDS, 100 S. Harrell, Madisonville TX 77864. Owner: T.F. Irby. General Manager: Dede Irby. Record company. Estab. 1977. Plans 2 singles in 1978 and 2 singles and 1 album in 1980. Works with musicians and songwriters on contract. Payment negotiable on accepted material.
How to Contact: Submit demo tape and lead sheet. Prefers 7½ ips reel-to-reel with 3-6 songs on demo. SASE. Reports in 1 month.
Music: C&W; country/pop; and bluegrass. Recently released "So Many Teardrops," by Country Road Express Band (C&W); and "I Don't Need You," by Country Road Express Band (country pop).

DELTA SOUND RECORDS, 814 W. Claiborne St., Box 672, Greenwood MS 38930. (601)453-3302. Labels include Cindy Boo. Owner: Mack Allen Smith. Record company and music publisher. Estab. 1967. Released 3 singles and 2 albums in 1978; plans 5 singles and 2 albums in 1979, 10 singles and 6 albums in 1980. Works with musicians and songwriters on contract. Pays 3-5% royalty to artists on contract; statutory royalties to songwriters on contract.
How to Contact: Submit demo tape and lead or lyric sheet. Prefers 7½ ips reel-to-reel or cassette with 1-5 songs on demo. "On reel-to-reel put leaders between songs and send typed or printed copy of words." SASE. Reports in 1 month.
Music: C&W; rock; and top 40/pop. Recently released "Carroll County Blues," by Mack Allen Smith (country single); and "Mean Ole Frisco," by Smith (country rock single).
Tips: "Submit songs that have strong lyrics with a good hook. I think a song should tell a story people can relate to.

DERBYTOWN RECORDS, 2061 Edgewood Dr., Charlestown IN 47111. (812)256-6183. A&R Director: Kenny Sowder. President: Brenda Sowder. Record company and music publisher. Estab. 1967. Released 1 single and 2 albums in 1977; plans 3 singles and 3 albums in 1979. Works with musicians and songwriters on contract. Pays 3-5% royalty to artists on contract; 2¢/song royalty to songwriters on contract. Buys some material outright.
How to Contact: Arrange personal interview or submit demo tape and lead sheet. Prefers 7½ ips reel-to-reel. SASE. Reports in 1 month.
Music: Bluegrass; C&W; and gospel. Recently released "Lonely Street," by Rex Allen Jr. (C&W single); and "To Keep from Dreaming," by Al Henderson (C&W single).

DIRECTION RECORDS, INC., 7250 Victoria Park Ave., Markham, Ontario, Canada. (416)495-0203. President: John J. Williams. Record company and music publisher. Estab. 1977. Released 42 singles and 7 albums in 1977. Works with musicians and songwriters on contract. Pays variable royalty. Buys some material outright; payment varies. Charges for some services.
How to Contact: Submit demo tape and lead sheet. Prefers 7½ ips half-track reel-to-reel or cassette. Include photo and bio. SAE and International Reply Coupons. Reports in 1 month.
Music: C&W; disco; folk; MOR; progressive; rock; and top 40/pop. Recently released "Magic Fly," by Kebekelektrik (disco single); "You Really Got Me," by Eclipse (rock/disco single); and *Gotham*, by Gotham (MOR/pop LP).

DOMINION BLUEGRASS RECORDINGS, Box 993, 211 E. 4th St., Salem VA 24153. (703)389-3190. Labels include Dominion and JRM Records. President: Rick Mullins. Vice President: Jack Mullins. Record company and music publisher. Estab. 1971. Released 4 singles and 7 albums in 1978; plans 6 singles and 10 albums in 1979, 6 singles and 12 albums in 1980. Works with musicians on salary and contract; songwriters on contract. Pays 5% royalty to artists on contract.
How to Contact: Submit demo tape and lead sheet. Prefers 7½ ips reel-to-reel with 1-12 songs on demo. SASE. Reports in 1 month.
Music: Bluegrass. Recently released *Virginia Where It Began*, by McPeak Brothers; *I Get High on Bluegrass*, by Jim Eanes; and *Bluegrass Western Swing Style*, by Burke Barbour and Troy Brammer (bluegrass LPs).

DOMINO RECORDS, 37 Odell Ave., Yonkers NY 10701. (914)969-5673. Vice President/General Manager: Joe Bollon. Record company. Estab. 1970. Works with musicians and songwriters on contract. Pays musicians' scale to artists on contract; Pays 2¢/single or 5¢/LP royalty to songwriters on contract. Buys some material outright; pays $50 minimum/song.
How to Contact: Submit demo tape and lead sheet. Prefers cassette or 45 rpm disc with 2-4 songs on demo. SASE. Reports in 2 weeks.
Music: Disco; easy listening; and MOR. Recently released "Give My Broken Heart a Break," "Old-Fashioned Baby" and "Say You Love Me," by Elsie Tucker (easy listening/pop singles).

DOMINO RECORDS, LTD., (fromerly Front Row Records), 222 Tulane St., Garland TX 75043. Labels include Front Row Records and Domino. Owner: D.E. Summers. Record company and music publisher. Estab. 1966. Released 5 singles and 2 albums in 1978; plans 6 singles and 5 albums in 1979 and 12 singles and 8 albums in 1980. Works with musicians and songwriters on contract. Pays 4% royalty to artists on contract; 50% royalty to songwriters on contract.
How to Contact: Prefers letter of introduction. Submit demo tape. Prefers only cassette or 8-track cartridge with 1-3 songs on demo. Does not return unsolicited material. SASE. Reports in 2 months.
Music: C&W; R&B; rock (soft); top 40/pop; and '50s material. Recently released "Southern Car Rocks On" ('50s rock single) and "Do Ya Think I'm Sexy?" by Gene Summers (C&W/MOR single); "Jimmy Carter Always Tells The Truth" (C&W/novelty single) and "A Beautiful Love Affair," by Joe Hardin Brown (C&W/MOR single)
Tips: "If you own masters of 1950s rock & roll-a-billy, contact us first! We will work with you on percentage basis for overseas release. We have active releases in Holland, Switzerland, Australia and England at the present. We need original masters. You must be able to prove ownership of tapes before we can accept and firm a deal. We're looking for little-known, obscure recordings."

DYNAMIC ARTISTS RECORDS, Box 25654, Richmond VA 23260. (804)282-6690. President: Joseph J. Carter Jr. Record company, music publisher, booking agency, management firm and production firm. Estab. 1976. Released 4 singles and 2 albums in 1978. Works with musicians on salary or contract; songwriters on contract. Pays 5% royalty to artists on contract.
How to Contact: Submit demo tape. Prefers 7½ ips reel-to-reel with 1-8 songs on demo. SASE. Reports in 2 weeks.
Music: Disco; rock; soul; and top 40/pop. Recently released "Out of the Ghetto" and "Almost Insane," by Starfire (singles).

E.L.J. RECORD CO., 1344 Waldron, St. Louis MO 63130. President: Eddie Johnson. Record company and music publisher. Estab. 1950. Released 6 singles and 2 albums in 1978; plans 12 singles and 3 albums in 1979, 12 singles and 3-4 albums in 1980.
How to Contact: Submit demo tape or submit demo tape and lead sheet. Prefers 7½ ips reel-to-reel or cassette with 4 songs on demo. SASE. Reports in 2 weeks.
Music: Blues; easy listening; soul; and top 40/pop. Recently released "Burning Flame of Love," by Tub Smith (single); "You Got Me," by the Eddie Johnson Trio (single); and *Jesus Knows*, by the Morning Star Church (LP).

EARWAX RECORDS, 226 Waysons Court, Lothian MD 20820. (301)627-5830. Labels include Bee Jay Records. President: Robert M. Johnson. Record company, music publisher and record producer. Estab. 1975. Released 1 single and 1 album in 1978; plans 2 albums in 1979, 2 singles in 1980. Works with musicians and songwriters on contract. Pays standard royalties to songwriters on contract.
How to Contact: Submit demo tape or submit acetate disc. Prefers 7½ or 15 ips reel-to-reel or cassette with 1-25 songs on demo. SASE. Reports in 1 month.
Music: Bluegrass; C&W; and rock. Recently released "A House Called Earth," by Ray Clauson (MOR/country); and "Rainy Days," by Clauson (MOR).

EDUCATOR RECORDS, INC., 1921 Walnut St., Philadelphia PA 19103. (215)561-1283. President: Cathleen O'Druyer. Musical Director: Bart Arntz. Record company and music publisher. Estab. 1976. Released 25 singles and 10 albums in 1978. Works with musicians on salary and contract; songwriters on contract. Pays negotiable royalty to artists on contract; standard royalty to songwriters on contract. Buys some material outright.
How to Contact: Submit demo tape. Prefers 7½ ips reel-to-reel or cassette with 3-8 songs on

demo. "Tape must be clearly audible. We are constantly seeking strong instrumentals of all types of music. We are also interested in license agreements on finished masters." SASE. Reports in 3 weeks.
Music: Children's (character songs); disco; soul; and show music of the '30s and '40s. "We are primarily a dance record company (tap, jazz and ballet). We also produce R&B material." Recently released *JoJo's Dance Factory*, by JoJo Smith (jazz dance LP); *Ballet in Colour*, by Don Farnworth (ballet instruction LP); and *Ron Daniels Makes You Feel Like Dancin'*, by Ron Daniels (tap dance LP).

EL CHICANO MUSIC, 20531 Plummer St., Chatsworth CA 91311. (213)998-0443. Labels include Dorn Records and Aztec Records. A&R Director: A. Sullivan. Record company, music publisher and booking agency. Estab. 1969. Released 2 singles in 1978; plans 4 singles and 1 album in 1979. Works with musicians and songwriters on contract. Payment negotiable.
How to Contact: Submit demo tape and lead sheet. Prefers 7½ ips reel-to-reel or cassette. SASE. Reports in 3 weeks.
Music: Bluegrass; blues; C&W; disco; easy listening; jazz; MOR; progressive; rock; soul; and top 40/pop. Recently released "Blood From My Hand" (R&B single) and "It Feels Good" (rock single), by Quicksand.

ELEKTRA/ASYLUM/NONESUCH RECORDS, 962 N. La Cienega Blvd., Los Angeles CA 90046. Head of A&R: Stephen Barncaro. Needs vary; query about needs and submission policy.

ELEKTRA/ASYLUM/NONESUCH RECORDS, 665 5th Ave., New York NY 10022. (212)355-7610. Contact: A&R Department. Record company.
How to Contact: Submit demo tape and lyric sheet. Prefers reel-to-reel or cassette with 1-4 songs on demo. SASE. Reports in 2-3 months.
Music: Classical (on Nonesuch only); disco; MOR; progressive; R&B; rock; and top 40/pop. Recently released albums by Linda Ronstadt, Cars, Queen, Judy Collins and Joni Mitchell.

EMBER RECORDS, INC., 747 3rd Ave., 27th Floor, New York NY 10017. (212)688-8170. Labels include Ember and Bulldog. Head of A&R: Howard Kruger. President: J.S. Kruger. Record company. Estab. 1960. Released 20 singles and 27 albums in 1978. Works with musicians and songwriters on contract. Pays 5-8% royalty to artists on contract; 50% royalty to songwriters on contract.
How to Contact: Submit demo tape and lead sheet. Prefers cassette with 2-6 songs on demo. SASE. Reports in 1 month.
Music: Disco; soul; and top 40/pop. Recently released "Fabulous Babe," by Kenny Williams (European pop single); and "I Don't Want to Put a Hold on You," by Berni Flint (United Kingdom pop single).
Tips: "We operate more in Europe than in the US, so allow time for material to flow overseas."

EMI-AMERICA/UNITED ARTISTS, 6920 Sunset Blvd., Los Angeles CA 90028. (213)461-9141. A&R Manager: Gary Gersh. Record company. Estab. 1979. Released 10 singles and 5 albums in 1978. Works with musicians on contract.
How to Contact: Submit demo tape. Prefers 7½ ips reel-to-reel or cassette with 3-5 songs on demo. SASE. Reports in 2 weeks.
Music: Bluegrass; blues; disco; easy listening; folk; jazz; MOR; progressive; R&B; rock; soul; and top 40/pop. Recently released *Sanctuary*, by J. Geils (LP); and *St. Vincent's Court*, by Kim Karnes (LP).

ENDANGERED SPECIES RECORDS, 1037 W. 4th St., Erie PA 16507. President: Paul L. Tatara. Record company, management firm and record producer. Estab. 1977. Released 2 singles in 1977; plans 3 singles and 1 album in 1979. Works with musicians on salary; songwriters on contract. Pays standard royalty to songwriters on contract.
How to Contact: Query or submit demo tape. Prefers 7½ ips reel-to-reel with 2-6 songs on demo. SASE. Reports in 3 weeks.
Music: Progressive and rock. Recently released "Don't Say Love Unless You Mean It," by Paul Tatara (progressive single); "Heart Throb," by Pistolwhip (punk rock single); and "Gotta Lotta Lose," by the Bradley Harrington Band (punk rock single).

FANFARE RECORDS, Box 2501, Des Moines IA 50315. (515)285-6564. President: Art Smart

Stenstrom. Estab. 1975. Released 2 singles and 1 album in 1978; plans 3 singles and 1 album in 1979, 3 singles and 2 albums in 1980. Works with musicians on contract. Payment negotiable.
How to Contact: Submit demo tape and lead sheet. Prefers cassette. SASE. Reports in 2 weeks.
Music: Rock and top 40/pop. Recently released *Sailing On Fantasies* (top 40 LP) and "Don't Feel Bad" (top 40 single), by Silver Laughter.

FANTASY/PRESTIGE/MILESTONE/STAX RECORDS, 10th and Parker, Berkeley CA 94710. (415)549-2500. Associate Director A&R: Hank Cosby. Record company. Works with musicians and songwriters on contract.
How to Contact: Submit demo tape. Prefers 7½ ips reel-to-reel or cassette. SASE. Reports in 3 weeks.
Music: Disco; easy listening; jazz; MOR; progressive; R&B; soul; and top 40/pop. Recently released "Disco Heat," by Sylvester (disco single); and "You Make Me Feel Mighty Real," by Sylvester (disco single).

FARR RECORDS, Box 1098, 350 Grove St., Somerville NJ 08876. (201)526-6310. Labels include Farr Records and Seminole Records. Vice President: Daniel G. Glass. Record company and music publisher. Estab. 1974. Released 6 singles and 2 albums in 1977; plans 15 singles and 3 albums in 1979. Works with musicians and songwriters on salary or contract. Payment negotiable.
How to Contact: Arrange personal interview or submit demo tape and lead sheet. Prefers 7½ ips reel-to-reel or cassette. SASE. Reports in 2 weeks.
Music: C&W; disco; easy listening; MOR; soul; and top 40/pop. Recently released "Theme From *Looking for Mr. Goodbar*," by the New Marketts (pop single); "You Say Something Nice," by Trini Lopez (MOR single); and *Silver, Platinum & Gold*, by Silver, Platinum and Gold (R&B LP).

FIRE LITE RECORD CO., 11344 Woodmont, Detroit MI 48227. (313)273-5828. Owner: Eugene Satterfield. Record company and music publisher. Estab. 1976. Works with musicians on salary or contract; songwriters on contract. Pays 5-10% royalty to artists and songwriters on contract.
How to Contact: Submit demo tape. Prefers reel-to-reel or cassette with 3-6 songs on demo. SASE. Reports in 1 week.
Music: Bluegrass; C&W; easy listening; and folk.

FIRST AMERICAN RECORDS, 65 Marion St., Seattle WA 98104. (206)625-9992. Labels include First American, Music is Medicine, Picadilly, and The Great Northwest Music Company. Chairman of the Board: Jerry Dennon. Record company and music publisher. Estab. 1976. Released 6 singles and 26 albums in 1978; plans 8 singles and 20 albums in 1979, 10 singles and 20 albums in 1980. Works with musicians and songwriters on contract. Payment negotiable.
How to Contact: Submit demo tape or submit demo tape and lead sheet. Prefers 7½ ips reel-to-reel or cassette with 2-6 songs on demo. SASE. Reports in 2 months.
Music: Blues; easy listening; folk; jazz; MOR; progressive; rock; soul; and top 40/pop. Recently released "Sitting in Limbo," by Don Brown (top 40/pop single).

FIST-O-FUNK, LTD., 293 Richard Court, Pomona NY 10970. (914)354-7157. President: Kevin Misevis. Record company, music publisher and management firm. Estab. 1976. Released 4 singles in 1977; plans 4 singles and 4 albums in 1979. Works with songwriters on contract. Pays negotiable royalty. Buys some material outright; payment negotiable.
How to Contact: Submit demo tape and lead sheet. Prefers 7½ ips reel-to-reel or cassette with 1-10 songs on demo. Does not return unsolicited material. Reports in 1 month.
Music: Blues; classical; disco; jazz; soul; and top 40/pop. Recently released "New York Strut," "Dance All Over the World" and "Keep on Dancin'," by T.C. James and Fist-O-Funk Orchestra (disco/pop singles).

FLEURETTE RECORDS, Box 43, Chester PA 19016. Record company and music publisher. Estab. 1958. Works with songwriters on contract. Pays standard royalties.
How to Contact: Submit acetate disc and lead sheet. SASE. Reports in 1 month.
Music: Blues; C&W; disco; easy listening; MOR; R&B; and top 40/pop. Recently released *In a New-Nostalgic Mood*, by Dick Durham (MOR LP).
Tips: "Submit good commercial material on an acetate disc with a singer and piano or guitar.

Songwriter's Market Close-Up

A commonplace problem of the new songwriter is the tendency to write "epics," says songwriter Patsy Bruce, shown here accepting a Nashville Songwriters Association International (NSAI) award with husband Ed for their collaboration, "Mamas Don't Let Your Babies Grow Up to Be Cowboys." "A lot of new songs are six or seven minutes long," with extraneous lines and "17 too many choruses," she says. President of NSAI, Bruce advises you to keep the song succinct. Too many songwriters try to "paint a mural, and not a little picture" when writing a song.

4-STAR RECORDS, INC., Kemper Music Co., 49 Music Square W., Nashville TN 37203. Contact: David Byers. Needs vary; query about needs and submission policy.

FRANNE RECORDS, Box 8135, Chicago IL 60680. (312)787-8220. Labels include Franne and Superbe Records. A&R Director/Executive Producer: R.C. Hillsman. Record company, music publisher and producer. Estab. 1977. Plans 10 singles and 4 albums in 1979. Works with musicians and songwriters on contract. Pays 3½% royalty to artists and songwriters on contract.
How to Contact: Arrange personal interview or submit demo tape and lead sheet. Prefers 7½ or 15 ips quarter-inch reel-to-reel or cassette with 4-6 songs on demo. "By registered mail only." SASE. Reports in 3 weeks.
Music: Church/religious; C&W; disco; gospel; jazz; MOR; rock; and top 40/pop. Recently released "He's Love" and "You Better Get Right," by Allen Duo (gospel singles).

FREE FLIGHT RECORDS, 6363 Sunset Blvd., Los Angeles CA 90028. (213)468-4185. West Coast A&R Manager: Tony Brown. Record company. Estab. 1979. Plans 4 singles in 1979. Works with musicians on contract.
How to Contact: Query, submit demo tape, or submit demo tape and lead sheet. Prefers 7½ ips reel-to-reel or cassette. SASE. Reports in 5 weeks.
Music: Blues; easy listening; jazz; MOR; progressive; R&B; rock; soul; and top 40/pop. Recently released "Neon Dreams," by Mychael (rock single); "So Close," by Sheron Wyley (MOR single); and "Boogie With Me Baby," by Debbie Peters (disco single).

FREEWAY RECORDS, INC., 10535 Wilshire Blvd., Suite 714, Los Angeles CA 90024. (213)340-7069. President: Joe Molina. Record company. Estab. 1978. Released 1 single in 1978; plans 2 albums in 1979. Works with musicians and songwriters on contract.
How to Contact: Submit demo tape and lead sheet. Prefers 7½ ips reel-to-reel or cassette with 1-100 songs on demo. SASE. Reports in 1 week.
Music: Progressive; rock; and top 40/pop. Recently released "Dizzy," by Garth Evans (pop single); and *Los Angeles Radio,* by 20 Artists (LP).

FRETONE RECORDS, INC., 3114 Radford Rd., Memphis TN 38111. (901)327-8187. Director A&R: Steve Gatlin. Record company, music publisher, record producer and management firm. Estab. 1972. Released 12 singles in 1978; plans 12 singles and 3 albums in 1979, 24 singles and 6 albums in 1980. Works with songwriters on contract. Pays negotiable royalties. Pays songwriters standard 50/50 split less agency licensing fees.

How to Contact: Submit demo tape or submit demo tape and lead or lyric sheet. Prefers 7½ ips reel-to-reel with 1-4 songs on demo. SASE. Reports in 1 month.
Music: Disco; and top 40/pop. Recently released "Disco Duck," by Rick Dees (disco novelty); "Fold Out Girl," by Pat Taylor (top 40/pop); and "Wookie," by Sam the Sham (top 40/pop).
Tips: "Submit only tunes that are of caliber to be 'A' side on 45 rpm record for AM radio play on top 40-type stations, very few ballads and no album cuts."

FRIENDSHIP STORE MUSIC RECORDS, Box M777, Gary IN 46401. (219)885-7401. Artist Director: Joseph Cohen. Record company, music publisher and record and demo producer. Estab. 1974. Plans 2 singles and 1 albums in 1979, 6 singles and 3 albums in 1980. Works with songwriters on contract. Pays variable royalties; statutory royalties to songwriters on contract.
How to Contact: Query or submit demo tape. Prefers 7½ ips reel-to-reel tape with 1-3 songs on demo. "All songs must be copyrighted before being submitted to us." SASE. Reports in 3 weeks.
Music: Folk; MOR; and top 40/pop. Recently released "Rainbow," by Joe Cohen.

FULL SAIL RECORDS, Full Sail Productions, 1126 Boylston St., Boston MA 02215. (617)262-7880. President: Fred Berk. Estab. 1976. Works with musicians on contract; songwriters on royalty contract. Pays 5-7% royalty to artists on contract; standard royalties to songwriters on contract. Buys some songs outright; pays $1-150/song.
How to Contact: Submit demo tape. Prefers 7½ ips reel-to-reel or cassette with 1-10 songs on demo. SASE. Reports in 1 month.
Music: Children's; C&W; disco; rock; soul; and top 40/pop.

G.R.T. Record Group, 9034 Sunset Blvd., Los Angeles CA 90069. (213)275-5002. President: Larry Welk. Record company, music publisher and record producer. Estab. 1967. Pays standard royalties.
How to Contact: Submit demo, lyric or lead sheet and a brief resume. "Copywritten material only." SASE. Reports in 1 week.
Music: Choral; church/religious; C&W; disco; easy listening; gospel; MOR; progressive; R&B; rock; and top 40/pop. Recently released "Oh Honey," by the Delegation (R&B/pop single); "What a Lie," by Sammi Smith (C&W single); and "Simple Little Words," by Cristy Lane (C&W single).

GALABALL, 7141 Rutland St., Philadelphia PA 19149. (215)728-1699. Labels include Galahad and Camelot. Owner: Phil Gaber. Record company, music publisher, record producer and management firm. Estab. 1963. Released 1 single in 1978; plans 1 single and 1 album in 1979. Works with musicians on contract and salary; songwriters on contract. Pays 2% minimum royalty to artists on contract.
How to Contact: Arrange personal interview or submit demo tape and lead sheet. Prefers 7½ ips reel-to-reel or cassette with 2 songs minimum on demo. Will return material "on request." SASE. Reports in 3 weeks.
Music: Blues; disco; easy listening; jazz; MOR; R&B; rock; soul; and top 40/pop. Recently released "Nite Ride" and "Lady," by Idyll Passion (disco singles).

GAMMA RECORDS, LTD., 9375 Meaux, St. Leonard, Quebec, Canada (514)327-5010. A&R Director: Dan Lazare. Record company and music publisher. Estab. 1965. Released 25 singles and 6 albums in 1977. Works with musicians and songwriters on contract. Pays negotiable royalty to artists and songwriters on contract.
How to Contact: Submit demo tape and lyric sheet.

GARLIN SOUND PRODUCTIONS, 7021 Hatillo Ave., Canoga Park CA 91306. (213)347-3902. Owner: Norman Pringle. Record company. Estab. 1960. Released 1 single in 1978; plans 3 singles in 1979.
How to Contact: Submit demo tape. Prefers 7½ ips reel-to-reel with 2 songs on demo. SASE.
Music: Country and MOR rock.

GHOST RECORDS, 1905 Pesos Place, Kalamazoo MI 49008. (616)375-2641. Labels include Ghost and Jobie. President: Don Jobe. Record company. Estab. 1967. Released 8 singles and 1 album in 1978; plans 5 singles and 1 album in 1979. Works with musicians and songwriters on contract. Buys some material outright; pays $100 minimum/song.
How to Contact: Submit demo tape and lead sheet. Prefers 7½ ips reel-to-reel. SASE. Reports in 1 month.

Music: Easy listening; rock; soul; and top 40/pop. Recently released "(Just Like) Romeo and Juliet" (top 40 single) and "Hey Lover" (easy listening single), by Don Jobe; and "Get a Little Bit Lonely," by the Ghosters (top 40 single).

GLOBAL RECORD CO., Box 207, Manistique MI 49854. President: Reg B. Christensen. Record company and music publisher. Estab. 1956. Released 15 singles and 2 albums in 1978; plans 20 singles and 5 albums in 1979. Works with musicians and songwriters on contract. Pays 10% royalty to artists on contract; 3¢/song royalty to songwriters on contract.
How to Contact: Submit demo tape and lead sheet. Prefers cassette with 2-5 songs on demo. SASE. Reports in 1 month.
Music: Bluegrass; C&W; gospel; MOR; and soul. Recently released "Heart, You Fool," by Louie Moore (C&W single); and "Woodstock" and "Crumbling Pyramids," by Paul Johnson (folk singles).

GLORI RECORDS, INC., 110 Academy St., Jersey City NJ 07302. (201)435-5266. Labels include Glori and Reborn Records. Vice President: Steven Herman. Record company and music publisher. Estab. 1972. Released 10 albums in 1977. Works with musicians on salary or contract; songwriters on contract. Pays 5% royalty to artists on contract; negotiable royalty to songwriters on contract.
How to Contact: Submit demo tape and lead sheet.

GOLD MIND RECORDS, 126 E. Mayland St., Philadelphia PA 19144. President: Norman Harris. Executive Vice President: Caryl Blockwell. Record company, music publisher and production company. Estab. 1976. Released 6 singles and 6 albums in 1978; plans 8 singles and 8 albums in 1979, 8 singles and 10 albums in 1980. Works with musicians on salary or contract; songwriters on contract. Payment negotiable.
How to Contact: Submit demo tape and lead sheet. Prefers 7½ ips reel-to-reel or cassette. SASE. Reports in 1 month.
Music: Blues; disco; easy listening; MOR; rock; soul; and top 40/pop. Recently released *Let Me Party With You*, by Bunny Sigler (LP); "Cheaters Never Win," by Love Committee (single); and "Dr. Love," by First Choice (single).

GOLDBAND RECORDS, Box 1485, Lake Charles LA 70602. Labels include Goldband, TEK, TIC TOC, ANLA, JADOR and LUFFCIN Records. President: Eddie Shuler. Record company and music publisher. Estab. 1944. Released 25 albums in 1978. Works with musicians on salary and contract; songwriters on contract. Pays standard rate to songwriters on contract.
How to Contact: Arrange personal interview. Prefers cassette with 1-6 songs on demo. SASE. Reports "when we have the time."
Music: Novelty songs in all music categories.

GOLDMONT MUSIC, INC., 24 Music Square E., Nashville TN 37203. (615)254-3725. Labels include Comet and Goldmont Records. Vice President/Manager: Betty McInturff. A&R Director: Bill McInturff. Record company, music publisher and recording studio. Estab. 1962. Released 20 singles and 5 albums in 1978; plans 30 singles and 5 albums in 1979. Works with musicians and songwriters on contract. Pays 10% royalty to artists on contract; 5% royalty to songwriters on contract.
How to Contact: Submit demo tape and lead or lyric sheet. "Song material should be accompanied by at least one instrument." Prefers 7½ ips reel-to-reel with 2-6 songs on demo, "but we will review other ips speeds, and cassettes." SASE. Reports in 1 month.
Music: Bluegrass; blues; children's; church/religious; C&W; easy listening; folk; gospel; jazz; MOR; progressive; rock (country); soul; and top 40/pop. Recently released "Miss Pauline," by Henry Briggs (C&W single); "Kamikaze Trail," by Sam Little (C&W single); and "Lonesome Highway," by Steve Krug (folk/C&W single).

GOLDUST RECORD CO., 115 E. Idaho Ave., Las Cruces NM 88001. (505)524-1889. Owner: Emmit H. Brooks. Record company, music publisher and recording studio. Estab. 1959. Released 5 singles and 8 albums in 1978; plans 8 singles and 8 albums in 1979; 12 singles and 12 albums in 1980. Works with musicians and songwriters on salary or contract. Pays 4-6% royalty to artists on contract; statutory royalty to songwriters on contract. Charges for some services: "Many of our studio customers have their own labels, and we record on a custom basis."
How to Contact: Submit demo tape. Prefers 7½ ips reel-to-reel or cassette with 1-5 songs on demo. "We do not wish to review material which has been previously released." SASE. Reports in 1 month.

Music: C&W; easy listening; MOR; rock (soft or country); top 40/pop; and fiddle instrumentals. Recently released *Fiddlin' Around*, by Junior Daugherty (country instrumental LP); and *Enchanted Mesa*, by Moon Pie Dance Band (country-rock LP).

GOSPEL RECORDS, INC., Box 90, Rugby Station, Brooklyn NY 11203. (212)773-5910. President: John R. Lockley. Record company. Estab. 1958. Works with musicians on contract. Payment negotiable.
How to Contact: Submit demo tape and lead sheet. Prefers cassette with 1-4 songs on demo. SASE. Reports in 3 weeks.
Music: Gospel. Recently released *Glorifying Jesus*, by the Lockley Family Spiritual Music Ensemble (gospel LP).

GREAT SOUTHERN RECORD CO., INC., Box 13977, New Orleans LA 70185. Labels include Great Southern and New Orleans Sound. President: John Bertholot. Public Relations Director: Rose Marie Costanza. Record company and music publisher. Estab. 1970. Works with musicians and songwriters on contract. Pays 2-4% royalty to artists on contract; statutory royalty to songwriters on contract.
How to Contact: Submit demo tape or submit demo tape and lead or lyric sheet. Prefers 7½ ips reel-to-reel or cassette with 1-4 songs on demo. SASE. Reports in 1 month.
Music: C&W (with MOR potential); jazz; MOR; soul; and top 40/pop. Recently released "Catch Me if You Can," by Porgy Jones (soul/jazz single); and "The Roach" (MOR/soul/jazz single) and "The Streetcar Song," by Alvin Thomas (MOR/jazz single).

GROUSE MUSIC, 173 Pemberton Ave., North Vancouver, British Columbia, Canada V7V 1R5. (604)986-1727. General Manager: William R. Snow. Record company, music publisher and recording studio. Estab. 1976. Released 3 singles in 1977. Works with musicians and songwriters on contract. Pays artists "as per contract"; 2½¢/side royalty to songwriters on contract.
How to Contact: Submit demo tape and lead sheet. Prefers reel-to-reel or cassette. SAE and International Reply Coupons. Reports in 1 month.
Music: C&W; easy listening, folk; MOR; and rock.

GULD RECORD, 7046 Hollywood Blvd., Hollywood CA 90028. (213)462-0502. Vice President: Harry Gordon. Record company, music publisher and record producer. Released 20 singles and 15 albums in 1978; plans 20 singles and 10 albums in 1979.
How to Contact: Submit demo tape or submit acetate disc. Prefers 7½ ips reel-to-reel with 2 songs minimum on demo. SASE. Reports in 1 week.
Music: C&W; gospel; R&B; rock; soul; and top 40/pop.

GUSTO RECORDS, Box 8188, Nashville TN 37207. (615)226-6080. Vice President: Tommy Hill. Record company and music publisher. Estab. 1973. Works with musicians/artists on contract. Pays standard royalties to artists on contract; standard royalties to songwriters on contract.
How to Contact: Arrange personal interview. Prefers 7½ reel-to-reel with 2 songs on demo. SASE. Reports in 1 month.
Music: Bluegrass; blues; C&W; disco; easy listening; folk; gospel; R&B; rock; soul; and top 40/pop. Recently released "Teddy Bear," by Red Sovine (country single); and "While the Feeling's Good" and "Honey Hungry," by Mike Lunsford (country single).
Tips: "I can not stress enough that we will not accept unsolicited material. The songwriter must call and make an appointment in order to get his tapes to us."

H&L RECORDS CORP., 532 Sylvan Ave., Englewood Cliffs NJ 07632. (201)567-8100. Vice President/A&R Director: Landy McNeal. Record company and music publisher. Estab. 1968. Released 16 singles and 20 albums in 1978; plans 12-20 singles and 20-30 albums in 1979. Works with musicians on contract; songwriters on contract or salary. Pays 5% royalty to artists on contract; 1½¢/record royalty to songwriters on contract.
How to Contact: Submit demo tape and lead or lyric sheet. Prefers 7½ ips reel-to-reel or cassette with 1-2 songs on demo. SASE. Reports in 1 month.
Music: Disco; jazz; rock; soul; and top 40/pop. Recently released "Wonder Woman," by the Stylistics (R&B/pop); "You Are My Love/Play With Me," by Sandy Mercer (R&B/pop); and "Trust Me," by Milt Matthews (R&B).

HANK'S MUSIC ENTERPRISES, INC., 11746 Goshen Ave., Suite 7, Los Angeles CA 90045. (213)479-6091. President: Hank Haldeman. Record company, record producer and music

publisher. Estab. 1977. Released 1 single in 1978. Works with songwriters on contract.
How to Contact: Query. Prefers 7½ ips reel-to-reel with 1-4 songs on demo. SASE. Reports in 1 month.
Music: C&W; easy listening; MOR; rock; and top 40/pop. Recently released "Maybe Baby," by Vicki Thomas (top 40/pop single).
Tips: "We're only looking for singles. Please send only professionally produced demos."

HAPPY DAY RECORDS, INC., 800 N. Ridgeland, Oak Park IL 60302. Vice President: Vince Ippolito. Record company, music publisher and TV/radio commercial producer. Estab. 1973.
How to Contact: Submit demo tape and lead sheet. Prefers 7½ ips reel-to-reel or cassette with 2-4 songs on demo. SASE.
Music: Disco; easy listening; jazz; MOR; progressive; rock; soul; and top 40/pop.

HARLEQUIN RECORDS, Box 665, Lemon Grove CA 92045. (714)462-6538. Owner: Dick Braun. Record company, music publisher and booking agency. Estab. 1959. Released 2 albums in 1978; plans 2 albums in 1979. Works with songwriters on contract. Pays negotiable royalty.
How to Contact: Submit lead sheet. Does not return unsolicited material. Reports on solicited material in 1 month.
Music: Easy listening; jazz; and big band. "We're interested in big band jazz or swing style music."

HEART RECORDS, Northern Productions, Ltd., Box 3713, Station B, Calgary, Alberta, Canada T2M 4M4. (403)274-8638. Labels include Heart and Stagecoach Records. President: Ron Mahonin. Record company, record producer, music publisher and management firm. Estab. 1975. Released 7 singles in 1978; plans 8 singles and 3 albums in 1979, 8 singles and 5 albums in 1980. Works with musicians on salary and contract; songwriters on contract. Pays negotiable royalty to artists and songwriters on contract.
How to Contact: Submit demo tape and lead sheet. Prefers 7½ ips reel-to-reel or cassette with 1-4 songs on demo. SASE. Reports in 1 month.
Music: C&W; easy listening; MOR; progressive; rock; and top 40/pop. Recently released "Close to Your Love," by Ron Mahonin (MOR single); "Angel in the Night," by Time Machine (MOR single); and "Queen of Hearts," by Bootleg (rock single).

HEAVY SOUND PRODUCTIONS, Box 2875, Washington DC 20013. Labels include Ben, LA and Rose Records. President: Ben Smalls. Vice President: Joe Holt. Record company and production company. Estab. 1973. Released 2 singles in 1977; plans 4 singles in 1979. Works with musicians and songwriters on contract. Pays 2% royalty to artists on contract; negotiable royalty to songwriters.
How to Contact: Submit demo tape and lead sheet. Prefers reel-to-reel or cassette with 2-4 songs on demo. SASE. Reports in 1 month.
Music: MOR; rock; soul; and top 40/pop. Recently released "Broken Hearted Clown," by Nat Hall (MOR single); "Soul Children," by the Ascots (soul single); and "Love Knows No Color," by the Children of the Night (soul single).

THE HERALD ASSOCIATION, INC., Drawer 218, Wellman Heights, Johnsonville SC 29555. Labels include Herald, Klesis and Mark Five Records. President: H. Ervin Lewis. Record company, music publisher and record producer. Estab. 1975. Released 4 singles and 8 albums in 1978; plans 6 singles and 9 albums in 1979, 8 singles and 6 albums in 1980. Works with musicians and songwriters on contract. "Several songwriters are under exclusive contract." Pays 4-6% royalty to artists on contract; statutory royalty to songwriters on contract.
How to Contact: Submit demo tape and lead sheet. Prefers 7½ ips reel-to-reel or cassette with 4-8 songs on demo. "Plainly mark outside of package with contents and identify each demo and lead sheet with name and address." SASE. Reports in 1 month.
Music: Choral; church/religious; and gospel. Recently released "Breaker, Breaker, Sweet Jesus," by Jerry Arhelger (C&W/gospel single); *Images*, by Rick Eldridge (gospel LP); and *Word Pictures*, by Erv Lewis (gospel LP).

HICKORY RECORDS, 2510 Franklin Rd., Nashville TN 37204. (615)385-3031. Vice President: John R. Brown. Record company. Estab. 1942. Works with musicians on contract.
How to Contact: Query. "Letter must be addressed to a person here whom you have previously contacted." Prefers 7½ ips reel-to-reel with 2-4 songs on demo. SASE. Reports in 1 month.
Music: C&W.

HILLSIDE RECORDS, 5275 N. Dixie Dr., Dayton OH 45414. Labels include Industry Records, Swap Bird Records and Country Gold Records. Owner: Dave Franer. Record company, music publisher and record producer. Estab. 1960. Released 10 singles and 4 albums in 1978. Works with musicians and songwriters on contract. Pays negotiable royalties to artists on contract; statutory royalties to songwriters on contract.
How to Contact: Submit lyrics. "Always send what you feel are the most outstanding lyrics you have. We have no use for good, fair and album cut songs. We are looking for hits." SASE. Reports in 2 weeks.
Music: Country; easy listening; MOR; rock; and top 40/pop. Recently released "Loving You," by Ray Sanders (MOR/country single); "I Can't Make It Without You," by Curtis Potter (country LP); and *Country Gold*, by Nashville Singers (country LP).

HOLLY RECORDS, 332 N. Brinker Ave., Columbus OH 45204. (614)279-5251. Script Manager: Jetta Brown. Record company, music publisher, record producer, management firm and booking agency. Estab. 1958. Released 32 albums in 1978; plans 50 singles and 50 albums in 1978, 500 singles and 100 albmus in 1980. Works with musicians and songwriters on contract; musicians and songwriters on salary. Pays 2-33⅓% royalty to artists on contract; statutory royalties to songwriters on contract. Buys some songs outright; pays $5-500/song.
How to Contact: Query, arrange personal interview, submit demo tape, submit demo tape and lead sheet, submit lead sheet or arrange in-person audition. Prefers 7½ or 15 ips reel-to-reel or cassette. Does not return unsolicited material. Reports in 3 weeks.
Music: Bluegrass; blues; church/religious; C&W; folk; gospel; MOR; and top 40/pop. Recently released "Don't Lock the Door," "Sittin on Top of the World" and "Darlin' What Am I Gonna Do?," by Walt Cochran (C&W singles).

HORIZON RECORDS, 1416 N. La Brea, Los Angeles CA 90028. (213)469-2411. A&R Director: Noel Newbolt. Record company.
How to Contact: Submit demo tape. Prefers 7½ ips reel-to-reel or cassette with 2-5 songs on demo. SASE.
Music: Blues; disco; easy listening; jazz; MOR; progressive; R&B; rock; and top 40/pop.
Tips: "Submit a clean demo with lyrics and melody line clearly understandable."

IBC RECORDS, 50 Music Square W., Suite 902, United Artists Tower, Nashville TN 37203. (615)329-0714. Executive Producer: Walter Haynes. Record company, music publisher and record producer. Estab. 1978. Plans 10 singles in 1979. Works with musicians and songwriters on contract. Pays standard royalties to artists on contract; statutory royalties to songwriters on contract. Sometimes buys material outright; payment negotiable.
How to Contact: Query or arrange personal interview. Prefers cassette with 3-4 songs on demo. SASE if time allows. Reports "as time allows."
Music: Modern country.

INTERMODAL PRODUCTIONS, LTD., Box 2199, Vancouver, British Columbia, Canada V6B 3V7. (604)688-1820. President: John Rodney. Record company and management firm. Estab. 1972. Released 12 singles and 4 albums in 1978; plans 12 singles and 4 albums in 1979, 24 singles and 8 albums in 1980. Works with musicians and songwriters on contract. Pays 4-14% royalty to artists and songwriters on contract. Charges for some services: "depends on the type of contract the artist is comfortable with, and how much independence he wishes in the creative area."
How to Contact: Submit demo tape. Prefers 7½ ips reel-to-reel with 1-6 songs on demo. SAE and International Reply Coupons. Reports in 1 month.
Music: Classical; C&W; MOR; and top 40/pop. Recently released "Love Is to Be a Stinging Bee," by Karmen; and "Kootenay Serenade," by Georges LaFleche.

ISLAND RECORDS INC., 7720 Sunset Blvd., Los Angeles CA 90046. (213)874-7760. President: Marshall Blonston. Record company.
How to Contact: Query. "We are not actively looking for outside material." SASE.
Music: Disco; jazz; progressive; R&B; rock; top 40/pop; and reggae.
Tips: "The better quality demo, the better."

ISLAND RECORDS, 444 Madison Ave., New York NY 10022. Labels include Mango (reggae) and Antilles (reggae and disco). Director of Special Markets: Alex Masucci. Assistant: Linda Giarrantani. Record company, music publisher and record producer.
How to Contact: Submit demo tape. Prefers cassette with 1-3 songs on demo. SASE. Reports in 1 month.
Music: Disco; rock; and reggae.

JAMES S. ENTERPRISES, 3190 Hallmark Court, Salinan MI 48603. (517)792-7889. Labels include Chivalry Records. President: J.S. Leach. Record company. Estab. 1973. Released 2 singles in 1977; plans 3 singles in 1978, 3 singles in 1979. Works with musicians and songwriters on contract. Pays 2% royalty to artists on contract; 2% royalty to songwriters on contract.
How to Contact: Submit demo tape and lead sheet. Prefers 7½ ips reel-to-reel or cassette with 3-5 songs on demo. SASE. Reports in 2 weeks.
Music: C&W; disco; easy listening; MOR; rock (country rock); and top 40/pop. Recently released "Nothin' Better to Do," by the John Brown Band (top 40/disco); "If You Can't Be Good," by Magic (top 40); and "Walkin' in the Country," by the Zoo (top 40).

JANUS RECORDS, 9034 Sunset Blvd., Los Angeles CA 90069. "No guarantee on time when tapes will be returned. Cassettes preferred. Emphasis on rock and roll."

JAY BIRD RECORD CO., 1313 Washington, Box 140, Parsons KS 67357. (316)421-1666. Manager/A&R Director: Albert H. Monday. Record company and music publisher. Estab. 1965. Released 3 singles in 1978; plans 3 singles in 1979, 4-5 singles and 1 album in 1980. Works with musicians and songwriters on contract. Pays 9% royalty to artists on contract; 2% royalty to songwriters on contract.
How to Contact: Submit demo or master tape and lead sheet. Prefers 7½ ips reel-to-reel or cassette with 2-4 songs on demo. Tapes should be in stereo. SASE. Reports in 1 month.
Music: Bluegrass; choral; C&W; and easy listening. Recently released "Reading My Heart" and "Big Time Joe."

JEMKL RECORD CORP., 1100 NE 125th St., Box 680460, Miami FL 33168. (305)891-0633. Labels include Children's World, JEMKL and Moonstone Records. A&R Director: James Novak. General Manager: Rosalie Petitte. Record company. Estab. 1970. Released 4 singles and 1 album in 1977; plans 10 singles and 4 albums in 1979. Works with musicians on salary or contract. Pays 5-10% royalty to artists on contract. Charges for some services: "if they want a recording out fast and are not under contract to us as a recording artist."
How to Contact: Submit demo tape and lead sheet. Include photo and bio. Prefers 7½ ips reel-to-reel with 1-4 songs on demo. SASE. Reports in 3 weeks.
Music: Children's; C&W; disco; folk; gospel; MOR; rock (hard); soul; and top 40/pop. Recently released "Disco Fever," by Leroy Morrison (disco single); "I'm Foot Loose and Fancy Free," by Cal Devlin (C&W single); and "When You Look Me Over," by Carole Shaw (MOR single).

JENERO RECORD CO., Box 121, Soda Springs ID 83276. President: Ronald Watts. Record company and music publisher. Estab. 1976. Released 3 singles and 2 albums in 1978; plans 4 singles and 2 albums in 1978, 6 singles and 3 albums in 1980. Works with musicians and songwriters on salary or contract. Pays 3-5% royalty to artists on contract; 0-2% royalty to songwriters on contract. Charges for some services: "If a demo tape is cut in company studio, studio time is charged to the songwriter."
How to Contact: Submit demo tape and lead sheet. Prefers cassette with 4-8 songs on demo. "All material must be submitted by registered mail." SASE. Reports in 3 weeks.
Music: C&W; easy listening; MOR; rock (soft or country); and top 40/pop. Recently released *Mem'rys* and *Yesterday and Today*, by Bill Corbett (easy listening LPs).

JERREE RECORDS, 1469 3rd Ave., New Brighton PA 15066. (412)847-0111. Labels include Candy, Buckshot, Green and Dolphin. Owners: Jerry Reed, Don Garvin. Record company and music publisher. Estab. 1962. Released 15 singles and 4 albums in 1978. Works with songwriters on contract. Pays 10-50% royalty to artists on contract; standard royalties to songwriters on contract.
How to Contact: Query or submit demo tape and lead sheet. Prefers 7½ ips reel-to-reel or cassette with 1-3 songs on demo. SASE. Reports in 2 weeks.
Music: C&W; disco; easy listening; MOR; R&B; soul; and top 40/pop. Recently released *Dancin' Man*, by Q (top 40 LP); "Mama Lied," by Frank Pellino (top 40 single); and *I Love My Music*, by Wild Cherry (top 40 LP).

JERSEY COAST AGENTS, LTD., 72 Thorne Place, Hazlet Township NJ 07734. (201)787-3891. Label include World, Karass, Granfalloon, Anomaly, Stonehedge, Output and BMA. President: Joe McHugh. Vice President, A&R: D.W. Griffiths. Record company, booking agency, music publisher and management firm. Estab. 1966. Released 8 albums in 1978; plans 10 albums in 1979, 8 in 1980. Works with musicians on salary or contract. Pays

varying royalty percentages that are "higher than average."
How to Contact: Call or write, describing material first. Prefers cassette with 3-4 songs on demo. SASE. Reports "as soon as work load permits."
Music: Bluegrass; folk; progressive; rock; and AOR. Recently released *Conspiracy, Vol. III, Live,* by Southern Conspiracy; and *Breakstone's Free,* by Informed Source.

JET RECORDS, INC., 2049 Century Park E., Suite 414, Los Angeles CA 90067. (213)553-6801. Director of A&R: Pat Siciliano. Record company. Estab. 1976. Released 7 singles and 4 albums in 1978; plans 11 singles and 11 albums in 1979. Works with musicians on contract.
How to Contact: Prefers cassette with 3 songs maximum on demo. "Put name and address on cassette as well as envelope." SASE. Reports in 10 weeks.
Music: C&W; disco; easy listening; progressive; rock; and top 40/pop. Recently released *Out of the Blue* and *Ole,* by Electric Light Orchestra (rock LPs).
Tips: "Include lyrics, bio, photos and best songs. If you have a good lawyer, call us. We listen to everything that comes in."

JEWEL RECORD CORP., Box 1125, 728 Texas St., Shreveport LA 71163. (318)222-0673. President: Stanley J. Lewis. Executive Vice President: F.R. Lewis. National Promotions Director: Jo Wyatt. Record company and music publisher.
How to Contact: Submit demo tape or submit demo tape and lead sheet. Prefers 7½ reel-to-reel, cassette or 8-track cartridge. SASE. Reports in 1 month.
Music: C&W; gospel; and soul.

JODY RECORDS, 2226 McDonald, New York NY 11223. (212)373-4468. Labels include Atlas and Jody Records. Vice President: Martin Pomerantz. Promotion: Tony Graye. A&R Director: Vincent Vallis. Record company and music publisher. Estab. 1969. Released 50 singles and 28 albums in 1978; plans 50 singles and 30 albums in 1979. Works with musicians and songwriters on contract. Pays 6% royalty to artists on contract; statutory royalty to songwriters on contract. Charges for some services: custom master sessions or demos.
How to Contact: Submit demo tape, arrange personal interview, submit demo tape and lead sheet, or submit lead sheet. Prefers 7½ ips reel-to-reel or cassette with 2-4 songs on demo. SASE. Reports in 2 weeks.
Music: Blues; C&W; disco; jazz; rock; and soul; Recently released "Hustle Bustle," Abracadabra; and "Do the Hammer," by Eddie Hailey.

JORAL RECORDS, 200 Noll Plaza, Huntington IN 46750. (219)356-8400. Director: Ray Repp. Record company and music publisher. Estab. 1977. Plans 12 albums in 1979. Works with musicians and songwriters on contract. Pays 5% minimum royalty to artists on contract; standard royalty to songwriters on contract. Buys some material outright; payment negotiable.
How to Contact: Submit demo tape. Prefers 7½ ips rees-to-reel or cassette with 4-6 songs on demo. SASE. Reports in 1 month.
Music: Children's; choral; church/religious; classical; C&W (religious); folk (religious); gospel; rock (religious); and top 40/pop (religious). Recently released *Life is a Fountain—And Other Psalms,* by Lorraine Louvat (church/religious LP).

JUPITER RECORDS, INC., 1017 N. La Cienega, Los Angeles CA 90069. (213)657-8730. Labels include Sue International. President: Juggy Murray. Record company, music publisher, record producer and management firm. Estab. 1975. Released 3 singles and 2 albums in 1978; plans 4 singles and 4 albums in 1979, 10 singles and 10 albums in 1980. Works with musicians and songwriters on contract.
How to Contact: Submit demo tape, submit demo tape and lead sheet, or submit acetate disc and lead sheet. Prefers reel-to-reel or cassette. SASE. Reports in 1 week.
Music: Blues; disco; gospel; jazz; progressive; R&B; and soul. Recently released "Inside America," "Disco Extraordinaire" and "Come On Do It Some More," by Juggy Murray Jones (disco).

KAJAC RECORD CORP., Box B, 155 1st St., Carlisle IA 50047. (515)989-0876. Labels include Kajac, KRC, Ven-Jence, Vision, and Red Rock Records. President: Harold L. Luick. A&R Director: Jim Phinney. Record company, music publisher and recording studio. Released 16 singles and 3 albums in 1978; plans 20 singles and 19 albums in 1979, 45 singles and 28 albums in 1980. Works with musicians on salary or contract; songwriters on contract. Pays standard rate to artists and songwriters on contract.

How to Contact: Submit demo tape and lead sheet or arrange personal interview. Prefers 7½ ips reel-to-reel with 1-3 songs on demo. "For a personal interview, set up an appointment. We allow 10 minutes. For submissions by mail, include SASE return mailer with proper postage. Otherwise, we dispose of the tape if we are not interested." Reports in 3 weeks.
Music: Bluegrass; children's; church/religious; C&W; disco; easy listening; gospel; MOR; rock (hard, country or punk); and top 40/pop. Recently released "Waylon, Sing to Momma," by Darrell Thomas (C&W single); "I've Had Enough of Loneliness," by Graham Fee (MOR single); and *Ballads of Deadwood South Dakota*, by Don Laughlin (C&W LP).

KANSA RECORDS, 1920 Hampton Dr., Box A-20, Lebanon TN 37087. (615)444-3753. General Manager: "Kit" Johnson. Record company and music publisher. Estab. 1974. Released 2 singles and 2 albums in 1978. Works with musicians and songwriters on contract. Payment negotiable.
How to Contact: Submit demo tape or submit demo tape and lead sheet. Prefers 7½ ips reel-to-reel or cassette with 3-4 songs on demo. SASE. Reports in 3 weeks.
Music: C&W; MOR; progressive; and top 40/pop. Recently released "A Little Something on the Side" and "Coldest Toes in Town," by Pat Garrett (singles); and "Married in Las Vegas (Divorced in Mexico)" and "Man with the Mandolin," by Debbie Dierks (singles).

K-D MUSIC CO., 111 Valley Rd., Wilmington DE 19804. (302)655-7488. A&R: Ed Kennedy. General Manager: Shirley Kay. Record company. Estab. 1950. Released 2 singles and 8 albums in 1978. Works with musicians on salary or contract; songwriters on contract. Payment negotiable. Buys some material outright. Charges for some services: to "outside producers or publishers only."
How to Contact: Submit demo and lead sheet. Prefers acetate disc. SASE. Reports in 2 weeks.
Music: Bluegrass, blues; children's; choral; church/religious; classical; C&W; easy listening; folk; gospel; jazz; MOR; rock; and top 40/pop. Recently released "Fortunes in Memories" and "I Cry," by Bob Freeman (C&W singles); and *Burlaky*, by Roman Lewycky (choral LP).

KEN KEENE INTERNATIONAL, Box 1830, New Orleans LA 70053. Labels include Briarmeade, Burlap, Keeta, Sea Cruise (UK), and Speedy. President Ken Keene. Vice President: Frankie Ford. Record company, booking agency, music publisher and management firm. Estab. 1970. Released 17 singles and 4 albums in 1978; plans 25 singles and 10 albums in 1979, 25 singles and 10 albums in 1980. Works with musicians and songwriters on contract. Pays 5% royalty to artists on contract; 2% royalty to songwriters on contract.
How to Contact: Submit demo tape and lead sheet. Prefers 7½ ips reel-to-reel on 5- or 7-inch reel (no 3-inch reels) or cassette with 2-6 songs on demo. SASE. Reports in 1 month.
Music: Blues; children's; church/religious; C&W; disco; easy listening; gospel; MOR; rock (easy, hard or country); soul; top 40/pop; and "foreign language hits." Recently released *The Memphis Session*, by Billy Joe Duniven (rockabilly LP); *The Best Performance of My Life*, by Denny Barberio (pop LP); "Foxy Man," by Billy Joe Duniven (pop single); "Halfway to Paradise," by Frankie Ford (pop single); and "Holy Roller," by Phil Enloe (country/gospel single).

KESS RECORDS, Box 2316, Nashville TN 37214. (615)889-6675. Estab. Owner: Jimmy Kish. Record company and music publisher. Pays negotiable royalties.
How to Contact: Submit demo tape and lead sheet. Prefers 7½ ips reel-to-reel or cassette. SASE. Reports in 2 weeks.
Music: C&W and gospel. Recently released "I Dare to Dream" and "That's What Makes a Heartache" (by Jimmy Kish and Les Peterson) and "Nite Plane to Nashville" (by Kish and Red River Dave), all recorded by Jimmy Kish (C&W).

KICKING MULE RECORDS, INC., Box 3233, Berkeley CA 94703. (415)452-1248. Labels include Sonet USA, Transatlantic USA and Sierra Wave. Head of A&R: Stefan Grossman, 125 Studdridge St., London SW 6, England. Record company and music publisher. Estab. 1972. Released 20 albums in 1978; plans 25 albums in 1979, 25 albums in 1980. Works with musicians on contract. Pays 10-16% royalty to artists on contract; statutory royalties to songwriters on contract.
How to Contact: Submit demo tape. Prefers reel-to-reel or cassette with 3-5 songs on demo. SASE. Reports in 1 month.
Music: All types. Recently released *Stefan Grossman and John Renbourn*, by Grossman and Renbourn (guitar instrumental LP); *Melodic Clawhammer Banjo*, by Bob Carlin (banjo instrumental LP); and *Rock and Roll Guitar Styles*, by David Bennett Cohen (rock instrumental LP).

KING OF KINGS RECORD CO., 38603 Sage Tree St., Palmdale CA 93550. Manager: L.R. Pritchett. Record company and music publisher. Estab. 1950. Released 1 album in 1978; plans 1 album in 1979. Works with musicians and songwriters on contract. Pays 5% royalty to artists on contract; "standard minimum" royalty to songwriters on contract.
How to Contact: Submit lead sheet. "If the lead sheet is of interest, a tape may be requested." Prefers 3¾ or 7½ ips reel-to-reel with 1-5 songs on demo. SASE. Reports in 1 month.
Music: Gospel; MOR; soul; and top 40/pop. Recently released *Another Dawn*, by Charles Vickers (gospel LP); and "Johnny Blue," by Niki Stevens (single).

DON KIRSHNER RECORDS, 1370 Avenue of the Americas, New York NY 10019. (212)489-0440. Record company and music publisher. Estab. 1972. Released 4 singles and 3 albums in 1978. Works with musicians on contract; songwriters on salary.
How to Contact: Query or submit demo tape. Prefers 7½ ips reel-to-reel or cassette with 2-3 songs on demo. SASE. Reports in 2 weeks.
Music: All types. Recently released "Dust," by Kansas (rock single); and "Sinner Man," by Sarah Dash (disco).

SID KLEINER MUSIC ENTERPRISES, (formerly Happy House Music), 3701 25th Ave. SW, Naples FL 33999. Labels include Musi-Poe, Top-Star, This Is It, Token, and Country-King. Owner: Sid Kleiner. Record company and consulting firm to music industry. Estab. 1949. Released 6 singles and 1 album in 1978; plans 12 singles and 2 albums in 1979, 20 singles and 6 albums in 1980. Works with musicians and songwriters on contract. Pays 2¢/record royalty to artists and songwriters on contract. Charges for some services: "We may, at our option, charge *actual* production expense. We are not get-rich-quickers or rip-off artists. But we are too small to pay all of these bills!"
How to Contact: Submit demo tape and lead sheet. Prefers cassette. SASE, "otherwise materials aren't returned." Reports in 3 weeks.
Music: Bluegrass; C&W; easy listening; folk; jazz; and "banjo and guitar soloists and features." Recently released *Burd Boys on Stage* (country LP) and *Chartbusters and Other Hits* (country LP), by the Burd Boys; and *Find a Simple Life*, by Dave Kleiner (folk/rock LP).

KNEPTUNE INTERNATIONAL RECORDS, Box 5236, Vancouver, British Columbia Canada V6B 4B3. US office: 1880 Century Park E., Suite 1411, Los Angeles CA 90067. (604)531-9331. Labels include Kneptune Records, Pyramid Records and Van Records. A&R Director: Kenny Harris. Record company and music publisher. Estab. 1970. Released 2 singles and 1 album in 1978; plans 3 singles and 3 albums in 1979. Works with musicians and songwriters on contract. Pays 5-15% royalty to artists and songwriters on contract.
How to Contact: Submit demo tape and lead sheet. Prefers 7½ ips reel-to-reel or cassette. Does not return unsolicited material. Reports in 2 weeks.
Music: Bluegrass; blues; children's; choral; church/religious; classical; C&W; disco; easy listening; folk; gospel; jazz; MOR; progressive; rock; soul; and top 40/pop. Recently released *Dr. Bundolo Volume Three* (comedy album); and "Funky Lady," by Gunnar.

KOUNTRY "44", Box 4126, Warrington FL 32507. (904)455-9845. President: Jimmy Welch. Record company, booking agency and music publisher. Estab. 1970. Released 2 singles and 1 album in 1977; plans 3 singles and 1 album in 1979. Works with musicians on salary or contract; songwriters on contract. Pays 4¢/song royalty to artists and songwriters on contract.
How to Contact: Submit demo tape and lead sheet. Prefers 7½ ips reel-to-reel or cassette. SASE. Reports in 1 month.
Music: Bluegrass; blues; and C&W. Recently released "Somebody Always Blows My Deal" and "Happy Anniversary Day," by Jimmy Welch (C&W/blues singles); and "Go Go Girls," by Don Hogen (C&W single).

L.M.I. (LEE MAGID, INC.), 19657 Ventura Blvd., Tarzana CA 91356. (213)996-6620. Owner: Lee Magid. Record company and music publisher. Estab. 1969. Released 20 singles in 1977. Works with musicians and songwriters on contract. Pays 3-6% royalty to artists and songwriters on contract.
How to Contact: Arrange personal interview, submit demo tape or submit demo tape and lead sheet. Prefers reel-to-reel or cassette with 3-8 songs on demo. SASE. Reports in 3 weeks.
Music: Bluegrass; blues; disco; easy listening; folk; jazz; and rock.

L.S. RECORDS, 120 Hickory St., Madison TN 37115. (615)868-7171. Labels include L.S. Records and V.E.C. Records. Publishing Director: Michael Radford. Record company and music publisher. Estab. 1975. Released 9 singles in 1977. Works with musicians and songwriters on contract. Pays 3-5¢/song royalty to artists on contract; 2¾¢/song royalty to songwriters on contract.

How to Contact: Submit demo tape and lyric sheet or arrange personal interview. Prefers 7½ ips reel-to-reel or cassette with 2-10 songs on demo. SASE. Reports in 1 month.

Music: C&W (modern); easy listening; MOR; rock (soft); and top 40/pop. Recently released "Let Me Down Easy" and "I'm Gonna Love You Anyway," by Cristy Lane (modern country singles).

LADD MUSIC CO., 401 Wintermantle Ave., Scranton PA 18505. (717)343-6718. Labels include White Rock Records. President: Phil Ladd. Record company, music publisher and producer. Estab. 1967. Released 12 singles and 1 album in 1978; plans 24 singles and 3 albums in 1979. Works with musicians and songwriters on contract. Payment varies for artists on contract; 3% royalty to songwriters on contract. Buys some material outright; payment varies.

How To Contact: Submit demo tape and lead sheet. Prefers cassette with 1-6 songs on demo. SASE. Reports in 2 weeks.

Music: Blues; children's; choral; C&W; easy listening; MOR; rock; soul; and top 40/pop. Recently released "You Want Love," by Frantic Freddie (single); "Honky Tonk Man," by Clyde Stacy (single); and "Try a Little Tenderness," by Eura Bailey (single).

LAKE COUNTRY RECORDS, Box 1073, Graham TX 76046. (817)549-5118. General Manager: Mark House. Record company, booking agency and music publisher. Estab. 1975. Works with musicians on contract. Payment negotiable.

How to Contact: Submit demo tape and lead sheet. Prefers 7½ ips reel-to-reel with 1-3 songs on demo. SASE. Reports in 1 month.

Music: C&W. Recently released "Feeling Right, Doing Wrong" and "Hurting Me," by Larry Quinten (C&W singles); and "It's Not That Easy to Lie," by Larry Wampler (C&W single).

LAND O' ROSES RECORDS, Box 45, Thomasville GA 31792. (912)226-7911. Labels include Rosebud Records and Soul O Records. Vice President: Emery T. Evans. Record company, music publisher, record producer and recording studio. Estab. 1974. Released 8 singles and 12 albums in 1978; plans 10 singles and 12 albums in 1979, 12 singles and 12 albums in 1980. Works with songwriters on contract; musicians on salary and artists for custom production of records. Pays standard royalties to songwriters on contract.

How to Contact: Query, arrange personal interview, submit demo tape, or submit demo tape and lead sheet. Prefers 7½ ips reel-to-reel or cassette with 1-3 songs on demo. SASE. Reports in 2 weeks.

Music: Bluegrass; church/religious; C&W; folk; and gospel. Recently released *Jesus is Real*, by Crownsmen (gospel LP); *Satisfied With Jesus*, by Holy Mighty Crusaders (spiritual LP); and "The Farmer's Lament," by Dawson Mathis (patriotic single).

LANOR RECORDS, Box 233, 329 N. Main St., Church Point LA 70525. (318)684-2176. Labels include Lanor and Joker Records. Owner: Lee Lavergne. Record company and music publisher. Released 7 singles and 2 albums in 1978. Works with artists and songwriters on contract. Pays 3% royalty to artists on contract; 1¢/song royalty to songwriters on contract.

How to Contact: Submit demo tape. Prefers 7½ ips reel-to-reel or cassette with 2-6 songs on demo. SASE. Reports in 2 weeks.

Music: C&W; rock; and soul. Recently released "Funky Grasshopper," by Hugh Boynton (soul single); and "Make-Believe Boy," by Becky Richard (country rock single).

LASALLE RECORDING CO., 8959 S. Oglesby Ave., Chicago IL 60617. (312)375-4276. Labels include Fay, LaSalle and Planet. Vice President: Armond Jackson. Record company, music publisher and booking agency. Estab. 1950. Works with musicians and songwriters on contract. Pays 1%/record side royalty to artists and songwriters on contract.

How to Contact: Submit demo tape, or submit demo tape and lead sheet. Prefers 7½ ips reel-to-reel or cassette with 12 songs minimum on tape. SASE. Reports in 2 weeks.

Music: Blues; church/religious; gospel; and top 40/pop. Recently released "Midnight Shuffle," by Jump Jackson (R&B single).

LEONA RECORDS, Box 3818, 704 S. 7th, Temple TX 76501. (817)773-1775. Labels include Buena Suerte Records. General Manager: Alberto Lopez. Record company, music publisher, record producer and booking agency. Estab. 1968. Released 10 singles and 4 albums in 1978; plans 24 singles and 10 albums in 1979, 24 singles and 10 albums in 1980. Works with musicians and songwriters on contract; musicians on salary. Pays 5-10% royalty to artists on contract: statutory royalties to songwriters on contract.

How to Contact: Query or submit demo tape. Prefers 7½ ips reel-to-reel or cassette with 5-20 songs on demo. SASE. Reports in 1 month.
Music: Latin/Spanish. Recently released *El Corazon De La Nacion*, by Big Lu (Tex-Mex LP); *Sea La Paz La Fuenja*, by Little Joe (Tex-Mex LP); and *La Voz De Aztlian*, by Little Joe (Tex-Mex LP).

LITTLE DAVID RECORDS, INC., 9200 Sunset Blvd., Los Angeles CA 90069. (213)278-7975. Labels include Hidden Records. Vice President: Ben Hurwitz. Record company. Estab. 1969. Released 1 album in 1978; plans 4 albums in 1979. Works with musicians and songwriters on contract.
How to Contact: Query. SASE.
Music: Blues; disco; easy listening; folk; jazz; MOR; progressive; R&B; rock; soul; and top 40/pop. Recently released *Indecent Exposure, On the Road* and *Evening with Wally Londo*, by George Carlin (comedy LPs); and *The Kenny Rankin Album*, by Kenny Rankin (LP).

LITTLE GEM MUSIC, INC., 38 Music Square E., Suite 114, Nashville TN 37203. President: Jack Stillwell. Record company, music publisher and independent producer. Released 20 singles and 6 albums in 1978; plans 24 singles and 6 albums in 1979. Works with musicians on salary or contract; songwriters on contract. Pays 5-9% royalty to artists on contract; statutory royalty to songwriters on contract. Charges for some services: "We charge recording fees to the artist, never to the songwriter."
How to Contact: Submit demo tape with lyric or lead sheet. Prefers 7½ ips reel-to-reel with 2-4 songs on demo. "Use new tape." SASE. Reports in 3 weeks.
Music: C&W and MOR. Recently released "Raggedy Ann," by Little Jimmy Dickens (C&W single); "Goodbye Bing, Elvis and Guy," by Diana Williams (C&W/Christmas single); and "Love Song for Jesus," by Lee Cummins (C&W single).

LITTLETOWN RECORDS, Box 851, Fall River MA 02722. President: Don Perry. Record company, booking agency and music publisher. Estab. 1965. Released 3 singles in 1977. Works with musicians and songwriters on contract. Payment negotiable.
How to Contact: Submit demo tape and lead sheet. Prefers cassette. SASE. Reports in 3 weeks.
Music: C&W; disco; easy listening; rock; and top 40/pop. Recently released "Pretty," by Carl Leslie (top 40 single); "Lovely Lies," by Cal Ray (C&W single); and "Want Ad," by Tympiece (disco single).

LONDON RECORDS, 539 W. 25th St., New York NY 10001. Labels include Le Joint. A&R Directors: Bob Paiva, Walt Maguire, Garrison Laykam. Record company. Estab. 1945.
How to Contact: Submit demo tape and lyric sheet. Prefers 7½ ips reel-to-reel or cassette with 1-4 songs on demo. SASE. Reports in 2 weeks.
Music: Disco; R&B; soul; and AOR. Recently released "Dancin' in the Sheets," by Hodges, James and Smith (disco single).

LONG NECK RECORDS, 6004 Bull Creek Rd., Austin TX 78757. President: Bobby Earl Smith. Record company and music publisher. Estab. 1973. Released 1 album in 1978; plans 4 albums and 6 singles in 1979. Works with musicians and songwriters on contract. Pays negotiable royalty to artists and songwriters on contract.
How to Contact: Submit demo tape or submit demo tape and lead sheet. Prefers 7½ ips reel-to-reel or cassette. Does not return unsolicited material.
Music: Blues; children's; C&W; easy listening; gospel; MOR; progressive; rock; soul; and top 40/pop. Recently released *Alvin Crow and the Pleasant Valley Boys*, by Alvin Crow (C&W LP); and "Nyquil Blues" and "All Night Long" by Alvin Crow (singles).

LOVE/PEACE/SERVICE RECORDS, INC., 2140 St. Clair St., Bellingham WA 98225. (206)733-3807. President: Renie Peterson. Record company and music publisher. Estab. 1970. Released 3 albums in 1978; plans 1 album in 1979 and 1 album in 1980. Works with musicians and songwriters on contract. Pays standard royalty to artists and songwriters. Current artists are under contract but songwriters are not.
How to Contact: Submit demo tape and lyric sheet. Prefers 7½ ips reel-to-reel or cassette with 1-4 songs on demo. SASE. Reports in 2 weeks.
Music: Inspirational; MOR; and top/40. "Similar style to Evie Tornquist's music." Recently released *Transformed*, by Tina Allen (inspirational/gospel LP).

LOYPRIQUAN, LTD., 39 W. 55th St., New York NY 10019. (212)586-3350. Labels include LPG Records and Marina Records. A&R Director: Nathaniel Adams. Controller: Debra

Martinez Franqui. Record company and music publisher. Released 10 singles and 6 albums in 1978; plans 24 singles and 12 albums in 1979. Works with musicians and songwriters on contract. Pays negotiable royalty to artists and songwriters on contract.
How to Contact: Submit demo tape and lead sheet. Prefers reel-to-reel or cassette. SASE. Reports in 2 weeks.
Music: MOR and top 40/pop. Recently released *The Nominee*, by Lloyd Price (pop LP); *Peaceful*, by Al Johnson (pop/R&B LP); and "Pulse," by Pulse (R&B single).

LUCIFER RECORDS, INC., Box 263, 37 Woodside Ave., Hasbrouck Heights NJ 07604. (201)288-8935. President: Ron Luciano. Record company, booking agency and music publisher. Estab. 1968. Works with musicians and songwriters on salary or contract. Buys some material outright.
How to Contact: Arrange personal interview. Prefers cassette with 4-8 songs on demo. SASE. Reports in 3 weeks.
Music: Disco; easy listening; MOR; rock; soul; and top 40/pop. Recently released "Look Into My Eyes," by Charles Lamont; and "That'll Be the Day," by Diamond Jym (rock singles).

LUCKY MAN MUSIC, The Home Place, Mount Juliet TN 37122. Labels include American Cowboy Songs. President: Alfred LeDoux. Record company and music publisher. Estab. 1972. Released 2 singles and 2 albums in 1978; plans 2 albums in 1979. Works with songwriters on contract. Pays standard royalties.
How to Contact: Submit demo tape and lead sheet. Prefers 7½ ips reel-to-reel with 1-5 songs on demo. SASE. Reports in 2 weeks.
Music: C&W; easy listening; and folk (about the West). "We are only interested in *authentic* songs about cowboys and the West. No Gene Autry stuff." Recently released *Life as a Rodeo Man* and *Songbook of the American West*, by Chris LeDoux (LPs).

LUNA RECORDS CO., 434 Center St., Healdsburg CA 95448. (707)433-4138. Labels include Luna, Lugar, Yuriko and Sony Records. President: Abel De Luna. Record company, booking agency and music publisher. Estab. 1976. Released 15 singles and 12 albums in 1978; plans 50 singles and 25 albums in 1979, 50 singles and 25 albums in 1980. Works with musicians and songwriters on contract. Pays 8% royalty to artists on contract; 2½% royalty to songwriters on contract.
How to Contact: Submit demo tape and lead sheet. Prefers cassette with 5-10 songs on demo. Does not return unsolicited material. Reports in 3 weeks.
Music: Children's and Latin. Recently released "Son Tus Perjumenes Mujer," by Los Huracanes Del Norte; "El Trage de Eva," by Grupo Chicaly; and "Ruego de Amor," by Ray Camacho (Latin singles).

M.R.C. RECORDS, Box 2072, Waynesboro VA 22980. (703)942-0106. Labels include MRC, Lark and Echo Records. President: John Major. Record company, music publisher and recording studio. Estab. 1965. Released 24 singles and 10 albums in 1978; plans 24 singles and 10 albums in 1979. Works with musicians on contract; songwriters on salary or contract. Payment negotiable. Buys some material outright; payment negotiable.
How to Contact: Submit demo tape and lyric sheet. Prefers 7½ ips reel-to-reel with 1-4 songs on demo. SASE. Reports in 2 weeks.
Music: Bluegrass; C&W; disco; easy listening; gospel; MOR; rock (country or hard); soul; and top 40/pop. Recently released "Afraid You'd Come Back," by Kenny Price (C&W single); "Deeper Water," by Brenda Kaye Perry (C&W single); and "Carlena and Jose Gomes," by Billy Walker (C&W single).
Tips: "Don't submit songs with tunes purchased from advertisements."

McKINNON PICTURES/RECORD CO., Box 691, Reading PA 19601. (215)372-7361. Labels include McKinnon, Slide, Holy Cross, Reading, Tar Heel, Movieland, Atlanna, Black Treasure and Ohiophone. President: Lenny McKinnon. Record company. Estab. 1964. Works with musicians on salary or contract; songwriters on contract. Pay 3-6% royalty to artists on contract; 5% maximum royalty to songwriters on contract.
How to Contact: Submit demo and lead sheet. Prefers 7½ ips reel-to-reel or disc with 2-6 songs on demo. SASE. Reports in 1 month.
Music: Blues; C&W; disco; easy listening; gospel; jazz; rock (soft); soul; and top 40/pop. Recently released "Potato Slide," recorded by Bobby Newton (disco).

MAINLINE RECORDS, 1440 Kearny St. NE, Washington DC 20017. (202)635-0464. Vice President A&R: Rodney Brown. Record company, music publisher and record producer.

Estab. 1974. Released 4 singles and 1 album in 1978; plans 3 singles and 1 album in 1979, 8 singles and 2 albums in 1980. Works with musicians and songwriters on contract. Pays 4-5% royalty to artists on contract; statutory royalties to songwriters on contract.
How to Contact: Submit demo tape. Prefers 7½ ips reel-to-reel or cassette with 2-4 songs on demo. SASE. Reports in 1 month.
Music: Disco; R&B; and soul. Recently released *Sweetest Piece of the Pie*, by Bobby Thurston (soul LP); "I Can't Take It," by Ricky Irving and Instant Replay (soul single); and "Baby Waldo," by Baby Waldo (soul single).

MAJEGA RECORDS, 240 E. Radcliffe Dr., Claremont CA 91711. (714)624-0677. President: Gary K. Buckley. Record company. Estab. 1976. Plans 6 singles and 4 albums in 1979. Works with musicians on salary or contract; songwriters on contract. Payment negotiable to artists on contract; pays statutory royalty to songwriters on contract.
How to Contact: Submit demo tape or submit demo tape and lead sheet. Prefers 7½ ips reel-to-reel or cassette with 1-4 songs on demo. SASE. Reports in 3 weeks.
Music: Children's; C&W; easy listening; gospel; MOR; rock (country or pop); and top 40/pop. Recently released *To God, With Love* and *Country Love*, recorded by Jerry Roark (gospel/C&W LPs); and "Songwriter," by Rick Buche (pop single).

MANQUIN, Box 2388, Toluca Lake CA 91602. (213)985-8284. Labels include Quinto Records. Co-Owner: Quint Benedetti. Record company, music publisher, record producer, management firm and public relations firm. Estab. 1979. Plans 2 albums in 1979. Works with musicians and songwriters on contract. Pays standard royalty to artists on contract; statutory royalties to songwriters on contract.
How to Contact: Query or submit demo tape and lead sheet. Prefers 7½ ips reel-to-reel or cassette with 2-3 songs on demo. SASE. Reports in 1 month.
Music: Novelty and Broadway musical.

MARANTA MUSIC ENTERPRISES, Box 1005, Englewood Cliffs NJ 07632. Labels include Eclipse, Spear, Maranta and Beagle Records. President/A&R Director: Clancy Morales. General Manager: Jackie Morales. Record company, music publisher and record producer. Estab. 1972. Plans 10 singles and 5 albums in 1979. Works with musicians and songwriters on contract. Does "master leasing and releasing of songs and recording acts based on royalties." Pays 10% royalty to artists on contract; 50% royalty to songwriters on contract. Charges for some services: "when we act as a consulting firm, contracted by an individual artist, songwriter or producer for selection of professional material, engineer, studio, studio musicians, arrangers and copyist (for projects contracted on other than our own record labels)."
How to Contact: Submit demo tape and lead sheet. Prefers 7½ ips reel-to-reel with 2-4 songs on demo. "We prefer a professionally recorded demo on 4, 8 or 16 tracks with enough instrumentation and singers. Song titles and the writer's name, as well as sender information, should be stamped on reel box and on the tape itself. All demos and lead sheets will be returned only if accompanied by SASE big enough for all material sent."
Music: Disco; jazz; progressive; rock (jazz); Latin salsa; and Latin pop. Recently released "Besame Otra Vez," by Jeniffer (crossover/Latin pop single); and "Happy Song," by the Blues Brothers (soul/top 40 single).

MARINA RECORDS, 39 W. 55th St., New York NY 10019. (212)586-3350. A&R Director: Nate Adams Jr. Record company and music publisher. Estab. 1970. Released 2 singles and 3 albums in 1978; plans 4 singles and 6 albums in 1979, 8 singles and 12 albums in 1980. Works with musicians and songwriters on contract. Pays standard royalties to songwriters on contract.
How To Contact: Submit demo tape or submit demo tape and lead sheet. Prefers 7½ or 15 ips reel-to-reel or cassette with 2 songs minimum on demo. SASE. Reports in 2 weeks.
Music: R&B; soul; and top 40/pop. Recently released *Peaceful*, by Al Johnson (pop LP); *Pulse*, by Pulse (soul LP); and *The Nominee*, by Lloyd Price (pop LP).

MARMIK, 135 E. Muller Rd., East Peoria IL 61611. (309)699-7204. President: Martin Mitchell. Record company and music publisher. Estab. 1972. Released 10 albums in 1978. Works with musicians and songwriters. Pays negotiable royalties. Sometimes buys material from songwriters outright; payment negotiable.
How to Contact: Query, submit demo tape, or submit demo tape and lead sheet. Prefers reel-to-reel or cassette with 2-10 songs on demo. "With first submission include an affidavit of ownership of material." SASE. Reports in 2 weeks.
Music: Blues; children's; choral; church/religious; C&W; easy listening; gospel; and MOR.

┌Songwriter's Market Close-Up─

Collaboration is a process that can't be forced, says composer/lyricist Lamont Dozier. "There has to be certain chemistry," says Dozier, whose chemistry in the team of Holland/Dozier/Holland produced hits for a variety of artists from the Supremes to the Doobie Brothers. "It's a very personal thing. And when you try to interject your feelings on somebody else and they're not receptive, then you've got chaos."—Photo by Jill Williams

MARVEL RECORDS CO., 852 Elm St., Manchester NH 03101. Labels include Banff, Marvel, Rodeo International, W&G and Melbourne Records. Executive Director: James N. Parks. Record company. Estab. 1946. Plans 12 singles and 6 albums in 1979. Works with musicians on salary or contract; songwriters on salary. Payment negotiable. Buys some material outright.
How to Contact: Submit lead sheet.

MAZINGO'S, INC., Box 11181, Charlotte NC 28209. (704)375-1102. President: Ben W. McCoy. Record company. Estab. 1954. Payment negotiable.
How to Contact: Query or submit demo tape and lead sheet. Prefers cassette or 8-track cartridge with 2-8 songs on demo. SASE. Reports in 1 month.
Music: Bluegrass; blues; children's; choral; church/religious; classical; C&W; folk; gospel; jazz; polka; progressive; soul; and top 40/pop.

MCA RECORDS, INC., 100 Universal City Plaza, Universal City CA 91608. (213)985-4321. Labels include Infinity; distributes Butterfly and Source. A&R Directors: Denny Rosencrantz, Harvey Kupernick. Record company. Released 200 singles and 100 albums in 1978. Works with musicians on contract.
How to Contact: Submit demo tape and lead sheet or lyric sheet. Prefers cassette with 5-10 songs on demo. SASE. Reports in 4 months.
Music: C&W; disco; easy listening; jazz; MOR; progressive; R&B; rock; and top 40/pop. Recently released *Totally Hot*, by Olivia Newton-John (rock LP); *Who Are You?*, by the Who (rock LP); and *A Single Man*, by Elton John (rock LP).
Tips: "The more professionally produced the package, the better. We'd like to see demos go beyond piano and vocal."

MCA RECORDS, 2409 21st Ave. S., Nashville TN 37212. (615)385-0840. Contact: A&R Department. Record company. Released 60 singles and 30 albums in 1978; plans 60 singles and 30 albums in 1979, 60 singles and 30 albums in 1980. Works with musicians/artists on contract.
How to Contact: Query. Prefers 7½ reel-to-reel with 2-4 songs on demo. SASE.
Music: Recently released "Ya'll Come Back Saloon," by the Oak Ridge Boys (country single); "Tulsa Time," by Don Williams (country single); and "If Loving You is Wrong," by Barbara Mandrell (country single).

MDK COMMUNICATIONS LTD., c/o Paul Kigar, Amcongen Sao Paulo, APO Miami FL 34030. (011)203-6692 (Sao Paulo Brazil). Owner: Malcolm Forest. Record company, music publisher and record producer. Estab. 1973. Released 2 singles in 1978; plans 2 singles and 1 album in 1979, 6 singles and 2 albums in 1980. Works with songwriters on contract. Pays standard royalties.
How to Contact: Submit demo tape and lead sheet or submit demo tape and lyric sheet. Prefers reel-to-reel or cassette with 1-4 songs on demo. SASE. Reports in 1 month.
Music: Disco; easy listening; MOR; progressive; R&B; rock; soul; and top 40/pop. Recently released "Silent Evenings" and "A Stupid Way" (ballad singles) and "Disco Lady" (disco single), by Malcolm Forest.
Tips: "We are constantly looking for hit potential (disco, AOR, etc.) titles for our gold artist, Malcolm Forest."

MELLOW MAN RECORDS, 1180 Forestwood Dr., Suite 304, Mississauga, Ontario, Canada L5C 1H9. Labels include Mellow Man, Foxy Lady, Rapper and Sweet Thing Records. Director: William Moran. Record company, music publisher and management firm. Estab. 1970. Plans 48 singles and 36 albums in 1979. Works with musicians and songwriters on salary or contract. Pays 8-10% royalty to artists on contract; 50% royalty to songwriters on contract. Buys some material outright; pays $300-1,000/song. "All studio and musician costs are an advance against sales."
How to Contact: Submit demo tape and lead sheet. Include bio and photo. Prefers 7½ ips reel-to-reel or cassette with 1-12 songs on demo. SAE and International Reply Coupons. Reports in 2 weeks.
Music: Blues; disco; easy listening; jazz; rock (country); soul; and top 40/pop. Recently released "Where Did the Good Times Go?", by Jeff Addams (easy listening single); "I Love to Sing," by Terry Logan (jazz single); and "It Happened One Night," by Jeff and Jackie (top 40 single).

MERRITT & NORMAN MUSIC, Rt. 5, Box 368-A, Yakima WA 98903. (509)966-6334. Labels include Tell International Records. General Manager: Hiram White. Record company, music publisher and recording studio. Works with musicians and songwriters on contract. Pays standard royalty to songwriters on contract; 6¢/sheet for sheet music. Buys some material outright.
How to Contact: Submit demo tape and lead sheet. Prefers 15 ips reel-to-reel or cassette with 1 song on tape. SASE. Reports in 2 months.
Music: Bluegrass; blues; C&W; disco; folk; jazz; and rock. Recently released "I Can't Get the You Out of Me," by Barbara Jean Taylor (C&W single); and "I'm Too Shy," by Penny Stadler (C&W single).

MICHAL RECORDING ENTERPRISES, Box 2194, Memphis TN 38101. (901)774-5689. Labels include Gospel Express, Hub City, Del My and Bishop. President: Bishop J.B. Cole. Vice President: Michal Cole. Record company, music publisher and booking agency. Estab. 1968. Plans 12 albums and 6 singles in 1979; 12 albums in 1980. Works with musicians and songwriters on contract. Pays 4% royalty to artists on contract; 2½% royalty to songwriters on contract.
How to Contact: Submit demo tape. Prefers 7½ ips reel-to-reel or cassette. SASE. Reports in 2 months.
Music: Blues; church/religious; gospel; and soul.

MIGHTY RECORDS, 5800 S. Central; Phoenix AZ 85040. Labels include Poormans, Hefty, Darlene and Bluestown Records. President: Mike Lenaburg. General Manager: Vero Duffins. Record company, music publisher and record producer. Estab. 1969. Released 9 singles and 1 album in 1978; plans 16 singles and 4 albums in 1979, 25 singles and 10 albums in 1980. Works with musicians on contract or salary; songwriters on contract. Pays 3% minimum to artists on contract; standard royalties to songwriters on contract.
How to Contact: Query, submit demo tape, submit demo tape and lead sheet, submit acetate disc or submit acetate disc and lead sheet. Prefers cassette. SASE. Reports in 1 month.
Music: Blues; disco; gospel; and R&B. Recently released *Blues Like They Used To Be*, by Oklahoma Zeke (blues LP); "Lord Won't You Help Me To Believe," by the Mighty Stars of Faith (gospel single); and "Mama's Baby, Daddy's Maybe," by Michael Liggins (blues single).
Tips: "We also lease masters, especially blues, gospel and oldies ('50s/'60s)."

MIR-A-DON RECORDS, 5333 Astor Place SE, Washington DC 20019. (301)891-3638. Labels include Mir-a-Don, Solid Soul and Trip City. A&R Director: Elwood Tobe. Record company,

music publisher and booking agency. Estab. 1965. Plans 10 singles and 8 albums in 1979. Works with musicians and songwriters on contract. Pays 3% royalty to artists on contract; 1½% royalty to songwriters on contract.
How to Contact: Submit demo tape and lead sheet. Prefers cassette with 4 songs minimum on tape. SASE. Reports in 2 weeks.
Music: Disco; gospel; and soul. Recently released "Miss Heartbreaker," by the Ascots (soul); and "How Blessed You Are," by the Wilson Sisters (gospel).

MIRROR RECORDS, INC., 645 Titus Ave., Rochester NY 14617. (716)544-3500. Labels include Mirror and House of Guitars Records. Vice President: Armand Schaubroeck. Record company and music publisher. Estab. 1967. Released 5 singles and 3 albums in 1978. Works with musicians on salary or contract; songwriters on contract. Pays 33% royalty to artists on contract; variable royalty to songwriters on contract. Buys some material outright; pays $100 minimum/song.
How to Contact: Submit demo tape. Prefers 7½ ips reel-to-reel or cassette. Include photo with submission. SASE. Reports in 2 months.
Music: Folk; progressive; rock; and punk.

MITCHELL RECORDING & MUSIC PUBLISHING CO., INC., Route 7, Box 67, Ridge Rd., Columbus MS 39701. Labels include Vimla, Mitchell and His-Way Records. President/Owner: W.B. Mitchell. Vice President: M.A. Mitchell. Director, Creative Division: Van T. Mitchell. Talent Acquisition/Press Relations: Karen L. Mitchell. Administrator, Wilmit Music Producers: Bert A. Mitchell. Record company and music publisher. Estab. 1973. Plans 30 singles and 10 albums in 1979. Works with musicians and songwriters on contract. Pays 5% royalty to artists on contract; statutory royalty to songwriters on contract.
How to Contact: Submit demo tape or submit demo tape and lead sheet. Prefers cassette with 1-3 songs on demo. SASE. Reports in 1 month.
Music: Blues; disco; easy listening; gospel; MOR; rock; soul; "satin soul"; and top 40/pop. Recently released "She Ain't No Brick House" (disco), "Another Heartache Like This Again" (pop) and "Feather Against the Wind" (disco), by Keith Mitchell and the Delta Sounds; "Love Strike," by Dorothy Lewis (disco); "Not Even in a Mansion" (pop); "I Could Be Happy," by Willie Boyd (blues); "Promise Me Love," by Edna Echols; "Run From Tomorrow, by Samuel T. Robinson with the Magnolia Charms (pop/soul); and "Take Time to Go Crazy," by Samuel T. Robinson (rock).
Tips: "Submit all demos to our publishing division, Wilmit Music Producers (BMI), at the same address."

MODERN SOUND PRODUCTIONS, Box 1345, Crowley LA 70526. (318)783-1601. Labels include Blues Unlimited, Kajun, Wildwood, Par T, and Showtime. General Manager: Mark Miller. Partner: Jay Miller. Record company, music publisher and recording studio. Estab. 1972. Works with musicians on salary or contract; songwriters on contract. Pays 4-5% royalty to artists on contract; 5% royalty to songwriters on contract. Charges for some services: "We charge for making audition tapes of any material that we do not publish."
How to Contact: Submit demo tape and lead sheet. Prefers 7½ ips reel-to-reel. SASE. Reports in 1 month.
Music: Blues; church/religious; C&W; disco; folk; gospel; MOR; progressive; rock; and soul. Recently released "Touch Me" (progressive C&W single), *At Last* (progressive C&W LP) and "Mama Don't Care" (C&W single), by Warren Storm.

MOLLY RECORDS, Jeffro Plaza, Suite 206, 2655 Philmont Ave., Huntingdon Valley PA 19006. (215)947-7743. Labels include LuMar Records, Stage 21 Records and LeRoi Records. President: Danny Luciano. Vice President: Ray Royal. A&R Director: Bill Mathias. Record company, music publisher, record producer, management firm and booking agency. Estab. 1974. Released 2 singles in 1978; plans 2 singles and 1 album in 1979, 4 singles and 2 albums in 1980. Works with musicians and songwriters on contract; musicians and songwriters on salary. Pays negotiable royalties.
How to Contact: Submit demo tape and lead sheet or submit acetate disc and lead sheet. Prefers 7½ or 15 ips reel-to-reel or cassette with 4-8 songs on demo. "Reel-to-reel should be leadered and should be sent with an accompanying title list." SASE. Reports in 1 month.
Music: Blues; disco; easy listening; jazz; MOR; R&B; rock; soul; and top 40/pop.

MOTHER BERTHA MUSIC, INC., Box 69529, Los Angeles CA 90069. (213)846-9900. Labels include Warner-Spector, Phil Spector, Phil Spector International and Philles Records. Administrative Director: Donna Sekulidis. Record company, music publisher and production

company. Estab. 1961. Works with musicians and songwriters on salary or contract. Payment negotiable for artists and songwriters on contract. Buys some material outright. Charges for some services.
How to Contact: Submit demo tape and lead sheet. Prefers 7½ ips reel-to-reel, cassette, or disc. "A writer should only include what he feels is important." SASE. "All material must have a return self-addressed and prepaid envelope enclosed, even though there is no guarantee any material will be returned. No material will be considered without SASE." Reports "as soon as possible."
Music: Bluegrass; blues; children's; choral; church/religious; classical; C&W; disco; easy listening; folk; gospel; jazz; MOR; progressive; rock; soul; top 40/pop; and "all forms of music." Recently released "Da Doo Ron Ron," by Shaun Cassidy (pop single); "Then She Kissed Me," by Kiss (rock single); and "Death of a Ladies' Man," by Leonard Cohen (single).

MOTHER CLEO PRODUCTIONS, Box 521, By-Pass 76, Newberry SC 29108. (803)276-0639. Labels include Mother Cleo, Cleo and Cub. Producer/Director: Hayne Davis. Studio Manager: Polly Davis. Record company, music publisher, recording studio, and production company producing music for films, features and commercials. "Mother Cleo Productions is a unique, small (but multifaceted) company engaged in numerous activities for the communications/entertainment industry." Estab. 1970. Works with musicians on salary or contract; songwriters on contract. "We also work with co-producers, supplying our facility and talent for outside use for a front fee. We hire talent (vocalists, musicians and writers) of varying types, styles and capabilities at varying intervals, depending on the requirements and frequency of the work project and the individual's capabilities." Pays 5-20% royalty to artists and songwriters on contract. Charges for some services: offers studio facilities for rental by "outside" songwriters, producers and publishers.
How to Contact: Submit demo tape and lead sheet. Prefers cassette with 2-8 songs on demo. "We are not responsible for return of tapes, lead sheets, etc. on unsolicited material. If, however, appropriate packaging and return postage is included, we make every effort to return materials and notify the sender by personal letter." SASE. Reports in 2 weeks.
Music: C&W (modern country); disco; easy listening; MOR; rock; and top 40/pop. Recently released "Sheila," by James Meadows (modern country single); "Too Far Gone," by Curt Bradford (modern country single); and *Cooks in 1 Minute*, by the J. Teal Band (rock LP).

MOTOWN RECORDS CORP., 6255 Sunset Blvd., Los Angeles CA 90028. (213)468-3589. Labels include Tamla, Gordy, Soul, Rare Earth, Prodigal, Hitsville, Kudu, Natural Resources and Hit Disco. Assistant to the Vice President, Creative Division: Tom DePierro. Record company. Works with musicians on contract; songwriters on contract.
How to Contact: Submit demo tape. Prefers 7½ ips reel-to-reel or cassette with 3-5 songs on demo. "All original tunes must be copyrighted beforehand."
Music: Blues; disco; jazz; R&B; rock; and top 40/pop. Recently released *Greatest Hits*, recorded by the Commodores (R&B LP); *Here My Dear*, recorded by Marvin Gaye (R&B LP); and *Come Get It*, recorded by Rick James (punk/funk LP).
Tip: "We accept anything where you can get your lyric and music across. We understand that people don't have a lot of money to spend on demos."

MSI RECORDING STUDIOS, Box 164, Pennsauken NJ 08110. Labels include Ocean Records. Producers: Andy Ditaranto, Anthony J. Papa. Vice President/Chief Engineer: Anthony J. Papa. Record company and music publisher. Estab. 1970. Plans 5 singles and 5 albums in 1979. Works with musicians and songwriters on contract. Pays 3% royalty to artists on contract; 2% royalty to songwriters on contract.
How to Contact: Submit demo tape. Prefers 7½ ips reel-to-reel with 2-6 songs on demo. Does not return unsolicited material. Reports in 2-4 weeks.
Music: Disco; easy listening; MOR; rock (hard); and top 40/pop. Recently released "Wet T-shirts" and "School's Back," by Philadelphia (hard rock singles); and "Lady Love," by Joe Ricci (MOR single).
Tips: "Try to get at least 2-4 hooks, either musically or lyrically, into each song."

MUSHROOM RECORDS INC., 9000 Sunset Blvd., Suite 710, Los Angeles CA 90069. (213)550-4502. Labels include Chanterelle Disco. Director of A&R: Marc Gilutin. Record company. Estab. 1974 in US. Released 3 singles and 4 albums in 1978; plans 6 albums in 1979.
How to Contact: Submit demo tape and lyric sheet. Prefers cassette with 2-4 songs on demo. SASE. Reports "as time permits."
Music: Rock; top 40/pop; progressive; jazz; and disco (on Chanterelle only). Recently

released "Shake It" and "Don't Hang Up Your Dancing Shoes," by Ian Matthews (rock singles).

MUSIC ADVENTURES RECORDS, INC., 12501 Madison Ave., Cleveland OH 44107. (216)521-1222. Labels include Ohio Records. Vice President A&R: Jon Baruth. Record company, music publisher, record producer, management firm and promoter. Estab. 1972. Released 5 singles in 1978; plans 10 singles and 2 albums in 1979, 10 singles and 6 albums in 1980. Works with musicians on contract. Pays 10-20% royalty to artists on contract; standard royalties to songwriters on contract.
How to Contact: Submit demo tape and lead sheet. Prefers 7½ ips reel-to-reel with 2-4 songs on demo. SASE. Reports in 3 weeks.
Music: Folk; progressive; R&B; rock; and top 40/pop. Recently released "With You in My Eyes," by Coyote (country rock single); "Disco Rapist," by the Other Half (rock single); and "This Time to the End," by Great Lakes Band (pop rock single).

MUSIC RESOURCES INTERNATIONAL CORP., 161 W. 54th St., Suite 601, New York NY 10019. (212)265-6420. Labels include MRI Records. President: Andy Hussakowsky. Director: A&R: Gene O'Brien. Record company and music publisher. Estab. 1979. Released 10 singles and 4 albums in 1978; plans 10 singles and 5 albums in 1979, and 10 singles and 6 albums in 1980. Works with musicians and songwriters on contract. Pays 5% royalty to artists on contract; standard royalties to songwriters on contract. Buys some material outright. "We are interested in distribution of finished masters for US and foreign releases."
How to Contact: Arrange personal interview or submit demo tape and lead sheet. Prefers 7½ ips reel-to-reel with 1-10 songs on demo. SASE. Reports in 1 month.
Music: Disco; rock; top 40/pop; and R&B. Past hits include: "More, More, More," by Andre True Connection; "New York You Got Me Dancing" by Goody, Goody; and "Sharing the Night Together," by Dr. Hook.

MUSIC RESOURCES INTERNATIONAL CORP., Los Angeles Office, 1100 N. Alta Loma Rd., Los Angeles CA 90069. Director of Coast Operations: Steve Brodie. See Music Resources International Corp., New York office for details.

MYSTIC RECORDING STUDIOS, 6277 Selma Ave., Hollywood CA 90028. (213)464-9667. Labels include Mystic Records, Solar Records, Clock Records and Sassafras Records. President: Doug Moody. Coordinator: Nancy Faith. Record company, music publisher and production firm. Also originates film and TV music. Estab. 1968. Released 8 singles and 3 albums in 1978; plans 10 albums and 20 singles in 1979. Works with musicians on salary or contract; songwriters on contract. Pays "standard rates; some advances."
How to Contact: Submit demo tape or submit demo tape and lead sheet. Prefers 7½ ips quarter-track reel-to-reel, 15 ips reel-to-reel or cassette. SASE. Reports in 1 month.
Music: Blues; C&W; easy listening; gospel (modern, rock or pop); MOR; rockabilly; soul; top 40/pop; and "spoken word plays (up to 1 hour)."

NASHVILLE INTERNATIONAL MUSIC CORP., 20 Music Square W., Nashville TN 37203. (615)256-2885. Labels include Phoenix Records, Nashville International Records and Air-Trans Records. President: Reggie M. Churchwell. General Manager, Music Group: Bob May. Record company and music publisher. Estab. 1971. Released 10 singles and 4 albums in 1978; plans 10 singles and 4 albums in 1979. Works on "per song" basis.
How to Contact: Submit demo tape and lead sheet, attention Bob May. Prefers 7½ ips reel-to-reel with 2-6 songs on demo. SASE. Reports in 4 weeks.
Music: C&W; gospel; MOR; progressive; and top 40/pop. Recently released "The American Hamburger Way," by Howard Lips (country/rock); "I Haven't Loved There Yet," by John Wells (country/pop); "It's Hard To Be a Cowboy These Days," by Conrad Pierce (country); "Little Tear Drops" (gospel) and "I Hope We Walk the Last Mile Together (country gospel), by the Singing Holley's; and "The Legend of the Duke," by Tom Destry (country/pop).

NATURAL GROOVE RECORDS, INC., 3588 Big Tree Cove, Memphis TN 38128. (901)525-9468. Labels include Natural Groove, Hot, Beale St. Blues, Truth of the Matter and Memphis International. A&R Director: Ron Townsend. Record company, music publisher, booking agency and management firm. Estab. 1972. Plans 25 singles and 10 albums in 1979. Works with musicians and songwriters on contract or salary. Pays 4% royalty to artists on contract; 1% to songwriters on contract.
How to Contact: Arrange personal interview, submit demo tape, submit demo tape and lead sheet, or submit lead sheet. Prefers 7½ ips reel-to-reel, cassette or disc with 5-10 songs on

demo. "Make sure each song is listed on the tape box according to the order it appears on the tape." SASE. Reports in 3 weeks.
Music: Blues; children's; church/religious; classical; C&W; disco; easy listening; folk; gospel; jazz; MOR; progressive; rock; soul; and top 40/pop. Recently released "Super Soul City," by Alfred Brown (soul); "Turn Me On," by Numbers (soul); and "Don't Walk Away," by Chained Reactions (pop/soul).

NEW WORLD RECORDS, 2309 N. 36th St., Suite 11, Milwaukee WI 53212. (414)445-4872. President: Marvell Love. Record company, music publisher and record producer. Estab. 1976. Released 4 singles in 1978; plans 8 singles and 1 album in 1979, 12 singles and 2 albums in 1980. Works with musicians and songwriters on contract. Pays 2½-3½% royalty to artists on contract; standard royalties to songwriters on contract.
How to Contact: Submit demo tape. Prefers 7½ ips reel-to-reel or cassette with 5 songs minimum on demo. SASE. Reports in 3 weeks.
Music: Disco; soul; and top 40/pop. Recently released "Don't Break the Rule," by Marvell Love (soul single); "Yesterday's Love," by J.D. Jones (ballad single); and "Comin' at Cha," by Jones (blues single).

NIC-LYN MUSIC CO., 1033 Little East Neck Rd., West Babylon NY 11704. (516)669-1872. Labels include White Card Records. A&R Director: Karolyn Summo. Record company and music publisher. Estab. 1977. Plans 6 singles and 4 albums in 1979. Works with musicians and songwriters on contract. Pays 2-5% royalty to artists and songwriters on contract.
How to Contact: Submit demo tape and lead sheet. Prefers 7½ ips reel-to-reel or cassette with 3-8 songs on demo. SASE. Reports in 1 month.
Music: Disco; R&B; rock; and top 40/pop. Recently released "Rock 'n Roll Years," by Cardell and White (rock); "I Do the Best I Can With What I Got," by Rose Marie McCoy (R&B/disco); and "What Is This Magic Feeling?", by Gus Colletti (disco).

N-M-I PRODUCTIONS, CORP., 516 W. 75th St., Kansas City MO 64114. (816)333-9617. Labels include N-M-I, Cory and E.B.C. Records. President: Eugene Gold. Record company and music publisher. Estab. 1969. Released 3 singles and 2 albums in 1978; plans 3 albums in 1979, 3 albums in 1980. Works with musicians and songwriters on contract. Pays 2% royalty to artists on contract; 4% royalty to songwriters on contract.
How to Contact: Arrange personal interview or submit demo tape and lead sheet. Prefers 7½ ips reel-to-reel with 6 songs minimum on tape. SASE. Reports in 1 month.
Music: Blues; disco; gospel; jazz; MOR; soul; top 40/pop. Recently released *Talking About Jesus* by Royal Dixie Wonder (gospel LP); "I'm Checking Out," by John Green and the Redneck (C&W single); and "Give in to the Power of Love," by the Committee (R&B single).

THE NORTH COUNTRY FAIRE RECORD CO., 314 Clemow Ave., Ottawa, Ontario, Canada K2S 2B8. (613)234-6992. Labels include North Country Faire Records. President: T. Peter Hern. Record company, booking agency and music publisher. Plans 10 singles and 10 albums in 1979. Works with musicians and songwriters on salary or contract. Payment negotiable.
How to Contact: Arrange personal interview or submit demo tape and lead sheet. "We prefer personal contact after initial mail or phone contact." Prefers 7½ ips quarter- or full-track stereo reel-to-reel or cassette with 4 songs on demo. SAE and International Reply Coupons. Reports in 2 weeks.
Music: Disco; easy listening; progressive; and top 40/pop. Recently released "Happy Song" and "I Can Smile," by Peter Hern (pop/MOR singles).

NRS RECORDS AND TAPES, INC., Suite 116, Music Park Bldg., Box 22653, Nashville TN 37202. (615)885-0713. Labels include Rising Star, NRS and Music of America. President: Dave Mathes. Record company and music publisher. Estab. 1975. Works with musicians on contract; songwriters on salary or contract. Pays standard royalty to artists on contract; $1.37/song royalty to songwriters on contract.
How to Contact: Submit demo tape and lyric sheet. Prefers 7½ ips reel-to-reel with 3-5 songs on demo. SASE; "enclose $1 to help defray postage and handling costs." Reports in 2 weeks.
Music: Bluegrass; blues; C&W; disco; easy listening; gospel; MOR; progressive; rock (country); soul; top 40/pop; and instrumental. Recently released *Baby You Know How I Love You*, by Jim Ed Brown and Helen Cornelius (C&W LP); and *The Last Goodbye*, by Faron Young (C&W LP).

OAKRIDGE MUSIC RECORDING SERVICE, 2001 Elton Rd., Haltom City TX 76117.

Labels include Oakridge, Crossfire and Arrowhead. President: Homer Lee Sewell. Record company and music publisher. Estab. 1961. Plans to release 10 singles and 10 albums in 1979. Works with musicians on salary or contract; songwriters on contract. Pays 4¢ minimum/song royalty to artists on contract; 5¢ minimum/song royalty to songwriters on contract.
How to Contact: Submit demo tape. Prefers 7½ ips mono or stereo reel-to-reel with 2-4 songs on demo. SASE. Reports in 6 weeks.
Music: Bluegrass; church/religious; C&W; and gospel. Recently released "Stand Up America," by Shel Price (C&W single); "The Pain of Love Is Not Free," by Bill Hensley (C&W single); and "Break of Day," by Lee Sawyer (C&W single).

ODLE RECORDS, 8431 Howard Dr., Houston TX 77017. (713)649-5579. Labels include Merry Records. President: M.F. Odle. Record company, music publisher and record producer. Estab. 1965. Released 4 singles and 2 albums in 1978; plans 2 albums in 1979. Works with musicians and songwriters on contract. Pays standard royalty to artists on contract; statutory royalties to songwriters on contract.
How to Contact: Query, arrange personal interview, submit demo tape, submit demo tape and lead sheet, submit acetate disc, submit acetate disc and lead sheet, or submit lead sheet. Prefers 7½ ips reel-to-reel or cassette with 4 songs on demo. SASE. Reports in 2 weeks.
Music: Blues; children's; church/religious; C&W; disco; easy listening; folk; gospel; jazz; MOR; R&B; rock; and soul.

OLD HAT RECORDS, Box 54, Man's Field TX 76063. (817)477-2897. Labels include Old Hat and T-2-Topple Records. President: James Michael Taylor. Record company, booking agency, music publisher and production company. Estab. 1975. Plans to release 6-8 albums in 1979. Works with musicians on salary or contract. Pays 1% minimum royalty to artists and songwriters on contract.
How to Contact: Submit demo tape, arrange personal interview, submit demo tape and lead sheet, or submit lead sheet. Prefers 3¾ or 7½ ips reel-to-reel or cassette with 6-12 songs on demo. SASE. Reports in 1 week.
Music: Children's; choral; C&W; folk; rock; and top 40/pop. Recently released *Feathers in the Wind*, by Snowgeese (progressive/folk LP); *First Unk*, by Bob French (folk LP); and "What to Do With the Pictures," by James M. Taylor (C&W single).

OMNISOUND, INC., Delaware Water Gap PA 18327. (717)476-0550. Manager: Yoshio Inomata. Record company and music publisher. Released 10 albums in 1978; plans 1 single and 10 albums in 1979, 10 albums in 1980. Works with songwriters on contract. Pays standard royalties to songwriters on contract.
How to Contact: Submit demo tape and lead sheet, or submit lead sheet. Prefers cassette. SASE. Reports in 2 weeks.
Music: Children's; choral; church/religious; classical; easy listening; folk; gospel; MOR; and top 40/pop. Recently released *Good News*, by the Glory Singers and Fred Bock (gospel LP); *Alone and Live*, by John Coates Jr. (jazz LP); and *Enjoy Jesus*, by the Hour of Power Choir (religious LP).
Tips: "Send material for review suitable for use in schools or churches or for publication/recording for gospel market."

OPAL RECORDS, 8872 Hwy. 166, Winston GA 30187. (404)489-2909. Labels include A.R.P. Records. Owner: Danny Mote. Record company, music publisher and record producer. Estab. 1975. Released 4 singles and 2 albums in 1978; plans 10 singles and 6 albums in 1979, 15 singles and 10 albums in 1980. Works with musicians and songwriters on contract; musicians on salary. Pays 4-7% to artists on contract; standard royalties to songwriters on contract.
How to Contact: Arrange personal interview, submit demo tape, or submit acetate disc. Prefers 7½ or 15 ips reel-to-reel tape with 1-10 songs on demo. Does not return unsolicited material. Reports in 1 month.
Music: Children's; church/religious; C&W; gospel; rock; and top 40/pop. Recently released "Who is Santa Claus," by Troy Crumpton Jr. (Christmas single); "Full Time Christian," by Tommy Godwin (gospel LP); and "Crying Eyes," by Danny Mote (country single and LP).

ORBIT RECORDS, 100 Harvard Ave., Gadsden AL 35901. (205)546-6906. President: Ray McGinnis. A&R Director: Chuck McGinnis. Record company and music publisher. Estab. 1967. Works with musicians on salary or contract; songwriters on contract. Pays 5% royalty to artists on contract; 3% royalty to songwriters on contract.
to songwriters on contract.

How to Contact: Submit demo tape and lead sheet. Prefers 7½ ips reel-to-reel or 8-track cartridge with 2-6 songs on demo. SASE. Reports in 3 weeks.
Music: C&W; rock (hard or country); and soul. Recently released "Sand Mountain Woman" (soft rock single) and "Alabama Home Grown Wine" (hard rock single), by the Malibus; and "Going Down," by Norm Peterson (country rock single).
Tips: "Be original and be simple. We look for songs that people in the same situation can identify with. Leave room for improvisation."

OVATION RECORDS. 1249 Waukegan Rd., Glenview IL 60025. A&R Director: David Webb. Record company and music publisher. Estab. 1969. Released 15 singles and 12 albums in 1978. Works with musicians and songwriters on contract. Payment negotiable. Buys some material outright; payment negotiable.
How to Contact: Submit demo tape. Prefers 7½ ips reel-to-reel with 1-3 songs on demo. SASE. Reports in 2 weeks.
Music: C&W (Kendalls-type); MOR (David Gates/Jackson Browne-type); progressive (Elvis Costello-type); rock (Boston-type); and top 40/pop (Jay Ferguson-type). Recently released "Heaven's Just a Sin Away" and "Just Like Real People," by the Kendalls (C&W).

OVATION RECORDS, 803 18th Ave. S., Nashville TN 37203. (615)327-4871. Vice President A&R: Brien Fisher. Publishing Director: Michael Kosser. Estab. 1969. Works with artists and writers on contract.
How to Contact: Submit demo tape and lyric sheet to Kosser or Robert John Jones. Prefers 7½ ips reel-to-reel or cassette with 1-3 songs on demo.
Music: Country and pop. Recently released "Heaven's Just a Sin Away," by the Kendalls; and "Old Flames Can't Hold a Candle to You," by Joe Sun (country singles). Country artists include the Kendalls, Joe Sun, the Cates and Sheila Andrews. Pop artists include Tantrum and Mark Gaddis, and disco artist, Cleveland Eaton.

LEE MACE'S OZARK OPRY RECORDS, INC., Box 242, Osage Beach MO 65065. (314)348-2702. Labels include Kajac, Ven Jence, Vision, KRC and Red Rock. General Manager: Harold L. Luick. Record company, music publisher and record producer. Estab. 1953. Released 31 singles and 18 albums in 1978; plans 45 singles and 25 albums in 1979, 75 singles and 50 albums in 1980. Works with musicians on salary. Pays 3-8% royalty to artists on contract; statutory royalties to songwriters on contract.
How to Contact: Arrange personal interview or submit demo tape and lead sheet. Prefers 7½ ips reel-to-reel or cassette with 2-4 songs on demo. SASE. Reports in 2 weeks.
Music: Bluegrass; blues; church/religious; C&W; gospel; and R&B. Recently released *Ballads of Deadwood SD*, by Bob Everhart (country LP); "Mama Worked the Rocks and Clay," by Darrell Thomas (country single); "It Sets Me Free," by Jack Paris (country single); and "I've Had Enough of Loneliness," by Graham Fee (MOR single).

PARASOUND, INC., 680 Beach St., San Francisco CA 94121. (415)673-4544. President: Bernie Krause. Vice President: Sid Goldstein. Record company and music publisher. Estab. 1968. Plans 3 singles and 3 albums in 1979. Works with musicians and songwriters on contract. Payment negotiable.
How to Contact: Submit demo tape and lead sheet. Prefers 7½ ips reel-to-reel with 3-6 songs on demo. SASE. Reports in 3 weeks.
Music: MOR; rock; and top 40/pop.

DON PARK MUSIC, INC., 190 Don Park Rd., Markham, Ontario, Canada L3R 2V8. (416)495-1710. Labels include Country, Heavenly Jukebox, Cheyenne, Kodiak, Boo, Riga and Dirty Ditty. President: John C. Irvine. Record company, music publisher, booking agency and management firm. Estab. 1967. Released 10 singles and 30 albums in 1978. Works with musicians and songwriters on contract. Pays 0-10% royalty to artists on contract; statutory royalty to songwriters on contract.
How to Contact: Submit demo tape and lead sheet, submit demo tape, or arrange personal interview. Prefers 7½ or 15 ips reel-to-reel or cassette, with 2 songs minimum on tape. SAE and International Reply Coupons. Reports in 2 weeks.
Music: Bluegrass; blues; children's; C&W; folk; gospel; jazz; and "esoteric" music. Recently released *Short Turn*, by Short Turn (Canadian folk/country LP); and *Malton & Hamilton*, by Malton and Hamilton (comedy LP).

PASSPORT RECORDS, INC., 3619 Kennedy Rd., South Plainfield NJ 07080. (201)753-6100. Labels include Passport and Visa Records. A&R Director: Phylis Pannone. Record company

and music publisher. Estab. 1973. Works with musicians on contract. Payment negotiable.
How to Contact: Submit demo tape. Prefers 7½ ips reel-to-reel or cassette with 2-6 songs on demo. SASE. Reports in 2 weeks.
Music: Folk; jazz; progressive; rock; pop; and new wave/punk. Recently released *Livestock*, by Brand X (jazz/rock LP); *From Rats to Riches*, by the Good Rats (rock LP); and *Intergalactic Touring Band*, by various artists (science fiction rock/fantasy LP).

FRANK PAUL ENTERPRISES, Box 113, Woburn MA 01801. (617)933-1474. Labels include Casa Grande Records, Don-Mar and Strawnut. General Manager: Frank Paul. Record company, booking agency and music publisher. Estab. 1950. Released 10 singles and 10 albums in 1978. Works with musicians and songwriters on contract. Pays 3% minimum royalty to artists and songwriters on contract.
How to Contact: Submit demo tape and lead sheet. Prefers cassette with 3-6 songs on demo. SASE. Reports in 1 month.
Music: Blues; children's; choral; church/religious; classical; C&W; disco; easy listening; folk; gospel; MOR; rock; soul; and top 40/pop. Recently released "Happy, Happy Birthday Baby," by the Timeweavers (R&B single); and "God Said He Would Fight My Battle," by the Fabulous Bullock Brothers (gospel single).

PEDIGREE RECORDS, 13615 Victory Blvd., Suite 216, Van Nuys CA 91401. (213)997-9100. Labels include Funnybone Records. Director A&R: Paul Armstrong. Record company, music publisher and record producer. Estab. 1975. Released 3 singles in 1978; plans 6 singles and 1 album in 1979, 9 singles and 3 albums in 1980. Works with musicians and songwriters on contract. Pays 4-7% royalty to artists on contract; statutory royalties to songwriters on contract.
How to Contact: Submit demo tape and lead sheet. Prefers 7½ ips reel-to-reel or cassette with 3-6 songs on demo. "Include typed lyric sheet." SASE. Reports in 3 weeks.
Music: C&W; disco; easy listening; MOR; R&B; rock; soul; and top 40/pop. Recently released "Love Makin' Love," by Dean Whitney (country/rock single); "Feet Back on the Ground," by Eddie Howard (country single); and "Jewish Country Singer," by Arnold Rosenthal (novelty single).

PEER-SOUTHERN ORGANIZATION, 6922 Hollywood Blvd., Hollywood CA 90028. (213)469-1667. Labels include Spark Records. Professional Manager: Roy Kohn. Record company and music publisher. Estab. 1928. Released 25 singles and 10 albums in 1978. Works with musicians and songwriters on contract. Pays standard royalty to artists and songwriters on contract.
How to Contact: Submit demo tape and lead sheet or arrange personal interview. Prefers 7½ ips reel-to-reel or cassette with 2-5 songs on demo. SASE. Reports in 1 month.
Music: C&W; disco; easy listening; MOR; rock; and top 40/pop. Recently released "Superman," by Celi-Bee (disco single); "Return to Me," by Marty Robbins (country single); and "Walk Right In," by Dr. Hook (top 40/pop single).

PELLEGRINO MUSIC CO., INC., 311 Brook Ave., Bay Shore, Long Island NY 11706. (516)665-1003. Labels include Ivory Gold Records. President: Joseph V. Pellegrino Jr. Record company, music publisher and production company. Estab. 1971. Released 2 singles in 1977; plans 8 singles and 10 albums in 1979. Works with musicians and songwriters on contract. Pays 4% royalty to artists on contract; 50% royalty to songwriters on contract. Buys some material outright; pays $125-850.
How to Contact: Submit demo tape and lead sheet. Prefers 7½ ips reel-to-reel or cassette with 3-6 songs on demo. SASE. Reports in 1 week.
Music: Church/religious; gospel; and oldies. Recently released "Skyline of Manhattan," by Jade Four (oldies single); "Every Daze," by Calhoon (rock single); and "Tomorrow (He'll Be Coming Home)," by Steeple Peeple (top 40/pop single).
Tips: "Songs must be copyrighted. Artists, put the best songs you have on first, some original and some standards. Songwriters, just original material."

PERRYAL PRODUCTIONS, INC., Box 1162, Buffalo NY 14240. (716)894-3115. Labels include Solar Sounds Records and Tapes. President/Executive Producer: Barney Perry. Record company and music publisher. Estab. 1975. Plans 3-4 singles and 2-3 albums in 1979. Works with musicians on salary or contract; songwriters on contract. Pays 5% minimum royalty to artists on contract; 1½% royalty to songwriters on contract.
How to Contact: Submit demo tape and lead sheet. Prefers 7½ ips reel-to-reel or cassette. "Please be sure to outline songs, writers and any other information on all containers." SASE. Reports in 2 months.

Music: Blues; choral; church/religious; classical; disco; easy listening; gospel; jazz; MOR; progressive; rock; soul; and top 40/pop. Recently released *Nightlife*, by Blair (R&B/jazz fusion LP).

PHAROAH RECORDS, 1260 E. Main, Meriden CT 06450. (203)728-5639. Labels include Pharoah and Hardtimes Records. President: Bruce Lloyd. Vice President/A&R Director: John M. Calone. Record company and music publisher. Estab. 1974. Plans 20 albums in 1979. Works with musicians on salary or contract; songwriters on contract. Pays 3% royalty to artists on contract; 2% royalty to songwriters on contract. Buys some material outright.
How to Contact: Submit demo tape and lead sheet. Prefers cassette with 3-6 songs on demo. SASE. Reports in 1 week.
Music: Bluegrass; blues; C&W; disco; folk; jazz; and progressive. Recently released *Starting All Over Again*, by David Liska (bluegrass LP); and "Ballad of Patty Hearst," by Sue Lloyd (top 40 single).

PHONOGRAM, INC., 2000 Madison Ave., Memphis TN 38104. (901)726-6000. Labels include Mercury Records. Director of Southern A&R: Jud Phillips. Record company. Estab. 1946. Works with musicians on contract.
How to Contact: Submit demo tape. Prefers cassettes. Copyrighted material only. SASE. Reports in 2 weeks.
Music: Disco; easy listening; MOR; rock; soul; and top 40/pop. "Absolutely no country music accepted." Recently released LPs by Confunkshun, the Barkays and 10CC.

PHONOGRAM/MERCURY RECORDS, INC., 6255 Sunset Blvd., Los Angeles CA 90028. (213)466-9771. Contact: A&R Department.
How to Contact: Submit demo tape. Prefers 7½ ips reel-to-reel or cassette. SASE. Reports in 2 weeks.
Music: C&W; disco; easy listening; jazz; MOR; progressive; R&B; rock; soul; and top 40/pop. Recently released "Heartaches," by Bachman-Turner Overdrive (rock single); "Shake," by Gap Band (R&B single); and "Dancing Fool," by Frank Zappa (rock single).

PHONOGRAM/MERCURY RECORDS, 810 7th Ave., New York NY 10019. Also distributes DJM, Zappa and De Lite Records. Vice President, A&R: Steve Katz. Record company. Mercury estab. 1947. Phonogram/Mercury estab. 1971.
How to Contact: Submit demo tape. Prefers cassette with 1-4 songs on demo. SASE. Reports in 2 weeks.
Music: Disco; jazz; MOR; progressive; R&B; rock; and top 40/pop. Recently released *Whiteface*, by Whiteface (rock LP).

PICKWICK RECORDS, 9200 Sunset Blvd., Los Angeles CA 90069. A&R Director: Don Shain. Needs vary; query about needs and submission policy.

PLANTATION RECORDS, 3106 Belmont Blvd., Nashville TN 37212. (615)385-1960. Labels include Sun International Records and SSS Records. Contact: A&R Director. Record company and music publisher. Estab. 1967. Pays standard royalties.
How to Contact: Query, then submit demo tape. Prefers cassette. SASE. Reports "as soon as possible."
Music: Bluegrass; blues; C&W; disco; easy listening; folk; gospel; jazz MOR; progressive; R&B; rock; soul; and top 40/pop. Recently released "Chatanooga Choo Choo," by Rita Remington (single); "Happy Cajun," by Jimmy C. Newman (single); and "Cold Cold Heart," by Jerry Lee Lewis (single).
Tips: "We do not accept unsolicited material. Songwriters should not submit material to us through the mail."

PLEIADES MUSIC, The Barn, North Ferrisburg VT 05473. (802)425-2111. Labels include Phil0 Records and Fretless Records. Vice President: Bill Schubart. Record company and music publisher. Estab. 1975. Works with musicians and songwriters on contract. Pays variable royalty to artists on contract; 50% royalty to songwriters on contract.
How to Contact: Submit demo tape. Prefers 7½ ips reel-to-reel or cassette with 1-3 songs on demo. SASE. Reports in 1 month.
Music: Blues; children's; classical; C&W; folk; jazz; progressive; rock; soul; and top 40/pop. Recently released *Old Friends*, by Mary McCaslin (pop LP); *Moments of Happiness*, by Rosalie Sorrels (pop LP); and *Sunday Street*, by Dave Van Ronk (folk LP).

POLKA TOWNE RECORDS, 211 Post Ave., Westbury NY 11590. President: Teresa Zapolska. Record company, music publisher, record producer and booking agency. Estab. 1963. Works with artists and songwriters on contract.
How to Contact: Submit demo tape. Prefers cassette with 1-3 songs on demo. SASE. Reports in 1 month.
Music: Polkas and waltzes.

POLYDOR RECORDS INC., 6255 Sunset Blvd., Hollywood CA 90028. (213)466-9574. Labels include MGM Records. A&R Director: Steve Duboff. Record company. Works with musicians on contract.
How to Contact: Submit demo tape and lyric sheet. Prefers 7½ ips reel-to-reel or cassette with 1-4 songs on demo. SASE. Reports in 1 week.
Music: Disco; folk; jazz; MOR; progressive; R&B; rock; and top 40/pop. Recently released *2 Hot*, by Peaches and Herb (R&B LP); *Love Tracks*, by Gloria Gaynor (disco LP); and *Danger Money*, by U.K. (rock LP).
Tip: "Do the best production you can on demos, but keep it simple."

POLYDOR RECORDS, 810 7th Ave., New York NY 10019. (212)399-7051. A&R: Stu Fine. Record company. Works with artists and songwriters on contract.
How to Contact: Submit demo tape and lead sheet. Prefers 7½ or 15 ips reel-to-reel or cassette. SASE.
Music: Disco; folk; jazz; MOR; progressive; rock; soul; and top 40/pop. Recently released *Champagne Jam*, by the Atlanta Rhythm Section, and LPs by Millie Jackson and U.K.

PORTRAIT RECORDS, CBS, 1801 Century Park W., Los Angeles CA 90067. (213)556-4806. Vice President, A&R: Lorne Saifer. Record company. Estab. 1976. Works with musicians on salary or contract; songwriters on contract. Pays negotiable royalty. Buys some material outright.
How to Contact: Submit demo tape or submit demo tape and lead sheet. Prefers 7½ or 15 ips reel-to-reel or cassette with 3-4 songs on demo. SASE. Reports "as soon as possible."
Music: Disco; folk; MOR; progressive; rock; soul; and top 40/pop. Recently released "Stand Tall," by Burton Cummings (MOR/pop single); and *Magazine* by Heart (rock/pop LP).
Tips: "Keep the tape as simple as possible."

PRAISE RECORDS, 6979 Curragh Ave., Burnaby, British Columbia, Canada V5J 4V6. Labels include New Born, Little People, Praise, Faith, Horizon and Quest. Manager: Paul Yaroshuk. Record company, music publisher and recording studio. Estab. 1967. Released 25 singles and 38 albums in 1978; plans 45 singles and 42 albums in 1979. Works with musicians and songwriters on contract. Pays 18% royalty to artists on contract; 2% royalty to songwriters on contract. Buys some material outright.
How to Contact: Submit demo tape. Prefers reel-to-reel with 12 songs on demo. SAE and International Reply Coupons. Reports in 2 weeks.
Music: Bluegrass; children's; choral; church/religious; C&W; folk; and gospel.

PRELUDE RECORDS, 200 W. 57th St., Suite 403, New York NY 10019. (212)581-4890. Contact: A&R Director. Record company. Estab. 1977. Released 8 albums in 1978; plans 15 albums in 1979. Works with musicians on contract.
How to Contact: Submit demo tape. Prefers 7½ ips reel-to-reel or cassette. SASE. Reports in 3 weeks.
Music: Disco; and soul. Recently released *Keep on Jumpin'*, by Musique (disco LP); *Come on Dance, Dance*, by the Saturday Night Band (disco LP); and *I'm a Man*, by Macho (disco LP).

PRIVATE STOCK RECORDS, LTD., 40 W. 57th St., New York NY 10019. (212)397-1600. A&R Director: Steven Scharf. Record company. Estab. 1974. Plans 30 singles and 18 albums in 1979. Works with musicians and songwriters on contract. Payment negotiable.
How to Contact: Submit demo tape, arrange personal interview, or submit demo tape and lead sheet. Prefers 7½ or 15 ips half-track reel-to-reel with 2-4 songs on demo. SASE. Reports in 1 month.
Music: Disco; easy listening; folk; MOR; progressive; rock; soul; and top 40/pop. Recently released "Emotion," by Samantha Sang (pop/R&B single); "Let's All Chant," by the Michael Zager Band (disco/R&B single); and *Robert Gordon & Link Wray*, by Robert Gordon and Link Wray (rock LP).

QCA RECORDS, INC., 2832 Spring Grove Ave., Cincinnati OH 45225. Labels include QCA,

Chime, QCA New Day, QCA Rejoice and QCA Redmark. Contact: A&R Dept. Record company, music publisher, custom pressing firm and recording studio. Estab. 1971. Works with musicians and songwriters on contract. Pays 5% royalty to artists on contract. Charges for some services: "if you record something for yourself not in connection with our releases or publishing."
How to Contact: Submit demo tape and lead and lyric sheet. Prefers 7½ ips reel-to-reel or cassette with 1-6 songs on demo. SASE. Reports in 1 month, "or longer at times."
Music: C&W; gospel; jazz; and soul (R&B).

QUINTO RECORD PRODUCTIONS, Box 2388, Toluca Lake CA 91602. (213)985-8284. Labels include Quinto, Suzi, BenRod, ManQuin, Fun, Top 'n' Bottom and Cloverleaf Records. Owner: Quint Benedetti. Record company, music publisher and demo producer. Estab. 1977. Released 3 singles and 2 albums in 1977. Works with musicians on salary or contract; songwriters on contract. Pays standard royalty to artists and songwriters on contract. Charges for some services; to produce demo records.
How to Contact: Submit demo tape and lead sheet. Prefers cassette with 2-4 songs on demo. SASE. Reports in 1 month.
Music: Musical comedy and novelty. Recently released *Chocalonia*, by original cast (rock musical LP); *The Lavender Lady*, by Agnes Moorehead (one-woman show LP); and "Cuyusos by the Sea," by Arnold Best (C&W single).

RAE-COX & COOKE MUSIC CORP., 1697 Broadway, Suite 702, New York NY 10019. Labels include Rae-Cox and Enrica Records. A&R Director: William Gray. Record company and music publisher. Released 8 singles and 6 albums in 1978; plans 7 singles and 7 albums in 1979, 10 singles and 9 albums in 1980. Works with musicians and songwriters on contract. Pays 2% royalty to artists and songwriters on contract.
How to Contact: Submit demo tape and lead sheet or submit lead sheet. Prefers reel-to-reel or cassette with 2-3 songs on demo. SASE. Reports in 2 weeks.
Music: Gospel; jazz; progressive; soul; and top 40/pop.

RAM RECORDS, Box 2802, Corpus Christi TX 78403. (512)992-5126. Contact: Bruce Taylor, John Davis. Estab. 1972. Released 2 singles and 1 album in 1978; plans 6 singles and 2 albums in 1979, 16 singles and 4 albums in 1980. Works musicians on contract; salary and songwriters on contract. Pays standard royalty to artists on contract; statutory rate to songwriters on contract. Sometimes buys songs outright for $50-500/song.
How to Contact: Submit demo tape. Prefers 7½ ips reel-to-reel or cassette with 2-5 songs on demo. Does not return unsolicited material. Reports in 2 weeks.
Music: Recently released "El Capitan," "Like Old Times Again," and "If I Don't Drink Myself to Death (I'm Gonna Drown Tryin')," by the Gary Davis Band (progressive/country singles).

RAM RECORDS, 4307 Saundersville Rd., Old Hickory TN 37138. (615)847-4419. Labels include Ram Records, "K," Pearl, Swingline, Jo and WLS. Contact: Professional Manager. President: Mira Ann Smith. Record company and music publisher. Estab. 1955. Plans 9 singles and 6 albums in 1979. Works with musicians and songwriters on contract. Pays 3% royalty to new artists on contract.
How to Contact: Submit demo tape with lyrics or demo tape and lead sheet. Prefers 7½ ips reel-to-reel on a 5-inch reel with 1-5 songs on demo. "We would like each song leadered." SASE. "We prefer material to be sent regular fourth class mail on the special sound recording rate and not special delivery, certified or registered mail. Send only duplicate tapes and never the master." Reports in 1 month.
Music: Bluegrass; blues; C&W; disco; easy listening; folk; gospel; jazz; MOR; progressive; rock; soul; top 40/pop; and "spoken word with original music." Recently released "Red Beans and Rice," by Scat Man Patin (rock); "Loneliness," by Bobby Page (soft rock); and "Easy Living," by Jon Legnon (soft rock).
Tips: "We also deal in 'collector's editions' of the '50s rock/country releases. Any writers, producers or former small independent label owners interested in rereleases or new recording releases of material they may have had out during the '50s or early '60s may contact us in this interest. Material is distributed on long-playing albums only."

RANDALL RECORDS, 29 Elaine Rd., Milford CT 06460. (203)878-7383. President: Gerald Randall. Record company, music publisher and record producer. Estab. 1972. Released 2 singles and 1 album in 1978; plans 12 singles and 4 albums in 1980. Works with musicians and

songwriters on contract. Pays 3-5% royalty to artists on contract: statutory royalties to songwriters on contract.
How to Contact: Submit demo tape and lead sheet. Prefers 3¾ or 7½ ips reel-to-reel or cassette with 1 song on demo. SASE. Reports in 1 month.
Music: Easy listening; MOR; and top 40/pop. Recently released "Why is Your Love Haunting Me?", by Samuel Turiano (easy listening); and "Zodiac Zoo" and "Sahib Sam," by the Satyrs (rock).

RAY'S SOUNDS, Box 103, East New York Station, Brooklyn NY 11207. (212)827-2582. Producer: Ray Smith. Record producer. Released 3 singles in 1978; plans 5 singles and 10 albums in 1980. Works with songwriters on contract. Pays standard minimum royalty to artists on contract; statutory royalties to songwriters on contract.
How to Contact: Query, arrange personal interview, submit demo tape, or submit demo tape and lead sheet. Prefers cassette with 2-4 songs on demo. SASE. Reports in 2 weeks.
Music: Disco; easy listening; and reggae. Recently released "Nine O'Clock," by A. Smith (reggae); "Christmas," by A.J. Smith (disco); and "I'm in Love with You," by Y. Johnson (disco).

RCA RECORDS, 6363 Sunset Blvd., Los Angeles CA. (213)468-4000. Head of A&R: Warren Schatz, 1133 Avenue of the Americas, New York NY 10036. Record company. Estab. 1929. Works with musicians and songwriters on contract.
How to Contact: Submit demo tape. Prefers 7½ ips reel-to-reel or cassette with 1-3 songs on demo. SASE. Reports in 8 weeks.
Music: Classical; disco; jazz; progressive; R&B; rock; soul; and top 40/pop. Recently released "Shame," by Evelyn Champagne King (disco single); "Count on Me," by Jefferson Starship (rock single); and "It's a Laugh," by Hall and Oates (rock single).
Tips: "We're interested in a simple demo with piano and voice for songs. For artists, the same applies, but get vocals out front."

RCA RECORDS, 806 17th Ave. S., Nashville TN 37203. (615)244-9880. A&R Director: Roy Dea. Record company. Works with musicians on contract or salary. Pays negotiable royalties.
How to Contact: Arrange personal interview or submit demo tape and lyric sheet. Prefers 7½ ips reel-to-reel or cassette with 2-3 songs on demo. SASE. Reports in 3 weeks.
Music: C&W and top 40/pop. Recently released "Heartbreaker," by Dolly Parton (pop single); "Only One Love in My Life" and "Long Way Around the World," by Ronnie Milsap (easy listening); and "Burgers and Fries," by Charlie Pride (C&W).

RCI RECORDS/SOUND STUDIOS, INC., Box 126, 4 William St., Elmsford NY 10523. (914)592-7983. Labels include RCI, Thomas and Aster Records. A&R/Vice President: Ray Roberts. Record company, music publisher and recording studio. Estab. 1965. Released 57 singles and 21 albums in 1978; plans 60 singles and 25 albums in 1979, 60 singles and 25 albums in 1980. Works with musicians and songwriters on salary or contract. Pays 10% royalty to artists on contract; 5% royalty to songwriters on contract.
How to Contact: Submit demo tape and lead sheet and lyrics, or "leave tape off at office and we will contact you." Prefers 7½ ips reel-to-reel with 1-12 songs on demo. SASE. Reports in 2 weeks.
Music: Bluegrass; church/religious; C&W; disco; easy listening; folk; gospel; jazz; rock; MOR; soul; top 40/pop; Latin; polka; and R&B. Recently released "Why Don't You Believe Me?", by Donna Stark (C&W/pop single); *Mario Tacca and Orchestra Play Your International Favorites*, by Mario Tacca (Italian/Latin album); *Fill My Cup, Lord*, by Harriet Edwards (gospel/religious album); "The Missing Link," by the Living Truth (Latin single); and "Better Days," recorded by J.J. Ronter Group (rock single).

RED BALL RECORD CO., 711 Saint Stephens Rd., Prichard AL 36610. (205)457-9431. Professional Manager: Ruben Hughes. Record company, music publisher, record producer and booking agency. Estab. 1967. Released 1 single in 1978; plans 4 singles in 1979, 7 singles in 1980. Works with artists and songwriters on contract. Pays 10-12% royalty to artists on contract; standard royalties to songwriters on contract.
How to Contact: Arrange personal interview, submit demo tape and lead sheet, submit acetate disc, submit acetate disc and lead sheet, or submit lead sheet. Prefers reel-to-reel or cassette with 2-4 songs on demo. Does not return unsolicited material. Reports in 3 weeks.
Music: Blues; church/religious; C&W; gospel; R&B; and soul.

REDEEMER RECORD CO., Box 55943, Houston TX 77055. (713)686-1749. President: Gary R. Smith. Record company, music publisher, record producer, management firm and booking agency. Estab. 1972. Released 2 albums in 1978; plans 5 albums in 1979, 5 albums in 1980. Works with musicians and songwriters on contract.
How to Contact: Arrange personal interview. Prefers reel-to-reel or cassette with 3-10 songs on demo. SASE. Reports in 1 month.
Music: Church/religious and gospel. Recently released *Comin' Home/I Found the Way*, by Gary R. Smith (contemporary gospel LP); and *More About Jesus*, by Greg S. Page (contemporary gospel LP).

REGENCY RECORDS, 9454 Wilshire Blvd., Suite 500, Beverly Hills CA 90212. (213)274-5857. President: Lloyd Segal. Managing Director: John Delgatto. Record company. Estab. 1976. Released 2 albums in 1978; plans 10 albums in 1979. Works with musicians and songwriters on contract. Pays 7-8% royalty to artists and songwriters on contract. Buys some material outright.
How to Contact: Submit demo tape or submit demo tape and lead sheet. Prefers cassette with 2-5 songs on demo. SASE.

REN-MAUR MUSIC CORP., 663 5th Ave., New York NY 10022. (212)757-3638. Labels include R&R Records and Ren Rome Records. Producers: Billy Nichols, Rena L. Feeney, Lenny Bailey. Record company, music publisher and production company. Estab. 1968. Released 2 albums in 1978; plans 2 albums in 1979. Works with musicians and songwriters on contract. Pays 4% royalty to artists and songwriters on contract.
How to Contact: Submit demo tape and lead sheet. Prefers 7½ ips reel-to-reel with 4-8 songs on demo. SASE. Reports in 1 month.
Music: Disco; jazz; MOR; rock; soul; and top 40/pop. Recently released "High Time," by Charles Hudson (MOR single); "Love a Little Longer," by Rena Romano (top 40 single); "Do It with Me," by the Lenny Bailey Orchestra (disco single); and "Everybody Let's Party," by Joe Rivers (disco single).

REQUEST RECORDS, 3800 S. Ocean Dr., 2nd Floor, Hollywood FL 33019. (305)456-0847. Labels include Request, Afro, Sounds of Caribbean, Euphoria, Oasis, Classical Excellence and Demand Records. President: Gene Settler. Executive Vice President: John Pudwell. Record company and music publisher. Estab. 1949. Plans 48 singles and 220 albums in 1979. Works with musicians on contract; songwriters on salary or contract. Pays negotiable royalty. Buys some material outright; payment negotiable.
How to Contact: Submit demo tape, arrange personal interview, or submit demo tape and lead sheet. Prefers 7½ ips reel-to-reel or cassette with 6-12 songs on demo. SASE. Reports in 2 weeks.
Music: Bluegrass; blues; children's; choral; church/religious; classical; C&W; disco; easy listening; folk; gospel; jazz; MOR; progressive; rock; soul; and top 40/pop. Recently released *Freddy Cole Sings*, by Freddy Cole (MOR LP); "Sweet Symphony," by Brown Sugar (disco/R&B single); and *Lighthouse*, by Johnny Porrazzo (gospel LP).

REVONAH RECORDS, Box 217, Ferndale NY 12734. (914)292-5965. Owner: Paul Gerry. Record company and booking agency. Estab. 1968. Released 5 albums in 1978; plans 5 albums in 1979, 4-5 in 1980. Works with musicians and songwriters on contract. Pays negotiable royalty to artists and songwriters on contract. Buys some material outright; payment negotiable.
How to Contact: Submit demo tape and lead sheet or arrange personal interview. Prefers reel-to-reel, cassette or 8-track cartridge. SASE. Reports in 1 month.
Music: Bluegrass; C&W; folk; and gospel. Recently released *West Virginia My Home*, by Mountain Grass; *Travelin' On*, by the Dixie Travelers; *Fred Pike & the Flat Top Guitar*; *Red Rector & Friends*; and *Orrtanna Home Companion*, by the West Orrtanna String Band.

RICHEY RECORDS, 7121 W. Vickery, Fort Worth TX 76116. (817)731-7375. Labels include Ridge Runner, Flying High, and Grass Mountain Records. President: Slim Richey. Estab. 1975. Record company and music publisher. Released 12 albums in 1978; plans 6 albums in 1979. Works with musicians on salary or contract; songwriters on contract. Pays 6% royalty to artists on contract; 2¾% royalty to songwriters on contract.
How to Contact: Submit demo tape and lead sheet.

RICHMOND RECORDS, Short Pump Associates, Box 11292, Richmond VA 23230. (804)355-4117. President: Ken Brown. Vice President: Dennis Huber. Record company and

music publisher. Estab. 1977. Released 2 singles and 1 album in 1978; plans 4 singles and 2 albums in 1979, 6 singles and 3 albums in 1980. Works with musicians on salary or contract; songwriters on contract. Pays 11% royalty to artists on contract; 8% royalty to songwriters on contract.
How to Contact: Submit demo tape and lead sheet. Prefers cassette with 3-6 songs on demo. SASE. Reports in 2 weeks.
Music: Country rock and rock 'n roll. Recently released "Sweet Virginia" and "Looking for a Sunny Day," by Robert Thompson.

RICHTOWN/GOSPEL TRUTH RECORDS, Box 7552, Richmond VA 23231. (804)226-0424. Labels include Cardinal, Richtown/Sire, Richtown/Gospel, Truth and Charity. Chairman of the Board: R.A. Charity. Record company. Estab. 1977. Plans 3 singles and 1 albums in 1979. Works with songwriters on contract. Buys some material outright; payment negotiable.
How to Contact: Submit demo tape and lead sheet or arrange personal interview. "We also accept master tapes." Prefers 7½ ips reel-to-reel or cassette with 2-4 songs on demo. "Be sure material is copyrighted and sent by registered mail." SASE. Reports in 1 month; "we copy all material and return the original to the songwriter."
Music: Bluegrass; blues; children's; choral; church/religious; classical; C&W; disco; easy listening; folk; gospel; jazz; MOR; progressive; rock; soul; and top 40/pop.

ROBBINS RECORDS, Rt. 3, Box 277, Leesville LA 71446. Labels include Headliner Stars Records and Robbins Records. Contact: Virginia Angel. President: Sherree Scott. Record company and music publisher. Estab. 1962. Released 2 singles and 3 albums in 1978; plans 6 singles and 3 albums in 1979. Works with musicians and songwriters on contract. Pays standard royalty to artists and songwriters on contract.
How to Contact: Submit demo tape and lead sheet. Prefers cassette. Does not return unsolicited material. Reports in 1 month.
Music: Bluegrass; church/religious; C&W; easy listening; folk; gospel; MOR; and top 40/pop. Recently released "There's a Cross" and "I Saw the Light," by Sherree Scott (religious singles).

ROTA RECORDS, 5305 Church Ave., Brooklyn NY 11203. (212)498-7111. Labels include Nilkam Records, Cartoon Records and K.G. Records. President: William R. Kamorra. Record company, music publisher and record producer. Estab. 1976. Released 3 singles and 2 albums in 1978; plans 3 singles and 2 albums in 1979, 3 singles and 2 albums in 1980. Works with musicians and songwriters on contract; musicians on salary. Pays 2-5% royalty to artists on contract; standard royalties to songwriters on contract. Buys some material; pays $200-1,000/song.
How to Contact: Query, submit demo tape and lead sheet, or submit acetate disc and lead sheet. Prefers 7½ ips reel-to-reel or cassette with 3-6 songs on demo. SASE. Reports in 2 weeks.
Music: Disco; MOR; R&B; rock; soul; and top 40/pop. Recently released *Unity*, by Future 2,000 (disco LP); *The Rules*, by Denis Lopsler (MOR LP); and "Answer to a Dream," by Misty (disco single).
Tips: A songwriter wishing to deal with this company "should first of all have all his music copyrighted, then send copies to us with a short letter about himself. If there is not much to write about send us a resume. We will return all the unusable material with a letter explaining why we can't use the product. Should we find something we can use, we will contact him immediately."

ROULETTE RECORDS, INC., 1790 Broadway, 18th Floor, New York NY 10019. Labels include Pyramid. A&R Director: Phil Kahl.
How to contact: Submit demo tape and lyric sheets. Prefers 7½ ips reel-to-reel or cassette with 1-3 songs on demo. SASE. Reports in 1 month.
Music: Blues; choral; C&W; disco; easy listening; folk; jazz; MOR; progressive; R&B; rock; soul; and top 40/pop. Recently released *Confessions*, by D.C. LaRue (disco LP distributed by Casablanca Records)

ROYAL T MUSIC, Box 54, Man's Field TX 76063. (817)477-2897. Labels include Old Hat and TZ Topple. President: James Michael Taylor. Record company, music publisher and booking agency. Estab. 1973. Released 2 singles and 2 albums in 1978. Works with musicians and songwriters on contract. Pays ½% royalty to artists and songwriters on contract.
How to Contact: Submit demo tape, submit demo tape and lead sheet, submit lead sheet, or arrange personal interview. Prefers 3¾ or 7½ ips reel-to-reel or cassette with 6-12 songs on demo. SASE. Reports in 1 week.
Music: Children's; choral; C&W; folk; MOR; rock; top 40/pop. Recently released "Feathers

in the Wind," by Snowgeese (country/rock/pop); and "First Link," by Bob French (folk/country).

ROYALTY RECORDS OF CANADA, LTD., 9229 58th Ave., Edmonton, Alberta Canada T6E 0B7. (403)436-0665. Contact: R. Harlan Smith. Record company, music publisher, record producer and management firm. Estab. 1966. Released 12 singles and 4 albums in 1978; plans 15 singles and 6 albums in 1979, 20 singles and 10 albums in 1980. Works with songwriters on contract; musicians on salary. Pays standard royalties.
How to Contact: Arrange personal interview, submit demo tape, or submit demo tape and lead sheet. Prefers 7½ ips reel-to-reel or cassette with 5-8 songs on demo. "Also include a written statement verifying that publishing is available internationally on the material submitted." Does not return unsolicited material. Reports in 1 month.
Music: C&W; easy listening; MOR; rock; and top 40/pop.

RSO RECORDS, INC., 8335 Sunset Blvd., Los Angeles CA 90069. (213)650-1234. Labels include Custom Records. Contact: A&R Department. Record company. Estab. 1976. Released 12 albums in 1978. Works with musicians on contract.
How to Contact: Submit demo tape. Prefers 7½ ips reel-to-reel or cassette with 3-5 songs on demo. SASE. Reports in 2 months.
Music: Blues; children's; disco; easy listening; folk; jazz; progressive; R&B; rock; soul; and top 40/pop. Recently released *Saturday Night Fever* and *Spirits Having Flown*, by the Bee Gees (LPs); and *Grease* (soundtrack LP).

SAGITTAR RECORDS, 1311 Candlelight Ave., Dallas TX 75116. President: Paul Ketter. Record company and music publisher. Estab. 1973. Released 4 singles and 2 albums in 1978; plans 6 singles and 3 albums in 1979, 6 singles and 12 albums in 1980. Works with musicians on salary or contract; songwriters on contract. Pays 5¢/record to artists on contract; 2¢/record to songwriters on contract.
How to Contact: Submit demo tape and lead sheet. Prefers 7½ ips reel-to-reel with 3-6 songs on demo. SASE. Reports in 3 weeks.
Music: C&W; MOR (country); and Christmas. Recently released "Theodore (Santa's Helper)," by Dave Gregory (Christmas single); "Games Grownups Play," "How High Is Your Mountain?" and "Diamonds Only Shine," by Bunnie Mills (C&W singles).

ST. LOU-E BLU RECORDS, 4412A Natural Bridge, St. Louis MO 63115. (314)385-8956. President: Morman Keaton. Record company. Estab. 1976. Plans 10 singles and 6 albums in 1979. Works with musicians and songwriters on contract. Pays 3% royalty to artists and songwriters on contract. Buys some material outright; pays $100-1,000/song.
How to Contact: Submit demo tape and lead sheet. Prefers 15 ips reel-to-reel or cassette with 2-6 songs on demo. SASE. Reports in 1 week.
Music: Disco; easy listening; soul; and top 40/pop. Recently released "She Didn't Know," by Runette Roberts (top 40 single); and "Bumpin' Bus Stop," by the Playboys (disco single).

SANDCASTLE RECORDS, 157 W. 57th St., New York NY 10019. (212)582-6135. Labels include Tara, Coby and Sandcastle Records. President: Mark Cosmedy. Record company. Estab. 1973. Released 10 singles and 7 albums in 1978; plans 14 singles and 10 albums in 1979. Works with musicians and songwriters on contract. Payment negotiable. Buys some material outright.
How to Contact: Submit demo tape and lead sheet. Prefers 7½ ips reel-to-reel or cassette with 2-4 songs on demo. SASE. Reports in 1 month.
Music: C&W; easy listening; folk; jazz; MOR; progressive; rock; and top 40/pop. Recently released "Eres Tu," by Mocedades (top 40 single); "Unicorn," by the Irish Rovers (top 40 single); and "Vodka and Tonic," by the Dukes of Dixieland (jazz single).

SAN-SUE RECORDING STUDIO, 1309 Celesta Way, Sellersburg IN 47172. (812)246-2959. Labels include Basic Records. Owner: Buddy Powell. Record company, music publisher and recording studio. Estab. 1968. Released 8 singles and 4 albums in 1978. Works with musicians and songwriters on contract. Pays 8% royalty to artists on contract.
How to Contact: Submit demo tape. Prefers 7½ ips reel-to-reel or cassette with 2-4 songs on demo. "Strong vocal with piano or guitar is suitable for demo, along with lyrics." SASE. Reports in 2 weeks.
Music: Church/religious; C&W; and MOR. Recently released "Little People," by Sue Powell (MOR single); and "I Missed You Again Today," by Jerry Baird (C&W single).

SAVOY RECORDS, Box 279, 342 Westminister Ave., Elizabeth NJ 07208. Contact: Helen Gottesmann, Milton Biggham. Record company and music publisher. Estab. 1940.
How to Contact: Query. Reports in 2 weeks.
Music: Gospel and traditional gospel.

SCOTT RECORDS, Box 148, Hollywood CA 90028. President: Scott Fredrickson. Record company and music publisher. Estab. 1977. Plans 7 albums in 1979. Works with songwriters on contract. Pays negotiable royalty to songwriters on contract.
How to Contact: Submit demo tape and lead sheet. Prefers cassette with 3-5 songs on demo. SASE. Reports in 1 month.
Music: Choral; church/religious; easy listening; gospel; jazz; MOR; and Latin (bossa nova, etc.). Recently released *Vocal Jazz Series*, by Great Feelin' (vocal jazz LP).

SEIDEL-LEHMAN PRODUCTIONS, 8537 Sunset Blvd., #2, Los Angeles CA 90069. (213)657-8852. Labels include Reuben Records. Contact: Travis Lehman. Record company, music publisher and management company. Estab. 1977. Works with musicians and songwriters on contract. Pays standard royalty to songwriters on contract.
How to Contact: Submit demo tape. Prefers 7½ ips quarter-track reel-to-reel or cassette. SASE. Reports in 3 weeks.
Music: C&W; rock (hard); and top 40/pop. Recently released "One Step Away" and "I Wish It Would Rain," by Rick Ellis (C&W singles).

SEMINAR RECORDS, Box 15094, New Orleans LA 70175. (504)282-8209. Labels include Down South, Flambo, New Orleans Soul, Proud Cock, and Port of Orleans Records. A&R Director: Tad Jones. Advertising Manager: Shelia Goines. Record company. Estab. 1962. Plans 25 singles and 10 albums in 1979. Works with musicians and songwriters on contract. Pays 4% royalty to artists on contract.
How to Contact: Submit demo tape and lead sheet. Prefers 7½ or 15 ips reel-to-reel or cassette. SASE. Reports in 3 weeks. "We will consider leasing completed professional master recordings, but it is only necessary to submit reel or cassette demo of the master tape."
Music: Blues; church/religious; C&W; easy listening; folk; gospel; jazz; MOR; rock (country); soul; and top 40/pop. Recently released "Let's Make a Better World," by Levon Helm (MOR); "Time for the Sun to Rise," by Earl King (R&B); and "Big Chief," by Dr. John (R&B).

SHELBY RECORD CO., Box 128, Bono AR 72416. Owner: Larry D. Gillihan. Record company, music publisher and record producer. Estab. 1972. Released 1 single and 1 album in 1978; plans 2 singles and 2 albums in 1979, 10 singles and 4 albums in 1980. Works with songwriters on contract. Pays negotiable royalties to artists on contract; standard royalties to songwriters on contract.
How to Contact: Query or submit demo tape. Prefers reel-to-reel or cassette. "Please include a written copy of lyrics with each song submitted." SASE. Reports in 1 month.
Music: C&W; disco; gospel; MOR; and top 40/pop. Recently released "Poor Crazy Sally," by Jess Mobley (country single); "Trying to Get to You" (rock single); *Lightning Strikes Again* (rockabilly LP) and "Thank You, Music Lovers" (MOR LP), all by Larry Donn.

SHILOH RECORDS, Box 737, Lexington TN 38351. (901)968-9323. President: W.R. Morris. Record company. Estab. 1978. Labels include Majesty. Plans 10 singles and 5 albums in 1979, 15 singles and 8 albums in 1980. Works with artists on contract. Payment negotiable. Charges for some services. "We charge if an artist wants record produced and we feel material is not suitable for our market."
How to Contact: Submit demo tape and lead sheet. Prefers 7½ reel-to-reel or cassette with 2-4 songs on demo. SASE. Reports in 1 month.
Music: C&W; gospel; and bluegrass. Recently released "Billy G.," by Eddie Bond.

SIERRA/BRIAR, Box 5853, Pasadena CA 91107. Record company and music publisher. Estab. 1971. Plans 15 singles and 25 albums in 1979. Works with musicians and songwriters on contract. Pays 4-7% royalty to artists on contract.
How to Contact: Submit demo tape. Prefers 7½ ips reel-to-reel with 3-6 songs on demo. SASE. Reports in 2 weeks.
Music: Bluegrass; C&W; and folk. Recently released *Toulussions*, by Toulouse Engelhardt (folk LP); and *Kentucky Colonels*, by the Kentucky Colonels (bluegrass LP).

SINGSPIRATION RECORDS, 1415 Lake Dr., Grand Rapids MI 49508. Labels include New

Dawn, Milk n' Honey, Sunshine, Music Mountain and Everlasting Spring. Director of Publications: Don Wyrtzen. National Music Coordinator: Phil Brower. Record company and music publisher. Estab. 1928. Released 25 albums in 1978; plans 30 albums in 1979. Works with musicians on contract; songwriters on salary or contract. Pays 5% royalty to artists on contract; 2% royalty to songwriters on contract.
How to Contact: Submit demo tape or submit demo tape and lead sheet. Prefers cassette with 3-5 songs on demo. Does not return unsolicited material. Reports in 1 month.
Music: Church/religious; easy listening; gospel; MOR; and rock. Recently released *Back Home*, by Christine Wyrtzen (contemporary LP); *A Touch of Forever*, by Ben Markley (gospel LP); and *God's Kids*, by Rick Powell.

SIR LION RECORDS, 455 W. Hanover St., Trenton NJ 08618. (609)989-9202. Contact: Eddie Toney. Record company and music publisher. Estab. 1969. Released 3 singles and 4 albums in 1978. Works with musicians and songwriters on contract. Pays 3% royalty to artists on contract.
How to Contact: Arrange personal interview. Prefers 7½ ips reel-to-reel with 1-2 songs on demo. SASE. Reports in 1 month.
Music: Church/religious; disco; and progressive. Recently released "Tell Like it Is," by Oscar Weather (top 40/pop single).

SIVATT MUSIC PUBLISHING CO., Box 7172, Greenville SC 29610. (803)269-5529. Labels include Pioneer, Brand-X and Accent Records. President: Jesse B. Evatte. Secretary: Sybil P. Evatte. Record company and music publisher. Estab. 1974. Released 4 singles and 11 albums in 1979; plans 6 singles and 20 albums in 1978, 10 singles and 25 albums in 1980. Works with musicians and songwriters on contract. Pays standard royalty to musicians and songwriters on contract.
How to Contact: Submit demo tape and lead sheet. Prefers cassette with 2-6 songs on demo. SASE. Reports in 1 month.
Music: Bluegrass; choral; church/religious; C&W; easy listening; folk; and gospel. Recently released *Down Home Singing*, by the Roy Knight Singers (country gospel LP); *Sincerely*, by Joyce and the Rogers Brothers (gospel LP); and *Down Home Guitar*, by Bob Dennis (instrumental gospel LP).

THE SMILE MUSIC GROUP, 1659 Bayview Ave., Suite 102, Toronto, Ontario, Canada M4G 3C1. (416)485-1157. President: Dave Coutts. Vice President: John D. Watt. Record company and music publisher. Estab. 1972. Plans 4 singles and 3 albums in 1979. Works with musicians and songwriters on contract. Pays negotiable royalty to artists on contract; 50% royalty to songwriters on contract.
How to Contact: Submit demo tape or arrange personal interview. Prefers 7½ ips reel-to-reel with 1-6 songs on demo. SAE and International Reply Coupons. Reports in 3 weeks.
Music: Top 40/pop; C&W; disco; easy listening; MOR; progressive; and rock. Recently released "Lazy Love," by New City Jam Band (rock single); "Set the Night on Fire," by John Lovesin (rock single); and *Consider the Heart*, by Tony Kosinec (MOR LP).

SONATA RECORDS, 4304 Del Monte Ave., San Diego CA 92107. (714)222-3346. President: Paul DiLella. Record company. Estab. 1962. Released 3 albums in 1978; plans 14 albums in 1979. Works with musicians and songwriters on contract. Pays 5% royalty to artists on contract; 2¢/record to songwriters on contract.
How to Contact: Submit demo tape and lead sheet or submit lead sheet. Prefers 7½ ips reel-to-reel or cassette with 6-12 songs on demo. SASE. Reports in 1 month.
Music: Church/religious; classical; C&W; disco; easy listening; gospel; MOR; rock; and top 40/pop. Recently released "Now Is the Time," by Lisa Paz (contemporary single); *Two Hundred Years of America*, by George J and the Nomads (easy listening LP); and "Songs of Hawaii," by Cathy Foy (easy listening single).

SONYATONE RECORDS, Box 567, Santa Barbara CA 93102. Labels include Sonyatone and Hen Cackle Records. Manager: Peter F. Feldmann. Record company. Estab. 1974. Released 6 albums in 1978; plans 10 albums in 1979, 10 albums in 1980. Works with musicians and songwriters on contract. Pays 3-12% royalty to artists and songwriters on contract. Charges for some services: "We sometimes divide recording and production costs and charge against royalties."
How to Contact: Submit demo tape. Prefers 7½ ips reel-to-reel or cassette with 1-6 songs on demo. SASE. Reports in 2 weeks.
Music: Bluegrass (traditional); children's; and folk (American/Middle-Eastern). "We are interested mainly in traditional-oriented folk, old-time country, bluegrass and similar music."

─Songwriter's Market Close-Up─

"Listen to every new song and album released," advises Molly-Ann Leikin, writer of the lyrics for "The Other Side of the Mountain II" and "Eight is Enough." "Be objective, even if you don't like a particular song," she says, and urges songwriters to apply that same objectivity to their own songs. "After you have written a song, distance yourself from it for several weeks, and then see if you can approach it as a craftsman and not its creator."

Recently released *How to Play Country Fiddle*, by Peter Feldmann (country instruction LP); *Hard Times in the Country*, by the Floyd County Boys (bluegrass LP); and *Girls of the Golden West*, by Mildred and Dorothy Good (early country LP).

SOUL SOUNDS UNLIMITED RECORDING CO., Box 24230, Cincinnati OH 45224. President: Alvin Don Chico Pettijohn. Record company and music publisher. Estab. 1976. Works with musicians and songwriters on contract. Pays negotiable royalty to musicians and songwriters on contract. Charges for some services: "We will make demo tapes for songwriters for their own use. If we feel that a writer or musician is best suited for our needs in the recording field, we will offer a recording contract."
How to Contact: Submit demo tape. Prefers 15 ips reel-to-reel, cassette or 8-track cartridge. SASE. "All tapes will become the property of Soul Sounds if return postage is not included." Reports in 3 weeks.
Music: Disco and soul. Recently released "Loving You," by the Devotions (easy listening soul single).

SOUNDS OF WINCHESTER, Box 574, Winchester VA 22601. (703)667-9379. Labels include Alear Records, Winchester and Real McCoy. Owner: Jim McCoy. Contact: Bertha McCoy. Record company, music publisher and recording studio. Estab. 1971. Released 12 singles and 4 albums in 1978. Works with musicians on salary or contract; songwriters on contract. Pays 2% royalty to artists and songwriters on contract.
How to Contact: Submit demo tape or arrange personal interview. Prefers 7½ ips reel-to-reel with 4-12 songs on demo. Does not return unsolicited material. Reports in 1 month.
Music: Bluegrass; C&W; gospel; rock (country); and top 40/pop. Recently released "The Other Lover," by David Elliott (C&W single); "Mr. Blue Grass Here's to You," by the Carroll County Ramblers (bluegrass single); and "Sweet Woman," by Larry Sutphin (C&W single).

SPEEDWAY RECORDS, Box 4192, Huntsville AL 35803. (205)881-7976. Labels include Speedway, Fireside, New Day and Springwater. Owner: George Wells. Record company and music publisher. Estab. 1971. Plans 10 singles in 1979. Works with musicians on salary or contract; songwriters on contract. Payment negotiable to artists and songwriters on contract.
How to Contact: Submit demo tape and lyric sheet or arrange personal interview. Prefers 7½ ips reel-to-reel with 1-3 songs on demo. SASE. Reports in 1 month.
Music: C&W; gospel; and MOR. Recently released "The Men Who Race for the Checkered

Flag," by Neil Bonnett (country single); "Greenie the Christmas Tree," by the Regents (country single); and "New Morality," by the Joymen (gospel single).

THE STACY-LEE LABEL, 425 Park St., Suite 3, Hackensack NJ 07601. (201)488-5211. Labels include Banana, Cuddles, Lions Den, Riot, Safari, Sampler and Inner Circle Records. President: Johnny Miracle. Vice President: Aileen Joy. Record company and music publisher. Estab. 1970. Works with musicians on salary or contract; songwriters on commission or contract. Pays 2% royalty to artists and songwriters on contract. Buys some material outright; pays $5 minimum.
How to Contact: Submit demo tape or submit demo tape and lead sheet. Prefers 7½ ips reel-to-reel or cassette with 2-6 songs on demo. "Try not to arrange songs. Just send in basic tunes." SASE. Reports in 2 weeks.
Music: Children's; church/religious; C&W; easy listening; folk; and gospel. Recently released "Pizzaman," by Tiny (novelty single); "Memories I Hold of You," by Sam Starr (C&W single); and "The Ashes Are Still Warm," by Al and Carrol (C&W single).

STAGE PRODUCTIONS RECORDS, 189 W. Madison St., Suite 303, Chicago IL 60602. (312)346-3173. President: Willie Nance. Record company and music publisher. Works with musicians and songwriters on contract. Pays 7% royalty to artists on contract; 2% royalty to songwriters on contract.
How to Contact: Arrange personal interview or submit demo tape and lead sheet. Prefers cassette. SASE. Reports in 3 weeks.

STAN RECORDS, INC., 2024 S. Cooper St., Arlington TX 76010. Labels include Bilmar Records. Manager: Bill Stansell. Record company and music publisher. Estab. 1973. Plans 4 singles in 1979, 10 singles in 1980. Works with songwriters on contract. Pays standard royalties.
How to Contact: Query. Prefers cassette with 1 song on demo. "First request permission to submit any material." SASE. Reports in 1 month.
Music: Children's novelty; C&W; and gospel. Recently released "I Loved You Now You're Gone," "Blue Yesterdays," "Words on Paper," and "Broken Hearted Lovers," by Bill Stansell (singles).

STANDY RECORDS, INC., 760 Blandina St., Utica NY 13501. (315)735-6187. Labels include Standy and Kama. President: Stanley Markowski. Record company and custom pressing firm. Estab. 1965. Works with musicians and songwriters on contract. Pays standard royalty to artists on contract.

STARCREST PRODUCTIONS, INC., 2516 S. Washington St., Grand Forks ND 58201. (701)772-6831. Labels include Meadowlark Records and Minn-Dak Records. President: George J. Hastings. Record company, management firm and booking agency. Estab. 1972. Released 2 singles and 1 album in 1978; plans 5 singles and 2 albums in 1979, 6 singles and 2 albums in 1980. Works with musicians and songwriters on contract. Payment negotiable.
How to Contact: Query or submit demo tape and lead sheet. Prefers 7½ ips reel-to-reel with 1-6 songs on demo. SASE. Reports in 1 month.
Music: C&W and top 40/pop. Recently released "Country Monday," by Mary Joyce (country single) and *Mary Joyce Sings Country Gospel*, by Mary Joyce (LP).

STARK RECORDS & TAPE CO., 628 South St., Mount Airy NC 27030. (919)786-2865. Labels include Stark, Hello, Pilot and Sugarbear. Owner: Paul E. Johnson. Record company and music publisher. Estab. 1960. Released 10 singles and 12 albums in 1978; plans 20 singles and 15 albums in 1979, 30 singles and 25 albums in 1980. Works with musicians and songwriters on contract. Pays 10% royalty to artists and songwriters on contract.
How to Contact: Submit demo tape and lead sheet. Prefers 7½ ips reel-to-reel with 3-5 songs on demo. SASE. Reports in 1 month.
Music: Bluegrass; church/religious; C&W; easy listening; folk; gospel; MOR; rock (country); and top 40/pop. Recently released "The Legend of Charlie Monroe" and "Truck Driver's Vow," by the Baux Mountain Boys (bluegrass singles); and "Freedom Bound," by the Four Souls (pop single).

STARLINE RECORDS & VIDEO WORKS, INC., Box 2818, Newport Beach CA 92663. (714)497-3758. President: Joseph Nicoletti. Vice President: Cheryl Lee Gammon. Record company, music publisher and record producer. Estab. 1976. Released 1 single and 1 album in 1978; plans 3 singles and 3 albums in 1979, 4 singles and 4 albums in 1980. Works with musicians on salary or contract; songwriters on contract. Pays 5% royalty to artists on contract;

2¾¢/record royalty to songwriters on contract.
How to Contact: Submit demo tape and lead sheet. Prefers 7½ ips reel-to-reel or cassette with 1-3 songs on demo. SASE. Reports in 1 month.
Music: Disco; easy listening; MOR; rock; soul; and top 40/pop. Recently released *Joseph Nicoletti*, by Joseph Nicoletti (MOR/rock LP).

STARR RECORDS, INC., Box 1037, Des Plaines IL 60018. (312)297-3376. President: Mary L. Starr. Record company.

STARTIME RECORDS, Box 643, LaQuinta CA 92253. (714)564-4823. Labels include Western Americana Records. General Manager: Robert Rice. Record company, music publisher and record producer. Estab. 1958. Released 1 single and 1 album in 1978. Works with musicians and songwriters on contract. Pays 8-12% royalty to artists on contract; standard royalties to songwriters on contract
How to Contact: Submit demo tape and lead sheet. Prefers cassette with 1-2 songs on demo. Does not return unsolicited material. Reports in 6 weeks.
Music: Country; rock; top 40/pop; and novelty. Recently released *God is Alive*, by Wayne Newton (inspirational LP); "The Hawk and the Dove," by Jim Kearce (folk/country single); and "Bad Boy," by Nico Princely (rock single).

STASH RECORDS, INC., Box 390, Brooklyn NY 11215. (212)965-9407. Labels include Stash and Jive Records. President: Bernard Brightman. Record company and music publisher. Estab. 1975. Plans 6 albums in 1979, 6 albums in 1980. Works with musicians on salary or contract; songwriters on contract. Payment negotiable.
How to Contact: Submit demo tape. Prefers cassette with 4 songs minimum on demo. Does not return unsolicited material. Reports in 1 month.
Music: Blues; jazz; and MOR. Recently released *Dialogue*, by Slam Stewart and Bucky Pizzarelli (jazz LP); and *Songs for New Lovers*, by Dardenelle (jazz/MOR LP).

STINSON RECORDS, Box 3415, Granada Hills CA 91344. (213)368-1316. President: Jack M. Kall. Record company. Estab. 1938. Released 6 albums in 1978; plans 10-12 albums in 1979, 12 albums in 1980. Works with musicians and songwriters on contract. Pays negotiable royalty to artists on contract; 1-2¾¢/record side to songwriters on contract.
How to Contact: Submit demo tape. Prefers reel-to-reel or cassette with 1-3 songs on demo. Does not return unsolicited material. Reports in 1 month.
Music: Bluegrass; folk; and jazz.

STONE DIAMOND PRODUCTIONS, 6255 Sunset Blvd., Hollywood CA 90028. (213)468-3400. Vice President: Jay Lowy. Record company and music publisher. Estab. 1958. Released 2 singles in 1978; plans 3 singles in 1979. Works with musicians on contract; songwriters on salary.
How to Contact: Submit demo tape and lead or lyric sheet. Prefers 7½ or 15 ips reel-to-reel or cassette with 3 songs on demo. SASE. Reports in 1 month.
Music: Bluegrass; blues; children's; choral; church/religious; classical; C&W; disco; easy listening; folk; gospel; jazz; MOR; progressive; R&B; rock; soul; and top 40/pop.

STONE POST RECORDS/MUSIC, Box 1213, Emporia KS 66801. (316)343-2727. President: Richard Bisterfeldt. Record company and music publisher. Estab. 1975. Released 3 singles and 1 album in 1978; plans 5 singles and 3 albums in 1979, 7 singles and 5 albums in 1980. Works with musicians and songwriters on contract. Pays 25% royalty to artists on contract; 3½-7¢/song royalty to songwriters on contract; payment negotiable.
How to Contact: Submit demo tape. Prefers 7½ ips reel-to-reel or 8-track cartridge with 3-5 songs on demo. SASE. Reports in 2 weeks.
Music: Progressive (country); rock (progressive/hard); and top 40/pop. Recently released "Make It Good" (rock single) and *Pyromancy*, by Fyre (rock LP).

STORM RECORDS, Rt. 2, Box 45B, Mead WA 99021. Manager: Ed Raney. Record producer and music publisher. Estab. 1967. Released 1 album in 1978; plans 3 singles and 1 album in 1979, 3 singles and 1 album in 1980. Works with musicians on contract. Pays 1-2% royalty to artists on contract.
How to Contact: Query, submit demo tape, or submit acetate disc. Prefers 7½ ips reel-to-reel tape with 2-4 songs on demo. SASE. Reports in 6 weeks.
Music: C&W; folk; and top 40/pop. Recently released *Songs of the Sky Soldier*, by Ed Raney (western/folk LP).

STYLETONE/HOOKS RECORDS, 254 E. 29th St., Los Angeles CA 90011. (213)661-7182. Labels include Ground Hog, J&J and Hooks Brothers Records. President: Jerry Hooks. Record company. Estab. 1937.

SUNCOUNTRY PRODUCTIONS, INC., 14 E. 2nd St., Tucson AZ 85705. (602)792-3194. Labels include Bandolier Records. President: Fred Knipe. Record company, music publisher and record producer. Estab. 1975. Released 2 singles and 2 albums in 1978. Works with musicians and songwriters on contract. Pays standard royalties to artists and songwriters on contract.
How to Contact: Submit demo tape and lyric sheet. Prefers cassette with 1-4 songs on demo. "Leader is appreciated." SASE. Reports in 1 month.
Music: C&W (modern country); disco; rock (not heavy metal or blues); soul; and top 40/pop. Recently released *Honky Tonk Music*, by the Dusty Chaps (LP) and "Get Up and Get Out," by Force (single).

SUNDOWN RECORDS, Rt. 1, Box 258, Carriere MS 39426. (601)798-7099. President: Vern Pullens. Vice President: Bruce Dixon. Record company and music publisher. Estab. 1973. Released 8 singles in 1978; plans 10 singles in 1979. Works with musicians on salary or contract; songwriters on contract. Pays 5% royalty to artists on contract. Charges for some services: session costs.
How to Contact: Submit demo tape and lead sheet. Prefers 7½ ips reel-to-reel with 4-12 songs on demo. SASE. Reports in 2 weeks.
Music: C&W; gospel; rock (country). Recently released "Breaker Breaker," by Roger Rainy (C&W single); "Dad and the Old Folks' Home," by Vern Pullens (C&W single); and "Stay with Me," by Sue Stuart (C&W single).

SUN-RAY RECORDS, 1662 Wyatt Pkwy., Lexington KY 40505. (606)254-7474. Labels include Sun-Ray and Sky-Vue. President: James T. Price. Record company and music publisher. Estab. 1950. Released 4 singles and 1 album in 1978; plans 6 singles and 1 album in 1979. Works with musicians on salary; songwriters on contract. Payment negotiable.
How to Contact: Submit demo tape or submit demo tape and lead sheet. Prefers 7½ ips reel-to-reel with 2-6 songs on demo. SASE. Reports in 3 weeks.
Music: Bluegrass (sacred or C&W); church/religious; C&W; and gospel. Recently released "Flat Top Box," by Tommy Jackson (country single); "We Will Cross Over," by Sherman Smith (sacred single); and *The Crucifixion of Christ*, by the Kelley Family (sacred bluegrass LP).

SUNSHINE COUNTRY RECORDS, Box 31351, Dallas TX 75231. (214)690-8875. Labels include SCR. Producer: "The General." A&R Director: Mike Anthony. Record company and music publisher. Estab. 1970. Works with musicians and songwriters on contract; "we also work with songwriters on royalty contract for other productions." Pays 6% royalty to artists on contract; 50% royalty to songwriters on contract.
How to Contact: Submit demo tape and lead sheet. Prefers 7½ ips reel-to-reel with 1-4 songs on demo. "We must have a copy of the words along with the tape." SASE. Reports in 1 month.
Music: C&W and gospel. Recently released "Lord, If I Make It to Heaven, Can I Bring My Own Angel Along?" and "You Read Between the Lines," by Billy Parker (C&W singles); and "Some Day I'd Like to Love You When You're Mine," by Doug Collins (C&W single).

SUNSHINE SOUND ENTERPRISES, INC., Box 1780, Hialeah FL 33011. Contact: Preliminary Screening Committee. Manager: Don Foster. Record company and music publisher. Estab. 1976. Released 10 singles and 5 albums in 1978; plans 50 singles and 25 albums in 1979. Works with musicians and songwriters on contract. Pays 3% minimum royalty to artists on contract; standard royalties to songwriters on contract.
How to Contact: Submit demo tape and lead sheet. Prefers 7½ ips reel-to-reel or cassette with 1-3 songs on demo. SASE. Reports in 6-8 weeks. "No reports issued unless material is accepted or unless we wish additional material for review."
Music: Disco; progressive; rock; soul; and top 40/pop. Recently released "Dance Across the Floor," by Jimmy "Bo" Horne (R&B/pop/disco single); and "Deeper in Love," by Fire (R&B/pop/disco single).

SUSAN RECORDS, Box 4740, Nashville TN 37216. (615)361-5356. Labels include Denco Records. A&R Director: Russ Edwards. Record company and music publisher. Estab. 1975. Released 2 singles and 1 album in 1978; plans 20 singles and 3 albums in 1979, 12 singles and 5 albums in 1980. Works with musicians and songwriters on contract. Pays 6¢/record to artists

on contract; 3¢/record to songwriters on contract. Buys some material outright; payment varies.
How to Contact: Submit demo tape and lead sheet. Prefers 7½ ips reel-to-reel with 1-6 songs on demo. SASE. Reports in 2 weeks.
Music: Blues; C&W; disco; easy listening; folk; gospel; jazz; MOR; rock; soul; and top 40/pop.

SWEETSONG RECORDING STUDIO, Box 2041, Parkersburg WV 26101. (304)485-0525. Labels include Mansion and Sweetsong. Owner: Roger Hoover. Record company and recording studio. Estab. 1977. Released 15 singles and 20 albums in 1978; plans 15 singles and 25 albums in 1979, 25 singles and 40 albums in 1980. Works with musicians on salary or contract. Pays royalty to artists and songwriters on contract. Buys some material outright; pays $25 minimum. Charges for some services: freelance demo work.
How to Contact: Submit demo tape and lead sheet "preferably in person but, if not, send a demo and lead sheet that need not be returned." Prefers 7½ ips reel-to-reel with 1-12 songs on demo. Does not return unsolicited material. Reports in 2 weeks.
Music: Church/religious (contemporary and conventional); C&W (modern); easy listening ("Barbra Streisand style"); gospel (contemporary); rock; soul; and top 40/pop. "Clean lyrics only. Sweetsong Records is looking for about 35 good gospel artists to handle, record, produce and promote. We need mainly contemporary gospel but some Southern or quartet gospel. We especially need several good female soloists, and groups." Recently released *Just in Time*, by the Singing Gospelaires (LP); and *Touching Jesus*, by the Golden Chords (LP).

T.F. RECORDS, INC., 14926 Ward, Detroit MI 48227. (313)933-4480, 81. President: Dennis Tally. A&R Director: Harold Jones. Record company and music publisher. Estab. 1968. Works with musicians and songwriters on contract. Pays 3-5% royalty to artists on contract; 2% royalty to songwriters on contract.
Music: Choral; church/religious; C&W; disco; easy listening; gospel; jazz; rock; soul; and top 40/pop.

TAKE HOME TUNES, Box 496, Georgetown CT 06829. (203)544-8288. Labels include Take Home Tunes and Broadway Baby. Owners: Doris Yeko, Bruce Yeko. Record company and music publisher. Estab. 1976. Released 6 albums in 1978; plans 7 albums in 1979, 8 albums in 1980. Works with musicians and songwriters on contract. Royalty payment varies for artists on contract; pays 5-10% royalty to songwriters on contract. Buys some material outright; payment negotiable.
How to Contact: Submit demo tape. Prefers cassette. SASE. Reports in 1 month.
Music: Children's and Broadway-type show tunes. No pop or rock. Recently released *Baker's Wife*, by Stephen Schwartz (show LP); *Snow White*, by Michael Valenti and Elsa Rael (children's LP); and *Robber Bridegroom*, by Waldman and Uhry (7-inch EP record).

TALISMAN RECORDS, INC., 6435 E. Corvette St., Los Angeles CA 90040. (213)475-7383. A&R Director: David Levine. Estab. 1978. Record company and production company.
How to Contact: Submit demo tape. Prefers cassette with 3-10 songs on demo. SASE. Reports in 3 weeks.
Music: Disco; easy listening; folk; MOR; progressive; R&B; rock; soul; and top 40/pop. Recently released *Pretty Girls*, by Lisa Del Bello.
Tip: "We're not looking for finished masters, but 8-track recordings give some depth for material. Submit clear piano/guitar vocal demos."

TALISMAN RECORDS, INC., 4800 Dufferin St., Downsview, Ontario, Canada. Contact: Tom Wilson. Record company and production company.
How to Contact: Submit demo tape. Prefers cassette with 3-10 songs on demo. SASE. Reports in 3 weeks.
Music: Disco; easy listening; folk; MOR; progressive; R&B; rock; soul; and top 40/pop.

TAPPAN ZEE RECORDS, 888 7th Ave., Suite 1901, New York NY 10019. (212)765-0580. Administrative Assistant: Didier C. Deutsch. President: Bob James. Record company and music publisher. Plans 10 albums in 1979. Works with musicians on contract. Pays negotiable royalty.
How to Contact: Submit demo tape and lead sheet. Prefers cassette with 1-4 songs on demo. SASE. Reports in 2 weeks.
Music: Blues; classical; disco; jazz; progressive; rock; and soul. Recently released *Heads*, by Bob James (progressive LP); and *Tightrope*, by Steve Khan (progressive LP).

TELEMARK DANCE RECORDS, 6845 Elm St., Suite 614, McLean VA 22101. Owner: Richard S. Mason. Record company. Estab. 1962. Released 5 singles and 3 albums in 1977; plans 10 singles and 5 albums in 1979. Works with musicians on contract. Pays 10-15% royalty to artists on contract.
How to Contact: Submit demo tape. Prefers 7½ ips reel-to-reel, cassette (include 1 song/side) or 8-track cartridge. SASE. Reports in 2 weeks.
Music: Disco; easy listening; and MOR. "We are interested in any good tunes that can be arranged in ballroom dance tempos, especially tunes written in ¾ time, suitable for medium tempos—30-36 measures/minute." Recently released *Isn't She Lovely?*, by Charles Barlow Orchestra; *Dancing Till Dawn*; and *Some Satin, Some Latin*, by the Hugo Strasser Orchestra (ballroom dance LPs).

TELL INTERNATIONAL RECORD CO., Rt. 5, Box 368-A, Yakima WA 98903. (509)966-6334. A&R Director: Hiram White. Record company. Estab. 1970. Released 15 singles and 2 albums in 1978. Works with musicians on contract. Pays standard royalty to artists on contract.
How to Contact: Submit demo tape and lead sheet. Prefers cassette with 1-4 songs on demo. SASE. Reports in 1 month.
Music: Bluegrass; blues; C&W; disco; folk; jazz; MOR; and rock. Recently released "Billie Joe" and "Georgia Wine," by Barbara Jean Taylor (C&W singles); and "I'm Too Shy," by Penny Stadler (C&W single).

TEROCK RECORDS, Box 4740, Nashville TN 37216. (615)361-5356. Labels include Terock and Curtiss Records. President: Wade Curtiss. Secretary: S.D. Neal. Record company and music publisher. Estab. 1974. Released 5 singles and 2 albums in 1978; plans 10 singles and 3 albums in 1979, 20 singles and 5 albums in 1980. Works with musicians and songwriters on contract. Pays 5¢/record to artists on contract; 3¢/record to songwriters on contract. Buys some material outright; payment varies.
How to Contact: Submit demo tape and lead sheet. Prefers 7½ ips reel-to-reel with 1-6 songs on demo. SASE. Reports in 2 weeks.
Music: Bluegrass; blues; C&W; disco; easy listening; folk; gospel; jazz; MOR; progressive; rock; soul; and top 40/pop. Recently released "That's Why I Love You," by Dixie Dee (C&W); "Born to Bum Around," by Curt Flemons (C&W); and "Big Heavy," by the Rhythm Rockers (rock).

THANKS RECORDS, Box 400843, Dallas TX 75240. (214)690-8165. President: Michael Stanglin. Record company and music publisher. Estab. 1968.
How to Contact: Submit demo tape. Prefers 7½ ips reel-to-reel or cassette with 1-3 songs on demo. SASE. Reports in 3 weeks.
Music: C&W; disco; easy listening; and top 40/pop. Recently released "I Hate Disco Music," by Rick Ramirez; and "Hokey Pokey/Happy Birthday" (for skating rinks).

TK RECORDS, 65 E. 55th St., New York NY 10028. (212)752-0160. Labels include Clouds, Dash, Alston, Marlin, Inphasion, Muscle Shoals Sound, Glades and Sunshine Sound. Vice President: Larry Lambert. Record company and music publisher. Estab. 1968. Released 50 singles and 25 albums in 1978; plans 75 singles and 35 albums in 1979, 75 singles and 35 albums in 1980. Works with musicians and songwriters on contract; songwriters on salary. Pays standard royalties to songwriters on contract.
How to Contact: Query or submit demo tape and lyric sheet. Prefers cassette with 1-3 songs on demo. SASE. Reports in 2 weeks.
Music: C&W; disco; R&B; rock; soul; and top 40/pop. Recently released *Get Off*, by Foxy (R&B/disco LP); *Bobby Caldwell*, by Bobby Caldwell (R&B/pop LP); and *Voyage*, by Voyage (disco LP).

TORTOISE INTERNATIONAL RECORDS, 15855 Wyoming, Detroit MI 48238. President: Don Davis. Record company, music publisher and record producer. Estab. 1968. Released 7 singles and 5 albums in 1978. Works with musicians on contract; songwriters on contract or salary. Pays standard royalties.
How to Contact: Query, submit demo tape, submit demo tape and lyric sheet, submit acetate disc or submit acetate disc and lyric sheet. Prefers 7½ ips reel-to-reel or cassette with 1-5 songs on demo. SASE. Reports in 3 weeks.
Music: Blues; disco; easy listening; MOR; progressive; R&B; rock; soul; and top 40/pop. Recently released *Love Transfusion*, by the Rockets (rock & roll LP); *Love at First Fire*, by First Fire (pop LP); and *Reflections*, by Johnnie Taylor (R&B LP).

TRAFIC RECORDS, 23 Av. Parc S., Ste. Julie, Quebec, Canada J01 2S0. (514)649-6853. Director: Rancourt Rahjan. Record company, music publisher, record producer and management firm. Estab. 1972. Released 6 singles and 3 albums in 1978; plans 5 singles and 3 albums in 1979, 10 singles and 5 albums in 1980. Works with musicians and songwriters on contract. Pays 5-15% royalty to artists on contract; standard royalties to songwriters on contract.
How to Contact: Query, arrange personal interview, submit demo tape, submit demo tape and lead sheet, submit acetate disc, submit acetate disc and lead sheet, or submit videocassettes. Prefers 7½ ips reel-to-reel, cassette or videocassette with 2 songs minimum on demo. Does not return unsolicited material. Reports in 1 month.
Music: Disco; easy listening; folk; MOR; rock; soul; and top 40/pop. Recently released *Berceuse Pour un Lion*, by Daniel Lavoie (folk/rock LP); *Contes Musicaux*, by Michej Ripoche (jazz rock LP); and *Robert Wood*, by Robert Wood (jazz rock LP).

ART TREFF PUBLISHING CO., 846 7th Ave., New York NY 10019. Labels include Steady, Phonosonic, Premier and Casset Majors Records. President: Art Trefferson. Record company and music publisher. Estab. 1968. Released 22 singles and 10 albums in 1977; plans 12 albums in 1979. Works with musicians on salary or contract; songwriters on contract. Pays standard royalty to songwriters on contract. Buys some material outright.
How to Contact: Submit demo tape and lead sheet. Prefers cassette. SASE. Reports in 1 month.
Music: Children's; classical; disco; folk; jazz; progressive; rock; soul; top 40/pop; and reggae. Recently released *Reggae's Greatest Hits Vols. I & II* (reggae LP).

TREND RECORDS, Box 201, Smyrna GA 30081. (404)432-2454. Labels include Trendsetter Records, Atlanta Records, Trend Records and Stepping Stone Records. President: Tom Hodges. Record company, music publisher, record producer and management firm. Estab. 1965. Released 6 singles and 2 albums in 1978; plans 10 singles and 5 albums in 1979, 10 singles and 8 albums in 1980. Works with musicians on contract. Pays 5-7% royalty to artists on contract; standard royalties to songwriters on contract.
How to Contact: Submit demo tape and lead sheet. Prefers cassette with 3-6 songs on demo. SASE. Reports in 3 weeks.
Music: Bluegrass; C&W; gospel; MOR; rock; and soul. Recently released "Only a Step," by Jo Ann Johnson (C&W single); "Say Welcome Home," by Souljers (blues single); and "Be Bop Alula," by Jimmy Dempsey (C&W single).

TRIANGLE RECORDS, INC., Box 23088, Nashville TN 37202. Music Editor: Morgan Lowry. Vice President/General Manager: Elwyn Raymer. Record company and music publisher. Estab. 1975. Works with musicians and songwriters on contract. Payment negotiable.
How to Contact: Submit demo tape and lead sheet. Prefers 7½ ips reel-to-reel or cassette with 1-3 songs on demo. SASE. Reports in 2 months.
Music: Children's; choral; church/religious; classical; and gospel. Recently released *The Way I Feel*, by Cynthia Clawson (sacred MOR LP).

TRUCKER MAN RECORDS, Centerline Rd., Cruz Bay, St. John VI 00830. (809)776-6814. Labels include One Number 18. President: Llewellyn Adrian Sewer. Record company, music publisher, record producer, management firm and booking agency. Estab. 1977. Released 5 singles and 2 albums in 1978; plans 10 singles and 4 albums in 1979, 20 singles and 10 albums in 1980. Works with musicians and songwriters on contract; musicians on salary. Pays 5-10% royalty to artists on contract; standard royalties to songwriters on contract.
How to Contact: Submit demo tape and lead sheet, or submit lead sheet. Prefers cassette with 2-4 songs on demo. SASE. Reports in 3 weeks.
Music: Church/religious; disco; R&B; soul; and top 40/pop. Recently released *Time is Running Out*, by Eddie and the Movements (calypso/reggae/disco LP); "Cota Zafei," by Julien and Daniel (French single); and *Mandingo Brass*, by Mandingo (calypso/reggae LP).

TRUSTY RECORDS, Rt. 1, Box 100, Nebo KY 42441. (502)249-3194. President: Elsie Childers. Record company and music publisher. Estab. 1970. "We have just reactivated this label and don't have any particular number of releases set yet." Works with musicians and songwriters on contract. Pays 2% royalty to musicians and songwriters on contract.
How to Contact: Submit demo tape and lead sheet. Prefers 7½ ips reel-to-reel or cassette with 2-4 songs on demo. SASE. Reports in 1 month.
Music: Blues; church/religious; C&W; disco; easy listening; folk; gospel; MOR; soul; and top 40/pop.

Tips: "We are particularly interested now in masters for release on our label."

TUMAC MUSIC (Incorporated with Spin-Chek R&D Co.), 2097 Vistadale Ct., Tucher GA 30084. Record company, record distribution and promotion, music publisher and booking agency. Estab. 1975. Pays standard royalty to artists and songwriters on contract.
How to Contact: Submit demo tape and lead. Prefers 7½ ips reel-to-reel or cassette with 2 songs on demo. SASE. Reports in 3 weeks.
Music: C&W; MOR; country rock; disco; and top 40/pop. Recently distibuted and promoted "Who's Larry," by Doyle Holly.

TYRE RECORDS, 903 Penn Circle Dr., 503 A, King of Prussia PA 19406. (800)251-9530. Vice President: Eric L. Ward. Record company and music publisher. Estab. 1973. Works with musicians and songwriters on contract; musicians on salary.
How to Contact: Query, arrange personal interview, submit demo tape, or submit demo tape and lead sheet. Prefers cassette with 4-6 songs on demo. SASE. Reports in 1 month.
Music: Blues; children's; choral; classical; disco; easy listening; gospel; jazz; MOR; R&B; soul; and top 40/pop.

UMBRELLA PRODUCTIONS, LTD., 7033 Transcanadian Hwy., Room 221, St. Laurent, Quebec, Canada. Labels include Umbrella and Magique Records. President: Yves Ladouceur. Record company and music publisher. Estab. 1975. Released 10 singles and 5 albums in 1977; plans 20 singles and 8 albums in 1979. Works with musicians and songwriters on contract. Pays 5-16% royalty to artists on contract; "we pay the usual share to the writers." Buys some material outright; pays $100-500/song.
How to Contact: Submit demo tape. Prefers 7½ or 15 ips reel-to-reel or cassette. SAE and International Reply Coupons. Reports in 1 month.
Music: R&B; disco; rock (country or soft); and top 40/pop. Recently released *Lindbergh II*, by Toulouse (R&B/disco LP); "It Always Happens This Way," by Toulouse (R&B/disco single); and "Aimes-Tu La Vie," by Boule Noire (R&B/disco single).
Tips: "We're bilingual; we accept material in English or French."

VELVET PRODUCTIONS, 517 W. 57th St., Los Angeles CA 90037. (213)753-7893. Labels include Velvet, Kenya, Normar, and Stoop Down Records. Manager: Aaron Johnson. Record company, booking agency and promoter. Estab. 1964. Released 2 singles and 1 album in 1978; plans 3 singles and 2 albums in 1979, 4 singles and 2 albums in 1980. Works with musicians and songwriters on contract. Pays 5% royalty to artists on contract; 2% royalty to songwriters on contract.
How to Contact: Submit demo tape, arrange personal interview, submit demo tape and lead sheet, or submit lead sheet. Prefers cassette with 3-5 songs on demo. SASE. Reports in 2 months.
Music: Blues; gospel; rock; soul; and top 40/pop. Recently released "Did You Mean It?", by Arlene Bell (single).

VIDEO RECORD ALBUMS OF AMERICA, 1224 N. Vine St., Hollywood CA 90038. (213)462-5860. Labels include VRA Records. Vice President: Ken Harper. A&R Director: W. Brown. Record company. Estab. 1972. Works with musicians and songwriters on contract, and producers with existing masters. Pays 5% royalty to artists on contract; 2½% royalty to songwriters on contract.
How to Contact: Submit demo tape and lead sheet. Prefers cassette with 2-4 songs on demo. SASE. Reports in 1 month.
Music: Blues; church/religious; C&W; disco; easy listening; and top 40/pop. Recently released "I'm on Fire," by Priscilla Cory (rock/disco single).

VOKES MUSIC PUBLISHING & RECORD CO., Box 12, New Kensington PA 15068. (412)335-2775. Labels include Vokes and Country Boy Records. President: Howard Vokes. Record company, booking agency and music publisher. Estab. 1954. Released 8 singles and 5 albums in 1978; plans 8 singles and 5 albums in 1979. Works with musicians and songwriters on contract. Pays 2½-4½¢/song royalty to artists and songwriters on contract.
How to Contact: Submit demo tape and lead sheet. Prefers reel-to-reel, cassette or 8-track tapes. SASE. Reports in 2 weeks.
Music: Bluegrass; C&W; and gospel. Recently released *Saturday Night/Sunday Morning*, by Ron Mesing (bluegrass LP); "Pretty Flowers," by Billy Wagner (bluegrass single); and "West of the Yukon," by Howard Vokes (country single).

VOLARE RECORDS, Box 325, Englewood NJ 07631. (201)567-7538. President: Clyde Otis. Record company, music publisher and record producer. Estab. 1956. Works with musicians on salary; songwriters on contract. Pays standard royalties.
How to contact: Submit demo tape and lead sheet. Prefers 7½ ips reel-to-reel with 1-3 songs on demo. SASE. Reports in 1 month.

W.A.M. MUSIC CORP., LTD., 901 Kenilworth Rd., Montreal, Quebec, Canada H3R 2R5. (514)341-6721. Labels include WAM Records and Disques Pleiade. President: Leon Aronson. Record company, music publisher and record producer. Estab. 1975. Released 18 singles and 4 albums in 1978. Works with musicians and songwriters on contract. Pays 5% minimum royalty to artists on contract; standard royalties to songwriters on contract.
How to Contact: Query or submit demo tape and lead sheet. Prefers 7½ ips reel-to-reel tape with 1-4 songs on demo. SAE and International Reply Coupons. Reports in 3 weeks.
Music: Disco; MOR; rock; and top 40/pop. Recently released "Lie to Myself," by Marty Butler (MOR/top 40 single); *Diane Tell*, by Diane Tell (pop LP); and "We've Gone Too Far," by Sharon Lee Williams (pop/disco single).

WALTNER ENTERPRISES, 14702 Canterbury, Tustin CA 92680. (714)731-2981. Labels include Sunbird and Daisy. Owner/President: Steve Waltner. Record company and music publisher. Estab. 1971. Released 3 singles in 1978. Works with musicians and songwriters on contract. Pays 5-10% royalty to artists on contract; 50% royalty to songwriters on contract.
How to Contact: Submit demo tape and lead sheet. Prefers 7½ ips reel-to-reel or cassette with 2-4 songs on demo. SASE. Reports in 3 weeks.
Music: C&W; easy listening; MOR; and top 40/pop. Recently released "Nashville Lady," by Tim Morton (country/pop single); "Boogie Man," by Jason Chase (top 40 single); and "Last Train Out," by Steve Shelby (country/pop single).

WARNER BROS. RECORDS, INC., 3300 Warner Blvd., Burbank CA 91510. (213)846-9090. General Manager: Roberta Petersen. Record company. Estab. 1958. Works with musicians and songwriters on contract.
How to Contact: Submit demo tape. Prefers 7½ ips reel-to-reel or cassette. SASE. Reports in 8 weeks.
Music: Bluegrass; blues; children's; choral; church/religious; C&W; disco; easy listening; folk; gospel; jazz; MOR; progressive; R&B; rock; soul; and top 40/pop. Recently released *Van Halen II*, by Van Halen (rock LP); *Minute by Minute*, by the Doobie Brothers (rock LP); and *Rumours*, by Fleetwood Mac (rock/pop LP).

WAVE RECORDS, 5635 Verona Rd., Verona PA 15147. (412)793-9503. President: James F. O'Leary Jr. Vice President/A&R Director: P.C. O'Leary. Record company and music publisher. Estab. 1975. Released 7 singles and 2 albums in 1978; plans 10 singles and 2 albums in 1979. Works with musicians and songwriters on contract. Payment negotiable.
How to Contact: Arrange personal interview or submit demo tape and lead sheet. Prefers 7½ ips reel-to-reel with 1-4 songs on demo. "Put leader between selections." SASE. Reports in 1 month.
Music: Blues; C&W; easy listening; MOR; rock; and top 40/pop. Recently released "Gift of Love," by Fauns Bell (blues single); "Lay That Rhythm Down," by Night Owl Band (rock/disco single); and "(Year of) 69," by Denny Marek (country-rock single).

WAYLON RECORDS, Summer Duck Publishing Co., 1216 Granby St., Norfolk VA 23510. (804)625-0534. President: D.H. Burlage. Record company and music publisher. Estab. 1977. Released 2 singles and 1 album in 1978; plans 4 singles and 2 albums in 1979. Works with musicians and songwriters on contract. Payment negotiable for artists on contract; pays 50% royalty to songwriters on contract.
How to Contact: Submit demo tape, submit demo tape and lead sheet, or submit lead sheet. Prefers 7½ or 15 ips reel-to-reel or cassette. SASE. Reports in 2 weeks.
Music: Bluegrass; C&W; easy listening; MOR; rock (hard or country); and top 40/pop. Recently released "Don't Diguise" and "Virginia Feelin' " (country rock singles); and "Shine the Light" (rock single), all by the Seabird Band.

WESJAC RECORD ENTERPRISES, Box 743, 317 S. Church St., Lake City SC 29560. A&R Director: W.R. Bragdton Jr. Record company and music publisher. Estab. 1972. Released 3 singles in 1977; plans 10 singles and 2 albums in 1979. Works with musicians on salary or contract; songwriters on contract. Pays 5% royalty to artists and songwriters on contract.
How to Contact: Submit demo tape and lead sheet. Prefers 7½ or 15 ips reel-to-reel with 2

songs minimum on tape. SASE. Reports in 1 month.
Music: Church/religious and gospel. Recently recorded "I'm Glad I Wasn't Made by Man" and "Every Now and Then," by the Gospel Songbirds (gospel singles); and "I Can't Stop Loving God," by the Traveling Four (gospel single).

WESTWOOD RECORDS, 125 Taylor St., Jackson TN 38301. (901)427-7714. Owner: Charlie Roach. Record company and music publisher. Estab. 1959. Released 2 singles and 2 albums in 1978; plans 2 singles and 2 albums in 1979, 2 singles and 2 albums in 1980. Works with musicians on contract. Pays 2-artists on contract: standard royalties to songwriters for each record sold.F4How to Contact: Query or submit demo tape. Prefers 7½ ips reel-to-reel or cassette with 4-10 songs on demo. "We will want to hear work that is copyrighted." SASE. Reports in 1 month.
Music: Bluegrass; blues; church/religious; C&W; gospel; R&B; rock; and soul. Recently released "Move Over Rover" (rock); "Tornado Twist" (rock); and "I Hate to Leave You" (rock).
Tips: "As of now I am leasing master tapes. I am looking for material and masters that were made between 1950 and 1970: rock, blues, R&B, country and western with a rockabilly touch to it. But we will listen to all that has a chance of making a good seller, no matter what type of music or when it was recorded. We are also looking for some new Hawaiian music suitable for recording."

WHEELSVILLE RECORDS, INC., 17544 Sorrento, Detroit MI 48235. (313)341-3538. Labels include Wheelsville and Purcal Records. President: Will Hatcher. Contact: Sharon Hatcher. Record company and music publisher. Estab. 1975. Works with musicians and songwriters on contract. Pays 5% royalty to artists on contract; 4% royalty to songwriters on contract.
How to Contact: Submit demo tape and lead sheet. Prefers 7½ ips reel-to-reel with 2-4 songs on demo. SASE. Reports in 2 weeks.
Music: Disco; gospel; soul; and top 40/pop. Recently released "Soul Sonata," by Firebirds (top 40 single); and "Who Am I Without You Baby," by W.C. Hatcher (soul single).

WHITE EAGLE PUBLISHING, INC., Box 2446, Toluca Lake CA 91602. (213)763-2300. Labels include Lotus Records. President: H. Lyman. Record company, music publisher and management firm. Estab. 1974. Works with songwriters on contract. Pays 2½¢/record to songwriters on contract. Buys some material outright; pays $100 minimum/song.
How to Contact: Submit demo tape and lead sheet. Prefers reel-to-reel or cassette with 2 songs on demo. SASE. Reports in 3 weeks.
Music: C&W; rock (country); and top 40/pop. Recently released "Play the Game" and "I'll Do the Same for You," by Lynnell Mitchell (blues/C&W singles).

WHITE ROCK RECORDS, INC., 401 Wintermantle Ave., Scranton PA 18505. (717)343-6718. President: Phil Ladd. Record company, music publisher and record producer. Estab. 1960. Released 4 singles in 1978; plans 8 singles and 2 albums in 1979, 16 singles and 4 albums in 1980.
How to Contact: Query or submit demo tape and lead sheet. Prefers cassette with 2 songs minimum on demo. SASE. Reports in 3 weeks.
Music: Children's; C&W; easy listening; R&B; rock; and top 40/pop. Recently released "Scotch 'n Soda," by Clyde Stacy (ballad single); "Rock 'n Roll Record Girl," by Bobby Brant (rock single); and "Tenderness," by Evra Bailey (ballad single).

WILDFIRE RECORDS, 1415 N. Hudson Ave., Hollywood CA 90028. Owner: Sam Weatherly. Record company, music publisher and production firm. Estab. 1969. Released 2 singles and 2 albums in 1978; plans 4 singles and 3 albums in 1979, 6-8 singles and 3-6 albums in 1980. Works with musicians and songwriters on contract. Pays 5-8% royalty to artists on contract.
How to Contact: Submit demo tape, or submit demo tape and lead sheet. Prefers 7½ ips quarter-track reel-to-reel with 1-3 songs on demo. SASE. Reports "as soon as possible."
Music: Blues (not hard/torch-type); C&W (soft/crossover); disco (vocal-oriented); easy listening; MOR; rock (not hard); top 40/pop; and jazz/rock. Recently released "Christmas in L.A.," by Jonathan Arthur (Christmas single).

WILDWOOD ENTERTAINMENT, 223 Broadway, Rensselaer NY 12144. Labels include Black & White and Millville Records. Co-Owner: Vincent Meyer II. Estab. 1975. Plans 4 singles and 2 albums in 1979, 4 albums in 1980. Works with musicians on contract and salary; songwriters on contract. Pays standard royalties.

How to Contact: Query, submit demo tape, submit demo tape and lead sheet, submit acetate disc, submit acetate disc and lead sheet or submit lead sheet. Prefers 7½ ips reel-to-reel or cassette with 2 songs minimum on demo. SASE. Reports in 3 weeks.
Music: Children's; disco; folk; jazz; progressive; rock; and top 40/pop.

MARTY WILSON PRODUCTIONS, INC., 185 West End Ave., New York NY 10023. (212)580-0255. Labels include D&M Sound and Cyma Records. President: Marty Wilson. Record company and music publisher. Estab. 1966. Released 4 singles and 6 albums in 1978. Works with musicians on salary for in-house work; songwriters on contract. Payment varies for artists on contract; pays statutory royalty to songwriters on contract.
How to Contact: Submit demo tape and lead sheet. Prefers 7½ or 15 ips reel-to-reel or cassette with 1-3 songs on demo. SASE. Reports in 1 month.
Music: Easy listening; jazz; MOR; and top 40/pop. Recently released "Love for Sale," by the Vast Majority (single); "Boop Boop a Hustle," by Camp Galore (single); and "Help Is on the Way," by Tanden Hayes (single).

WILWIN RECORDS, Box 1669, Carlsbad CA 92008. (714)729-8406. Owner: Denny Tymer. Record company. Estab. 1976. Released 1 album in 1978. Works with musicians and songwriters on contract. Pays 5-9% royalty to artists on contract; statutory royalty to songwriters on contract.
How to Contact: Arrange personal interview or submit demo tape and lead or lyric sheet. Prefers 7½ ips reel-to-reel or cassette with 1-3 songs on demo. "Demos should be simple and each song should not be over 3 minutes, 20 seconds long. Put leader between each song on tape." SASE. Reports in 3 weeks.
Music: C&W and top 40/pop. Recently released *It's About Tymer*, by Denny Tymer (C&W LP).
Tips: "We work with musicians according to the American Federation of Musicians (AFM) Phonographic Labor Agreement, and with vocal background singers in agreement with the American Federation of Television and Radio Artists (AFTRA)."

WINDSONG RECORDS, 1901 Avenue of the Stars, Suite 740, Los Angeles CA 90067. Vice President, A&R: Denny Diante. Director/Artist Development: Larry Hamby. Record company, music publisher and management firm. Estab. 1970. Works with musicians on contract. Payment negotiable.
How to Contact: Submit demo tape. Prefers 7½ ips quarter-track reel-to-reel or cassette with 1-3 songs on demo. SASE. Reports "as soon as possible."
Music: MOR; progressive; rock; and top 40/pop. Recently released *Lead Me On*, by Maxine Nightingale (LP); *Blind Date*, and by Blind Date (LP).

WOODRICH RECORDS, Box 38, Lexington AL 35648. (205)247-3983. President: Woody Richardson. Record company and music publisher. Estab. 1959. Released 8 singles and 15 albums in 1978; plans 10 singles and 20 albums in 1979, 15 singles and 25 albums in 1980. Works with musicians on salary or contract; songwriters on contract. Pays 5% royalty to artists on contract; 1-3/8¢/song royalty to songwriters on contract.
How to Contact: Submit demo tape. Prefers 7½ ips reel-to-reel or cassette with 2-4 songs on demo. SASE. Reports in 1 month.
Music: Bluegrass; blues; children's; choral; church/religious; C&W; easy listening; folk; gospel; jazz; MOR; progressive; rock; soul; and top 40/pop. Recently released *High on Bluegrass*, by the Madison County Ramblers (bluegrass LP).

WOODSHED RECORDS, LTD., Rt. 1, Emsdale, Ontario, Canada P0A 1J0. (705)636-5684. President: David Essig. Record company and music publisher. Estab. 1972. Plans 6 albums in 1979. Works with musicians and songwriters on contract. Payment negotiable.
How to Contact: Submit demo tape. Prefers 7½ ips reel-to-reel with 3-5 songs on demo. SAE and International Reply Coupons. Reports in 1 month.
Music: Bluegrass; blues; C&W; folk; and rock (country). Recently released *Hobo's Taunt* and *Cathy Fink & Duck Donald*, by Willie P. Bennett (country); and *Stewart Crossing*, by David Essig (country/folk LP).

WORD, INC., 4800 W. Waco Dr., Waco TX 76703. (817)772-7650. Labels include Word, Myrrh, Dayspring and Canaan. Assistant Director of A&R/Music Publishing: Don Cason. Director of A&R: Buddy Huey. Record company and music publisher. Estab. 1952. Plans 70 albums in 1979, 70 albums in 1980. Works with musicians and songwriters on contract.
How to Contact: Submit demo tape and lead sheet. Prefers 7½ ips reel-to-reel or cassette with

3-7 songs on demo. SASE. Reports in 2 months.
Music: Children's; choral (gospel); church/religious; disco (gospel); easy listening (gospel); folk; gospel (all kinds); jazz; MOR; progressive (gospel); rock (country or hard); soul (gospel); and top 40/pop (gospel). Recently released "Home Where I Belong," by B. J. Thomas (pop single); "Mirror," by Evie (MOR single); and *Sail On*, by the Imperials (contemporary gospel LP).

YATAHEY RECORDS, Box 31819, Dallas TX 75231. (214)690-8875. Owner: Pat McKool. A&R: Mike Anthony. Record company and music publisher. Estab. 1974. Works with artists and songwriters on contract. Pays 8% royalty to artists on contract.
How to Contact: Submit demo tape and lead sheet or submit demo tape and lyric sheet. Prefers 7½ ips reel-to-reel with 1-4 songs on demo. SASE. Reports in 1 month.
Music: C&W and gospel. Recently released "I'm the Man," by Dugg Collins (C&W single); and "Bill's Hillbilly Bar," by Dave Farley (C&W single).

ZONE RECORD CO., 2674 Steele, Memphis TN 38127. (901)357-0064. Owner: Marshall E. Ellis. Record company, music publisher and record producer. Estab. 1957. Released 5 singles in 1978; plans 5 singles in 1979, 10 singles in 1980. Works with songwriters on contract. Pays 3¢/record royalty to artists on contract; statutory royalties to songwriters on contract.
How to Contact: Submit demo tape. Prefers 7½ ips reel-to-reel or cassette with 4 songs on demo. "Be sure the words are clear. Don't try to make a master—just a good clean tape." Reports in 2 weeks.
Music: Blues; church/religious; C&W; easy listening; progressive; and R&B. Recently released "Was it All That Bad?", by Patti Faith (country-rock single); "Words Softly Spoken," by the Wrane Show (country single); and "Baby You Don't Love Me Anymore," by J. Pullman (country single).

Throughout 1979, the editors and correspondents of *Songwriter's Market* contacted all important American and Canadian record companies at least once—and in some cases, two or three times. Most major record companies responded to our information requests. Some, however, chose not to give us information. Publishers in the following list declined to give us information for one of the following reasons:

• They are not actively seeking new artists or material from songwriters.
• They *will* listen to material, but believe that they receive sufficient material without listing in *Songwriter's Market*.
• They are a branch office that concentrates on marketing or other business endeavors, and leaves selection selection of artists and songs to branches in other cities.
• They work only with artists or songwriters recommended to them from other sources.
• They are staffed with in-house songwriters.
• They don't have a staff large enough to handle the increased number of submissions a listing would create.
• They are concerned with copyright problems that might result if they record a song similar to one they've reviewed and rejected.
• They have once listed with another songwriter directory and were deluged with inappropriate submissions.

Though many of the following firms will review material, we suggest that you not send demo tapes. Write a brief query letter describing your material and asking about the company's current submission policies. Always use a self-addressed, stamped envelope or post card for such queries (see "Proper Submission Methods" for details).

Arista Records, 38 Music Square E., Nashville TN 37203.

Amherst Records, 9229 Sunset Blvd., Los Angeles CA 90069.

Birthright Records, 3101 S. Western, Los Angeles CA 90018.

Capitol Records, 38 Music Square E., Nashville TN 37203.

Capitol Records, Inc., 1370 Avenue of the Americas, New York NY 10019.

Capricorn Records, Inc., 4405 Riverside Dr., Burbank CA 91505.

CBS Records, Inc., 51 W. 52nd St., New York NY 10019.

Children's Records of America, Inc., 1 Lincoln Plaza, New York NY 10023.

Claridge Records, 6381 Hollywood Blvd., Suite 318, Los Angeles CA 90028.

Columbia Records, 51 W. 52nd St., New York NY 10019.

Elektra/Asylum, 1216 17th Ave. S., Nashville TN 37212.

Epic Records, 51 W. 52nd. St., New York NY 10019.

Fantasy/Prestige/Milestone/Stax, Suite 600, Mid Memphis Tower, 1407 Union, Memphis TN 38104.

Fantasy/Prestige/Milestone/Stax, 1776 Broadway, Suite 617, New York NY 10019.

Lifesong Records, 9229 Sunset Blvd., Los Angeles CA 90069.

Millenium Records, 3 W. 57th St., New York NY 10019.

Monument Records, 21 Music Square E., Nashville TN 37203.

Nashboro Record Co., 1011 Woodland St., Nashville TN 37206.

Phonogram, Inc., 10 Music Circle S., Nashville TN 37203.

Polydor, Inc., 21 Music Circle E., Nashville TN 37203.

Polygram Corp., 450 Park Ave., New York NY 10022.

RCA Records, 1133 Avenue of the Americas, New York NY 10036.

Republic Records, 5858 Sunset Blvd., Hollywood CA 90028.

Republic Records, 815 18th Ave. S., Nashville TN 37203.

RSO Records, Inc., 1775 Broadway, New York NY 10019.

RSO Records, Inc., 3747 Moss Rose Dr., Nashville TN 37203.

Scorpio Enterprises Inc., 38 Music Square E., Nashville TN 37203.

United Artists Records, Inc., 6920 Sunset Blvd., Los Angeles CA 90028.

United Artists Records, Inc., 50 Music Square W., Nashville TN 37203.

United Artists Records, Inc., 729 7th Ave., New York NY 10019.

Vee Jay International Music, 131 E. Magnolia Blvd., Burbank CA 91502.

Warner Bros. Records, 1706 Grand Ave., Box 12646, Nashville TN 37212.

Record Producers

A successful song typically follows a path that leads it from publisher to producer to record company. Some songwriters, however, like to skip ahead and deal directly with the record producer, who controls virtually every aspect of recording a song from choosing the right material for his artists to deciding the song's arrangement, from finding the best musicians and vocalists for the recording session to supervising the final mixing of the record.

The producer is also a talent scout, always looking for fresh material for his artists. Today, the producer is nearly as active as the publisher in searching for the next big hit. Producer Shane Wilder recommends approaching record producers first, "as most producers are publishers, and you stand a better chance of getting the song recorded."

"The easiest way to get anything accomplished," says another producer, "is to go directly to the independents. Major companies are so inundated with material that it's really hard to get your songs listened to. They might have a secretary listening to tapes and what kind of day she's had will affect her evaluation. The producer gives a fairer evaluation."

Other advantages of approaching a producer first, in the eyes of a variety of producers, include openness to new ideas, contacts, and willingness to invest more time and money into a song. Independent producers are now the ones taking chances. They record new acts with new material, then try to sell finished masters to record companies. Producers also seek contracts with record companies to produce specific acts already signed with the record companies. Either the way, producers need material.

"It's good for a writer to directly contact a producer," says John Braheny, co-director of the Alternative Chorus Songwriter's Showcase. "It's always good for writers to try to make any contacts they can with producers and recording artists."

As mentioned before, many producers also run publishing branches, as well as record labels and management firms. Braheny says offering producers a portion of the publishing rights to your material increases your chances of getting recorded. "If you can go to a producer or an artist and say, 'Record this song and I'll give you the publishing rights'—that producer is more likely to cut your song than to take an equally good song from another publisher. The producer gets more out of that deal." Yet, Braheny warns, "The only pitfall is that unless the song is recorded by a major artist who's really going to get out and plug the song, the writer may end up having given his rights to a person that is not a fulltime publisher, but is a producer first. This producer may not have the wherewithall to further exploit your songs."

Still, one producer says, "I'll promote the tune that I publish; that's the priority. . . . What I have is a reversion clause in my contracts. After one year, if the tune does nothing, the rights revert back." Ask for a reversion clause in any producer contracts you sign (for more on such a clause, see "Negotiating Your Contract" in the introductory material of this book).

Other producers feel that songwriters, especially new songwriters who don't understand the intricacies of publishing, should stick with the publishers. They believe a publisher's contacts—including contacts with producers—can be valuable to a songwriter. "A publisher does his job to place good songs and a producer to create a good product," says Gary Buckley, president of FYDAQ Productions. "I've never accepted or rejected a job because I was able to get the publishing as part of the package. In the long run, I'd like my songs to be with a good publisher, and my records handled by a good producer."

Still others are neutral (one said he

takes an MOR stand) on the matter. Whoever is excited about your material should handle it, they say. If a producer can work your material harder than a publisher, then so be it.

Producers surveyed recently by *Songwriter's Market* note that they'd rather deal with good songwriter/artists, and that good songwriters are in demand. Producers, therefore, are willing and eager to listen to your material.

Producers are paid in several ways. Producers contract for a percentage royalty on records sold, receive a set fee from a record company to produce one of their artists, or receive a set fee from the artist or songwriter. A combination of any of these three may also be used.

Follow the same guidelines when submitting to producers as you do to publishers or record companies. Most prefer reel-to-reel demos with lead sheets. Include a list of the song order. A typed copy of your lyrics is helpful. Check the following listing for specific submission policies of individual producers.

Study the listings to determine the types of music the producers handle. Watch producer names on record charts (in *Billboard*, *Record World*, and *Cashbox*) to see what producers are currently doing, as well as which producers handle which artists. "Zero in on what type of material/artist the company is looking for and gear your efforts in that direction before making your approach," says a representative of Camillo/Barker Enterprises.

Inquiring about the producer's interest by mail is a good way to start. "I tried just doing the rounds with phone calls, but that doesn't work," says one producer. "I found that sending a letter and then showing my face worked. I advocate persistence. Sit in the office and wait. Get to know the secretaries, because that's a large part of the game." But "never deliver any material in person unless you have an appointment set up first," says Diane Jean Klusowski of Paul Wolfe Productions.

Don't give up on a producer if he rejects a song or two. "Continue to send fresh new material as long as the company is willing to listen seriously," says Gene Huddleston, who owns Huddleston's Recording Studio. A rejection doesn't mean the producer doesn't want to work with you; it simply means the particular songs didn't fit his needs.

Above all, "Be willing to listen and work hard to achieve goals," says Hayne Davis, producer/director of Mother Cleo Productions/DaviSound. "Realize there is no 'magic wand' for success—just talent, hard work and common sense."

EUGENE ADAMS PRODUCTIONS, Box 47578, Los Angeles CA 90047. President/A&R: Eugene Adams. Record producer and management firm. Estab. 1977. Deals with artists. Produced 4 albums and 10 singles in 1978; plans 8 albums and 16 singles in 1979. Fee derived from sales royalty.
How to Contact: Query or submit demo tape and lead sheet. Prefers cassette with 4-6 songs on demo. SASE. Reports in 3 weeks.
Music: Blues; church/religious; disco; gospel; rock (hard or country); and soul. Recently produced "This Masquerade," by Mary Love (soul single, Message Records); and "All About Love," by Eugene Adams (soul single, Message Records).

APPLE/CHIPETZ MANAGEMENT, 1808 Ludlow St., Philadelphia PA 19103. (215)567-0287. Contact: Steve Apple. Estab. 1977. Deals with artists and songwriters. Fee derived from sales royalty.
How to Contact: Submit demo tape. Prefers cassette with 4 songs maximum on demo. SASE. Reports "as soon as possible."
Music: Disco; rock (hard AOR); and top 40/pop.

ARGONAUT MUSIC, Box 32044, San Jose CA 95152. (408)258-6000. President: Eric R.

Hilding. Music publisher and record producer. Estab. 1976. Interested in songwriters and artists. Royalty basis contracts.
How to Contact: Query or submit demo tape and lyric or lead sheet. Prefers cassettes but will accept 7½ ips reel-to-reel with 1-3 songs on tape. SASE. Reports in 3-5 weeks.
Music: Contemporary "hit" singles material a la top 40/pop (crossover); disco; easy listening/MOR; gospel/Christian; C&W (pop country); rock; and soul.

THE WILLIAM ASHWOOD CORP., 256 S. Robertson Blvd., Beverly Hills CA 90211. (213)659-4210. Director, New Artist Development: Margeaux Levy. General Manager: Mel Zimmerman. Record producer, music publisher and management firm. Estab. 1967. Deals with artists and songwriters. Produced 8 albums in 1978; plans 8 albums in 1979. Fee derived from sales royalty and publishing licenses.
How to Contact: Submit demo tape and lead sheet. Prefers cassette with 3-5 songs on demo. "Demos should be acoustic: the simpler, the better. No elaborate production." Does not return unsolicited material. Reports "as soon as possible."
Music: Bluegrass (new grass or electric); blues (R&B or soul); children's; C&W; disco; rock; and top 40/pop. Recently produced "A Collector's Item," by Star Spangled Washboard (novelty/new grass single, Flying Fish Records); "Fast and Loose," by the Max (rock single, United Records); and "You Light Up My Life," by Andreya Reynolds (ballad single, Talobit Records).

ASTRAL PRODUCTIONS, INC., (A division of the Earthraker Corp.), 214 W. 6th St., Suite AA, Box 4527, Topeka KS 66604. (913)233-9716. Executive Vice President: Kent Raine. Record producer and talent promoters. Other corporate divisions include record companies, music publishers and a management and booking firm. Estab. 1976. Deals with artists and songwriters. Plans 4 albums and 8 singles in 1979; 6 albums and 12 singles in 1980. Fee derived from sales royalty.
How to Contact: Submit demo tape and lead sheet. Prefers cassette "although 7½ ips is acceptable" with 2-6 songs on demo. SASE. Reports in 1 month.
Music: Rock; country rock; C&W; disco; jazz; MOR; blues; soul; and top 40/pop.

ATLAS RECORDS, Harvey Levy Productions, 1345 W. Estes, Chicago IL 60626. (312)338-6729. President: Harvey Levy. Record producer, booking agency and music publisher. Estab. 1967. Deals with artists and songwriters. Produced 2 albums and 5 singles in 1978; plans 3 albums and 8 singles in 1979. Fee derived from sales royalty.
How to Contact: Query or submit demo tape. Prefers cassette with 2-6 songs on demo. Does not return unsolicited material. Reports in 3 weeks.
Music: Blues; C&W; easy listening; MOR; rock (country); and top 40/pop. Recently produced "Gweee," by Richard Fudoli (jazz single, Date Records); "Streakin'," by Red Garter Band (easy listening single, Atlas Records); and "My Fine Feathered Friend," by Jim Beyers (C&W single, Maestro Records).

AZTEC PRODUCTIONS, 20531 Plummer St., Chatsworth CA 91311. (213)998-0443. General Manager: A. Sullivan. Record producer, music publisher and management firm. Estab. 1968. Deals with artists and songwriters. Produced 1 album and 2 singles in 1978; plans 3 albums and 4 singles in 1979. Fee derived from sales royalty.
How to Contact: Submit demo tape and lead sheet. Prefers 7½ ips reel-to-reel or cassette with 6 song maximum on demo. SASE. Reports in 2 weeks.
Music: Blues; disco; easy listening; MOR; rock; and top 40/pop. Recently produced "El Chicano" (top 40, Dorn Records); "With You," by Abraas (top 40, Dorn Records); and "Summer Nites," by Newstreet (rock, Dorn Records).

BAKER-HARRIS-YOUNG PRODUCTIONS, INC., Lewis Tower Bldg., Suite 817-819, 225 S. 15th St., Philadelphia PA 19102. (215)569-1496. Vice President: Ron Baker. Record producer and music publisher. Estab. 1972. Deals with artists and songwriters. Produced 16 albums in 1978. Fee derived from sales royalty. Charges for some services: "50% production advance."
How to Contact: Query or submit demo tape and lead sheet. Prefers 7½ ips reel-to-reel or cassette with 1-3 songs on demo. "Include name, address and telephone number with area code." SASE. Reports in 4-6 weeks.
Music: Disco; soul; and top 40/pop. Recently produced "Disco Inferno," by the Trammps (disco single, Atlantic Records); "Cheaters Never Win," by Love Committee (disco single, Gold Mind Records); and "Our Love," by the Dells (R&B single, Mercury Records).

bARTISTIC MUSIC, 1921 Walnut St., Philadelphia Pa 19103. (215)561-1283. Music Director:

Bart Arntz. Record producer, music publisher and management firm. Estab. 1975. Deals with songwriters and dancers. Produced 6 albums and 45 singles in 1978. Fee derived from sales royalty.
How to Contact: Submit demo tape. Prefers 7½ ips reel-to-reel or cassette with 1-4 songs on demo. SASE. Reports in 3 weeks.
Music: Disco; soul; and top 40/pop. Recently produced *JoJo's Dance Factory*, by JoJo Smith (disco/funk LP, Education Records); *Ron Daniels Makes You Feel Like Dancin'*, by Ron Daniels (MOR LP, Education Records); and *Ballet in Colour*, by Don Farnworth (classical LP, Education Records).

AL BASI PRODUCTIONS, 93 Bedford St., New York NY 10014. Professional Manager: Richard A. Lo Cicero. Estab. 1976. Deals with artists and songwriters. Produced 12 singles in 1978; plans 6 singles in 1979. Fee derived from outright fee from record company.
How to Contact: Submit demo tape only. Prefers 7½ ips or cassette with 1-6 songs on demo. SASE. Reports in 1 month.
Music: C&W; disco; easy listening; gospel; MOR; rock (any type); soul; and top 40/pop. Recently produced "I Got Soul Love," by Seaboard Coastliners (R&B, Mayhams Collegiate Records); "We'll Build A Bungalow," by Seaboard Coastliners (disco, Mayhams Collegiate Records); "Go/Don't Say Love," by Ian York (rock, JEM Records); and "But the Dance Goes On," (disco, Mayhams Collegiate Records).

THOM BELL PRODUCTIONS, 2212 4th Ave., Seattle WA 98121. (206)682-5278. Contact: JoDee Omer. Record producer. Estab. 1968. Deals with artists. Fee derived from sales royalty or outright fee from record company.
How to Contact: "Representative contact either from record company or management. New artists with an established label deal or label deal pending only, or already established artists." Prefers 7½ ips reel-to-reel or cassette. Send resume and previous LPs or singles if released.
Music: Classical; C&W; disco; easy listening; folk; gospel; jazz; MOR; progressive; rock; soul; and top 40/pop. Recently produced material by the Spinners (Atlantic Records); the O'Jays (P.I.R. Records); and MFSB (P.I.R. Records).

ART BENSON PRODUCTIONS, 1560 N. La Brea, Hollywood CA 90028. A&R/Pop Producer: Art Benson. R&B Producer: Sonny Craver. Deals with artists and songwriters. Plans 48 albums and 75 singles in 1979. Fee derived from sales royalty.
How to Contact: Query or submit demo tape and lead sheet. Prefers 7½ or 15 ips reel-to-reel or cassette with 3-12 songs on demo. SASE. Reports in 1 month.
Music: Bluegrass; blues; church/religious; C&W; disco; easy listening; gospel; jazz; MOR; rock; soul; and top 40/pop. Recently produced *Energy Crisis*, by King Solomon (R&B LP, Celestial Records); *Universe Rock*,by Captain DJ (disco LP, Celestial Records); and *Country Dreaming*, by Tommy Cooper (C&W LP, Celestial Records).

BIG MIKE MUSIC, 408 W. 115th St., 2W, New York NY 10025. (212)222-8715. President: Bill Downs. Estab. 1957. Deals with songwriters. Produced 6 albums in 1978; plans 10 albums and 12 singles in 1979. Fee derived from sales royalty.
How to Contact: Submit demo tape and lead sheet. Prefers cassette with 3 songs on demo. SASE. Reports in 1 month.
Music: Blues; disco; jazz; and soul. Recently produced Chris Bantley (soul, Right On Records); and Supreme Court (soul/disco, Big Mike Records).

JACK BIELAN PRODUCTIONS, 6381 Hollywood Blvd., Suite 509, Hollywood CA 90028. Contact: Jack Bielan. Record producer and music publisher. Estab. 1971. Deals with artists and songwriters. Produced 2 albums and 4 singles in 1978. Fee derived from sales royalty or outright fee from record company.
How to Contact: Submit demo tape or submit demo tape and lead sheet. Prefers 7½ or 15 ips reel-to-reel or cassette with 1-3 songs on demo. "Send no more than three songs on reel-to-reel. Leader them. Cassettes are fine. Lyric sheets are acceptable in place of lead sheets. Please don't send long letter of life history. A brief resume is acceptable. Put 'Song Material Enclosed' on outside of envelope." SASE. Reports in 3 weeks.
Music: Disco; rock; soul; and top 40/pop. Recently produced "Nadia's Theme," by Sounds of Sunshine (ballad single, Ranwood Records); "The Amazing Spiderman Disco Theme," by Steamroller Big Band (disco single, Warner-Curb Records); and "Can I Have You?", by Spring Fever (pop/ballad single, Warner-Curb Records).
Tips: "Send samples of what you're best at. If you're a singer, show your most commercial point. It you're a writer, categorize your material relating to today's commercial market so that

the producer has some idea of where you're at. Strong Sedaka/Kristofferson/Mac Davis-style lyrics with good repeating choruses are needed. Barry Manilow-style songs are also needed."

BIG DEAL RECORDS CO., Box 60-A, Cheneyville LA 71325. President: Launey Deal. Record producer, music publisher, booking agency and management firm. Estab. 1965. Deals with artists and songwriters. Produced 20 albums and 7 singles in 1978; plans 50 albums and 10 singles in 1979. Fee derived from sales royalty or outright fee from songwriter/artist.
How to Contact: Query, arrange personal interview, submit demo tape or submit demo tape and lead sheet. Prefers 7½ ips reel-to-reel or cassette with 4-20 songs on demo. SASE. Reports in 1 week.
Music: Blues; C&W; disco; gospel; rock (hard or country); and soul. Recently produced "Somebody Have Mercy" (blues/soul single, Soul-Cat Records), and "Sometime Losers Win" (blues single, Soul-Cat Records), by Rocking Lonnie; and "No-Way," by the Reverend L. Allen (gospel single, Gospel Soul Train Records).

BISHOP & MICHAL ENTERPRISES, Box 2194, S. 3rd St., Memphis TN 38101. President: Bishop Cole. Record producer, booking agency and management firm. Estab. 1978. Deals with artists and songwriters. Produced 4 singles and 6 albums in 1978; plans 12 albums in 1979. Fee derived from sales royalty.
How to Contact: Submit demo tape and lead sheet. Prefers cassette. SASE. Reports in 1 month.
Music: Blues; church/religious; disco; gospel; jazz and soul. Recently produced "Rock My Soul," by Lula Collins (gospel, Gospel Express Records); "Phone Call From Heaven," by The Bishop (gospel, Gospel Crusade Records); and "Stop That," by Lee Porter (rock, Michal Records).

BOUQUET-ORCHID ENTERPRISES, Box 4220, Shreveport LA 71104. (318)686-7362. President: Bill Bohannon. Record producer, music publisher and management firm. Estab. 1977. Deals with artists and songwriters. Produced 1 album and 3 singles in 1978; plans 2 albums and 4 singles in 1979, 2 albums and 4 singles in 1980. Fee derived from sales royalty.
How to Contact: Submit demo tape and lead sheet. Prefers 7½ ips reel-to-reel or cassette with 2-5 songs on demo. SASE. Reports in 1 month.
Music: C&W; church/religious; and top 40/pop. Recently produced "Gonna Be a Brighter Day" and "I Need You Today," by Shan Wilson (C&W singles, Bouquet Records).

STAN BRONSON PRODUCTIONS, INC., Box 162, Provo UT 84601. (801)224-1775. President: Stan Bronson. Record producer and music publisher. Estab. 1975. Deals with artists and songwriters. Fee derived from sales royalty, outright fee from record company or outright fee from songwriter/artist. "If I choose an artist for my roster, I arrange financing. My production services and facilities are also available to artists and songwriters who arrange their own financing."
How to Contact: Query or submit demo tape and lead sheet. Prefers cassette with 2 songs on demo. SASE. Reports in 1 month.
Music: Bluegrass; children's; church/religious; C&W; easy listening; folk; MOR; rock (soft or country); and top 40/pop. Recently produced *Proud Earth*, by Chief Dan George (easy listening LP, Salt City); "Sugartime Dan," by Bryan Edgar (pop single, Salt City); and "Sail Away From Me," by Johnny Whitaker (pop single).

BROTHER LOVE PRODUCTIONS, Box 852, Beverly Hills CA 90213. (213)980-9271. Producer: Jeremy McClain. Secretary: S. Roshay. Record producer and music publisher. Estab. 1970. Deals with artists and songwriters. Produced 5 albums and 5 singles in 1978; plans 8 albums and 8 singles in 1979. Fee derived by royalty or outright fee from record company.
How to Contact: Query with letter of introduction, arrange personal interview or submit demo tape and lead sheet. Prefers cassette with 4 songs on demo. SASE. Reports in 3 weeks.
Music: C&W; disco; easy listening; MOR; rock (commercial top/40); and top 40/pop. Recently produced *Happy Days*, by Pratt and McClain (top 40, Warner Bros. Records); *What Ever Happened*, by Tom Gillon (country, Brother Love Records); and *Pratt & McClain*, by Pratt and McClain (top 40, ABC Records).

BENNIE BROWN PRODUCTIONS, 3011 Woodway Lane, Box 5702, Columbia SC 29206. (803)788-5734. Owner: Bennie Brown Jr. Estab. 1968. Deals with artists, songwriters and music publishers. Produced 4 albums and 12 singles in 1978; plans 4 albums and 14 singles in 1979, 6 albums and 15 singles in 1980. Fee derived from sales royalty.
How to Contact: Query, submit demo tape, or submit demo tape and lead sheet. Prefers 7½ ips

reel-to-reel with 2-4 songs on demo. SASE. Reports in 3 weeks.
Music: C&W (pop country); disco; gospel; MOR; soul; and top 40/pop. Recently produced "She's Blowing My Mind," by the Soul Agents (disco single, Nu-Tone Records).

RON BROWN MANAGEMENT, 319 Butler St., Pittsburgh PA 15223. (412)781-7740. Producer: Ron Brown. Estab. 1969. Deals with artists and songwriters. Produced 3 albums and 10 singles in 1978. Fee derived from sales royalty or outright fee from record company.
How to Contact: Submit demo tape or submit demo tape and lead sheet. Prefers 7½ ips reel-to-reel or 8-track cartridge. SASE. Reports in 2 weeks.
Music: Blues; disco; easy listening; MOR; progressive; rock; soul; and top 40/pop. Recently produced "Gimmy Some," by Fun (top 40 single, Buddah Records); and " 'Cause I Say I Do," by Sha-Zamm (top 40 single, Fat Man Records).

STEVE BUCKINGHAM, Box 754, Roswell GA 30077. (404)993-0871. Producer: Steve Buckingham. Estab. 1978. Deals with artists and songwriters. Produced 2 albums and 2 singles in 1978, 3-5 albums and 4-6 singles in 1979. Fee derived from sales royalty and outright fee from record company.
How to Contact: Submit demo tape or submit demo tape and lead sheet. Prefers 7½ ips reel-to-reel or cassette with 1-3 songs on demo. SASE. Reporting time varies.
Music: Country (contemporary); disco; MOR; rock (any form); soul; and top 40/pop. "Any well structured commercial song." Recently produced "I Love the Nightlife," by Alicia Bridges (top 40/disco/R&B, Polydor Records) and *Alicia Bridges*, by Alicia Bridges (top 40/disco/R&B LP, Polydor Records).

BUCKSKIN PRODUCTIONS, INC., 7800 Woodman Ave., #19A, Panorama City CA 91402. (213)786-3324. Producer: Jeffrey Wheat. Record producer, music publisher and management firm. Estab. 1969. Deals with artists and songwriters. Produced 3 singles and 2 albums in 1978; plans 4 singles and 3 albums in 1979. Fee derived from sales royalty.
How to Contact: Submit demo tape. Prefers 7½ ips reel-to-reel or cassette with 4-6 songs on demo. SASE. Reports in 1 month.
Music: Rock (hard or country) and top 40/pop. Recently produced "Gotta Move," by October Young (hard rock single, Buckskin Records); "Fort Wayne," by Pearl Alley (rock single, Epic Records); and "Captain, Captain," by Dee Carstensen (folk/rock single, Buckskin Records).

C.R.S., INC., 5624 Chew Ave., Philadelphia PA 19138. (215)844-9528. President: Curtis R. Staten. Record producer and music publisher. Estab. 1969. Deals with artists and songwriters. Produced 12 singles in 1978; plans 4 albums and 8 singles in 1979. Fee derived from sales royalty.
How to Contact: Submit demo tape and lead sheet. Prefers 7½ ips reel-to-reel or cassette with 2-8 songs on demo. SASE. Reports in 2 weeks.
Music: Blues; disco; easy listening; gospel; jazz; MOR; rock; soul; and top 40/pop. Recently produced "Sometime Alone," by Frankie Allen (easy rock single, C.R.S. Records); "Thinking of You," by the Butlers (rock single, C.R.S. Records); and "When You See What You Want," by Al Berry (rock/jazz single, C.R.S. Records).

CHARLES CALELLO PRODUCTIONS, LTD., Box 562, Livingston NJ 07039. President: Charles Calello. Music arranger and music publisher. Estab. 1963. Deals with artists and songwriters. Produces 4-6 albums a year. Fee derived from royalties or outright fee from record company.
How to Contact: Submit demo tape and lead sheet. Prefers reel-to-reel or cassette with 1-5 songs on demo. SASE. Reports in 2 weeks.
Music: Pop songs. Recently produced *Sooner or Later*, recorded by Rex Smith (Columbia Records); *American Standard Band* (Island Records); *Calello* (Mid-Song International); *Desmond Child and Rouge* (Capitol Records); and *Bat Out of Hell*, recorded by Meat Loaf.

CAMILLO/BARKER ENTERPRISES (formerly Venture Sounds, Inc.), 121 Meadowbrook Dr., Somerville NJ 08876. (201)359-5110. Producers: Tony Camillo, Cecile Barker. Record producer, music publisher and production company. Estab. 1964. Deals with artists and songwriters. Produced 3 albums and 12 singles in 1978; plans 5 albums and 20 singles in 1979. Fee derived from sales royalty or outright fee from record company.
How to Contact: Query or submit demo tape and lead sheet. "Send as complete a package as possible." Prefers cassette with 2-5 songs on demo. SASE. Reports in "1 month or longer depending on schedule."

Music: Disco; soul; MOR; top 40/pop; "excellent material only." Recently produced *Funked Up*, by Creme D' Cocoa (R&B/soul/disco LP, Venture Records); *The Need to Be*, by Sandra Feva (R&B/soul/disco LP, Venture Records); *If You Want It You Got It*, by Sandra Feva (12" disco LP, Venture Records); *Baby Don't You Know*, by Creme D' Cocoa (12" disco LP, Venture Records); and various singles.

CHEMICAL PRODUCTIONS, 1037 W. 4th St., Erie PA 16507. President: Paul L. Tatara. Record producer, management firm and record company. Estab. 1977. Deals with artists and songwriters. Produced 1 album and 2 singles in 1978; plans 3 albums and 5 singles in 1979. Fee derived from sales royalty.
How to Contact: Query or submit demo tape. Prefers 7½ ips reel-to-reel with 2-6 songs on demo. SASE. Reports in 3 weeks.
Music: Progressive and rock. Recently produced "Don't Say Love Unless You Mean It," by Paul Tatara (progressive/rock single, Endangered Species Records); "Heart Throb," by Pistolwhip (punk rock single, Endangered Species Records); and "Gotta Lotta Lose," by the Bradley Harrington Band (punk rock single, Endangered Species Records).

CITISOUNDS COMMUNICATIONS CORP., 37 Riverside Dr., Suite 7-A, New York NY 10023. Contact: Jean Edwards. Record producer, music publisher and management firm. Estab. 1973. Deals with songwriters and recording artists. Produced 3 albums and 3 singles in 1978; plans 5 albums and 5 singles in 1979. Fee derived from sales royalty, outright fee from record company, or outright fee from songwriter/artist. Charges for some services: "If we place a song, expenses are necessary."
How to Contact: Query. Prefers cassette with 2 songs minimum on demo. SASE. Reports in 3 weeks.
Music: Blues; disco; gospel; jazz; and progressive. Recently produced "Thank You Baby," by Leon Thomas (disco single, Bareback); "Miss Universe Song," by Count Robin (calypso single, Camille Records); and "Sweet Caroline," by Phil Abner (disco single, Camille Records).

CLAY PIGEON PRODUCTIONS, Box 20346, Chicago IL 60620. (312)476-2553. A&R Director: V. Beleska. Record producer. Estab. 1975. Deals with artists and songwriters. Produced 5 albums and 10 singles in 1978; plans 15 albums and 25 singles in 1979. Fee derived from sales royalty or outright fee from record company.
How to Contact: "We cannot consider any material without a written inquiry first, describing self and material." Prefers 7½ ips reel-to-reel or cassette with 1-5 songs on demo. SASE. Reports in 2-8 weeks.
Music: Bluegrass; blues; children's; choral; church/religious; classical; C&W; disco; easy listening; folk; gospel; jazz; MOR; progressive; rock; soul; top 40/pop; avant-garde; and punk rock. Recently produced "All for You," by Christopher (MOR single, Clay Pigeon International Records); "Disco People," by Roto Applicators (punk rock single, Broken Records); and *Tricentennial 2076*, by Vyto B (avant-garde LP, Clay Pigeon International Records).

COLEMAN, KESTIN AND SMITH PRODUCTIONS, LTD., 7507 Sunset Blvd., Suite 1, Hollywood CA 90046. (213)935-5786. President: K.H. Smith. Vice President of Creative Services: Linda Lou Kestin. Record producer, music publisher and record company. Estab. 1976. Deals with artists. Produced 1 album and 4 singles in 1978; plans 3 albums and 10 singles in 1979. Fee derived from sales royalty or advances against royalties.
How to Contact: Query or submit demo tape and lead sheet. Prefers cassette with 1-8 songs on demo. SASE. Reports in 2 weeks.
Music: Blues; C&W; disco; easy listening; folk; jazz; MOR; progressive; rock; soul; and top 40/pop. Recently produced "Train of Desire," by Total Force and John Blouin (disco/top 40/pop single, CKS-Claridge); "Love and Life," by Lee Rogers (disco/blues single, Motown-Gwen Glen); and "Go for it Sucker," by R.G. Ingersoll (disco single, Motown).

COUSINS MUSIC, 211 Birchwood Ave., Upper Nyack NY 10960. President: Lou Cicchetti. Estab. 1950. Produced 5 singles in 1978; plans 5 singles in 1979. Fee derived from sales royalty.
How to Contact: Submit demo tape only. Prefers 7½ or 15 ips reel-to-reel or cassette with 2 songs minimum on demo. SASE. Reports in 2 weeks.
Music: C&W (any); and rock. Recently produced "Wall Between Us," by the Earls (soul/rock, Dakar Records) and "One More Heartache," by CoCo (C&W, Daisy Records).

LARRY COX PRODUCTIONS, INC., Box 2266, Van Nuys CA 91404. President: Larry Cox. Record producer and music publisher. Estab. 1971. Deals with artists and songwriters.

Songwriter's Market Close-Up

Songwriter Ed Bruce believes that songwriters should respond to natural creative processes. "Trying too hard to finish the song is the biggest mistake you can make," he says. "When it hits you, do it then." Bruce speaks from experience; the idea for the Grammy-winning "Mamas Don't Let Your Babies Grow Up to Be Cowboys" (co-written with his wife, Patsy, on the right) hit him while driving down the freeway. Yet, Bruce doesn't believe you can waste time waiting for divine inspiration. When asked how you beat a writer's slump, he says, "Letters from collection agencies help."

Produced 2 albums and 6 singles in 1978. Fee derived from sales royalty or outright fee from record company.
How to Contact: Submit demo tape and lead sheet. Prefers 7½ ips reel-to-reel or cassette with 3-6 songs on demo, or disc. "State the specific reason for the submission and whether artist/material/songwriter is currently committed in any way." Does not return unsolicited material. Reports in 1 month.
Music: Blues; C&W (progressive); MOR; rock (no acid rock); soul; and top 40/pop. Recently produced *Red Octopus*, *Spitfire*, *Dragonfly* and *Earth*, by Jefferson Starship (rock LPs, Grunt).

COYOTE PRODUCTIONS, 14002 Palawan Way, Marina Del Rey CA 90291. (213)822-7905. President: Leonard Sachs. Estab. 1974. Deals with artists and songwriters. Produced 4 singles and 2 albums in 1978; plans 25 singles and 50 albums in 1979, 50 singles and 100 albums in 1980. Fee derived from sales royalty or outright fee from record company.
How to Contact: Query or arrange personal interview. Prefers 7½ ips reel-to-reel with 3-4 songs on demo or cassette. SASE. Reports in 2 weeks.
Music: Pop, soul, disco, jazz and MOR. Recently produced "Shack Up," by Banbarra (pop/R&B/disco single, United Artists Records); "Sun and Steel" and "Scorching Beauty," by Iron Butterfly (rock singles, MCA Records).

DANCER PRODUCTIONS, LTD., 1638 R St. NW, Washington DC 20009. (202)234-8860. President: David Carpini. Record producer. Estab. 1976. Deals with artists and songwriters. Produced 2 albums and 4 singles in 1978; plans 3 albums and 6 singles in 1979. Fee derived from sales royalty.
How to Contact: Submit demo tape and lyric sheet. Prefers 7½ ips reel-to-reel or cassette.

DAVIS PRODUCTS, 3203 E. 130th St., Cleveland OH 44120. (216)752-7732. President: Robert Davis. Estab. 1970. Deals with artists and songwriters. Produced 3 albums and 3 singles in 1978; plans 8 albums and 6 singles in 1979, 15 albums and 8 singles in 1980. Fees derived from sales royalty.
How to Contact: Query or submit demo tape and lead sheet. Prefers cassette. SASE. Reports in 1 month.
Music: Blues; disco; gospel; jazz; MOR; pop; and soul. Recently produced *Enough of Love*, by Danny Cocco (MOR LP, Image Records).

DAWN PRODUCTIONS, Cloud 40, Paradise PA 17562. President: Jay Welz. Estab. 1963-65. Deals with artists and songwriters. Plans 3 albums and 6 singles in 1979. Fee derived from sales

royalty or outright fee from record company.
How to Contact: Submit demo tape. Prefers 7½ ips reel-to-reel or cassette with 6-12 songs on demo. Does not return unsolicited material. Reports in 1 month. "We hold material in files and use when appropriate."
Music: Blues; C&W; disco; easy listening; folk; MOR; progressive; rock; and top 40/pop. Recently produced "Rippen' 'Em Off in the Name of Love," by New Wave Comets (punk, Disco Records); "Sir Duke at the Hop," by The Comet Revival (Disco Records).

LOU DeLISE PRODUCTIONS, 6123 Reach St., Philadelphia PA 19111. (215)725-6388. Owner: Lou DeLise. Record producer and music publisher. Estab. 1974. Deals with artists, songwriters, producers and record companies. Plans 4 albums and 15 singles in 1979. Fee derived from sales royalty, outright fee from record company, or outright fee from songwriter/artist.
How to Contact: Submit demo tape and lead sheet. Prefers 7½ ips reel-to-reel or cassette. SASE. Reports in 3 weeks.
Music: Church/religious (pop); C&W (pop); disco; easy listening; MOR; soul; and top 40/pop. Recently produced "Trinidad," by John Gibbs U.S. Steel (disco single, Makossa Records); "When Did You Stop?", by the J's (disco single, Dante Records); and "Figures," by William DeVaughn (R&B/pop single, Farr Records).

STEVE DIGGS PRODUCTIONS, 20 Music Square W., Nashville TN 37203. (615)259-4024. Producers: Steve Diggs, Stan Gunselman. Record producer, music publisher and jingle production. Estab. 1972. Deals with artists and songwriters, and clients looking for musical advertising. Fee derived from sales royalty or outright fee from record company.
How to Contact: Query or submit demo tape and lead sheet. Prefers 7½ ips reel-to-reel with 2-4 songs on demo. SASE. Reports in 1 month.
Music: Bluegrass; children's; church/religious; C&W; easy listening; folk; MOR; rock; and top 40/pop. Recently produced *I Feel Love*, by Saxons (MOR LP, Kyte Records); and *Memories*, by Insiders (MOR LP, Kyte Records).

DUANE MUSIC, INC., 382 Clarence Ave., Sunnyvale CA 94086. (408)739-6133. President: Garrie Thompson. Estab. 1966. Deals with artists and songwriters. Fee derived from sales royalty.
How to Contact: Submit demo tape only. Prefers 7½ ips reel-to-reel or cassette with 1-5 songs on demo. SASE. Reports in 1 month.
Music: Blues; C&W; rock; soul; and top 40/pop. Recently produced "Wichita," (C&W, Hush Records) and "Syndicate of Sound," (rock, Buddah Records).

DYN-O-MITE RECORDS, Box 194, Violet LA 70092. (504)682-4149. Contact: Freddie Sanchez. Estab. 1979. Deals with artists, songswriters and promotions. New company. Fee derived from sales royalty.
How to Contact: Query or submit demo tape and lead sheet. Prefers cassette with 10-12 songs on demo. SASE. Reports in 2 weeks.
Music: Disco; gospel; soul; and dixieland.

EASTEX MUSIC, 8537 Sunset Blvd., #2, Los Angeles CA 90069. (213)657-8852. Owner: Travis Lehman. Record producer and music publisher. Estab. 1977. Deals with songwriters. Plans 6 singles in 1979. Fee derived from sales royalty.
How to Contact: Submit demo tape. Prefers 7½ ips reel-to-reel or cassette. SASE. Reports in 3 weeks.
Music: Recently produced "Tear in Your Eye" and "Another Place in Time," by Rick Ellis (C&W singles, Reuben Records).

EBB-TIDE PRODUCTIONS, Box 2544, Baton Rouge LA 70821. (504)925-2603. President: E.K. Harrison. Estab. 1978. Deals with artists and songwriters. Fee derived from sales royalty.
How to Contact: Submit demo tape and lead sheet. Prefers cassette with 4-6 songs on demo. SASE. Reports in 2 weeks.
Music: Bluegrass; church/religious; C&W; and folk. Recently produced "Cryin', Cryin'," by Evie Laborde (C&W single, Deb's Country Records); "Son of Sam," by Ernest Thomas (soul single, C.I.T.S. Records); and "Cryin' in the Streets," by the Silver Stars (soul single, C.I.T.S. Records).

ESPRIT RECORDS, 2141 Pemberton Rd. SW, Atlanta GA 30331. (404)349-1459. A&R Director: Gordon Boykin. Record producer and music publisher. Estab. 1968. Deals with

artists and songwriters. Plans 8-10 albums in 1979. Fee derived from sales royalty and publishing royalty.
How to Contact: Submit lead sheet. Prefers 7½ ips reel-to-reel with 4-8 songs on demo. SASE. Reports in 3 weeks.
Music: Blues; church/religious; disco; easy listening; gospel; jazz; rock; soul; and top 40/pop. Recently produced "African Strutt," by L. Westbrook (soul single, Esprit Records); "Funky Fingers," by R. Marks (jazz single, Esprit Records); and "It's So Sad," by B. Geddis (gospel single, Esprit Records).

ESQUIRE INTERNATIONAL, Box 6032, Station B, Miami FL 33123. (305)547-1424. President: Jeb Stuart. Record producer, music publisher and management firm. Estab. 1973. Deals with artists and record labels. Produced 5 singles in 1978; plans 5 singles in 1979. Fee derived from sales royalty or independent leasing of masters and placing songs. Charges for some services: "We charge artist management or backers, not particularly songwriters."
How to Contact: Query, submit demo tape and lead sheet or telephone. Prefers cassette with 2-4 songs on demo, or disc. SASE. Reports in 1 month.
Music: Blues; church/religious; C&W; disco; gospel; jazz; rock; soul; and top 40/pop. Recently produced "Can't Count the Days" (R&B single, Kent Records); "Sitba" (R&B single, King Records); and "Hung up on Your Love" (disco single, Esquire Records), all by Jeb Stuart.

FRANK EVANS PRODUCTIONS, Box 6025, Newport News VA 23606. (804)595-9000. President: Frank Evans. Estab. 1967. Deals with artists and songwriters. Produced 2 albums and 3 singles in 1977, 2 albums and 2 singles in 1978; plans 1 album and 2 singles in 1979. Fee derived from sales royalty.
How to Contact: Submit demo tape and lead sheet. Prefers cassette with 3-5 songs on demo. "Also submit brief resume of former musical works with your name, address and age." SASE. Reports within 90 days.
Music: Choral; C&W; disco; easy listening; folk; MOR; and top 40/pop. Recently produced "Bryan's Song," by Laurie Wilson (MOR, Premiere Artist Records); "Without You," by Wayne Baxter Trio (MOR, Old Dominion Records); and "Butterfly" by Steve Cook (MOR, Premiere Artist Records).

FIST-O-FUNK, LTD., 293 Richard Ct., Pomona NY 10970. (914)354-7157. President: Kevin Misevis. Record producer, music publisher, management firm and record company. Estab. 1976. Deals with artists and songwriters. Produced 3 albums and 2 singles in 1978; plans 3 albums and 2 singles in 1979, 3 albums and 3 singles in 1980. Fee derived from sales royalty.
How to Contact: Submit demo tape and lead sheet. Prefers 7½ ips reel-to-reel with 3-10 songs on demo. SASE.
Music: C&W; disco; jazz; MOR; and top 40/pop. Recently produced "Keep on Dancin' " and "Dance All Over the World," by T.C. James (pop/disco); "To Hear My Daddy Pray" and "Our America," by the Country Congregation (gospel, Majega Records); "Steppin' Out," by the Gospelmen (gospel, Majega Records); and "We're Working Together" and "My Only Love," by Dusk (top 40, Fuban Records).

ROB FRABONI PRODUCTIONS, Box 695, Beverly Hills CA 90213. (213)457-9744. Producer/Owner: Rob Fraboni. Producer: Tim Kramer. Record producer. Estab. 1975. Deals with artists and songwriters. Produced 4 albums 1978; plans 3 albums in 1979, 3 albums in 1980. Fee derived from sales royalty.
How to Contact: Query or submit demo tape. Prefers cassette with 1-5 songs on demo. Does not return unsolicited material. Reports in 1-2 months.
Music: Blues; progressive; rock; and top 40/pop. Recently produced *Rick Danko*, by Rick Danko (LP, Arista Records); "No Reason to Cry," by Eric Clapton (LP, RSO Records); *Stingray*, by Joe Cocker (LP, A&M Records); *Milton*, by Milton Nascimento (LP, A&M Records); *Blondie Chaplin*, by Blondie Chaplin (LP, Asylum Records); *Life in the Food Chain*, by Tonio K. (LP, Epic/Full Moon Records); *The Last Waltz*, by The Band, Bob Dylan, Joni Mitchell, Van Morrison, Eric Clapton, Muddy Waters and Neal Young (LP, Warner Bros. Records); and *Shot Through the Heart*, by Jennifer Warnes (LP, Arista Records).

FYDAQ PRODUCTIONS, 240 E. Radcliffe Dr., Claremont CA 91711. (714)624-0677. President: Gary K. Buckley. Record producer. Estab. 1970. Deals with artists, songwriters and record companies. Produced 4 albums and 2 singles in 1978; plans 5 albums and 4 singles in 1979. Fee derived from sales royalty, outright fee from record company, or outright fee from songwriter/artist.

How to Contact: Query, arrange personal interview, submit demo tape, or submit demo tape and lead sheet. Prefers 7½ ips reel-to-reel or cassette with 1-4 songs on demo. SASE. Reports in 3 weeks.

Music: Children's; church/religious; C&W; disco; easy listening; folk; gospel; MOR; rock; soul; and top 40/pop. Recently produced *Buche*, by Rick Buche (top 40/MOR LP, Paradise Records); *To God, With Love*, by Jerry Roark (gospel LP, Majega Records); and *Country Love*, by Jerry Roark (C&W LP, Majega Records).

PHIL GABER RECORD PRODUCTION AND PERSONAL MANAGEMENT, 7141 Rutland St., Philadelphia PA 19149. (215)728-1699. Owner: Phil Gaber. Record producer, music publisher, management firm and record company. Estab. 1961. Deals with artists and songwriters. Produced 1 album and 8 singles in 1977; plans 4 singles in 1978. Fee derived from sales royalty or outright fee from record company.

How to Contact: Query, arrange personal interview, or submit demo tape. "If you're an artist, include photo." Prefers 7½ ips reel-to-reel or cassette with 2 songs minimum on tape, or disc. "It's best to call late (after 10 pm EST)."

Music: Blues; disco; easy listening; jazz; MOR; rock; soul; and top 40/pop. Recently produced "Nite Ride" and "Puttin' it Down," by Idyll Passion.

GALLANT ROBERTSON, INC., 1115 Sherbrooke St. W., Suite 2504, Montreal, Quebec, Canada H3A 1H3. (514)288-8880. Vice President: Ian Robertson. Record producer and music publisher. Estab. 1972. Deals with artists and songwriters. Produced 4 singles and 2 albums in 1978; plans 4 albums 1979 and 6 albums in 1980. Fee derived from sales royalty or outright fee from record company.

How to Contact: Query, arrange personal interview or submit demo tape. Prefers 7½ ips reel-to-reel or cassette with 1-3 songs on demo. SAE and International Reply Coupons. Reports in 1 month.

Music: Disco; MOR; rock (top 40); and top 40/pop. Recently produced *Will You Give Me Your Love?* (top 40 LP, Attic Records); *Patsy* (disco/top 40, Attic Records); and *Are You Ready for Love?* (top 40 LP, EMI Records), by Patsy Gallant.

THE GENERAL PRODUCTION, Box 31819, Dallas TX 75231. (214)690-8874. Producer: Mike Anthony. Record producer. Estab. 1975. Deals with artists and songwriters. Fee derived from sales royalty.

How to Contact: Query or arrange personal interview. Prefers 7½ ips reel-to-reel with 2-4 songs on demo. Include lyric or lead sheet. SASE. Reports in 1 month.

Music: Church/religious; C&W; and gospel. Recently produced *Man From Galilee* by Billy Parker (gospel LP, SCR Records); "Baby, Baby, Who Do You Always?", by Janet Sue (C&W single, SCR Records); and "Wildlife," by Dale Noe (C&W single, SCR Records).

GOLD GIANT MUSIC, Valley Forge Plaza, Suite 605, King of Prussia PA 19406. (215)783-7243. Vice President: James E. Sauls. Record producer and music publisher. Estab. 1977. Deals with artists, songwriters, producers and arrangers. Produced 12 albums in 1978; plans 20 albums and 3 singles in 1979. Fee derived from sales royalty.

How to Contact: Query with letter of introduction, phone, arrange personal interview, submit demo tape and lead sheet. Prefers 7½ ips reel-to-reel or cassette with 1-5 songs on demo. "The main objective is to make personal contact."

Music: Blues; C&W; disco; easy listening; MOR; rock; and top 40/pop.

WALT GOLLENDER ENTERPRISES, 12 Marshall St., Suite 8Q, Irvington NJ 07111. (201)373-6050. Executive Director: Walt Gollender. Record producer, music publisher and management firm. Estab. 1963. Deals with artists, songwriters and producers. Produced 4 singles in 1978; plans 3-5 singles in 1979. Fee derived from sales royalty, outright fee from record company, or outright management fee from songwriter/artist.

How to Contact: Arrange personal interview or submit demo tape. Prefers 7½ ips mono reel-to-reel or cassette with 1-4 songs on demo. SASE. Reports in 2 weeks.

Music: Blues; C&W; disco; easy listening; folk; MOR; rock (pop or soft); soul; and top 40/pop. "Responsible for putting together in 1968-69 the now world-famous songwriting team of Irwin Levine and Larry Brown. Now producing Tina Sanderson (Spring Records) and several other acts being recorded by major industry producers such as Denny Randell."

GOLLY MUSIC, Penthouse A, 12 Marshall St., Irvington NJ 07111. (201)373-6050. President: Walt Gollender. Estab. 1966. Deals with artists, songwriters, producers, agents, publishers, backers, other managers, theatrical photographers and the industry at large. Produced 3 singles

in 1978; plans 4-6 singles in 1979. Fee derived from sales royalty, outright fee from record company or outright fee from songwriter/artist.
How to Contact: Arrange personal interview. "Send or bring me demo tape. Call any evening 5-8 p.m. EST." Prefers 7½ ips reel-to-reel, cassette or dubs with a maximum of 4 songs on demo. SASE. Reports in 3 weeks.
Music: Blues; C&W; disco; easy listening; folk; MOR; rock (medium to light); soul; and top 40/pop. Recently produced "I'm Not the Other Woman," by Mary Lee Martin (C&W, Golly Records); "Misty Morning in Missouri," by Chuck Ehrmann (C&W, Golly Records); and "It's All Over," by Ben Wiggins (soul/bump, Golly Records).

GOSPEL EXPRESS, 1899 S. 3rd, Box 2194, Memphis TN 38101. (901)774-5689. President: Bishop Cole. Estab. 1970. Deals with artists and songwriters. Produced 8 albums and 2 singles in 1978; plans 5 albums and 4 singles in 1979. Fee derived from sales royalty.
How to Contact: Submit demo tape and lead sheet. Prefers cassette. SASE. Reports in 3 weeks.
Music: Blues; church/religious; disco; and gospel.

JOE GRACEY PRODUCTIONS, 6004 Bull Creek Road, Austin TX 78757. (512)451-1747. Vice President, A&R: Bobby Earl Smith. Record producer. Estab. 1977. Deals with artists and songwriters. Produced 1 album in 1978; plans 5 albums and 10 singles in 1979. Fee derived from sales royalty.
How to Contact: Submit demo tape. Prefers 7½ ips reel-to-reel or cassette with 1-3 songs on demo. Does not return unsolicited material.
Music: Blues; C&W; rock; and top 40/pop. Recently produced *Double Trouble*, *Freda & the Firedogs* and *The Skunks*, by Double Trouble (LPs, Big Wheel Records).

GRAMEX RECORDS, INC., 749 Peachtree, Atlanta GA 30308. (404)874-4451. Vice President: Sidney Goldberg. Producer: Eric Sutoris. Record producer, music publisher, management firm and record company. Estab. 1974. Deals with artists, songwriters and producers. Produced 2 albums and 3 singles in 1978; plans 4 albums and 10 singles in 1979. Fee derived from sales royalty.
How to Contact: Submit demo tape. Prefers 7½ ips reel-to-reel with 1-5 songs on demo. "Tape should specify quarter-track or half-track stereo." SASE. Reports in 2 weeks.
Music: Disco; rock (hard or soft); and top 40/pop. Recently produced "The Disco," by the Chicken and the Egg (disco single, Gramex Records); and "Rock 'n Roll Freedom" and "Better Way," by the Balls Brothers Band (top 40 singles, Gramex Records).
Tips: "We are only interested in material with top 40 hit potential. We cut nothing unless we have the publishing on unknown writers."

GREAT PYRAMID, LTD., 10 Waterville St., San Francisco CA 94124. Contact: Joseph Buchwald. Record producer, music publisher and management firm. Estab. 1973. Deals with artists and songwriters. Produced 1 album in 1978; plans 2 in 1979, 2 in 1980. Fee derived from sales royalty, outright fee from record company, or outright fee from songwriter/artist.
How to Contact: Query or submit demo tape and lead sheet. Prefers cassette with 3-6 songs on demo. Does not return unsolicited material. Reports "as soon as possible."
Music: Rock. Recently produced *Jesse Barish*, by Jesse Barish (ballad LP, RCA Records).

ABNER J. GRESHLER PRODUCTIONS, INC., 9200 Sunset Blvd., #909, Los Angeles CA 90069. (213)278-8146. President: Abner J. Greshler. Vice President: Steve Greshler. Record producer and booking agency. Estab. 1950. Deals with artists and songwriters. Plans to produce 10 albums and 6 singles in 1978, 20 albums and 12 singles in 1979. Fee derived from sales royalty.
How to Contact: Query or submit demo tape and lead sheet. Prefers cassette with 2-4 songs on demo. Does not return unsolicited material. Reports in 1 month.
Music: Rock (hard or country) and soul.

GRUSIN/ROSEN PRODUCTIONS, 408 Holly Place, Northvale NJ 07647. (201)768-7292. Contact: Larry Rosen. Estab. 1976. Deals with artists and songwriters. Produced 8 albums in 1978; plans 8 albums in 1979. Fee derived from sales royalty or outright fee from record company.
How to Contact: Query. Prefers reel-to-reel or cassette with 2-5 songs on demo. SASE. Reports in 1 month.
Music: Jazz. Recently produced *One of a Kind*, by Dave Grusin (LP, Polydor); *Havana Candy*, by Patty Austin (LP, CTI); and *Finger Paintings*, by Earl Klugh (LP, Blue Note).

GEORGE GUESS PRODUCTIONS, 2250 Bryn Mawr Ave., Philadelphia PA 19131. (215)477-7122. A&R Director: Ted Brown. Record producer. Estab. 1969. Deals with artists and songwriters. Produced 2 albums and 3 singles in 1978; plans 3 albums and 5 singles in 1979.
How to Contact: Query with letter of introduction or submit demo tape. Prefers 7½ ips reel-to-reel or cassette with 5 songs on demo. SASE. Reports in 3 weeks.
Music: Disco; soul; and top 40/pop. Recently produced "So Doggone Good," by Ecstasy (R&B/disco, Ari-Star Records); "Ain't We Had Enough," by Ronnie Williams (R&B/disco, Voyage Records); and "Red Hot Lovin'," by Harry Moon (R&B/disco, Pearl Harbor Records).
Tips: "If a writer, be consistant with creativity of original compositions. Stay on top of what's musically happening."

JOHN HARVEY PUBLISHING CO., Box 245, Encinal TX 78019. President: John Harvey. Record producer and music publisher. Estab. 1969. Deals with artists and songwriters. Produced 3 singles and 1 album in 1978; plans 3 singles and 1 album in 1979, 6 singles and 2 albums in 1980. Fee derived from sales royalty.
How to Contact: Submit demo tape and lead sheet. Prefers cassette with 2-6 songs on demo. "Include letter giving brief resume of artist/songwriter with submission. Also indicate what type of plans or goals the artist/songwriter has for his songs." Does not return unsolicited material. Reports in 1 month.
Music: Children's; C&W; easy listening; and folk. Recently produced "Take These Chains" and "Cold, Cold Heart," by Johnny Gonzales (C&W singles, CBS/Columbia Records); and "Sincere Love," by John Harvey (easy listening, Harvey Records).

RON HITCHCOCK PRODUCTIONS/PINELLAS MUSIC, 21315 Ibanez Ave., Woodland Hills CA 91364. (213)992-4922. President: Ron Hitchcock. Record producer. Estab. 1976. Deals with artists and songwriters. Fee derived from sales royalty.
How to Contact: Submit demo tape and lead sheet. Prefers cassette with 3-5 songs on demo. SASE. Reports in 1 month.
Music: MOR; rock; and top 40/pop. Recently produced "Anymore" and "Easy Street," by Dave Munyon (MOR singles, April/Blackwood Records); "Hillside Strangler," by the Hollywood Squares (new wave single, Square Records); *It's Live*, by Melissa Manchester (unreleased MOR LP, Arista Records); and *Les Demerle & Transfussion*, by Les Demerle (jazz/rock LP, Rogue Records).

HOOKS & MYSTIC RECORDS, 6277 Selma Ave., Hollywood CA 90028. (213)464-9667. President/A&R Director: Jerry Hooks. Coordinator: Nancy Faith. Record producer. Estab. 1979. Deals with artists and songwriters. Plans 10 albums and 5 singles in 1979. Fee derived from sales royalty.
How to Contact: Submit demo tape or submit demo tape and lead sheet. Prefers 7½ ips reel-to-reel or cassette. SASE. Reports in 1 month.
Music: Blues; church/religious; rock; and soul. "No drug or sex lyrics." Recently produced "Send It On Down," by the Long Beach Southernairs (gospel, Hooks-Mystic Records); "Our Lord's Prayer," by Eddie LeJay (religious, Mystic Records); "Non Support," by Ironing Board Sam (blues, Hooks Records); and "My Girl Ruth," by Ron McFarrin (C&W, Solar Records).

HUDDLESTON'S RECORDING STUDIO, 11819 Lippitt Ave., Dallas TX 75218. (214)328-9056. Owner: Gene Huddleston. Engineer: Jimmy Burch. Record producer, music publisher and recording studio. Estab. 1970. Deals with artists and songwriters. Produced 2 albums and 8 singles in 1978; plans 3 albums and 12 singles in 1979, 5 albums and 15 singles in 1980. Fee derived from sales royalty or outright fee from record company. Charges for some services: Recording studio facilities are available to songwriters/artists for their own use.
How to Contact: Query with bio and photo or submit demo tape and lead sheet. Prefers 7½ ips reel-to-reel with 3-5 songs on demo. "Submit the best quality recording on the demo that is financially possible for the writer." SASE. Reports in 1 week.
Music: C&W; easy listening; gospel (contemporary); progressive (country); rock; and top 40/pop. Recently produced "You Better Get Straight," by Laurie Hollingsworth (disco single, Missle Records); "Songwriting Dream," by Jimmy Massey (country single, Missle Records); and *Today, Tomorrow, Tonight*, by Larry Randall (LP, Texas Domino Records).

INMUSIC PRODUCTIONS INC., 6255 Sunset Blvd., Suite 709, Los Angeles CA 90028. (213)467-5108. Producer/Professional Manager: Barry Oslander. Deals with songwriters on contract.

How to Contact: Submit demo tape and lyric sheet. Prefers cassette with 3-5 songs on demo. SASE. Reports in 2 weeks.
Music: Children's; choral; church/religious; disco; easy listening; folk; gospel; MOR; R&B; rock; soul; and top 40/pop.

THE INNOVATION ORGANIZATION, 6684 Charing St., Simi Valley CA 93063. (213)882-0177. Owner: Ron Lewis. Record producer and jingle company. Estab. 1970. Deals with artists and songwriters. Produced 6 singles in 1978; plans 2 albums and 6 singles in 1979. Fee derived from sales royalty.
How to Contact: Submit demo tape. Prefers 7½ ips reel-to-reel or cassette 2 songs minimum on tape. SASE. Reports in 1 month.
Music: Disco; easy listening; MOR; rock; soul; and top 40/pop. Recently produced "Big Ben," by Kathi Pinto (top 40, INV Records); "Skateboard Wizard," by Kathy Berry (top 40, INV Records); and "Happiness Place," by Marlyn O'Brien (top 40, INV Records).

INTERNATIONAL MARKETING AND MANAGEMENT CORP., 3310 Lebanon Rd., Hermitage TN 37076. (615)889-7100. President: Dallas Corey. Record producer, music publisher, management firm and jingle and commercial agency. Estab. 1971. Deals with artists, songwriters, authors and poets. Produced 15 albums and 50 singles in 1978; plans 20 albums and 50 singles in 1979. Fee derived from sales royalty, outright fee from record company, or outright fee from songwriter/artist.
How to Contact: Query, arrange personal interview, or submit demo tape and lead sheet. Prefers 7½ ips reel-to-reel with 5-10 songs on demo. SASE. Reports in "3-4 months depending on schedule."
Music: Bluegrass; blues; children's; church/religious; C&W; easy listening; folk; gospel; MOR; progressive; rock; soul; and top 40/pop. Recently produced *Country Hospitality*, by the Stonemans (bluegrass LP, RCA Records); "Man on Page 602," by Zoot Fenster (novelty single, Antique Records); and "Would You Take the Chance Again?", by Jack Barlow (C&W single, Crescent Records).

ALEXANDER JANOULIS PRODUCTIONS (AJP), Box 13584, Atlanta GA 30324. (404)872-0266. Independent record producer. Estab. 1960. Deals with artists and songwriters. Produced 2 albums and 10 singles in 1978; plans 3 albums and 6 singles in 1979. Fee derived "depends on particular situation and circumstance. If the songwriter/artist is not signed to me, a minimum fee of $500/song or $5,000/album is charged plus travel expenses."
How to Contact: Query or submit demo tape. Prefers cassette with 2-3 songs on demo. Does not return unsolicited material. Reports in 6 weeks.
Music: Blues; C&W; disco; jazz; MOR; progressive; rock (new wave); and top 40/pop. Recently produced "So Much" and "The Way It Used to Be," by Little Phil and the Night Shadows (top 40/pop singles, ABC Dot Records); "Another Day" and "Don't Take It Out On Me," by Starfoxx (top 40/new wave singles, Hottrax Records); and "Love Generator" and "Silver Grill Blues," by Diamond Lil (disco, Glamour & Grease Records).

JED RECORD PRODUCTION, 39 Music Square E., Nashville TN 57203. (615)255-6535. President: John E. Denny. Record producer, music publisher, management firm and production company. Estab. 1962. Deals with artists and songwriters. Fee derived from sales royalty, production, publishing and management.
How to Contact: Submit demo tape and lead sheet. Prefers 7½ ips mono reel-to-reel with 4 songs on demo. SASE. Reports in 6 weeks.
Music: Bluegrass; C&W; gospel; and MOR.

QUINCY JONES PRODUCTIONS, 1416 N. La Brea Ave., Hollywood CA 90028. General Manager: Beverly Giddens. Record producer and music publisher. Estab. 1976. Deals with artists and songwriters. Produced 2 albums and 6 singles in 1977; plans 3 albums and 9 singles in 1978, 4-5 albums and 8-10 singles in 1979. Fee derived from sales royalty.
How to Contact: Submit demo tape (and lead sheet, if possible). Prefers 7½ ips reel-to-reel or cassette with 3-6 songs on demo. SASE. Reports in 1 month.
Music: Disco; jazz; soul; and top 40/pop. Recently produced "Right on Time" and "Look Out for Number 1," by Brothers Johnson (R&B singles, A&M Records); and "I Heard That," by Quincy Jones (jazz single, A&M Records).

BOB KARCY PRODUCTIONS, 437 W. 16th St., New York NY 10011. (212)989-1989. President: Bob Karcy. Vice President: Jack Arel. Record producer, music publisher and management firm. Estab. 1971. Works with artists, songwriters, publishers and record

companies. Produced 3 albums and 11 singles in 1977; plans 5 albums and 20 singles in 1978, 8 albums and 30 singles in 1979. Fee derived from "negotiable package."
How to Contact: Query or submit demo tape and lead sheet. "No interview without prior appointment." Prefers cassette with 1-6 songs on demo. SASE. Reports in 3 weeks.
Music: Disco; easy listening; MOR; rock (all except hard, acid and punk); and top 40/pop. Recently produced "Melody Lady," by Sunshine (top 40 single, Carrere Records); "Spimbi Theme," by Julie Jacobs (top 40/disco single, Phillips Records); and "Magician," by Royal Flush (top 40 single, A&B Records).

KARRIC PRODUCTIONS, INC., 1227 Spring St. NW, Atlanta GA 30309. (404)875-1440. President: Babs Richardson. Record producer and music publisher. Deals with artists and songwriters. Produced 10 albums in 1978. Fee derived from sales royalty.
How to Contact: Arrange personal interview or submit demo tape and lead sheet. Prefers 7½ ips reel-to-reel or cassette with 2-5 songs on demo. SASE. Reports in 1 month.
Music: Disco; easy listening; gospel (traditional/contemporary); MOR; rock (all); and top 40/pop. Recently produced *Sammy Duncan*, by Sammy Duncan (jazz LP, Down Home Cookin' Records); *Troy Ramey & Soul Searchers*, by Troy Ramey and the Soul Searchers (gospel LP, Nashboro Records); and *Ivory Roads*, by Mac Frampton (MOR/easy listening LP, Triumvirate Records).

RICK KEEFER PRODUCTIONS, 319 North 85th St., Seattle WA 98103. (206)783-2524. Manager: Donna-Alexa Keefer. Estab. 1971. Deals with artists and songwriters. Produced 10 albums and 14 singles in 1978; plans 2 albums and 4 singles in 1979 "so far." Fee derived from sales royalty, outright fee from record company or outright fee from songwriter/artist, "depending on the particulars of the project."
How to Contact: Query or submit demo tape. Prefers 15 ips reel-to-reel or cassette. SASE. Reports in 1 month.
Music: Disco; rock; and top 40/pop. Recently produced "Livin' It Up Friday Night," by Bell & James (top 40, A&M Records); "Soul Butterfly," by Heart (Portrait Records); and *Magazine*, by Heart (rock LP, Mushroom Records).

KING HENRY PRODUCTION, 1855 Fairview Ave., Easton PA 18042. (215)258-4461. President: Hnery Casella. Estab. 1967. Deals with artists and songwriters. Produced 1 album and 2 singles in 1978; plans 1 single in 1979. Fee derived from sales royalty.
How to Contact: Submit demo tape and lead sheet. Prefers cassette with 2-4 songs on demo. SASE. Reports in 1 month.
Music: Bluegrass; C&W; disco; easy listening; MOR; and top 40/pop. Recently produced "Christmas in the City," by Rick Peoples (MOR, VPO Records); *VOS Live*, by VOS Trio (easy rock LP, Valley Sound Records); and "Wanted," by American Show Band (MOR, KHP Records).

KOOL DEAL JAMS, 3203 E. 130th St., Cleveland OH 44120. (216)752-7732. President: Robert Davis. Estab. 1970. Deals with artists and songwriters. Produced 3 album and 3 singles in 1978; plans 8 albums and 6 singles in 1979, 15 albums and 8 singles in 1980. Fee derived from sales royalty.
How to Contact: Query or submit demo tape and lead sheet. Prefers cassette. SASE. Reports in 1 month.
Music: Blues; church/religious; disco; gospel; jazz; and soul. Recently produced "I Love You Still" and "There Is You," by Cash (disco single, Old World Records).

L.A.R. PRODUCTIONS, INC., 23 Lincoln St., Roseland NJ 07068. Director: Lou Robertella. Record producer and management firm. Estab. 1968. Deals with artists and songwriters. Produced 2 singles in 1978; plans 2 in 1979, 2 albums and 6 singles in 1980. Fee derived from sales royalty.
How to Contact: Submit demo tape. Prefers 7½ ips reel-to-reel or cassette with 2-6 songs on demo. SASE. Reports in 3 week.
Music: MOR; rock (soft); and top 40/pop. Recently produced "Children," by Chris Breeden (MOR single, Keefe-Jay); and "Dreams of a Crazy Man," by Bruce Grilli (MOR single, L.A.R.).

LAS VEGAS RECORDING STUDIO, INC., Terry Richards Productions, 3977 Vegas Valley Dr., Las Vegas NV 89121. (702)457-4365. Vice President: Hank Castro. President/Producer: Terry Richards. Record producer, music publisher, management firm and record company. Estab. 1972. Deals with artists and songwriters. Produced 2 albums and 6 singles in 1978; plans

Songwriter's Market Close-Up

To Felice and Boudleaux Bryant, songwriters are not trend-setters, but trend interpreters. "If a songwriter has a song that he thinks affects the world, it's because it's already in the air, and that's how he got it," says Felice. "So the world was already going in that direction."

"Occasionally, through some intuitive process, somebody anticipates a trend just by a hair, and in doing so, gets a monstrous hit that sets a trend," Boudleaux adds. "After the trend is set, then the bandwagon is in motion and people jump on it all over the world and wear it out—wear the wheels down to the axles."

Felice and Boudleaux Bryant know a lot about songwriting; their hits include such classics as "Wake Up Little Susie" and "Bye Bye Love" recorded by the Everly Brothers, and more contemporary recordings, such as "Raining in My Heart" recorded by Leo Sayer and "Devoted to You" recorded by Carly Simon and James Taylor.

Felice and Boudleaux realize that songwriting means responding to public tastes. "The truth is that nobody in this business knows anything about the business, because it's purely dependent on the whimsy of the record-buying public," says Boudleaux.

4 albums and 10 singles in 1979. Fee derived from sales royalty, outright fee from record company, or outright fee from songwriter/artist. "We do not charge songwriters for their demos, but we do ask for publishing if we place the material."
How to Contact: Arrange personal interview, submit demo tape or submit demo tape and lead sheet. Include lyric sheet. Prefers reel-to-reel or cassette. SASE. Reports as soon as possible.
Music: Bluegrass; blues; church/religious; C&W; disco; easy listening; folk; gospel; jazz; MOR; progressive; rock; soul; top 40/pop; and instrumental. Recently produced "Platters Reborn," by the Platters (disco, Pye/Polydor Records).

LEON AND GEE PRODUCTIONS-DON LEONARD PRODUCTIONS, 8 Cherry Hill Court, Reisterstown MD 21136. (301)833-3816. Producer: Don Leonard. Estab. 1950. Deals with artists and songwriters. Produced 10 albums and 45 singles in 1978; plans 10 albums and 23 singles in 1979. Fee derived from sales royalty. Changes fee "if hired to produce and the artist or writer wants to pay for own session. I do not charge if I see a strong potential in an artist—no fee for songs of chart possibility."
How to Contact: Query, arrange personal interview, submit demo tape only or submit demo tape and lead sheet. Prefers cassette or 8-track cassette. SASE. Reports in 1 month.
Music: C&W; disco; easy listening; jazz; MOR; progressive; rock; soul; and top 40/pop. Recently produced "Roll Away Heartaches," by Eddie Farrel.

MIKE LEWIS/STUART WEINER ENTERPRISES, LTD., 747 Pontiac Ave., Suite 101, Cranston RI 02910. (401)781-0554. President: Mike Lewis. Vice President: Stuart Weiner. Record producer, music publisher and management firm. Estab. 1966. Deals with artists and

songwriters. Produced 4 singles and 3 albums in 1978; plans 5 singles and 4 albums in 1979, 6 singles and 6 albums in 1980. Fee derived from sales royalty.
How to Contact: Submit demo tape and lead sheet. Prefers 7½ ips quarter-track reel-to-reel with 1-8 songs on tape. SASE. Reports in 3 weeks.
Music: Easy listening; folk; MOR; progressive; rock; soul; and top 40/pop. Recently produced *A Painting*, by Neal Fox (MOR LP, RCA Records); *Rhythm*, by Rhythm (R&B LP, RCA Records); and *Ken Lyon and Tombstone*, by Ken Lyon and Tombstone (progressive LP, Columbia Records).

DANNY LUCIANO PRODUCTIONS, 1 Jeffro Plaza, 2655 Philmont Ave., Suite 206, Dept. SM, Huntingdon Valley PA 19006. (215)947-7743. President: Danny Luciano. Record producer, music publisher and management firm. Estab. 1974. Deals with artists, songwriters and composers. Fee derived from sales royalty "plus percentage."
How to Contact: Query or submit demo tape and lead sheet. Prefers 7½ ips reel-to-reel or cassette (no 8-track cartridges) with 4-6 songs on tape. "Provide leader (3 minutes or more) when possible." SASE. Reports in 1 month.
Music: Disco; jazz; MOR; rock; soul; and top 40/pop. Recently produced "The Sun Came Out Today," by Sharon Gale (top 40/pop single, Molly Records); "Ting-A-Ling Double Play," by Larry Bowa and Dave Cash (novelty single, Molly Records); and "I'm Gonna Love You Baby," by the Three of Us (top 40/pop single, Molly Records).
Tips: "We're also affiliated with the Ray Royal Agency, which provides bookings on a national level."

MAC TALENT ASSOCIATES, 140 Main St., Box 202, Metuchen NJ 08840. (201)494-8166. President: John J. MacIver. Estab. 1978. Deals with artists and songwriters. Produced 2 albums and 3 singles in 1978; plans 2 singles in 1979. Fee derived by outright fee from songwriter/artist or management contract.
How to Contact: Arrange personal interview or submit demo tape. Prefers 7½ ips reel-to-reel or cassette with 1-2 songs on demo. SASE. Reports in 2 weeks.
Music: Blues; C&W; disco; easy listening; folk; MOR; progressive; soul; and top 40/pop. Recently produced *Almost Live*, by Lou Caddy and the Panics (comedy/music LP, Jac Lyn Records); "What Are We Going To Do," by Young & Wright and "Later On Now," by Young & Wright (pop, MTA Records).

MACK McCORMICK ASSOCIATES, 9023 Autauga, Houston TX 77080. Producer: L.O. Williams. Independent production company. Estab. 1959. Deals with artists and songwriters. Produced 4 albums in 1978; plans 6 albums in 1979. Fee derived from sales royalty.
How to Contact: Submit demo tape. Prefers 7½ ips reel-to-reel or cassette. Does not return unsolicited material. Reports in 1 month.
Music: "We are concerned with sound documentary recordings involving songs, slang, music, jokes, toasts, recitations, traditional stories or other cultural expressions from regions of the United States, Mexico or the Caribbean." Bluegrass; blues; children's; church/religious; classical; gospel; jazz; polkas; sacred harp; corridos; junkanoo; and spoken narratives. Recently released *Settler's Reunion*, by People of Tierra Amarilla, New Mexico (narrative, Private Records); *Border Music: Corridos*, by various artists (corridos, Vicuna Records); and *Ray Baca/Czech Tex*, by Ray Baca (traditional Czech, Reprise Records).

JOHN MADARA ENTERPRISES, INC., 3146 Arrowhead Dr., Hollywood CA 90068. (213)461-4756. Vice President: John J. Madara. Record producer and music publisher. Estab. 1964. Deals with artists and songwriters. Produced 2 singles and 2 albums in 1978; plans 2 singles and 2 albums in 1979. Fee derived from sales royalty.
How to Contact: Submit demo tape and lead sheet. Prefers 7½ or 15 ips reel-to-reel or cassette with 2-5 songs on demo. SASE. Reports in 3 weeks.
Music: Disco; jazz; MOR; progressive; rock; soul; and top 40/pop. Recently produced *Rick Sandler Band*, by the Rick Sandler Band (top 40); *Gino Cunico*, by Gino Cunico (top 40); and *TSLA*, by TSLA (disco).

MAN QUIN, Box 2388, Toluca Lake CA 91602. (213)985-8284. Producer: Quint Benedetti. Estab. 1979. Deals with artists and songwriters. Fee derived from sales royalty.
How to Contact: Submit demo tape and lead sheet. Prefers cassette with 2-4 songs on demo. SASE. Reports in 1 month.
Music: C&W; easy listening; broadway; and novelty.

MANDALA INTERNATIONAL, 112 Maureen Dr., Hendersonville TN 37075. (615)824-7144.

President: Louis Lofredo. Estab. 1977. Deals with U.S. and foreign artists. Produced 13 albums total 1977, 1978 and 1979. Fee derived from outright fee from record company.
How to Contact: Query or submit demo tape and lead sheet. Prefers 7½ ips reel-to-reel or cassette with a maximum of 4 songs on demo. SASE. Reports in 1 month.
Music: Children's; disco; MOR; progressive; rock; and top 40/pop. Recently produced "Sweet & Funky Gold," by Sam & Dave (soul, Gusto Records); Grass Roots (pop, Gusto Records); B.J. Thomas (pop, Gusto Records); and "Looks Like a Job for Superman," by Hargrove Effect (disco, Epic Records).

EARLE MANKEY, 1645 Fremont, Thousand Oaks CA 91360. (805)497-9953. Producer: Earle Mankey. Deals with artists and songwriters. Produced 4 albums and 8 singles in 1978; plans 4 albums and 8 singles in 1979. Fee derived from sales royalty or outright fee from record company.
How to Contact: Submit demo tape and lead sheet. Prefers 1-4 songs on demo. SASE. Reports in 3 weeks.
Music: Rock and top 40/pop. Recently produced *Queens of Noise*, by the Runaways (rock LP, Mercury Records); *Ear Candy*, by Helen Reddy (MOR LP, Capitol Records); and *Paley Brothers*, by the Paley Brothers (rock LP, Sire Records).

MARC MUSIC AND MEDIA, 310 Franklin St., Boston MA 02110. (617)423-3544. 427 Broadway, Everett MA 02149. (617)387-3373. President: Marv Cutler. Record producer, music publisher and management firm. Estab. 1972. Deals with artists and songwriters. Produced 6 albums and 18 singles in 1978; plans 10 albums and 25 singles in 1979. Fee derived from sales royalty.
How to Contact: Query or submit demo tape and lead sheet. Prefers 7½ ips reel-to-reel or cassette with 2-6 songs on demo. Does not return unsolicited material. Reports in 1 month.
Music: Blues; children's; C&W; disco; easy listening; jazz; MOR; progressive; rock (light); soul; and top 40/pop. Recently produced "As Dreams Take Flight," by Vega 79 (easy listening single, Marc Records); "Donna/Sincerely," by Bob Carter (rock single, White House Records); and "Rockin' Rhymes," by Scott Cutler (rock/children's single, Marc Records).

MARK RECORDING STUDIOS, 7326 Biscayne Blvd., Miami FL 33138. (305)751-6296. President: Milt Schnapf. Estab. 1978. Deals with artists and songwriters. Produced 2 albums and 2 singles in 1978; plans 3 albums in 1979. Fee derived from various options. "Songwriter charged for services before he'll work with them when they require special marketing techniques."
How to Contact: Query or submit demo tape and lead sheet. Prefers cassette with 4-6 songs on demo. SASE. Reports in 2 weeks.
Music: All material heard.

BOBBY MARTIN PRODUCTIONS, 6367 W. 6th St., Los Angeles CA 90048. Publishing Coordinator: Ron Woodmansee. Record producer. Estab. 1974. Deals with artists and songwriters. Produced 5 albums and 10 singles in 1978; plans 5 albums and 10 singles in 1979. Fee derived from sales royalty.
How to Contact: Query. Prefers 7½ ips reel-to-reel or cassette with 2-6 songs on demo. Does not return unsolicited material. Reports in 1 month.
Music: Disco; jazz; progressive; soul; and top 40/pop. Recently produced "Something to Love," by LTD (soul single, A&M Records); "I Had to Fall in Love," by Jean Terrell (soul single, A&M Records); and "There's No Good in Goodbye," by the Manhattans (soul single, CBS Records).

MARULLO PRODUCTIONS, 1121 Market St.; Galveston TX 77550. President: A.W. Marullo Sr. Vice President: A.W. Marullo Jr. Record producer and music publisher. Estab. 1952. Deals with artists, songwriters and master owners. Produced 4 singles in 1978. Plans 7 singles in 1979. Fee derived from sales royalty.
How to Contact: Submit demo tape. Prefers 7½ ips reel-to-reel, cassette or demo dub with 12 songs maximum on demo. SASE. Reports in 1 month.
Music: C&W; disco; rock; soul; and top 40/pop. Recently produced "Don't Forget to Write," by Joe D'Ambra (rock single, Mercury Records); "Restless Man," by David Yeamans (C&W single, Ro Tab Records); "Lonely Night #7," by George Lee (rock single, Red Dot Records); "Me and My Guitar," by Joe Dymon (C&W single, RDS Records); and "Made to be Played," by Michael Wilde (rock single, RDS Records).
Tips: "You record it, we will lease it. Consultations and negotiations to place your masters with the major record companies and the music publishers."

MASTERSOURCE PRODUCTIONS, 440 N. Mayfield, Chicago IL 60644. (312)921-1446. President: Charles Thomas. Record producer. Estab. 1977. Deals with artists and songwriters. Produced 8 albums in 1978; plans 12 albums in 1979. Fee derived from outright fee from record company or outright fee from songwriter/artist.
How to Contact: Query or submit demo tape and lead sheet. Prefers cassette with 1-5 songs on demo. Does not return unsolicited material. Reports in 2 weeks.
Music: Church/religious; MOR; progressive; rock and Christian rock. Recently produced *Terry Robbins*, by Terry Robbins (MOR/religious, Burlap Records); *God Gave a Song*, by LeAne Courvesier (gospel, Burlap Records); *Sunrise* (Pinebrook Records); *Relayer* (MSP Records); and *Manna* (Pinebrook Records).

MASTER AUDIO, INC., 1227 Spring St. NW, Atlanta GA 30309. (404)875-1440. President: Babs Richardson. Record producer and music publisher. Deals with artists and songwriters. Produced 10 albums in 1978. Fee derived from sales royalty.
How to Contact: Arrange personal interview or submit demo tape and lead sheet. Prefers 7½ ips reel-to-reel or cassette with 2-5 songs on demo. SASE. Reports in 1 month.
Music: Disco; easy listening; gospel (traditional or contemporary); MOR; rock; and top 40/pop. Recently produced *Sammy Duncan*, by Sammy Duncan (jazz LP, Down Home Cookin' Records); *Troy Ramey & Soul Searchers*, by Troy Ramey and the Soul Searchers (gospel LP, Nashboro Records); and *Ivory Roads*, by Mac Frampton (MOR/easy listening LP, Triumvirate Records).

MASTERVIEW MUSIC PUBLISHING CORP., Ridge Rd. and Butler Lane, Perkasie PA 18944. (215)257-9616. General Manager: Thomas Fausto. President: John Wolf. Record producer, music publisher, record company and management firm. Estab. 1963. Deals with artists and songwriters. Produced 3 albums and 15 singles in 1978. Fee derived from sales royalty.
How to Contact: Arrange personal interview or submit demo tape and lead sheet. Prefers 7½ or 15 ips reel-to-reel with 2-6 songs on demo. SASE. Reports in 2 weeks.
Music: Disco; folk; gospel; and rock. Recently produced "Hollywood Girl" and "100 Years," by Sugar Cane (rock singles, Masterview); and "Rubber Spider," by Tommy Hutton (ballad single, Masterview).

JAY MILLER PRODUCTIONS, 413 N. Parkerson Ave., Crowley LA 70526. (318)783-1601. Owner: Jay Miller. Manager: Mark Miller. Record producer and music publisher. Estab. 1946. Deals with artists and songwriters. Produced 11 albums and 2 singles in 1977. Fee derived from sales royalty.
How to Contact: Query, arrange personal interview or submit demo tape. Phone calls accepted. Prefers 7½ ips reel-to-reel or cassette with 4 songs on demo. SASE. Reports in 1 month.
Music: Blues; C&W; disco; folk; gospel; MOR; rock; soul; top 40/pop; and comedy. Recently produced *Back Sounds of Rockabilly*, by Al Ferrin (country LP, Showtime); "Laughing With Jeb and Cousin Easy," by Jeb and Cousin Easy (comedy single, Par T); and "That's What You're Doing," by Wayne Morse (country single, Wildwood).

BILL MILLER'S PRODUCTIONS, 347 Litchfield Ave., Babylon NY 11702. (516)661-9842. Producer: William H. Miller. Record producer and music publisher. Estab. 1955. Deals with artists, songwriters and arrangers. Produced 1 album and 2 singles in 1978; plans 2 albums and 4 singles in 1979, 2 albums and 8 singles in 1980. Fee derived from sales royalty or outright fee from record company.
How to Contact: Submit demo tape and lead sheet. Prefers cassette with 4 songs minimum on tape. SASE. Reports in 1 month.
Music: Blues; C&W; disco; rock (all); soul; and top 40/pop. Recently produced "Daddy's Home," by Permonations (soul/pop single, Tassie Records); "I'm Going to Get to You," by Allan Turner (top 40 single, Tassie Records); and *Permonations*, by Permonations (soul LP, Tassie Records).

MILLS AND MILLS MUSIC, 2502 W. Cheltenham Ave., 2nd Floor, Philadelphia PA 19150. (215)927-7866. Vice President: Aubrey A. Gravatt. Record producer and music publisher. Estab. 1975. Deals with artists and songwriters. Produced 3 albums and 6 singles in 1978; plans 5 albums and 8 singles in 1979. Fee derived from sales royalty but "we are willing to negotiate."
How to Contact: Query, arrange personal interview, or submit demo tape and lead sheet. Prefers cassette. "Mail tapes certified mail, with return receipt, so you can be sure that we

receive the material." SASE. Will return unsolicited material "if requested." Reports in 1 week. **Music:** Blues; C&W; disco; easy listening; gospel; jazz; MOR; progressive; rock; soul; and top 40/pop. Recently produced *Smooth Talk* (pop/R&B LP, RCA Records); *Music Box*, by Evelyn Champagne King (LP, RCA Records); material for Phyllis Hyman; and the Beck Family on London Records.

MIMOSA RECORDS PRODUCTIONS, 4920 Maiden Lane, La Mesa CA 92041. (714)464-0910. Producer: Stephen C. LaVere. Record producer and music publisher. Estab. 1973. Deals with artists. Fee derived from sales royalty.
How to Contact: Query or submit demo tape and lead sheet. Prefers 7½ ips reel-to-reel. SASE. Reports in 1 month.
Music: Blues; folk; gospel; jazz; and rock. Recently produced "Goin' Away Baby," by Joe Hill Louis (blues single, Mimosa); It's Too Bad, by Joe Willie Wilkins (blues LP, Adamo); and "Rock a Little Baby," by Harmonica Frank (rock 'n roll single, Mimosa).

CLANCY MORALES & FRIENDS, LTD., Box 1055, Englewood Cliffs NJ 07632. President/A&R Director: Clancy Morales. Associate Producers: Marty Sheller, Larry Spencer, Billy Jones. Record producer, music publisher and record company. Estab. 1972. Deals with artists, songwriters, studio musicians and producers. Produced 3 albums and 2 singles in 1978; plans 3 albums and 3 singles in 1979, 4-5 albums and 5 singles in 1980.
How to Contact: Submit demo tape and lead sheet. Prefers 7½ ips reel-to-reel with 2-4 songs on demo. "All tape boxes should be properly identified with titles and authors, address and phone number. The SASE should be big enough for material to be returned." SASE. Reports in 1 month.
Music: Disco; easy listening; jazz; progressive (rock and jazz); rock; soul; Latin salsa; and Latin pop. Recently produced *Dawn*, by Mongo Santamaria (Latin/jazz LP, Fania Records); *Shades in Creation*, by Brother to Brother (disco/soul LP, Turbo Records); *Baclash*, by Brother to Brother (soul/disco/rock LP, All Platinum Records); *Nasty*, by Jack McDuff (soul/disco/jazz LP, Chess Records); and *Enter Paradise*, by Clancy Morales (soul/jazz/Latin, Maranta Records).

JOEL W. MOSS, 12826 Landale St., Studio City CA 91604. (213)766-7617. Producer/Engineer: Joel W. Moss. Record producer, music publisher, engineer, audio and video production consultant. Estab. 1968. Deals with artists and songwriters. Produced 5 albums and 5 singles in 1978; plans 5 albums and 5 singles in 1979. Fee derived from sales royalty or outright fee from record company.
How to Contact: Query, arrange personal interview, or submit demo tape and lead sheet. Prefers cassette with 1-4 songs on demo. "Name and address on tape box." SASE. Reports in 3 weeks.
Music: Blues (R&B); children's; classical (for application with video or animation); C&W; disco; easy listening; folk; gospel (R&B); jazz (no long, free-form solo); MOR; progressive; rock (not too hard); soul; and top 40/pop. Recent work: *Comin' Down With Love*, by Joe Ramano (pop/jazz LP, Baby Grand Records); *Gotham Odyssey*, by Fanfair (MOR/big band LP, Pelican Records); *Living at the Mission*, by Ron Fair (pop LP, Baby Grand Records); and "Disco Walk, Don't Run," by the Ventures (disco single, United Artists Records). Bobby Hatfield engineered portions of the *L.A. Light Album*, by the Beach Boys (rock LP, CBS Records).

MOTHER CLEO PRODUCTIONS/DAVISOUND, Bypass 76/Sunset, Box 521, Newberry SC 29108. (803)276-0639. Studio Manager: Polly Davis. Producer/Director: Hayne Davis. Record producer, music publisher and production company. Estab. 1970. Deals with artists and songwriters. Produced 2 albums and 5 singles in 1978; plans 2 albums and 6 singles in 1979, 3 albums and 6 singles in 1980. Fee derived from sales royalty, outright fee from record company, or outright fee from songwriter/artist. Charges for some services: "In special cases, where the songwriter/artist is simply booking our studio facilities, there is a charge. Also, if an artist/writer wishes us to produce him with himself as co-producer, we share profits on a 50/50 basis but at the same time, expenses of production are also shared 50/50."
How to Contact: Submit demo tape. Prefers 7½ ips reel-to-reel or cassette with 4-8 songs on demo. SASE. Reports in 2 weeks.
Music: C&W (contemporary); disco; easy listening; MOR; rock (all); and top 40/pop (all). Recently produced "Sheila," by James Meadows (C&W/rock single, Mother Cleo Records); "Too Far Gone," by Curt Bradford (C&W/rock single, Mother Cleo Records); and "Brainwasher," by J. Teal Band (rock single, Mother Cleo Records).

BOB W. MOTTA PRODUCTIONS, 9411 Shore Rd., Apt 2-6, Brooklyn NY 11209. President:

Songwriter's Market Close-Up

"A great song touches something, illuminates some kind of truth, has an originality—something that's never been said that way before," says Marilyn Bergman, who, with her husband Alan, wrote Academy Award-winners "The Way We Were" and "Windmills of Your Mind," and, most recently, the Neil Diamond/ Barbra Streisand hit, "You Don't Bring Me Flowers Anymore." How do you know if your writing is truly original? "It is essential to have conversance with the literature of popular music which has preceded them," says Bergman. "A student of architecture studies that which has endured. He *is not* going to study a motel on Santa Monica Boulevard. He *is* going to study the Colosseum—its style, structure and aesthetics. The lack of awareness of the music before the '60s appalls me. Particularly lyric writers should study the masters— Porter, Mercer, Harburg, Lerner, Al Dugan. You can't turn on the radio and hear them. You have to go to them. How can you know where you're going, if you don't know where you've been?"

Bob W. Motta. Estab. 1972. Deals with artists and songwriters. Produced 2 singles in 1978; plans 1 album and 3 singles in 1979. Fee derived from sales royalty.
How to Contact: Submit demo tape and lead sheet. Prefers 7½ ips quarter-track stereo reel-to-reel or cassette with 1-4 songs on demo. SASE. Reports in 1 month.
Music: Disco; soul; and top 40/pop. Recently produced "Disco Lucy," by The N.Y. Rubber Rock Band (disco, Henry Street Records); and "Hello Stranger," and "Put Your Love in My Hands," by Rubber Rock featuring Colleen Heather (disco/soul, Henry Street Records).

MOVIN' IN, 313 McKnight NE, Albuquerque NM 87102. A&R Director: Budd Lurero. Record producer and booking agency. Estab. 1970. Deals with artists and songwriters. Fee derived from sales royalty or outright fee from record company.
How to Contact: "Submit demo tape, 8x10 photo, and letter explaining concept of record and act." Prefers cassette. SASE. Reports in 1 month.
Music: Disco; soul; top 40/pop; and Latin disco and top 40. Recently produced "Friends," by ZoZobra (Latin disco single); "Take It in Stride," by T.J. and Wolfee (soul single); and "Jussy," by Eddie San (disco single).

MUSCADINE PRODUCTIO⌐S, INC., 297 Bass Rd., Macon GA 31210. President: Paul Hornsby. Record producer .nd music publisher. Estab. 1977. Deals with artists and songwriters. Produced 4 albums in 1978; plans 5 albums in 1979, 5 albums in 1980. Fee derived from "advance and royalty from sales."
How to Contact: Submit demo tape and lead sheet. Prefers reel-to-reel or cassette. SASE. Reports in 1 month.
Music: Rock (hard or country); and top 40/pop. Recently produced *Volunteer Jam*, by Charlie Daniels, Willie Nelson, and others (Epic Records); *Good Brothers* (RCA Records); *Cooder Browne*, by Cooder Browne (Lone Star Records); *Two Guns* (Capricorn); and *Missouri* (Polydor).

THE NEXT CITY CORP., Box 1085, Ansonia Station, New York NY 10023. (212)873-2403. Vice President, A&R: Ric Browde. Record producer, music publisher and management firm.

Estab. 1970. Deals with artists and songwriters. Produced 4 albums and 5 singles in 1978; plans 4 albums and 8 singles in 1979, 5 albums and 8 singles in 1980. Fee derived from sales royalty.
How to Contact: Submit demo tape. Prefers 7½ ips reel-to-reel or cassette. SASE. Reports in 2 weeks.
Music: Progressive, rock, new wave and pop. Recently produced *Weekend Warriors, Double Live Gonzo,* and *Cat Scratch Fever,* by Ted Nugent (rock LPs, Epic Records); *Dirty Angels,* by the Dirty Angels (rock LP, A&M Records); *Tea Break Over—Back On Your Head,* by If (jazz/rock LP, Capitol Records); *Wanna Meet the Scruffs,* by the Scruffs (rock/new wave LP, Line/Teldec Records).

NISE PRODUCTIONS, INC., Box 5132, Philadelphia PA 19141. (215)276-0100. President: Michael Nise. Record producer, music publisher, management firm and recording studio. Estab. 1969. Deals with artists and songwriters. Plans to produce 15 albums and 30-40 singles in 1979. Fee derived from sales royalty.
How to Contact: Submit demo tape. Prefers 7½ ips reel-to-reel or cassette with 1-3 songs on demo. SASE. Reports in 1 month.
Music: Blues; children's; church/religious; disco; easy listening; folk; gospel; soul; and top 40/pop. Recently produced "100 South of Broadway," by Philadelphia Society (R&B/disco single, Gull); "Instead How Are You," by Coalitions (R&B single, Phi-La of Soul); "Not Easy to Say Goodbye," by Ghetto Children (R&B single, Roulette); and the TV theme to *Mork and Mindy.*

NOURREDIM RECORDS, 217 Dorsey Ave., Cincinnati OH 45210. (513)241-4369. President: Khalid Nourredim. Estab. 1971. Deals with artists and songwriters. Fee derived from sales royalty.
How to Contact: Submit demo tape. Prefers 7½ ips reel-to-reel or cassette with 3 songs minimum on tape. SASE. Reports in 3 weeks.
Music: C&W; disco; soul; and top 40/pop. Recently produced "Always and Forever," by Billy Starr (soul single, Nourredim Records); "All I Ever Wanted Was You," by Tex Colin (C&W single, Nourredim Records); and "In My World," by B.R.E. (disco single, Nourredim Records).

O.T.L. PRODUCTIONS, 63 Main St., Maynard MA 01754. (617)897-8459. Chief Producer: David Butler. Estab. 1975. Deals with artists, songwriters; publishers and managers. Produced 2 albums and 4 singles in 1978; plans 5 albums and 10 singles in 1979. Fee and royalty received.
How to Contact: Arrange personal interview, submit demo tape only. "Personal contact necessary to serious consideration. Audition live if possible." Prefers 7½ ips reel-to-reel or cassette with 3-10 song on tape. SASE. Reports in 1 month.
Music: Bluegrass; disco (disco funk); folk; gospel; jazz; MOR; progressive; rock (country/classical); and soul. Recently produced "I'm Gonna Make You Love Me," by Blend (rock, MCA Records); "Helene," by Kevan Michaels (pop/MOR, Nordice Records); "Burning Fire," Donny Johnson (disco/funk, Handsum Records); and "Good News/Rainbow Reign," by Carolina Edwards (pop/gospel, Great Northern Records).

PALOMA PRODUCTIONS CXA, 2920 Clark Rd., Suite 104, Sarasota FL 33581. President: Stephen R. Hatch. Estab. 1976. Deals with artists and songwriters. Produced 9 albums and 15 singles in 1978; plans 3 albums and 3 singles in 1979. Fee derived from outright fee from record company.
How to Contact: Submit demo tape. Prefers cassette with 5-12 songs on demo. Does not return unsolicited material. Reports in 3 weeks.
Music: Disco (Latin); soul (Latin); and salsa and merengue. Recently produced "Taxi Driver," by Juan Felipe (disco, Enbajabor Records); "Puta Linda," by Juan Felipe (disco, Paloma Records); and "Paloma Blanca," by Frine Fernadez (disco/rock, Paloma Records).

PARASOUND, INC., 680 Beach St., Suite 414, San Francisco CA 94109. (415)673-4544. President: Bernie Krause. Vice President: Sid Goldstein. Record producer and music publisher. Estab. 1967. Deals with artists and songwriters. Produced 4 singles in 1978; plans 1 in 1979. Fee derived from sales royalty.
How to Contact: Submit demo tape and lead sheet. Prefers cassette with 3-6 songs on demo. SASE. Reports in 3 weeks.
Music: Folk; MOR; rock; and top 40/pop. Recently produced *Citadels of Mystery,* by Bernie

Krause (Chrysalis Records); and *Linda Laurie*, by Linda Laurie (20th Century Records).

BRANDY PASCO PRODUCTIONS, Box 32, Minersville PA 17954. (717)544-2404. President: Brandy Pasco. General Manager: Celia Johnson. Record producer and music publisher. Deals with songwriters. Fee derived from sales royalty or standard AGAC contract.
How to Contact: Query. Prefers 7½ ips reel-to-reel or cassette with 1-4 songs on demo, or disc. Include lyric sheets. SASE. Reports in 1 month.
Music: Blues; C&W; gospel; MOR; rock (country); and top 40/pop. Recently produced "Too Sad to Laugh, Too Hurt to Cry," by Cecelia Bucko (ballad, Horizons Unlimited Records); and "Casey at the Bat," by Foster Brooks (narration single, Horizons Unlimited Records).
Tips: "No pay melodies accepted. Do not submit only copy and make sure your songs are protected."

RICHARD PODOLOR PRODUCTIONS, INC., 11386 Ventura Blvd., Studio City CA 91604. President: Richard Podolor. Vice President: Bill Cooper. Record producer, music publisher and recording studio. Estab. 1958. Deals with artists, songwriters, musicians, engineers and producers. Produced 5 albums ion 1978; plans 3-5 in 1979. Fee derived from sales royalty, outright fee from record company, or outright fee from songwriter/artist. Charges for some services: "Podolor Productions charges a production fee in advance for an artist it produces that a label owns, plus a royalty rate. Each independent production situation is treated and negotiated individually. We are always looking for good songs for the artists we are involved with."
How to Contact: Submit demo tape and lead sheet. Prefers 7½ ips quarter-track reel-to-reel or cassette with 1-5 songs on demo. "Please try to send only tapes that don't have to be returned, or at least enclose SASE." Reporting time "depends on reaction to songs."
Music: Easy listening; MOR; rock; and top 40/pop. Recently produced *Rubicon*, by Rubicon (rock LP, 20th Century Records); *Gettin' Lucky*, by Head East (rock LP, A&M Records); *Ain't Life Grand*, by Black Oak Arkansas (rock LP, Atlantic Records); and *Souther-Hillman-Furay Band*, by Souther-Hillman-Furay Band (C&W/rock, Asylum Records).

PRODUCCIONES PALOVESY PALOMES, 2920 Clark Rd., Suite 104, Sarasota FL 33595. President: Stephen R. Hatch. Record producer and management firm. Estab. 1969. Deals with artists and songwriters. Produced 5 albums and 7 singles in 1978; plans 9 albums and 18 singles in 1979, 9 albums in 1980. Fee derived from sales royalty or outright fee from songwriter/artist.
How to Contact: Query or submit demo tape. Prefers cassette with 6-12 songs on demo. Does not return unsolicited material. Reports in 3 weeks.
Music: Disco (sal and soul); soul; salsa; and merengue.

QUADRAPHONIC TALENT, INC., Box 630175. Miami FL 33163. (305)472-7757. President: Jack P. Bluestein. Record producer and music publisher. Estab. 1973. Deals with artists and songwriters. Produced 5 singles in 1978; plans 1 single in 1979. Fee derived from sales royalty.
How to Contact: Query, submit demo tape (artist), submit demo tape and lead sheet (songwriter). Prefers 7½ ips reel-to-reel with 1-4 songs on demo. SASE. Reports in 1 month.
Music: Blues; C&W; easy listening; folk; gospel; jazz; MOR; rock; soul; and top 40/pop. Recently produced "Three Things" and "A Miracle in You," by Ray Marquis (C&W singles, Twister Records); and "Red Velvet Clown" and "Love Day," by Dottie Leonard (pop singles, AMG Records)."

QUINTO RECORDS, Box 2388, Toluca Lake CA 91602. (213)985-8284. Producer: Quint Benedetti. Estab. 1977. Produced 2 albums and 1 single in 1978; plans 2 albums and 2 singles in 1979. Deals with artists and songwriters. Fee derived from sales royalty.
How to Contact: Submit demo tape and lead sheet. Prefers cassette with 2-4 songs on demo. SASE. Reports in 1 month.
Music: C&W; MOR; and novelty-Broadway. Recently produced "Rock & Roll Heaven" and "A Dim Cafe," by Leti (MOR/C&W, Quinto Records).

R&R RECORDS, INC., 663 5th Ave., New York NY 10022. (212)757-3638. Producer/President: Rena L. Feeney. Producers: Billy Nichols, Lenny Bailey. Record production and music publishing. Estab. 1968. Deals with artists, songwriters and producers. Produced 4 albums and 8 singles in 1978; plans 6 albums and 12 singles in 1979. Fee derived from sales royalty.
How to Contact: Submit demo tape. Prefers 7½ ips reel-to-reel with 4-8 songs on demo. SASE. Reports in 1 month.

Music: Disco; easy listening; MOR; rock; soul; and top 40/pop. Recently produced "Love a Little Longer," by Rena Romano (rock single, R&R-Ren Rome Records); "High Time," by Charles Hudson (MOR single, R&R-Ren Rome Records); "Everybody Let's Party," by Joe Rivers (disco single, R&R-Ren Rome Records); and "Do It With Me," by the Lenny Bailey Orchestra (disco single, R&R-Ren Rome Records).

RAINBOW RECORDING STUDIOS, 2322 S. 64th Ave., Omaha NE 68132. (402)554-0123. Producer: Lars Erickson. Estab. 1976. Deals with artists, songwriters in production of "commercial jingles." Fee derived from outright fee from record company or songwriter/artist.
How to Contact: Query or submit demo tape. Prefers 7½ ips reel-to-reel or cassette with 4 songs maximum on demo. SASE. Reports in 1 month.
Music: Any style acceptable.

RARE MAGNETISM MUSIC/BAD BOY MUSIC, 6000 Sunset Blvd., Los Angeles CA 90028. (213)466-9131. Owner: Kim Fowley. Record producer, music publisher and management. Estab. 1959. Deals with artists, songwriters and co-publishers. Plans to produce 50 albums in 1979. Fee derived from sales royalty, outright fee from record company or outright fee from songwriter/artist.
How to Contact: Submit demo tape and lead sheet. Prefers cassette. Does not return unsolicited material. Reports "when I hear a hit."
Music: Disco; easy listening; MOR; rock (radio/top 40); soul; and top 40/pop. Recently produced "You're My World" and "Happy Girls," by Helen Reddy (MOR, Capitol Records); and "Streettalk," by Streettalk (AOR, Asylum [Newzea] Records).

REAL TO REEL PRODUCTIONS, 98 Benz St., Ansonia CT 06401. (203)735-5883. Owners: Marty Kugell, Sharon Kugell. Record producer, music publisher and management firm. Estab. 1955. Deals with artists, songwriters, managers and agents. Produced 4 albums and 4 singles in 1978; plans 4 albums and 4 singles in 1979. Fee derived from sales royalty or outright fee from record company.
How to Contact: Submit demo tape and lead sheet. Prefers 7½ ips reel-to-reel leadered with 1-2 songs on demo. SASE. Reports in 3 weeks.
Music: Disco; easy listening; MOR; rock (medium); soul; and top 40/pop. Recently produced "I'll Be Seeing You," by Jeff Evans (disco, Pickwick Records); "Tears Tears Tears," by Black Satin (disco, Buddah Records); "Romeo & Juliet," by Jimmy Jackson (top 40, Buddah Records; and "Train," by Herman's Hermits (top 40, Buddah Records).

RICH AND FAMOUS PRODUCTIONS, 1645 Fremont Dr., Thousand Oaks CA 91360. Producer: Earle Mankey. Record producer and recording studio. Estab. 1978. Deals with artists and songwriters. Produced 2 albums and 6 singles in 1978; plans 2 albums and 6 singles in 1979. Fee derived from sales royalty or outright fee from record company.
How to Contact: Submit demo tape. Prefers cassette with 4 songs maximum on demo. SASE. Reports in 1 month.
Music: Rock and top 40/pop. Recently produced "You Drive Me Ape (You Big Gorilla)," by the Dickies (loud pop single, A&M Records); *Mondo Deco*, by the Quick (loud pop LP, Mercury Records); *Paley Brothers*, by the Paley Brothers (pop LP, Sire Records); and *Pop!*, by Pop! (pop LP, Arista Records).

DAN RUPERT ORGANIZATION, 2514 Dexter Ave. N., #8, Seattle WA 98109. (206)285-7479. Consultant: Delbert Finchley. President: Dan Rupert. Record producer. Estab. 1974. Deals with artists and songwriters. Produced 8 albums and 4 singles in 1978; plans 10 albums and 4 singles in 1979; 12 albums and 5 singles in 1980. Fee derived from sales royalty or outright fee from songwriter/artist. Charges for some services: "Sometimes requires fee after initial consultation."
How to Contact: Submit demo tape and lead sheet. Prefers cassette with 2-4 songs on demo. SASE. Reports in 3 weeks.
Music: Choral; church/religious; C&W; folk; gospel; jazz; MOR; progressive; rock; soul; and top 40/pop. Recently produced *Portrait*, by the Fry Family (sacred LP, Homestead Records); "Hello," by Ruthie, Clarke and George (disco single, Bagdad Records); and "Children's Christmas," by Ric Hall (MOR single, Dark Horse Records).

RUSTRON MUSIC PRODUCTIONS, 200 Westmoreland Ave., White Plains NY 10606, main office. (914)946-1689. Executive Director: Rusty Gordon. Director A&R: Ron Caruso. Estab. 1970. Deals with artists and songwriters. Produced 3 albums and 3 singles in 1978; plans

4 albums and 8 singles in 1979. Fee derived from sales royalty and outright fee from record company.
How to Contact: Query, arrange personal interview, submit demo tape and lead sheet and submit promotional material and photos. Prefers 7½ ips reel-to-reel, "with leader tape between all songs and at beginning and end of tape" or cassette with 3-6 songs on demo. "Interviews are held in the evenings Monday through Thursday from 7-10 p.m. We specialize in singer/songwriter package for promotion and publishing. We will also review songs from non-performing writers." SASE. Reports in 1 month.
Music: R&B; country (popular and progressive); disco (salsa, popular, swing); easy listening; folk (rock and folk/country); MOR; rock (country/rock and rock & roll); and pop (standards). Recently produced *Lois Britten Project*, by Lois Britten (pop/rock/disco LP/Rustron Records); *Sign Painter*, by Christian Camilo Veda and the Tingalayo Rhythm Band (salsa/disco/American pop LP, FM Records); and "Amor Mio," by Christian Camilo Veda and the Tingalayo Rhythm Band (Spanish ballad single, FM Records).

SAGITTAR RECORDS, 1311 Candlelight Ave., Dallas TX 75116. (214)298-9576. President: Paul Ketter. Record producer, record company and music publisher. Estab. 1973. Deals with artists and songwriters. Plans 1-2 albums and 6 singles in 1979. Fee derived from sales royalty.
How to Contact: Submit demo tape and lead sheet. Prefers 7½ reel-to-reel with 3-12 songs on demo. SASE. Reports in 1 month.
Music: C&W; folk; MOR (country); and progressive (country). Recently produced "Diamonds Only Shine," "Games Grownups Play" and "How High is Your Mountain," by Bunnie Mills (C&W singles, Sagittar Records).

STEVEN C. SARGEANT, 31632 2nd Ave., South Laguna Beach CA 92677. Producer: Steven C. Sargeant. Record producer. Estab. 1970. Deals with artists and songwriters. Fee derived from sales royalty.
How to Contact: Query or submit demo tape. Prefers 7½ ips reel-to-reel or cassette with 3-5 songs on demo. SASE. Reports in 3 weeks.
Music: Folk; jazz; rock (country or hard); and top 40/pop.

SHALYNN PRODUCTIONS, Box 34131, Dallas TX 75234. (214)242-6152. General Manager: Linwood Henderson. Promotion Manager: Rick Jackson. President: Stephen Kedlarchuk. Record producer, music publisher and management firm. Estab. 1977. Deals with artists and songwriters. Plans 10 albums and 20 singles in 1979. Fee derived from outright fee from record company or outright fee from songwriter/artist.
How to Contact: Query, arrange personal interview, or submit demo tape and lead sheet. Prefers 7½ ips reel-to-reel with 2-4 songs on demo. SASE. Reports in 2 weeks.
Music: Bluegrass; church/religious; C&W; disco; easy listening; gospel; MOR; progressive; rock; soul; and top 40/pop. Recently produced "Sunlight in Her Hair" and "Flower Song," by Shalynn (top 40/pop singles, Ice Records); and "Dime a Dozen Man" and "Trouble in the Last Frontier," by Watkins and Lamb (country/rock/top 40 singles, Ice Records).

SHOWROOM COMMUNICATIONS, INC., Valley Forge Plaza, Suite 605, King of Prussia PA 19406. (215)265-7569. President: Eric L. Ward. Record producer, booking agency, music publisher and management firm. Estab. 1976. Deals with artists and songwriters. Produced 3 albums and 7 singles in 1978; plans 9 albums and 8 singles in 1979, 13 albums and 12 singles in 1980. Fee derived from sales royalty.
How to Contact: Query or arrange personal interview. Prefers cassette with 4-8 songs on demo. SASE. Reports in 1 month.
Music: Bluegrass; blues; children's; choral; church/religious; classical; C&W; disco; easy listening; folk; gospel; jazz; MOR; progressive; rock; soul; and top 40/pop. Recently produced *I'll Get Over It*, by the Thompsons (R&B LP, BCW Records).

THE SHUKAT CO., LTD., 25 Central Park W., New York NY 10023. (212)582-7614. Contact: Scott Shukat, Larry Weiss. Record producer, music publisher and management firm. Estab. 1972. Deals with artists, songwriters and producers. Produced 1 album in 1978; plans 1 in 1979, 1 in 1980. Fee derived from sales royalty.
How to Contact: Submit demo tape and lead sheet. Prefers reel-to-reel or cassette with 3-15 songs on demo. SASE.
Music: Folk; rock; and top 40/pop.

SOFTWARE MEDIATRICS USA, INC., Box 476, Calabasas CA 91302. Music Manager: Nanci Schultz. Record producer and music publisher. Estab. 1971. Deals with artists and

songwriters. Produced 3 albums in 1977; plans 5 albums in 1978. Fee derived from sales royalty or outright fee from record company.
How to Contact: Query or submit demo tape. Prefers 7½ ips reel-to-reel or cassette. Does not return unsolicited material.
Music: Disco; MOR; progressive; rock (punk); and top 40/pop.

SOLID RECORDS, 6101 Ridgeview Ave., Baltimore MD 21206. (301)254-7354. General Manager/A&R Director: George Brigman. Record producer and music publisher. Estab. 1974. Produced 1 single and 1 album in 1978; plans 1 album and 2 singles in 1979, 1 album and 2 singles in 1980. Fee derived from sales royalty. "We don't charge for anything. If someone wants me to produce independently (from Solid Records) and I feel the band and material is worth it, I'd expect a retainer plus a percentage of the royalties."
How to Contact: Query, arrange personal interview, submit demo tape, submit demo tape and lead sheet, or submit lead sheet. Prefers 7½ or 15 ips reel-to-reel with 2-6 songs on demo. SASE. Reports in 2 weeks.
Music: Blues; easy listening; jazz; progressive; and rock (hard or soft). Recently produced "Drifting" and "Blowin' Smoke," by Split (jazz/hard rock singles, Solid Records); and *Jungle Rot*, by George Brigman (rock LP, Solid Records).

SOLID SOUL AND ATMOSPHERE PRODUCTIONS, 3282 E. 119th St., Cleveland OH 94120. (216)752-1904. Executive Vice President: Sylvester A. Luke. Producer: Robert Davis. Record producer, booking agency and management firm. Estab. 1969. Deals with artists. Fee derived from sales royalty or outright fee from record company.
How to Contact: Query, arrange personal interview or submit demo tape. Prefers reel-to-reel or cassette with 4-12 songs on demo. Reports in 1 month.
Music: Blues; church/religious; disco; gospel; jazz; rock; and soul. Recently produced "Makin' Music and I Mean," recorded by Chill Wills and Kinsman Dazz (soul/disco single, 20th Century Records); *Los Nombres*, recorded by Nombres (Latin soul LP, Lorain Sound Records); and "City People," recorded by Danny Cocco (soul single, Daywood Records).

SOUNDS OF WINCHESTER, Box 574, Winchester VA 22601. (703)667-9379. Owner: Jim McCoy. Record producer and music publisher. Estab. 1968. Deals with artists and songwriters. Produced 8 albums and 10 singles in 1978; plans 10 albums and 15 singles in 1979, 12 albums and 20 singles in 1980. Fee derived from sales royalty.
How to Contact: Submit demo tape and lead sheet. Prefers 7½ ips reel-to-reel with 4-10 songs on demo. SASE. Reports in 1 month.
Music: Bluegrass; C&W; gospel; MOR; and rock.

SPECTRA SOUND RECORDS, 4847 N. Milwaukee Ave., Chicago IL 60630. (312)777-7186. President: Dan Belloc. Record producer and music publisher. Estab. 1958. Deals with artists and songwriters. Plans 2 albums and 2 singles in 1979. Fee derived from sales royalty.
How to Contact: Submit demo tape and lead sheet or submit lead sheet. Prefers reel-to-reel. SASE. Reports in 1 month.
Music: C&W; easy listening; MOR; and top 40/pop. Recently produced *Cowboy & the Lady*, by Eddie Douglas (C&W LP, Spectra Sound Records).

SHANE WILDER PRODUCTIONS, 1680 N. Vine St., Suite 313, Hollywood CA 90028. (213)467-1958, 467-1959. President: Shane Wilder. Record producer and music publisher. Estab. 1958. Deals with artists and songwriters. Produced 14 albums and 31 singles in 1978; plans 15 albums and 25 singles in 1979, 15 albums and 25 singles in 1980. Fee derived from sales royalty.
How to Contact: Query. Prefers cassette with 3-8 songs on demo. SASE. Reports in 2 weeks.
Music: C&W; easy listening; MOR; rock; and top 40/pop. Recently produced *Meet Crystal Blue* and *South of the Border*, by Crystal Blue (Network Records). Presently producing LPs by Laurie Loman and Susan Rhodes.

STARKWEATHER, QUINN & GILBERT, 7800 Woodman Ave., #19A, Panorama City CA 91402. (213)786-3324. Producer: Jeffrey Starkweather. Record producer, music publisher and management firm. Estab. 1969. Deals with artists and songwriters. Plans 3 albums and 5 singles in 1979. Fee derived from sales royalty.
How to Contact: Submit demo tape and lead sheet. Prefers 7½ ips reel-to-reel or cassette with 4-6 songs on demo. SASE. Reports in 1 month.
Music: Rock (country or hard) and top 40/pop. Recently produced "Sweet Country Air," by Wheels (country/rock single, Buckskin Records); "St. Louis," by Rain (hard rock single, RCA

Records); and "A Chance to Love," by Gary Quinn (top 40 single, Buckskin Records).

STONE DIAMOND PRODUCTIONS, 6255 Sunset Blvd., Hollywood CA 90028. (213)468-3400. Vice President/General Manager: Jay Lowy. Record production company and music publisher. Estab. 1958. Released 2 singles in 1978; plans 3 singles in 1979. Works with musicians on contract; songwriters on salary.
How to Contact: Submit demo tape and lead sheet or lyric sheet. Prefers 7½ or 15 ips reel-to-reel or cassette with 1-3 songs on demo. SASE. Reports in 1 month.
Music: Blues; disco; easy listening; jazz; MOR; R&B; rock; soul; and top 40/pop.

SUMAC MUSIC, 1697 Broadway, New York NY 10019. (212)246-0575. President: Susan McCusker. Record producer and music publisher. Estab. 1975. Deals with artists and songwriters. Fee derived from sales royalty.
How to Contact: Submit demo tape and lead sheet. Prefers 7½ ips reel-to-reel with 2-5 songs on demo. Does not return unsolicited material. Reports in 1 month.
Music: Disco; soul; and top 40/pop. Recently produced "Let's All Chant," by Michael Zager Band (disco single, Private Stock).

SUNBURST MUSIC PRODUCTIONS, 26949 Chagrin Blvd., Suite 209, Beachwood OH 44122. Executive Producer: Jim Quinn. Associate Producer: Otto F. Neuber. Record producer, music publisher and management firm. Estab. 1976. Deals with artists and songwriters. Produced 2 album and 4 singles in 1978; plans 2 albums and 4 singles in 1979. Fee derived from sales royalty.
How to Contact: Submit demo tape. Prefers 7½ ips reel-to-reel or cassette with 1-3 songs on demo. SASE. Reports in 3 weeks.
Music: MOR and top 40/pop. Recently produced *Glory*, by Glory (progressive LP, United Artists Records); *I Don't Care*, by I Don't Care Band (jazz LP, Buddah Records); and "Struttin'," by All Nite Strutter (progressive single, Black Vinyl Records).

SUNCAT RECORDS, Suncat Entertainment, Box 66, Manhattan Beach CA 90266. (213)973-1999. President: Gary Young. Vice President/A&R Director: Larry Thatt. Record producer, music publisher and management firm. Estab. 1970. Deals with artists and songwriters. Produced 15 albums and 20 singles in 1977; plans 10 albums and 30 singles in 1978, 15 albums and 40 singles in 1979. Fee derived from sales royalty.
How to Contact: Arrange personal interview or submit demo tape. Prefers 7½ ips reel-to-reel or cassette with 3-10 songs on demo. SASE. Reports in 1 month.
Music: Blues; C&W; disco; easy listening; folk; gospel; MOR; progressive; rock (pop or country); soul; and top 40/pop. Recently produced *California Discovery*, by California (boogie-rock LP, RCA Records); *Creation of Sunlight*, by Sunlight (pop/rock LP, Pirate Records—BASF South America); and *Kissin' My Memories*, by Buck Taylor (C&W LP, Wind Records).

SUNDAY PRODUCTIONS, INC., 705 Western Ave., Urbana IL 61801. President: Michael Day. Record producer, music publisher and recording studio. Estab. 1973. Deals with artists and songwriters. Plans 3 albums and 6 singles in 1979. Fee derived from sales royalty.
How to Contact: Query or submit demo tape and lead sheet. Prefers 7½ ips quarter-track reel-to-reel or cassette with 1-3 songs on demo. SASE. Reports in 6 weeks.
Music: C&W; disco; easy listening; MOR; rock; soul; and top 40/pop. Recently produced *Thirsty or Not, Choose Your Flavor*, by Coalkitchen (soul/pop LP, Epic Records); and *Michael Day*, by Michael Day (pop LP, Columbia Records).

TIGER RECORDS, C.I.T.S. Records, Box 2544, Baton Rouge LA 70821. (504)925-2603. Producer/A&R Director: "Ebb-Tide." President: E.K. Harrison. Record producer, music publisher and record company. Estab. 1978. Deals with artists, songwriters and composers. Plans to produce 3 albums and 12 singles in 1978, 6 albums and 34 singles in 1979. Fee derived from sales royalty.
How to Contact: Submit demo tape and lead sheet. Prefers cassette with 4-6 songs on demo. SASE. Reports in 2 weeks.
Music: Folk; MOR; rock (pop); and top 40/pop. Recently produced "S.O.S. I Love You," by Pamela Marie (rock/pop single, Tiger Records).

TIVEN PRODUCTIONS (formerly Big Sound Records), 2 Washington Square Village, #7D, New York NY 10012. Director/Producer: Jon Tiven. Record producer, music publisher, management firm and record company. Estab. 1977. Deals with artists. Produced 2 albums and

┌ Songwriter's Market Close-Up

Songwriting has been a matter of persistence to Randy Bachman, formerly of the Guess Who and Bachman-Turner Overdrive, and now with Iron Horse. He wrote "Takin' Care of Business," BTO's best-known single, when he was 15. He tried to get the song on every Guess Who album he worked on, but couldn't. It wasn't until he formed BTO that he finally got the song recorded—and even then the song appeared on BTO's *second* LP.

Songwriting is also a matter of hooks to Bachman. He maintains a large record collection, but a record doesn't enter the collection if it doesn't grab him in the first four bars. He realizes that many music industry people judge songs by those same four bars, so Bachman always gets the hook—a grabber—in the very beginning of the song.

1 single in 1978; plans 2 albums and 2 singles in 1979, 2 albums and 3 singles in 1979. Fee derived from sales royalty.
How to Contact: Submit demo tape. Prefers cassette with 1-12 songs on demo. SASE. Reports in 2 weeks.
Music: Blues (rock); progressive; rock; and top 40/pop. Recently produced *Bionic Gold,* by various artists (Phil Spector LP, Big Sound Records); *Are You Serious*, by Van Duren (Beatlesque LP, Big Sound Records); and "Lost Johnny," by Mick Farren (punk single, Ork Records).

TNT & THRUST PRODUCTIONS, 3472 E. 116th St., Cleveland OH 44120. (216)561-5681. President: Robert Miller. Estab. 1970. Deals with artists and producers. Produced 1 single in 1977; plans 1 single in 1978. Fee derived from sales royalty.
How to Contact: Query. Reports in 1 month.
Music: Blues; disco; jazz; rock; and soul. Recently produced "Love Will Turn You Around," by Entertains (disco single, Steeltown Records).

TRACKDOWN RECORD DISTRIBUTORS, 542 S. Dearborn, Suite 1102, Chicago IL 60605. (312)486-2989. Vice President: T.J. Wacker. Record producer, booking agency, music publisher and management firm. Estab. 1952. Produced 100 albums and 400 singles in 1978; plans 500 albums and 700 singles in 1979, 1,000 albums and 1500 singles in 1980. Payment negotiable.
How to Contact: Submit demo tape or submit demo tape and lead sheet. Prefers 7½ ips reel-to-reel or 8-track with 10-100 songs on demo. SASE. Reports in 1 month.
Music: Bluegrass; blues; church/religious; classical; C&W; disco; easy listening; folk; gospel; jazz; MOR; progressive; rock; soul; and top 40/pop. Recently produced "So-Called Friend," by Lee Mitchell (soul single, Full Speed Ahead).

SCOTT TURNER PRODUCTIONS, 524 Doral Country Dr., Nashville TN 37221. Executive Producer: Scott Turner. Record producer and music publisher. Estab. 1977. Deals with artists and songwriters. Produced 15 albums in 1978. Fee derived from outright fee from record company or outright fee from songwriter/artist. "It depends on whether or not I am producing a major act for a major label, or if I place a custom session with a label."

How to Contact: Submit demo tape and lead sheet. Prefers cassette with 1-4 songs on demo. SASE. Reports in 2 weeks.
Music: C&W; easy listening; folk; MOR; progressive; rock; and top 40/pop. Recently produced material for Nilsson, Del Reeves, Sonny Throckmorton and Rosemary Clooney.

WILLIAM F. WAGNER AGENCY, 13437 Ventura Boulevard, Suite 223, Sherman Oaks CA 91423. (213)995-4277. Owner: Bill Wagner. Record producer, music publisher and management firm. Estab. 1957. Deals with artists and songwriters. Produced 3 albums and 4 singles in 1978; plans 4 albums and 2 singles in 1979, 6 albums and 2 singles in 1980. Fee derived from sales royalty, outright fee from record company, or outright fee from songwriter/artist.
How to Contact: Query or submit demo tape and lead sheet. Prefers 3¾ or 7½ ips reel-to-reel, 2- or 4-track mono or cassette with 1-8 songs on demo. SASE. Reports in 3 weeks.
Music: Blues; C&W; easy listening; jazz; MOR; progressive; and top 40/pop. Recently produced *This Time Around,* by Bruce Kosaveach (folk/pop LP, BK Records); *Earth Song* by Sioux City Zoo (MOR/pop LP, Medi-Arts Records); and *All the Children Cried,* by John Klemmer (progressive jazz LP, Chess Records).
Tips: "Try to exercise some judgment on type of tunes submitted, and please, if acoustic piano is used, tune it."

KENT WASHBURN, 10622 Commerce Ave., Tujunga CA 91042. Owner: Kent Washburn. Record producer and music publisher. Estab. 1974. Deals with artists and songwriters. Produced 2 albums and 5 singles in 1978; plans 3 albums and 6 singles in 1979, 3 albums and 6 singles in 1979. Fee derived from sales royalty or outright fee from record company.
How to Contact: Query or submit demo tape and lead sheet. Prefers 7½ ips reel-to-reel or cassette with 1-4 songs on demo. SASE. Reports in 1 month.
Music: Disco; easy listening; jazz; MOR; soul; and top 40/pop. Recently produced *Turnin' On,* by High Inergy (pop LP, Motown Records); "Ride a Wild Horse," by Ernie Fields (disco single, Motown Records); "Never Thought I'd Be Losing You," by Major Lance (R&B single, Motown); "Passion Flower," by Kenny Cupper (pop single, Motown); and *Dependable,* by Charles Drain (R&B LP, RCA).

WATERMELON PRODUCTIONS, Box 530, Cooper Station, New York NY 10003. President/Producer: Paul Wade. Record producer and music publisher. Estab. 1976. Deals with artists and songwriters. Plans 10 albums and 20 singles in 1979. Fee derived from sales royalty.
How to Contact: Query or submit lead sheet. Prefers cassette with 2-3 songs on demo. "Send lead sheet. We'll ask for a tape if we want one. However, if tape is sent with SASE, we'll return it. We are interested in music with no lyrics also." SASE. Reports in 2 weeks.
Music: Children's; disco; easy listening; MOR; rock; soul; and top 40/pop. Recently produced "L.A. Baby" and "Box of Tissues," by Elements (top 40 singles, House Records); and "I Took a Chance," by Ana Leonard (top 40 single, House Records).

WHITEWAY PRODUCTIONS, INC., 65 W. 55th St., New York NY 10019. President: Eddie White. Record, play, film and concert producer. Estab. 1959. Deals with artists and actors. Fee derived from sales royalty.
How to Contact: Query, arrange personal interview or submit demo tape. "We advertise or send out calls when we are doing a show." SASE. Reports in 1 week.
Music: Musical shows. Recently produced *Birmingham Rag* and *Dixieland Blues,* by Sunny Gale.

WILHOS MUSIC PUBLISHING, Box 3443, Hollywood CA 90028. (213)291-0539. President: Willie E. Hoskins Jr. Record producer and music publisher. Estab. 1962. Deals with artists and songwriters. Produced 7 albums and 12 singles in 1978; plans 12 albums and 18 singles in 1979. Fee derived from sales royalty.
How to Contact: Submit demo tape and lead sheet. Prefers cassette with 2-4 songs on demo. SASE. Reports in 3 weeks.
Music: Disco; soul; and top 40/pop. Recently produced "All About You," by La Tefa (top 40/pop single, Cassan); "You Are the One," by Jerri Albano (top 40/pop single, Cassan); and "Why Should We Stop," by Natural Four (soul single, ABC).

WINDCHIME PRODUCTIONS, INC., 1201 16th Ave. S., Nashville TN 37212. (615)320-7927. President: Johnny Slate. Record producer and music publisher. Estab. 1972.

Deals with artist and songwriters. Fee derived from sales royalty or outright fee from record company.
How to Contact: Submit demo tape. Prefers 7½ ips reel-to-reel with 1-4 songs on demo. SASE. Reports in 1 month.
Music: Disco; easy listening; rock; and soul. Recently produced "Love Is on the Air," by Larry Henley (soft rock single, Epic Records); and "Shotgun Rider," by Blue Jug (rock single, Ariola Records).

PAUL WOLFE PRODUCTIONS, Box 262, Abe Lincoln Station, Carteret NJ 07008. (201)541-9422. Vice President: Gary Hills. A&R Director: Joyce McRae. Estab. 1965. Deals with artists, songwriters and record companies. Produced 17 albums and 42 singles in 1978; plans 25 albums and 47 singles in 1979; 35 albums and 42 singles in 1980. Fee derived from sales royalty or outright fee from record company.
How to Contact: Query or submit demo tape and lead sheet with background information and photographs. Prefers 7½ ips reel-to-reel, cassette or 8-track with 6-12 songs on demo. SASE. Reports in 1 month.
Music: Children's; C&W; disco; easy listening; folk; jazz; MOR; progressive; rock; soul; top 40/pop; and ethnic. Recently produced *Sonny Ray & the Del-Rays Live In Concert* (oldies LP, Buddah Records). "I am currently working in the studio with the 1910 Fruitgum Company on their new LP, and some live Jackie Wilson recording sessions for Brunswick Records."

DAN ZAM PRODUCTIONS, 183 Thompson St., New York NY 10012. (212)982-1374. President: Dan Zam. Record producer. Estab. 1978. Deals with artists and songwriters. Fee derived from sales royalty.
How to Contact: Submit demo tape or submit demo tape and lead sheet. Prefers 7½ or 15 ips reel-to-reel (no Dolby) with 3 songs minimum on tape. SASE. Reports in 3 weeks.
Music: Pop/rock (new wave, country and other genres).

Play Producers and Publishers

"American theater gains much of its distinctive quality from the excellence of the American musical," says ElizaBeth King, literary manager of Actors Theatre of Louisville.

"Some of the most exciting theatrical innovations have come to be through musicals," adds Thomas Edward West, assistant artistic director of the Asolo State Theater in Florida.

Musicals are "absolutely vital" to modern theater, says West. What's more, they're important to audiences. "There is *always* an audience for a good story, song and dance," says King.

"Good musicals are in demand," says a representative of the Performance Publishing Company. "Therefore, good composers are very important and difficult to find."

The lesson? Play producers and publishers need you.

The theater game has no rules, yet you must play it by the book. The "book" is the nonmusical part of a play: the dialog and stage directions, which, contrary to the opinions of some songwriters, are not unnecessary mumblings that move the audience from one song to another. "Start from the book," advises one script editor. "Music should serve necessary dramatic functions," such as moving the plot forward. The music should be so well integrated into the play that the script wouldn't make sense if the songs were cut out of it.

Meshing music and script into a single, unified entity is difficult, especially since musicals are often products of collaboration. Playwright and songwriter must share not only work schedules, but also a concept of the goals and direction of the product they're co-writing. Collaborate with a person with whom you can work creatively, yet efficiently.

Finding that person can sometimes be difficult, though you'll certainly find a collaborator if you seek one logically and systematically. Check the drama department of the local college or university, for instance. Better yet, join a local theater group. Among the actors, directors, and even stage hands you meet and work with will certainly be a struggling playwright, perhaps one that's looking for *you*.

That last idea is not a suggestion; it's a requirement. Even if you already have a collaborator lined up, you should work closely with at least one theater group to get a look at theater operations. "Go to the theater," advises Cedric Vendyback of Brandon University. "See how it works." No successful musical has been written by someone lacking direct, intimate contact with the theater. Working with a local group—in any capacity—will give you a pragmatic grounding in what you can and can't do on a stage. Close contact with such a group will also allow you to accomplish three out of producer Eugene Cassasa's four steps to success: "Learn all the problems of the producer/director. Recognize that music is to be enjoyed by the *audience*. Keep the story line clear. Marry someone rich." (Chances are that you won't achieve that fourth step by joining a theater group, as no rich people seem to be involved with the theater.)

Second in preference to working on plays is watching them. Attend as many musicals (nonmusicals, too) as possible. "It's very important to see a lot of plays and see professionals doing them, because professionals are doing what's current," says Lawrence R. Harbison, assistant editor of Samuel French, a major play publishing company. Regional theaters and dinner theaters abound, giving you plenty of opportunity to witness high-quality productions. Public television stations often broadcast superb theatrical presentations, as well.

"If you can't see them, read them," says Harbison. Write play publishers, request copies of their catalogs, and order a few playscripts to study. Although reading a musical doesn't allow you to hear the music, it will give you an idea of how song lyrics relate to the rest of the show, how and when songs are woven into the show, and the number of songs used.

Read theater magazines, as well. One good one is *Theatre Profiles* (355 Lexington Ave., New York City 10017). The Theatre Communications Group publishes a market list called *Information for Playwrights* (355 Lexington Ave., New York City 10017). You can also get useful information by joining the American Theatre Association (ATA, 1029 Vermont Ave. NW, Washington D.C. 20005), which publishes various theater and membership directories; and the Dramatist's Guild (234 W. 44th St., New York City 10036), which publishes a newsletter that covers, as do the other periodicals mentioned here, contests, producers, markets and trends.

Knowing as much as possible about trends is important, not so much so you can tell where theater is going, but so you can determine where it's been. Producers and publishers won't tell you where theater is going, because they want *you* to tell *them*. "The best plays we find are not the ones that imitate the trends, but the ones that try to set their own trends," says Harbison. "We want tomorrow's trends."

Few trends remain in effect long enough for you to exploit them. One recent trend, however, will continue to have its effect on theater: inflation.

Rising costs force producers and directors to seek material that can be produced simply and inexpensively. Extravaganzas are still being produced, but, like the dinosaurs they're beginning to resemble, they're flirting with extinction.

"Keep it simple," says Randall J. Buchanan, chairman of Texas A&I's Department of Communication and Theatre Arts. "Because of costs today, the big show is just too expensive to produce."

Shirley Bell of the Cockpit in Court Summer Theater agrees: "Begin with small-cast, simple-set shows that can be done by little theaters with limited facilities and limited funds. Music

should sound good when played by two or three musicians."

That's not to say that you should write only spare, two-character, bare-stage plays. Instead, provide flexibility by giving it room for trimming—or for embellishments. A musical is an outline—not a blueprint—followed by the director, choreographer, etc. "Supply material from which magic can be made," says Cedric Vendyback, "stuff capable of being developed by creative minds."

Keeping the play versatile will also give you a shot at any of a wide variety of theatrical markets. Professional casts can handle complex songs and arrangements, but remember that Broadway need not be your ownly goal. Many nonprofessional groups—such as dinner theaters, children's theaters, high school and college groups, and community theaters—provide outlets for musicals, and their casts will appreciate less complex material. Play publishers are another good outlet for material; nonprofessional groups are the primary patrons of the publishers. One publisher, for instance, deals primarily in "young people's plays." Regarding the plays in the publisher's catalog, "as the age level advances, so does the musical complication," according to one of its editors. Shoot first for production of the play. A successful production can lead to publication (both producers and publishers are included in the following market list). "If you get it produced first, the publication is just gravy," says Lawrence Harbison.

The most important element of success, however, is writing a good show with solid, appealing songs. "Musical numbers must be strong enough to grab the listener on first hearing," says one director. That one hearing may be the only time the audience will hear the song, leaving little time for songs to "grow" on it. Songs must be immediately appealing.

The pacing of songs is also important. "Each scene/act should have one 'catchy' tune," says Ralph Tabakin, a director with Theatre Profiles' Productions. Another director asks playwrights/composers to keep songs "clean, bright and hummable."

You'll find doing this will be easier if you, as Cedric Vendyback suggests, "write about something you *care* and know about." Don't, however, write a musical about composers trying to write musicals. Neil Simon has already teamed up with Marvin Hamlisch and Carole Bayer Sager to do just that. The name of the show? *They're Playing Our Song*, of course.

ACTORS THEATRE OF LOUISVILLE, 316 W. Main, Louisville KY 40202. (502)584-1265. Literary Manager: ElizaBeth King. Play producer. Estab. 1964. Produces "19 equity shows, including 8-10 new plays per year." Produced 2 musicals in 1978; plans 2 in 1979, 2 in 1980. "Actors Theatre is a resident equity professional theater operating for a 35-week season, from September to June. Subscription audience of 18,000 from extremely diverse backgrounds. Repertoire spans classics to contemporary, all genres. There are two theaters: a 640-seat thrust, and a 200-seat three-quarter arena." Payment negotiable. Submit complete ms, score and cassette tape of songs. SASE. Reports in 4 months.
Musicals: "Should be full-length (two or more acts) with a strong story line and a basically positive lifeview. Story can be either original or an adaptation; music any style. Of foremost importance is a literate book with strong characterizations and dialogue. No situation comedies or absurdist work." There are two theaters. "For the small theater, musicals should be very small: 8 actors or less, 1 or 2 pianos. For the large theater: 5 actors or less, 3- or 4-piece ensemble. We cannot produce multimedia shows. Multiple set shows are difficult for us."
Recent Productions: *Getting Out*, by Marsha Norman (woman's first day out of prison); *The Gin Game*, by D.L. Coburn (two nursing home residents confront each other while learning gin rummy); *Andronicus*, by Jon Jory and Jerry Blatt (rock music version of Shakespeare's *Titus Andronicus*); *Lone Star*, by James McLure; *Matrimonium*, by Peter Ekstrom (musical based on Shaw comedies); *Crimes of the Heart*, by Beth Henley (three sisters fight family battles in Mississippi); *Gold Dust*, by Jon Jory and Jim Wann (musical of Old West prospector trying tp hoard money and son's girl).

ALLENBERRY PLAYHOUSE, Boiling Springs PA 17007. (717)258-6120. Managing Director: Nelson Sheeley. Play producer. Estab. 1948. Produces 11 plays/year. Produced 3 musicals in 1978; plans 2 in 1979. Pays according to property. Query with synopsis. SASE. Reports as soon as possible.
Musicals: "Other than established material, we are looking for small cast, 4-10 characters, simply produced musicals—they should run between 2-2¼ hrs in length. Take into account that we are in a conservative, religiously oriented part of the country. Four letter words are fairly taboo, but then again, it depends on the four letter word! Stay away from what middle America finds objectionable: excessive dwelling on any violation of the Ten Commandments, slurs on the country (not necessarily the government), nudity, or esoteric subject matter."
Recent Productions: *South Pacific*, by Rogers and Hammerstein; and *I Do, I Do*, by Schmidt and Jones.

ASOLO STATE THEATER, Drawer E, Sarasota FL 33578. (813)355-7115. Assistant Artistic Director: Thomas Edward West. Play producer. Estab. 1960. Produces 15 plays/year. Produced 1 musical in 1978; plans 1 in 1979, 2 in 1980. Plays are performed at the Asolo Theater (325-seat proscenium house), the Asolo Stage Two (180-seat thrust stage), or by the Asolo Touring Theater (6-member company touring the Southeast). Pays 5% minimum royalty. Query. SASE. Reports in 3 months.
Musicals: "We want nonchorus musicals only. They should be full-length, any subject, with not over 30 in the cast. There are no restrictions on production demands; however, musicals with excessive scenic requirements may be difficult to consider. Submit finished works only."
Recent Productions: *Travesties*, by Tom Stoppard; *The School for Wives*, by Moliere; and *Richard III*, by Shakespeare.
Tips: "Musicals are produced infrequently here due to the 'classical' basis of Asolo's repertory and inability to 'job-in' musical-theater talent."

B.M.R. CONCEPTS, INC., 234 W. 44th St., New York NY 10036. Production Consultant: Michael May. Play producer. Estab. 1976. Produces 2 plays/year. Produced 2 musicals in 1978; plans 2 in 1979. "Although we do not produce exclusively for the European market, this is the mainstay of our operation. Our audiences are international and the productions are musicals, mostly of the Broadway type. Houses range from 250-1,800." Pays Drama Guild minimum but "other arrangements are possible." Submit complete ms, score and tape of songs. Prefers cassette but will accept 7½ ips reel-to-reel on a 7-inch reel. SASE. Reports in 1 month.

Musicals: "We produce musical comedies or musical revues dealing with particular periods in history, but will consider works in a contemporary vein providing the music and book form a cohesive unit. Up numbers are always desirable but contrasting moods are essential. We will consider any material within the framework of musical and dramatic quality. We prefer anywhere between 8 and 14 songs. These can range from simple piano accompaniment to full orchestrations. A strong story line is essential. The cast should be no larger than 22 and no smaller than 5. Scene changes should be integral with action so maximum effect can result from minimal sets, even though they may be intricate and extravagant. A visual spectacle is possible if the work is strong enough to support it."

Recent Productions: *Bubbling Brown Sugar*, by Lofton Mitchell; *Love*, by Dennis Rosa, Howard Morren and Susan Birkinhead; *The Club*, by Eve Merriam; and *A Life in the Theatre*, by David Mamet.

BARTER THEATRE, STATE THEATRE OF VIRGINIA, Abingdon VA 24210. (703)628-2281. Producing Director: Rex Partington. Business Manager: Pearl Hayter. Play Producer. Estab. 1932. Produces 12 plays/year. Produced 2 musicals in 1978. Plays performed in Barter Theatre. Pays minimum 5% royalty. SASE. Reports in 3 months.

Musicals: Full length, all styles and topics, small casts, basic instrumentation and minimal set requirements. "Keep it small. Think in relavent and reomantic subjects."

Recent Productions: *I Do! I Do!*; *Oh Coward*; and *The Apple Tree*.

DAVID BLACK, 251 E. 51st St., New York NY 10022. (212)753-1188. Producer: David Black. Play producer. Estab. 1961. Produces 2 plays/year. Plays are performed on Broadway, Off-Broadway and in London. Pays 2% royalty of "gross weekly box office plus $500 average advance." Query with synopsis. SASE. Reports in 2 weeks.

Musicals: "I'm interested in all types of musicals. Playwrights should write for themselves, not me."

Recent Productions: *A Funny Thing Happened on the Way to the Forum*, by Bert Shevelove (musical comedy); and *George M!*, by Michael Stewart (musical).

BROAD RIPPLE THEATRE CENTRE, 916 E. Westfield Blvd., Indianapolis IN 46220. (317)253-2072. Managing Director: Diane Malone. Play producer. Estab. 1978. Produces 12 plays/year. "A new intimate theater with seating capacity approximately 75. Interested in small musicals, revues with limited cast and orchestration." Pays 5% minimum royalty. Submit complete ms, score and cassette tape of songs. SASE. Reports "as soon as possible."

Musicals: "Any style as long as it's small; no more than 12 in cast. We have a platform thrust stage—no wings no flies." Does not want big cast, many sets or spectacular effects.

Recent Productions: *Steambath*, by Bruce Jay Friedman (life and death); *The Runner Stumbles*, by Milan Stitt (religion/murder); and *Starting Here, Starting Now*, by Richard Maltby Jr. and David Shire (musical revue/young love).

EUGENE S. CASASSA, Ashby West Rd., Fitchburg MA 01420. (617)342-6592. Producer: Eugene S. Casassa. Play producer. Estab. 1962. Produces 8 plays/year. Produced 1 musical in 1978; plans 1 in 1979. Plays are produced in an arena with thrust type stage; resident company and small house (120). Pays $150-200 for unknown work. Query with synopsis. Does not return unsolicited material. Reports as soon as possible.

Musicals: "We have done a wide variety with success. We are essentially looking for low set requirements; should use piano and or small combo. Musical should have strong story line."

CHILDREN'S THEATRE OF RICHMOND, INC., 6317 Mallory Dr., Richmond VA 23226. (804)288-6634. Director: Frank Howarth. Play producer. Estab. 1926. Produces 4-5 plays/year. Produced 2 musicals in 1978; plans 2 in 1979, 2 in 1980. For children 5-12 years old. Plays performed in 700-seat auditorium with proscenium stage. Pays negotiable royalty or by negotiable rate/performance. Query with synopsis then submit complete ms and score. SASE. Reports in 2 months.

Musicals: Wants "children's musicals with playing time of one hour in any style, hopefully reflecting current musical tastes. New approaches to old fairy tales are welcomed, new stories too." Does not want "pedantic, sing-song musicals. Both story and songs should be clear and have only as much complication as necessary. Songs should not be long. Any romantic passages must move swiftly. No more than 15-22 cast members. No other limits."

Recent Productions: *Aesop's Falables*, by Ed Graczyk (musical); *Christmas Carol*, by Frank Howarth and Bill Roper (musical); *Golden Crane*, by Mary Mulder; and *Penny and the Magic Medallion*, by Joseph Robinette and James Shaw (musical).

COCKPIT IN COURT SUMMER THEATRE, Essex Community College, Baltimore MD 21237. (301)682-6000. Managing Director: F. Scott Black. Play producer. Estab. 1973. Produces 7 plays/year. Produced 3 musicals in 1978; plans 3 in 1979. "We operate three separate theaters on our campus. Broadway type musicals are performed in a well-equipped, beautiful theater. Cockpit, upstairs, is a cabaret theater. Classics are performed outdoors in the courtyard with stylized sets and full makeup." Pays through rental and royalty agreement with firms who control rights. Submit complete ms and score. SASE. Reports in 1 month.
Musicals: "Wholesome shows which are suitable for audiences of all ages. Musical score should be of top quality. We use a full orchestra in the pit. Large casts are OK. We like good leading and supporting roles." No material that is politically controversial, vulgar or offensive to the audience. "We prefer a cast of 20-30 for most of our summer musicals with some doubling. We use wagon sets, no turntables or revolving stages."
Recent Productions: *Kiss Me Kate*, by Cole Porter; *I Do, I Do*, by Tom Jones and Harvey Schmidt (*The Fourposter* with music); and *West Side Story*, by Leonard Bernstein (modern day *Romeo and Juliet*).

DAVID J. COGAN, 350 5th Ave., New York NY 10003. (212)563-9562. Contact: David Cogan. Play producer. Estab. 1958. Produces 1 play/year. Plans 1 musical in 1978; plans 1 in 1979. Produces musical comedy in New York. Pays on a royalty basis, or buys script outright for $5,000 maximum. Query. SASE. Reports in 1 month.
Musicals: Interested only in completed projects.
Recent Productions: *A Raisin in the Sun*, by Hannesbury (drama); and *The Odd Couple*, by Neil Simon (comedy).

GLENN CRANE, 6260 Birdland Dr., Adrian MI 49221. (517)263-3411. Producing Director: Glenn Crane. Play producer. Produces 2-4 new plays/year. Produced 1 musical in 1978; plans 1 in 1979. Pays by royalty or buys scripts outright for $200 minimum. Submit complete ms, score and tape of songs. Prefers 7½ ips reel-to-reel or cassette. SASE. Reports in 1 month.
Musicals: "Any creative, clever, original treatment—full-length or 1-act. We are especially interested in children's musicals and plays with small cast (6-8 major roles) for the adult musicals and large cast for children's musicals."
Recent Productions: *Without a Song*, by Young and Hurley (variety of love); *The Whistler's Christmas*, by Harbison and Ames (folk tale); and *Young Willow*, by Gastleton and Ames (Civil War romance).

THE CRICKET THEATRE, 345 13th Ave. NE, Minneapolis MN 55413. (612)379-1411. Artistic Director, Works in Progress: Sean Dowse. Play producer. Estab. 1971. Produces 14 plays/year (7 main season, 7 works-in-progress). Produced 2 musicals in 1978; plans 1 in 1979. Plans for 1980 "depend on plays submitted." Royalty negotiable; pays $500 minimum for main season. Submit complete ms and cassette tape of songs. SASE. Reports in 3-6 months.
Musicals: "We seek musical plays by American playwrights and songwriters. We do not seek mainstream, escapist, 'huge production' musicals like *Music Man*, *Hello Dolly* or *1776*, but 'medium production' musicals in the 'new play tradition' of *Promenade*, *Subject to Fits* and *The Club*. Small orchestras only." Maximum cast size: 3.
Recent Productions: *Subject to Fits*, by Robert Montgomery (musical/dramatic version of Dostoevsky's *The Idiot*); *The Club*, by Eve Merriam (musical set in an exclusive men's club in early 1900s); and *The D.B. Cooper Project*, by John Orlock (musical about the USA's only successful skyjacking for ransom).

CYPRESS COLLEGE THEATER ARTS DEPARTMENT, 9200 Valley View St., Cypress CA 90630. (714)821-6320. Theater Arts Department Chairman: Kaleta Brown. Play producer. Estab. 1966. Produces 5-6 plays/year. Produced 1 musical in 1978; plans 1 in 1979. "Our audience at Cypress College is basically a middle- class, suburban audience. We have a continuing audience that we have built up over the years. Our plays now are produced in our Campus Theater (seating capacity 623) or workshop theater (maximum seating capacity 250)." Pays $50-125/performance. Submit complete ms, score and 7½ ips reel-to-reel tape of songs. SASE. Reports in 1 month.
Musicals: "We must do large-cast shows because the shows are done as a class. Because we are on a limited budget, we must look carefully at scenery requirements, costume requirements and props. No small-cast shows or nude shows."

Recent Productions: *The Crucible,* by Arthur Miller (about Salem witch trials); *A Cry of Players,* by William Gibson (Shakespeares' England); *Devour the Snow,* by Abe Polsky (Donner Party); *Oklahoma,* by Rodgers and Hammerstein; *Follies* and *Company,* by Stephen Sondheim; and *The Physicists,* by Friedrich Durrenmatt.

DEPARTMENT OF COMMUNICATION AND THEATRE ARTS, Texas A&I University, Kingsville TX 78363. (512)595-3401. Department Chairman: Randall J. Buchanan. Play producer. Produces 6 musicals/year. Audience composed of University students, townspeople, highschool students and elementary students for children's theater. Plays performed in one of three theaters: 400-seat proscenium; 240-seat proscenium; or 100-seat flexible. Produced 2 musicals in 1978; plans 2 in 1979. Pays $75-250/performance. Query. SASE. Reports in 3 weeks.
Musicals: "Generally light, small-cast shows with a minimum of setting demands. We try to do them either in a dinner theater situation or they are done in a flexible setting. We do not have sufficient room to accomodate large setting shows. For the dinner format the show must be entertaining, fast-paced and not demanding of the voice. We recently did *Side by Side by Sondheim*. This was the style that we will continue to look for. Maximum cast size would be 10 for dinner theater format, and 25 for nondinner theater musical. Staging in each case should be simple. Either a one-set or a flexible setting. Simple choreography. None that are heavy on message or demand a number of excellent voices."
Recent Productions: *Side by Side by Sondheim,* by Stephen Sondheim (musical review); *Three Penny Opera,* by Bertolt Brecht (man's condition); *Oh, God,* by Neil Simon (Job's story); *A View From the Bridge,* by Arthur Miller (love and immigration); and *A Midsummer Night's Dream,* by William Shakespeare (love and confusion).

EAST WEST PLAYERS, 4424 Santa Monica Blvd., Los Angeles CA 90029. (213)660-0366. Artistic Director: Mako Iwamatsu. Administrator: Norman Cohen. Play producer. Estab. 1965. Produces 4 plays/year. "We have produced original musical revues and some children's musicals in our theater which is a 99-seat Equity waiver house. Our actors are professional actors. We are an Asian-American theater and consequently the audience is primarily ethnic in make up." Pays 5% minimum royalty. Query with synopsis. SASE. Reports in 1 month.
Musicals: "We look for material dealing with Asian-American culture and produce adult and children's musicals in book and/or revue form. We make no limitations on the writing approach. We look for theme and above all originality. We primarily produce shows with casts under 15. The stage is not huge and has certain limitations; however, we do have a turntable at our disposal."
Recent Productions: *Asian-American Hearings,* by various authors (topical review); and *Once Upon in America,* by various authors (Japanese immigration).

ENTERTAINMENT UNLIMITED, INC. (formerly Doug Jenson Enterprises), 444 Ruxton Ave., Manitou Springs CO 80829. (303)685-5104. Secretary: Sharon Rose. Play producer. Estab. 1962. Produces 4 plays/year. Audiences are seasonal, comprised primarily of families. Buys script outright for $125-300. Submit complete ms and score. SASE. Reports in 3 weeks.
Musicals: "We want old-fashioned (late 1800s) comedy "mellerdrammers" in a western style; song parodies; sight gags; zany characters; lots of humor; fast moving; simple plot, props and staging; and simple costumes and sets. May be slightly risque but not vulgar. Simple choreography may be included when we perform it; music provided by a piano. No more than four songs (comedy songs) or eight cast members. We don't want to see anything serious or set in contemporary times."
Recent Productions: *The Charge of Heaven's Ethic,* by Phil Arrow (on the Civil War); *Lily, the Virtuous Seamstress,* by Alice McDonald (comedy melodrama); and *The Chips Are Down,* by Schubert Fendrich (western comedy/melodrama).

ETC. COMPANY, Jackson Community College, 2111 Emmons Rd., Jackson MI 49203. (517)787-0800. Director: G.L. Blanchard. Play producer. Estab. 1929. Produces 4-6 plays/year. Produced 1 musical in 1978; plans 1 in 1979. Plays are produced in a new proscenium theater with thrust capabilities seating 367, or a multiform theater seating 100-200 depending on arrangement. Pays $100-200/performance. Query with synopsis. SASE. Reports in 2 weeks.
Tips: "We lean in the direction of shows with casts in the area of 20 or under, with 'moderately sensible' staging."

FESTIVAL PLAYHOUSE, Kalamazoo College, Kalamazoo College MI 49007. (616)383-8509. Artistic Director: Clair Myers. Play producer. Estab. 1964. Productions attended by city and regional audience as well as student body. Three theaters available: 406-seat open stage; 306-seat thrust stage; and 100-seat experimental stage. Produces 3-4 plays/year. Produced 1 musical in 1978; plans 2 in 1979. Pays $75-150/performance. Query. SASE. Reports in 1 month.

Musicals: "There is no limit on type of musical except those which are operas or require excessive scenic elements. Plays with casts in excess of 30 are prohibited, as are those with excessive scenery."

Recent Productions: *Candide*, by Bernstein, et al; *Streetcar Named Desire*, by Williams; and *Texas Triology*, by Jones.

THE FIRST ALL CHILDREN'S THEATRE, INC., 37 W. 65th St., New York NY 10023. Producer: Meridee Stein. Estab. 1969. Produces 5 plays/year. "For children, ages two and up, teenagers and their families. These plays are developed with and for our special company to appeal to an audience of young theatergoers." Pays 5% maximum royalty; buys script outright for $750 maximum, or pays $15/performance. Query or submit complete ms and score; "outline is best. If we like it, then we help develop it with the author. All pieces must be created especially for our company." SASE. Reports in 8-10 weeks.

Musicals: "ACT musicals are 45-50 minutes in length and include 8-10 songs with incidental music. We do plays in all genres featuring many kinds of music, i.e., commedia dell' arte, baroque musical fairy tales, modern pop, old tales made new, and originals with challenging, meaningful messages. We do not want material unsuitable for children and their families. The music must be a very important part of the work. Harmonies, arrangements and selection of a band are all done later. Plays include 15-35 children and teenagers. Props, staging can be creative and challenging, though not unrealistic. We have as many as nine pieces in our orchestra."

Recent Productions: *Three Tales at a Time*, by C. Crisman, S. Dias, M. Kaplowitz, M. Stein, T. Stein, J. Thomas, D. Kalvert and D. Nelson (a trilogy of shapes); *Clever Jack and the Magic Beanstalk*, by Judith Thomas and John Forster (fast and funny version of the well-known tale); and *The Pushcart Fables*, by Betsy Shevey (3 Grimms fairy tales revolving around the lives of people on the lower East Side); *The Incredible Feeling Show* by Eliz Swados.

Tips: "Our theater stresses excellence and professionalism. Flexibility on everybody's part is the key to our success. The work we produce is extremely creative and highly original. Each production is developed and nurtured over a long period of time—sometimes as long as two years. Each show has a team of adult theater professionals who direct and supervise the entire production."

FOOLKILLER ETC., 2 W. 39th St., Kansas City MO 64111. (816)756-3754. Chairman: Bill Clause. Play producer. Estab. 1971. Produces 7-15 plays/year. Pays negotiable royalties. "Foolkiller is an excellent exposure showcase for new talent." Query with synopsis or contact by phone. SASE. Reports in 2 months.

Musicals: "We consider everything but prefer topics dealing with problems aimed at working and middle-class people — comedies and political and social commentaries. We prefer material that doesn't last more than one hour. Our stage is about 15x35; cast should be 2-15 people. We don't want to see any slick, sophisticated kinds of writing that may go over everyone's head, or anything terribly pessimistic."

Recent Productions: *Drop Hammer*, by Manny Fried (labor unions); and *Turn of the Century Vaudeville*, by Joyce Constant, Don Carlson and Carol Smith (historical vaudeville musical).

Tips: "The Foolkiller is an organization that has many facets. It is a showcase for new talent. Musicians have frequent public jam sessions and walk-on talent is encouraged. Freedom of expression is emphasized in all activities. There is a large public following and community support. All material is original."

SAMUEL FRENCH, INC., 25 W. 45th St., New York NY 10036. (212)582-4700. Assistant Editor: Lawrence R. Harbison. Play publisher. Estab. 1830. Publishes 80-90 scripts/year. Published about 10 musicals in 1978. Plays used by community, stock and dinner theaters, regional repertories, and college and high school markets. Pays 10% royalty on play scripts sold, and a per-performance royalty depending on various factors. "We take 10-20% agency fee. Submit only the libretto (book). If we like it, we may ask to see and/or hear music." SASE. Reports in 10 weeks minimum.

Musicals: "We publish primarily New York-based musicals, though we do occasionally bring out a show which has not had a New York City production. These are intended primarily for children's and community or dinner theaters. No religious material, or anything unstageworthy."

Recent Titles: *Chicago*, by Fred Ebb and Bob Fosse (on the jazz age); *The Club*, by Eve

Merriam (on male chauvinism); and *Cowardly Custard*, by Noel Coward (revue).

THE GOODMAN THEATRE, 200 S. Columbus Dr., Chicago IL 60603. Artistic Director: Gregory Mosher. Play producer. Estab. 1925. Produces 15 plays/year. Plans 1 musical in 1980. "The Goodman has a six-play Mainstage season and a three-play Stage Two subscription season. It also hosts a new play conference consisting of staged readings." Pays on a royalty basis. Submit complete ms and cassette tape of songs. SASE. Reports in 4 months.
Musicals: "The Goodman seeks musicals with serious musical and literary purpose and merit; those that seek to be more than light entertainment. Except under extraordinary circumstances, cast size must be 12 or under. Physical production demands should not be great. Emphasis should be on the script, music and actors, not the physical production values."
Recent Productions: *Lone Canoe*, by David Mamet, with music and lyrics by Alaric (Rokko) Jans.

GREEN MOUNTAIN GUILD, White River Junction VT 05001. (802)295-7016. Managing Director: Marjorie O'Neill-Butler. Play producer. Estab. 1971. Produces 18 plays/year. Produced 6 musicals in 1978; plans 9 in 1979. Produces plays for a summer theater audience in 3 locations in Vermont: Stowe, Killington and Mt. Snow. Pays $75 minimum/performance. Query with synopsis. SASE. Reports in 1 month.
Musicals: We are looking for musicals with "a small cast, a good story line, well-developed characters, songs and music that come naturally out of the story and music that works with piano and drums only." No frivolous material. Prefers one-set shows.
Recent Productions: *Shenandoah* (about Civil War farm family); *Carousel*, by Rogers and Hammerstein; and *Pippin*, by Stephen Schwartz.

HILL COUNTRY ARTS FOUNDATION, Box 176, Ingram TX 78025. (512)367-5121. Director, Point Theatre: Jim Weisman. Play producer. Estab. 1959. Produces 8 plays/year. Produced 1 musical in 1978; plans 4 in 1979. Plays are produced in a theater seating 500 and musicals run for 15 performances. Audience is primarily from small towns and rural communities. Plays are produced in an outdoor theater on the banks of the Guadalupe River in the summer and in an indoor pavilion in the winter. Pays $25-125/performance. Query with synopsis. SASE. Reports in 1 month.
Musicals: "I am looking for full-length musicals (2 or 3 acts, about 2 hours in length) which would have Texan or Southwestern interest or emphasis. The play must be suitable for a family audience. I will consider both historical and contemporary plays, and the major figure need not be of public importance. I am looking for plays in a variety of styles. I would be particularly interested in seeing historical shows which are not in a realistic style." Prefers instrumentation which has a Southwestern flavor: piano, guitar, steel guitar, banjo, accordian, harmonica, etc. Prefers 35- member cast maximum.
Recent Productions: *South Pacific*, by Rogers and Hammerstein; *Hello, Dolly*, by Jerry Herman; and *Texas Hill Country*, by Dorothy Dodd and Mort Stine (about boyhood of Lyndon B. Johnson).

HOWARD UNIVERSITY DEPARTMENT OF DRAMA, Washington DC 20059. (202)636-7050. Chairperson: Henrie Edmonds. Play producer. Estab. 1909. Produced 3 musicals in 1978; plans 2 in 1979. Pays $75-100/performance. Submit complete ms and cassette of songs. SASE. Reports in 4 months.

WILLIAM E. HUNT, 801 West End Ave., New York NY 10025. Contact: William E. Hunt. Play producer/director. Estab. 1947. Produces 4 plays/year. Produced 1 musical in 1978. "I produce and direct musicals for adult audiences only. No children's shows. No one-acts. Plays have been performed in stock, regional theater and Off-Broadway. Large-cast musicals with many sets are not for me." Pays 5% minimum royalty. "There is usually, but not always, a small royalty advance." Submit complete ms, score and cassette tape of songs. SASE. Reports in 1 month.
Musicals: "Only musicals as good as *The Threepenny Opera*, *Guys and Dolls*, *Of Thee I Sing*, and *The King and I*. However, use smaller casts, fewer sets. Taboo topics: religion and historical pageants. Nothing smirky. Out and out sexy, yes. Gay, yes. But if it's sexy let it be out and out sexy, not leering. I am not by nature a rock fan. One-act musicals are almost impossible to put on anywhere."
Recent Productions: *Jerome Kern at the Hartman*, by Jerome Kern and William E. Hunt (evening of Kern music); *The Sunshine Train*, by various authors (evening of gospel music); and *You Never Know*, by Cole Porter (romance; book adapted from play *By Candlelight*).

THE INNER CITY CULTURAL CENTER, 1308 S. New Hampshire Ave., Los Angeles CA 90006. (213)387-1161. Executive Director: C. Bernard Jackson. Administrative Director: Elaine Kashiki. Play producer. Estab. 1967. Produces 4-6 plays/year. Produced 2 musicals in 1978; plans 2 in 1979, 2 in 1980. "The Inner City Cultural Center is a multi-ethnic, multi-cultural arts organization primarily aimed at the community in which it is located." Query with synopsis. Does not return unsolicited material. Reports in 1 month.
Recent Productions: *Wanted: Experienced Operators*, by C.B. Jackson and Estela Scarlata (illegal aliens); *Shaka Zulu*, by James Bronson (Zulu nation); and *Second City Flat*, by Momoko Iko (black/Asian love story).

INTERNATIONAL ARTS RELATIONS, INC., Box 788, Times Square Station, New York NY 10036. (212)247-6776. Artistic Director: Max Ferra. Play producer. Estab. 1966. Produces 5-6 plays/year. Plays are performed in New York City. Buys script outright for $75-250. Query, submit complete ms and score, or send resume. SASE. Reports in 1 month.
Musicals: "We are seeking material for children's comedies and dramas." Length: 1-1½ hours.
Recent Productions: *Carmencita*, by Manuel Martin (based on *Carmen*); and *The Dumb Lady*, by Lope de Vega (a classical Spanish comedy).

JEWISH COMMUNITY CENTER OF GREATER WASHINGTON, 6125 Montrose Rd., Rockville MD 20852. (301)881-0100. Director, School of Theatre: Bruce S. Silver. Play producer. Estab. 1969. Produces 4-6 plays/year. Produced 2 musicals in 1978; plans 2 in 1979. Produces plays in a 300-seat theater. Pays by outright purchase of $200. Query. SASE. Reports in 1 month.
Musicals: "We produce popular and original musicals and dramas performed by teens and adults, especially with a Jewish flavor."
Recent Productions: *Hello Dolly*, *Oliver*, *Fiddler on the Roof*, *Ellis Island* and *The Skin of Our Teeth*.

LIBRE PUBLISHING CO., 512 Brooks Bldg., Scranton PA 18503. Publisher: John J. White. Play publisher. Estab. 1977. Publishes 8-10 plays/year. Published 2 in 1978; plans 3 in 1979. Pays 2½-18% royalty. Query with synopsis. Does not return unsolicited material.

LORETTO-HILTON REPERTORY THEATRE, 130 Edgar Rd., St. Louis MO 63119. (314)962-8410. Literary Consultant: Thomas Breyer. Play producer. Estab. 1967. Produces 8 plays/year. "We produce two seasons: one of five established (or, occasionally, new) works of broad appeal, the other of three new plays or classical works of relatively narrow appeal. The former are presented in a 724-seat thrust theater for 30-odd performances; attendance runs about 90% of capacity, 80% season subscribers. Audiences are cross-sectional, with a distinct bias towards upper-income and high eduction. We could consider 'experimental' musicals for the second season, but it's not likely." Pays 4% royalty "and up on a sliding scale." Query or query with synopsis. SASE. "Plays/librettos that are obviously outside our range are returned fairly soon (say, six weeks); others are held until we start planning in February for the following fall. Setting the season generally takes us until July or August."
Musicals: "Dramatic values are paramount; intellectual and/or artistic qualities rank well ahead of entertainment. We are primarily an acting company, not a musical one. Emphasize characterization and theme. We are at our best expressing the complexity and depth of real characters in humanly significant (not necessarily real—fantasy is acceptable) situations; at our worst in inventing or pretending to three-dimensionality where the playwright's imagination has failed. We look more kindly on scores that call for relatively small orchestras. As to mise-en-scene, we regard that by and large as the designer's problem, not the playwright's. Likewise, 'business if not dramatically integral, is the concern of actors and directors."
Recent Productions: *Tom Jones*, by Arrick and Damashek (adaptation of Fielding's novel); *Canterbury Tales*, by Starkie, Coghill, Hall and Hankins (adaptation of Chaucer's epic); and *Have I Stayed Too Long at the Fair* (a look at the St. Louis World's Fair of 1904).

MARIONETTES MERINAT, 1315 21st Ave. NW, Calgary, Alberta, Canada T2L 1M5. (403)282-2226. Artistic Director: Eric Merinat. Play producer. Estab. 1969. Produces 2 plays/year. Buys script outright for $300 minimum or pays $20/performance. Query with synopsis. SAE and International Reply Coupons. Reports in 1 month.
Musicals: "We need musicals for adults in high schools and universities and for children in elementary schools. In both cases, they must be musicals with songs and script or operas. Lengths may vary from 30 minutes to 90 minutes depending on style and audience. Plays must have been conceived for marionettes and puppets and must use all the possibilities of this art. The puppeteers can be invisible and the play on magnetic tape, or they can be visible and act

with the puppets on stage. Generally we employ three or four puppeteers."
Recent Productions: *Idepop*, by Monika Merinat (fantasy); *Once in the Past*, by Isabelle Grenier (bygone customs); and *Mosaic* by Eric Merinat (music-hall).
Tips: "Caution: The art of puppets is very specific; don't send us musicals for living actors! All information about this is available from us at any time."

MEMPHIS STATE UNIVERSITY, Theatre Department, Memphis TN 38152. (901)454-2565. Director of Theatre: Dr. Richard A. Rice. Play producer. Estab. 1945. Produces 12 plays/year. Produced 2 musicals in 1978; plans 4 in 1979. Audience is the faculty, students and townspeople of Memphis. Pays 10-15% of gate or $20-100/performance. Query with synopsis. SASE. Reports in 1 month.
Musicals: "We are most interested in noncommercial, nonformula works. We can also handle difficult music and large cast demands. We do both extravaganza and studio type productions. No pageants, historical epics or satires on satires."
Recent Productions: *The King is a Fink*, by Kennedy and Caldwell (based on the comic strip, *The Wizard of Id*); *Back County Crimes*, by Robertson (a kind of *Spoon River Anthology* set in Oklahoma); and *The Sword in the Stone*, by White and Queener (whimsical version of King Arthur's youth).

MILWAUKEE REPERTORY THEATER, 929 N. Water St., Milwaukee WI 53202. (414)273-7121. Artistic Director: John Dillon. Play producer. Estab. 1954. Produces 11 plays/year. Produced 1 musical 1978; plans 1 in 1979. "We havemainly a subscription audience." Pays negotiable royalty. Submit ms and cassette tape of songs. SASE. Reports "as soon as possible."
Musicals: "We seek small cast musicals suitable for resident theater productions. We're interested in quality material (not froth) performable in a 500-seat three-quarter round theater."
Recent Productions: *Island*, by Peter Link; *Fighting Bob*, by Tom Cole; and *The Taming of the Shrew*.

NASHVILLE ACADEMY THEATRE, 724 2nd Ave., South and Lindsley, Box 7066, Nashville TN 37210. (615)254-9103. Director: Thomas C. Kartak. Play producer. Estab. 1931. Produces 8 plays/year. Plays are performed in a 696-seat theater for audiences ranging in age from kindergarten through high school. Pays $15-50/performance. Submit complete ms and score. SASE. Reports "after play-reading committee is through."
Musicals: "We want wholesome entertainment for various age groups, e.g. *Cinderella* for the very young, *Tom Sawyer* for teens and pre-teens and *Man of La Mancha* for high schoolers. Average cast size is 15. We do not want to see any poorly written, sensational or pornographic materials."
Recent Productions: *1984*, by George Orwell (future); *Ten Little Indians*, by Agatha Christie (revenge); and *Really Rosie*, by Maurice Sendak (imagination).

THE NEW PLAYWRIGHT'S THEATRE OF WASHINGTON, 1742 Church St. NW, Washington DC 20036. (202)232-1122. Script Evaluations: Robert Schulte. Musical Director: Thom Wagner. Play producer. Estab. 1972. Produces 6 plays/year. Produced 2 musicals in 1978; plans 2 in 1979, 2 in 1980. For general audience with interest in new works. Payment individually negotiated; averages $600/work. Submit complete ms and cassette tape of music. Score is optional. SASE. Reports in 3-5 months.
Musicals: Seeks all types: revues, musical comedies and musical theater. Does not want material that has had major, fully professional prior production. Instrumental forces should be chamber-size; no more than 12 musicians. Cast can be up to 15."
Recent Productions: *Nightmare*, by Tim Grundmann (satiric musical comedy); *Sweet and Hot*, by Ken Bloom (Harold Arlen revue); *Canticle*, by Michael Champagne and William Penn (music-drama); *A Whitman Sonata*, by Paul Hildebrand Jr. and Thom Wagner (chamber drama); and *Eddie's Catchy Tunes*, by Tim Grundmann (musical comedy).

OFF CENTER THEATRE, 436 W. 18th, New York NY 10011. (212)929-8299. Producer: Abigail Rosen. Play producer. Estab. 1968. Produces 4 plays/year. Produced 1 musical in 1978; plans 2 in 1979, 3 in 1980. The plays are performed "Off-Broadway." Pays percentage of box office receipts after initial expenses have been recouped. Submit complete ms, score and type of songs. SASE. Reports in 1 week.
Musicals: "We're interested in any and all types of musicals but prefer a small cast."
Recent Productions: *The Last Vaudeville Show at Radio City Music Hall*, by Seidman, Rosen and Field (vaudeville).

OKLAHOMA THEATER CENTER, 400 W. Sheridan, Oklahoma City OK 73102. (405)239-6884. Artistic Director: Gordon Greene. Play producer. Estab. 1972. Produces 12 plays/year. Plays are performed for families and general audiences. Plays are performed in 590-seat thrust or 240-seat arena stage. Pays $25-50/performance. Submit complete ms, score and tape of songs. Submit through agent only. Prefers cassette only. SASE. Reports in 3-6 months "depending on the backlog."

Musicals: "We want full-length (two-hour) plays only. Material should be suitable for family entertainment and have strong plot, good character development and good female roles. Musical numbers should be strong enough to grab the listener on the first hearing. Any tasteful treatment of any topic in most any style is acceptable, but we do not want any nude shows, excessively violent material, verse plays or shows requiring multiple sets. We want modest-sized cast and single sets suitable for arena production."

Recent Productions: *I Do, I Do*, by Jones and Schmidt (musical); and *A Funny Thing Happened on the Way to the Forum*, by Gelbart, Shevelove and Sondheim (musical comedy).

OMAHA COMMUNITY PLAYHOUSE, 6915 Cass St., Omaha NE 68132. (402)553-4890. Associate Director: Christopher Rutherford. Play producer. Estab. 1926. Produces 10 plays/year. Plays are produced in a "500-seat main stage auditorium for general community audiences of all ages with a preference for 'Broadway style' shows. Also a 150-seat studio theater for smaller experimental shows and reviews." Pays standard rates or prize for the Jane L. Gilmore Playwriting Contest. Query or request contest information and entry form. SASE. Reports in 2 weeks.

Musicals: "Primary means of submitting unpublished work is through our contest. Authors should request entry form before submission of manuscript intended for contest." Musicals must be accompanied by full score and available arrangements. Also include cassette tape with the music in order in which it appears in the play.

Recent Productions: *Cabaret*, by Masteroff, Kander and Ebb; *Christmas Carol*, by Charles Jones; and *How to Succeed in Business*, by Burrows and Loesser.

PERFORMANCE PUBLISHING CO., 978 N. McLean Blvd., Elgin IL 60120. (312)697-5636. Editor: Virginia Butler. Play publisher. Estab. 1973. Publishes 30-50 plays/year. Published 4 musicals in 1978; plans 6 in 1979. Plays are used by children's theaters, junior and senior high schools and colleges. Pays standard royalty/performance. Submit complete ms and score; or submit complete ms, score and cassette tape of songs. SASE. Reports in 3 months.

Musicals: "We prefer large cast, contemporary musicals which are easy to stage and produce. Costume and nostalgia shows are popular. We like children's musicals if the accompaniment is fairly simple. Plot your shows strongly, keep your scenery and staging simple, your musical numbers and choreography easily explained and blocked out. Originality and style are up to the author. We want innovative and tuneful shows but no X-rated material. We are very interested in the new writer and believe that, with revision and editorial help, he can achieve success in writing original musicals for the amateur market."

Recent Titles: *Rock-n-Roll*, by Michael Fingerut and David Cotherall; *She's at Sea*, by Jim Seay and Henry Conrad; and *Frankenstein Follies*, by Peter Walker and Katherine J. Leslie.

PERFORMING ARTS DEPARTMENT, Avila College, 11901 Wornall Rd., Kansas City MO 64145. (816)942-8408. Chairman, Performing Arts: Dr. William J. Louis. Play producer. Estab. 1930. Produces 5 plays/year. Produced 1 musical in 1978; plans 1 in 1979. Plays are produced in a 500-seat thrust stage theater. To date, only well known musicals have been produced. Original shows would have to be individually contracted for. Submit through agent. SASE. Reports in 2 months.

Musicals: "We prefer shows 2 hours in length and topics for a liberal school but still a Catholic-sponsored institution. No crass, vulgar scripts that have no redeeming qualities. We prefer cast not larger than 25."

Recent Productions: *Paint Your Wagon*, *Man of La Mancha*, *Brigadoon*, *Of Thee I Sing*, *Oklahoma* and *The Mikado*.

MRS. PAUL REDINGER, Box 275, Dover OH 44622. (216)364-5111. Contact: Rachel Redinger. Play producer. Estab. 1970. Produces 2 plays/year. Produced 2 musicals in 1978; plans 2 in 1979 "Produces *Trumpet in the Land*, an outdoor hisorical drama during July and August of each year in Schoenbronn Amphitheatre and a children's show or a musical in either the 1,400-seat amphitheater or the 300-seat pavilion." Pays 5% minimum royalty or salary for season. Query with synopsis. SASE. Reports in 1 month.

Musicals: "We produce children's musicals with unusual plots written for an audience of both children and adults (with intelligent dialogue, such as *Reynard the Fox*)." No heavy serious

musical drama. "We have a strong choral group with some outstanding voices and our dancers are more athletic than balletic. Our amphitheater requires simple staging and sets and realistic props and costuming."
Recent Productions: *Trumpet in the Land*, by Paul Green (history of Tuscarawas Valley in Ohio); *Toad of Toad Hall*, by A.A. Milne (children's play); and *Hollywood Heartbreak*, by David Gibson (about the '30s).

ROCHESTER CIVIC THEATRE, Mayo Park, Rochester MN 55901. (507)282-7633. President: David Richardson. Play producer. Estab. 1952. Produces 6-8 plays/year. Produced 2 musicals in 1978; plans 2 in 1979, 2 in 1980. Pays "standard" fees. Submit complete ms, score, and cassette or 3¾ or 7½ ips reel-to-reel tape of songs. SASE. Reports when the results of an annual playwriting contest are decided in August.
Musicals: Adaptable for a small orchestra, if possible.
Recent Productions: *A Little Night Music*; *Amorous Flea*; and *Gypsy*.
Tips: "We offer a prize of $1,000 in 1980 for the best new play (musical or otherwise) by an American author. The winning play will be produced by RCT. Small consolation prizes are also offered."

ST. NICHOLAS THEATER, 2851 N. Halsted St., Chicago IL 60657. Contact: Assistant Artistic Director. Play producer. Estab. 1972. Produces 10 plays/year. Submit complete ms, score and tape of songs. SASE. Reports in 3 months.
Musicals: Wants "theatrical" musicals with small casts.

SHOWBOAT MAJESTIC, Foot of Broadway, Cincinnati OH 45202. (513)241-6550. Producing Director: F. Paul Rutledge. Play producer. Estab. 1967. Produces 7 plays/year. Produced 5 musicals in 1978; plans 5 in 1979. Plays are produced on the Showboat Majestic, the last of the original floating theaters located on the Ohio River. Query. SASE. Reports in 1 month.
Musicals: "We are seeking original songs, musical comedies no longer than two hours with an intermission, revues and small cast shows." No avant-garde or experimental scripts. Cast should be less than 10.

SUSQUEHANNA UNIVERSITY THEATRE, Susquehanna University, Selinsgrove PA 17870. (717)374-9700. Producer: Larry D. Augustine. Play producer. Estab. 1968. Produces 13 plays/year. Produced 1 musical in 1978; plans 1 in 1979. Plays are produced in 1,500-seat auditorium and in a 160-seat theater to a general audience of high school students through senior citizens. Query with synopsis. SASE. Reports in 3 weeks.

THEATER DEPARTMENT BLACKBURN COLLEGE, Carlinville IL 62626. (217)854-3231. Chairman: Tom Anderson. Play producer. Estab. 1970. Produces 5-6 plays/year. Produced 1 musical in 1978; plans 1 in 1979. Plays produced in a college theater. Query with synopsis. SASE.
Recent Productions: *Forum*, *Fantasticks* and *Stop the World*.

THEATER EXPRESS, 4615 Baum Blvd., Pittsburgh PA 15213. (412)621-5454. General Manager: Caren Harder. Artistic Director: William Turner. Play producer. Estab. 1976. Produces 5 plays/year. Produced 4 musicals in 1978. Audience is in "the 25-40 age range, although there is a complete cross-section." Pays $10-50 royalty. Query. SASE. Reports in 3 weeks.
Musicals: "Types which influence the contemporary American sensibility in some new and innovative way." Does not want big production musicals. Cast size: no more than 3 women and 4 men, with minimal number of sets and props.
Recent Productions: *Assassins*, by Charles Gilbert Jr.; *Made by Two*, by Gertrude Stein and William Turner; *The Elephant Man*, by William Turner; and *Hotel for Criminals*, by Richard Foreman and Stanley Silverman.

THEATER 3, 10426 95th St., Edmonton, Alberta, Canada T5H 2C1. (403)426-6870. Artistic Director: Keith Digby. Play producer. Estab. 1970. Produces 6-9 plays/year. Plays are performed in a 250-seat, theater. Payment negotiable. Query. SAE and International Reply Coupons. Reports in 1 month.
Musicals: "Ours is not basically a musical theater. Occasionally a high quality, profile musical is performed. Family orientations are preferred for the Christmas season. Small casts and back-up musicians groups are essential. Simple unit staging is also necessary."

Recent Productions: *Godspell*, by Stephen Schwartz and John Michael Tebelak; *Vanities*, by Jack Heifner (drama); and *A Taste of Honey*, by Shelagh Delaney (drama).

THEATRE ARTS DEPARTMENT OF CARROLL COLLEGE, 100 N. East Ave., Waukesha WI 53186. (444)547-1211. Managing Director: David Molthen. Play producer. Estab. 1896. Produces 3 mainstage and 18 one-act plays/year. Produced 1 mainstage in 1978; plans 1 mainstage and 1 one-act in 1979. Plays are performed in a 250-seat mainstage auditorium with flexible staging and new studio theater with black box staging. Plays to a campus/community Midwestern audience. Pays by contract: straight royalty amount per run plus, if applicable, residency on campus $100-1,200. Query with synopsis. SASE. Reports in 2 weeks.

THEATRE ARTS CORP., Box 2677, Santa Fe NM 87501. General Director: Marianne de Pury-Thompson. Play producer. Estab. 1963. Produces 12 plays/year. "We perform in various spaces around Santa Fe, but our main theater is a tiny little theater which cannot seat more than 50 people. Our other theater seats 200 and has a very large performing area." Pays 10% maximum royalty "payable after the last performance." Submit complete ms and score. SASE. Reports in 2 months.
Musicals: "We are interested in new forms, new music and/or any good musicals. We would be interested in collaborating with the author(s) if we decide to produce the musical. Clear writing of the script and score is the most important element. Often, piano solo arrangement with indications of other instruments helps when readers are not too knowledgeable in musical writing. We don't want any more than eight or so performers or five to six performers per band."
Recent Productions: *Harry and Sylvia*, by Richard Strand (a clown's life); *Lonely's 66*, by Grubb (a garage in Gallup with strange happenings); and *Oompapah*, by de Pury-Grubb-Thompson (a series of songs relating to Santa Fe).

THEATRE DEPARTMENT, Centenary College, Shreveport LA 71104. (318)869-5242. Chairman: Robert R. Boseick. Play producer. Estab. 1955. Produces 6 plays/year. Produced 3 musicals in 1978; plans 3 in 1979. Plays are produced in a 350-seat playhouse to college and community audiences. Submit ms and score. SASE. Reports in 1 month.
Recent Productions: *The Boy Friend, Camelot, Applause* and *Philemon*.

THEATRE FOR YOUNG AMERICA, 7204 W. 80th St., Shawnee Mission KS 66208. Artistic Director: Gene Mackey. Play producer. Estab. 1974. Produces 8 plays/year. For children, preschool to high school. Query with synopsis. SASE. Reports in 1 month.
Musicals: 1-1½ hour productions with small cast oriented to children and high-school youths.
Recent Productions: *Tom Sawyer*, by Mark Twain.

THE THEATRE OF THE BIG BEND, Sul Ross State University, Alpine, Alpine TX 79830. (915)837-3461. Director of Theatre: Chet Jordan. Play producer. Estab. 1947. Produces 6 plays/year. Produced 1 musical in 1978; plans 2 in 1979. Plays are produced for community and tourists to the area in a theater which seats 400 and has a permanent stage shell. Pays $20-150/performance. Query with synopsis. SASE. Reports in 3 weeks.
Musicals: "Generally we seek small-cast musicals (up to 20) and avoid heavy costuming. Our shows should last no more than 2 hours running time. We use a variety of set patterns though we have no way to use drops or change them and have no space for wagons in the permanent shell." No nudity or foul language. "We do not have a large music staff in the summers, but what we do have is of professional quality. Cast should be no larger than 20. The shell is solid with four door entrances and an 8x6 sliding door entrance in the rear. We have two side stage areas and a pit. The lighting system is not very flexible."
Recent Productions: *Godspell*, by Stephen Schwartz (Sunday school lesson); *You're a Good Man, Charlie Brown*, by Clark Gessner; and *Stop the World*, by Bricusse and Newley.
Tips: "Work with both theater and music people; have portions of it presented in a studio situation to check the validity of development; and seek production of the completed work in a theater such as ours."

THEATRE OF THE RIVERSIDE CHURCH, 490 Riverside Dr., New York NY 10027. (212)864-2929. Coordinating Director: David Manion. Play producer. Estab. 1965. Produces 6 plays/year. Plays are produced for black and Hispanic audiences in New Jersey and New York. Pays $125. Submit complete ms, score and tape of songs. Prefers cassette. SASE. Reports in 1-3 months.
Musicals: "All types are accepted, full-evening or one-act. We are very involved with Hispanic and black themes and are specifically searching for an American Indian show. We favor

smaller casts (under ten) and do not want to see sexual overtness or nudity for no purpose."
Recent Productions: *Fixed*, by Robert M. Riley (a beauty parlor in Detroit in the 1930s); *Corral*, by Allan Albert (musical saga of the West); and *A Broadway Musical*, by William F. Brown, Charles Strouse and Lee Adams.
Tips: All submissions should be as brief as possible and include a resume and synopsis.

THEATRE PROFILES' PRODUCTIONS, 4930 Cordell Ave., Bethesda MD 20014. (301)652-7999. Director: Ralph Tabakin. Play producer. Estab. 1971. Produces 15 plays/year. Produced 8 musicals in 1978; plans 10 in 1979. Plays are performed on tour before young audiences sponsored by schools, recreational activities and community groups. Pays 8-12% royalty or $12-25/performance. Query with synopsis. SASE. Reports in 3 weeks.
Musicals: For use in open (no stage) areas (playgrounds, large halls). Minimum costume, just indication of the character; semi-historical and folk-lore type. Cast: 6-8 with roles than can be doubled. No plays requiring major orchestration, music that can't be taped, or material requiring special effects.
Recent Productions: *Long-Live Ice Cream*, by Kathy Herr (all ice-cream disappears); *Always the Queen*, by R. Ralf (young student wanting to be school principal); *Alice, Mr. Oz and Friends*, by R. Ralf (an Oz-type adventure); and *3 Pigs and the Oriental Wolf* and *Let's Go Backstage*, by R. Ralf.
Tips: "Put production to an in-depth reading by same age bracket of potential audience. Each scene/act should have 1 catchy tune and scene of physical activity. Rewrite! Stay away from rehearsals. Get it on stage even if you must change script/lyrics. There's nothing 'holy' about a new piece of material. Don't mother it to death, and get it produced by helping the producer and director 'visualize' it through their eyes."

THEATRE-IN-THE-PARK, 66 Norton St., #45, New Haven CT 06511. (203)624-5989. Producer/Artistic Director: Thom J. Peterson. Play producer. Estab. 1975. Produces 3 plays/year. Plays are produced for outdoor musical comedy theater. Pays $1,500-2,900 for 6-8 performances. Query or submit complete ms and score. SASE.
Musicals: "We produce full-length standard musicals. Generally for our audience the family-type show is the most successful. We don't want to see any rock or nudity."
Recent Productions: *I Do, I Do*, by Schmidt and Jones; *King and I* and *Carousel*, by Rodgers and Hammerstein; *Music Man*, by Meridith Wilson; *Mame*, by Jerry Herman; and *Cabaret*, by Kander and Ebb.

13th STREET THEATRE REPERTORY CO., 50 W. 13th St., New York NY 10011. Managing Director: David Rappoport. Artistic Director: Edith O'Hara. Play producer. Estab. 1970. Produces 20 plays/year. Pays 6% royalty for Off-Broadway productions; does not pay for workshop productions. Submit complete ms, score and cassette or reel-to-reel tape of songs. SASE. Reports in 1-6 months.
Musicals: "Open to anything but prefer small casts, and simple sets, costumes and technical requirements. However, we will do anything if it's good enough. We'd love to see some experimental musicals that work. The writer should keep in mind current producing costs, if he has an expectation of the show moving Off-Broadway. We are the only nonprofit theater in New York dedicated to producing original works for the American musical theater as a primary focus. We do not want musicals on a gay theme, unless they're exceptionally well-done."
Recent Productions: *Boy Meets Boy*, by B. Solly and D. Ward ('30s spoof); *Line*, by I. Horovitz (power); *Joan and the Devil*, by S. Reiter and D. Hyman (Americana satire); and *Movie Buff*, by J. Raniello and H. Taylor ('30s movies).

UNIVERSITY OF ARKANSAS AT PINE BLUFF, Dept. of Speech and Dramatic Arts, Pine Bluff AR 71603. (501)535-6700. Chairperson: H.D. Flowers II. Play producer. Estab. 1970. Produces 6 plays/year. Produced 3 musicals in 1978; plans 3 in 1978, 3 in 1980. "Audience is basically black, but it depends on the show." Pays $0-100/performance. Submit complete ms, score, and tape of songs. SASE. Reports as soon as possible.
Musicals: Uses one-act and full-length musicals and revues. No "choiry" scripts. Accepts "raw scripts."
Recent Productions: *Michael: A King*, by Al Boswell (about Martin Luther King); and *The Clock*, by Emmanuel Robles (drama).

UNIVERSITY OF MAINE AT FORT KENT, Pleasant St., Fort Kent ME 04743. (207)834-3162. Director of Performing Art: Charles Closser. Play producer. Estab. 1975. Produces 5 plays/year. Produced 2 musicals in 1978; plans 2 in 1979. Plays are produced in a

university theater to university and community audience. Pays $300 maximum. Query with synopsis. SASE. Reports in 1 month.
Musicals: We are looking for musicals of 2 hours "for general audience family theater. No strong language, nudity or shows with more than six sets."
Recent Productions: *Pippin*, *Carnival* and *Once Upon a Mattress*.

THE UNIVERSITY OF MICHIGAN PROFESSIONAL THEATRE PROGRAM. The Michigan League, 227 S. Ingalls, Ann Arbor MI 48109. (313)763-5213. General Manager: J. Roland Wilson. Musical theater contest. Estab. 1977. Gives 1 major award each year. $2,000 award for an original full length musical. Submit ms, score and cassette of songs. Does not return unsolicited material. Reports in May of each year.

UNIVERSITY THEATRE, Oregon State University, Corvallis OR 97331. Coordinator, Theatre Arts: C.V. Bennett. Play producer. Estab. 1920. Produces 8 plays/year. Produced 1 musical in 1978. Produces plays in 2 theaters seating 80 and 426 to an audience of faculty, students and townspeople. Pays flat royalty fee of $25-150 and by performance: $25-50 for first performance and $10-35 for each additional performance. Submit complete ms and score. SASE. Reports in 2 weeks.
Recent Productions: include *Stop the World*, by Bricusse and Newley; *Music Man*, by Willson; *Charlie Brown* by Gesner; and *Celebration* by Schmidt and Jones.

CEDRIC VENDYBACK, Brandon University, Brandon, Manitoba, Canada R7A 6A9. (204)728-9520. Professor: C. Vendyback. Play producer. Estab. 1950. Produces 2-6 plays/year. Audience is urban and rural, middle-class, faculty and students. Query with synopsis. SASE. Reports in 1 month.
Musicals: Prefers "one- to three-act; social comment, smallish cast. We also like simple props and staging. Nothing lavish."
Recent Productions: *All My Sons*, by Miller (social conscience); *The Love of Four Colonels*, by Ustinov (good vs evil); and *Getting Married*, by Shaw (social awareness).

WABASH COLLEGE THEATER, Wabash College, Crawfordsville IN 47933. (317)362-0677. Chairman/Theater Department: Dr. Robert Zyromski. Play producer. Estab. "early 1900s." Produces 4 plays/year. "Musicals are produced occasionally as schedule and personnel permit. Audience is small college town and the male student body of the college. We have two theaters: a 370-seat intimate proscenium with lift for stage; and a black box, seating up to 250." Pays standard royalty. Query with synopsis or submit complete ms and score. SASE. Reports as soon as possible.
Music: Any type. Plays require mostly male characters with small- to medium-size orchestra and up to 25-30 in cast.
Recent Productions: *Guys and Dolls*, *Cabaret*, *Fantasticks* and *Canterbury Tales*.

WALDO ASTORIA PLAYHOUSE, 5028 Main, Kansas City MO 64112. Producer: Richard Carothers. Associate Producer: Karen Hennessy. Play producer. Estab. 1972. Produces 12 plays/year. For general audience. Pays negotiable royalty. Submit complete ms. SASE. Reports in 1 month.
Musicals: Wants musical comedy. "No special format, just appeal to public taste. Three acts, 40-40-40 maximum, rated G. Do not exceed 15 in cast with minimal orchestra; we have a relatively small stage. Not interested in burlesque."
Recent Productions: *Okahoma*, *Cactus Flower*, and *The Latest Mrs. Adam* (comedies).

WATERLOO COMMUNITY PLAYHOUSE, Box 433, Waterloo IA 50704. (319)235-0367. Managing Director: Charles Stilwill. Play producer. Estab. 1916. Produces 9 plays/year. Produced 2 musicals in 1978; plans 1 in 1979, 1 in 1980. "Our audience prefers solid, wholesome entertainment, nothing too risque or with much strong language. We perform in Hope Martin Theatre, a 368-seat house." Pays $150 maximum/performance. Submit complete ms, score and tape of songs on cassette. SASE. Reports "within six months."
Musicals: "Casts may vary from as few as 6 people to 54."
Recent Productions: *My Fair Lady*, *Annie Get Your Gun*, *A Funny Thing Happened on the Way to the Forum*, *You're A Good Man Charlie Brown*, and *Man of La Mancha*.

WESTERN COLLEGE, 900 Otay Lakes Rd., Chula Vists CA 92010. (714)421-6700. Artistic Director: W. Virchis. Play producer. Estab. 1964. Produces 7 plays/year. Produced 4 musicals in 1977, 5 in 1978. Query with synopsis. SASE. Reports in 3 weeks.

Awards: Outstanding Young Man of America—American College Theatre; Festival Regional Winner *Pippin*—Film Coordinator—Mime Ent.

YORK COLLEGE OF PENNSYLVANIA, Country Club Rd., York PA 17405. Director of Theatre: Richard D. Farrell. Play producer. Estab. 1974. Produces 2-4 plays/year. Plans 1 musical in 1979. Plays are produced in a college theater to a college and community audience. Pays royalty through publishing house. Submit complete ms, score and tape of songs. SASE. Reports in 1 month.
Recent Productions: *Man for All Seasons*, by Robert Bolt; *The Corn is Green*, by Emlyn Williams; *You're a Good Man Charlie Brown*, by Charles Schultz: and *The Veldt*, by Ray Bradbury.

Advertising Agencies

"There is *money* to be made" in the advertising field, according to Blair Advertising's John Brown. "Sixty percent of all retail advertisers use music. And they demand *good* music."

"The work is there," agrees Michael Orton, creative director of Blue Sky Thinking. "Because extravagent budgets are a thing of the past, the independent is in a better position than ever to get involved." Using an independent jingle-writer or composer has more than just an economic advantage, however. Independent songwriters can provide an agency with the versatility and talent an agency needs when preparing a series of campaigns for clients.

"All producers look for talented jinglewriters, and I see a lot of good ideas and concepts coming from independents," says Marc W. Johnson, production director of Vandecar, DePorte & Johnson. The thought is echoed by Kathleen Silvestri of Stauch-Vetromile-Gilmore: "Jingles and compositions are imperative in maintaining and supporting a creative campaign effort, to provide a more powerful impact on the selling effort as a whole."

Composers interested in advertising must realize that "jingles" *per se* are less important than solid compositions. The days of "You'll wonder where the yellow went when you brush your teeth with . . ." have given way to the new era of "You deserve a break today. . . ." "'Jingles' in the old-style reference are not as important as music itself today," says Peter Banning, vice president/creative director of Schindler & Howard Advertising. "Music—either of a timely (e.g., disco beat) nature or perfectly matched to the setting or goals of commercials and ad programs—plays a big role in attracting listeners/viewers and increasing impact and recall." A representative of John Paul Itta, Inc. prefers the word *composer* to *jinglewriter* because " 'jinglewriter' is, to me, an old-fashioned concept and term used in old-fashioned advertising."

This has opened the advertising field to using a variety of musical styles, a trend intensified by a common agency policy of producing variations of commercials to match the styles of the media in which they're broadcast. For example, a deodorant ad to be played on a rock radio station might use the same sell copy, but different background music than an ad to be played on a disco station. Some companies use a clearly identifiable song as a base which is varied from one campaign to another ("Coke adds life" was recorded in rock, C&W and other styles). "From a strong original concept, a truly great jingle writer can prepare all sorts of new re-scores and re-sings of the original melody—*a la* McDonald's," says Tim Loy of the Patton Agency. "No client likes to abandon a good campaign." When submitting a demonstration of your work, therefore, present music in a variety of styles. "Use your imagination when developing material," says Peter Banning. "Music/lyrics could change pace dramatically from attention-getting mood to closing appeal. Perhaps employ a style quite different from bulk of stuff currently being aired."

This call for variety doesn't invite *everything* from composers. You won't place a "song" in the strict sense of the word with an advertising agency. In fact, many agencies complain about composers who don't understand advertising and deluge them with the wrong types of material. "Don't write songs—write jingles," says Chip Miller, media and music director of American Media. "Compose with a market—not your own artistic standards—in mind." A common fault of composers new to the field is "being wrapped up in music inappropriate to the advertising field," says Marc Johnson. "Too often I see a person with talent to write good music not able to transfer that talent into *sell*." And that, above all, is the purpose of advertising.

That's not to say that you can get away with mediocre material. Composers "must avoid the attitude that 'It's just advertising,'" says Steven Hicks, copy director of Advertising & Marketing, Inc. "The people who make a killing in the business are the people who come up with fresh approaches, not tired, formula pablum." Advertising music must sell, yes, but it must do it in the most artistic way possible. It can't come on strong. For example, "Intrusive or blatantly commercial musical sell doesn't work," says Peter Banning.

Intrusive songwriters don't work, either; that is, they don't get work. Be persistent when approaching agencies, but don't be pushy. Politely follow up on all submissions, but don't fume and raise a ruckus if the agency doesn't report back to you within the week. Many agencies keep tapes on file to be prepared when a project suitable to your talents arises. That project may not come up for months.

Also, don't intrude into the client list of an agency you're working with if you feel the agency isn't handling your music properly. "Be careful of pitching an agency client directly," says Walt Harrell, broadcast manager of Freedman, Inc. "Granted, many agencies may be afraid to suggest something, but some have a very good reason for saying 'yes' or 'no' to the efforts of the composer, so don't screw up chances for a sale some time in the future."

Harrell also recommends that you detail your prices to the agency *before* doing any actual work. "Get *all* charges on paper out front," he says. "No surprises." This is especially important considering that price is one of the reasons agencies turn to independents. One pitfall a composer should avoid is

charging too much. On the other hand, "Make sure you don't sell yourself too cheap," says Loren Comitor, executive vice president of Rod/Com Advertising & Marketing. "No one works without you—make sure you're paid well for your talent." You must be certain that your working on a project is profitable for both you *and* the agency.

"Cost is important anywhere," says a spokesperson of one agency, "but more so in a small agency." Small agencies, therefore, are good places to start. "Don't aim too high to start," says Fred Sherwood of Weber, Cohn & Riley. "Establish credentials and get experience on small local work, then go after accounts. Don't oversell when making contacts or claim the ability to produce any kind of 'sound.' Producers believe only what they hear on sample reels."

Producers would like to hear contemporary material on sample reels. For example, some producers note the trend toward the use of "big sound: lots of strings, horns, background vocals and everything under the sun to achieve the 'New York' sound," says Marc Johnson. "Beginning jingle writer/composers must know how to arrange those sounds (or know someone who can do it for them)." Listen carefully to commercial music. Monitor trends. Work up a good demonstration tape of samples (compose some samples of imaginary campaigns if you're just starting out). Submit the tape. Make contacts. And never get discouraged. Remember that "the field is open, and always looking for fresh talent," says Fred Sherwood. "Advertising constantly needs new music."

ACT, 1719 Wyandotte, Kansas City MO 64108. (816)474-5222. Owner: Dolores Gage. Advertising agency. Estab. 1955. Serves retail and financial clients. Uses jingles and background music in commercials. Commissions 2 pieces/year. Payment negotiable. Buys one-time rights.
How to Contract: Query. Prefers cassette. SASE. Reports "as soon as possible."

ADELANTE ADVERTISING, INC., 588 5th Ave., New York NY 10036. (212)869-1470. Vice President: David Krieger. Advertising agency. Estab. 1973. Estab. 1973. Serves soft goods, entertainment, wines, financial, and other consumer products clients. Uses jingles and background music in commercials, demonstration and sales films, and audiovisuals. Pays

$25-3,000/job. "Speculative demos to be determined." Buys all rights.
How to Contact: Submit demo tape of previous work. Prefers 7½ ips reel-to-reel or cassette with 3-15 songs on tape. Does not return unsolicited material. Reports in 2 weeks.
Music: "We are an ethnic advertising agency. Our needs are to fulfill the music needs of the black and Spanish communities to enforce sales via radio and TV. We use R&B, jazz, disco, salsa, merenque, etc."

ADVERTISING, INC., 588 5th Ave., New York NY 10036. (212)869-1470. Vice President: David Krieger. Advertising agency. Estab. 1973. Serves soft goods, entertainment, wines, financial, and other consumer products clients. Uses jingles and background music in commercials, demonstration and sales films, and audiovisuals. Pays $25-3,000/job. "Speculative demos to be determined." Buys all rights.
How to Contact: Submit demo tape of previous work. Prefers 7½ ips reel-to-reel or cassette with 3-15 songs on demo. Does not return unsolicited material. Reports in 2 weeks.
Music: "We are an ethnic advertising agency. Our needs are to fulfill the music needs of the black and Spanish communities to enforce sales via radio and TV. We use R&B, jazz, disco, salsa, merengue, etc."

ADVERTISING & MARKETING, INC., 1 LeFleur's Square, Box 873, Jackson MS 39205. (601)981-8881. Copy Director: Steven Hicks. Advertising agency. Estab. 1975. Serves financial, service and package goods clients. Uses jingles and scores in broadcast commercials. Commissions 10-15 pieces/year. Pays $1,000-15,000/job. Prefers to buy all rights, but will negotiate for top quality work.
How to Contact: Submit demo tape of previous work. Prefers 7½ ips reel-to-reel with 5-15 songs on demo. "Where possible, identify cost of production for each piece of music on reel." Does not return unsolicited material.
Music: Both long-term corporate jingles and short-term music for single campaigns. Adamantly opposed to "re-treads."
Tips: "Avoid condescension; we may be in Jackson, Mississippi, but we know what's good and what isn't. We have used major national sources in the past, and will in the future."

ADVERTISING CONCEPTS, INC., 1221 Baltimore, Kansas City MO 64105. Copywriter: Selma Stuck. Advertising agency. Estab. 1974. Serves retail clients. Uses jingles and background music in commercials. Commissions 1 piece/year. Payment negotiable. Buys one-time rights.
How to Contact: Query. Prefers cassette with 2-10 songs on demo. SASE. Reports in 2 weeks.
Music: MOR with popular appeal.
Tips: "We don't purchase much material. However, tapes are kept on file and, if a client wants to use music, we would go to those files and perhaps call someone who had submitted material."

ALLVINE ADVERTISING ASSOCIATES, Suite 516, Security National Bank Bldg., Kansas City KS 66101. (913)281-0222. President: Jon Phelps. Advertising agency. Estab. 1964. Primarily serves financial clients. Uses jingles and background music in commercials. Commissions 3-5 pieces/year. Pays $500-4,000/job. Buys all rights.
How to Contact: Submit demo tape of previous work. Prefers cassette with 5 songs minimum on tape. "Include statement of what the songwriter is available to do, whether he needs outside lyrics, etc. Material is kept on file." SASE. Reports in 2 weeks.

ALPINE ADVERTISING, INC., 2244 Grand Ave., Box 30895, Billings MT 59107. (406)652-1630. President: James F. Preste. Advertising agency. Estab. 1973. Serves financial, automotive and food clients. Uses jingles. Commissions 20 pieces/year. Pays $650-3,500/job. Buys all rights.
How to Contact: Submit demo tape of previous work. Prefers 7½ ips reel-to-reel with 5-12 songs on demo. Does not return unsolicited material. Reports in 1 month.

ALPINE ADVERTISING, INC., 311 Haggerty Lane, Bozeman MT 59715. (406)586-4931. President: James F. Preste. Advertising agency. Estab. 1973. Serves automotive, dairy, industrial, food and financial clients. Uses jingles. Commissions 20 pieces/year. Pays $650-3,500/job. Buys all rights.
How to Contact: Submit demo tape of previous work. Prefers 7½ ips reel-to-reel with 6-12 songs on demo. Does not return unsolicited material. Reports in 1 month.
Music: Needs music for financial, food, automotive and industrial purposes. Musician will "formulate jingle from established concept from agency."

AMERICAN MEDIA, INC., 29 Park Ave., Rutherford NJ 07070. (201)438-3055. Vice President/Media & Music Director: Chip Miller. Advertising Director: Hans Boyesen. Advertising agency. Estab. 1974. Serves industrial, pharmaceutical, medical, consumer and land development clients. Uses jingles, background music for commercials and films. Commissions 20 pieces/year. Pays $45 minimum/hour. Buys all rights.
How to Contact: Query with resume or submit demo tape of previous work. Prefers 7½ ips reel-to-reel with 3-6 songs on demo. "Send lyric sheets, when applicable." SASE. Reports in 3 weeks.
Music: Needs jingles ("catchy, good solid lyrics; contemporary, folk- or rock-oriented, with hooks"); and film and commercial scoring (dramatic or lightly orchestrated arrangements). Avoid "overproduction, pretentiousness and slickness."
Tips: "Don't write songs, write jingles. Compose with a market in mind not your own artistic standards."

AMVID COMMUNICATIONS SERVICES, INC., 2100 Sepulveda Blvd., Manhattan Beach CA 90266. (213)545-6691. Production Manager: Bob Chick. Producer: Florence L. Dann. Estab. 1974. Uses services of music houses for background music. Pays by the job.
How to Contact: Query with resume of credits. Prefers 7½ ips reel-to-reel. Does not return unsolicited material.
Music: Background music written to convey specific moods.

ANDERSON & PARTNERS, INC., 1015 Chestnut St., 5th Floor, Philadelphia PA 19107. (215)925-8903. Account Executive: Mark A. Fresh. Advertising agency. Estab. 1976. Serves financial, entertainment and dining clients. Uses jingles. Commissions 2 pieces/year. Pays $100 minimum/job. Rights purchased vary.
How to Contact: Query. Prefers cassette with 3-15 songs on demo. SASE. Reports in 1 month.
Music: Easy listening and MOR.
Tips: "Do not oversell your product."

APPLE DESIGN, 4800 Rainbow St., Suite 102, Shawnee Mission KS 66205. (913)677-5666. Owner: Michael C. Broadway. Advertising agency. Estab. 1976. Serves print media, retail, publishing and industrial clients. Uses jingles and background music in commercials. Pays $250-500/job. Buys one-time rights.
How to Contact: Query. Prefers cassette with 1-5 songs on demo. Tapes are kept on file. SASE. Reports in 1 week.

WARD ARCHER ADVERTISING, 11 S. Orleans, Memphis TN 38103. Writer/Producer: Guy Rose. Advertising agency and public relations firm. Estab. 1952. Serves industrial, consumer and banking clients. Uses jingles. Commissions 4-5 pieces/year. Pays $800-1,200/job. Buys all rights.
How to Contact: Submit demo tape of previous work. Prefers 7½ ips reel-to-reel with 3-5 songs on demo. SASE. Reports in 2 weeks. "No lengthy sales calls, please."

ARH ADVERTISING AND MARKETING, INC., 8686 W. 96th St., Overland Park KS 66212. (913)381-5727. President: Jack Hurley. Advertising agency. Estab. 1976. Serves retail clients. Uses jingles and background music in commercials. Commissions 2-3 pieces/year. Pays on a per-job basis. Buys all rights.
How to Contact: Query or submit demo tape of previous work. Prefers cassette. SASE. Reports in 1 week.
Music: Simple jingles.

ASSOCIATED ADVERTISING AGENCY OF ROANOKE INC., Box 104, 22 W. Luck Ave., Roanoke VA 24002. (703)344-3206. Operations Manager: Jim Webster. Advertising agency. Estab. 1960. Serves financial and industrial clients. Uses jingles. Commissions 4 pieces/year. Pays $750-4,000/job. Buys all rights.
How to Contact: Query. Prefers 7½ ips reel-to-reel with 3-15 songs on demo. SASE. Reports in 1 month.
Music: "We have used all types of music (rock, big band, jazz). Our needs vary with clients and products."
Tips: "Avoid that 'sameness' of sound, especially on the demo tape. Demonstrate variety, not only in types of music, but with lyrics, instrumentation and arrangements. Projects are usually submitted to two or three houses/writers. We usually expect a rough demo (one voice with guitar or piano). A project would be assigned on the basis of this demo. Usually writers are supplied with a theme line, then given a free hand. Studio facilities and quality of talent are as

important in final selection as music and lyrics." ·

AYER/PRITIKIN & GIBBONS, 27 Maiden Lane, San Francisco CA 94108. Creative Director/Vice President: Dick Fenderson. Advertising agency. Estab. 1971. Serves bank, restaurant, consumer and industrial clients. Uses jingles and background music for commercials. Commissions 6 pieces/year. Pays $200 minimum/job. Buys all rights.
How to Contact: Submit demo tape of previous work. Prefers 7½ ips reel-to-reel with 5-12 songs on demo. Does not return unsolicited material. Reports in 1 month.

BALLARD CANNON, INC., 506 2nd W., Box 9787, Seattle WA 98119. (206)284-8800. Vice President/Creative Services: Dick Rosenwald. Advertising agency. Estab. 1950. Serves financial, retail, travel, entertainment/food and insurance clients. Uses jingles and background music for commercials. Commissions 3 pieces/year. Pays $1,000 minimum/job. Rights purchased vary.
How to Contact: Query with resume of credits or submit demo tape of previous work. Prefers 7½ ips reel-to-reel with 4-12 songs on demo. "Include a brief description of involvement in each project, total costs, objectives and use of material." Does not return unsolicited material.
Tips: "Do not try to prepackage jingles. You must approach each one individually to solve specific communication/image needs."

BARRETT-YEHLE, INC., 2727 Main St., Kansas City MO 64108. Creative Director: Dick Hopkins. Advertising agency. Estab. 1961. Serves retail, financial and service clients. Uses jingles and background music in commercials. Commissions 5 pieces/year. Pays $3,000-12,000/job. Rights purchased vary.
How to Contact: Submit demo tape of previous work. Prefers 7½ ips reel-to-reel with 7-10 songs on demo. Does not return unsolicited material. "Barrett-Yehle rarely reports back on material. If the material is good, we keep it on file. If I want to use the writer, I'll call. Otherwise, don't expect a reply."

BATZ-HODGSON-NEUWOEHNER, INC., VFW Bldg., 406 W. 34th St., Kansas City MO 64111. Creative Director: Jim Sheiner. Advertising agency. Estab. 1952. Uses jingles and background music in commercials. Commissions 1 piece/year. Payment arranged through AFTRA. Rights purchased vary.
How to Contact: Submit demo tape of previous work. Prefers 7½ ips reel-to-reel with 7-8 songs on demo. SASE. Reports in 1 week.

BB&W ADVERTISING, 1106 State St., Boise ID 83702. (208)343-2572. Producer: Bob Rudd. Advertising agency. Estab. 1963. Serves corporate, industrial, retail and financial clients. Uses jingles and background music in commercials. Pays $100-4,500/job. Buys all rights.
How to Contact: Submit demo tape of previous work. Prefers 7½ ips reel-to-reel with 5-25 songs on demo. Does not return unsolicited material. "We keep demo tapes on file, and contact songwriters when there is a need for their services."

BBDO WEST, 10960 Wilshire Blvd., Los Angeles CA 90024. (213)879-1673. Creative Director: Don Spector. Advertising agency. Estab. 1895. Uses jingles and background music for commercials. Pays by the job.
How to Contact: Submit demo tape of previous work. Prefers 7½ ips reel-to-reel. SASE.

BEAR ADVERTISING, 1424 N. Highland Ave., Los Angeles CA 90028. (213)466-6464. Vice President: Bruce Bear. Estab. 1960. Serves sporting goods, fast foods and industrial clients. Uses jingles and background music in commercials. Pays by the job.
How to Contact: Submit demo tape of previous work. Prefers cassette. SASE. Reports "as soon as possible."
Music: Needs vary.

BELL OF THE CAPE ADVERTISING, Box 23, East Dennis MA 02641. (617)385-2334. Vice President: Robert G. Fish. Advertising agency. Estab. 1972. Serves attractions, financial, insurance, light industry, cable TV and restaurant clients. Uses jingles and background music for commercials. Commissions 3 pieces/year. Pays $300 minimum/job. "We purchase only when the client accepts." Buys all rights.
How to Contact: Submit demo tape of previous work. Prefers 7½ ips reel-to-reel with 5-15 songs on demo. SASE. Reports in 2 weeks.
Music: "We work with jingles and one-shot or full series music backgrounds. Persons willing to work on spec are most valuable to us. We deal with a medium market and most clients prefer

specs. Closings are better following such specs."

BENSON/RATHKE & ASSOCIATES, INC., Suite 307, 810 E. State St., Rockford IL 61104. (815)963-5373. Broadcast Director: Webb Kerns. Advertising agency. Estab. 1972. Serves industrial, financial, retail and national consumer clients. Uses jingles and background music for commercials and industrial films. Commissions 8 pieces/year. Pays $500-2,200/job. Buys all rights.
How to Contact: Submit demo tape of previous work. Prefers 7½ ips reel-to-reel or cassette. SASE. Reports in 1 week.
Music: "We have a continuing need for new jingle packages, primarily, and we occasionally have a need for film music."
Tips: Have a wide variety of music samples. Also, "have the common sense to pay close attention to what the client and/or agency wants, yet also have the courage to deviate from those guidelines when there are compelling, creative reasons to do so."

BERGER, STONE & RATNER, INC., 666 5th Ave., New York NY 10019. President: Joseph Stone. Advertising agency. Estab. 1962. Serves automobile, bank, jewelry, optical, corporate financial and institutional clients. Uses jingles and background music for commercials. Commissions 10 pieces/year. Pays $1,000-4,000/job. "We mainly buy orchestration and production of commercials we write." Buys all rights.
How to Contact: Query with resume. Prefers reel-to-reel or cassette, or videotape or 16mm film. Does not return unsolicited material. "Never reports, unless interested in the material."
Tips: "Realize that jingles are advertising; they must fill marketing needs within marketing plans. Learn what makes advertising work, and write that kind of material into the jingle."

BERNARD & CO., 605 E. Algonquin Rd., Suite 410, Arlington Heights IL 60005. (312)593-8131. Account Executive: Timothy Daro. Advertising agency. Estab. 1976. Serves industrial clients. Uses soundtracks for films. Commissions 2-3 pieces/year. Pays $250 minimum/job. Buys one-time rights.
How to Contact: Query. Prefers cassette with 1-3 songs on demo. SASE. Reports in 1 week.
Music: "We're looking for distinctive background music for occasional use."

BERNSTEIN, REIN & BOASBERG, 800 W. 47th St., Kansas City MO 64112. (816)756-0640. Creative Director: Jeff Bremser. Advertising agency. Estab. 1964. Uses jingles and background music in commercials. Commissions 10-20 pieces/year. Pays $15,000 maximum/job. "We buy complete production, not just songs."
How to Contact: Submit demo tape of previous work. Prefers reel-to-reel with 5 songs minimum on tape. SASE. "We keep tapes on file; we do not report."
Music: "All styles for use as jingles and commercial scores."

BLAIR ADVERTISING, INC., subsidiary of BBDO International, 96 College Ave., Rochester NY 14607. (716)473-0440. Copy Chief: John R. Brown. Advertising agency. Estab. 1960. Serves financial, industrial and consumer clients. Uses jingles, background music for commercials and music for sales meeting presentations. Commissions 10 pieces/year. Pays $1,000-10,000/job. Buys all rights.
How to Contact: Query. Prefers 7½ ips reel-to-reel with 5-20 songs on demo. Does not return unsolicited material.
Music: "We need every type. Often, lyrics will be supplied. We're seriously interested in hearing from good production sources. We have at hand some of the world's best working for us, but we're always ready to listen to fresh, new ideas."

BLUE SKY THINKING, Box 24510, Los Angeles CA 90024. Creative Director: Michael Orton. Advertising agency and public relations firm. Estab. 1972. Serves small business clients, along with some motion picture accounts. Uses jingles, background music for commercials and motion picture scores. Pays $25/hour or $200 minimum/job. Buys all rights or one-time rights.
How to Contact: Submit demo tape of previous work. Prefers cassette with 3 songs on demo. "Submit credentials/references/resume with tape; other queries will not be reviewed." Does not return unsolicited material.
Music: Needs "contemporary material for audiovisual presentations, plus soundtracks for commercials, radio/TV and film."
Tips: "We are an extremely small operation with three or four projects a year. Our people are energetic, and remain so after working with us."

JOHN BORDEN ADVERTISING AGENCY, 5841 73rd Ave. N., #102, Brooklyn Park MN

55429. (612)566-4515, 227-8345. Owner/Account Executive: John Borden. Estab. 1955. Serves industrial, financial, medical, insurance and food manufacturing clients. Uses jingles. Pays $200-2,000/job. Rights purchased vary.
How to Contact: Submit demo tape of previous work. Prefers cassette. Does not return unsolicited material. Reports in 1 month.

BROCHURES, INC., 9104 Bond St., Shawnee Mission KS 66214. President: Larry Owark. Advertising agency. Estab. 1973. Serves all types of clients. Uses jingles and background music in commercials. Payment negotiable. Buys all rights.
How to Contact: Query. Prefers cassette with 2 songs minimum on demo. SASE. Reports "as soon as possible."

BRUCE-GREEN ADVERTISING, #3 Felton Place, Box 940, Bloomington IL 61701. (309)827-8081. Media Supervisor: Becki Hart Engle. Advertising agency. Estab. 1966. Serves consumer, industrial and agricultural clients. Uses jingles and background music for commercials. Pays $100 minimum/job. Buys all rights.
How to Contact: Query with resume or submit demo tape of previous work. Prefers cassette. SASE. Reports in 1 week.

SAL BUTERA ASSOCIATES ADVERTISING, 1824 Whipple Ave. NW, Canton OH 44708. Broadcast Services Supervisor: Mark Heil. President: Sal Butera. Advertising agency. Estab. 1962. Serves consumer clients. Uses jingles and background music for commercials. Commissions 5 pieces/year. Pays on a per-bid basis. Buys all rights or one-time rights.
How to Contact: Submit demo tape of previous work. Prefers 7½ ips reel-to-reel or cassette with 6-12 songs on demo. Does not return unsolicited material. Reports in 1 month.

CALLAHAN & DAY, INC., Wellington Square, Pittsburgh PA 15235. (412)372-4700. Contact: Bill Baker. President: G.R. Day. Advertising agency. Estab. 1941. Serves financial, consumer product and industrial clients. Uses jingles and background music in commercials. Commissions 12-30 pieces/year. Payment negotiable. Buys all rights.
How to Contact: Submit demo tape of previous work. Prefers 7½ ips reel-to-reel.

CHARLES R. CARR ADVERTISING, 4210 Johnson Dr., Mission KS 66205. (913)384-3492. Creative Director: Jerry Mahlik. President: Charles R. Carr. Advertising agency. Estab. 1975. Serves retail and manufacturing clients. Pays on a per-job basis. Buys all rights.
How to Contact: Arrange personal interview. Prefers cassette with 3 songs minimum on tape. SASE. Reports in 1 week.
Music: Needs "lyrics rather than melody." No overproduction.

CASA ADVERTISING, INC., 1046 Town & Country Rd., Orange CA 92668. (714)835-3377. Vice President/Creative: Rex Couch. Chairman: Ted Knorr. Advertising agency. Estab. 1970. Serves financial, consumer and industrial clients. Uses jingles and background music for commercials. Commission 1-2 pieces/year. Pays $100 minimum/job. Buys all rights.
How to Contact: Query. Prefers cassette with 3-10 songs on demo. SASE. "We're not doing very much now, but we hope to build volume over the next few years."

CHARLES AGENCY INC., 2530 N. Calvert St., Baltimore MD 21218. (301)467-5200. President: Paul Silver. Vice President: Joseph Herman. Advertising agency and public relations firm. Estab. 1972. Serves industrial, entertainment and financial clients. Uses jingles and background music in commercials. Pays by the job. Buys all rights or one-time rights.
How to Contact: Query. Prefers cassette. SASE. Reports in 1 week.

CHIAT/DAY ADVERTISING, 517 S. Olive, Los Angeles CA 90013. (213)622-7454. Vice President/Senior Art Director: Lee Clow. Creative Secretary: Barbara Silbert. Serves stereo equipment, home loan, life insurance, food, beverage and hotel clients. Uses background music in commercials. Commissions 1 piece annually. Pays by the job.
How to Contact: Submit demo tape of previous work. Prefers 7½ ips reel-to-reel. SASE. Reports "as soon as possible."

CHRISTENSON, BARCLAY AND SHAW, INC., 3130 Broadway, Kansas City MO 64111. Account Executive: Bob Shaw. Creative Director: Jim Ragan. Advertising agency. Estab. 1954. Serves industrial clients. Uses jingles and background music in commercials. Commissions 1 piece/year. Pays $300-4,000/job. Buys all rights.
How to Contact: Query. Prefers 7½ ips reel-to-reel with 6-12 songs on demo. SASE.

CLINE, INC., Box 1399, Boise ID 83701. Creative Director: Vernon Melander. Advertising agency. Estab. 1935. Serves industrial and financial clients. Uses jingles and background music for commercials. Commissions 4 pieces/year. Pays $1,000-5,000/job. Buys all rights.
How to Contact: Submit demo tape of previous work. Prefers 7½ ips reel-to-reel.

COADCO, 1412 Knox, Kansas City MO 64116. (816)471-4800. Advertising Director: Ron Juergensen. Advertising agency. Estab. 1955. Serves retail and industrial clients. Uses jingles and background music in commercials. Commissions 2 pieces/year. Payment negotiable. Buys all rights.
How to Contact: Query. Prefers cassette with 6 songs minimum on tape. SASE. Reports in 2 weeks.
Music: "We're the in-house agency for Cook Paint, and most of our needs are for Cook Paint commercials."

COAST TO COAST ADVERTISING, INC., 1500 N. Dale Mabry, Box 22601, Tampa FL 33622. (813)871-4731. Vice President: Charles R. Bisbee Jr. Advertising agency. Estab. 1961. Serves retail clients. Uses jingles. Commissions 3 pieces/year. Pays on a per-job basis. Buys all rights.
How to Contact: Query. Prefers reel-to-reel. SASE. Reports "immediately if material is solicited. If it's unsolicited, I may not report back."

COLE & WEBER, INC., 220 SW Morrison, Portland OR 97204. Writer/Producers: Tom Wiecks, Dave Newman, Rick McQuiston, Dave Youmans. Advertising agency. Estab. 1932. Serves financial, fashion, packaged goods, industrial and consumer electronics clients. Uses jingles. Commissions 4 pieces/year. Pays $1,000-10,000/job. Buys all rights.
How to Contact: Prefers 7½ ips reel-to-reel with 8-20 songs on demo. SASE. Reports in 3 weeks.
Music: "Take theme line written by agency, set it to music; or take 'rough' lyrics written by agency, rewrite lyrics as suitable and set to music. Avoid putting together a reel with little pieces of jingles. We prefer each jingle in its entirety. We look for exceptionally good melodies, tight production, and good matching of lyrics to music."

COLLIE & McVOY ADVERTISING, INC., 601 Broadway, Suite 400, Denver CO 80203. Broadcast/Production Director: James R. Withers. Advertising agency. Estab. 1946. Uses jingles and background music for commercials. Commissions 5-10 pieces/year. Pays $1,200-3,500/job. Buys all rights.
How to Contact: Query with resume or submit demo tape of previous work. Prefers 7½ ips reel-to-reel with 3-12 songs on demo. SASE. Reports "immediately if requested; otherwise, they are kept on file."
Music: "Big sound, mostly donuts. Some 'full sing' and contemporary."
Tips: "You should be willing to offer free or inexpensive 'spec' cuts to demo the concept; if not, forget it."

COMMUNICATIONS TEAM, INC., 3875 Heaton Rd., Huntingdon Valley PA 19006. (215)322-9390. President: Charles Tucker. Advertising agency. Estab. 1978. Serves real estate, graphics, casino, perfume, insurance, automobile, paint and varnish manufacturer and hospital clients. Uses jingles. Commissions 6-8 pieces/year. Pays $500-5,000/job. Buys all rights.
How to Contact: Query with resume of credits or submit demo tape of previous work. Prefers cassette with 4-6 songs on demo. SASE. Reports in 1 month.
Music: "We need jingles for our accounts, most of whom are real estate oriented, selling entire communities."

COMMUNICATIONS II, INC., Box 48, 115 W. Lexington, Independence MO 64051. President: Ruth Zimmer. Vice President: Linda Lindell. Advertising agency and public relations firm. Serves industrial, entertainment and financial clients. Uses jingles and background music in commercials. Commissions 5 pieces/year. Pays varying rates/job. Buys one-time rights.
How to Contact: Query with resume. Prefers cassette with 3 songs minimum on tape. SASE. Reports in 2 weeks.
Music: "We're interested in 30- and 60-second spots. Our musical needs vary from C&W to classical."

ROBERT W. CONRADI ADVERTISING, INC., 7777 Bonhomme, Suite 1010, St. Louis MO 63105. Media Director: Donna Vorhies. Account Services: Charlotte Becker. Advertising

agency, public relations firm and marketing firm. Estab. 1966. Serves financial, automotive, retail ladies wear and hotel clients. Uses jingles and background music for commercials. Payment negotiable. Buys all rights.
How to Contact: Submit resume. Prefers cassette with 4-5 songs on demo. SASE. Reports in 1 month.

COONS, SHOTWELL & ASSOCIATES, 1614 W. Riverside Ave., Spokane WA 99201. Advertising agency and public relations firm. Estab. 1959. Serves industrial, retail, media, financial, public utility, medical insurance and automotive clients. Uses jingles and background music for commercials. Commissions 4-8 pieces/year. Pays $1,500-5,000/job. Buys all rights.
How to Contact: Submit demo tape of previous work. Prefers 7½ ips reel-to-reel with 7-15 songs on demo. "The cost of submitted productions would be helpful." Does not return unsolicited material. Reports "immediately, if we have a need."
Tips: "We're not interested in hearing from songwriters *per se*. We usually deal with music houses that are in the business of selling music for radio and TV commercials."

CREATIVE ADVERTISING, 1003 Walnut, Kansas City MO 64106. Purchasing Agent: Rick Philhour. Advertising agency. Serves financial clients. Uses jingles and background music in commercials. No recent commissioned pieces; "we are currently building a file for future use." Pays by the job. Buys all rights.
How to Contact: Query. Prefers cassette with 5-10 songs on demo. SASE. Reports in 3 weeks.

CREATIVE HOUSE ADVERTISING, INC., 24370 Northwestern Hwy., Suite 300, Southfield MI 48075. (313)353-3344. Vice President/Creative Director: Robert G. Washburn. Advertising agency and graphics studio. Estab. 1965. Serves commercial, retail, consumer, industrial and financial clients. Uses jingles and background music for radio and TV commercials. Commissions 2 pieces/year. Pays $1,500-7,000/job. Buys all rights.
How to Contact: Submit demo tape of previous work. Prefers 7½ ips reel-to-reel with 6-12 songs on demo. SASE. Reports in 1 month.
Music: "The type of music we need depends on clients. The range is multi, from contemporary to disco to rock to MOR and traditional."

JOHN CROWE ADVERTISING AGENCY, 1104 S. 2nd St., Springfield IL 62704. (217)528-1076. President: John F. Crowe. Advertising agency. Estab. 1953. Clients include industrial, financial, commercial, aviation, retail, state and federal agencies. Uses jingles and background music in commercials. Commissions 3-6 pieces/year. Pays $500-3,000/job. Buys all rights.
How to Contact: Submit demo tape of previous work. Prefers cassette with 2-4 songs on demo. Does not return unsolicited material. Reports in 1 month.

CUMMINGS/McPHERSON/JONES & PORTER, INC., 510 N. Church St., Suite 204, Rockford IL 61103. (815)962-0615. President: W.W. Jones. Advertising agency. Estab. 1925. Serves industrial clients. Uses background music in commercials.

DE MARTINI ASSOCIATES, 414 4th Ave., Haddon Heights NJ 08035. President: Alfred De Martini. Advertising agency. Estab. 1950. Serves industrial, consumer and food clients. Uses jingles and background music for commercials and educational filmstrips. Commissions 12-15 pieces/year. Pays $100-400/job. Buys all rights.
How to Contact: Submit demo tape of previous work. Prefers cassette with 5-10 songs on demo. SASE. Reports in 1 month.
Music: Background music for filmstrips and audiovisual purposes, plus jingles. "Synthesizer music welcome."

DELTA DESIGN GROUP, INC., 518 Central, Greenville MS 38701. (601)335-6148. President: Noel Workman. Advertising agency. Estab. 1969. Serves industrial, financial, agricultural and retail commercial clients. Uses jingles and background music in commercials. Commissions 6 pieces/year. Pays $500-1,500/job. Buys "rights which vary geographically according to client. Some are all rights; others are rights for a specified market only."
How to Contact: Submit demo tape of previous work. Prefers 7½ ips reel-to-reel with 3-6 songs on demo. "Include typed sequence of cuts on tape on the outside of the reel box." SASE. Reports in 2 weeks.
Music: Needs "30- and 60-second jingles for banks, savings and loans, home improvement centers, fertilizer manufacturers, auto dealers, furniture retailers and chambers of commerce."

DELVE COMMUNICATIONS, INC., 5091 Miller Rd., Flint MI 48507. President: James F. McIntosh. Advertising agency. Estab. 1978. Serves industrial and retail clients. Uses jingles and background music in commercials and slide shows. Pays by the job. Buys all rights.
How to Contact: Query with resume of credits or submit demo tape of previous work.

DKG ADVERTISING, INC., 1271 Avenue of the Americas, New York NY 10020. (212)489-7300. Producers: Frank DiSalvo, Vic Wiengast, Mindy Gerber. Advertising agency. Estab. 1963. Uses jingles and background music for commercials. Pays $2,000-5,500/job. Buys all rights.
How to Contact: Submit demo tape of previous work. Prefers 7½ ips reel-to-reel with 1-12 songs on demo. SASE. Reports in 1 week.
Music: Background, underscore for TV commercials.
Tip: "Being too aggressive will turn people off. Show consistent good work, with a successful track record."

THE DREYFUS AGENCY, 10100 Santa Monica Blvd., Los Angeles CA 90067. (213)879-2114. Senior Art Director: Jerry Bonar. Advertising agency. Estab. 1965. Serves audio-products, financial and retail clients. Uses jingles and background music in commercials. Pays by the job.
How to Contact: Submit demo tape of previous work. Prefers cassette. SASE. Reports in 2 weeks.
Music: "Send your best material. Be versatile."

DUNSKY ADVERTISING, LTD., 1640 Albert St., Regina, Saskatchewan, Canada S4P 2S6. Manager: Jean Johnson. Advertising agency and public relations firm. Estab. 1973. Serves governmental, business and consumer clients. Uses jingles and background music in commercials. Commissions 8 pieces/year. Pays $3,000-7,000/job. Buys all rights.
How to Contact: Submit demo tape of previous work. Prefers reel-to-reel with 6-10 songs on demo. "We would like cost of songs submitted and information on the demo breakdown." Does not return unsolicited material.
Music: "Our needs vary. We usually need songs describing special government programs with room for copy or dialogue or testimonials. Usually full instrumental, intro, extro and donut; varying donut lengths. We are looking for warmth, originality, and suitability to client and program."

EASTMAN ADVERTISING AGENCY, 6842 Van Nuys Blvd., Suite 703, Van Nuys CA 91405. (213)787-3120. Account Executive: Frank Hovore. Advertising agency. Estab. 1955. Serves savings and loan clients. Uses jingles and background music for commercials. Commissions 1 piece/year. Pays $1,800 maximum/job. Buys all rights.
How to Contact: Query or submit demo tape of previous work. Prefers 7½ ips reel-to-reel or cassette. SASE. Reports in 2 weeks.
Music: "Big beat or country rock orchestration acceptable for presentation, but we prefer upbeat full orchestral arrangements." No rock. Agency sets slogan line or theme for campaign. "Vocals open and close music beds for announcer/copy inserts."
Tips: Target audience is 35-55, "so find out as much as possible about the needs of our prospects."

EATOUGH ASSOCIATES ADVERTISING, 4700 Bellview St., Kansas City MO 64112. Creative Director: Win Johnston. Advertising agency. Estab. 1973. Serves "almost all types of clients." Uses jingles. Pays $500 minimum/job. Buys all rights.
How to Contact: Query. Prefers cassette. SASE. Reports in 1 month.
Music: Contemporary, C&W and easy listening.

EHRLICH-MANES & ASSOCIATES, 4901 Fairmont Ave., Bethesda MD 20014. (301)657-1800. Creative Director: Bill de Vasher. Advertising agency. Estab. 1968. Serves industrial, financial, multi-chain retail and national associations clients. Uses jingles and background music for commercials. Commissions 5-10 pieces/year. Pays $1,000-6,000/job. Rights purchased vary.
How to Contact: Query with resume or submit demo tape of previous work. Prefers 7½ ips reel-to-reel with 5-25 songs on demo. Does not return unsolicited material. "We will contact with specific jobs in mind."
Music: "Musical identity packages for both radio and TV use. Style and instrumentation will vary depending upon the client and use."
Tips: "Be accurate with all estimates. Don't miss deadlines, and do sensational work."

THOMAS ERWIN & ASSOCIATES, 300 St. Andrews Rd., Saginaw MI 48603. (517)793-6551. Media Director: Scott Richards. Advertising agency. Estab. 1968. Uses jingles. Commissions 2 pieces/year. Pays $500-5,000/job. Buys all rights.
How to Contact: Query. Prefers reel-to-reel or cassette.

EXCLAMATION POINT ADVERTISING, 411 Stapleton Bldg., Billings MT 59101. (406)245-5819. Media Director: Bernie Nelson. President: Janet Cox. Advertising agency. Estab. 1969. Serves financial, real estate, retail clothing and lumber clients. Uses jingles. Pays on a per-job basis. Buys all rights.
How to Contact: Submit demo tape of previous work. Prefers reel-to-reel. Does not return unsolicited material.
Music: 30-second jingles.

FIRST MARKETING GROUP, 912 Baltimore St., Kansas City MO 64105. President: John Strecker. Administrative Assistant: Jean Wolf. Advertising agency and public relations firm. Estab. 1977. Serves financial, hotel, convention and electronics clients. Uses jingles and background music in commercials. Commissions 1-2 pieces/year. Pays on a per-job basis. Buys one-time rights.
How to Contact: Query. Prefers 7½ ips reel-to-reel with 3 songs minimum on demo. "Through the mail only; no calls or personal appearances." SASE. Reports in 1 month.
Music: MOR.

FISHER, WALTKE & HAGEN, 9369 Oliver, #100, St. Louis MO 63132. (314)991-3370. Chairman: Harry N.D. Fisher. Advertising agency and public relations firm. Estab. 1963. Serves industrial, financial and retail clients. Uses jingles and background music for commercials. Commissions 4-6 pieces/year. Pays $1,500-2,500/job. Buys all rights.
How to Contact: Query with resume or submit demo tape of previous work. Prefers reel-to-reel or cassette with 1-3 songs on demo. SASE. Reports in 2 weeks.
Tips: "Don't submit too much; we'll understand from a simple idea whether to orchestrate and how much fill-in of what type is needed. Also, an advance briefing of material needed often helps something get off on the right foot."

FOX CENTURY ADVERTISING AND FOX CENTURY PLAZA RECORDS, 1920 Chestnut St., Philadelphia PA 19103. Director of Music: Perry Stevens. Advertising agency, direct mail service company and recording company. Estab. 1976. Serves direct mail, management consultants, financial investors and music-oriented companies. Uses services of recording companies, publishing companies, singers and lead sheets. Commissions 400 pieces/year. Pays $10-32/job. Buys one-time rights.
How to Contact: Submit demo tape and lyric sheet of previous work. Prefers cassette. SASE. Reports in 2 weeks.
Music: Needs "any type of music or lyrics. Assignments could include lead sheet preparation, singing, and possibly assisting clients with the distribution of their songs."
Tip: "This firm does not work with jingles. We are primarily here to assist and service songwriters who are interested in entering the music/record business."

ALEX T. FRANZ, INC., 35 E. Wacker Dr., Chicago IL 60601. (312)782-9090. Vice President/Creative Director: J.N. Wilson. Advertising agency. Estab. 1943. Serves industrial and bank clients. Uses jingles and background music for commercials. Commissions 2-3 pieces/year. Pays $200-1,000/job. Buys one-time rights.
How to Contact: Submit demo tape of previous work.

FREEDMAN, INC., 118 William Howard Taft Rd., Cincinnati OH 45219. (513)861-4000. Broadcast Manager: Walt Harrell. Advertising agency. Estab. 1959. Clients include retail, financial and some industrial companies. Uses jingles and background music in commercials. Commissions 2 pieces/year. Pays $150 minimum/job. Prefers to buy all or area rights.
How to Contact: Submit demo tape of previous work. Prefers 7½ ips reel-to-reel with "as many songs as possible" on tape. "We may be contacted by phone, by mail or in person." SASE. Reports "as soon as possible."
Music: Uses jingles/songs for radio and television.
Tips: "Be careful of pitching an agency client direct. Granted, many agencies may be afraid to suggest something, but some have a very good reason for saying yes or no to the efforts of the composer, so don't mess up chances for a sale some time in the future. Get *all* charges on paper out front. No surprises."

FREMERMAN-MALCY & ASSOCIATES, INC., 106 W. 14th St., Kansas City MO 64105. Advertising agency. Chairman: Marvin Fremerman. Estab. 1959. Serves retail, financial and public service clients. Uses jingles and background music in commercials. Commissions 5-7 pieces/year. Pays $500-3,800/job. Buys all rights.
How to Contact: Submit demo tape of previous work. Prefers 7½ ips reel-to-reel with 8-10 songs on demo. Does not return unsolicited material; keeps material on file.

FROZEN MUSIC, INC., Suite B, 812 Howard St., San Francisco CA 94103. (415)543-5146. Production Director: Don Goldberg. Media consultants. Estab. 1976. Serves entertainment, industrial and recreational clients. Uses jingles, background music in commercials and theme songs. Commissions 4-5 pieces/year. Pays $100 minimum/job. Buys all rights.
How to Contact: Query with resume. Prefers cassette with 5-15 songs on demo. "Send only high quality tapes, edited for time and content. No splices. We prefer examples which have been used in productions, with a list of credits." Does not return unsolicited material. Reports in 2 weeks.
Music: "Hard/soft rock, jazz, MOR and country rock. Assignments are commercials mostly for the radio market, with some TV and independent movie scoring."

GALLAGHER GROUP, INC., 477 Madison Ave., New York NY 10022. (212)751-6700. President: James Gallagher. Executive Vice President: Nate Rind. Creative Director: Roy McKecknie. Advertising agency. Estab. 1972. Serves automotive, entertainment and other clients. Uses jingles and background music in commercials. Commissions 5-6 pieces/year. Pays $500-2,000/job. Buys all rights.
How to Contact: Query with resume of credits. Prefers 7½ ips reel-to-reel.

GALVIN-FARRIS-ROSS, INC., 2 E. 33rd St., Kansas City MO 64111. (816)531-5300. Creative Director: Gary Mallen. Advertising agency. Estab. 1953. Uses jingles and background music in commercials. Commissions 2-3 pieces/year. Pays on per-job basis. Rights purchased vary.
How to Contact: Query. Prefers reel-to-reel. SASE. Doesn't report back, but does keep a file for future reference and will call a songwriter if agency is interested.

GILLHAM ADVERTISING, 15 E. 1st S., 5th Floor, Desert Plaza, Salt Lake City UT 84111. (801)328-0281. Producers: Bob Parchman, Verlene Kelsey. Advertising agency. Estab. 1911. Serves financial, real estate, fast food, tourist and automobile dealer clients. Uses jingles and background music for commercials. Commissions 4-6 pieces/year. Payment negotiable. Buys all rights.
How to Contact: Submit demo tape of previous work. Prefers 7½ ips reel-to-reel with 6-12 songs on demo. Does not return unsolicited material. "We like to know who is available to do what, but please don't call and bug us twice a month. We're happy to meet people and review their work, but we don't like being hounded. An occasional (semiannual) contact is enough. If we like your work, we'll call you."
Music: "Financial jingles are our largest market."
Tips: "Keep us up-to-date on your work with occasional demo tapes and inquiries about our needs. You might also send us demos when you know it's a product we're heavy in."

GILPIN, PEYTON & PIERCE, INC., Box 13129, Orlando FL 32809. TV/Radio Producer: Michael P. Doyle. Advertising agency and public relations firm. Estab. 1960. Uses jingles and background music for commercials. Pays $1,000 minimum/job. Buys all rights.
How to Contact: Submit demo tape of previous work. Prefers 7½ ips reel-to-reel.

GOLDEN QUILL, Drawer 444, Executive Plaza, Nokomis FL 33555. (813)488-9999. Vice President: Charles Buchanan. Advertising agency and public relations firm. Estab. 1928. Serves various commercial clients. Commissions "over 100" pieces/year. Pays a "flat fee and/or royalty." Rights purchased vary.
How to Contact: Query. Prefers cassette. "Suggestions sent by letter are given first and full consideration." SASE. Reports in 2 weeks.

GOODWIN, DANNENBAUM, LITMAN & WINGFIELD, INC., 7676 Woodway, Houston TX 77063. (713)977-7676. Creative Director: Jack Douglas. Advertising agency. Estab. 1938. Serves multi-market, retail, financial, real estate and food products clients. Uses jingles and background music for commercials and audiovisual presentations. Commissions 20 pieces/year. Pays $2,500-5,000/job. Buys commercial use rights.
How to Contact: Submit demo tape of previous work. Prefers 7½ ips reel-to-reel with 10-20 songs on demo. SASE. Reports in 1 week.

Music: "We want music that enhances the selling message or image building efforts for our clients. Send proof of performance on tape, showing how you helped solve a marketing problem with your music. Send costs."

GRIFFITH & SOMERS ADVERTISING AGENCY, LTD., 330 Frances Bldg., Suite 206, Sioux City IA 51101. (712)277-3343. President: Margaret Holtze. Advertising agency. Estab. 1966. Uses jingles. Commissions 4 pieces/year. Pays $700-5,000/job. Buys all rights.
How to Contact: Submit demo tape of previous work. Prefers reel-to-reel or cassette with 3-5 songs on demo. SASE. Reporting time varies.
Music: 30- to 60-second jingles.

GROUP TWO ADVERTISING, 2002 Ludlow St., Philadelphia PA 19103. (215)561-2200. Broadcast Director: Marian V. Marchese. Advertising agency. Estab. 1970. Serves industrial, entertainment, financial, real estate, hotel/motel and retail clients. Uses jingles. Pays $800 minimum/job. Buys one-time rights.
How to Contact: Submit demo tape of previous work. Prefers 7½ ips reel-to-reel or cassette with 5 songs minimum on demo. "We prefer to keep material on file for future reference. We'll contact the person when a job comes up. A price list (no matter how general) is also helpful for us to keep on file."
Music: "Due to the variety of clients we handle, with various budgets, assignments can be of any nature."

ALVIN GUGGENHEIM & ASSOCIATES, INC., 3130 Broadway, Kansas City MO 64111. (816)531-0994. Account Executive: Gloria Drummond. Advertising agency. Estab. 1975. Serves entertainment, industrial and retail clients. Uses jingles. Pays $400 minimum/job. Buys all rights.
How to Contact: Arrange personal interview or submit demo tape of previous work. Prefers cassette with 10 songs minimum on demo. "Please call first to explain your capabilities before sending a tape." SASE. Reports in 2 weeks.
Tips: "Be willing to do demo tapes according to our needs, and have a price list when you first come to see us. Don't come in without an appointment, don't try to anticipate our needs, and don't try to judge our accounts."

GUMPERTZ, BENTLEY & FRIED, 5900 Wilshire Blvd., Los Angeles CA 90036. (213)931-6301. Creative Director: Mikeo Osaki. Art Director: Darryl Shimazu. Advertising agency. Serves stock brokers, visitors' bureau, bank, tape recorder manufacturer and food clients. Uses jingles and background music in commercials. Pays on a per-job basis.
How to Contact: Submit demo tape of previous work. Prefers 7½ ips reel-to-reel or cassette. SASE. Reports "as soon as possible."
Music: Needs vary.

HAINES, WILSON, LUKENS AND GRADY ADVERTISING, INC., Suite 530, MNB Bldg., Muncie IN 47305. (317)284-6375. Radio/TV Director: B. K. Wilson. Advertising agency. Estab. 1959. Serves financial, industrial and consumer clients. Uses jingles. Commissions 4-8 pieces/year. Pays $800-3,800/job. Buys all rights.
How to Contact: Submit demo tape of previous work. Prefers 7½ ips reel-to-reel with 3-10 songs on demo. Sometimes returns unsolicited material. Reports "whenever possible."

THE HARRINGTON GROUP, 5515 Southwyck Blvd., Toledo OH 43614. (419)865-1341. Creative Director: Robert Beach. Advertising agency. Estab. 1965. Serves industrial and consumer clients. Uses jingles, background music in commercials and "sales meeting themes." Commissions 4-6 pieces/year. Pays on a per-job basis. Buys all rights.
How to Contact: Submit demo tape of previous work. Prefers cassette. Does not return unsolicited material; "we would like to keep it on file." Reports in 2 weeks.
Music: "We use commercial jingles for radio and TV, background for slide shows or industrial films, and theme songs and music for sales meetings. We need suppliers in fairly close geographic proximity for a good working relationship. Toledo is a small market, so budgets are small and media residuals are impossible to sell. We need a wide variety of styles and sounds."

CLAUDE HARRISON AND CO., 7 Mountain Ave. SE, Box 2780, Roanoke VA 24001. (703)344-5591. President: Claude Harrison. Advertising agency and public relations firm. Estab. 1948. Serves industrial and financial clients. Uses jingles and background music in commercials. Commissions 6 pieces/year. Pays $500 minimum/job, "depending upon the client's budget. Fee must include scratch track, which must be approved by the client." Buys all rights.

How to Contact: Query. Prefers reel-to-reel. SASE. Reporting time "depends upon decision by client."

HEPWORTH ADVERTISING CO., 3403 McKinney Ave., Dallas TX 75204. (214)526-7785. President: S.W. Hepworth. Advertising agency. Estab. 1952. Serves financial, industrial and food clients. Uses jingles. Pays on a per-job basis. Buys all rights.
How to Contact: Query. Prefers cassette. SASE. Reports in 1 week.

HERMAN ASSOCIATES, 488 Madison Ave., New York NY 10022. Creative Director: Richard Murnak. Advertising agency. Serves industrial, travel, insurance, garment, fashion, automotive and photographic clients. Uses background music for commercials and audiovisual presentations. "To date, we have never purchased original music." Pays $250 minimum/job. Buys one-time rights.
How to Contact: Query with resume of credits. Prefers cassette with 3-6 songs on demo. SASE. Reports in 3 weeks.
Music: Possible assignments related to travel, photography or fashion: "primarily speculative generic music is also of interest. Music influenced by foreign destinations might be needed."
Tips: "Don't over-orchestrate. The simpler, the better. Plan pieces that are adaptable to audiovisuals, not simply commercials."

HOLLAND-WALLACE, 1880 Union National Plaza, Little Rock AR 72207. (501)372-3191. Copy Director: Leonard Stern. Advertising agency. Estab. 1970. Serves appliance and food clients. Uses jingles, background music for commercials and audiovisual accompaniment. Commissions 4-5 pieces/year. Pays $500-5,000/job. Buys all rights.
How to Contact: Query with resume. Prefers reel-to-reel with 5-15 songs on demo. Does not return unsolicited material. Reports in 2 weeks.

HOOD, HOPE & ASSOCIATES, 6440 S. Lewis, Tulsa OK 74136. (918)749-4454. Vice President/Creative Director: B. Bowers. Advertising agency and public relations firm. Estab. 1970. Serves industrial, entertainment and financial clients. Uses jingles, background music in commercials and original tracts for sales films. Commissions 3-4 pieces/year. Pays by the job. Buys all rights.
How to Contact: Submit demo tape of previous work. Prefers 7½ ips reel-to-reel. SASE.

E.T. HOWARD CO., 850 3rd Ave., New York NY 10022. (212)832-2000. Vice President/Creative Director: Leo Fassler. Advertising agency. Estab. 1877. Serves consumer goods clients. Uses jingles and background music in commercials. Commissions 10 pieces/year. Pays on a per-job basis. Buys broadcast or sales meeting use rights.
How to Contact: Query by phone.

INGALLS ASSOCIATION, INC., 857 Boylston St., Boston MA 02116. (617)261-8900. Producer: Ilene Greenberg. Advertising agency. Estab. 1911. Serves retail industrial, financial and retail clients. Commissions 5-10 pieces/year. Pays $7,500 maximum/job. Buys all rights and residuals.
How to Contact: Submit demo tape of previous work, then call. Prefers 7½ ips reel-to-reel with 5-12 songs on demo. SASE.
Music: Needs commercial jingles in all styles.
Tip: "Put together a demo which reflects an ability to write a variety of types of commercial music."

JOHN PAUL ITTA, INC., 680 5th Ave., New York NY 10019. Administrative Assistant: Barbara Klish. Advertising agency. Estab. 1969. Serves package goods clients. Uses jingles and background music for commericals. Commissions 15 pieces/year. Payment negotiable. Rights purchased vary.
How to Contact: Submit demo tape of previous work. Prefers 7½ ips reel-to-reel. Does not return unsolicited material.

JONATHAN ADVERTISING, INC., 866 3rd Ave., New York NY 10013. President: Jonathan Gubin. Advertising agency. Estab. 1974. Serves consumer products clients. Uses jingles and background music for commercials. Commissions 2 pieces/year.

JONES, ANASTASI & MITCHELL, 3715 Poplar St., Erie PA 16508. (814)864-3048. Vice President: Len Tobin. Advertising agency. Estab. 1975. Serves financial, industrial and packaged goods clients. Uses jingles and background music in commercials. Commissions 3-5

pieces/year. Pays minimum $1,800/job. Buys all rights.
How to Contact: Submit demo tape of previous work. Prefers 7½ ips reel-to-reel with 8-24 songs on demo. Does not return unsolicited material. Reports "as job requires."

KEYE/DONNA/PEARLSTEIN, 9440 Santa Monica Blvd., Los Angeles CA 90210. (213)273-9920. Creative Director: Paul Keye. Art Director: Len Zimmelman. Advertising agency. Estab. 1968. Serves financial, fashion, electronics, food and wine clients. Uses jingles and background music in commercials. Pays on a per-job basis.
How to Contact: Submit demo tape of previous work. Prefers 7½ ips reel-to-reel. Does not return unsolicited material. Reports in 1 month.

KEILER & McKINLAY ADVERTISING, 304 Main St., Farmington CT 06032. (203)677-8821. Broadcast Director: Lee Allen Hill. Advertising agency and public relations firm. Estab. 1973. Serves industrial, corporate, financial and consumer clients. Uses jingles and background music for commercials and audiovisual presentations. Pays $500 minimum/job.
How to Contact: Submit demo tape of previous work. Prefers reel-to-reel or cassette with 5-10 songs on demo. SASE. Reports in 1 month.
Music: "The types of music we require vary according to the product or service we are promoting. Versatility, therefore, is extremely important."

KETCHUM, MACLEOD & GROVE, 4 Gateway Center, Pittsburgh PA 15222. (412)456-3700. Assistant Broadcast Manager: Daryl Warner. Creative Director: Raymond Werner. Advertising agency. Estab. 1922. Serves industrial, financial and consumer clients. Uses jingles and background music for commercials. Commissions 15-20 pieces/year. Pays $250-1,200 minimum/job. Buys all rights.
How to Contact: Query with resume of credits or submit demo tape of previous work. Prefers 7½ ips reel-to-reel with 7-15 songs on demo. Does not return unsolicited material.
Music: "We use a wide range of styles with memorable melodies and excellent production. Assignments from us are generally original, specific and with excellent lyrics supplied as a direction."

KIZER & KIZER ADVERTISING/COMMUNICATIONS, 900 NE 63rd St., Oklahoma City OK 73105. (405)840-3321. Associate Creative Director: Bill Landers. President: Dennis Kizer. Advertising agency. Estab. 1971. Serves fast food, food service and financial clients. Uses jingles. Commissions 5 pieces/year. Pays $500-5,000/job. Buys all rights or one-time rights.
How to Contact: Query with resume of credits or submit demo tape of previous work. Prefers 7½ ips reel-to-reel. SASE. Reports in 2 weeks.
Tips: "Don't be too persistent. We'll yell when we're ready."

LANE & HUFF ADVERTISING, 707 Broadway, Suite 1200, San Diego CA 92101. (714)234-5101. Executive Vice President: Robert V. Maywood. Traffic Manager: Peggy Toth. Advertising Agency. Estab. 1962. Serves financial clients. Uses background music for commercials. Commissions 8 pieces/year. Pays $2,500-30,000/job. Buys all rights.
How to Contract: Submit demo tape of previous work. Prefers reel-to-reel with 8 songs on demo. SASE. Reports in 1 month.
Music: Full lyric jingles.

LD&A ADVERTISING CORP., 717 Main St., Batavia IL 60510. (312)879-2000. President: Leo Denz. Advertising agency, public relations firm and audiovisual company. Estab. 1955. Serves consumer and industrial clients. Uses jingles and background music in commercials and audiovisual shows. Payment depends on use. Buys one-time rights or all rights.
How to Contact: Query with resume of credits or submit demo tape of previous work. Prefers cassettes. "Don't mix 'types' on a single cassette; for example, don't put jingles on the same tape as background music." SASE. "We'll keep material on file for client review. We like to let our clients have a hand in choosing talent for their commercials and films. Usually we select three and let them make the final choice."
Music: "Jingles: We will furnish the points to cover and their relative importance. Background: We will furnish the edited film with a description sheet of what the music is to accomplish."

AL PAUL LEFTON CO., 71 Vanderbilt Ave., New York NY 10017. (212)689-7470. Director of Broadcast: Joe Africano. Estab. 1929. Advertising agency. Clients include financial, industrial and consumer products clients. Uses jingles and background music in commercials. Commissions 15 pieces/year. Pays $200 minimum/hour or $200 minimum/job. Buys all rights.

How to Contact: Submit demo tape of previous work. Prefers 7½ ips reel-to-reel with 5 songs minimum on demo. SASE. Reports in 3 weeks.

LESSING-FLYNN ADVERTISING, INC., 3106 Ingersoll, Des Moines IA 50312. (515)274-9271. Creative Director: Joe Rosenberg. Advertising agency. Estab. 1907. Serves industrial, retail, consumer and financial clients. Uses jingles and background music for commercials. Commissions 5-7 pieces/year. Pays $800-3,500/job. Buys all rights.
How to Contact: Submit demo tape of previous work. Prefers 7½ ips reel-to-reel with 5-10 songs on demo. "Send a letter along with the tape and follow up with phone calls." SASE. Reports in 1 week.
Music: "Jingles for use as client identifiers. Some audiovisual backgrounds. Please don't try to sell us jingle 'packages' with our client's name inserted at the end."
Tips: "Don't get hung up on singing the message of the client. Music, not words, should carry the message. No need to try and verbalize the whole package of goods or services in a song."

J. LIPSEY & ASSOCIATES, 430 Continental Bldg., Omaha NE 68102. (402)342-7676. President: Robert Lipsey. Advertising agency. Estab. 1947. Serves retail, industrial and financial clients. Uses jingles and background music in commercials. Commissions 15 pieces/year. Pays $250-3,500/job. Buys all rights.
How to Contact: Submit demo tape of previous work. Prefers 7½ ips reel-to-reel with 10 songs minimum on demo. Does not return unsolicited material. Reports in 2 weeks.

LONDON & ASSOCIATES, 6666 N. Western Ave., Chicago IL 60645. Creative Director: Kaye Britt. Advertising agency. Estab. 1960. Serves retail, consumer products and trade clients. Uses jingles and background music in commercials. Commissions 6 pieces/year. Pays $500-3,000/finished job. Buys all rights.
How to Contact: Submit demo tape of previous work. Prefers 7½ ips reel-to-reel with 6-12 songs on demo. SASE. Reports in 2 weeks.
Music: "We need highly identifiable music/jingles. The type depends on clients. Be willing to work on small budget for spec tape."

LONG, HAYMES & CARR, INC., 2006 S. Hawthorne Rd., Box 5627, Winston-Salem NC 27103. (919)765-3630. Vice President/Creative Director: Bill Kent. Advertising agency. Estab. 1949. Clients cover "broad spectrum: from foods, to hosiery, to banking, to industrial." Uses jingles and background music in commercials and films. Commissions 10-15 pieces/year. Pays on a per-job basis. Buys all rights.
How to Contact: Query with resume of credits. Prefers 7½ ips reel-to-reel. SASE. Reports "as soon as possible."
Music: "Primarily jingles for TV: usually for 30-second spots."

LORD, SULLIVAN & YODER, INC., 196 S. Main St., Marion OH 43302. (614)387-8500. Producer: Neil Pynchon. Advertising agency. Estab. 1965. Serves industrial and consumer clients. Uses jingles and background music for commercials. Commissions 6-10 pieces/year. Pays $3,500-15,000/job. Buys all rights.
How to Contact: Query with resume of credits. Prefers 7½ reel-to-reel with 6-12 songs on demo. SASE. Reports in 2 weeks.
Music: Jingles.
Tips: "Submit fresh, non-jingly ideas. Show an understanding of what commercial music should do. Stress strong enunciation in lyrics. Remember that music can't exist for itself alone, but has to help sell something, and sometimes creative genius—but never musicianship—has to be sacrificed for the sake of the message."

AL MAESCHER ADVERTISING, INC., 230 S. Bemiston, Clayton MO 63105. (314)727-6981. President: Al Maescher. Advertising agency. Estab. 1954. Serves industrial, retail and financial clients. Uses jingles. Pays on a per-job basis. Buys one-time rights, for exclusive use in service area.
How to Contact: Submit demo tape of previous work. Prefers 7½ ips reel-to-reel or cassette.

MAISH ADVERTISING, 280 N. Main, Marion OH 43302. (614)382-1191. Creative Director: John Hoffman. Advertising agency. Estab. 1916. Serves industrial, financial and home building products clients. Uses jingles. Commissions 4-6 pieces/year. Payment negotiable for complete packages, including production. Buys all rights.
How to Contact: Submit demo tape of previous work. Prefers 7½ ips reel-to-reel.

JOHN MALMO ADVERTISING, Commerce Title Bldg., Memphis TN 38103. Copywriters: Robin McCuddy, Greg Jungheim. Advertising agency. Estab. 1968. Serves consumer, industrial and financial clients. Uses jingles. Commissions 4-5 pieces/year. Pays $50-14,000/job. Buys all rights.
How to Contact: Submit demo tape of previous work. Prefers 7½ ips reel-to-reel with 4-10 songs on demo. SASE. Reports in 1 week "if interested."
Music: Needs "music that will suit the personality of a given client, but it's impossible to say what that might be until marketing and research techniques have been employed."
Tips: "Don't call us; we'll call you if we like your reel and can use you."

MANDABACK & SIMMS, INC., 20 N. Wacker Dr., Suite 3620, Chicago IL 60606. (312)236-5333. Creative Director: Anje Berger. Office Manager: Joan M. Graef. Advertising agency. Estab. 1952. Serves industrial, financial and consumer clients. Uses jingles and background music for commercials. Commissions 10 pieces/year. Pays union scale. Rights purchased dependent upon client's needs.
How to Contact: Submit demo tape of previous work. Prefers 7½ ips reel-to-reel with 6 songs minimum on demo. Does not return unsolicited material.
Music: All types for TV, radio and audiovisual presentations.
Tips: "Don't pester us. We'll listen to your tapes and make decisions. Do not tell us you are non-union when we need union talent. Don't assume we don't know the music business."

MAP ADVERTISING AGENCY, INC., 212 W. McDaniel, Box 1836 SSS, Springfield MO 65805. (417)866-2779. Vice President, Creative: Raymond D. Bradshaw. Time Buyer: Jean Cates. Advertising agency. Estab. 1969. Serves financial, food service, automotive and agricultural clients. Uses jingles and background music in commercials. Commissions 4-6 pieces/year. Pays $750-5,000/job. Buys all rights.
How to Contact: Submit demo tape of previous work. Prefers 7½ ips reel-to-reel. SASE. Reports in 1 month.
Music: "Concentrate on that ring of a cash register; it's the most important music the client hears. Winning awards would be great, but it's always secondary to that cash register ring. Try to produce what we (and our tin-eared clients) want, rather than what you as a songwriter want to sell. We're a message-oriented shop, and we rely on musical treatment for client identification only."

MARS ADVERTISING CO., 18470 W. Ten Mile, Southfield MI 48075. (313)559-0300. Creative Director: Marilyn Reese. Advertising agency. Estab. 1972. Serves supermarket and retail clients. Uses jingles. Commissions 4-6 pieces/year. Pays $1,000-1,500/job. Buys all rights.
How to Contact: Arrange personal interview or submit demo tape of previous work. Prefers cassette with 10-25 songs on demo. SASE. Reports in 3 weeks.
Music: "We're constantly looking for retail jingles that have a type of nursery rhythm. Also, we're looking for catchy lyrics that 'turn on the listener' to the supermarket. We're not looking for sophisticated pieces of music."

LYNN MEDBERRY ASSOCIATION, 9229 Sunset Blvd., Los Angeles CA 90069. (213)274-8684. Creative Directors: Terry Galanoy, Dick Hendler. President: Lynn Medberry. Advertising agency. Estab. 1978. Serves wine, food, swimwear, clothing, toiletries, fashion, financial and spa manufacturing clients. Uses jingles and background music in commercials. Pays on a per-job basis.
How to Contact: Submit demo tape of previous work. Prefers 7½ ips or cassette. SASE. Reports "as soon as possible."
Music: Needs vary.

MELDRUM & CAMPBELL ADVERTISING, 1717 E. 9th St., Suite 2121, Cleveland OH 44114. (216)696-3456. Director, Radio/TV: Charles E. Ford Jr. Advertising agency. Estab. 1970. Serves financial, utilities, direct response, car dealers, and industrial clients. Uses jingles, background music in commercials, and song stories. Commissions 1 piece/year. Pays $250-4,000/job. Buys all rights for regional or local use only.
How to Contact: Submit demo tape of previous work. Prefers 7½ ips reel-to-reel with 5-15 songs on demo. SASE. Reports in 2 weeks.
Music: "Includes program themes, commercial instrumental underscoring, song stories. Primarily MOR sound; some country and contemporary."

MEREDITH & BROTHERS, INC., 4819 NW Coves Dr., Kansas City MO 64151. (816)741-6400. President: Dick Halstead. Advertising agency. Estab. 1973. Serves all types of

clients. Uses jingles and background music in commercials. Commissions 2 pieces/year. Pays $600 minimum/job. Buys all rights.
How to Contact: Submit demo tape of previous work. Prefers cassette. SASE.

MINTZ & HORE, INC., 10 Tower Lane, Avon CT 06001. Broadcast Manager: Ms. Leslie Ring. Advertising agency and public relations firm. Estab. 1971. Serves industrial retail, financial, telephone company and entertainment clients. Uses jingles. Commissions 4 pieces/year. Payment depends on client's budget. Buys all rights.
How to Contact: Submit demo tape of previous work. Prefers 7½ ips reel-to-reel with 5-10 songs on demo. "Tape submitted should show a wide vareity of styles." Does not return unsolicited material. Reports "when I have a jingle coming up."
Music: "We give writer the type of feeling that we want, the slogan and, possibly, all the lyrics."
Tips: "Avoid calling me constantly. I'll call when and if I have something."

MITHOFF ADVERTISING, INC., 4105 Rio Bravo, El Paso TX 79902. Producer Radio/TV: Debby Shepard. Advertising agency. Estab. 1936. Serves financial, supermarket and rifle equipment clients. Uses jingles, background music in commercials and soundtracks. Commissions 5-10 pieces/year. Pays $2,000-5,000/job. Buys regional rights or all rights.
How to Contact: Prefers 7½ ips reel-to-reel with 5-15 songs on demo. SASE. Reports in 2 weeks.
Music: "We need development of musical concepts. We usually provide the lyrics."

MOHAWK ADVERTISING CO., 149 4th St. SW, Mason City IA 50401. (515)423-1354. Vice President/Production Manager: Jim Clark. Advertising agency. Estab. 1956. Serves financial and industrial clients, agricultural industries, fast-food restaurants and insurance companies. Uses jingles and background music in commercials. Commissions 4-10 pieces/year. Payment negotiable; supply fee estimate. Prefers to buy one-time rights.
How to Contact: Submit demo tape of previous work. Prefers 7½ ips reel-to-reel or cassette with 5-10 songs on demo. SASE. Reports in 3 weeks.

NEALE ADVERTISING ASSOCIATES, 7060 Hollywood Blvd., Suite 1204, Los Angeles CA 90028. (213)464-4184. President: Ted Neale. Advertising agency. Estab. 1946. Serves financial, manufacturing, mail order and retail clients. Uses jingles and background music in commercials. Pays on a per-job basis. Buys all rights.
How to Contact: Query. Submit demo tape of previous work. Prefers 7½ ips reel-to-reel. Does not return unsolicited material. Reports "as soon as possible."
Music: Needs vary.

BURTON NELSON, INC., 3201 Gillham Plaza, Kansas City MO 64109. Vice President: Burton Nelson III. Advertising agency. Estab. 1962. Serves retail and financial clients. Uses jingles and background music in commercials. Commissions 2 pieces/year. Pays $2,000 maximum/job. Buys all rights.
How to Contact: Submit demo tape of previous work. Prefers cassette. SASE. Reports in 2 weeks.
Music: 30- and 60-second jingles for radio and TV.

NOWAK VOSS ADVERTISING, 214 S. Warren St., Syracuse NY 13202. (315)422-0255. Broadcast Production Director: Marnie Blount. Advertising agency. Estab. 1952. Serves industrial, financial and retail clients. Uses jingles. Commissions 5 pieces/year. Pays $50 minimum/job. Buys all rights.
How to Contact: Query with resume of credits. Prefers cassette with 3 songs minimum on demo. SASE. Reports in 1 month.

PALM AND PATTERSON, INC., Fidelity Bldg., 1940 E. 6th St., Cleveland OH 44114. (216)696-0111. Executive Vice President: Harry Gard Shaffer Jr. Advertising agency. Estab. 1946. Serves industrial, consumer and retail clients. Use jingles and background music in commercials. Commissions 10 pieces/year. Pays $2,500 maximum/job. Buys all rights.
How to Contact: Submit demo tape of previous work. Prefers 7½ ips reel-to-reel or cassette with 5-15 songs on demo. SASE. Reports in 2 weeks.

THE PATTON AGENCY, 1800 N. Central, Phoenix AZ 85004. (602)258-8211. Director, Client Services: Tim Loy. Advertising agency and public relations firm. Estab. 1960. Serves retail, auto, financial and dairy clients. Uses jingles and background music in commercials.

Commissions 5 pieces/year. Pays on a per-job basis or by "applicable charges from house/writer." Buys all rights.
How to Contact: Submit demo tape of previous work. Prefers cassette with 5-10 songs on demo. SASE.
Tips: "Do not send samples of any work in which the lyrics are not totally clear and understandable. From a strong original concept a truly great jingle writer can propose all sorts of new re-scores and re-sings of the original melody, a la McDonald's. No client likes to abandon a good campaign, but, unfortunately, they tire of it before the market as a whole."

PEARSON, CLARKE & SAWYER ADVERTISING & PUBLIC RELATIONS, 5640 S. Florida Ave., Box 5400, Lakeland FL 33803. (813)646-5071. Copywriters: Carolyn Black, Jim Natherson. Advertising agency and public relations firm. Estab. 1963. Serves industrial, financial, fast food, shelter and packaged goods clients. Uses jingles and music for audiovisual presentations. Commissions 1-3 pieces/year. Pays $500-5,000/job. Buys all rights.
How to Contact: Submit demo tape of previous work.

PETZOLD AND ASSOCIATES, INC., 1800 SW 1st Ave., Portland OR 97201. (503)221-1800. Broadcast Producers: Carol Brodsky, Leighton Smith. Vice President: Fred Delkin. Advertising agency. Estab. 1970. Serves fast food chain, real estate, resort and travel clients. Uses jingles and background music in commercials. Commissions 4-6 pieces/year. Pays $1,500 minimum/job. Buys all rights.
How to Contact: Query with resume of credits or submit demo tape of previous work. Prefers 7½ ips reel-to-reel with 6 songs minimum on demo. "Note production costs for each cut on tape." SASE. Reports in 1 month.

PRO/CREATIVES, 25 W. Burda Place, Spring Valley NY 10977. President: David Rapp. Advertising and promotion agency. Estab. 1973. Serves consumer products and services, sports and miscellaneous clients. Uses background music in TV and radio commercials. Payment negotiable.
How to Contact: Query with resume of credits. SASE.

RALEIGH COMMUNICATIONS, INC., 575 Madison Ave., New York NY 10022. (212)371-1934. President: Philip Radin. Advertising agency. Estab. 1977. Serves industrial, entertainment and financial clients. Uses jingles and background music for commercials. Commissions 6 pieces/year. Pays $250 minimum/job. Buys all rights.
How to Contact: Query. Prefers cassette. SASE. Reports in 1 month.
Tips: "Have previous exposure to our clients' requirements."

READ POLAND, INC., 411 Adolphus Tower, Dallas TX 75202. Associates/Account Executives: Howard Adkins, David Dunnigan. Advertising agency. Estab. 1915. Serves political, corporate, public service, retail and trade clients. Uses jingles and background music for commercials. Payment negotiable; "it depends on the job and the client—we usually aim for mid-range prices." Rights purchased vary.
How to Contact: Query with resume; "include information so that sample tapes can be obtained when and if we have a need." Prefers cassette with 30-second to 2-minute songs on demo. SASE. Reports in 1 month.

ROD/COM ADVERTISING & MARKETING, 666 N. Lakeshore Dr., Chicago IL 60611. (312)337-2992. Executive Vice President: Loren Comitor. President: Lawrence A. Rodkin. Advertising agency. Estab. 1968. Serves retail and consumer product clients. Uses jingles. Commissions 300 pieces/year. Pays on a per-job basis. Buys all rights.
How to Contact: Submit demo tape of previous work. Prefers 7½ ips reel-to-reel with 3-5 songs or 6-10 jingles on demo. SASE. Reports in 1 month.
Music: Needs "all types, from disco to marches."
Tips: "Make sure you don't sell yourself too cheap. No one works without you; make sure you're paid well for your talent."

RUBEN-MONTGOMERY & ASSOCIATES, INC., 1812 N. Meridian St., Indianapolis IN 46202. (317)924-6271. Copy Chief: Allan P. Godshall. Advertising agency. Estab. 1950. Uses jingles. Commissions 10-15 pieces/year. Pays $500-1,000/year for demo only. Package payment for final versions needed from demo. Buys all rights.
How to Contact: Submit demo tape of previous work. Prefers 7½ ips reel-to-reel with 10-15 songs on demo. SASE. Reports "as needed."
Music: Needs vary.

SCG ADVERTISING, 6901 W. 63rd St., Overland Park KS 66202. (913)384-4444. Senior Writers/Producers: Scott Nelson, Ken Segall. Advertising agency. Estab. 1975. Serves national and regional consumer clients. Uses jingles and background music in commercials. Commissions 3 pieces/year. Pays $1,000-7,000/job. Buys all rights.
How to Contact: Submit demo tape of previous work. Prefers 7½ ips reel-to-reel with 6-12 songs on demo. "More original materials and less variations on established themes by other composers would be appreciated." SASE. Reports when writer contacts them within 2 weeks.
Music: All styles (rock, folk, C&W, pop, classical, mood, etc.).

SCHINDLER & HOWARD ADVERTISING, INC., Suite 118, 7710 Reading Rd., Cincinnati OH 45237. Vice President/Creative Director: Peter Banning. Advertising agency and public relations firm. Estab. 1955. Serves "60% industrial, with the balance including financial and consumer goods" clients. Uses jingles and background music in commercials. Commissions 2 pieces/year. Pays $350-1,500/job. Buys all rights.
How to Contact: Query or submit demo tape of previous work. Prefers 7½ ips reel-to-reel with 3-7 songs on demo. "Anything but cold calls will be considered. Hype or too much hard sell turns us off. The work can speak for itself." SASE. Reports in 3 weeks.
Music: "Our most recent job using music was a 21-minute 16mm color motion picture on house construction. No lyrics, but original music arranged to suit action. The remainder of jobs in the past 18 months have been 30-second VTR TV spots and 60-second radio spots, all for local airing."
Tips: "If possible, have an idea of our client list, make proposals, even though of a sketchy and speculative nature, for specific accounts. We are not looking for 'free' ideas, but appreciate creative/thoughtful salesmanship. In the demo reel, show how you can work for different client categories, audiences and needs. We prefer to work with composer/songwriter from the beginning. In most instances, we would write the lyrics, or at least inspire them."

ROBERT D. SCHOENBROD, INC., 919 N. Michigan Ave., Chicago IL 60611. (312)944-4774. Vice President: Jerry R. Germaine. Advertising agency. Estab. 1971. Serves all types of clients. Uses jingles and background music in commercials and trade shows. Payment negotiable; "usually music writers have their own schedules." Buys all rights.
How to Contact: Query. Prefers 7½ ips reel-to-reel. "Do not submit unsolicited material."

ANN NOLAN SCOTT ADVERTISING, INC., Suite 1005-06, Frank Nelson Bldg., 205 N. 20th St., Birmingham AL 35203. (205)252-8271. Music Productions Manager: Cheryl Kilpatrick. President: A.N. Scott. Advertising agency and public relations firm. Estab. 1976. Uses jingles and background music in commercials. Payment negotiable. Rights purchased vary.
How to Contact: Submit demo tape of previous work or arrange personal interview. Prefers 7½ ips reel-to-reel or cassette with "8 jingles maximum on one tape; 30 and/or 60 seconds each in length." SASE. Reports in 2 weeks.
Music: C&W and soul.

SHAILER DAVIDOFF ROGERS, INC., Heritage Square, Fairfield CT 06430. (203)255-3425. Broadcast Manager: Barbara Boyd. Advertising agency. Estab. 1967. Serves consumer, financial and food clients. Uses jingles and background music for commercials. Commissions 6-8 pieces/year. Pays $400-4,500/job. Rights purchased vary.
How to Contact: Submit demo tape of previous work. Prefers 7½ ips reel-to-reel with 4 songs on demo. Does not return unsolicited material.

SILTON/TURNER ADVERTISING, 320 Statler Office Bldg., Boston MA 02116. (617)542-9460. President: Ramon H. Silton. Administrative Assistant: Helen C. Beyer. Advertising agency and public relations firm. Estab. 1947. Serves consumer, industrial and financial clients. Uses jingles and background music in commercials. Pays $500-5,000/job. Rights purchased vary.
How to Contact: Query with resume of credits or submit demo tape of previous work. Prefers cassette with 3 songs minimum on demo. SASE. Reports in 3 weeks.

SIMONS ADVERTISING & ASSOCIATES, 29429 Southfield Rd., Southfield MI 48076. Creative Director: Bill Keller. Owner: Steven Simons. Advertising agency. Estab. 1972. Serves retail clients. Uses jingles and background music for commercials. Pays $750 minimum/job. Buys all rights.
How to Contact: Query with resume or submit demo tape of previous work. Prefers 7½ ips reel-to-reel.

SIVE ASSOCIATES, INC., 712 Broadway, Cincinnati OH 45202. (513)421-3000. Contact: Jean Burkhart. Advertising agency. Estab. 1938. Serves consumer and industrial clients. Uses jingles and background music for commercials. Commissions 50 pieces/year. Buys all rights or one-time rights.
How to Contact: Submit demo tape of previous work. Prefers 7½ ips reel-to-reel with 15-20 short segments on tape. SASE. "We don't report back on submitted review materials. The songwriters recontact us."
Tips: "Don't push us too hard. Be straightforward and direct. Play us things that have been sold and are working. Watch the costs. Make buy-outs available. Avoid 'hype' approaches."

SOUND IDEAS, 224 Bellevue Ave., Haddonfield NJ 08033. Owner: Frank Knight. Advertising agency. Estab. 1966. Serves consumer clients. Uses jingles and background music in commercials. Commissions 10 pieces/year. Pays union fees plus $1,000 for jingles. Rights purchased vary.
How to Contact: Submit demo tape of previous work. Prefers 7½ ips reel-to-reel or cassette. Does not return unsolicited material.
Music: Commercial lead-ins, and jingles or related materials concerning banks and financial clients.

SPACE AND TIME, 4638 J.C. Nichols Pkwy., Kansas City MO 64112. (816)931-9955. Owner: Karen Smith. Media buying service. Estab. 1976. Serves retail clients. Uses jingles and background music in commercials. Commissions 3 pieces/year. Pays on a per-job basis. Buys one-time rights.
How to Contact: Submit demo tape of previous work. Prefers cassette with 1-12 songs on demo. SASE.
Music: "Original music that may or may not be adaptable with lyrics."

EDGAR S. SPIZEL ADVERTISING, INC., 1782 Pacific Ave., San Francisco CA 94109. (415)474-5735. President: Edgar S. Spizel. Advertising agency, public relations firm and TV/radio production firm. Estab. 1950. Serves consumer clients "from jeans to symphony orchestras, from new products to political." Uses background music in commercials. Pays $1,500 minimum/job. Buys all rights.
How to Contact: Query. Prefers cassette with 3-5 songs on demo. SASE. Reports in 3 weeks.

STAUCH-VETROMILE-GILMORE, INC., 49 Weybosset St., Providence RI 02903. (401)331-2436. Copywriter: Kathy Silvestri. Advertising, marketing and public relations firm. Estab. 1971. Serves industrial, amusement, financial, retail and consumer clients. Uses jingles and background music for commercials. Payment negotiable. Rights purchased negotiable.
How to Contact: Query with resume, arrange personal interview or submit demo tape of previous work. Prefers cassette with 1-10 songs on demo. SASE. Reports in 2-3 weeks.
Music: "Interested in music for fine jewelry retail spots (romantic, mellow, contemporary-sounding backgrounds with appeal for both youth and adult markets) and amusement spots (snappy, catchy, fun-sounding kiddie-oriented tunes)."

STEPHENSON ADVERTISING AGENCY, INC., 1610 Fourth National Bank Bldg., Tulsa OK 74119. (918)587-1200. Broadcast Director: Tom Twomey. Advertising agency. Estab. 1971. Serves regional and national retail, industrial and institutional clients. Uses jingles and background music in commercials. Commissions 3-10 pieces/year. Pays "per job bid, $500 and up." Buys all rights.
How to Contact: Query with resume or submit demo tape of previous work. Prefers 7½ ips reel-to-reel with 3-7 songs on demo. "Tell what involvement you had with each piece." SASE. Reports in 2 weeks.
Music: Needs jingles and background music that runs 30 and/or 60 seconds for commercials and up to 20 minutes for audiovisual presentations.

STEVENS, INC., 809 Commerce Bldg., Grand Rapids MI 49502. (616)459-8175. Creative Director: Burl Robins. Advertising agency. Estab. 1923. Uses jingles and background music for commercials. Commissions 1-3 pieces/year. Pays $2,000 minimum/job. Buys all rights.
How to Contact: Submit demo tape of previous work. Prefers 7½ ips reel-to-reel with 5 songs on demo. SASE. Reports in 3 weeks.

CHARLES SWEENEY & ASSOCIATES, 600 S. Commonwealth, Los Angeles CA 90005. (213)386-5050. Art Director: Steve Sugarman. Advertising agency. Estab. 1971. Serves jewelry, food, cameras, toys and assorted products clients. Pays by the job.

How to Contact: Submit demo tape of previous work. Prefers 7½ ips .reel-to-reel or cassette with 1-3 songs on demo. "Call Tuesday mornings between 9 and 12." SASE. Reports "as soon as possible."
Music: "All types. It depends upon the assignment."

THOMAS ADVERTISING, Box 17015, Los Angeles CA 90017. (213)651-5991. President: Thomas Waller. Media Buyer: Linda Ward. Advertising agency. Estab. 1973. Serves entertainment and publishing clients. Uses jingles, background music for commercials and movie scores. Commissions 50 pieces/year. Pays $125 minimum/job or 1-2% royalty. Buys all rights.
How to Contact: Submit demo tape of previous work. Prefers cassette with minimum 3 songs on demo. SASE. Reports in 2 weeks.
Music: C&W and MOR.

JERRE R. TODD & ASSOCIATES, 1800 CNB Bldg., Fort Worth TX 76102. Vice President: Greg Regian. Advertising agency and public relations firm. Estab. 1963. Serves financial, oil and gas, and automobile dealership clients. Uses jingles. Commissions 5-6 pieces/year. Pays $1,000-15,000/job. Buys all rights.
How to Contact: Submit demo tape of previous work. Prefers 7½ ips reel-to-reel or cassette. Does not return unsolicited material. "We might hold for future use."
Music: "Needs jingles for financial, car dealers and other clients with assortment of full-sing and donuts in both 30- and 60-second lengths."

CALDWELL VAN RIPER, 1314 N. Meridian, Indianapolis IN 46202. (317)632-6501. Creative Director: John Anthony. Advertising agency and public relations firm. Estab. 1910. Serves industrial, financial and consumer/trade clients. Uses jingles and background music for commercials. Commissions 25 pieces/year. Buys all rights.
How to Contact: Submit demo tape of previous work. Prefers 7½ reel-to-reel. SASE.

VANDECAR, DEPORTE & JOHNSON, 255 Lark St., Albany NY 12210. (518)463-2153. Production Director: Marc W. Johnson. Advertising agency. Estab. 1960. Serves financial, automotive, consumer and other clients. Uses jingles, background music in commercials and filmtracks. Commissions 20 pieces/year. Pays on a per-job basis. Rights purchased vary.
How to Contact: Submit demo tape of previous work. Prefers 7½ ips reel-to-reel with 3 songs minimum on demo. SASE. Reports in 2 weeks.
Music: Jingle work, music tracks, demo work, chart writing, conceptualization and assistance on assignments.
Tips: "Avoid the common fault of being wrapped up into music inappropriate for the advertising field. Too often I see a person with talent to write good music but not able to transfer that talent into selling."

Z.F. VARKONY, INC., 1420 Walnut St., Allentown PA 18102. Director of Public Relations: Tibor T. Egervary. Advertising agency and public relations firm. Estab. 1971. Serves industrial, consumer and entertainment clients. Uses jingles and background music in commercials. Pays $500-1,500/job. Buys all rights.
How to Contact: Submit demo tape of previous work. Prefers 7½ ips reel-to-reel with 5-20 songs on demo. Does not return unsolicited material. Reports "after client contact."
Music: "60- and 30-second beds and 5-second identity spots. Mostly consumer and service jingles, and some specialty work."

WAGNER CORP., 1 Financial Plaza, Hartford CT 06103. (203)278-7675. Copy Supervisor: Wil Bradford. Advertising agency. Estab. 1977. Serves industrial and financial clients. Uses jingles and background music for commercials. Commisssions 6 pieces/year. Pays $600 minimum/job. Buys all rights.
How to Contact: Submit demo tape of previous work. Prefers 7½ ips reel-to-reel with 3-15 songs on demo. SASE. Reports in 1 month.
Music: Needs "upbeat and distinctive" music for a wide variety of assignments, mostly consumer.

WARWICK, WELSH & MILLER, 375 Park Ave., New York NY 10022. (212)751-4700. Broadcast Manager: Don Rann. Advertising agency. Estab. 1939. Serves consumer products clients. Uses jingles and background music for commercials. Commissions 50 pieces/year. Pays $250-7,500/job. Buys all rights.
How to Contact: Submit demo tape of previous work. Prefers 7½ ips reel-to-reel tape, 5-7

minutes long. Does not return unsolicited material.

ERWIN WASEY, 5455 Wilshire Blvd., Los Angeles CA 90036. (213)931-1211. Associate Producer: Ellen Fox. Executive Creative Director: John Wagner. Advertising agency. Estab. 1914. Serves consumer package goods clients. Uses jingles and background music in commercials. Pays by the job.
How to Contact: Submit demo tape of previous work. Prefers 7½ ips reel-to-reel or cassette. SASE. Reports as soon as possible.

WEBER, COHN & RILEY, 444 N. Michigan Ave., Chicago IL 60611. Creative Director: Fred Sherwood. Advertising agency. Estab. 1968. Serves real estate, financial and food clients. Uses jingles and background music for commercials. Commissions 3-5 pieces/year. Pays $1,000 minimum/job. Rights purchased vary.
How to Contact: Submit demo tape of previous work. Prefers 7½ ips reel-to-reel with 3-8 spots on tape. "We listen to and keep a file of all submissions, but generally do not reply unless we have a specific job in mind."
Music: "We expect highly original, tight arrangements that contribute to the overall concept of the commercial. We do not work with songwriters who have little or no previous experience scoring and recording commercials."
Tips: "Don't aim too high to start. Establish credentials and get experience on small local work, then go after bigger accounts. Don't oversell when making contacts or claim the ability to produce any kind of 'sound.' Producers only believe what they hear on sample reels."

WEBSTER & HARRIS ADVERTISING AGENCY, 1313 Broadway, Suite 1, Lubbock TX 79401. (806)747-2588. Account Executive: Doug Hodel. Advertising agency and public relations firm. Estab. 1947. Serves financial, industrial, automobile, pharmaceutical and agricultural clients. Present client list: 40. Uses jingles and background music for commercials. Commissions 5 pieces/year. Pays $1,200 maximum/job. Buys all rights.
How to Contact: Submit demo tape of previous work. Prefers 7½ ips reel-to-reel with 1-10 songs on demo. SASE. Reports in 1 week.
Music: "We need all types of music—C&W, top 40, etc. Before any songwriter could begin working for us, they'd have to know the client inside out, the problems involved and what type of background music/jingles would fit the products. To gain this, they would have to work closely with us and the client."

WESTON ADVERTISING, 176 S. River Rd., Manchester NH 03102. Associate Creative Director: Ted Sink Jr. Advertising agency. Estab. 1949. Uses jingles. Payment negotiable. Buys all rights.
How to Contact: Query. Prefers 7½ ips reel-to-reel with 3-5 songs on demo. SASE. Reports in 1 month.

WILCOX/MYSTROM ADVERTISING, INC., Box 80252, 509 Wilcox Ave., Fairbanks AK 99708. (907)479-4401. President: Brenda Wilcox. Advertising agency. Estab. 1974. Serves retail and industrial clients. Uses jingles. Commissions 5 pieces/year. Pays $600-2,000/job. Buys all Alaskan rights, with option to obtain rights for the other 49 states.
How to Contact: Query. Prefers 7½ ips reel-to-reel with 5 songs minimum on demo. SASE. Reports in 2 weeks.
Music: "Preferably jingles for small clients with low budgets. They should be catchy, and not too upbeat."

WILDRICK & MILLER, INC., 1 Rockefeller Plaza, New York NY 10020. (212)977-8080. President: Donald Wildrick. Vice President: Roy Gorski. Advertising agency. Estab. 1935. Serves industrial clients. Uses background music in commercials. "We have just begun to buy music." Pays on a per-job basis. Buys all rights.
How to Contact: Query. "We do not accept unsolicited material and we neither evaluate it nor or return it."

WORLD WIDE AGENCY, INC., 111 S. Bemiston, Clayton MO 63105. (314)726-5900. Regional Manager: J. Kathleen Cavasher. Creative Director: Shelley Heeley-Smith. Advertising agency. Estab. 1949. "We primarily do personnel recruitment advertising, although we're beginning to branch into institutional and product campaigns." Uses jingles and background music for commercials. Pays "per job, based on AFM scale and recording scale locally, plus rights negotiation." Buys all rights.
How to Contact: Submit demo tape of previous work. Prefers cassette with 2-6 songs on demo.

"Show varied skills, from rhythm section bed to full orchestration, using examples of previously recorded music." SASE. Reports in 1 month.
Music: "We would primarily need identity jingles and background bed for radio and TV."
Tips: Make sure initial estimates are accurate, and that any additional costs are reviewed before they occur. "In addition, most of these projects have a very limited time-span. We often work on tight deadlines and need a fast turnaround production time."

ED YARDANG & ASSOCIATES, 1 Romana Plaza, San Antonio TX 78205. (512)227-8141. Assistant Producer: Katie A. Keller. Advertising agency. Estab. 1972. Uses jingles and background music for commercials. Commissions 10-15 pieces/year. Payment varies with job. Buys all rights.
How to Contact: Query with resume of credits or submit demo tape of previous work. Prefers 7½ ips reel-to-reel or cassette with 2-10 songs on demo. Does not return unsolicited material. Reports in 3 weeks. "If we don't like the material, it is unlikely that we'll report back."
Music: Jingles and instrumentals. "We're especially interested in Latin and Hispanic ethnic style. We like jingles with a lot of liveliness and memorability."
Tips: "We like lyricists and songwriters who are willing to work very closely with us and are sensitive to our needs."

YECK & YECK ADVERTISING, Box 225, Dayton OH 45406. (513)294-4000. Vice President: Tom Tumbusch. Advertising agency. Estab. 1949. Serves retail, industrial and financial clients. Uses jingles and background music in commercials and for audiovisual productions. Commissions 3-5 pieces/year. Pays $800-4,000/job. Buys all rights.
How to Contact: Submit demo tape of previous work. Prefers cassette or 7½ ips reel-to-reel with 6-8 songs on demo. Does not return unsolicited material.
Music: "Types vary. We provide a guideline sheet that specifies the types of products wanted. Don't try to sell me a stock track or rewrite to some other hot jingle in another market."

YOUNG & RUBICAM, SPECIAL MARKETS DIVISION, INC., 100 Park Ave., New York NY 10017. Executive Producer: Roger Brann. Advertising agency. Estab. 1924. Serves industrial, corporate, consumer and entertainment industry clients. Uses jingles, background music in commercials, and music for documentary and industrial films. Commissions 10 pieces/year. Pays $300-10,000/job. Buys all rights.
How to Contact: Query with resume of credits or submit demo tape of previous work. Prefers 7½ ips reel-to-reel with 8-15 songs on demo. "No unsolicited phone calls." Does not return unsolicited material. Reports "as soon as possible."
Music: Uses variety of jingles and mood scoring.

YOUNG & RUBICAM INTERNATIONAL, 1155 Dorchester W., Montreal, Quebec, Canada H3B 3T2. Creative Director: Pierre Dupuis. Advertising agency. Serves "consumer-oriented, mostly packaged goods clients." Uses jingles and background music in commercials and audiovisual presentations. Pays $700-3,000/job "including speculative demo work." Buys all rights.
How to Contact: Submit demo tape of previous work. Prefers 7½ ips reel-to-reel with 5-20 songs on demo. SAE and International Reply Coupons. Reports in 1 week.
Music: Possible assignments include writing lyrics for existing music, translating lyrics from French, writing music for specific radio/TV requirements, or executing an advertising concept using sound.

Audiovisual Firms

The audiovisual field is "wide open to those with considerable talent," says Sid Glenar, vice president of production of Maxfilms. "For those with moderate talent, the going will be difficult indeed. But if the talent is there, the possibilities are unlimited."

Two obstacles face the composer who wants to work in the audiovisual field, making it difficult for all but the extremely talented. The first is the budget cuts facing educational facilities, which are a primary consumer of slide shows, film strips and movies. AV producers are often held to strict budgets, which rarely have large allocations for music. "To be honest," says one producer, "music is not the main thrust of our productions."

Related to budgets is the second obstacle facing songwriters: competition from music libraries, which are collections of canned music. Dozens of firms in this country and hundreds overseas offer thousands of songs in all styles. An AV producer can choose anything in stock, listen to it before committing himself, and pay for only what he uses. Payment is per needle-drop (per song used), ranging from $75-300, and the library takes care of all royalty payments. "Take your place in line, except if your work is excellent and the price is competitive with the libraries," says Larry Randall Vincent, producer/director of Marvin Productions.

Yet, it's this very reliance on music libraries that also works in the freelancer's favor. "There's a real need for fresh material because of the over-reliance on mechanical music," says Jack Gauvitte, producer for Direction Films. Indianer Multi-Media's David Gravel concurs: "Most production music is pre-recorded, but custom work requires original scores.

Gauvitte sees recording costs as the main obstacle to using original music because of the union scale wage that must be paid to musicians. "But, if a songwriter can perform his own music, he greatly improves his chances for a sale. In fact, any way that a songwriter can help keep costs under budget will heighten his sales."

Another way to heighten sales is to remember that audiovisual firms seek versatile songwriters who can compose music for a range of materials ranging from vocational training filmstrips to sales presentations to documentary films. "Submit a tape that would cover a fairly wide scope of musical styles and approaches," advises producer Larry Nicholson.

"Send a *quantity* of *short* samples in the format required," adds Pat Stephenson, manager of creative services of Multimedia Forum Productions. Study the following listings for the tape format preferred by each firm. Additional names and addresses of firms can be found in *Audio Visual Market Place* (R.R. Bowker), though submission details aren't covered. Be sure the tape is leadered and is accompanied by an explanatory letter; if any selection on your demonstration tape has been used in an AV product, point it out.

Above all, keep in mind how your music will eventually be used, and submit appropriate material. In audiovisuals, music is used in the background to maintain interest and set mood. "We don't use 'songs,'" Gauvitte points out. "We use instrumental/orchestral compositions designed to illustrate visual continuity." In fact, one of the most frequent complaints voiced by producers is the submission of songs. "No boss, hit-bound singles," says John Fippin, chief engineer of Magnetic Studios.

Some firms will want to meet you; others frown on personal visits. If you are asked to meet with a producer, make certain you give as good a first impression as your demonstration tape. "No dirty fingernails," one producer grumbles.

When you eventually receive that AV assignment, keep one point foremost in your mind: Music exists to complement the visuals. As one producer points out, "Visual communication is our primary concern; verbal communication is our secondary concern; and the music is strictly icing. In the majority of cases, the music is superfluous, so if a songwriter wants to sell the the AV market, he has to fit our specialized needs, or we're not interested."

ALLISON PRODUCTIONS, INC., The 1833 Kalakaua Bldg., Suite 404, Honolulu HI 96815. (808)955-1000. President: Lee Allison. Estab. 1966. Clients include advertising agencies in Hawaii and Asia, and businesses. Uses services of music houses, songwriters and stock music libraries for background music in commercials and films. Commissions 50-100 pieces/year. Pays $50-2,500/job. Buys one-time rights.

ARZTCO PICTURES, INC., 15 E. 61st St., New York NY 10021. (212)753-1050. President/Producer: Tony Arzt. Estab. 1974. Clients include industry, government and advertising agencies. Uses services of music houses and songwriters for film scores. Commissions 20-50 pieces/year. Pays $150-6000/job, or $25-750 royalty. Buys all rights or one-time rights.
How to Contact: Submit demo tape of previous work. Prefers 7½ ips reel-to-reel or cassette with 6-12 songs on demo. SASE. Reports "immediately, if appropriate for a job on hand."
Music: "We generally prefer small group sound—no large orchestras with too much brass and strings. Good beat and melody are important."

AUDIO VISUAL PRODUCTIONS, INC., 1233 N. Ashland Ave., Chicago IL 60622. (312)276-1400. President: R. Rubel. Estab. 1962. Clients include television, business and industrial firms. Uses services of songwriters for film scores and background music. Pays $200-5,000/job. Buys all rights or one-time rights.
How to Contact: Submit demo tape of previous work. Prefers reel-to-reel or cassette. SASE. Reports in 1 month.
Tips: "Only those writers with the ability and contacts to provide performance, as well as writing, should contact us."

AUDIOVISUAL RESULTS, 334 E. 31st St., Kansas City MO 64108. (816)931-4103. Partner: Rob Runnels. Estab. 1974. Clients include industrial firms. Uses services of songwriters for thematic scores in films and filmstrips. Payment negotiable. Buys all rights.
How to Contact: Query with demo tape of previous work. Prefers reel-to-reel or cassette. Keeps tapes on file.
Music: Broad range of musical styles for industrial, sales training and promotional shows.

AVC CORP. (Jabberwocky), #4 Commercial Blvd., Novoto CA 94947. (415)883-7701. President: Robert D. Lewis. Estab. 1972. Clients include the general educational market, some retail and radio. Uses services of songwritersfor background music. "Occasionally, productions include songs done by various characters in the story (as in *The Wizard of Oz* or *The Hobbit*)." Commissions 5-20 pieces/year. Pays $200-500/job. Buys all rights.
How to Contact: Submit demo tape of previous work. "Contact us if you are interested in composing original music for forthcoming projects. We will then negotiate." Prefers reel-to-reel or cassette with 5-20 songs on the tape. "Contact us *before* sending tape. No unsolicited tapes!" SASE. Reports in 1 month. Free catalog.
Music: "Mostly mood, transition, and general background built around one or two central themes, depending on the story recorded. Music should be composed with single instruments and small groups in mind. No big musical scores!"

BACHNER PRODUCTIONS, INC., 45 W. 45th St., New York NY 10036. (212)354-8760. President: A. Bachner. Estab. 1972. Clients include users of TV film and videotape commercials and industrial and sales training films. Uses services of music houses and songwriters for commercial jingles and background music for TV and in-house use. "Assignments are for music only or music and lyrics for commercials. Background music is scored to film." Commissions 6-10 pieces/year. Pays $750-5,000/job. Buys all rights or one-time rights.

How to Contact: Query with resume of credits. Prefers 7½ or 15 ips reel-to-reel. Does not return unsolicited material. Reports in 1 month.

BARR FILMS, 3490 E. Foothill Blvd., Pasadena CA 91107. (213)793-6153. Producer: Ronald B. Underwood. Estab. 1938. Clients include schools, public libraries, and business and industrial firms. Uses services of songwriters for film scores and background music. Commissions 6-12 pieces/year. Pays "according to the complexity of the job." Rights purchased "depend upon the needs of the job."
How to Contact: Submit demo tape of previous work with letter and resume. Prefers 7½ ips reel-to-reel with 4-15 songs on demo. "The absolute best demo is seeing a film itself, to see how the music works with the picture." SASE. Reports in 1 month. Catalog $1.

BELLE STREET PRODUCTIONS, 3620 Bell St., Kansas City MO 64111. (816)753-4376. Producer: Bill Foard. Chief Engineer: Larry Johnson. Estab. 1975. Clients include business and promotional firms. Uses services of songwriters for music in radio commercials. Commissions 24 pieces/year. Payment negotiable. Rights purchased ·vary.
How to Contact: Arrange personal interview or submit demo tape of previous work. Prefers 7½ ips reel-to-reel or cassette with 4-5 songs on demo. SASE. Reports in 1 week.

BERNING-BURCH PRODUCTIONS, INC., 327 Dauphine St., New Orleans LA 70112. (504)581-2996. Sales Director: Buddy Burch. Estab. 1976. Clients include advertising agencies, industrial firms and corporations. Uses services of music houses and songwriters for background music, TV and radio commercials, international sales films, and safety/training films. Pays on a per-job basis. Buys all rights or one-time rights.
How to Contact: Submit demo tape of previous work or query with resume of credits. Prefers 7½ ips reel-to-reel with 4 songs minimum on tape. SASE. Reports in 1 month.

BORDEN PRODUCTIONS, INC., Great Meadows Rd., Box 520, Concord MA 01742. President: Richard Borden. Estab. 1950. "We're producers of motivational, educational, documentary and television films—emphasis onsports, outdoors, natural history, recreation and wildlife." Uses services of music houses and songwriters for film themes and background music. Commissions 1-2 pieces/year. Pays on a per-job basis. Rights purchased vary.
How to Contact: Query with resume of credits or submit demo tape of previous work. Prefers 7½ or 15 ips reel-to-reel tape illustrating 5-6 moods/styles. "Be aware that we buy very little, but might buy more in the future. The costs of original scores often drive clients away, even though we push for them." SASE. Reports in 2 weeks.
Music: "We have produced three major documentaries on wildlife/environmental subjects with original scores—moody, full orchestral sound. We also need ballads and title themes. Show us a way to produce full sound without 50 sidemen; e.g., be good at double- and triple-tracking. In addition, music that speaks for itself is the best for us."

CALVIN COMMUNICATIONS, INC., 1105 Truman Rd., Kansas City MO 64106. (816)471-7800. Music Director: Bucky Weishaar. Sound Engineer: Richard Stobaugh. Estab. 1930. Clients include industry and commercials. Uses services of music houses and songwriters for background music in films. Pays "union scale." Buys all rights.
How to Contact: Submit demo tape of previous work. Prefers 7½ ips reel-to-reel. "Leave something to let us know where you can be contacted. We file material until the need arises." Does not return unsolicited material.
Music: Needs underscore instrumentals for films and themes.

CINE/COM SERVICES, INC., 639 Wellons Village, Durham NC 27703. Audio Specialist: Ray St. Clair. President: Kent Evans. Estab. 1978. Clients include schools, state government, industry and film producers. Uses services of songwriters and music libraries for background music in films and for film scores. Commissions 3-10 pieces/year. Buys one-time rights. Rates negotiable.
How to Contact: Query with resume of credits or submit demo tape of previous work. Prefers 7½ ips reel-to-reel or cassette with 3-10 songs on demo. "We suggest demo tapes be sent to be kept on file so our clients may hear the types of music done." SASE. Reports in 1 week "unless we can keep it on file."
Music: "We use original, contemporary background music for solo instruments in a 'pop' sound. Most of our clients listen to audition tapes with a specific 'sound' in mind, often solo guitar, flute or other simple instruments."

CLARUS MUSIC, LTD., 340 Bellevue Ave., Yonkers NY 10703. (914)375-0864. President:

Selma Fass. Estab. 1976. Clients include educational and retail markets. Pays standard royalties. Buys all rights.
How to Contact: Query with resume of credits or submit demo tape of previous work. Prefers 7½ ips reel-to-reel or cassette with 3-20 songs on the tape. SASE. Reports in 3 weeks. Free catalog.
Music: Various kinds of music.
Tips: "Submit material for consideration; no assignments until we've communicated and an agreement is made between our company and the writer(s)."

CLEAR LIGHT PRODUCTIONS, INC., Box 391 Newton MA 02158. (617)969-3456. President: Don Andreson. Estab. 1971. Clients include religious organizations, business, and industrial and professional firms. Uses services of songwriters and music libraries for multi-image presentation background music. Commissions 1-10 pieces/year. Pays $100-500/job. Buys all rights or one-time rights.
How to Contact: Submit demo tape of previous work. Prefers cassette with 1-5 songs on demo. Does not return unsolicited material. Reports in 1 month.
Music: Needs contemporary music with lush backgrounds, and simple vocals.

COCONUT GROVE PRODUCTIONS, 3100 Carlisle, #107, Dallas TX 75204. (214)748-2755. Producer: Tim Pugliese. Estab. 1975. Clients include business firms. Uses services of music houses for background music and TV/radio commercials. Commissions 3-4 pieces/year. Pays $500-2,500/job. Buys all rights.
How to Contact: Submit demo tape of previous work with cover letter explaining prices. Prefers 7½ ips reel-to-reel with 5-10 songs on demo. Does not return unsolicited material. Reports "only if we are going to use the person."
Music: Needs "anything from full instrumentals to synthesized music."

COLEMAN FILM ENTERPRISES, INC., 9101 Barton St., Shawnee Mission KS 66214. Vice President Production: Maurice Prather. Estab. 1967. Clients include educational and industrial firms. Occasionally uses services of songwriters for television jingles. Payment negotiable. Buys all rights.
How to Contact: "Query first. Do not send unsolicited material." SASE. Reports in 1 month.

COMMUNICATIONS WORKSHOP, Campbell-Mithun, Inc., 1000 Northstar Center, Minneapolis MN 55402. (612)339-7383. Audio Production Manager: Jim Maloney. Estab. 1933. Clients include advertising agencies, and business and industry. Uses services of in-house composers and stock music libraries for multimedia presentations and demo commercials. Commissions 1-5 pieces/year. Pays $50 minimum/job. Buys all rights.
How to Contact: Submit demo tape of previous work. Prefers 7½ ips reel-to-reel with 5-10 songs on demo. SASE. Reports "when selected." Free catalog.

THE COMMUNICATORS, INC., Pomfret Center CT 06259. (203)928-7766. Vice President: Marcia Ryan. Estab. 1962. Clients include industry (motion pictures, slide shows, filmstrips), educational institutions (filmstrips—grades K-12), and business (strip and slide formats). Uses services of music houses and independent musicians for background and underscoring. Commissions 50 pieces/year. Pays $250-600/motion picture; $50-100/educational training. Buys all rights.
How to Contact: Query by phone or submit demo tape of previous work. Prefers 7½ or 3¾ ips reel-to-reel or cassette with 6-10 songs on demo (per side, if cassette). SASE. Reports in 2 weeks.
Music: Children's: generally 4- 10- minute single instrument; business or industrial: "progress" type orchestrations, varied to 20 minutes.

MARK CRAIG ASSOCIATES, 7062 Paxton Rd., Boardman OH 44512. (216)743-1492 Vice President Production: C. Conroy. Estab. 1963. Clients include business-restaurant chains. Produces education films, industry and safety films, filmstrips, TV spots, travelogues and politicals. Uses services of music houses and songwriters for radio and TV jingles and background music in industrial and educational films. Commissions 12-15 pieces/year. Pays $50 minimum/job or on royalty basis. Usually buys all rights, but "one-time rights for politicals depending on use."
How to Contact: Query. Prefers 7½ ips reel-to-reel or cassette. SASE. Reports in 3 weeks. Free catalog.

CREATIVE PRODUCTIONS, 20 E. 53rd St., New York NY 10022. (212)935-1111. President:

Chuck Kambourian. Estab. 1969. Clients include ad agencies, industry and government. Uses services of music houses for "stock music unless jingles are required." Commissioned "2 pieces in 9 years." Pays on a per-job basis. Buys all rights.

CREATIVE PRODUCTIONS, INC., 221 N. LaSalle, Chicago IL 60601. (312)332-4076. President: Leo Cummins. Estab. 1961. Clients include business and industrial firms. Uses services of music houses and songwriters for background music for films, slide shows and radio/TV spots. Commissions 100 pieces/year. Pays "by needle drop or selection from library, $20-45 each." Rights purchased vary.
How to Contact: Submit demo tape of previous work. Prefers 7½ ips reel-to-reel with 5-10 songs on demo. Does not return unsolicited material. Reports in 2 weeks.
Music: Needs backgrounds for a variety of business, educational and industrial films. "Be wide-ranging in your ability to adapt to the producer's needs and budget."

D4 FILMS STUDIOS, INC., 109 Highland Ave., Needham Heights MA 02194. (617)444-0226. President: Stephen Dephoure. Estab. 1935. Clients include educational, industrial and medical firms, and governmental agencies. Uses services of music houses and songwriters for background music.

DIRECTION FILMS, 1523 Valders Ave. N., Minneapolis MN 55427. (612)544-2367. Producer: Jack Gauvitte. Estab. 1971. Clients include other production firms, and general industry and business firms. Uses services of music houses for films, radio and TV commercials, slide films and live programs. Commissions 300-400 pieces/year. Pays $25-800/job. Buys one-time rights.
How to Contact: Submit demo tape of previous work. Prefers 7½ ips reel-to-reel with 8-20 songs on demo. SASE. Reports in 1 month.
Music: "Film production music (instrumental) of all types, particularly busy 'underscore' and opening and closing titles. Some acid rock and industrial/mechanical material."

DOCUMENTARY PRODUCTIONS, INC., 6087 Sunset Blvd., Hollywood CA 90028. (213)465-7692. Vice President: Wendell C. Stewart. Estab. 1967. Clients include business and industry. Uses services of songwriters for music tracks forhalf-hour motion pictures.

JAN EDEN SOUND SERVICE, 4709 W. 30th St., Indianapolis IN 46222. (317)297-1658. Owner: Jan Eden. Estab. 1952. Clients include display manufacturers, advertising agencies, and commercial and industrial firms. Uses services of songwriters for commercials, jingles and background music. Pays "scale" on a per-job basis. Buys all rights or one-time rights, "as deemed necessary by the job and client."

CHARLES ELMS PRODUCTIONS, INC., 163 Highland Ave., North Tarrytown NY 10591. (914)631-7474. Producer/General Manager: Charles D. Elms. Estab. 1952. Clients include business and industry. Uses services of music houses for background or opening, bridges, closing for film strips, and scores for films. Pays on a per-job basis. Buys one-time rights.
How to Contact: Query with resume of credits. "Do not send material until requested." Reports after client has indicated preference.
Music: "I do not like singing commercials—I use music for mood. Other than opening, closing and bridges the level should be kept so low that you do not realize it is there. I do not produce 'screaming Meemies' commercials!"

ENTERTAINMENT PRODUCTIONS, INC., 1137 2nd St., Suite 210, Santa Monica CA 90403. (213)451-5505. Motion picture production company. President: Edward Coe. Estab. 1975. Clients include distributors/exhibitors. Uses services of music houses and songwriters for background and theme music for films. Commissions/year vary. Pays scale/job. Rights purchased vary.
How to Contact: Query with resume of credits. Prefers reel-to-reel. "Demo records/tapes sent at own risk—nonreturnable." Reports only if interested.
Tips: "Have resume on file."

ENT/GATES FILMS, INC., 200 Chicago St., Buffalo NY 14204. (716)856-3220. Production Manager: John Coniglio. President: J.V. Gates. Estab. 1972. Clients include industrial firms. Uses services of music houses for opening, closing and background music in films. Pays on a per-job basis. Buys all rights.
How to Contact: Query with resume of credits or submit demo tape of previous work. Prefers reel-to-reel. SASE. Reports in 2 weeks. Free catalog.

EQUINOX FILMS, 50 Kearney Rd., Needham MA 02194. Vice President, Music Services: Daniel A. Radler. Marketing Director: Peter Quintiliani. Estab. 1976. Clients include local and federal government, schools, and business and industrial firms. Uses services of music houses and songwriters for film scores and commercials. Pays $25 minimum/job. Buys all rights. **How to Contact:** Submit demo tape of previous work. Prefers 7½ ips reel-to-reel with 3-5 songs on demo. SASE. Reports in 1 week. Free catalog.

F.E.L. PUBLICATIONS, LTD., 1925 Pontius Ave., Los Angeles CA 90025. (213)478-053. Treasurer: James D. Boyd. Estab. 1967. Clients include the religious folk liturgical market. Uses services of songwriters. Commissions 20-50 pieces/year. Pays 4-7% royalty. Buys all rights.
How to Contact: Submit demo tape of previous work. Prefers cassette with 10-15 songs on demo. SASE. Free catalog.
Music: Religious folk hymns and songs.

FILM ASSOCIATES LTD., INC., 1321 N. Meridian St., Executive Suite 210, Indianapolis IN 46202. (317)632-2244. Production Manager: Robert C. Holstein. President: Ed Resener. Estab. 1976. Clients include advertising agencies, the state and federal government and industrial firms. Uses services of music houses and songwriters for film scores and background music. Commissions 30-45 pieces/year. Pays $300 minimum/job. Buys all rights.
How to Contact: Query with resume of credits, arrange personal interview, or submit demo tape of previous work. Prefers 7½ ips reel-to-reel with 10-25 songs on demo. SASE. Reports in 2 weeks. Catalog for #10 SASE.
Music: "The material we use depends on the job requirement. Ninety percent of our scored music is for motion pictures (TV commercials). The other 10% is for background music in industrial films." Most work is for local, regional and national TV spot commercials.

THE FILM WORKS (a division of Patterson & Hall), 1250 Folsom St., San Francisco CA 94103. Vice President: Thomas F. Hall. Estab. 1921. Uses services of independent songwriters for films, audiovisual shows and occasional live shows. Commissions 2 pieces/year. Pays on a per job basis. Buys all rights, unless otherwise specified.
How to Contact: Submit demo tape of previous work. Prefers reel-to-reel or cassette with optional number of songs on demo. SASE.
Music: "Very tight TV spots, 6-10 minute sales films, to a 20-25 minute industrial film."

FOUNTAIN FILMS, 959 N. Seward, Hollywood CA 90038. (213)465-0404. President: Ned Shaheen. Estab. 1969. Clients include theaters and television markets. Uses services of songwriters for scoring films. Payment negotiable. Buys all rights.
How to Contact: Query with resume of credits. Prefers cassette with 4-7 songs on demo. SASE. Reports in 1 month.
Music: Needs "original scores for background vocals; ballads, etc."

FOURNIER FILMCOM, INC., Outer Winthrop Rd., Hallowell ME 04347. President: Paul J. Fournier. Estab. 1970. Clients include federal and state government agencies, business and industry, medical associations, television networks and promotional agencies. Uses services of music houses and songwriters for thematic backgrounds for films, multimedia audiovisual programs and filmstrips. Commissions 5-10 pieces/year. Pays $50 minimum/job. Buys one-time rights.
How to Contact: Query or submit demo tape of previous work. Prefers 7½ ips reel-to-reel or cassette with 1-5 songs on demo. SASE. Reports in 3 weeks.
Music: Needs outdoor themes: scenic; pastoral; environmental; outdoor sports action (skiing, whitewater canoeing); light industrial (lab work, electronic); and heavy industrial (power plant construction).

ROSS GAFFNEY, INC., 21 W. 46th St., New York NY 10036. Vice President: Paul Burggraff. Estab. 1955. Clients include television networks, film companies and government agencies. Uses services of "independent composers" for background music for sound filmstrips and musical scores in films. Pays $300-25,000/job. Buys all rights.
How to Contact: Query with resume of credits. Prefers 15 ips reel-to-reel with 1-4 songs on demo. Does not return unsolicited material.

GANUNG, INC., 6061 W. 3rd St., Los Angeles CA 90036. (213)939-1185. President: Art GaNung. Sound Engineer: Barry Draper. Estab. 1965. Clients include business and industriy. Uses services of music house for background and theme music and lyrics. Commissions 4

pieces/year. Pays $150-500/job. Buys all rights or one-time rights.
How to Contact: Submit demo tape of previous work. Prefers 7½ ips reel-to-reel with 3-5 songs on the tape. SASE. Reports in 1 month.
Music: Background and theme music and lyrics for sales and marketing presentations.

JOHN N. GEKAS FILM PRODUCTIONS, 2305 Bissonnet, Houston TX 77005. (713)528-4965. President: John Gekas. Estab. 1954. Clients include business and industrial firms; "we also consult for other producers and our in-house industrial audiovisual departments." Uses services of songwriters and lab libraries for film scores and background music. Pays on a per-job basis: $1-250/film reel; or a negotiable fee for original scores. Buys all rights or one-time rights.
How to Contact: Query with resume of credits or submit demo tape of previous work. Prefers 7½ ips reel-to-reel or cassette with 3-6 songs on demo. SASE. Reports in 4 weeks.
Music: Needs "custom music appropriate to basic industrial and business film scripts" and "original film scores, as needed. Contact us to determine our needs and check in periodically."

GEORGETOWN STUDIOS, INC., Box 136, Georgetown CT 06829. Production Assistant: Harry D. Buch. Estab. 1973. Clients include educational firms. Uses songwriters and "occasional in-house production" for original scores for filmstrips and 16mm motion pictures Commissions 12 pieces/year. Pays $50 minimum/minute of music. Buys all rights.
How to Contact: Submit demo tape of previous work. Prefers 7½ or 15 ips reel-to-reel with 4-10 minutes of songs on demo. SASE. Reports in 2 weeks.
Music: "Instrumental music played by a small ensemble. No 'pop' or rock; music is generally semi-classical and occasionally folk and light jazz. Typical assignment length: 3-6 minutes. Strict timing cues for dramatic dialogue and screen action."

GOTTABE MUSIC, Box 9073, Chattanooga TN 37412. (615)624-6185. President: W. Stanley Hall Jr. Pays $25 minimum.
How to Contact: Query or submit demo and lead sheet and "letter of explanation as to what I might have to offer Gottabe in the way of new and 'commercial' ideas within the parameters set forth above." SASE. Reports in 1 month.
Music: "We are always interested in novel ideas for concepts (jingles) as well as commercial material."

HERALD HOUSE/INDEPENDENCE PRESS, 3225 S. Nolan Rd., Independence MO 64055. (816)252-5010. Director, Electronic Media Division: Jerry Riegle. Clients include religious markets. Uses services of songwriters for musical backgrounds. Commissions 1 piece/year. Payment negotiable. Buys one-time rights.
How to Contact: Query. Prefers cassette with 3 songs minimum on tape. SASE. Reports in 2 weeks.
Music: "Almost exclusively religious music, gospel and church material."

IMAGE MEDIA, INC., 2930 Irving Ave. S., Minneapolis MN 55408. (612)827-6500. President: A. Michael Rifkin. Estab. 1973. Clients include retail firms, business and industry, and educational services. Uses services of music houses and songwriters for background music for radio/TV commercials and for films and slide presentations. Commissions 4-10 pieces/year. Pays $500 minimum/job. Buys all rights or one-time rights.
How to Contact: Query with resume of credits or submit demo tape of previous work. Prefers cassette. SASE. Reports in 2 weeks.

INDIANER MULTI-MEDIA, 16201 SW 95th Ave., Box 550, Miami FL 33157. (305)235-6132. Vice President Systems: David Gravel. President: Paul Indianer. Estab. 1965. Uses services of music houses and songwriters for background music scored to action. Commissions 40 pieces/year. Pays $50/finished minute. Buys all rights or one-time rights.
How to Contact: Submit demo tape of previous work. Prefers 7½ ips reel-to-reel with 5 songs minimum on tape. SASE. Reports in 3 weeks.

INTERNATIONAL FILM INDUSTRIES, 450 Main St., New Rochelle NY 10801. (914)576-3330. Associate Producer: Wendy Lidell. Estab. 1968. "We produce theatrical feature-length films." Uses services of songwriters for film scores and theme songs. "We score several films annually." Payment negotiable. Rights purchased vary.
How to Contact: Query with resume of credits or submit demo tape of previous work. Prefers cassette with 2-5 songs on demo. SASE. Reports in 6 weeks. "Songwriters should observe the

trade papers for indications of our current projects; e.g., ads, articles and casting notices'."
Music: "Background and/or current popular styles needed—rock, disco, ballads."

JACOBY/STORM PRODUCTIONS, INC., 101 Post Rd. E., Westport CT 06880. Vice President: Doris Storm. Estab. 1965. Clients include schools, publishers, business and industrial firms. Uses services of music houses and songwriters for film scores, background music and an occasional theme song. Commissions 2-3 pieces/year. Payment negotiable. Buys all rights or one-time rights.
How to Contact: Query with resume of credits or submit demo tape of previous work. Prefers 7½ or 15 ips reel-to-reel. SASE. Reports in 2 weeks. "Don't send any material without querying first."
Music: Needs songs and background music for films geared to elementary or high school students; also suitable for industrial and documentary films.

KEN-DEL PRODUCTIONS, INC., 111 Valley Rd., Wilmington DE 19804. (302)655-7488. A&R Director: Shirley Kay. General Manager: Jerry Smith. Estab. 1950. Clients include publishers, schools and industrial firms. Uses services of songwriters for film scores and title music. Pays on a per-job basis. Buys all rights.
How to Contact: Submit demo of previous work. Prefers acetate discs, but will accept tapes. SASE; "however, we prefer to keep tapes on file for possible future use." Reports in 2 weeks.

KEY PRODUCTIONS, INC., Box 2684, Gravois Station, St. Louis MO 63116. President: John E. Schroeder. Estab. 1956. Clients include churches, colleges, church schools, industry and festivals. Uses services of songwriters for stage and educational TV musical dramas, background music for filmstrips, some speculative collaboration for submission to publishers, and regional theatrical productions. Commissions "10 pieces/year, but selects up to 50 songs." Pays $50 minimum/job or by 10% minimum royalty. Buys one-time rights or all rights.
How to Contact: Query with resume of credits or submit demo tape of previous work. "Suggest prior fee scales." Prefers cassette with 3-8 songs on demo. SASE. Reports in 1 month.
Music: "We almost always use religious material; some contemporary Biblical opera; and some gospel, a few pop, blues, folk-rock and occasionally soul."

SANDY KIESEL, 3542 Main St., Kansas City MO 64111. (816)753-1197. President: Sandy Kiesel. Estab. 1975. Clients include educational and industrial firms. Uses services of music houses for background music in films. Pays on a per-job basis. Buys all rights.
How to Contact: Query with resume of credits. "Phone calls are acceptable." Prefers 7½ ips reel-to-reel. SASE. Reports in 2 weeks.

SID KLEINER MUSIC ENTERPRISES, 3701 25th Ave. SW, Naples FL 33999. (813)455-2693 or 455-2696. Managing Director: Sid Kleiner. Estab. 1972. Clients include the music industry. Uses services of songwriters for background music. Pays $20 minimum/job. Buys all rights.
How to Contact: Submit demo tape of previous work. Prefers cassette with 1-4 songs on demo. SASE. Reports in 3 weeks.
Music: "We generally need soft background music, with some special lyrics to fit a particular project."

KOESTER AUDIO-VISUAL PRESENTATIONS, Box 336, Far Hills NJ 07931. (201)766-2143. President: Ralph Koester. Estab. 1972. Clients include industrial and sales firms, schools and museums. Uses services of music houses and songwriters for opening, closing and background music for slide shows and films. Pays by license fee or contract. Buys all rights or nonexclusive one-time rights.
How to Contact: Contact by phone, query with resume of credits or submit nonreturnable demo tape. Prefers 7½ ips reel-to-reel with 3-10 songs on demo. Does not return unsolicited material. Reports in 3 weeks. "Leave demo tape, and we will call when the need arises."
Music: "We need openings, closings and backgrounds in both modern and classical moods. Usually, we use no vocals."

KUCHARO COMMUNICATIONS, INC., 4700 N. Central Ave., Suite #1, Phoenix AZ 85012. (602)263-5304. President: Mike Kucharo. Estab. 1973. Clients include advertising agencies, industrial and business firms. Uses services of music houses and songwriters for film scores, jingles and background music. Commissions 5-6 pieces/year. Pays $250 minimum/job. Buys all rights.
How to Contact: Submit demo tape of previous work. Prefers 7½ ips reel-to-reel with 5 songs

minimum on tape. Include listing of music, what it was written for, cost of music, and production costs, if known. SASE. Reports in 2 weeks.

Music: "We need TV jingles, primarily. Contemporary music, driving rhythm, uptempo. Songwriters must be willing to work with us and the ad agency, and be aware of any budget limitations, which would be made known up front."

LAVIDGE & ASSOCIATES, INC., 409 Bearden Park Circle, Knoxville TN 37919. (615)584-6121. Account Executive: R. Lyle Lavidge. Estab. 1950. "Full-service advertising agency with complete in-house film production facility." Uses services of music houses for jingles, musical commercials and audiovisual/film scores. Pays $1,000 minimum/job. Buys all rights or one-time rights, "depending on the client, market, etc."

How to Contact: Arrange personal interview or submit demo tape of previous work. Prefers 7½ ips reel-to-reel with 4-12 songs on demo. SASE. Doesn't report unless interested.

W.V. LEVINE ASSOCIATION, INC., 18 E. 48th St., New York NY 10022. (212)751-1880. President: W. Levine. Estab. 1967. Clients include industrial firms. Uses services of songwriters for live industrial presentations at sales meetings, conferences and trade shows. Pays $250-1,500/job. Buys one-time rights.

How to Contact: Query with resume of credits. Prefers 7½ ips reel-to-reel or cassette with 4-6 songs on demo. SASE. Reports in 3 weeks.

JACK LIEB PRODUCTIONS, 200 E. Ontario, Chicago IL 60611. (312)943-1440. Contact: Susan Schrier. President: W.H. Lieb. Estab. 1946. Clients include governmental agencies and industrial firms. Uses services of music houses and songwriters for background music and public service announcements. Pays on a per-job basis. Buys all rights.

How to Contact: Submit demo tape of previous work. Prefers 7½ ips reel-to-reel. Does not return unsolicited material.

HARLEY McDANIEL FILMPRODUCTION, INC., 4444 W. Capitol Dr., Milwaukee WI 53216. President: John R. McDaniel. Estab. 1975. Clients include colleges, national associations, TV stations and advertising agencies. Uses services of music houses and songwriters for film scores and background music. Commissions 10 original scores/year; 40-60 needle drops/year. Pays $1,500-12,000/job. Buys all rights.

How to Contact: Submit demo tape of previous work. Prefers 7½ or 15 ips reel-to-reel with 5-15 songs on demo. SASE. Reports in 3 weeks.

Music: "We need bright and catchy music that doesn't sound canned. Much of our music is used for TV promos. For longer films, we guide the music writing, but we rely on the writer's judgment."

Tips: "Make music easy to edit to different lengths."

MAGNETIC STUDIOS, Lindy Productions, Inc., 4784 N. High St., Columbus OH 43214. Chief Engineer: John Fippin. Estab. 1960. Clients include advertising agencies, industrial/consumer manufacturers, and educational publishers. Uses songwriters and music libraries for radio/TV commercial jingles; and background music for slide, filmstrip, motion picture and multi-image presentations. Commissions 5-10 pieces/year. Pays $150 minimum/job. Buys all rights.

How to Contact: Submit demo tape of previous work. "*No telephone queries.*" Prefers 7½ ips reel-to-reel with 3-10 songs on demo. Does not return unsolicited material. Reports "at our discretion."

MARVIN PRODUCTIONS, 3630 Barham Blvd., #Z-101, Los Angeles CA 90068. Producer/Director: Larry Randall Vincent, DGA. Estab. 1972. Clients include corporations, government and advertising agencies. Uses services of music houses and music libraries for background music. Commissions 10 pieces/year. Pays $50/needle drop. Buys all rights.

How to Contact: Submit demo tape of previous work. Prefers 7½ ips reel-to-reel with 5-10 songs on demo. Does not return unsolicited material. Replies "only if the writer calls." Free brochure.

Tips: "Our firm is a 'boutique'—one producer/director shop. We freelance out most of our production work, including music, occasionally."

ED MARZOLA & ASSOCIATES, 8831 Sunset Blvd., Suite 408, Hollywood CA 90069. (213)652-7481. Vice President/Creative Director: Bill Case. President: Ed Marzola. Estab. 1970. Clients include business/industry, schools, TV stations and theaters. Uses services of music houses and songwriters for background music and scoring. Commissions 3 pieces/year.

Pays $200-1,500/job, or by negotiable royalty. Buys all rights or one-time rights.
How to Contact: Query with resume of credits. Prefers cassette with 3-10 songs on demo.
SASE. Reports in 1 week.
Music: Uses "mostly background for industrial films and music for educational films."
Tips: "We are not heavy users; most of the time we try to pull music from libraries, stock, etc.
But sometimes we do use a good songwriter, provided we have a budget for it."

MAXFILMS, 2525 Hyperion Ave., Los Angeles CA 90027. (213)662-3285. Vice President,
Production: Sid Glenar. Production Assistant: Y. Shinn. Estab. 1971. Clients include
corporations, nonprofit organizations and schools. Also produces films for theatrical and
television release. Uses services of songwriters "for background on a theatrical or television
film. Occasionally, an original score will be contracted for use in a corporate or educational
film." Commissions 8-10 pieces/year. Pays $350-7,000/job. Buys all rights.
How to Contact: Query with resume of credits or submit demo tape of previous work. Prefers
7½ ips reel-to-reel or cassette with 1-6 songs on demo. "Tapes submitted should have some
background as to the type of picture or presentation the music was scored for." SASE. Reports
in 3 weeks.
Music: "Complete scoring, or a title song or intro to a film or audiovisual presentation. State
complete capabilities in terms of composing, arranging and performing with some indication of
the type of music that you handle best."

FORNEY MILLER FILM ASSOCIATES, 5 Timber Fare, Spring House PA 19477.
(215)643-4167. Owner: Forney Miller. Estab. 1969. Clients include institutions, industrial and
business firms. Uses services of songwriters and composers for film scores and background
music. Pays $200 minimum "for open/close music." Buys all rights or one-time rights.
How to Contact: Submit demo tape of previous work. Prefers cassette. SASE. Reports "as soon
as possible."
Music: Uses background music for business, promotional and documentary films.

WARREN MILLER PRODUCTIONS, 505 Pier Ave., Hermosa Beach CA 90254. Production:
Jim Greer. Estab. 1948. Clients include industrial, sports film, resort and airline firms. Uses
services of music houses for background music in films. Commissions 1 piece/year. Pays
$2,000 minimum/job; $25/needle drop. Buys one-time rights.
How to Contact: Submit demo tape of previous work. Prefers cassette with 1-10 songs on
demo, or disc. SASE. Reports in 3 weeks.
Music: Needs action, outdoors, symphonic, soft rock, "energy music that is light and
youthful."
Tips: "It is important to be in this area to score a film. The musician must work closely with
the editor. Be adept at scoring several instruments. Instrumentals will be better for us than
vocals."

MONOGRAM ENTERTAINMENT CORP., Box 18793, Irvine CA 92713. Producer/Director:
Robert C. Stone. Estab. 1978. Uses services of songwriters for industrial/sales firms. T.V.
commercials, feature films and commercial album and single recordings. Commissions 15-25
pieces/year. Pays $100-1,000 minimum/job. Buys all rights or one-time rights.
How to Contact: Query or submit demo tape of previous work. Prefers cassette with 2-4 songs
on demo. SASE.
Music: "Varied types are needed. Every project uses a different, specific type of music. Top
40/popular songs also needed for our record division."

JACK MORTON PRODUCTIONS, 830 3rd Ave., New York NY 10012. Vice President,
Production: Paul Kielar. Estab. 1948. Clients include business and industry. Uses songwriters
for musical scores for live dramatizations, sound filmstrips, films, etc. Commissions 500
pieces/year. Pays $1500-7500/job. Buys one-time rights.
How to Contact: Query with resume of credits, arrange personal interview or submit demo
tape of previous work. Prefers cassette with 3-6 songs on demo. Reports in 3 weeks.
Music: "Pop, rock, disco—the music being played today."

MOYNIHAN ASSOCIATES, 1717 S. 12th St., Milwaukee WI 53204. (414)645-8200.
Producer/Director: Diane Wittenberg. Clients include schools, non-profit organizations,
businesses and industrial firms. Uses services of music houses and songwriters for film title and
background music. Commissions 1-2 pieces/film. Buys all rights.
How to Contact: Submit demo tape of previous work. Prefers 7½ ips reel-to-reel with 5-7 songs
on demo. SASE. Reports in 2 weeks. Free catalog with SASE.

Music: Needs "bold, exciting music for industrial films. Light, easygoing background and credit music. Use music as an extension of the film visuals."

MULTIMEDIA FORUM PRODUCTIONS, 2450 Grand Ave., Suite 400, Kansas City MO 64108. (816)274-8321. Manager of Creative Services: Pat Stephenson. Estab. 1973. Clients include corporations. Uses services of music houses and libraries for "soundtracks for all media." Commissions 10 pieces/year. Pays $500-5,000/job. Rights purchased vary.
How to Contact: Submit demo tape of previous work. Prefers 7½ ips half- or full-track reel-to-reel. Does not return unsolicited material; "we keep the material on file."
Music: Needs jingles, custom lyrics, uptempo music, rock: "Pepsi-generation type things."

MULTI-MEDIA PRODUCTIONS, INC., 1393 S. Inca, Denver CO 80223. (303)722-2892. Audio Supervisor: Robert J. Taylor. Estab. 1972. Clients include business, industry, state and federal government, and schools. Uses music houses, songwriters and in-house talent for introduction, closing and background for slides, filmstrips, videotape, motion pictures, radio and TV. Pays per cut, or unlimited total usage per program, "e.g. $175/15-minute audiovisual presentation." Buys all rights and one-time rights.
How to Contact: Query with resume of credits, arrange personal interview or submit demo tape of previous work. Prefers 7½ reel-to-reel or cassette with 3 songs on demo. SASE. Reports in 1 week.
Music: "We'd like to expand our production of broadcast jingles and logo music."

MUSIC MARKET PLACE, INC., 4130 Aurora St., Coral Gables FL 33146. (305)448-2763. Creative Director: Rene Barge. Estab. 1976. Clients include advertising agencies. Uses services of music houses and songwriters for background music, and radio and TV commercials. Pays on a per-job basis. Rights purchased vary.
How to Contact: Query with resume of credits or submit demo tape of previous work. Prefers 7½ or 15 ips reel-to-reel with 5-10 songs on demo. SASE. Reports in 2 weeks. Free catalog.
Music: "We mainly do jingles, although we're trying to get into record production also."

JOHN MUTRUX PHOTOGRAPHY, 7415 Stearns St., Shawnee Mission KS 66203. President: John Mutrux. Estab. 1976. Clients include advertising, business and industrial firms. Uses services of music houses for sound synchronized slide presentations. Commissions 3 pieces/year. Pays on a royalty or per-job basis. Buys one-time rights.
How to Contact: Query with resume of credits. Prefers cassette with 1-5 songs on demo. SASE. Reports in 2 weeks.

N.F.L. FILMS, INC., 230 N. 13th St., Philadelphia PA 19107. (215)567-4321. Music Director: Phil Spieller. Estab. 1966. Clients include TV networks. Uses services of music houses and songwriters for film scores and background music. Commissions 25-50 pieces/year. Pays 10% royalty. Buys all rights.
How to Contact: Submit demo tape of previous work. Prefers cassette with 10-20 songs on demo. Does not return unsolicited material. Reports in 1 month.

LARRY NICHOLSON PRODUCTIONS, 2100 Stark, Kansas City MO 64126. President: Larry Nicholson. Estab. 1954. Clients include government, industrial and educational firms. Uses services of music houses and songwriters for background music, themes and jingles. Commissions 6-12 pieces/year. Pays on a per-hour, per-job or royalty basis. Buys one-time rights or all rights. Complete in-house sound recording studio.
How to Contact: Submit demo tape of previous work. Prefers reel-to-reel or cassette with 6-10 songs on demo. SASE. Prefers not to return material, but will if requested. Reports in 2 weeks.
Music: "Frequently looking for 'stingers,' 6- to 20-second pieces for bridges in transitions, openers and closers."

NODUS PRODUCTIONS, 47 W. 68th, New York NY 10023. (212)787-1066. President: Arthur Mills. Estab. 1969. Clients include TV networks, advertising agencies, film companies and industrial firms. Uses services of music houses and songwriters for film scores, and original material for performers and TV specials. Pays "participation in profits." Rights purchased vary.
How to Contact: Query with resume of credits or submit demo tape of previous work. Prefers cassette with 4-6 songs on demo. SASE. Reports in 1 month.
Music: "Anything from classical music to rock. We especially need music that can be adapted to film scores, and material for cabaret and nightclub performers. We also need songs for TV movies and specials, the legitimate theater, and industrial shows (live and film)."

PADDOCK PRODUCTIONS, INC., 9101 Barton, Shawnee Mission KS 66214. (913)492-9850. Sound Engineer: Keith Fariss. President: Chuck Paddock. Estab. 1961. Clients include industrial and educational firms. Uses services of music houses and songwriters for filmstrips, films, commercials and jingles. Commissions 50 pieces/year. Pays on a per-job basis. Buys one-time rights or all rights.
How to Contact: Submit demo tape of previous work. Prefers 7½ ips reel-to-reel with 5 songs minimum on demo. SASE. Reports "as soon as possible."

PENTACLE PRODUCTIONS, INC., 1408 W. 50th St., Kansas City MO 64112. President: John Altman. Estab. 1974. Clients include corporations. Uses services of music houses and songwriters for background music in documentary films. Commissions 2-3 pieces/year. Payment negotiable. Buys worldwide television and nontheatrical rights.
How to Contact: Query with resume of credits, arrange personal interview or submit demo tape of previous work. Prefers 7½ ips reel-to-reel under 15 minutes running time. SASE. Reports in 3 weeks.
Tips: "If you have a print of film that you have scored, that is helpful."

VERNE PERSHING, 824 Grove, San Francisco CA 94117. (415)346-7825. Estab. 1971. Clients include educational, documentary, commercial, promotional and theatrical firms. Uses services of songwriters. Commissions 5 pieces/year. Pays $50-1,500/job. Rights purchased vary.
How to Contact: Submit demo tape of previous work. Prefers cassette with 1-100 songs on demo. SASE. Reports in 2 weeks.

PHELAN PRODUCTIONS, INC., 146 W. 11th Ave., Denver CO 80204. (303)571-1163. Vice President/Producer: Larry Schreiner. Estab. 1975. Clients include corporations, advertising agencies and government agencies. Uses services of music houses and songwriters for commercials and film scores. Commissions 5-15 pieces/year. Pays $1,000 minimum/job. Buys all rights or one-time rights.
How to Contact: Query with resume of credits or submit demo tape of previous work. Prefers 7½ ips reel-to-reel with 5-12 songs on demo. SASE. Reports in 2 weeks.
Music: Themes that run from 30 seconds to 1 hour.

GERARD PICK, PRODUCER, AUDIO/VISUAL MEDIA, Box 3032, Santa Monica CA 90302. (213)459-5596. Producer/Owner: Gerard Pick. Estab. 1971. Clients include business and industrial firms. Uses services of songwriters for background music, and "sometimes front and end titles." Pays $500 minimum/job. Buys all rights.
How to Contact: Query with resume of credits. Prefers cassette. SASE. Reports "immediately, after submission has been discussed."
Music: One-instrument or electronic accompaniment.

HENRY PORTIN MOTION PICTURES, 709 Jones Bldg., Seattle WA 98101. (206)682-7864. Producer: Henry Portin. Estab. 1962. Clients include industrial, airline and touring firms. Uses services of songwriters for background music. Commissions 1 piece/year. Pays $500 minimum/job. Buys all rights.
How to Contact: Query with resume of credits. Prefers cassette with 2-4 songs on demo. SASE. Reports in 1 month.
Music: Background music for documentaries.

JOHN M. PRICE FILMS, INC., Box 81, Radnor PA 19087. President: John M. Price. Estab. 1962. Clients include business, government and ad agencies. Uses music houses for occasional background music and musical scores for films. Pays $100-500/job. Buys one-time rights.
How to Contact: "Mail description of work, and we will file information for future reference." Prefers 7½ ips reel-to-reel tape "but none until requested."

PRODUCTION GALLERY, 3101 Mercier, Suite 484, Kansas City MO 64131. (816)531-3900. President: Rick DeBlock. Production Manager: Eben Fowler. Estab. 1976. Clients include business, industrial, advertising and educational firms. Uses service of music libraries for audiovisual soundtracks. Commissions 50 pieces/year. Pays on a per-job basis. Buys music copyright releases.
How to Contact: Query with resume of credits or submit demo tape of previous work. Prefers 7½ ips reel-to-reel with 4-5 songs on demo; include "various styles, if available." SASE. Reports only "if we use the material."
Music: For radio/TV spots.

PROTESTANT RADIO & TV CENTER, INC., 1727 Clifton Rd. NE, Atlanta GA 30329. (404)634-3324. Chief Engineer: Jim Hicks. Estab. 1949. Clients include denominational projects, local churches, schools and colleges (educational needs), and social campaigns. Uses services of songwriters for film scores, commercials and radio programs. Payment negotiable. Rights purchased vary.
How to Contact: Query or submit demo tape of previous work. Prefers 7½ or 15 ips reel-to-reel or cassette with 2-8 songs on demo. Does not return unsolicited material. Reports in 1 month.
Music: Themes for radio, television, film and audiovisual productions.

QUENZER DRISCOLL DAWSON, INC., 320 Ward Ave., Suite 109, Honolulu HI 96814. (808)521-6961. President: Mique Quenzer. Estab. 1975. Clients include advertising agencies. Uses services of music houses for jingles, background music and film scores. Commissions 12 pieces/year. Pays $1,200-6,000/job. Buys all rights in individual local markets.
How to Contact: Submit demo tape of previous work. Prefers 7½ ips reel-to-reel with 8-15 songs on demo. SASE. Reports in 1 month.
Music: "Mostly commercial jingles, with a variety of approaches. Music must be able to re-create a contemporary Hawaiian feel, rhythm patterns, instrumentation, etc."

RAINY DAY PRODUCTIONS, INC., 16283 10th NE, Seattle WA 98155. (206)364-0682. Contact: Terri Wacker/Michael Wacker. Estab. 1975. Clients include industrial, advertising and public relations agencies, and independent producers. Uses services of songwriters and music libraries for commercials and films. Pays $100-1,000/job. Buys all rights or one-time rights.
How to Contact: Query with resume of credits or submit demo tape of previous work. Prefers 7½ or 15 ips reel-to-reel or cassette with 4-8 songs on demo. "We like to keep copies of demos for future reference." SASE. Reports "as soon as possible."

RICHTER McBRIDE PRODUCTIONS, INC., 150 E. 52nd St., New York NY 10022. President: Robert Richter. Estab. 1968. Clients include public and commercial TV, government agencies and nonprofit organizations. Uses services of music houses and songwriters for film scores and background music. Commissions 2 pieces/year. Pays on a per-job basis. Buys all rights or one-time rights.
How to Contact: Submit demo and resume of previous work. Prefers cassette with 2-5 songs on demo. SASE. "Also, put name, return address and phone number on the tape itself." Reporting time varies "according to our business rush."
Music: "We have varying needs—sometimes we need a musical score to which we cut the film; at other times, we need music for already edited film."

RIDDLE VIDEO & FILM PRODUCTION, INC., 507 5th Ave., New York NY 10017. (212)697-5895. President: William Riddle. Estab. 1954. Clients include industrial and television stations. Uses services of songwriters. Commissions 50 pieces/year. Pays "standard rates." Buys all rights.
How to Contact: Query or submit demo tape of previous work. Prefers cassette with 6-12 songs on demo. SASE. Reports in 1 month. Free catalog.

T.A. ROGERS, INC., 9101 Barton, Overland Park KS 66214. (913)492-9853. Production company. Owner: Teri Rogers. Estab. 1975. Clients include retail, business, education and industry. Uses services of music houses and songwriters for background music in soundstrips. Commissions 2 pieces/year. Pays $1,500 minimum/job. Buys all rights.
How to Contact: Submit demo tape of previous work. Prefers 7½ ips reel-to-reel with 5 songs minimum on demo. SASE. Reports in 2 weeks.
Music: All types from piano or guitar to full orchestra; some lyrics.

SENSORIUM, LTD., 1137 Fort Street Mall, Honolulu HI 96813. (808)531-0208, 531-0209. Audio Director: Bill Soares. Estab. 1972. Clients include special interest groups, business, industry, and users of self-originating entertainment/information packages. Uses services of songwriters for film scores. Commissions 3-4 pieces/year. Payment and rights purchased depend "upon agreements involved with the particular production."
How to Contact: Arrange personal interview and bring demo tape. Prefers 7½ ips reel-to-reel tape, 3-10 minutes in length. "Tape should illustrate a range of style and mood." SASE. Reports in 1 month.
Music: "We need music that complements moving images. For instructions, a rough framework of time and a verbal idea of mood is given. Depending on the project, I may watch

the music develop very closely or not at all."
Tips: "Don't write songs, but write music."

SEVEN OAKS PRODUCTIONS, 8811 Colesville Rd., Silver Spring MD 20910. (301)587-0030. Production Coordinator: Paula Blanche. Production Manager: M.A. Marlow. Estab. 1957. Clients include schools, government agencies and foreign film producers. Uses services of music houses and songwriters for film scores and background music. Commissions 20-30 pieces/year. Payment negotiable. Buys all rights or one-time rights.
How to Contact: Query with resume of credits or submit demo tape of previous work. "If possible, submit a film with soundtrack so we can judge if the score fits the film's mood." Prefers 7½ ips reel-to-reel or cassette tape with 3 songs minimum to 1 hour long maximum, or 16mm film. SASE. "We prefer to keep tapes on file, to select potential composers for our projects." Reporting time varies "with the demands of the project."
Music: Needs scores and theme songs for "family-type feature films and educational, documentary productions. Our production people rely heavily upon music to raise audience interest and make even the most pedantic subjects interesting."

SHEA MANAGEMENT, INC., 1326 Freeport Rd., Pittsburgh PA 15238. (412)782-1624. Director of Communications: William J. Devlin. Estab. 1944. Clients include association of industrial manufacturers. Uses producers for music for filmstrips. Pays on a per-job basis. Buys one-time rights.

SMF PRODUCTIONS, 41 Union Square W., New York NY 10003. (212)675-3298. President: Shel Freund. Estab. 1979. Clients include advertising agencies and advertisers. Uses services of songwriters for records, jingles and film scores. Pays "depending on assignment. Outside songwriters use AGAC guide." Buys all rights.
How to Contact: Submit demo tape of previous work. Prefers 7½ reel-to-reel with 1-5 songs on demo. "Mail with reel-to-reel leadered and lyric or lead sheets—copyrighted material only." SASE. Reports in 1 month.
Music: "Hit songs in all idioms (disco, country, etc.)."

SPECTRUM IV, 501 N. Interegional Hwy., Austin TX 78701. (512)477-2018. President: Hart Sprager. Estab. 1974. Clients include schools, governmental agencies and industrial firms. Uses services of songwriters for background music. Commissions 6-10 pieces/year. Pays $100-1,500/job. Buys all rights.
How to Contact: Submit demo tape of previous work. Prefers cassette with 3-6 songs on demo. SASE. Reports in 2 weeks. Catalog for 15¢ postage.
Music: Needs specific mood background pieces to fit films and audiovisuals of a specific length.

STAGE 3 SOUND PRODUCTIONS, 12 E. 39th St., Kansas City MO 64111. (816)531-1375. President: Don Warnock. Estab. 1968. Clients include business and advertising agencies. Uses services of songwriters for background music in productions. Pays AFTRA scale. Buys all rights.
How to Contact: Query. Prefers 7½ ips reel-to-reel. SASE. Reports "as soon as possible."

CARTER STEVENS STUDIOS, INC., 153 W. 24th St., New York NY 10011. President: Carter Stevens. Estab. 1973. Produces theatrical feature films and business documentaries. Uses services of music houses and songwriters for film scores. Commissions 40-60 pieces/year. Pays $250-1,000/job. Buys all rights or one-time rights.
How to Contact: Submit demo tape and lyric sheet of previous work, or query with resume of credits. "Do not call our office." Prefers cassette with 2-8 songs on demo. SASE. Returns material if totally unusable; "we keep everything for future reference if we feel the writer has any potential. Send a sample of as many styles and moods of music as possible."
Tips: "There is a 3- to 6-month lag time on our projects, as we are working at least one to two films ahead at all times."

TCA FILMS, 2841 Palos Verdes Dr. W., Palos Verdes Estates CA 90274. (213)326-6073. Contact: Tom Carr. Estab. 1973. Clients include business and industry. Uses services of songwriters for film scores and background music in filmstrips. Commissions 10-30 pieces/year. Pays $1,500-3,000/job. Buys all rights or one-time rights.
How to Contact: Query with resume of credits or submit demo tape of previous work. Prefers 7½ ips reel-to-reel with 3-5 songs on demo. SASE. Reports in 1 week.

TELESOUND, INC., Box 1900, San Francisco CA 94101. Manager, Creative Division: Karl

H. Sjodahl. Audiovisual firm and production company. Serves TV stations, production companies and commercial clients. Uses services of songwriters for commercial scores and identification jingles. Commissions 30 pieces/year. Pays $500 minimum/job or 5% minimum royalty. Purchases all rights or rights purchased vary with job.
How to Contact: Submit demo tape of previous work. Prefers 7½ ips reel-to-reel or cassette with 2-10 songs on demo. "Show as much variety as possible. We are particularly interested in material that will work visually." SASE.
Music: Specific commercial songs. "Write the kind of material that people can't stop humming."

TRIKON PRODUCTIONS, Box 21, La Jolla CA 92038. (714)459-5233. Owner: H. Lee Pratt. Estab. 1974. Clients include schools, industrial firms and businesses. Uses services of songwriters for film scores. Pays $250 minimum/job. Buys all rights.
How to Contact: Phone for interview. Prefers cassette tape, 3-15 minutes in length. "Music houses should call and send us a brochure; songwriters should call, plus send a resume and demo tape." SASE. Reports in 2 weeks.
Music: "Provide us with the music we want, when we want it. We need scores and backgrounds custom written, so know how to creatively enhance a project with music."

RICK TROW PRODUCTIONS, 3941 Commerce Ave., Willow Grove PA 19149. (215)659-8300. Contact: Sharon Lindsey. Estab. 1960. Clients include schools, business and industry. Uses music houses. "Currently, we use stock libraries, but we're open to suggestions. The music is almost exclusively background and supplementing vivid visuals and live narration. The production style is a fast-paced, unique blend of education and entertainment, and much of the shows' youthful energy is dependent on the music." Commissions 30-100 pieces/year. Pays $500-1,500/job, but will consider package deals. Purchases one-time rights on needle drops; all rights on original scores.
How to Contact: Submit demo tape of previous work. Prefers 7½ ips reel-to-reel or cassette with 5-15 cuts; cuts needn't be longer than 30 seconds apiece. "It would be helpful to receive standard rate sheets and other written information for filing and reference." SASE. Reports in 2 weeks. "We would prefer to keep the demo tape, but for reference purposes only."
Music: "Happy instrumentals with a solid rock beat are best for our editing style. Our supplier should exhibit a definite feel for the most current sound, yet be flexible enough for occasional flights into novelty or whimsy. To keep pace with our teenage audience, we are constantly seeking out new music and music sources."

TULSA STUDIOS, 6314 E. 13th St., Tulsa OK 74112. (918)836-8164. Business Manager: LaDonna Downs. General Manager: Tom Claiborne. Clients include schools, producers, industry, business and advertising agencies. Uses services of music houses and songwriters for jingles, arrangements, films scores and background music. Commissions 20 pieces/year. Pays $250-10,000/job, or 4% maximum royalty. Buys all rights or one-time rights.
How to Contact: Query with resume of credits and submit demo tape of previous work. Prefers 7½ or 15 ips reel-to-reel or cassette with 3-6 songs on demo. SASE. Reports in 1 month.
Music: Needs vary with client's desires. "We have our own staff for music scores, which we use most of the time. Therefore, very few writers are selected without showing unusual capabilities."

US GOVERNMENT, National Park Service, Division of Audiovisual Arts, Harpers Ferry Center, Harpers Ferry WV 25425. Chief Branch of Audio Production: Blair Hubbard. Estab. 1955. Clients include national parks, recreational areas and historic sites. Uses services of music houses and songwriters for thematic and background music for films and sound-slide and multimedia programs. Commissions 50 pieces/year. Pays $200-4,000/hour for film; or $25-500/job for stock music. Buys all rights.
How to Contact: Query with resume of credits or submit demo tape of previous work. Prefers 7½ or 15 ips reel-to-reel with 3-10 songs on demo. Does not return unsolicited material. We maintain a permanent file." Reports "when we have specific needs." Free catalog.
Music: "Needs vary; usually background for a film or a sound-slide program for a national park, recreational or historic area."

UNIVERSAL IMAGES, 6321 Blue Ridge Blvd., Kansas City MO 64133. (816)358-6166. Production Director: Ralph Papin. Estab. 1974. Clients include theater, TV and business firms. Uses services of music houses and songwriters for background music in films. Commissions 15-20 pieces/year. Pays on a per-job basis. Buys all rights.
How to Contact: Submit demo tape of previous work. Prefers 7½ ips reel-to-reel with 5-6 songs

on demo. SASE. Reports as soon as possible.

VIDEO ONE, INC., 1216 N. Blackwelder Ave., Oklahoma City OK 73106. (405)524-2111. Production Manager: Rick A. Lippert. President: Robert M. Howard. Estab. 1976. Clients include business, industry, institutions and advertising agencies. Uses services of music houses, songwriters and stock libraries for video training productions, background, transitions and open/close. Commissions 5-10 pieces/year. Pays $100 minimum/job. Buys all rights.
How to Contact: Query or submit demo tape of previous work. Prefers 7½ ips reel-to-reel or cassette with 3-10 songs on demo. "Cassettes should be recorded on Dolby system; reel-to-reel should not. We prefer quarter-track, but will accept half-track." SASE. Reports in 3 weeks.

NORM VIRAG PRODUCTIONS, 1220 Wild Turkey Lane, Lansing MI 48906. (518)374-8193. President: Norm J. Virag. Estab. 1977. Clients include government, advertising agencies and independent producers. Uses services of songwriters for background music in films, filmstrips and slide programs. Commissions 6 pieces/year. Pays $200-1,000/job. Buys all rights.
How to Contact: Query with resume of credits or submit demo tape of previous work. Prefers 7½ ips full-track reel-to-reel with 6-12 songs on demo. SASE. Reports in 2 weeks. Free catalog.

DORIAN WALKER PRODUCTIONS, 2000 P St. NW, Suite 608, Washington DC 20036. (202)452-1776. Producer: John Simmons. Estab. 1974. Clients include corporations and government agencies. Uses services of music houses and songwriters for animated corporation logos and film scores. Commissions 4 pieces/year. Pays $100-250/finished screen minute. Rights purchased vary.
How to Contact: Query with resume of credits or submit demo tape of previous work. Prefers 7½ ips reel-to-reel with 3-5 instrumental pieces on tape. SASE. Reports in 1 month.
Music: "We're looking for tasteful use of 3-4 instruments; we have a heavy accent on instrumentals. Our composer needs to be loose and flexible, ready to execute a musical idea coming from the producer. In addition, he must be able to convey a variety of moods from the same musical theme. It helps to have a wide repertoire of clear and simple musical effects."

WESTFALL PRODUCTIONS, INC., 271 Madison Ave., New York NY 10016. Development Dept.: Mary Cullen. Estab. 1971. Clients include major networks, advertising agencies and major studios. Uses services for background music for films, songs for animated musicals and film themes. Commissions "approximately 6 pictures' worth." Pays by royalty and on a per-job basis. Buys all rights.
How to Contact: Query with resume of credits or submit demo tape of previous work. Prefers cassette or disc. "Label clearly as to type, and possible use. Clearly mark all credits on music, lyrics, arrangements, etc. All information on original composition and rights must be included." SASE. Reports in 3 weeks.

CARL WIKMAN VIDEO/TAPE, Box 06237, 8243 SE 74, Portland OR 97206. (503)234-3562. Owner: Carl Wikman. Estab. 1973. Clients include business, government, schools and broadcasters. Uses services of songwriters and public domain material for background, narration and dynamic effects in documentation. Commissions 8-12 pieces/year. Pays $10/hour, $25 minimum/job, or participation in future profits. Buys all rights.
How to Contact: Query with resume of credits or submit tape of previous work. Prefers 15 ips reel-to-reel with 3-6 songs on demo. Reports in 1 week.
Music: "All types—jazz, C&W, rock, gospel, neo-classical and ethnic. Writers often brought in at start of project and given free reign. At other times, specific music style and length is dictated."

DICK WILLIS & ASSOCIATES, 4138 Broadway, Kansas City MO 64111. (816)931-2100. President: Dick Willis. Estab. 1965. Serves ad agencies. Uses services of music houses and songwriters for commercial jingles and background music in industrial films. Commissions 3 pieces/year. Payment negotiable. Rights purchased vary.
How to Contact: Submit demo tape of previous work. Prefers 7½ ips reel-to-reel with 8-10 songs on demo. SASE. Reports in 2 weeks.

WING PRODUCTIONS, 1600 Broadway, New York NY 10019. (212)265-5179. President: Jon Wing Lum. Estab. 1964. Clients include NBC and the New York State Education Department. Uses services of songwriters for film scores. Commissions 35 pieces/year. Pays $500 minimum/job. Buys all rights.
How to Contact: Submit demo tape of previous work. Prefers 7½ or 15 ips reel-to-reel or cassette with 5 songs on demo. SASE. Reporting time "depends on need." Free catalog.
Music: Needs dramatic and educational music.

Services and Opportunities

Contests and Awards

Songwriter or musician competitions can be a pleasant and sometimes lucrative endeavor. What's more, participation in contests is a good way of exposing your work and your talents. Some contests are judged by music publishers and other industry officials, guaranteeing a professional hearing for your material. Contacts, and sometimes contracts, result from a good showing in a major competition.

Contests may not seem to be a "market" in the usual sense, yet you are selling yourself and your work. Thus, marketing techniques shouldn't be forgotten. Each contest you enter, for example, should be studied so that you can slant your material to the award you seek.

Other competitions and contests can be found by reading music-related magazines.

ABA OSTWALD BAND COMPOSITION CONTEST, c/o Dr. Mark Hindsley, 1 Montclair Rd., Urbana IL 61801. For composers. Annual. Estab. 1956. Purpose: "to promote major original compositions for concert band." Deadline: November 1. Accepts unlimited number of entries. Entrants should send for free copy of contest rules. Composers retain all rights to winning entries. Losing entries will be returned.
Awards: Winner: "This year (the 25th anniversary of the Ostwald contest) the prize will be $5,000." Undergraduate student award $500. Contest judged by a panel of approximately 7 band directors who compare and listen to tapes of all entries and select winners.
Tips: "This is not a song or a march contest. We are looking for serious instrumental band compositions."

THE AMERICAN SONG FESTIVAL, 5900 Wilshire Blvd., Los Angeles CA 90036. (213)464-8193. Manager: Joe Willemse. Sponsor: Sterling Recreation Organization. Estab. 1974. Annual. "We are the world's largest international songwriting competition with categories for top 40 (rock/soul); easy listening; disco; country; folk; and gospel/inspirational. Open to amateur and professional songwriters. Awards presentation held in Los Angeles. Festival held in January. Average attendance: 400. Submit demo tape. Application deadline

June 4. Entry fee: $13.85 for first category, $8.25 for each additional category.
Musician Competitions: Vocal performance category for amateurs only. Awards $2,000 grand prize.
Songwriter Competitions: Awards 2 grand prizes (1 amateur and 1 professional), total cash award $10,000; 10 category winners (6 amateur and 4 professional), $2,000 each; 30 semi-finalists (3 from each category) $200 each; 350 quarter-finalists (250 amateur and 100 professional), $50 each; and 1,000 honorable mentions (amateurs only), scroll.

ASCAP FOUNDATION GRANTS TO YOUNG COMPOSERS, ASCAP Bldg., 1 Lincoln Plaza, New York NY 10023. (212)595-3050. Director of Grants: Martin Bookspan. For composers. Purpose: to provide grants to young composers to help them pursue their studies in music composition and develop their skills or talents.
Requirements: "Applicants must be citizens or permanent residents of the US who have not reached their 30th birthday by November 1. Applicants must submit professional recommendations; complete an application listing prior education, experience and background in the field of music; and submit 1-2 examples of their composition. Music of any style or category will be considered. Submissions must be original works and not previously published or winners of previous competitions or grants." Deadline: November 1. Send for application; samples required. "Submit copies only. Score reproductions and/or manuscripts may be submitted on regular music paper or reproduced by an accepted reproduction process. Tapes will be accepted also. Tapes must be on 5- or 7-inch reels, 7½ ips, head out."
Awards/Grants: ASCAP Foundation awards grants of $500-2,500. Length: 1 year. Applications judged by screening-panel of musical authorities.

BMI AWARDS TO STUDENT COMPOSERS, 40 W. 57th St., New York NY 10019. (212)586-2000. Director: James J. Roy Jr. For composers of "serious concert music." Annual. Estab. 1951. Purpose: "to pick outstanding young (25 or under) composers and make cash awards for furthering their musical education."
Requirements: Applicants must not have reached their 26th birthday by Dec. 31 of the year preceding the Feb. 15th contest deadline. "Serious concert music is preferred to popular songs, but all music is considered. All geographic locations of the world, but applicant must be a citizen or permanent resident of the western hemisphere enrolled in an accredited public, private or parochial secondary school, in an accredited college or conservatory of music, or engaged in private study with recognized music teachers." Deadline: Feb. 15. Number of entries/student: 1. Send for free application and rules. Rights retained. Entries returned, include SASE.
Awards: BMI Awards to Student Composers: "prizes totaling $15,000 ranging from $300 to $2,500 may be given to winning students, by check, with certificate of honor." Contest judged by "outstanding composers, music publishers and musicologists."

COMPOSERS GUILD, 2333 Olympus Dr., Salt Lake City UT 84117. (801)278-1745. President: Sharon Nielson. For songwriters and composers. "We are a nonprofit organization working to help the composer/songwriter. Each year we sponsor classes, workshops, seminars, a composition contest, and a performance at the University of Utah."
Requirements: "Annual membership of $15 entitles entry to contest. No other restrictions." Deadline: August 31. Send for application.
Awards/Grants: $2,000 distributed among 5 categories: keyboard, popular, choral, children's and instrumental. "Detailed critique is given to every contest entry. Applicants judged by professional, usually head of university music department or firmly established producer of performed music."
Tips: "Sloppy manuscripts will not be accepted by Composers Guild."

CONCERT ARTISTS GUILD COMPETITION, 154 W. 57th St., Studio 136, New York NY 10019. (212)757-8344. Auditions Chairman: Cheryl Kerr. For musicians. "CAG was founded to help young professionals of exceptional talent win recognition through a nationwide competition. Six to ten winners are chosen."
Requirements: "Applicants must be under 30 years of age, or 35 years old for vocalists." Deadline: February. Send for application. Samples required; prefers 7½ ips reel-to-reel of "good quality."
Awards/Grants: Concert Artists Guild Award: $250. Includes "debut in Carnegie Recital Hall, preview concert, major press coverage and all concert expenses are paid." Applications judged by panel screening tapes, "then three rounds of live auditions. Judging is based on programming, tone, intonation, technique, interpretation and musicality."

Tips: "Pay special attention to programming. Musicians need to choose pieces that will show off their talent."

CONCERTO COMPETITION OF THE ROME FESTIVAL ORCHESTRA, 170 Broadway, Suite 201, New York NY 10038. (212)349-1980. Contact: Chairman, Concerto Competition. For musicians. Annual. Estab. 1971. Purpose: "to provide performance opportunities in Rome, Italy and elsewhere in Italy during the summer for promising artists." Entrants must "perform on one of the following: violin, viola, cello, string bass, oboe or french horn." Deadline: January 15. Accepts unlimited number of entries. Query; rules and applications free on request.
Awards: Five first prizes, $500; Honorable Mention, $200. Contest judged by a panel of judges who evaluate submitted tapes. "All entries are judged subjectively."

THE DELTA OMICRON INTERNATIONAL MUSIC FRATERNITY COMPOSITION COMPETITION FOR WOMEN COMPOSERS, 405 Dudley Rd., Lexington KY 40502. Chairman: Dr. Katherine E. Longyear. For women composers only. Triennial. Estab. 1964. Purpose: to encourage women composers and further the cause of contemporary music. Applicants must be women of college age or over. Current category: "Music for a chorus of women, in three of four parts, a cappella or accompanied with piano or organ." Competition subject changes with each contest. Deadline: August 1. Deadline varies each triennium. No limitation on number of entries; each entry must be in separate envelope. Mss 10-15 minutes in length; not previously published or publicly performed. Send for rules; free on request. Entry fee: $5 for each ms; "covers postage to judges, and return of manuscript to composer." Rights retained; entries returned.
Awards: First prize; $500 and first performance at the 1980 Delta Omicron International Conference. "Three judges make independent decisions. The manuscript receiving the highest grading is the winner, unless none of the compositions submitted is of calibre warranting an award."
Tips: "Material submitted should be legibly written in ink or processed. It should be mailed in a flat package by insured, prepaid mail or express."

EAST & WEST ARTISTS, 310 Riverside Dr., #313, New York NY 10025. (212)222-2433. Founder/Director: Adolovni P. Acosta. For composers and performers. Purpose is to promote outstanding young performers and composers world-wide by sponsoring an annual auditions for young performers and an annual competition for composers.
Requirements: Applicants in young performers' auditions accepted to age 32 for instrumentalists; to 35 for singers. No age limit in composers' competition. Deadline: performers, February; composers, May. Send for application.
Awards: Annual Young Performers' Auditions: Carnegie Recital Hall debut. Annual Composers' Competition: First prize,$150 and performance at Carnegie Recital Hall; 2nd and 3rd prizes, performance in the same concert at Carnegie Recital Hall.

THE KOSCIUSZKO FOUNDATION-CHOPIN PIANO COMPETITION, 15 E. 65th St., New York NY 10021. (212)734-2130. For piano students. Purpose is to award money aimed at helping young pianists meet their schooling costs.
Requirements: Applicants must be between the ages of 15 and 21. Detailed requirements of the repertoire provided with application. Deadline: March. Send for application.
Awards: Three prizes: $1,000, $500 and $250.

MIDLAND-ODESSA NATIONAL YOUNG ARTIST COMPETITION, c/o Mrs. Doris Campbell, 2825 E. 17th St., Odessa TX 79761. (915)366-3868. Chairman: Mrs. Campbell. For musicians. Annual. Estab. 1963. Purpose: "to give recognition and encouragement to outstanding secondary school and college musicians." Entrants must be registered, resident students in secondary school, college, university or conservatory and must not have reached their 26th birthday before January 1, 1979. Any person launched on an active professional career under management is ineligible. Deadline: December 15. (Deadlines each year must be at least 6 weeks before the competition.) Accepts the "first 85 complete applications received before the deadline." Send for free rules and application. Charges $25 entry fee.
Awards: Performing winners, no less than $750; finalists, no less than $200; and winners, no less than $400. Performing winners return to perform with the Midland-Odessa Symphony Orchestra. Contest judged by nationally known specialists in the fields of piano, strings, woodwinds and college voice.

MUSIC CITY SONG FESTIVAL, Box 17999, 1014 16th Ave. S., Nashville TN 37217.

(615)244-3748. Festival Directors: Scott Spinka, Roy Sinkovich, Mick Lloyd. Songwriting and performance competition for amateurs. Assistant to the Directors: Alison Brockman. Deadline: August 15; gospel competition, November 30. Entrants must be amateurs. Write for complete information.

Awards: Separate awards in both the country and gospel categories will be given for songwriting, lyric writing and vocal performance. Prizes for a single award range from $50-10,000. Contest judged by persons active in the industry.

PIANISTS FOUNDATION OF AMERICA, 4811 Calle Chueca, Tucson AZ 85718. President: Ozan Marsh. Secretary: Patricia Meyer. For musicians. Purpose is "to open the way for young artists of exceptional talent at the outset of their careers."
Requirements: Information on request.
Awards/Grants: Various competitions and scholarships. May be renewed. Applications judged by the board of directors.

JULIUS STULBERG AUDITIONS, INC., 6488 S. Westnedge, Kalamazoo MI 49002. (616)342-9371. Chairman, Auditions Committee: Mrs. R.K. Jones, 1522 Meadowbrook, Kalazazoo MI 49008. For musicians. Purpose: "To inspire young string players to continue their studies; to afford the winner an opportunity to solo with an orchestra."
Requirements: Any string player who will be not over 19 the year of the auditions may enter with the permission of his/her teacher. Deadline: January. Send for application. Samples of work required with application: playing time not to exceed 10 minutes on a good quality standard cassette.
Awards: First prize; $500 and solo appearance with the Kalamazoo Junior Symphony Orchestra at their spring concert. Second prize, $300; third prize, $200. "Twelve finalists are chosen by a local panel of judges. These are judged in live auditions by nationally know musicians."

THREE RIVERS PIANO COMPETITION, 4802 5th Ave., Pittsburgh PA 15213. (412)622-1459. Managing Director: Eva Tumiel-Kozak. Purpose is "to encourage young pianists and provide them with opportunities to perform.
Requirements: Applicants must be under 30 years of age as of March 31, have had formal music training and meet the requirements of the prescribed repertoire. Deadline: March. Send for application; include 2 letters of recommendation.
Awards/Grants: 1st prize: 3 performances with the Pittsburgh Symphony, $5,000 and the Vesuvius Gold Award; 2nd prize: $3,000 and the Silver Award; 3rd prize: $2,000 and the Bronze Award; 4th prize: $1,000.

THE UNIVERSITY OF MICHIGAN PROFESSIONAL THEATRE PROGRAM, The Michigan League, 227 S. Ingalls, Ann Arbor MI 48109. (313)763-5213. General Manager: J. Roland Wilson. Musical theater contest. Estab. 1977. Gives 1 or more major award each year.
Awards: $2,000 maximum for an original full-length musical. Submit 3 manuscripts and cassettes of songs. Does not return unsolicited material. Reports in May of each year. Deadline: end of January. Entry fee: $35.

YOUNG ARTISTS COMPETITION, Performers of Southern Connecticut, 2-C Cross Hwy., Westport CT 06880. (203)227-6770. Coordinator: Heida Hermanns. December 1st and 2nd, for ensembles only; string, brass, woodwind, mixed with piano, mixed without piano. Annual. Estab. 1973. Purpose: "to provide outstanding young performers with the challenge of a professional competition." Applicants must be from or residents of Connecticut, or present or former students in any of the New England states. Only one member of ensemble need qualify. Age limit: 29 years. Deadline: November 1. Send for application and rules; free with #10 SASE. Entry fee: $25 per ensemble.
Awards: "First prize; New York Carnegie Recital Hall debut. Also other performance opportunities and cash awards. Finalists will be presented in public performance and will be included in talent referral listing." Applicants judged by individual juries in each category with finalists panel consisting of renowned area performers.

Managers and Booking Agencies

The manager is the artist's mentor, a confidant who guides, decides, pushes and promotes you as a talent package.

A manager should be chosen for whom he knows as much as for what he knows about the music business. The most important consideration, however, is finding a manager who unfailingly believes in your ability and your future. Your manager advises you in the selection of material, your stage performance, your publicity campaign, and your industry dealings. He's also your representative. His job is to get people to listen to you, to promote you as a first-class artist or songwriter. Your job is to prove him right; you must believe in yourself as much as the manager or booking agent does.

Self-confidence was one of the reasons Ross Todd & Associates decided to deal with writer/artist Dane Donahue. "He is sure of his material, and it reflects in his songs and performance," says John Todd. "In other words, he believed in himself." Other things that will attract a manager to you are your talent, originality, credits, dedication and professionalism. Demonstrate these qualities in your submission. "Prepare a press kit containing a high-quality, interesting, professional 8x10 publicity photo; a three- to four-paragraph bio sheet; a list of songs (both commercial and original material) performed; a list of engagement credits; a current itinerary; any relevent press clippings; and a live, unedited cassette tape of an actual performance," says Charles V. Steadham Jr., general manager of the Blade Agency.

Your submission package to managers and booking agencies will resemble your material for record companies and producers. In each case, you are auditioning. You want to include your best material, the most exciting part of your act.

In general, managers and booking agencies prefer to work with singer/songwriters. "Performers who write their own material seem to reflect a greater feel for it in their performance," says John Todd. Cherie Hanfelt of the Richard Lutz Entertainment Agency says that songwriter/artists "are always striving for a higher goal, constantly trying to better themselves and their music. They are not easily satisfied with just playing. They appreciate well-written music." Writer/artists are also appreciated because they can evoke a unique sound. Also, "They are, generally speaking, easier to sell to a record company, but who would turn down Olivia Newton-John or Linda Ronstadt because they don't write?" asks manager Bill Wagner.

Having a manager is particularly important when approaching a record company. The manager and the booking agency can set up performance dates that will give you experience and credits, help you develop a promotional package to present to record companies, and take care of business dealings. "A good business sense is essential," says Thom Trumbo, A&R director of Chrysalis Records. "You not only sign the artist, you sign the management, too. . . . Management is extremely important."

Managers, like record companies, can specialize in the types of acts or music they promote. Some deal only with rock bands, while others will take groups that play in bars and lounges.

The following listings include managers and booking agencies. The booking agent is a coordinator actively finding you work and performance opportunities. The booking agency finds you jobs; the manager guides your career development. A manager can, but doesn't necessarily, perform both tasks of promoting and booking. Each listing specifies whether or not the company is a booking agency, management firm, or both.

Managers and booking agents work on a commission basis. They receive a certain percentage of your gross income. The more you make, the more they make—a perfect incentive for doing their best to promote you. The minimum/maximum commission the companies charge is included in the listings. Both managers and agents can deal with solo artists, groups or songwriters. Some will specialize in promoting or booking one category, such as groups, while others will work with all three types. Make sure you submit to a manager or agent who handles your type of act or music. If a company works only in a specific region, the listing will tell you that. Otherwise, assume the company will deal with acts from across the country.

AAA-ALL AMERICAN AGENCY, ENTERTAINMENT CONSULTANTS, 1675 S. King St., Denver CO 80219. (303)934-4440. President: Lon Egbert. Management firm and booking agency. Estab. 1974. Represents professional individuals and groups from the Rocky Mountain, Southwestern and West Coast states; currently handles over 100 acts. Receives 15% commission. Entertainers pay marketing and publicity costs in addition to the 15% booking rate.
How to Contact: Query or submit demo tape and lead sheet. Prefers cassette. All inquiries should be in writing and include current references. SASE. Reports in 1 month.
Music: Bluegrass; blues (pop or easy listening); MOR; progressive; rock (country, hard or light); MOR; easy listening; and top 40/pop. Works primarily with rock/dance bands, lounge acts. nightclub acts, variety acts, concerts and speakers. Current acts include Electric Bass (MOR group); Middle of the Road (rock group); and Pear (rock and easy listening group).

ALL STAR TALENT AGENCY, Box 82, Greenbrier TN 37073. (615)643-4192. Owner/Agent: Joyce Brown. Booking agency. Estab. 1967. Represents professional individuals, groups and songwriters; currently handles 12 acts. Receives 15% commission.
How to Contact: Submit demo tape and lead sheet. Prefers reel-to-reel or cassette with 1-4 songs on demo. SASE. Reports as soon as possible.
Music: Bluegrass; C&W; gospel; MOR; rock (country); and top 40/pop. Works primarily with dance bands, club acts and concerts. Current acts include Bill Carlisle and the Carlisles (C&W group); Ronnie Dove (MOR/C&W artist); and Randy Parton (pop artist).

ALLIED BOOKING CO. 2250 3rd Ave., San Diego CA 92101. (714)234-8767. Associate: Jim Deacy. Booking agency. Estab. 1955. Deals with individuals in California and Arizona. Receives 10-20% commission.
How-to-Contact: Query or submit demo tape. Prefers cassette with 5-10 songs on demo. SASE. Reports in 2 weeks.
Music: MOR and top 40/pop. Works primarily with dance bands. "We book all types of musical groups, and many different ones throughout the year."

SAMUEL AIZER ENTERPRISES, 2 Boxwood Dr., Great Neck NY 11021. (212)989-4951. President: Samuel Aizer. Management agency. Estab. 1976. Represents individual artists, groups and songwriters; currently represents 4 acts. Receives 15-25% commission.
How to Contact: Arrange personal interview. Prefers cassette tape with 2-5 songs on demo. SASE. Reports in 1 week.
Music: Progressive; rock; and top 40/pop. Current acts include Screaming Mimi (rock group); Ben Candid (rock singer); Fantasy (rock group); and Dean Price (rock singer). "I am looking for professionals with desire for hard work. This is my method of working. I have strong contact with record companies."

AJAYE ENTERTAINMENT CORP., Box 6568, 2181 Victory Pkwy., Cincinnati OH 45206. (513)221-2626. Artist Relations: Dale Lewis. Booking agency. Estab. 1967. Represents artists and groups; currently represents 26 acts. Receives 10-20% commission.
How to Contact: Submit demo tape and write or call to explain the purpose of submission. Prefers 7½ ips reel-to-reel or cassette with 3-6 songs on demo. SASE. Reports ASAP.
Music: Progressive; rock; soul; top 40/pop. Current acts include The Raisins, Blaze, Wheels, Bell Jar, Relay, Spike, Krystal Kidd, Jackson Highway, Carefree Day, Sweetheart, Haymarket Riot and Sass, all rock groups.

ALEXIS ENTERPRISES, 681 Conina Dr., Cincinnati OH 45238. (513)451-1081. President:

Bob Hanneken. Booking agency. Estab. 1976. Represents groups. Receives 15% maximum commission.
How to Contact: Query or submit demo tape and lead sheet. Prefers 7½ ips reel-to-reel or cassette tape with 4 songs minimum on demo. SASE. Reports "as soon as possible."
Music: Disco; folk; progressive; rock; and top 40/pop. Current acts include Millennium (top 40/rock); Spike (hard rock); Albatross (top 40/rock); Charter Flight (top 40/pop); and Fanfare (top 40/disco).

ALIVE ENTERPRISES, 8600 Melrose Ave., Los Angeles CA 90069. (213)659-7001. Director of Creative Services: Bob Emmer. Management agency. Estab. 1968. Represents artists, groups and songwriters; currently represents 7 acts. Receives 20% minimum commission.
How to Contact: Query or submit demo tape and lead sheet. Prefers cassette with 2-6 songs on demo. SASE. Reports in 3 weeks.
Music: Rock (all types); soul; and top 40/pop/Works with "major record company signed artists." Current acts include Alice Cooper (rock); Teddy Pendergrass (R&B); and Yvonne Elliman (top 40).

ALTA CALIFORNIA ARTISTS, 150 Shoreline Highway, Suite B-28, Mill Valley CA 94941. (415)332-9592. President: Bill Allen. Management agency. Estab. 1977. Represents West Coast artists, group and songwriters; currently represents 7 acts. Receives 15-25% commission.
How to Contact: Arrange personal interview or submit demo tape and lead sheet.

AMERICANA CORPORATION, Box 47, Woodland Hills CA 91365. (213)347-2976. President: Steve Stebbins. Management and booking agency. Estab. 1947. Represents artists and groups; currently represents 6 artists and 8 bands. Receives 10-15% commission.
How to Contact: Submit demo tape only. Prefers cassette tape with 3-5 songs on demo. SASE. Reports in 1 month.
Music: C&W. Works with dance and bar bands. Current acts include Johnny & Jonie Mosby (country); Phillips Express Band (country); and Ron Wayne & Kountry Cookin Band (country).

AMERICAN ENTERPRISES, 610 White St., Houston TX 77007. (713)864-6561. Vice President: Jim Lawrence. Management firm and booking agency. Estab. 1945. Represents individuals and groups; currently handles 4 acts. Receives 10-20% commission.
How to Contact: Query or submit demo tape. Prefers cassette with 3-6 songs on demo. SASE. Reports in 2 weeks.
Music: C&W; disco; MOR; rock; and top 40/pop. Works primarily with rock, variety and C&W bands. Current acts include Mundo Earwood (C&W); Harts (variety); Actor (rock); and Neve (disco).

AMRON, HALPERN & MARGO PRODUCTIONS, INC., 8831 Sunset Blvd., Suite 406, Los Angeles CA 90069. (213)855-7061. Director West Coast Operations: Maureen Nemeth. Management firm, record producers and publishers. Estab. 1978. Represents artists, groups, songwriters, actors and actresses; currently handles 5 acts.
How to Contact: Submit demo tape and lead sheet. Prefers cassette tapes. SASE. Reports in 1 month.
Music: Disco; progressive; rock; soul; and top 40/pop. Current acts include Kristy and Jimmy McNichol (pop/top 40, disco); Bob Guilaume (disco/soul, pop); Frank Flippetti (rock); and Foy Hauser (R&B/pop/disco).

AMUSEX CORP., 970 O'Brien Dr., Menlo Park CA 94025. (415)324-1444. Artists Managers: David Elder and Jim Kalogrides. Management firm and booking agency. Estab. 1972. Represents artists, groups and songwriters; currently handles 10 acts. Negotiates commission.
How to Contact: Submit demo tape and lead sheet. Prefers cassette or video-VHS format with 2-10 songs on demo. SASE. Reports in 2 weeks.
Music: Disco; rock (all); and top 40/pop. Current acts include Santa Esmeralda (disco); Jimmy Goings (disco, pop, rock); and Gotcha (top 40/pop).

ARMAGEDDON TALENT ASSOCIATES, 1604 W. Juneway Terrace, Chicago IL 62301. (312)465-3373. Co-owners: Gail Smith and Fred Tieken. Management and booking agency and recording studio. Estab. 1971. Represents groups; currently represents 12 groups. Receives 10-20% commission.
How to Contact: Submit demo tape only. Prefers cassette with 2-6 songs on demo. SASE. Reports in 1 month.

Music: Rock (hard or new wave). Works with original rock and new wave bands. Current acts include The Swingers (new wave rock); Slip Mahoney (hard rock); and Jonny III (new wave).

ARMSTRONG & DONALDSON MANAGEMENT, INC., 2 East Read St., Suite 209, Baltimore MD 21202. (301)727-2220. President: Rod Armstrong. Estab. 1971. Represents artists, groups and songwriters; currently handles 4 acts. Receives 15-25% commission.
How to Contact: Submit demo tape and lead sheet. Prefers 7½ ips reel-to-reel or cassette with 2-4 songs on demo. SASE. Reports in 2 weeks.
Music: Disco; progressive; soul; and top 40/pop. Current acts include Walter Jackson, the Softones and First Class (stage and show acts).

ARTIST ENTERTAINMENT CORP., 2314 Peach St., Suite 1, Erie PA 16502. (814)455-7729. Executive Vice President: Frank J. Sonzala. Management firm, booking agency and Starcrescent Record Co. Estab. 1970. Represents artists, groups and songwriters; represents 300 acts. Receives 10-20% commission.
How to Contact: Submit demo tape and lead sheet. Prefers cassette with 3-6 songs on demo. SASE. Reports in 1 month.
Music: C&W; disco; folk; progressive; rock; soul; and top 40/pop. Works with recording, concert and lounge acts. Current acts include Easy (Southern rock); Justin Time (progressive rock); Michael Hamilton (folk/country); Laura Presutti (pop); and Guardian (rock).

ARTISTS ONE MANAGEMENT, 35 Brentwood Ave., Farmingville NY 11738. (516)698-7525. President: Philip Lorito. Management agency. Estab. 1977. Represents artists; currently represents 6 acts.
How to Contact: Submit demo tape. SASE. Reports in 2 weeks.
Music: Progressive; rock; and top 40/pop.

ARTISTS UNLIMITED, Box 206, Williamstown MA 01267. President: Steve Case. Management firm and booking agency. Estab. 1975. Represents artists and groups.
How to Contact: Submit demo tape only. Prefers cassette with 3-10 songs on demo. SASE. Reports in 2 weeks.
Music: Folk; MOR; rock; and top 40/pop.

ASCENSION ARTIST MANAGEMENT, LTD., Box 2484, Trenton NJ 08607. President: Robin Garb. Vice President: Bill Ring. Management agency and music publisher (Valsong). Estab. 1973. Represents artists, groups and songwriters; currently handles 3 acts. Receives 20% commission.
How to Contact: Query or submit demo tape only. Prefers cassette with 3-5 songs on demo. SASE. Reports in 2 weeks.
Music: Disco; MOR; rock (not hard); and top 40/pop. Works with individuals and original concert bands. Current acts include Frank Stallone (singer/songwriter); Bob Tangrea (singer/songwriter); and Peter Glassboro (singer/songwriter).

WILLIAM ASHWOOD ORGANIZATION, 230 Park Ave., New York NY 10017 or 256 S. Robertson Blvd., Beverly Hills CA 90211. (212)953-1999. Contact: Artist Relations or Producer Relations. Management agency and publishing/production film. Estab. 1923. Represents artists, groups, songwriters and record producers; currently represents 5 acts.
How to Contact: Query, arrange personal interview, submit demo tape only or demo tape and lead sheet. Prefers cassette with 3-5 songs on demo. SASE. Reports in 3 weeks.
Music: Blues; children's; disco; rock; and top 40/pop. Works with bands and songwriters of "unique individuality." Current acts include Star Spangled Washboard (musical comedy band); Crac (vocal rock); and John Lee Hooker (blues).

ATMOSPHERE & TNT CONCERT PROMOTION CONSULTANTS, 2526 E. 82nd St., Cleveland OH 44105. (216)231-0772. Director: Winston Craig. Public Relations: Tony Luke. Booking agency and management firm. Estab. 1969. Represents individuals and groups.
How to Contact: Send letter of introduction. Prefers cassette with 5-10 songs on demo. Reports in 1 month.
Music: Blues; disco; jazz; rock; and soul.

CLIFF AYERS PRODUCTIONS, 62 Music Square West, Nashville TN 37203. (615)256-1693. Vice President: Connie Wright. Management firm, booking agency, record production and distribution company, publisher. "We publish *Music City Entertainer* newspaper." Estab. 1959.

Represents artists, groups and songwriters; currently represents 76 acts. 15% minimum commission.
How to Contact: Submit demo tape and lead sheet or lead sheet. Prefers cassette with a maximum of 2 songs on demo. SASE. Reports in 1 week.
Music: Church/religious; C&W; disco; gospel; MOR; soft rock; and top 40/pop. Current acts include Ernie Ashworth (C&W, Grand Old Opry star); Tommy Sands (pop); and Candice Early (pop, portrays Donna on ABC-TVs *All My Children*).

AZTEC PRODUCTIONS, 20531 Plummer St., Chatsworth CA 91311. (213)998-0443. General Manager: A. Sullivan. Management firm and booking agency. Estab. 1969. Represents individuals, groups and songwriters; currently handles 7 acts. Receives 10-25% commission.
How to Contact: Submit demo tape and lead sheet. Prefers 7½ ips reel-to-reel or cassette. SASE. Reports in 3 weeks.
Music: Blues; C&W; disco; MOR; rock; soul; and top 40/pop. Works primarily with club bands, show groups and concert groups. Current acts include El Chicano (Latin/rock); Abraxas (MOR); Storm (show group); and Tribe (soul/R&B).

B.I.T.C.H.E.S., INC., 8720 Flower Ave., Silver Spring MD 20703. (301)565-0120. Executive Director: D. Napoleon Wood. Management firm. Estab. 1967. Represents individuals and groups; currently handles 12 acts. Receives 15-25% commission.
How to Contact: Query with resume and photos or submit demo tape. Prefers cassette with 2-4 songs on demo. Does not return unsolicited material. Reports in 3 weeks.
Music: Bluegrass; blues; children's; choral; church/religious; classical; C&W; disco; folk; gospel; jazz; MOR; opera; polka; progressive; rock (hard, soft or country); soul; and top 40/pop. Works primarily with dance bands, single vocalists, duos, jazz groups and R&B groups. Currents acts include "Experience Unlimited" (R&B group) and "Olavie Jones and Company" (jazz group).

BAND AID ENTERTAINMENT, INC., Box 3673, Baton Rouge LA 70821. (504)387-5709. President: Ed Patterson. Booking agency. Estab. 1969. Represents Southern groups; currently handles 6 acts. Receives 15-20% commission.
How to Contact: Query; prefers phone call. SASE. Reports in 2 weeks.
Music: Rock and pop. Current acts include Billy Pendleton and Earth (rock group); Orpheus (rock group); and Magenta (rock group).

BAUER-HALL ENTERPRISES, 138 Frog Hollow Rd., Churchville PA 18966. (215)357-5189. Contact: William B. Hall III. Booking agency. Estab. 1968. Represents individuals and groups; currently handles 6 acts. Receives 10-15% commission.
How to Contact: Query; "include photos, promo material, and record or tape." Prefers cassette. "Letter of inquiry preferred as initial contact." Does not return unsolicited material. Reports in 1 month.
Music: Children's; circus; ethnic; and polka. Works primarily with "unusual or novelty attractions in musical line, preferably those that appeal to family groups." Current acts include Coco's Musical Comix (all clown band); Philadelphia Mummers' String Bands (string bands); Ruth Daye (novelty xylophonist); Fred Wayne (circus bandmaster); Joseph Kaye (one-man band); and Generation Bridge (band).

BEAU-JIM AGENCY, INC., Box 758, Lake Jackson TX 77566. (713)393-1703. President: James E. "Buddy" Hooper. Management firm, booking agency and music publisher. Estab. 1972. Represents individuals, groups and songwriters. Currently handles 3 acts. Receives negotiable commission.
How to Contact: Query or submit demo tape and lead sheet. Prefers 7½ ips reel-to-reel or cassette with 3-5 songs on demo. SASE. Reports in 3 weeks.
Music: Blues; C&W; MOR; and top 40/pop. Works primarily with dance and showbands. Current acts include Donna Douglas, 7 other individuals, and 5 groups.

BEAVERWOOD TALENT AGENCY & RECORDING STUDIO, 133 Walton Ferry Rd., Hendersonville TN 37075. (615)824-2820. Owner/Manager: Clyde Beavers. Management firm, booking agency, music publisher and record company. Estab. 1969. Represents individuals, groups and songwriters; currently handles 15 acts. Receives 15% commission.
How to Contact: Query, arrange personal interview, submit demo tape, or submit demo tape and lead sheet. Prefers 7½ or 15 ips reel-to-reel or cassette with 1-5 songs on demo. SASE. Reports as soon as possible.
Music: Bluegrass; blues; children's; choral; church/religious; classical; C&W; disco; folk;

gospel; jazz; MOR; opera; polka; progressive; rock; soul; and top 40/pop. Works primarily with variety, C&W, gospel and top 40 acts. Current acts include Nick Nixon (C&W artist); Lois Johnson (C&W artist); and the Telestials (gospel group).

THE BELKIN MADURI ORGANIZATION, 28001 Chagrin Blvd., Suite 205, Cleveland OH 44122. (216)464-5990. Contact: Bruce Maduri or Jim Fox, A&R Department. Management firm and production company. Estab. 1965. Represents artists, groups and songwriters; currently handles 16 acts.
How to Contact: Query or submit demo tape and lead sheet. Prefers 7½ reel-to-reel or cassette with 3-5 songs on demo. "Send a tape and follow up with a phone call." SASE. Reports from 1-3 weeks.
Music: Disco; MOR; progressive; rock (pop/rock or progressive rock); soul; and top 40/pop. Works with commercial pop, R&B artists/songwriters. "Would like to pursue disco acts much more aggressively. We are involved in crossover acts, R&B/top 40, progressive rock/top 40 etc. Current acts include Wild Cherry (top 40/soul/disco); The Michael Stanley Band (rock/pop/top 40); Gabriel (rock/top 40/pop); Sly, Slick and Wicked (soul/pop); Breathless (rock/pop/top 40); and LaFlavour (top 40/soul/disco).

VIC BERI PRODUCTIONS, 1811 NE 53rd St., Fort Lauderdale FL 33308. (305)776-1004. President: Vic Beri. Management agency. Estab. 1959. Represents artists and groups; currently represents 10 acts. Negotiates commission.
How to Contact: Arrange personal interview. Prefers 7½ ips reel-to-reel and cassette tape. SASE. Reports ASAP.
Music: C&W; disco (soft); MOR; rock; and top 40/pop. Current acts include Both Sides Now (group); Tory Chance (vocalist); Christopher Contillo (pianist); Christian Brothers (disco top 40/pop); and Carrie McDowell (vocalist top 40/pop).

BIG "C" MUSIC, 2970 N. Pine Hill Rd., Suite 48, Orlando FL 32808. (305)293-6687. President: Bud Cutright. Management firm and booking agency. Estab. 1970. Represents individuals, groups and songwriters; currently handles 6 acts and 1 songwriter. Receives 10-20% commission.
How to Contact: Query (phone calls accepted), arrange personal interview, or submit demo tape. Prefers 7½ ips reel-to-reel with 1-3 songs on demo. SASE. Reports in 2 weeks.
Music: Bluegrass; C&W (country rock); folk; and MOR. Works primarily with C&W show bands, bluegrass show bands and bar bands. Current acts inclue B.C. and the Wheelers (C&W show); Harvest Gold (C&W show); Talismen (C&W show); Stone Mountain Boys (bluegrass show); and B.C. (songwriter).
arrpoximently

BIG SOUND RECORDS, 2 Washington Square Village, No. 7D, New York NY 10012. Contact: Sally Young. Record company. Estab. 1977. Represents artists, groups and songwriters; currently handles 25 acts. Negotiates commission.
How to Contact: Submit demo tape only. Prefers cassette. SASE.

BLADE AGENCY, Box 12239, Gainesville FL 32604. (904)372-8158, (904)377-8158. General Manager: Charles V. Steadham Jr. Management firm and booking agency. Estab. 1975. Represents professional individuals and groups; currently handles 36 acts. Receives 15% commission.
How to Contact: Query or submit demo tape. Prefers cassette with 3-5 songs on demo. SASE. Reports as soon as possible.
Music: Bluegrass; blues; C&W; disco; folk; MOR; rock (country); soul; top 40/pop; and comedy. Current acts include Gamble Rogers (C&W/folk artist); Peyton Brothers (contemporary bluegrass group); Tom Parks (comedian); Rambo Street (top 40/pop group); Mike Cross (contemporary folk artist); Johnny Shines (blues); Vigilante (top 40/disco); and Mike Reid (contemporary folk/blues).

RICK BLOOM'S OFFICES, (formerly Agency for the Performing Arts, Inc.), 16024 Ventura Blvd., Suite 116, Encino CA 91436. (213)995-3440. Agent/Owner: Rick Bloom. Estab. 1978. Represents individuals and groups in the jazz and contemporary field. Currently handles 7 acts. Receives minimum 15% commission.
Music: Jazz and progressive. Works only with self-contained performers. Current acts include Dabid Grisman, Willie Bobo, Eddie Henderson, Passport, and Tony Williams.

JAMES CIOE BOOGITTY BOOGITTY PRODUCTIONS, 3057 N. Town Hall, Traverse

City MI 49684. (616)941-0589. President: James Cioe. Management firm, booking agency and production/promotion company. Estab. 1976. Represents artists, groups and comedy/theater performers; currently handles 15 acts. Receives 5-15% commission.
How to Contact: Query, submit demo tape or call. Prefers cassette with 4 songs minimum on demo. SASE. Reports in 1 week.
Music: Bluegrass; blues; C&W ("outlaw" type); folk; jazz; progressive; rock (no hard rock); and comedy. Works with "hip, noncommercial single acts and bands—everything but disco and top 40." Current acts include Stuart Mitchell (single); Don Tapert; Buck's Stove and Range Co. (band); and Honeyboy (band).

BOUQUET-ORCHID ENTERPRISES, Box 4220, Shreveport LA 71104. (318)686-7362. President: Bill Bohannon. Management firm. Estab. 1977. Represents individuals and groups; currently handles 2 acts. Receives 15% minimum commission.
How to Contact: Submit demo tape. Prefers 7½ ips reel-to-reel or cassette with 2-5 songs on demo. SASE. Reports in 1 month.
Music: C&W; rock (country); and top 40/pop. Works primarily with solo artists and small combos. Current acts include Shan Wilson (C&W singer/songwriter); and the Bandoleers (top 40/pop group).

BOBBY BOYD, 2609 NW 36th St., Oklahoma City OK 73112. (405)942-0462. President: Bobby Boyd. Management agency. Estab. 1970. Represents artists and songwriters. Receives minimum 25% commission.
How to Contact: Submit demo tape and lead sheet. Prefers 7½ ips reel-to-reel with 5-6 songs on demo. "Send tapes that do not have to be returned." Does not return unsolicited material. Reports in 2 weeks.
Music: C&W; rock; soul; and top 40/pop. Current acts include Jim Whitaker (single); Dale Greear (single); and Belinda Eaves (single).

BENNIE BROWN PRODUCTIONS, 3011 Woodway Lane, Box 5702, Columbia SC 29206. (803)788-5734. President: Bennie Brown Jr. Management firm and booking agency. Estab. 1969. Represents artists, groups and songwriters.
How to Contact: Submit demo tape only or submit demo tape and lead sheet. Prefers 7½ ips reel-to-reel or cassette with 4-6 songs on demo. SASE. Reports in 3 weeks.
Music: C&W; disco; gospel; jazz; MOR; soul; top 40/pop. Works with dance bands mostly and groups like the Four Tops and Bee Gees. Current acts include Mandingo Band (top 40/pop, disco); Freestyle Band (soul); Anathy Smith (songwriter); Coleman Sistrunk (songwriter); and Linda Martell (country).

BOB BURTON/MIRAMAR MANAGEMENT, Box 3153, Austin TX 78764. Owner: Bob Burton. Management agency. Estab. 1975. Represents individuals, groups and songwriters; currently handles 1 act. Receives 15-30% commission.
How to Contact: Query. Prefers cassette with 2-5 songs on the tape. SASE. Reports in 1 month.
Music: Jazz and rock (melodic). Works with concert acts. Currently represents St. Elmo's Fire (melodic rock group).

TOBY BYRON MANAGEMENT, 225 Central Park West, New York NY 10024. (212)580-7210. President: Toby Byron. Management firm and publisher. Estab. 1976. Represents artists, groups, songwriters and producers; currently handles 2 groups.
How to Contact: Query or submit demo tape only. Prefers cassette with 4 songs minimum on demo. SASE. Reports in 1 month.
Music: Rock; jazz (rock); top 40/pop; soul; MOR; disco; and R&B. Current acts include Lenny White (jazz/rock); Nick Moroch (rock/pop/new wave); and Barry Goldberg (writer/producer).

C.F.A., Seabird Recording Studio, 415 N. Ridgewood Ave., Edgewater FL 32032. (904)427-2480. President: Dick Conti. Management firm and booking agency. Estab. 1973. Represents groups and songwriters from the South, the Midwest and the Southeast; currently handles acts "and a multitude of songwriters." Receives 10-30% commission.
How to Contact: Query, submit demo tape and lead sheet, or call. Prefers 7½ ips reel-to-reel or cassette. SASE. Reports in 1 month.
Music: Bluegrass; blues; children's; choral; church/religious; classical; C&W; disco; folk; gospel; jazz; MOR; rock; soul; and top 40/pop. Works primarily with large "Mike Curb Congregation" type groups, rock groups (black and white); and commercial/jingle writers and arrangers. Current act is the Conti Family.

THE CAMERON ORGANISATION, INC., 320 S. Waiola Ave., La Grange IL 60525. (312)352-2026. Vice President/General Manager: Jean M. Cameron. Management firm. Estab. 1973. Represents individuals, groups and songwriters; currently handles 6 acts.
How to Contact: Submit demo tape and lead sheet. Prefers 7½ ips reel-to-reel or cassette with 1-3 songs on demo, or acetates. SASE. Reports in 1 month.
Music: Blues; progressive; rock; soul; and top 40/pop. Current acts include Muddy Waters and Willie Dixon (blues); Mighty Joe Young (blues/rock); Skafish (rock); Wazmo Nariz (rock); and Bonnie Koloc (pop).

CAPITOL BOOKING SERVICE, INC., 13826 Beaver Rd., New Springfield OH 44443. (216)549-2155. Musical Dept.: David Musselman, Gary Wilms. Booking agency. Estab. 1968. Represents show groups; currently handles 11 acts. Receives 15-20% commission.
How to Contact: Query. Prefers cassette with 3 songs minimum on tape. "We would like references. We also have video equipment, and if artist has videotape, we would like to see this." SASE. Reports in 2 weeks.
Music: Church/religious; C&W; folk; gospel; and top 40/pop. Works primarily with "self-contained musical groups that play all-around music for mixed audiences." Current acts include Life (show group); Sunshine Express (show group); the Shoppe (music and comedy); Transition (show/dance group); and the Melodeers (show/dance group).

CARMAN PRODUCTIONS, INC., 15456 Cabrito Rd., Van Nuys CA 91406. President: Tom Skeeter. Manager: J. Eddy. Management firm. Estab. 1970. Represents individuals and groups; currently handles 8 acts. Receives 15-20% commission.
How to Contact: Query or submit demo tape and lead sheet. Prefers cassette with 1-6 songs on demo. SASE. Reports in 1 month.
Music: Jazz; MOR; progressive; rock; and top 40/pop. Works primarily with recording artists. Current acts include Rick Springfield (rock/MOR); Les Emmerson (rock/MOR); Lorence Hud (rock/C&W); and Jeff Silverman (rock/jazz).

CAROLINA ATTRACTIONS, INC., 203 Culver Ave., Charleston SC 29407. (803)766-2500. President: Harold Thomas. Vice President, A&R: Michael Thomas. Management firm. Estab. 1961. Represents only nationally known individuals, groups and songwriters; currently handles 5 acts. Receives 10-25% commission.
How to Contact: Submit demo tape. Prefers 7½ ips reel-to-reel or cassette. "Send cover letter with tape and any additional promo material (pictures, news releases, etc.) available. Bio if possible." SASE. Reports in 3 weeks.
Music: Disco; soul; and top 40/pop. Works primarily with artists for show and dance groups and concerts. Current acts include the Tams (show/concert group); Cornelius Brothers and Sister Rose (show/concert group); and the Original Drifters (show/concert group).

TONY CEE ASSOCIATES, 17 South St., Utica NY 13501. (315)735-2231. Agent: Tony Cee. Management firm and booking agency. Estab. 1968. Represents professional groups; currently handles 25 acts. Receives 15-25% commission.
How to Contact: Submit demo tape and lead sheet. Prefers reel-to-reel or cassette. SASE. Reports in 1 month.
Music: Current acts include All American Band (American 60s top 40 act); Carmen Canavo Show (top 40/Italian specialty act); and Frogs (X-rated rock act).

ED CHAMBERS TALENT ASSOCIATES, 11141 Georgia Ave., Suite A-1, Silver Spring MD 20902. (301)949-9500. Owner: Edward M. Chambers. Management firm and booking agency. Estab. 1971. Represents individuals, groups, and "magical and variety entertainment." Deals in the mid-Atlantic region only. Currently handles 40 acts. Receives 5-20% commission.
How to Contact: Query or submit demo tape and lead sheet. Prefers cassette with 4 songs minimum on tape. Include a photo if possible. SASE. Reports in 2 weeks.
Music: Blues; disco; folk; MOR; rock; and top 40/pop. Works primarily with dance bands. Current acts include Nite Hawks; Sinbad; and Nowhere Men (rock groups).

CHECK PRODUCTIONS, INC., 936 Moyer Rd., Newport News VA 23602. (804)877-0762. President: Wilson Harrell. Management firm and booking agency. Estab. 1965. Works with local individuals and groups; currently handles 10 acts. Receives 10-15% commission.
How to Contact: Query or submit demo tape. Prefers cassette with 5-10 songs on demo. "Submit song list, resume and 8x10 glossy." SASE. Reports in 1 month.
Music: Bluegrass; disco; folk; MOR; rock (country rock); soul; and top 40/pop. Works primarily with dance bands for lounges and private parties. Current acts include Harvest (top

40/disco group); Daybreak (top 40/disco group); and Brandy (top 40/commercial/disco group).

CTI RECORDS, A division of Creed Taylor, Inc., 1 Rockefeller Plaza, New York NY 10020. (212)489-6120. Professional Manager: Amy Roslyn.Estab. 1970. Represents artists and groups. Receives royalties according to contract.
How to Contact: Submit demo tape and lead sheet by mail or in person. prefers cassette with a minimum of 2 songs on demo. SASE. Reports in 2 weeks-1 month.
Music: Disco; jazz; progressive; soul; and top 40/pop. Works with solo artists mainly, screens songs for 2 singers and other material (pop, jazz and R&B) for instrumentalists. Uses studio musicians for albums. Current acts include Art Farmer (trumpet, flugelhorn, small group); Nina Simone jazz soloist); Patti Austin (jazz, R&B, pop); Hank Crawford (saxophone, small group); and Yuself Lateef (saxophone, woodwinds, R&B).

CLARK MUSICAL PRODUCTIONS, Box 299, Watseka IL 60970. President: Dr. Paul E. Clark. Management firm, booking agency and music publisher. Estab. 1971. Deals with artists in the Midwest and South. Represents individuals, groups and songwriters; currently handles 12 acts. Receives 10-20% commission.
How to Contact: Query or submit demo tape and lead sheet. Prefers cassette with 3-5 songs on demo. SASE. Reports in 1 month.
Music: Choral; church/religious; C&W; folk; gospel; rock (soft); and top 40/pop. Works primarily with acts for concerts, dances and club dates. Current acts include Mark Peterson (C&W solo artist); the Basic Basses (country and rock vocal quartet); and Pat Gould (top 40/pop solo artist).

CLOCKWORK MANAGEMENT, Box 1600, Haverhill MA 01830. (617)374-4792. President: Bill Macek. Management firm and booking agency. Estab. 1972. Deals with artists in New England only. Represents groups and songwriters; currently handles 6 acts. Receives 10-15% commission.
How to Contact: Query or submit demo tape only. Prefers cassette with 3-12 songs on demo. "Also submit promotion and cover letter with tape." SASE. Reports in 2 weeks.
Music: MOR; rock (all types); and top 40/pop. Current acts include The Skinny Kid Band (top 40/rocker); Renegade (FM rocker); Striker (top 40/rocker); and Boaz (funk/rocker).

BRUCE COHN MANAGEMENT/MUSIC, Box 878, Sonoma CA 95476. (707)938-4060. Manager: Bruce Cohn. Management firm and music publisher. Estab. 1975. Represents individuals, groups and songwriters. Receives negotiable commission.
How to Contact: Submit demo tape.
Music: C&W; disco; MOR; rock; soul; and top 40/pop. Works primarily with rock and roll groups and artists. Current acts include the Doobie Brothers.

MARK COLLIER ENTERPRISES, 1379 S. Beltline Hwy., Paducah KY 42001. (502)442-7341. Owner: Mark Collier. Management firm, booking agency and music publisher. Estab. 1973. Represents artists, musical groups and songwriters; currently handles 6 acts. Receives 10-15% commission.
How to Contact: Query or submit demo tape only. Prefers reel-to-reel or cassette with 3-5 songs on demo. SASE. Reports in 2 weeks.
Music: C&W; MOR; and top 40/pop. Works with dance bands, club bands and writers interested in placing their songs. Current acts include Mark Collier Show (4-piece country/pop band); Leon Barnett (4-piece country/pop band); and Today's Country (4-piece country band).

WAYNE COOMBS AGENCY, INC., 655 Deep Valley Dr., Suite 190, Rolling Hills Estates CA 90274. (213)377-0420. Vice President: Dave Peters II. Booking agency. Estab. 1969. Represents professional individuals; currently handles 30 acts. Receives 15-20% commission.
How to Contact: Query. Prefers cassette with 3-6 songs on demo. Does not return unsolicited material. Reports in 1 month.
Music: Gospel; MOR; soul; and top 40/pop. "We primarily handle major international and national artists in the gospel field." Current acts include Pat Boone; B.J. Thomas; Billy Preston; and Debby Boone.

CORNERSTONE MANAGEMENT, Box 480048, Los Angeles CA 90048. President: Martin Wolff. Management agency and publisher (3rd Street Music). Estab. 1977. Represents artists and songwriters; currently handles 3 acts. Receives 15-25% commission.

How to Contact: Query, submit demo tape and lead sheet. Prefers cassette. SASE. Reports in 2 weeks.
Music: Blues; children's; disco; folk; jazz; MOR; progressive; rock; soul; and top 40/pop. Current acts include Max Gronenthal (writer/recording artist) and Tim Goodman (writer/recording artist).

COUNTERPOINT/CONCERTS, INC., 10 Munson Ct., Melville NY 11746. (516)549-1443. Director: Peter Mallon. Management firm. Estab. 1965. Represents individuals and groups; currently handles 6 acts. Receives 10-25% commission.
How to Contact: Query or submit demo tape. Prefers 7½ ips reel-to-reel or cassette. SASE. Reports in 1 month.
Music: Blues; jazz; MOR; and top 40/pop. Works primarily with dance bands, commercial jazz and pop. Current acts include Lee Castle-Jimmy Dorsey Orchestra (jazz); Marty Napoleon-Louis Armstrong Alumni All Stars Band (jazz); Jersey Pops Jazz Symphony (jazz); and Soccer (disco).

COUNTRY SHINDIG PROMOTION CO., 394 W. Main St., C-18, Hendersonville TN 37075. (615)822-1817. Vice President: C.K. Spurlock. Promotion company. "We buy talent, then book a tour, doing all the things dealing with the show's production." Contracts with professional C&W individuals and groups. "After we pay all our acts and expenses, we keep the rest of each tour's revenue as our profit."
How to Contact: Query. "Our company deals with putting together a tour of acts we feel are 'hot' at the time—a package of everything from leasing the buildings to printing the tickets, from advertising to setting up the lights and sound systems." Prefers cassette with 2-3 songs on demo; "however, write first regarding interest, enclosing a biography and photo." SASE. Reporting time varies according to production schedule.
Music: C&W. Recently arranged tours for Loretta Lynn and Conway Twitty, Kenny Rogers and Ronny Milsap. "Understand that we do not manage or book these acts—we buy their talent from their booking agencies."

COYOTE PUBLISHING CO., Box 12523, Raleigh NC 27605. (919)832-7936. Artists Representative: Steve Lamb. Booking agency and promotional firm. Estab. 1978. Represents artists, groups and songwriters. Receives 0-25% commission.
How to Contact: Submit demo tape and lead sheet. Prefers cassette with 1-4 songs on demo. SASE. Reports back "if interested." Also submit photos if available.
Music: Bluegrass; choral; classical; C&W; jazz; and rock (all types). Works with artists for bars, universities and music festivals. Promotion and representation inherent to copyright protection and contracting with record labels.

CRASH PRODUCTIONS, Box 40, Bangor ME 04401. (207)794-6686. Manager: Jim Moreau. Booking agency. Estab. 1969. Represents individuals and groups; currently handles 3 acts. Receives 10-25% commission.
How to Contact: Query. Prefers cassette with 4-8 songs on demo. Include resume and photos. "We prefer to hear groups at an actual performance." SASE. Reports in 2 weeks.
Music: Bluegrass; C&W; rock (country); and top 40/pop. Works primarily with local night clubs. Current acts include New Hampshire (country rock); Ellie Eldridge Show (country rock); and the Kennebec Valley Boys (bluegrass).

CREATIVE CORPS, 6607 W. Sunset Blvd., Suite E, Hollywood CA 90028. President: Kurt Hunter. Management firm and music publisher. Estab. 1974. Represents songwriters and top 40 bands; currently handles 10 acts. Receives 10-20% commission.
How to Contact: Submit demo tape and lead sheet. Prefers cassette with 1-5 songs on demo. SASE. Reports in 3 weeks.
Music: Country; folk; and top 40/pop. Works primarily with original songwriters. Current acts include Denny Martin (songwriter); Norman Mezey (songwriter); Tom Barger (songwriter); and the Double Shuffle Band.

CREATIVE MINDS, INC., 1560 N. La Brea, Hollywood CA 90028. President: Art Benson. Management firm. Estab. 1969. Represents individuals, groups and songwriters; currently handles 5 acts. Receives 25% commission and "cash or a percentage of salary for promotion and publicity."
How to Contact: Arrange personal interview or submit demo tape. Prefers reel-to-reel or cassette. SASE. Reports in 1 month.
Music: Bluegrass; blues; children's; choral; church/religious; classical; C&W; disco; folk;

gospel; jazz; MOR; opera; polka; progressive; rock; soul; and top 40/pop. Current acts include Tommy Cooper (pop/MOR); King Solomon (R&B); and Al Jarvis (piano).

CROSBY MUSIC AGENCY, 7730 Herschel Ave., La Jolla CA 92037. (714)276-7381. Agent: Doug Fries. Booking agency. Estab. 1970. Deals with regional artists only. Represents artists and groups; currently handles 40 acts. Receives 10-20% commission.
How to Contact: Query. Prefers reel-to-reel or cassette with 1-6 songs on demo. SASE. Reports in 2 weeks.
Music: Jazz; rock (hard rock and country rock); and top 40/pop. Works with dance bands, club bands and concert bands. Current acts include Magick (hard rock); Serpentine Fire (disco rock); and Bob Crosby Orchestra (jazz).

DANIEL PROMOTION CORP., Box 1302, Cherry Hill NJ 08002. (609)665-2233. President: Conrad Daniel. Management firm, booking agency and concert promoter. Estab. 1978. Deals with artists in northeast U.S. region only. Represents artists and groups; currently handles 1 act. Receives 10-15% commission.
How to Contact: Submit demo tape only. Prefers reel-to-reel or cassette tape. SASE. Reports in 3 weeks.
Music: Disco; progressive; rock (all); and top 40/pop. Works with original acts with recording potential. Current acts include Reign (original rock).

CONNIE DENAVE MANAGEMENT, 162 W. 56th St., New York NY 10019. (212)582-7410. President: Connie DeNave. Management agency. Estab. 1978. Represents artists, groups and songwriters; currently handles 3 acts.
How to Contact: Query. Prefers cassette with 6 songs maximum on demo. SASE. Reports in 3 weeks.
Music: Disco; MOR; progressive; rock (all kinds); soul; and top 40/pop. Works with artists for concerts and recording. Current acts include Rhetta Hughes (pop/top 40/disco/R&B); Passengers (top 40/rock); and Mark Abel (top 40/rock).

DE SANTO ENTERPRISES, Box 4796, Nashville TN 37216. President: Duane De Santo. Management firm and booking agency. Estab. 1973. Represents individuals and groups; currently handles 5 acts. Receives 10-15% commission.
How to Contact: Submit demo tape. Prefers 7½ ips reel-to-reel.

DIAMONDACK MUSIC CO., 10 Waterville, San Francisco CA 94124. Administrator: Joseph Burchwald. Management firm and publishing company. Estab. 1973. Represents artists, groups and songwriters; currently handles 6 clients. Receives 10% minimum commission
How to Contact: Submit cassette and lead sheet. Prefers a minimum of 3 songs on demo. SASE. Reports ASAP.
Music: Rock. Current clients include Marty Balin.

TONY DIPARDO AGENCY, 2420 Pershing Rd., Suite 311, Kansas City MO 64108. (816)842-6787. Owner: Tony Dipardo. "Music and entertainment consultant." Estab. 1928. Handles mostly local individuals and groups "but some national acts when they come to Kansas City"; currently handles 10-12 acts. Receives 5-20% commission.
How to Contact: Submit demo tape and lead sheet. Prefers reel-to-reel or cassette with 6 songs minimum on tape. SASE. Reports in 2 weeks.
Music: Bluegrass; C&W; disco; folk; jazz; MOR; polka; progressive; rock (all types); soul; and top 40/pop. Works primarily with dance bands and lounge acts. Current acts include Frank Smith Trio (jazz); Karen Day and Charisma (MOR); and Gary Fike Trio (semi-rock).

DISCOVERY UNLIMITED, 3114 Radford Rd., Memphis TN 38111. (901)327-8187. Director: Ted Cunningham. Promotion, publicity and personal management. Estab. 1974. Represents individuals and groups; currently handles 5 acts. Receives 15-25% commission.
How to Contact: Submit demo tape and lead sheet. Prefers 7½ ips reel-to-reel with 1-4 songs on demo. SASE. Reports in 1 month.
Music: C&W; MOR; rock; and top 40/pop. Works primarily with concert and club groups. Current acts include Sam the Sham (top 40); Wolfpack (southern rock); Stephen (top 40); and Pat Taylor (top 40).
Tips: "We will audition material for Fretone Records and if we can't use it we will try to place it with another artist or company for a percentage."

DIVERSIFIED MANAGEMENT AGENCY, 17650 W. Twelve Mile Rd., Southfield MI 48076.

(313)559-2600. Mid-West Agent: Trip Brown. Advertising/Promo Director: Dale Ross. Booking agency. Estab. 1969. Represents individuals and groups; currently handles 25 acts. Receives 15-20% commission.
How to Contact: Submit "promo pack including song list, demo tape and photo of act." Prefers cassette with 3-6 songs on demo. Does not return unsolicited material. Reports in 2 weeks "if interested."
Music: Rock (hard or top 40 rock). Works primarily with "advanced bar bands and concert acts." Current acts include Ted Nugent; Nazareth; and Sammy Hagar.

DMR ENTERPRISES AGENCY, Suite 317, Wilson Bldg., Syracuse NY 13202. (315)471-0868. Owner: David M. Rezak. Booking agency. Estab. 1973. Represents individuals and groups; currently handles 20 acts. Receives 10-15% commission.
How to Contact: Submit demo tape and press kit. Prefers cassette with 1-4 songs on demo. SASE.
Music: Rock; blues; progressive; top 40/pop; and country rock. Works primarily with dance bands. Current acts include Moss Back Mule Band (progressive country rock); Alligators (pop/rock); Sandy Bigtree Band (R&B/progressive country rock); and 805.

DR. COOL PRODUCTIONS, 237 NE 3rd St., Room 10, Miami FL 33132. (305)374-9717. President: Dr. Cool. Management firm and booking agency. Estab. 1970. Represents artists and groups; currently handles 50 acts. Receives 10-15% commission.
How to Contact: Arrange persoal interview. Prefers cassette with 3-4 songs on demo. Reports in 3 weeks.
Music: Blues; disco; folk; gospel; and soul. Works with soul, blues, gospel bands and vocalists. Current acts include Sandra Cool and her Coolettes (soul); Charles 'King Kong' Butler (comic); Blues Boy Fleming (blues) and Baby King (blues).

THE BOB DOYLE AGENCY, 708 S. Pugh St., State College PA 16801. (814)238-5478. President: Bob Doyle. Booking agency. Estab. 1978. Deals with artists in Pennsylvania. Represents groups; currently handles 25 acts. Receives 15-25% commission.
How to Contact: Submit demo tape and lead sheet. Prefers cassette with 3-5 songs on demo. Does not return unsolicited material. Reports in 1 week. "I prefer a phone call first to see if this agency can work with the group. Then we like to have the promo and tape. We need to know if the group can work the markets we are involved with."
Music: Bluegrass; disco; folk (ethnic); and rock (country). Works fraternity markets and some clubs. Current acts include Buffalo Chipkickers (modern bluegrass); Whetstone Run (traditional bluegrass); Tracy & Elosie Schwarz (folk, old time); Hat Trick (funk rock); and Foxie (funk rock).

BUSTER DOSS PRESENTS, Box 927, Manchhac Station, Austin TX 78652. (512)282-4010. President: Buster Doss. Management firm and booking agency. Estab. 1957. Represents groups; currently handles 20 acts. Receives 15-20% commission.
How to Contact: Arrange personal interview or submit demo tape. Prefers 7½ ips reel-to-reel with 3-6 songs on demo. SASE. Reports in 2 weeks.
Music: C&W. Works primarily with dance bands. Current acts include Cooder Browne (C&W artist); Jess Demaine (C&W artist); and Sherry Bee and Summit Ridge (C&W group).

TOM DRAKE AGENCY, 1106 Westport Rd., Kansas City MO 64111. (816)531-1148. Owner: Tom Drake. Producer: Hazel Drake. Booking agency. Estab. 1925. Represents individuals and groups; currently handles 35 acts. "Acts are 'produced' by the agency, including wardrobe, stage show, etc. Payment is negotiated in advance."
How to Contact: Arrange personal interview, submit demo tape with pictures and bio or arrange live audition. Prefers cassette. SASE.
Music: Bluegrass; blues; children's; choral; church/religious; C&W; folk; gospel; MOR; and top 40/pop. Works primarily with show bands and grandstand stage bands. Current acts include Denny Eary (MOR show band); Buddy Young Show (full band); Straub Family (MOR show band); and Mass Transitt (MOR show band).

TIM DRAKE ASSOCIATES, Box 602, Woodcliff Lake NJ 07675. (201)666-5553. Vice President: Paul Freifuss. Management firm, booking agency and middle agency for college concert promotions. Estab. 1974. Deals with national talent from the East Coast. Represents artists, groups and songwriters; currently handles 4 acts. Receives 10-15% commission. "If we are the manager and also act as booking agent the commission will be 20%."

How to Contact: Submit demo tape. "If artist is well known, telephone call will do. If unknown, submit tape, biography, press clippings, etc." Prefers cassette with 3-10 songs on demo. SASE. Reports in 2 weeks.
Music: C&W; disco; folk (rock); progressive; rock; and top 40/pop. Works with singer-songwriters, touring rock groups and concert attractions. Current acts include Melanie (singer-songwriter with back up band); Billy Falcon (5-piece rock group); and Michael Ross (singer-songwriter).

BARRY DRAKE/JON IMS AGENCY, The Gables, Halcott Rd., Fleischmanns NY 12430. (914)254-4565. Contact: Barry Drake, Patricia Padla. Management firm and booking agency. Estab. 1974. Represents individuals, groups and songwriters; currently handles 2 acts. Receives 10-20% commission.
How to Contact: Query or submit demo tape. Prefers cassette with 2-4 songs on demo. SASE. Reports in 1 month.
Music: Bluegrass; blues; C&W; folk; MOR; progressive; rock; and top 40/pop. Works primarily with solo singer/songwriters. Current acts include Barry Drake and Jon Ims.

DYNAMIC TALENT AGENCY, Box 13584, Atlanta GA 30324. (404)872-0266. Vice President, Promotions: Bob Biser. President: Alex Janoulis. Booking Agency. Estab. 1969. Represents individuals and groups; currently handles 6 acts. Receives 10-15% commission.
How to Contact: Submit demo tape. Prefers cassette with 2-3 songs on demo. "Send photos and bio." Reports as soon as possible.
Music: Blues; jazz; rock (new wave). Works with top 40 bands. Current acts include The Wayne Chaffin Group (top 40/pop); Starfoxx (top 40/rock); and The Night Shadows (new wave).

EAGLE PRODUCTIONS, 1239 Conner St., Noblesville IN 46060. (317)773-5696. President: Steve Pritchard. Management firm and booking agency. Estab. 1975. Represents individuals, groups and songwriters; currently handles 15 acts. Receives 15-20% commission.
How to Contact: Submit demo tape. Prefers cassette with 5-12 songs on demo. SASE. Reports in 3 weeks.
Music: Bluegrass; disco; folk; jazz; MOR; rock; and top 40/pop. Works with "all types" of artists. Current acts include Bill Wilson; Carolyn Peyton; and J. Michael Henderson (solo artists).

EBB-TIDE BOOKING AGENCY, Box 2544, Baton Rouge LA 70821. (504)925-2603. President: E.K. Harrison. Booking agency. Estab. 1958. Represents professional individuals and groups; currently handles 3 acts. Receives 15% commission.
How to Contact: Query or submit demo tape along with photographs and biographical information. Prefers cassette tape. SASE. Reports in 1 month.
Music: Bluegrass; blues; children's; choral; church/religious; classical; C&W; disco; easy listening; folk; gospel; jazz; MOR; progressive; rock; soul; and top 40/pop. Current acts include George Perkins and the Silver Stars (soul act); and Paula Marie (rock/pop female artist).

STEVE ELLIS AGENCY, LTD., 250 W. 57th St., Suite 330, New York NY 10019. (212)757-5800. Vice President: Nanci Linke. Agent: Dan Brennan. Booking agency. Estab. 1978. Represents individuals and groups; currently handles 11 acts. Receives 10% commission.
How to Contact: Query. Prefers cassette with 3-6 songs on demo. Does not return unsolicited material. Reports in 3 weeks.
Music: Works with one night concert groups (vocalists w/band). Current acts include Chic (disco/pop group); Jerry Butler (soul); Cameo (disco/funk group); Staples (soul/MOR); and Enchantment (soul/MOR).

RICHARD LEE EMLER ENTERPRISES, 8601 Wilshire Boulevard, Suite #1000, Beverly Hills CA 90211. (213)659-3932. Owner: Richard Lee Emler. Management firm. Estab. 1975. Represents professional artists and songwriters; currently handles 6 acts. Receives 10-20% commission.
How to Contact: Query. Prefers cassette. SASE. Reports in 1 week.
Music: C&W; disco; folk; MOR; rock; soul; top 40/pop; and music for films and TV. Current acts include Peter Matz, Fred Warner and Henry Mollicone (composers/arrangers/conductors); Mitzie Welch (lyricist); Trisha Noble (vocalist); and Larry Dean (guitarist/vocalist).

ENCHANTED DOOR MANAGEMENT CO., INC., Box 1235, New Rochelle NY 10802. (914)961-7189. President: Joe Messina. Management firm. Estab. 1970. Represents professional individuals, groups and songwriters; currently handles 3 acts.
How to Contact: Submit demo tape and lead sheet. Prefers 7½ ips reel-to-reel or cassette tape. SASE. Reports as soon as possible.
Music: Rock; soul; and top 40/pop. Current acts include Spyder Turner (soul vocalist) and Wowii (rock group).

ENCORE ATTRACTIONS, 454 Wren Dr., Los Angeles CA 90065. (213)223-4212. Owners: Joe and Carolyn Dale. Booking agency. Estab. 1953. Represents individuals and groups, Vegas show groups and musical Broadway shows. Receives 10% minimum commission.
How to Contact: Query (include pictures and brochures), arrange personal interview, submit demo tape or submit demo tape and lead sheet. Prefers cassette. Reports "as soon as possible."
Music: Bluegrass; blues; C&W; disco; jazz; progressive; rock; soul; and top 40/pop.

BOB ENGLAR THEATRICAL AGENCY, 2466 Wildon Dr., York PA 17403. (717)741-2844. President: Bob Englar. Booking agency. Estab. 1967. Represents individuals and groups. Receives 10-15% commission.
How to Contact: Query or submit demo tape. Prefers 8-track cartridge with 5-10 songs on demo, or disc. Include photo. SASE. Reports in 3 weeks.
Music: Bluegrass; blues; children's; choral; church/religious; classical; C&W; disco; folk; gospel; jazz; polka; rock (light); soul; and top 40/pop. Works primarily with string quartets and dance bands.

ENTERTAINERS MANAGEMENT & BOOKING AGENCY, 421 Briabend Dr., Charlotte NC 28209. (704)527-1639. President: Thomas Lesesne. Management firm, booking agency and placement firm for "yet undiscovered talent." Estab. 1975. Deals with acts in Southeast region, unless group is a national recording act. Represents groups and songwriters; currently handles 8 acts. Receives 10-20% commission.
How to Contact: Query, arrange personal interview, submit demo tape only or if the group is established submit a complete promo package. Prefers 7½ ips reel-to-reel or cassette with 2-3 songs on demo. SASE. Reports in 3 weeks.
Music: Disco; jazz; rock; soul; and top 40/pop. Works with artists for nightclubs, colleges, major concerts, dances (high school). Current acts include Green Ice (disco, R&B); Continental Drive (top 40/pop); Gemi (rock); and Gary Toms Empire (disco).

ENTERTAINMENT SERVICES CONCEPT, Box 2501, Des Moines IA 50315. (515)285-6564. President: Art Smart Stenstrom. Management firm, booking agency, record company and music publisher. Represents groups and songwriters; currently handles 2 acts and books 10-20 acts. "We generally deal only with regional attractions, but we're interested in doing dates on groups from any area that might want to work this area." Receives 7½-25% commission.
How to Contact: Submit all promotional materials available, with song list and demo tape. Prefers cassette tape. "On a demo tape of a live performance, any number of songs. Telephoning prior to sending materials will ensure that materials get attention." SASE. Reports in 2 weeks.
Music: Rock (only material that is recognizable) and top 40/pop (commercial or nostalgia shows). Works primarily with "regional attractions that work club, small concert, college, high school and ballroom gigs." Current acts include Dahcotah (original rock and AOR material); Silver Laughter (original rock and AOR material); Impulse (rock and top 40); and the Mob (show group).

FANTASMA PRODUCTIONS, INC., 1675 Palm Beach Lakes Bldg., Suite 902, West Palm Beach FL 33401. (305)686-6397. Director of Booking: Gary Propper. President: Jon Stoll. Management firm, booking agency and promotion agency. Estab. 1970. Represents groups; currently handles 8 acts. Receives 10-20% commission.
How to Contact: Query or submit demo tape. Prefers 7½ ips reel-to-reel or cassette with 3-5 songs on demo. Include bio and photo. SASE. Reports in 1 month.
Music: Bluegrass; C&W; disco; folk; jazz; MOR; progressive; rock (country, hard or punk); soul; and top 40/pop. Current acts include True of America (comedy/show/top 40); Coconut (country/folk); Cactus (rock); Free Wheel (rock); and Harmony Grits (bluegrass).

FRED T. FENCHEL ENTERTAINMENT AGENCY, 2104 S. Jefferson Ave., Mason City IA 50401. General Manager: Fred T. Fenchel. Booking agency. Estab. 1965. Represents professional individuals and groups; currently handles 15 acts. Receives 15-20% commission.

How to Contact: Query. Prefers cassette. SASE. Reports in 3 weeks.
Music: C&W; rock; and top 40/pop. Current acts include Southern Kumfort (top 40 group); Cruise (top 40 group with "speciality features"); and Pearl (top 40 group).

JOAN FRANK PRODUCTIONS, Suite 228, 2 Turtle Creek Village, Dallas TX 75219. (214)522-3240. Manager: R.D. Leonard. Booking agency. Estab. 1934. Represents individuals and groups. Receives 15% minimum commission.
How to Contact: Query. SASE. Reports in 2 weeks.
Music: C&W and MOR. Works primarily with dance bands, combos and singles. Current acts include the Shoppe (instrumental/vocal/comedy lounge act); the Gary Lee Combo (dance music band); and Biff Murphy and the Plaids (dance music band).

FRASCO ENTERTAINMENT AGENCY, INC., 1208 Eastview, Jackson MS 39201. (601)969-1434. President: Greg Frascogna. Booking agency. Estab. 1968. Represents individuals and groups; currently handles 30 acts. Receives 15-20% commission.
How to Contact: Submit demo tape and lead sheet. Prefers 7½ ips reel-to-reel with 3-5 songs on demo. SASE. Reports in 3 weeks.
Music: Disco; rock; soul; and top 40/pop. Works primarily with rock groups. Current acts include Peggy Scott (MOR singer); Mississippi (rock group); and Th' Rugbys (rock group).

FREDDIE "C" ATTRACTIONS, 370 Market St., Box 333, Lemoyne PA 17043. (717)761-0821. Owner: Fred Clousher. Booking agency. Estab. 1971. Represents groups and comedy and novelty acts in Pennsylvania, Maryland, Virginia, West Virginia, New York, New Jersey and Ohio; currently handles approximately 75 acts. Receives 10-20% commission.
How to Contact: Query or submit demo tape. Include "photos, list of credits, etc." Prefers 7½ ips reel-to-reel, cassette or 8-track cartridge with 3-7 songs on demo. Does not return unsolicited material. Reports in 3 weeks.
Music: Bluegrass; C&W; gospel; polka; and top 40/pop. Works primarily with "commercial, commercial/rock, country and novelty show groups. Most dates are one-nighters." Current acts include the Hawaiian Review 79; (Hawaiian show group); Smokey Warren Show (C&W group); Jolly Knights (polka, German, etc.); and The Ronnie Allyn Show (tribute to Elvis).

FROST & FROST ENTERTAINMENT, 3985 W. Taft Dr., Spokane WA 99208. (509)325-1777. Owner/Agent: Dick Frost. Booking agency. Estab. 1969. Represents individuals and groups; currently handles 14 acts. Receives 10-15% commission.
How to Contact: Query. Prefers cassette with 5 songs minimum on tape. Include information on past appearances, as well as list of references. SASE. Reports in 2 weeks.
Music: C&W; MOR; and top 40/pop. Works primarily with dance bands, show bands and individual artists. Currently acts include Tex Williams (western act); Kay Austin (C&W/MOR act); Big Tiny Little, Frank Fara Show, Dick Frost, Magician, Sons of Pioneers, Stagecoach West, and West Side Street.

FUNKY P.O. MUSIC CORP., 712 SW Salmon St., Suite B, Portland OR 97205. (503)221-0288. Manager: Chad Debnam. Management firm and publishing and production company. Estab. 1974. Represents artists, groups and songwriters; currently handles 20 acts. Negotiates commission.
How to Contact: Submit demo tape only. Prefers cassette with 3-5 songs on demo. SASE. Reports in 3 weeks.
Music: Disco; jazz; rock (hard); soul; and top 40/pop. Works with concert groups. Current acts include Pleasure (progressive funk); Dennis Springer (jazz); and Gary Ogan (pop/folk).

GAIL AND RICE PRODUCTIONS, 11845 Mayfield, Livonia MI 48150. (313)427-9300. Vice President: Greg Purcott. Booking agency. Estab. 1931. Represents individuals and groups; currently handles 25 acts. Receives 10-20% commission.
How to Contact: Submit demo tape and lead sheet. Prefers cassette with 3-6 songs on demo. Does not return unsolicited material. Reports in 3 weeks.
Music: C&W; rock; soul; and top 40/pop. Works primarily with "self-contained groups (2-8 people), show and dance music and individual name or semi-name attractions." Current acts include Southern Comfort (show group); Trinidad Tripoli Steel Drum Band (show group); the Dazzlers (vocal/dance act); and Glenn Haywood (comedian/ventriloquist).

MICK GAMBILL PRODUCTIONS, 6051 Romaine St., Hollywood CA 90038. (213)466-9777. President: Mick Gambill. Management firm and booking agency. Estab. 1971. Represents West Coast groups; currently handles 30 acts. Receives 15-20% commission.

How to Contact: Submit demo tape. Prefers cassette with 3-6 songs on demo. SASE. Reports in 2 weeks.
Music: MOR and top 40/pop. Works primarily with top 40 groups. Current acts include Skogie; Afrodezia; and Ratchell Rumbleseat (top 40/pop groups).

LARRY GLICKMAN, 1215 Barry Ave., Los Angeles CA 90025. President: Larry Glickman. Management agency. Estab. 1976. Deals with local artists only. Represents artists, groups and songwriters; currently handles 5 acts. Receives 20% commission.
How to Contact: Submit demo tape and lead sheet. Prefers cassette with 6 songs on demo. Submission should include picture, resume. "All material *must* be written by artist." SASE. Reports in 2 weeks.
Music: Rock and top 40/pop. "I am currently a one man operation. I have major agency and legal experience. I would probably not be interested in new talent for about 6 months when I will be adding staff." Current acts include Choir (rock); Tezer (rock); Feast (rock); and Cece Bullard (pop-country actress).

ZACH GLICKMAN, 6430 Sunset Blvd., Hollywood CA 90028. (213)461-2988. President: Zach Glickman. Management agency. Estab. 1968. Represents artists, groups and songwriters; currently represents 4 acts.
How to Contact: Submit demo tape and lead sheet. Prefers reel-to-reel tape. SASE. Reports 1 month.
Music: Church/religious; disco; gospel; rock; soul; and top 40/pop. current acts include Dion (rock); Mighty Clouds of Joy (gospel); and Faragher Brothers (rock).

GLIMMER IMAGES/TCS MANAGEMENT, 115 E. Foothill Blvd. No. 6, Glendora CA 91740. (213)335-1216 or 849-BAND. Contact: Tom Soran. Management agency and production company. Deals with artists from Southern California only. Represents artists and groups; currently handles 350-400 acts. Negotiates fee paid.
How to Contact: Call first. Have press kit prepared. Query. Prefers cassette with 1-10 songs on demo. SASE. Reports in 2 weeks.
Music: C&W; disco; jazz; MOR; rock; and top 40/pop (new wave, cross-over). Works with "pop" and dance bands, cover and original. Current acts include The Renegades (3-4-10 piece casual and session band); Featherstitch (AOR, 6-piece, original); Yankee Rose (5-piece, English rock, original); and Silver Chance (5-piece, original power pop).

GOLDMAN-DELL MUSIC PRODUCTIONS, 421 W. 87th St., Box 8680, Kansas City MO 64114. (816)333-8701. Owner: Irv Goldman. Management firm and booking agency. Estab. 1962. Represents individuals, groups and songwriters; currently handles approximately 30 acts. Receives "minimum commission set by the union." Also contract producer of shows with local or national acts.
How to Contact: Arrange personal interview, submit demo tape and lead sheet or contact by phone. Bandleaders or acts send cassette tape and photo. Prefers reel-to-reel or cassette with 2 songs minimum on tape. SASE. Reports at once if acceptable.
Music: Bluegrass; blues; classical (guitar); C&W; disco; folk; gospel; jazz; MOR; rock; soul; and top 40/pop. Works primarily with variety and dance bands but accepts all types. Current acts include Classmen (show band); Butch Silver Band (top/40 pop/disco); and Brothers Heritage (show-dance-stage band).

WALT GOLLENDER ENTERPRISES, 12 Marshall St., Suite 8Q, Irvington NJ 07111. (201)373-6050. Executive Director: Walt Gollender. Management firm. Estab. 1966. Represents artist and songwriters. Receives sales royalty, outright fee from record company or outright fee from songwriter/artist.
How to Contact: Submit demo tape only. Prefers 7½ ips reel-to-reel (mono mix) or cassette with a maximum of 5 songs on demo. "Call any evening 5-8 p.m. EST." SASE. Reports in 3 weeks.
Music: Blues; C&W; disco; easy listening; folk; MOR; rock (light); soul; and top 40/pop. Works primarily with rock groups, vocalists, small combos, songwriters and C&W vocalists. Current acts include Dan and Bob (folk/pop duo); Mary Lee Martin (C&W vocalist); Chuch Ehrmann (C&W); Tina Sanderson (rock/disco); and Ben Wiggins (soul/disco).

GOOD KARMA PROUCTIONS, INC., 4218 Main St., Kansas City MO 64111. (816)531-3857. Co-Owner: Paul Peterson. Management agency. Estab. 1969. Deals with Midwest artists only. Represents artists and groups; currently handles 4 acts. Receives maximum 20% commission.

How to Contact: Submit demo tape only. Prefers 7½ ips reel-to-reel and cassette with 2-4 songs on demo. SASE. Reports in 2 weeks.
Music: Disco; progressive; rock (hard and country); and top 40/pop. Works with rock and country rock bands, concert and recording artists only and songwriters. Current acts include the Ozark Mountain Daredevils (country-rock recording artists); the Randle Chowning Band (rock recording group); and the St. Louis Sheiks (R&B/disco/rock group).

GOOD MUSIC MANAGEMENT, INC., Box 4087, Missoula MT 59806. President: Doug Brown. Booking agency. Estab. 1972. Represents artists and groups; currently handles 10 acts. Receives 15-20% commission.
How to Contact: Submit demo tape and press kit only. "Send all information possible, no phone calls please." Prefers cassette with a minimum of 5 songs on demo. Also send references on live performance. SASE. Reports in 3 weeks.
Music: C&W; rock; top 40/pop; and country rock. Current acts include Nina Kahlle (singer-songwriter); Mission Mountain Wood Band (bluegrass/country/rock); The Guess Who (rock); and Larry Raspberry (rock, R&B).

JOE GRAYDON & ASSOCIATES, Box 1, Toluca Lake CA 91602. (213)769-2424. President: Joe Graydon. Management firm. Estab. 1960. Represents artists, groups, songwriters and package shows for tours; currently handles 12 acts. Receives 10-15% commission.
How to Contact: Submit demo tape only. Prefers cassette tape. SASE. Reports in 1 week.
Music: Bluegrass; C&W; disco; MOR; soul; and primarily top 40/pop. Works with show groups that play Nevada lounges and individual singers, male and female. Current acts include Helen Forrest (singer); C.C. Jones (singer with road show); and The Boos Brothers (show group).

GREAT AMERICAN TALENT, INC., 12301 Wilshire Blvd., Los Angeles CA 90025. (213)820-6673. President: Jim Summers. Vice President: Burk Dennis. Management firm and booking agency. Estab. 1976. Deals with artists in California region only. Represents individuals, groups and songwriters; currently represents 50 acts. Receives 10-20% commission.
How to Contact: Query or submit demo tape and lead sheet. Prefers 7½ ips reel-to-reel with 3-10 songs on demo. SASE. Reports in 3 weeks.
Music: Bluegrass; C&W; disco; jazz; MOR; rock; soul; and top 40/pop. Works with concert acts. Current acts include Emperor (rock group); Morgania King (jazz singer); and Wolfman Jack (variety artist).

MALCOLM GREENWOOD, Box 4164, Jackson MS 39216. (601)354-1958. Personal Manager: Malcolm Greenwood. Management firm and booking agency. Estab. 1978. Represents individuals and groups; currently handles 2 acts. Receives negotiable commission.
How to Contact: Query by phone. Prefers 7½ ips reel-to-reel with 4-10 songs on demo. SASE. Reports in 1 week.
Music: Gospel (contemporary Christian). Works with contemporary Christian single artists and groups. Current acts include The Pat Terry Group (contemporary Christian group); and Glenn Garrett (contemporary Christian artist).

THE GROUP, INC., 1957 Kilburn Dr., Atlanta GA 30324. (404)872-0266. General Manager: Hamilton Underwood. Vice President: Robert Biser. Management agency. Estab. 1967. Represents individuals and groups. Receives 15-25% commission..
How to Contact: Submit demo tape only. Prefers cassette with 2-3 songs on demo. Include photo and bio. Doesn't return unsolicited material. Reports as soon as possible.
Music: Blues; jazz; progressive; rock; and top 40/pop. Works with total package groups (artists and songwriters). Current acts include Jazzo (jazz/rock); Starfoxx (top 40/rock); Little Phil and the Night Shadows (new wave); and Diamond Lil (female impersonator).

AMRON HALPERN ATTRACTIONS, INC., 8831 Sunset Blvd., Los Angeles CA 90069. (213)855-7061. Vice President West Coast: Maureen Nemeth. Management firm, record producers and publishers. Estab. 1978. Represents artists, groups, songwriters, actors and actresses; currently handles 5 acts. Receives 15-25% commission.
How to Contact: Submit demo tape and lead sheet. Prefers 7½ ips reel-to-reel, cassette tapes. SASE. Reports in 1 month.
Music: Disco; progressive; rock; soul; and top 40/pop. Current acts include Kristy & Jimmy McNichol (pop/top 40, disco); Bob Guillaume (disco/soul); and Frank Filipetti (rock).

JIM HALSEY CO., INC., 9000 Sunset Blvd., Suite 1010, Los Angeles CA 90069.

(213)278-3397. Vice President Music Operations: Larry Baunach. Estab. 1978. Management firm, booking agency, production company (White Buffalo Production, Inc.) and music publishing company (Bear Tracks Music, Inc.). Represents artists groups and songwriters; currently handles 20 acts. Negotiates commission.

How to Contact: Submit demo tape only or demo tape and lead sheet. Prefers 7½ ips reel-to-reel or cassette tapes. SASE. Reports in 3 weeks or less.

Music: C&W; folk; MOR; rock (all forms); and top 40/pop. Works with concert bands and artists.

THE JACK HAMPTON AGENCY, 226 S. Beverly Dr., Beverly Hills CA 90212. (213)274-6075. Artists' Manager/Agent: Robert Archibald. Management firm and booking agency. Estab. 1948. Represents artists, groups, songwriters, recording artists, entertainers and lecturers. Receives 10-20% commission. Percentage 50% if from acts as producer.

How To Contact: Arrange personal interview if in Los Angeles area. Prefers cassette with 3-5 songs to be mailed with resume, song list and photo to agency with proper amount of postage affixed. SASE. Reports in 2 weeks.

Music: Bluegrass; blues; children's; classical; C&W; disco; folk; jazz; MOR; progressive; rock (original, MOR, hard, soft); soul; top 40/pop and diverse instrumental and vocal acts. Works with dance and bar bands and original groups looking for recording contracts. Current acts include Buddy de Franco (jazz); Tilman Thomas (rock, original); Paul Cypress (classical guitarist); Rocket 88 (rock, clubs/original); Pacific Flyer (top 40/pop); and Paul Gann (lecturer).

GEOFFREY HANSEN & ASSOCIATES, INC., Box 63, Orinda CA 94563. (415)937-6469. Artist Relations: Stan Jacobson. Management agency. Estab. 1953. Represents artists, groups and songwriters; currently handles 5 acts. Receives 10-25% commission. Also paid on a contract (or double/contract) basis.

How to Contact: Submit demo tape and lead sheet. Prefers reel-to-reel and cassette. SASE. Reports in 1 month or longer.

Music: Blues; C&W; MOR; rock (and country rock); and top 40/pop. Works with top 40 and C&W artists. Current acts include Garmon Hines (C&W); and Liff Richard (top 40/MOR).

FOREST HAMILTON PERSONAL MANAGEMENT, 9229 Sunset Blvd., Suite 700, Los Angeles CA 90069. Manager: Forest Hamilton. Assistant Manager: Phil Casey.Management firm. Estab. 1973. Represents individuals and groups; currently handles 6 acts. Receives negotiable commission.

How to Contact: Submit demo tape and lead sheet. Prefers cassette with 3-6 songs on demo. Does not return unsolicited material. Reports in 1 month.

Music: Blues; disco; gospel; jazz; MOR; rock; soul; and top 40/pop. Works primarily with bands and solo artists. Current acts include the Dramatics (soul group); Side Effect (band); and David Oliver (solo artist).

HARMONY ARTISTS, INC., 8833 Sunset Blvd., Suite 200, Los Angeles CA 90069. (213)659-9644. President: Michael Dixon. Booking agency. Estab. 1975. Represents groups; currently handles 100 acts. Receives 10-15% commission.

How To Contact: Arrange personal interview. Prefers reel-to-reel or cassette with 3-5 songs on demo. SASE. Reports in 2 weeks.

Music: Disco; rock (hard rock); and top 40/pop. Current acts include Auracle, Ohio Players and Nick Gilder.

THE DAVID HARRIS AGENCY, 17100 Ventura Blvd., #226, Encino CA 91316. (213)955-1088. Contact: David Harris. Booking agency. Estab. 1976. Represents artists, groups and songwriters. Receives 10-15% commission.

How To Contact: Call. Prefers cassette with 3-5 songs on demo. Does not return unsolicited material.

Music: Disco; MOR; soul; and top 40/pop. Works with dance bands.

HARTMANN & GOODMAN, 1500 Cross Roads of the World, Hollywood CA 90028. (213)461-3461. Contact: Margaret Holmes. Management agency. Estab. 1973. Represents artists, group and songwriters (who also perform their work); currently handles 10 acts.

How To Contact: Submit demo tape. Prefers cassette with 1-4 songs on demo. "Please indicate whether the material is being submitted for our artists to record or for possible management." SASE. Reports in 1 month.

Music: MOR; rock (country rock, hard rock, etc.); and top 40/pop. Works with rock, acoustic rock and country rock individuals and bands. Also recording and concert acts. Current acts include America (group); Poco (group); and Dwight Twilley, David Crosby and Graham Nash.

HEATHER MANAGEMENT CO./A DIVISION OF PMA, INC., 8040 Roosevelt Blvd., Suite 119, Philadelphia PA 19152. (215)868-9050. President: Ben Rose. Vice President: Chuck Krase. Sec./Treasurer: John Kaye. Management firm, booking agency and production & publishing company. Estab. 1977. Represents artists, groups and songwriters; currently handles 34 acts. Receives 10-25% commission.
How To Contact: Query and submit demo tape and lead sheet. "All initial correspondence is to be handled by mail. No phone calls please. All material will be reviewed at the end of each week. All correspondence will be answered promptly." Prefers cassette with 3-6 songs on demo. SASE. Reports in 2 weeks.
Music: Blues; disco; jazz; MOR; progressive; rock; soul; and top 40/pop. Works with concert acts, nightclub and disco acts, single performers and non-performing songwriters. Current acts include Fuzzy Bunny (8-piece funk rock fusion concert act); Shuttlekract (8-piece jazz, funk, rock fusion concert act); Lunisphere (6-piece classical jazz, rock fusion theatrical concert act); Yevette Williams & Rory McDonald (R&B, top/40 pop singing/songwriting act); Mook Stanton Jr. (R&B singer/songwriter); and Larry Bond (singer/songwriter, theatrical, classical, jazz, rock).

JERRY HELLER AGENCY, 6430 Sunset Blvd., #1516, Hollywood CA 90028. (213)462-1100. President: Jerry Heller. Booking agency. Estab. 1969. Represents individuals, groups, songwriters and producers; currently handles 25 acts.
How to Contact: Query or arrange personal interview. Prefers 7½ ips reel-to-reel or cassette with 3-7 songs on demo. SASE. Reports as soon as possible.
Music: Folk; jazz; MOR; progressive; rock; and soul. Current acts include Joan Armatrading (vocalist); John Mayall (blues); and Cory Wells (pop).

GLENN HENRY ENTERTAINMENT AGENCY, 3887 State St., Suite 208, Santa Barbara CA 93105. (805)687-1131. Contact: Glenn Henry, Jerry Brown. Booking agency. Estab. 1960. Represents individuals and groups; currently handles 14 acts. Receives 10-15% commission.
How to Contact: Query or arrange personal interview. Prefers cassette or 8-track cartridge with 3-5 songs on demo.
Music: MOR and top 40/pop. Works with lounge and hotel bands "with a girl if possible." Current acts include Waterfall; Jet Lag; and Elysium (MOR bands).

RON HENRY MANAGEMENT AND CONSULTANTS, 7265½ Hollywood Blvd., Hollywood CA 90046. (213)851-8494. President: Ron Henry. Management agency. Estab. 1977. Represents artists, groups and songwriters; currently handles 4 acts. Receives 15-20% commission.
How To Contact: Prefers cassette with 2-5 songs on demo. SASE. Reports in 2 weeks.
Music: MOR; progressive; rock; and top 40/pop. Works with artists who write their own music. Current acts include Moon Martin (pop/rock 'n roll band); Fast Fontaine (pop/rock 'n roll band); and US Rock (pop band).

CHUCK HERNANDER, 808 S. Herbert Ave., Los Angeles CA 90023. (213)264-0715. Professional Manager: Chuck Hernander. Management firm. Estab. 1977.
How to Contact: Submit demo tape and lead sheet. Prefers 7½ ips reel-to-reel with 5-11 songs on demo. SASE. Reports in 3 weeks.
Music: Bluegrass; C&W; hard rock; and top 40/pop.
Tips: "Send demo, then call to get an appointment to discuss your material."

HIGH TIDE MANAGEMENT, INC., 180 Allen Rd. NE, Suite 120C, Atlanta GA 30328. (404)252-9140. President: Charles Brusco. Management firm and music publisher. Estab. 1976. Represents individuals, groups and songwriters; currently handles 2 groups and 3 songwriters. Receives 15-25% commission.
How to Contact: Submit demo tape and lead sheet. Prefers cassette with 4-8 songs on demo. Does not return unsolicited material. Reports in 2 weeks.
Music: MOR; progressive; rock; and top 40/pop. Works primarily with country rock and southern rock artists. Current acts include the Outlaws (country rock group); and Bill Lamb, and Freddy Salem (singer/songwriters).

KAZUKO HILLYER INTERNATIONAL, 250 W. 57th St., New York NY 10019.

(212)581-3644. President: Kazuko Hillyer. Vice President, North American Operations: Vincent Wagner. Management firm and booking agency. Estab. 1968. Represents professional individuals and groups; currently handles 124 acts. Receives 20% commission.
How to Contact: Submit lead sheet. Does not return unsolicited material. Reports "only if interested."
Music: Blues; choral; classical; folk; gospel; jazz; and opera. Current acts include Odetta (folk vocalist); Tokyo String Quartet (classical group); and Mario Escadero (flamenco guitarist).

HITCH-A-RIDE MUSIC, Box 201, Cincinnati OH 45201. Manager: J.H. Reno. Management firm. Estab. 1975. Represents professional individuals, groups and songwriters; currently handles 6 acts. Receives negotiable commission.
How to Contact: Query or submit demo tape. Prefers 7½ ips reel-to-reel with 1-5 songs on demo. SASE. Reports in 1 month.
Music: Bluegrass; C&W; and MOR. Current acts include Pam Hanna; Jack Reno; and Al Henderson (C&W vocalists); and Mary Ellen Tanner (MOR/C&W vocalist).

ROBERT HOLLIDAY & ASSOCIATES, Box 28613, Atlanta GA 30328. (404)973-0033. President: Robert Holliday. Management firm and booking agency. Estab. 1970. Represents groups and songwriters; currently handles 8 acts. Receives 10-25% commission.
How to Contact: Submit demo tape. Prefers 7½ ips reel-to-reel with 3-6 songs on demo. SASE. Reports in 1 month.
Music: Rock and top/40 pop. Works primarily with concert attractions. Current acts include William Bell (soul songwriter); Starbuck (top 40/pop group); and Beaverteeth (top 40/pop group).

GEORGE B. HUNT & ASSOCIATES, 8350 Santa Monica Blvd., Los Angeles CA 90069. (213)654-6600. Owner: George B. Hunt. Management firm and booking agency. Estab. 1949. Represents professional individuals and groups. Receives 10-15% commission.
How to Contact: Query. SASE. Reports in 1 month.
Music: Current acts include Sunshine 'n Rain (folk group); Scotty Plummer (banjo artist); and Dirk Arthur (magician). "In addition to the above, we book all types of acts for fairs, conventions, banquets, etc."

GEORGE B. HUNT & ASSOCIATES, 1009 22nd St., Sacramento CA 95816. Manager: Jackie O'Dell. Management firm and booking agency. See Hunt & Associates, Los Angeles office, for details.

GEORGE B. HUNT & ASSOCIATES, 1255 Post St., San Francisco CA 94109. Manager: Elizabeth Phillips. See Hunt & Associates, Los Angeles office, for details.

ICA TALENT, 113 N. San Vicente Blvd., Beverly Hills CA 90211. (213)550-0254. President: Chet Aetis. Management firm, booking agency and publicity and financial services. Estab. 1976. Represents artists, groups, songwriters and dance productions. Receives 10-20% commission.
How To Contact: Submit demo tape only and all press reviews and performance track record. Prefers cassette with 3-10 songs on demo. SASE. Reports in 1 month.
Music: Bluegress; blues; C&W; folk; disco; jazz; MOR; progressive; rock (all forms); soul; and top 40/pop. Works with concert bands, major showroom (i.e. Las Vegas) productions, bar bands. Current acts include Alan: A Tribute to Elvis (rock); Vince Vance & The Valiants (rock); Rain: A Tribute to the Beatles (rock); and Dazzle (broadway-disco dance revue).

ICR INTERNATIONAL CELEBERITY REGISTER, INC., (Music Division), 214 W. 6th St., Suite AA, Box 4527, Topeka KS 66604. (913)233-9716. Executive Vice President in charge of entertainmnet: Kent Raine. Estab. 1976. Management firm and booking agency, a division of the Earthraker Corporation. Represents artists, groups and songwriters; currently handles 8 acts. Receives 10-25% commission.
How to Contact: Query or submit demo tape and lead sheet. Photos and short biography helpful. Prefers 7½ ips reel-to-reel or cassette with 2-6 songs on demo. SASE. Reports in 1 month.
Music: Blues; C&W; disco; jazz; MOR; rock (and country rock); soul; and top; 40/pop. Works with artists for concert attractions and recording groups. "We're always on the look out for a promising young songwriter or artist, however, don't expect any miracles in this business."

IF PRODUCTIONS, 15 Glenby Lane, Brookville NY 11545. (516)626-0929. 22240 Schoenborn St., Canoga Park CA 91304. (213)883-4865. New York: Producer/Staff writer: Tom Ingegno. Los Angeles: Producer/Staff writer:Mike Frenchik. Management agency and production company. Estab. 1977. Represents individuals, groups and songwriters. Currently handles 4 acts. Receives 15-20% commission.
How to Contact: Query or submit demo tape only. Prefers 7½ ips reel-to-reel or cassette with 3-5 songs on demo. SASE. Reports in 3 weeks.
Music: MOR; progressive; rock; and top 40/pop. Current acts include Thrills (rock act); Tony Monaco (songwriter); and Dave Fullerton (songwriter).

INNOVATIVE ARTISTS MANAGEMENT, Box 246, Worcester MA 01613. (617)753-1318. President: Patrick George. Booking agency and management firm. Estab. 1968. Deals with artists in the Boston-Washington D.C. area, also Great Britain. Represents groups and songwriters; currently handles 25 acts. Receives 10-30% commission. "We also serve as career development and marketing consultants at $50/hour or will travel to artist's area for $250 per day plus expenses"
How To Contact: Submit demo tape, photo and resume. Prefers cassette with 3-10 songs on demo. SASE. "Send $1 to cover postage and handling if material is to be returned." Reports in 3 weeks.
Music: Top 40/pop. Works with dance bands, bar bands and pop concert acts. Current acts include Fate (original and copy pop/rock group with product); Circus (original and copy pop/rock group with product) and G.A. Wallace (songwriter).

INTERMOUNTAIN CONCERTS, Box 8252, Rapid City SD 57709. (605)342-7696. Contact: Ron Kohn or Steve Hughes. Management firm and concert production agency. Estab. 1978. Deals with artist from the upper-midwest region. Represents artists and group; currently handles 12 acts. Negotiates management fees.
How to Contact: Query or submit demo tape. Prefers cassette with 1-5 songs on demo. SASE. Reports in 2 weeks.
Music: Rock.

J.M.J. PRODUCTIONS, 934 Charles Hawkins Dr., Gary IN 46407. (219)882-4333. President: James Edward Dye. Management firm, booking agency and record placement company. Estab. 1971. Represents artists, groups and songwriters; currently handles 3 groups and 7 songwriters. Receives 20% commission.
How To Contact: Query or submit demo tape only. Prefers cassette with 2-5 songs on demo. SASE. Reports in 3 weeks.
Music: Disco; rock; soul; and top 40/pop. Works with groups, bands, solos and songwriters ready for introduction to and production for a major label. Current acts include Ultra High Frequency (self-contained 7-piece male group); The Bobby Brown Story (male vocalist); Sky's The Limit (4-piece male vocal group); and Grace Wise (female vocalist).

J & J PRODUCTIONS, Box 5522, Arlington TX 76011. (817)267-7475. Owner: Jim Dunegan. Management firm and booking agency. Estab. 1967. Represents individuals and groups; currently handles 15 acts. Receives 20% minimum commission "at the time of the engagement."
How to Contact: Query, arrange personal interview, submit demo tape, submit demo tape and lead sheet, or submit lead sheet. Prefers cassette with 1-3 songs on demo. SASE. Reports in 1 month.
Music: Blues; C&W; disco; gospel; jazz; MOR; and rock (country). Current acts include Jill Burge (C&W vocalist); and the Playmates.

JACKSON ARTISTS CORP., 5725 Nieman Rd., Suite E., Shawnee Mission KS 66203. (913)268-6666. Management firm, booking agency and music publisher. Estab. 1960. Represents individuals and songwriters; currently handles 40 acts. Receives 15% minimum commission from individual artists and groups; 10% from songwriters.
How to Contact: Query, arrange personal interview, submit demo tape, submit demo tape and lead sheet or phone. Prefers reel-to-reel or cassette. "We do most of our business by phone." Will return material if requested. SASE. Reports in 1 week.
Music: Bluegrass; blues; C&W; disco; MOR; progressive; rock (soft); soul; and top 40/pop. Works primarily with dance and show bands. Current acts include acts in all fields of entertainment—Ken & VanDel (C&W/MOR/pop); Jeff & Marsha (pop); Satin (disco/pop/top/40); Jimmy Caesar (comedy); and Freedom Road (pop/rock)."

RANDY JACKSON PRODUCTIONS, INC., 2165 Minnesota St., Baton Rogue LA 70802. (504)343-4257. President: Randy D. Jackson. Management agency and booking firm. Estab. 1978. Represents individuals, groups and songwriters; currently handles 27 acts. Receives minimum 20% commission.
How To Contact: Query or submit demo tape and lead sheet. Prefers cassette with a minimum of 3 songs on demo. Also prefers photo to accompany tape. SASE. Reports in 1 month.
Music: Blues; choral; church/religious; classical; disco; folk; gospel; jazz; MOR; opera; progressive (country); rock (hard); soul; and top 40/pop. Current acts include Topaz (disco-rock-soul); Greg Wright (hard rock); Butch Hornsby (country rock); and Jazz-Alive (fusion group).

JAYDE ENTERPRISES, 32 W. Randolph St., Chicago IL 60601. (312)726-0771. Owner: Melba R. Caldwell. Booking agency. Estab. 1960. Represents individuals and groups. Receives 15-20% commission.
How to Contact: Submit demo tape and lead sheet. Prefers cassette with 2-3 songs on demo. SASE. Reports in 1 month.
Music: Gospel; show tunes; soul; and top 40/pop. Works primarily with self-contained musical and singing acts for special club dates, benefits, and industrial/union shows. Current acts include Billy Wallace (comedian); Shelly Fisher (composer/singer/pianist); the Sunshine Festival (Jamaican/American revue); the Young Step Brothers (dance act); and the Third Generation Steps (dance act).

NADA C. JONES OPERATION MUSIC ENTERTAINMENT, 233 W. Woodland Ave., Ottumwa IA 52501. (515)682-8283. President: Nada C. Jones. Management firm and booking agency. Estab. 1968. Represents individuals, groups and songwriters; currently handles 8 acts. Receives 15% minimum commission.
How to Contact: Submit demo tape. Prefers 7½ ips reel-to-reel or cassette with 5-6 songs on demo. SASE. Reports in 1 month.
Music: Blues; C&W; rock (country); and soul. Works primarily with dance, bar and show groups. Current acts include Reesa K. Jones and Country Class (country rock); Gold Dust (50s/top 40 rock); and Jimmy R. Powers (C&W).

HELEN KEANE ARTISTS MANAGEMENT, 49 E. 96th St., New York NY 10028. President: Helen Keane. Management firm. Estab. 1962. Represents professional individuals and groups; currently handles 3 acts. Receives negotiable commission.
How to Contact: Query or submit demo tape. Prefers cassette. "Individuals may want to include some background information, e.g., previously published songs, affiliations." Does not return unsolicited material. Reports "only if we're really interested."
Music: Jazz; MOR; and progressive. "Basically we deal with jazz groups and singers performing their own and other people's material." Current acts include the Bill Evans Trio (jazz group); Kenny Burrell Trio (jazz group); and Morgana King (jazz/pop vocalist).

KEN KEENE INTERNATIONAL, Box 515, St. Louis MO 63166. (314)776-2278. President: Ken Keene. Management firm and booking agency. Estab. 1970. Represents individuals, groups and songwriters; currently handles 25 acts. Receives 10-20% commission.
How to Contact: Submit demo tape. Prefers 7½ ips reel-to-reel or cassette with 1-5 songs on demo. SASE. Reports as soon as possible. "We get a tremendous amount of material and sometimes it takes 2 months or longer."
Music: Blues; church/religious; C&W; disco; gospel; MOR; progressive; rock (hard/country); soul; and top 40/pop. Works with top 40 show groups and single artists in all of the above fields. Current acts include Frankie Ford (top 40 rock artist); Billy Joe Duniven ('50s style singer); and Tom Pallardy (Nashville singer/songwriter).

KESSLER-GRASS MANAGEMENT, 11925 Ventura Blvd., Studio City CA 91604. (213)506-1710. President: Clancy B. Grass III. Management firm, booking agency, production and publishing company. Estab. 1974. Represents individuals, groups and songwriters; currently handles 8 acts. Receives 15% commission.
How To Contact: Query or submit demo tape and lead sheet. Prefers cassette. SASE. Reports in 2 weeks.
Music: Blues; disco; rock; soul; and top 40/pop. Currently handles 5 acts.

CHUCK KRONZEK MANAGEMENT, 5857 Phillips Ave., Pittsburgh PA 15217. (412)422-7052. President: C.M. Kronzek. Management firm and booking agency. Estab. 1974.

Represents individuals and groups; currently handles 24 acts. Receives 10-25% commission: "partnerships with acts, hourly billing."
How to Contact: Query or submit demo tape and lead sheet. "Include bio, photo, availability, other affiliations and prices. Submit the promo by mail and cut us two weeks later." Prefers cassette with 3-7 songs on demo. Does not return unsolicited material. Reports in 2-3 weeks.
Music: Bluegrass; C&W; disco; jazz; MOR; progressive; rock (country); top 40/pop; and "motel circuit bands, etc. Most of our acts travel full time. We are strong with country rock and motel lounge bands. Most of our acts are exclusive." Current acts include Ezy Elmer (country rock); Daybreak (lounge/top 40); and Pearl (jazz).

JOSEPH LAKE AND ASSOCIATES, Charrington Square, 4525 South 2300 East, Suite 201B, Salt Lake City UT 84117. (801)277-3432. President: Joe Lake. Vice President: Virginia Larsen. Management agency. Estab. 1976. Represents individuals, groups, and songwriters; currently handles 25 acts. Receives 15-30% commission.
How To Contact: Query, arrange personal interview, submit demo tape only or send press material (photos, write-ups, etc.) Prefers cassette with 3-5 songs on demo. SASE. Reports in 2 weeks.
Music: Church/religious; disco; rock (country rock); and top 40/pop. Works with concert groups with full back-up band/some dance bands/songwriters. Current acts include SunShade 'n Rain (concert group); Change of Pace (recording and concert group); and Malibu Revue ('50s act).

LAKE FRONT TALENT AGENCY, Box 2395, Sandusky OH 44870. (419)626-4987. Owner/Manager: Larry Myers. Management firm and record company. Estab. 1968. Represents individuals, groups and songwriters from Ohio, Pennsylvania, West Virginia, Michigan and "possibly" other areas; currently handles 15% commission.
How to Contact: Query by mail or phone. Prefers 7½ ips reel-to-reel with 3-5 songs on demo.
Music: C&W; disco; rock (hard or country); and top 40/pop. Current acts include Llynn Stevens (country rock); West Fall (rock); and Anna Jane Allen Family Show (C&W/rock/polka/standard).

L & L TRACKDOWN RECORD DISTRIBUTORS, 542 S. Dearborn, Chicago IL 60605. (312)486-2989. Chairman of the Board: Hank Williams. Management firm, booking agency, publisher, record promoter, producer, record distributor, marketing and sales company. Estab. 1962. Represents artists, groups and songwriters; currently handles 30 acts.
How To Contact: Query, arrange personal interview or submit demo tape and lead sheet. Prefers 7½, 3¾ or 1⅞ ips reel-to-reel, cassette or 8-track with 4-7 songs on demo. SASE. Reports in 2 weeks.
Music: Bluegrass; blues; church/religious; C&W; disco; folk; gospel; jazz; MOR; rock (hard and country); soul; and top 40/pop. Works with dance bands. Current acts include Centralettes, Central Sounds, Centrallites (disco, R&B); Cisco (country); and Menler H. David (church/religious).

THE CHARLES LANT AGENCY, Box 1085, Cornwall, Ontario, Canada K6H 5V2. (613)932-1532. Contact: W. B. Lant. Booking agency. Estab. 1973. Represents individuals and groups. Receives 10-20% commission.
How to Contact: Query or phone. Prefers cassette with 3-10 songs on demo. SAE and International Reply Coupons. Reports as soon as possible.
Music: C&W and big bands. Works primarily with dance bands. Current acts include the Stardusters Orchestra (19-piece band).

STAN LAWRENCE PRODUCTIONS, 191 Presidential Blvd., Bala Cynwyd PA 19004. (215)664-4873. President: Stan Lawrence. Management agency. Estab. 1970. Represents individuals and groups on the East coast; currently handles 3 acts.
How to Contact: Query or arrange personal interview.
Music: Disco and top 40/pop. Current acts include Tonnee Collins (female vocal/disco); and Tony Branco and Innervisions (MOR group).

LE SUEUR MANAGEMENT, 803 1st Ave., Athens AL 35611. (205)232-5062. General Manager: Mike Lessor. Management firm, booking agency and promotion agency. Estab. 1973. Represents individuals; currently handles 12 acts. Receives 10-25% commission.
How to Contact: Submit demo tape and lead sheet. Prefers 7½ ips reel-to-reel or cassette with 2-12 songs on demo. SASE. Reports in 1 month.
Music: MOR; rock; soul; and top 40/pop. Works primarily with "singers and musicians who

write. We look for entertainment values. We don't do much folk type things." Current acts include Wayne Chaney (R&B/rock singer); Kelly Cline (MOR singer/songwriter); and Spook (horn band).

LEAN JEAN ENTERPRISES, 312 Sharon Ave., Marshalltown IA 50158. (515)752-3198. President: Alan Lund. Management firm, booking agency and sound and lighting company. Estab. 1975. Represents groups and songwriters; currently handles 10 acts. Receives 15% commission.
How To Contact: Query by mail or phone. Prefers 7½ ips reel-to-reel or cassette with 3-5 songs on demo. SASE. Reports "as soon as possible."
Music: Progressive; rock (all types); and top 40/pop. Works with mostly concert-oriented rock acts. Current acts include Hot Jam (concert rock act); Roxx (concert rock act); and Glitch (standard rock act).

BUDDY LEE ATTRACTIONS, INC., 38 Music Square E., Suite 300, Nashville TN 37203. (615)244-4336. Artists and Groups Contact: Tony Conway. Songwriters Contact: Jim Prater. Management firm and booking agency. Estab. 1968. Represents individuals and groups; currently handles 50 acts. "Principally, we deal with established name acts who have recording contracts with major labels." Receives 10-15% commission.
How to Contact: Submit demo tape and lead sheet. Prefers 7½ ips reel-to-reel with 4 songs minimum on tape. SASE. Reports as soon as possible.
Music: Bluegrass; C&W; MOR; rock; soul; and top 40/pop. Works primarily with concert attractions. Current acts include Danny Davis and the Nashville Brass (C&W/MOR instrumental); Del Reeves Show (C&W); and Billy ThunderKloud and the Chieftones (C&W/pop).

ED LEFFLER MANAGEMENT, 9229 Sunset Blvd., Suite 625, Los Angeles CA 90069. (213)550-8802. President: Ed Leffler. Management firm.
How to contact: Query by mail.
Music: Current acts include Sweet (Capitol); Sammy Hagar (Capitol); Juice Newton) (Capitol); Buckeye (Polydor); and Steve Harley (EMI).
Tip: "We are looking for established, self-contained artists with a track record."

LENTALENT PRODUCTIONS, Box 509, Kinston NC 28501. (919)523-6974. Owner: Len Loftin. Booking agency. Estab. 1970. Represents individuals and groups; currently handles 10 acts. Receives 15% commission.
How to Contact: Submit demo tape. Prefers cassette with 6-10 songs on demo. SASE. Reports in 2 weeks.
Music: C&W; disco; folk; jazz; MOR; progressive; rock; soul; and top 40/pop. Current acts include Pegasus; Warehouse; Starfire; the Waller Family; Mickey Murray; Super Grit Cowboy Band; the Arnold Chinn Group; David Allan Coe; Labamba; Spiral; Ripple; Magga Brain; and Anglo Saxon Brown.

JOHN LEVY ENTERPRISES, INC., 109 N. Almont Dr., Los Angeles CA 90048. (213)271-6244. President: John Levy. Management agency. Estab. 1951. Represents individuals and songwriters; currently handles 3 acts. Receives 10-20% commission.
How To Contact: Submit demo tape only or demo tape and lead sheet. Prefers 7½ ips or cassette with 1-5 songs on demo. SASE. Reports in 2 weeks.
Music: Jazz; soul; and top 40/pop. Current acts include Nancy Wilson (singer); Joe Williams (singer); and Randy Crawford (singer).

JERRY LEE LEWIS & CO., 1719 West End, Suite 1100, Nashville TN 37203. Manager: Robert Porter. Management firm and booking agency. Estab. 1970. Represents professional individuals; currently handles 2 acts. Receives 10-20% commission.
How to Contact: Submit demo tape and lead sheet. Prefers 7½ ips reel-to-reel with 1-4 songs on demo. Does not return unsolicited material. Reports as soon as possible.
Music: Bluegrass; blues; C&W; folk; gospel; rock (country); and top 40/pop. Current acts include Jerry Lee Lewis (C&W/pop vocalist); and Bill Littleton (C&W/pop vocalist).

LEW LINET MANAGEMENT, 7225 Hollywood Blvd., Hollywood CA 90046. (213)876-4071. President: Lew Linet. Management agency and independent record producer. Estab. 1971. Represents artists, groups and songwriters; currently handles 1 act. Receives 20% commission.
How To Contact: Submit demo tape and lead sheet. Prefers cassette with 3 songs on demo. Include lyrics sheet. SASE. Reports in 1 month.

Music: Folk; rock (country or hard); and top 40/pop. Works with recording artists. Current acts include Noel Butler & Cherokee (country rock).

LINETT MANAGEMENT, 1146 S. Hayworth Ave., Los Angeles CA 90035. President: Elaine Linett. Management firm. Estab. 1972. Represents individuals, groups and songwriters; currently handles 3 acts. Receives 15-25% commission.
How to Contact: Submit demo tape and lead sheet. Prefers 7½ ips reel-to-reel or cassette with 4-7 songs on demo. "Include photo and resume." SASE. Reports in 3 weeks.
Music: Disco; jazz; MOR; rock (pop); and soul.

RON LUCIANO MUSIC CO., Box 263, Hasbrouck Heights NJ 07604. (201)288-8935. President: Ron Luciano. Management firm and booking agency. Estab. 1967. Represents artists, group and recording/speciality acts; currently handles 7-8 acts. Receives 10-20% commission.
How To Contact: Query or submit picture and biography. Prefers 7½ ips reel-to-reel or cassette with 2-8 songs on demo. "Can also approach by sending a copy of their record release." SASE. Reports in 2-6 weeks.
Music: Disco; MOR; rock; soul; and top 40/pop. Works with 4- 5- piece,self-contained groups "that play in Holiday Inn, Sheratons, etc. We also book a lot of oldie groups like the Belmonts and Flamingos." Current acts include Voyage (top 40/disco); Legz (rock 'n roll); and Charles Lamont.

RICHARD LUTZ ENTERTAINMENT AGENCY, 5625 0 St., Lincoln NE 68510. (402)483-2241. General Manager: Cherie Hanfelt. Management firm and booking agency. Estab. 1964. Represents individuals and groups; currently handles 220 acts. Receives 15% minimum commission.
How to Contact: Query by phone or submit demo tape and lead sheet. Prefers cassette with 5-10 songs on demo. SASE. Reports in 1 week.
Music: C&W; MOR; and top 40/pop. Works primarily with lounge groups. Current acts include Cottonwood (C&W/pop); Big Al and Co. (top 40/pop); Dave Anderson (MOR); Jefferson Harper (MOR); Honey (top 40/pop); and Baker Street (MOR).

McDONALD & ASSOCIATES, 317 Clifton Ave., Suite 1, Minneapolis MN 55403. (612)871-0183. President: Guy McDonald. Management firm and booking agency. Estab. 1978. Deals with artists in the 5 state Midwest region and bookings and promotion for national acts. Represents groups and songwriters; currently handles 5 acts. Receives 10-20% commission and on occasion takes a percentage of gross door receipts at shows they promote.
How To Contact: Contact by telephone. Prefers 3-5 songs on demo. SASE. Reports in 1 week.
Music: Blues; rock. Works with original rock or blues, specifically for clubs and concerts. Current acts include Willie & The Bumblebees (original, rock & R&B); Marilyn (original rock); and Berlin (original hard rock).

McMEEN TALENT AGENCY, Box 40681, Nashville TN 37204. (615)329-9889. President: John McMeen. Booking agency. Estab. 1976. Represents individuals and groups; currently handles 4 acts. Receives 10-15% commission.
How to Contact: Submit demo tape. Prefers 7½ ips reel-to-reel with 2-6 songs on demo. SASE. Reports in 3 weeks.
Music: C&W and progressive (country). Current acts include Stella Parton (concert performer); and the Drifting Cowboys (concert performers).

MAD MAN MANAGEMENT, Box 54, Man's Field TX 76063. (817)477-2897. President: James Michael Taylor. Management firm, booking agency, publisher and recording company. Estab. 1974. Represents individuals, groups and songwriters; currently handles 3 acts.
How to Contact: Query, arrange personal interview, submit demo tape or submit demo tape and lead sheet. Prefers 7½ ips reel-to-reel or cassette with 12 songs maximum. SASE. Reports in 2 weeks.
Music: C&W; folk; and MOR. Current acts include Snow Geese (pop trio); Rick Babb (country single); and James Michael Tayler (singer/songwriter).

THE MANAGEMENT CO., 145 Newton St., Waltham Branch, Boston MA 02154. (617)891-7310. Contact: Joe Casey. Management firm, affiliated with DME, a booking agency. Estab. 1977. Deals with artists in New England-New York region only. Represents artists and groups; currently handles 2 acts. Receives 20-25% commission.
How To Contact: Submit demo tape.

MARANATHA! MUSIC RECORDS, Box 1396, Costa Mesa CA 92626. (714)979-8536. Production (Artist Liason): Bob Bennett. Record company. Estab. 1972. Deals with artists in California only. Represents artists, groups and songwriters; currently handles 17 artists, 3 groups and 4 major songwriters.
How To Contact: Query. "By mail give us details on backround experience, personal testimony, goals for future in every area." Prefers cassette with 2 songs on demo. SASE. Reports in unspecified time.
Music: Church/religious; C&W; folk (contemporary Christian); gospel; MOR; rock (country/soft); soul; and pop. "Our music has a message." Works with solo artists for colleges, universities, coffee houses, etc., bands and songwriters. Current acts include Leon Patillo (keyboard, vocalist, songwriter); Kelly Willard (singer/songwriter); Bob Bennett (songwriter, vocalist, guitarist); and Tom Coomes (songwriter, vocalist, guitarist and keyboard).

MARIS MANAGEMENT, 2007 Wilshire Blvd. #325. Los Angeles CA 90057. (213)484-9659. Owner: Stephen Mariscal. Booking agency and management complimentary. Estab. 1977. Represents individuals and groups. Currently handles 5 acts. Receives 10-20% commission.
How to Contact: Query by mail or phone. Prefers cassette with 2-4 songs on demo. "If they want their material returned they must send a SASE large enough to hold material. Otherwise, it will not be returned. They must not be too insistent." Reports in 2 weeks.
Music: Disco; MOR; and rock (hard and soft). Current acts include the David Lee Band (rock vocal/instrumental); Eileen Valentino (MOR); and Marc Garrett (MOR).

MARSAINT MUSIC, INC., 3809 Clematis Ave., New Orleans LA 70122. Management firm and publishing company. Estab. 1972. Represents artists, groups and songwriters; currently handles 10 acts. Receives 15-25% commission.
How To Contact: Submit demo tape only or demo tape and lead sheet. Prefers cassette with 1-10 songs on demo. SASE. Reports in 1 month.
Music: Blues; C&W; disco; folk; gospel; progressive; rock; soul; top 40/pop. Current acts include Chocolate Milk (R&B, pop); Meters (R&B, pop); and Lee Dorsey (R&B, pop).

MARSH PRODUCTIONS, INC., 1704 West Lake St., Minneapolis MN 55408. (612)827-6141. President: Marshall Edelstein. Management firm, booking agency and promotion company. Estab. 1962. Represents artists and groups; currently handles 44 exclusive acts and 25 songwriters. Receives 15-20% commission.
How To Contact: Query, arrange personal interview, submit demo tape or submit demo tape and lead sheet. Prefers 7½ ips reel-to-reel or cassette with 3-6 songs on demo. SASE. Reports in 2-4 weeks.
Music: Rock. "We have eight fulltime agents who have all been in the rock industry, that's our specialty." Works with dance, bar and concert bands. Current acts include Cain (hard rock); Fairchild Flight (hard rock); and Scott Jones (single, folk).

MASADA MUSIC, INC., 888 8th Ave., New York NY 10019. (212)757-1953. Vice President: Gene Heimlich. Management firm and production house. Estab. 1976. Deals with artists in East Coast region only. Represents artists, groups and songwriters; currently handles 3 acts. Receives 10-20% commission.
How To Contact: Query or arrange personal interview. Prefers 7½ ips reel-to-reel with 2-7 songs on demo. Does not return unsolicited material. Reports in 2 weeks.
Music: Bluegrass; blues; C&W; disco; folk; jazz; MOR; progressive; soul; and top 40/pop. Works with singer-songwriters and self contained bands. Current acts include Diane Snow (jazz, MOR); Whirlwind (disco); and Tom Williams (jazz).

MAXIMUM MANAGEMENT, Box 2118, Vineland NJ 08360. (609)327-3838. President: Dennis Hill. Management agency. Estab. 1976. Deals with artists in eastern United States. Represents artists and groups; currently handles 2 acts. Receives 12-18% commission.
How To Contact: Submit demo tape only. Prefers cassette with 3-6 songs on demo. SASE. Reports in 2 weeks.
music: Disco; jazz; MOR; progressive; rock; and top 40/pop. Current acts include Bill Barkin (folk/rock/MOR); and Trinity (progressive).

DOM MELILLO AGENCY, 1010 17th Ave. South, Nashville TN 37212. (615)327-4656. President: Dom Melillo. Booking agency. Estab. 1956. Deals with artists in mid-south region only. Represents artists, groups and songwriters; currently represents 10 acts. Receives 10-15% commission.

How To Contact: Submit demo tape and lead sheet. Prefers cassette with 2-4 songs on demo. SASE. Reports in 2 weeks.
Music: C&W; MOR; and top 40/pop. Current acts include Van Trevor (country artist/composer); Dale Houston (country artist/composer); Kenny Earl (pop artist/composer); The Joy Ford Show (country variety show); Peter and the Wolf (Duo); and Horizon featuring Terri Hollowell (recording artist with Con Brio Records).

CON MERTEN MANAGEMENT, 8927 Nevada Ave., Canoga Park CA 91304. President: Con Merten. Management agency. Estab. 1965. Deals with local artists only. Represents artists and groups; currently handles 4 acts. Receives minimum 20% commission.
How To Contact: "I must see them live. Artists should also submit photos." Prefers cassette with 3 songs on demo. SASE. Reports in 1 month.
Music: Disco; rock; and top 40/pop. Works with young, all male groups that are pop and disco oriented, Andy Gibb and Shaun Cassidy types.

MIKE'S ARTISTS MANAGEMENT LTD., 308 E. 51st, New York NY 10022. (212)759-9658. President: Michael J. Lembo. Management Director: Mike Bowe. Management agency. Estab. 1975. Represents artists, groups, songwriters and comics; currently handles 6 acts. Receives 20-25% commission.
How To Contact: Query, submit demo tape and head sheet or press, bio or any important information. "Write with info first." Prefers 15 ips reel-to-reel or cassette with 3-5 songs on demo. SASE. Reports within 2-3 weeks.
Music: Blues; MOR; progressive; rock; soul; and top 40/pop. Current acts include Baby Grand (rock 'n roll); NRBQ; Malcolm Tomlinson (white, R&B); and Peter C. Johnson (songwriter).

MOON-HILL MANAGEMENT, INC., Box 4945, Austin TX 78765. Vice President: T. White. Vice President: Larry Watkins. Management firm and booking agency. Estab. 1969. Represents professional individuals, groups and songwriters; currently handles 4 acts. Receives 15-30% commission.
How to Contact: Query. Prefers cassette with 1-4 songs on demo. Does not return unsolicited material. Reports in 2 weeks. "In general, we approach artists. So, it's best for the artist to create a market on his own; when the market is sufficient, then we'll be interested."
Music: Blues; C&W; disco; folk; gospel; jazz; MOR; progressive; rock; soul; and top 40/pop. Current acts include Rusty Wier; Traveler; the Tennessee Hat Band; and Vince Bell.

MOUSEVILLE NOSTALGIA, 5218 Almont St., Los Angeles CA 90032. (213)223-2860. President: Mr. Perez. Management firm and booking agency. "We sponsor, refer and represent only specialized oldies-but-goodies acts for rock 'n roll revue concert specials and other areas of live entertainment." Estab. 1978. Represents artists, groups, songwriters, "exclusively 1950s and early 1960s oldies-but-goodies nostalgia performers." Receives 20-25% commission, also negotiable union contracts.
How to Contact: Query, submit demo tape only or demo tape and lead sheet or promo kit, etc., with any current single or album. Prefers cassette tapes or records with 6-12 songs on demo. "Studios, A&Rs, recording labels, agents, managers and producers are invited to call, write or wire direct anytime." SASE. Reports in 1 week.
Music: Blues (deep and R&B); children's; C&W (plus 1950s rock-a-billy rock); folk (and folk-rock); MOR; polka; rock (all 1950s through 1960s styles and sounds, oldies but goodies vintage); soul; top 40/pop; Hawaiian; Polynesian; Latin; and mid 60s British Mersey and Liverpool R&R sounds.

MUSE PRODUCTIONS, INC., 1337 Chetworth Ct., Alexandria VA 22314. (703)549-2858. Artist's Representative: Alice Kimball. Management firm, booking agency and promotional packages producer. Estab. 1976. Represents artists, groups, songwriters, mimes and comedians; currently handles 24 acts. Receives 15-25% commission. "When we do promotional packages and other set services we get set fee, promo packages run from $250-1,500."
How To Contact: Query or submit promo, tapes and lyric sheets. Prefers cassette with 4-6 songs on demo. SASE. Reports in 3 weeks.
Music: Blues; classical; disco; rock (middle to hard); and top 40/pop. Also new wave. Works with bar bands, concert bands and solo artists. Current acts include Stuart Payne (classical transition to rock); Dick Anderson (lyricist); D Ceats (new wave rock); Michael Guthrie Band (British influence rock 'n roll); and Casse Culver and the Bell Star Band (rock 'n roll).

MUSKRAT PRODUCTIONS, INC., 59 Locust Ave., New Rochelle NY 10801. (914)636-0809.

Contact: Donna Ryder. Estab. 1970. Represents individuals and groups; currently represents 11 acts. Deals with artists in the New York City area. "We are a production company; we sell a package and buy the talent for a flat rate. We don't take a commission out of the amount we pay the artist."
How to Contact: Query. Prefers cassette with 3 songs minimum on tape. SASE. Reports "only if interested."
Music: "We specialize in old-time jazz and banjo music and shows." Current acts include Smith Street Society Jazz Band (dixieland jazz); Your Father's Mustache (banjo sing-along); and Harry Hepcat and the Boogie Woogie Band ('50s rock revival).

ARNIE NAIDITCH/BLACK DOG PRODUCTIONS, Box 14147, Atlanta GA 30324. (404)872-2133. President: Arnie Naiditch. Management agency. Estab. 1976. Represents individuals, groups and songwriters; currently handles 4 acts. Receives 20-25% commission.
How to Contact: Submit demo tape. Prefers 7½ ips reel-to-reel or cassette with 3-6 songs on demo. SASE. Reports in 3 weeks.
Music: Rock and top 40/pop. Works with concert and showcase attractions. Current acts include Jesse Winchester; Gary Bennett; and Crus-O-Matic.

NO-MOSS PRODUCTIONS, (formerly Larry Tremaine Enterprises), 115 E. Foothill Blvd., #6, Glendora CA 91740. (213)335-1216, 849-2263. Contact: Norman Windisch, Tom Soran Jr. Management firm, placement agency and musicians referral service. Estab. 1962. Represents professional individuals, groups and songwriters; currently handles 400 acts. Receives negotiable commission.
How to Contact: Query or submit demo tape and lead sheet. Prefers cassette. SASE. Reports in 2 weeks.
Music: Bluegrass; blues; church/religious; classical; C&W; disco; folk; gospel; jazz; MOR; progressive; rock (heavy metal or easy listening); soul; and top 40/pop (new wave or power pop). Current acts include the Dogs (new wave group); Silver Chalice (progressive power pop group); the Renegades (top 40/MOR group); and Parsec (progressive jazz, folk, rock).

NORTH COUNTRY FAIR TALENT, Box 11444, Kansas City MO 64112. (816)753-1600. Owner: Dave Maygers. Booking agency. Estab. 1974. Represents groups; currently handles 10 acts. Receives 15% minimum commission.
How to Contact: "Call first," then submit demo tape with bio and pictures. Prefers cassette with 3-4 songs on demo. SASE. Reports in 2 weeks.
Music: Progressive; rock (all); soul; and top 40/pop. Works primarily "with bands that have a song list of 50% radio material and 50% original material." Current acts include Morning Star (CBS Records); Justus (funk rock); and J.T. Cooke (progressive rock).

TROD NOSSEL PRODUCTIONS, INC., Box 57/10 George St., Wallingford CT 06492. (203)269-4465 or 265-0010. Management agency. Estab. 1968. Deals with artists in Northeast region only. Represents artists, groups and songwriters; currently handles 10 acts. Receives 10-30% commission.
How To Contact: Query. "A complete promotional package most helpful." Prefers cassette with 4-6 songs on demo. SASE. Reports in 1 month.
Music: Rock. "Our acts work club circuits as well as concert situations." Current acts include The Scratch Band (rock 'n roll); Roger C. Reale and Rue Morgue (rock 'n roll act); and Van Duren (singer/songwriter).

ONSTAGE MANAGEMENT, INC., 3227 River Dr., Columbia SC 29201. (803)765-0087. Agent: Key Thrasher. Booking agency. Estab. 1976. Deals with regional individuals in North and South Carolina. Represents artists and groups; currently handles 4 acts. Receives 10-15% commission.
How to Contact: Query. Prefers cassette with 3-6 songs on demo. SASE. Reports in 1 week.
Music: Bluegrass; folk; jazz (progressive); rock (country); and top 40/pop. Works primarily with acoustic artists, club bands, country rock and rock groups. Current acts include Rob Crosby (acoustic solo); Buddy Ray and the Easycome Band and Revue (country rock); Roadwork (top 40/rock); Bob Crosby (country rock group); and Nappy Patch (jazz, rock).

PATHFINDER MANAGEMENT, INC., Box 30166, Memphis TN 38130. (901)324-5385. Executive Secretary: Shirley Flowers. Management firm. Estab. 1969. Represents individuals, groups and songwriters; currently handles 9 acts. Receives 15-20% commission.
How to Contact: Submit demo tape and lead sheet. Prefers 7½ ips reel-to-reel or cassette with

1-4 songs on demo. SASE. Reports in 1 month.
Music: Blues; church/religious; gospel; rock; soul; and top 40/pop. Works primarily with dance bands. Current acts include Kim Tolliver (female vocalist); Ollie Nightingale (male vocalist); and Sugar Bush (5-piece group with 3 vocals).

HARRY PEEBLES AGENCY, Box 1324, Kansas City MO 66117. (913)596-1220. Owner: Harry Peebles. Booking agency. Estab. 1931. Represents individuals and groups; currently handles over 100 acts. Receives 15% minimum commission.
How to Contact: Submit demo tape with photos and bio. Prefers cassette or 8-track cartridge with 3 songs minimum on tape. SASE. Reports in 6 months.
Music: Bluegrass; blues; church/religious; C&W; gospel; jazz; MOR; rock; soul; and top 40/pop. Works primarily with show bands. Current acts include Sherwin Linton (C&W); and R.W. Blackwood (C&W).

PELICAN PRODUCTIONS, Room 10, 3700 East Ave., Rochester NY 14618. President: Peter Morticelli. Management firm and booking agency. Estab. 1972. Represents artists and groups from upstate New York; currently handles 2 acts. Receives 15-25% commission.
How to Contact: Query or submit demo tape. Prefers cassette with 3-6 songs on demo. SASE. Reports in 2 weeks.
Music: Rock (all kinds) and top 40/pop. Works with "any type of act as long as the songwriting ability is very strong." Current acts include Duke Jupiter (original rock artist); and Bat McGrath (singer/songwriter).

RITA CARTER PERRY, Box 12241, Jacksonville FL 32209. (904)768-6608, (912)384-1920. President: Rita Carter Perry. Management firm and booking agency. Estab. 1969. Deals with artists in Southeastern region only. Represents artists, groups and songwriters; currently handles 6 acts. Receives 10-20% commission.
How to Contact: Query or submit demo tape and lead sheet. Prefers 7½ ips reel-to-reel with 3-10 songs on demo. SASE. Reports in 1 month.
Music: Blues; church/religious; disco; gospel; jazz; MOR; rock; soul; and top 40/pop. Works with horn sections, jazz and disco bands, soul, rock and pop self contained units and single artists. Current acts include The Terry Perry Horns; The Jazz Keynotes (jazz); Sun City Jazz Band (jazz/rock); Kenobe (soul/rock); Nathaniel Huff (gospel); and KUDU (pop/soul/rock).

ROGER PERRY & ASSOCIATES, Box 480107, Los Angeles CA 90048. President: Roger Perry. Management firm and production company. Represents individuals, groups and songwriters; currently handles 4 acts. Receives 20% commission.
How to Contact: Submit demo tape. Prefers 7½ ips reel-to-reel or cassette with 4 songs on demo. Include lyric sheets, bio and photo. SASE. Reports in 2 weeks.
Music: C&W; folk; progressive; rock (country); and top 40/pop. "We work with solo artists and groups that generally can provide their own material. Solo artists must be self-accompanied. We prefer contemporary singer/songwriters and progressive country or country rock bands." Current acts include Janet Fisher (singer/songwriter); the Mike Pruet Band (rock); and Jim Barton (singer/songwriter).

MARTY PICHINSON MANAGEMENT, 518 N. La Cienega, Los Angeles CA 90048. (213)659-7491. Manager: John Babcock. Management firm. Estab. 1977.
How to contact: Query by mail.
Music: Current acts include Nigel Olsson; Jay Ferguson; and Jerry Doucette.
Tips: "Our clients are recording artists who have a strong track record. Unknown artists being signed are rare."

JERRY PLANTZ PRODUCTIONS, 1703 Wyandotte, Kansas City MO 64108. (816)471-1501. Agent: Jerry Plantz. Sub-Agents: Kevin Clark, Sue Benoit, Henry Thompson. Management firm and booking agency. Estab. 1976. Represents individuals, groups and songwriters from Missouri, Kansas, Iowa and Nebraska; currently handles 50 acts. Receives 10-15% commission.
How to Contact: Submit demo tape and lead sheet or contact by phone. Prefers reel-to-reel, cassette or 8-track cartridge with 10-15 songs on demo. SASE. Reports in 2 weeks.
Music: Bluegrass; blues; children's; classical; C&W; disco; folk; jazz; MOR; progressive; rock; soul; and top 40/pop. Works primarily with dance bands. Current acts include Danny Byrd (C&W); US (rock and roll); Roy Searcy (blues); and George Main (C&W).

PREFERRED ARTIST MANAGEMENT, INC., 9701 Taylorsville Rd., Louisville KY 40299. (502)267-5466. Vice President: Dan Green. Secretary: David H. Snowden. Management

agency. Estab. 1977. Deals with artists in eastern United States and Midwest states. Represents artists and groups; currently handles 12 acts. Receives 10-25% commission.
How to Contact: Query or submit demo tape and lead sheet. Prefers 7½ ips reel-to-reel or cassette with 2-4 songs on demo. SASE. Reports in 2 weeks.
Music: Disco; rock (funk, medium); and top 40/pop. Works with bar artists ranging from bar bands to both single and group concert acts. Current acts include Free Fall (rock/show act); Bob Brickley (lounge/show act); Solomon King (Vegas type show act/concerts); and Encore (disco lounge act).

PROCESS TALENT MANAGEMENT, 439 Wiley Ave., Franklin PA 16323, (814)432-4633. Contact: Norman Kelly. Management agency. Estab. 1960. Represents artists and groups; currently handles 20 acts. Receives 10-15% commission.
How to Contact: Query. Prefers 7½ ips reel-to-reel, cassette, 8-track cartridge also acceptable with 2-6 songs on demo. SASE. Reports in 2 weeks.
Music: Bluegrass; blues; C&W; disco; folk; gospel; jazz; MOR; polka; progressive; rock; soul; and top 40/pop. Works with C&W artists (70%), gospel (10%) and pop/rock etc. (20%). Current acts include Junie Lou (C&W); Sego Brothers and Naomi (gospel); Bonnie Baldwin (C&W); Virge Brown (C&W) and Tessa Carol (soul and jazz).

RAM TALENT, Box 2802, Corpus Christi TX 78403. (512)922-5126. Owner: Bruce Taylor. Management firm and booking agency. Estab. 1972. Deals with artists from South Texas region only. Represents artists, groups and songwriters; currently handles 5 acts. Receives 10-15% commission.
How To Contact: Submit demo tape.

WILLIAM REZEY MANAGEMENT CO., 11 N. Pearl St., Home Saving Bank Bldg., Albany NY 12207. (518)462-4462. President: Bill Rezey. Manager: John Conlin. Management firm. Estab. 1968. Represents individuals and groups; currently handles 12 acts. Receives "escalating scale of commission based on income."
How to Contact: Query, arrange personal interview, submit demo tape, submit demo tape and lead sheet, or submit lead sheet. Prefers 7½ ips reel-to-reel or cassette with 2-4 songs on demo. SASE. Reports in 2 weeks.
Music: Disco; jazz; rock (hard or country); soul; and top 40/pop. Works primarily with concert and college attractions. Current acts include Jaime Renato (cabaret artist); Hott (high-energy funk); and Hal David-Lauri Bono Band (rock band).

REDBEARD PRESENTS PRODUCTIONS, LTD., 3196 Maryland Pkwy., #212, Las Vegas NV 89109. (702)734-1992. President: Robert Leonard. Management firm, booking agency, production company and music publisher. Estab. 1960. Represents individuals, groups and songwriters; currently handles 12 acts. Receives 10-15% commission.
How to Contact: Query or submit demo tape and lead sheet. Prefers 7½ ips reel-to-reel or cassette with 4-12 songs on demo. "It is most helpful if the artist or group can arrange for me to see them work." SASE. Reports in 2 weeks.
Music: Blues; disco; jazz; MOR; progressive; rock (soft or country); soul; and top 40/pop. Works primarily with jazz "names"; Latin show and dance bands; rock 'n roll show groups; and Las Vegas show groups. Current acts include Jon Hendricks and Family (jazz vocal act); Stue Gardner (funk/jazz act); Vocal Point (Las Vegas show-dance group); Jose Luis-The Latin Touch (Las Vegas show group); Ruth Brown (jazz/blues pop singer, actress); Silk & Satin (Las Vegas show group—Marilyn McCoo-Billy Davis type); and Jimmy Witherspoon (blues artist).

REEL TO REAL PRODUCTIONS, 98 Benz St., Ansonia CT 06401. (203)735-5883. Owners: Marty Kugell, Sharon Kugell. Management agency, music publisher and record producer. Estab. 1955. Represents individuals, groups and songwriters; currently handles 1 act. Fee derived from sales royalty.
How to Contact: Submit demo tape and lead sheet. Prefers 7½ ips reel-to-reel with 1-10 songs on demo. "Unleadered tapes will not be listened to." SASE. Reports in 3 weeks.
Music: Disco; rock; soul; top 40/pop; and easy listening. Currently handles David Szpak (self-contained writer/vocalist/keyboardist).

RNJ PRODUCTIONS, INC., 11514 Calvert St., North Hollywood CA 91606. President: Rein Neggo Jr. Vice President: Roger Montesano. Management firm. Estab. 1967. Represents professional individuals and groups; currently handles 6 acts. Receives 15-20% commission.
How to Contact: Submit demo tape and lead sheet. Prefers 7½ ips reel-to-reel or cassette with 1-3 songs on demo. SASE. "Material is reviewed monthly."

Music: Folk; MOR; and top 40/pop. Works primarily with artists for concerts and tours. Current acts include Glenn Yarbrough (pop/folk artist with 9-piece back-up band); the Limeliters (folk group); and Mike Settle (singer/songwriter).

ROADSHOW ARTIST'S MANAGEMENT, 850 7th Ave., New York NY 10019. (212)765-8840. Vice President: Mrs. Wynne Smith. Management agency. Estab. 1978. Represents artists, groups and songwriters; currently handles 3 acts. Negotiates commission.
How to Contact: Submit demo tape and lead sheet. Prefers 7½ ips reel-to-reel or cassette with 5-8 songs on demo. SASE. Reports in 3 weeks.
Music: Gospel; jazz; MOR; rock; soul; and top 40/pop.

DAVID ROSE, 3250 Lowry Rd., Los Angeles CA 90027. (213)666-2569. President: David Rose. Management agency. Estab. 1976. Represents artists and groups; currently handles 2 acts. Receives minimum 20% commission.
How To Contact: Query or submit demo tape only. Prefers cassette tape. "Must have pictures also." SASE. Reports in 1 month.
Music: C&W; gospel; and top 40/pop.

ROSEBUD MUSIC AGENCY, Box 1897, San Francisco CA 94101. (415)566-7009. Contact: Mike Kappus. Management firm and booking agency. Estab. 1976. Represents artists and groups; currently handles 7 acts. Receives 10-25% commission.
How to Contact: Submit promo and tape or phone. Prefers cassette with 3-6 songs on demo. "Phone call should be followed by tape and promo." SASE. Reports in 2 weeks.
Music: Blues (traditional, acoustic and electric and blue wave); jazz; progressive; rock (progressive and non-punk new wave); soul; top 40/pop; contemporary; and pop. "We are an organization devoted to developing a limitednumber of artists to their greatest potential. We specialize in North American tours and work with the coordination of overseas tours." Current acts include Mose Allison Trio (jazz/blues); John Lee Hooker (blues); George Thorogood and the Destroyers (blues/rock & roll); Captain Beefheart and the Magic Band (progressive rock); and James Lee Stanley (contemporary pop).

NIEL ROSEN/RON MASON MANAGEMENT, 8170 Beverly Blvd., Los Angeles CA 90028. (213)653-4460. Contact: Niel Rosen, Ron Mason. Management firm, TV producer and play producer. Estab. 1967. Represents individuals, groups, songwriters and directors; currently handles 10 acts. Receives 15% minimum commission.
How to Contact: Performers submit demo tape, writers submit demo tape and lead sheet. Include photos, bios and reviews. Prefers cassette with 3 songs minimum on tape. SASE. Reports in 1 week.
Music: C&W; MOR; progressive; rock; soul; and top 40/pop. Works primarily with recording artists, main room attractions and TV performers. Current acts include Pat Paulsen (comedian); Philippe Wynn (soul group); and Donna Fargo (C&W vocalist).

HOWARD ROTHBERG, LTD., 1706 N. Doheny Dr., Los Angeles CA 90069. (213)273-9100. President: Howard Rothberg. Management firm. Estab. 1974. Represents individuals; currently handles 4 acts. Receives negotiable commission.
How to Contact: Query or submit demo tape.

SHELLY ROTHMAN, 15 Central Park W., New York NY 10023. (212)246-2180. Owner: Shelly Rothman. Booking agency. Estab. 1971. Represents individuals, groups and variety artists; currently handles 18 acts. Receives 10% commission.
How to Contact: Query or arrange personal interview. Prefers 7½ ips reel-to-reel with 1-3 songs on demo. Does not return unsolicited material. Reports in 2 weeks.
Music: C&W and MOR. Works primarily with variety club talent. Current acts include Paula Wayne (vocalist); Bunny Parker (vocalist); Corbett Monica (comedy act); and Julie Budd (vocalist).

DICK RUBIN, LTD., 60 W. 57th St., New York NY 10019. (212)541-6576. President: B. Richard Rubin. Management firm. Estab. 1962. Represents individuals and groups; currently handles 2 acts. Receives 10-15% commission.
How to Contact: Query. SASE. Reports in 1 month.
Music: Bluegrass; C&W; and progressive. Works primarily with show groups. Current acts include the Mission Mountain Wood Band.

RUSTRON MUSIC PRODUCTIONS, 35 S. Broadway, Suite B-3, Irvington NY 10533 (branch office and studio A&R). (914)591-6151. Contact: Ron Caruso. See Rustron Music Productions, White Plains NY office, for details.

RUSTRON MUSIC PRODUCTIONS, 200 Westmoreland Ave., White Plains NY 10606. (914)946-1689. Artists' Consultant: Rusty Gordon. Composition Management: Ron Caruso. Management firm, booking agency, music publisher and record producer. Estab. 1970. Represents individuals, groups and songwriters; currently handles 12 acts. Receives 10-25% commission for management and/or booking only.
How to Contact: Query, arrange personal interview, or submit in person or by mail demo tape and lead sheet. Prefers 7½ ips reel-to-reel, cassette with 3-6 songs on demo. SASE. Reports in 1 month.
Music: Disco; folk (contemporary/topical); MOR (pop style); and rock (folk/pop). Current acts include Gordon and Caruso (songwriter/producers); Rick McDonald (folk/rock singer/songwriter); Lois Britten (disco/rock/pop/singer/songwriter); Christian Camilo-Veda and the Tigalayo Rhythm Band (salsa-disco/pop); and Dianne Mower and Jasmine (modern jazz instrumental and vocal).

RUSTRON WEST, 2804 S. Baldwin Ave., Arcadia CA 91006. Contact: Mike Cohen. Marketing and promotion only; see Rustron Music Productions, White Plains NY office, for details.

S.R.O. PRODUCTIONS, INC., c/o Oak Manor, 12261 Yonge St., Box 1000, Oak Ridges, Ontario, Canada L0G 1P0. (416)881-3212. Chairman: Ray Danniels. President: Vic Wilson. A&A Director: Michael Tilka. Estab. 1973. Represents individuals, groups and songwriters; currently handles 6 acts. Receives commission based on individually negotiated contracts.
How to Contact: Submit demo tape with bio material. Prefers 7½ ips reel-to-reel or cassette with 3-6 songs on demo. SAE and International Reply Coupons. Reports in 6 weeks.
Music: Progressive; rock; and top 40/pop. Works primarily with rock concert acts. Current acts include Rush; Max Webster (rock act); and Ian Thomas and Wireless.

SAGITTARIAN ARTISTS INTERNATIONAL, 970 Aztec Dr., Muskegon MI 49444. (616)733-2329, 744-3256. Coordinator: Basil H. Ruhl. Director: G. Loren Ruhl. Management firm. Estab. 1965. Represents individuals and songwriters; currently handles 6 acts. Receives 15-25% commission.
How to Contact: Query or submit demo tape and lead sheet. Prefers cassette with 2-4 songs on demo, or record. SASE. Reports in 1 month.
Music: Blues; C&W; jazz; rock; and top 40/pop. Works primarily with dance bands and bar bands. Current acts include Ricky Briton (pop vocalist); Les Basilio (vocalist); and Tobie Columbus (pop vocalist).

PETE SALERNO ENTERPRISES, 317 Temple Place, Westfield NJ 07090. President: Pete Salerno. Management firm and booking agency. Estab. 1965. Represents professional individuals, groups and songwriters; currently handles 45 acts. Receives 15-25% commission.
How to Contact: Query, then submit demo tape and lead sheet.

JOHN SALVATO AGENCY, 111 W. 6th St., Bayonne NJ 07002. (201)339-5966. President: John Salvato. Management firm and booking agency. Estab. 1962. Represents individuals, groups and songwriters; currently handles 20 acts. Receives 15-25% commission.
How to Contact: Submit demo tape and lead sheet. Prefers cassette with 4-6 songs on demo. SASE. Reports in 2 weeks.
Music: Church/religious; disco; MOR; rock (country); soul; and top 40/pop. Works primarily with concert and club attractions. Current acts include the Imperials; the Duprees; and the Joneses (vocal group/variety attraction).

MICHAEL J. SANSONE, 1924 Genesee St., Utica NY 13502. (315)735-2020. Manager: Michael J. Sansone. Booking agency. Estab. 1972. Represents artists, groups and songwriters; currently handles 15 acts. Receives 10-20% commission.
How to Contact: Submit demo tape and lead sheet. Prefers cassette tapes. Does not return unsolicited material. Reports in 2 weeks.
Music: Disco; rock; soul; and top 40/pop. Works with dance and bar bands. Current acts include Band of Oz (concert); Sail (dance, disco, top 40); and Sixty-Six Inches (dance, top 40).

PHIL SCHAPIRO, INC., 157 W. 57th St., New York NY 10019. Executive Vice President: Hy Grill. Management firm and production company. Estab. 1967. Represents individuals, groups,

songwriters and all other types of performers/acts; currently handles 12 acts. Commission determined by "individual negotiation."
How to Contact: Submit demo tape and lead sheet. Prefers 7½ ips reel-to-reel or cassette with 1-4 songs on demo, or 45 or 33⅓ rpm disc. SASE. Reports in 1 week.
Music: Bluegrass; blues; C&W; disco; MOR; progressive; rock (country); and top 40/pop. Current acts include Jan Peerce; Claire Barry; and Harmony and Grits.

WALTER R. SCOTT, 6430 Sunset Blvd., Suite 821, Hollywood CA 90028. (213)461-4421. Contact: Walter Scott, H.B. Barnum, James Tolbert. Management firm. Estab. 1968. Represents individuals, groups and songwriters; currently handles 25 acts. Receives 15-25% commission.
How to Contact: Query or submit demo tape and lead sheet. Prefers cassette or 8-track cartridge with 2-4 songs on demo. SASE. Reports in 2 weeks.
Music: Blues; C&W; jazz; MOR; rock (soft or country); soul; and top 40/pop. Works primarily with 3- to 12-piece bands that "entertain, sing, and can play for dancing. Plus, individual singers, actors, actresses, writers and comedians." Current acts include Sandy Baron (actor/comedian); Bob Denver (actor/singer); Ann Howard (singer/actress); and Solid State (group).

SELECT ARTISTS ASSOCIATES, 7300 E. Camelback Rd., Scottsdale AZ 85251. (602)994-0471. President: Charles T. Johnston. Booking agency. Estab. 1967. Represents groups; currently handles 35 acts. Receives 15% minimum commission.
How to Contact: Query or submit demo tape and lead sheet. Prefers cassette with 3 songs minimum on tape. SASE. Reports in 1 month.
Music: Disco and top 40/pop. Works primarily with show/dance groups. Current acts include Gringo (top 40/disco lounge act); Quantrell (top 40/disco lounge act); and Phoenix Express (top 40/disco lounge act).

SHORT PUMP ASSOCIATES, Box 11292, Richmond VA 23230. (804)355-4117. President: Ken Brown. Vice President: Dennis Huber. Management agency. Estab. 1977. Deals with artists in the Virginia, North Carolina, Washington D.C. and Maryland region. Represents artists, groups and songwriters; currently handles 2 acts. Receives 10-20% commission.
How to Contact: Submit demo tape and lead sheet. Prefers cassette with 2-10 songs on demo. "Biographies and itineraries are helpful." SASE. Reports in 3 weeks.
Music: Disco; rock (country rock and hard rock); soul; and top 40/pop. Works with dance bands (usually 6-10 piece w/horns), concert, rock and country rock artists. Current acts include Robbin Thompson and the No Slack Band (rock-country rock); Andrew Lewis Band (top 40/soul/disco); and Eric Heiberg (rock).

SHOWCASE ATTRACTIONS, Box 6687, Wheeling WV 26003. (614)758-5812. President: R.H. Gallion. Management firm and booking agency. Estab. 1971. Represents individuals, groups and songwriters; currently handles 44 acts. Receives 15% minimum commission.
How to Contact: Query or submit demo tape. Prefers 7½ ips reel-to-reel with 2 songs minimum on demo. Does not return unsolicited material. Reports in 1 month.
Music: Bluegrass; C&W; folk; gospel; MOR; and top 40/pop. Works primarily with C&W and gospel artists and groups. Current acts include Bob Gallion (C&W); Patti Powell (C&W); and the Dixie Melody Boys (gospel group).

SIDARTHA ENTERPRISES, LTD., 1504 E. Grandriver Ave., Suite 101, East Lansing MI 48823. (517)351-6780. President: Thomas R. Brunner. Management firm and booking agency. Estab. 1970. Represents artists and groups. Receives 15-25% commission.
How to Contact: "Always make phone contact first." Submit demo tape and lead sheet.

SKYBLUE MANAGEMENT AGENCY, Box 1284, Venice CA 90291. (213)399-6986. President: Marc M. Dulberger. Management firm, booking agency and advertising agency. Estab. 1976. Represents individuals, groups and songwriters; currently handles 3 acts. Receives 5-20% commission.
How to Contact: Query or submit demo tape and lead sheet. Prefers cassette with 2-12 songs on demo. SASE. Reports in 1 month.
Music: Bluegrass; blues; disco (funk, European); folk; jazz (salsa progressive); MOR; progressive; rock (hard); soul (funk); top 40/pop; and electronic. Current acts include Howard Epstein (rock songwriter); Craza (rock group); Mark Paternostro (rock songwriter); Jack Le Torneau (rock songwriter); Tom Schroeder (rock songwriter); Gordon Elliot (rock songwriter);

Art Rapkin (rock songwriter); Mark Kruger (rock songwriter); Jay Livington; and Dan Sverdlin.

JAMES R. SMITH/HANK WILLIAMS JR. ENTERPRISES, Box 790, Cullman AL 35055. (205)734-8656. Manager: James R. Smith. Management firm and booking agency. Estab. 1974. Represents individuals and songwriters; currently handles 4 acts. Receives negotiable commission.
How to Contact: Query or submit demo tape and lead sheet. Prefers 7½ ips reel-to-reel or cassette with 1-3 songs on demo. Does not return unsolicited material.
Music: C&W; rock (country); and top 40/pop. Works primarily with vocal acts. Current acts include Hank Williams Jr. and the Bama Band (group); Merle Kilgore (singer); and Nate Harvell (singer).

SOLID SOUL PRODUCTIONS, 3282 E. 119th St., Cleveland OH 44120. (216)231-0772, 752-1904. Executive Vice President: Anthony Luke. Concert consultant and promotion. Estab. 1970. Represents individuals and groups.
How to Contact: Send letter of introduction. Prefers cassette with 6-12 songs on demo. SASE. Reports in 1 month.
Music: Blues; disco; rock; and soul.

SOUND '86 ENTERTAINMENT/CONCERTS/MANAGEMENT, Box 432, Rapid City, SD 57709. (605)343-9515. Owner: Kelly Hollister. Management firm and booking agency. Estab. 1974. Represents groups from the upper Midwest. Receives 15% commission.
How to Contact: Submit demo tape. Prefers cassette with 3-7 songs on demo. "Include band resume, including song list, equipment list and references."
Music: Rock (all types) and country rock. Current acts include Bold Lightning, Cartune, Ambush and Ivory.

SOUND III MANAGEMENT, 9046 Sunset Blvd., Los Angeles CA 90069. (213)271-7246. President: Bruce Berlow. Management firm. Estab. 1976. Represents individuals, groups and songwriters; currently handles 6 acts. Receives 20% commission.
How to Contact: Query, arrange personal interview or submit demo tape. Prefers 7½ ips reel-to-reel or cassette with 3-6 songs on demo. SASE. Reports in 2 weeks.
Music: C&W; progressive; rock (hard or country); and top 40/pop. Works primarily with solo artists or rock groups and with composers and singer/songwriters. Current acts include White Light (rock group); Chris Rhodes (solo artist); Bob Darcy/Ann Robbins (songwriters); and Mundell Lowe (composer).

SOUNDWAYS INTERNATIONAL INC., 1704 W. Lake St., Minneapolis MN 55408. (612)827-5533. Managing Director A&R: Steve Greenberg, Reid McLean and Marshall Eddstein. Management firm and record company. Estab. 1977. Represents artists, groups and songwriters. Negotiates contract.
How to Contact: Submit demo tape with lyric sheets. Prefers 7½ ips reel-to-reel and cassette with 1-5 songs on demo. SASE. Reports in 1 month.
Music: Disco; folk; jazz; MOR; rock (hard and country); soul; and top 40/pop. Current acts include Scott Jones (jazz/folk); Fairchild (progressive rock); and Halloween (hard rock).

SOUTHERN MANAGEMENT BOOKINGS, Box 262, Rt. 2, Landenberg PA 19350. Manager: Bob Paisley. Management firm and booking agency. Estab. 1976. Represents artists, groups and songwriters; currently handles 7 acts. Receives 10-15% commission.
How to Contact: Query, submit demo tape or demo tape and lead sheet. Prefers cassette with 3 songs on demo. SASE. Reports in 3 weeks.
Music: Bluegrass; C&W; and folk. Works with bar bands, festival bands and works with artists for recording sessions. Current acts include Southern Mountain Boys (bluegrass); Country Class (C&W); and Caroll County Boys (bluegrass).

SPIRIT PRODUCTIONS, 7308 Williamson Creek, Austin TX 78736. (512)288-0514. President: Cathy Thornton. Agent: Tom Thornton. Management firm and booking agency. Estab. 1971. Represents individuals, groups and songwriters from the Southwest; currently handles 5 acts. Receives 10-20% commission.
How to Contact: Query or submit demo tape. Prefers cassette with 3-6 songs on demo. SASE. Reports "only if we think we could do something with them."
Music: C&W; progressive; and rock (country). Works primarily with dance bands for dance halls and clubs. Current acts include T. Gosney Band (country rock dance band); Barrett

(country rock dance band); and Kurt Van Sickle (single artist).

STAR ARTIST MANAGEMENT, 30555 Southfield Rd., Southfield MI 48076. (313)645-0200.
President: Ron Geddish. Treasurer: Ken Cornett. Director of West Coast Operations: Ray
Shelide. Director of Canadian Operations: Brian Courtis. Director of Artist Relations: Chris
Best. General Counsellor: Tom Werner. Management firm. Estab. 1972. Represents
individuals, groups and songwriters, currently handles 5 acts. Receives 10-20% commission.
How to Contact: Submit demo tape. Prefers 7½ ips reel-to-reel or cassette with 3-5 songs on
demo. SASE. Reports in 1 month.
Music: Rock (hard or MOR). Works primarily with hard rock groups. Current acts include
Tilt; Toby Redd; and White Wolf (rock groups).

STAR REPRESENTATION, 4026 Bobby Lane, Schiller Park IL 60176. (312)678-2755.
President: James Stella. Management agency and production company. Estab. 1976.
Represents artists, groups and songwriters; currently handles 9 acts. Receives 15-25%
commission.
How to Contact: Arrange personal interview or submit demo tape and lead sheet. Prefers 7½
ips reel-to-reel or cassette with 2-6 songs on demo. SASE. Reports in 2-3 weeks.
Music: Children's; disco; MOR; progressive; rock (hard or melodic rock); soul; and top
40/pop. Works with dance and bar bands-looking for national potential. Current acts include
Europe (melodic rock); John Cesario (songwriter/artist); and Steve Busa (songwriter/artist).

STARCREST PRODUCTIONS, INC., 2516 S. Washington St., Grand Forks ND 58201.
(701)772-6831. President: George Hastings. Management firm and booking agency. Estab.
1970. Represents individuals, groups and songwriters; currently handles 4 acts. Receives
10-15% commission.
How to Contact: Query, then submit demo tape and lead sheet. Prefers 7½ ips reel-to-reel with
2 songs minimum on demo. SASE. Reports in 1 month.
Music: Classical; C&W; gospel; MOR; and top 40/pop. Current acts include Mary Joyce
(C&W vocalist); the Pioneers (C&W group); and Bob Angle (C&W songwriter).

STERLING ENTERTAINMENT AGENCY, 2726 Eden Lane, Rapid City SD 57701.
(605)342-2697. Owner: Lowell Sterling. Booking agency. Estab. 1965. Represents groups;
currently handles 24 acts. Receives 10% minimum commission.
How to Contact: Query. Prefers cassette. SASE. Reports in 1 week.
Music: C&W; rock (country or light); and top 40/pop. Works primarily with "dance singles,
duos and quartets and some show groups." Current acts include R. Tommy Roe and Strange
Magic (variety/dance); Diane Lee Show (C&W dance trio); and Rawhide (C&W dance
quartet).

RANDY STEWART ENTERPRISES, 11 Greendale Crescent, Kitchener, Ontario, Canada.
N2A 2R5. (519)893-0420. Owner/Agent: Randy Stewart. Sub-Agent: Lynn Bell. Management
firm, booking agency and concert promoter. Represents individuals and groups. Currently
handles 1 songwriter; represents "an unlimited number of artists and groups on an unexclusive
basis." Receives 20% maximum commission.
How to Contact: Query or arrange personal interview. "Send complete promo package with
open dates, prices, details, itinerary, band members' names and locals, plus where to contact."
Prefers 7½ ips reel-to-reel or cassette. Does not return unsolicited material "unless requested
after a period of time and nonuse."
Music: Bluegrass; C&W; disco; MOR; polka; rock (all); soul; and top 40/pop. Works with
dance and bar bands, concert attractions and recording groups. Current acts include Pigbone
(country rock show band); ELI (contemporary big band); and Randy Stewart
(singer/songwriter).

TOM STINNETTE ENTERTAINMENT AGENCY, Box 06404, Portland OR 97206.
(503)235-5988. President: Tom Stinnette. Production Manager: Bryce Lister. Management firm
and booking agency. Estab. 1971. Represents artists and groups; also handles special
promotions for clubs, fairs and concerts for businesses. Currently handles 30 agency and 3
management acts. Receives 10-20% commission or percentage of gross.
How to Contact: Submit demo tape and lead sheet. "Please include all pertainent details of
your act. Follow up with a phone call to make sure we received your material."

SUPER ASSOCIATES, Box 32, Willowdale, Ontario, Canada L3R 2V8. (416)495-1710. Vice
President: John W. Boswell. President: John C. Irvine. Management firm. Estab. 1965. Deals

with artists "mostly from Canada, some US." Represents individuals, groups and songwriters; currently handles 4 acts. Receives 10% minimum commission.

How to Contact: Query, submit demo tape or submit demo tape and lead sheet. Prefers 7½ or 15 ips reel-to-reel or cassette with 2 songs minimum on tape. Include bio and photo. SAE and International Reply Coupons. Reports in 3 weeks.

Music: Bluegrass; blues; children's; C&W; folk; gospel; jazz; and polka. Works primarily with C&W, folk, "esoteric," jazz and blues artists. Current acts include Short Turn (folk); Shot Jackson (C&W/bluegrass); Eddie Coffy (Newfoundland country); Smiley Bates (C&W); and Donna Darlene (C&W).

SUREFIRE PRODUCTIONS, Box 1808, Asheville NC 28802. President: Ron Weathers. Management firm and booking agency, Estab. 1977. Represents artists, groups and songwriters; currently handles 50 acts. Receives 15-20% commission.

How to Contact: Submit demo tape only. Prefers 7½ ips reel-to-reel with 5-10 songs on demo. SASE. Reports in 1 month.

Music: Disco; MOR; soul; and top 40/pop. Works with top 40 dance bands and show groups. Current acts include Toby King (top 40 and disco); Grand Slam (top 40 and disco); Celebrity Ball (top 40 and disco); and Hayes & Vyain.

SUTTON ARTISTS CORP., 2930 Turtle Creek Plaza, Dallas TX 75219. (214)521-6530. Regional Manager: H.D. McElroy. Booking agency. Estab. 1970. Represents artists and groups; currently handles 30 acts. Receives 10-20% commission.

How to Contact: Submit demo tape. Prefers cassette with 4 songs minimum on demo. "Phone first and describe original music, then mail demo." Does not return unsolicited material. Reports in 1 month.

Music: Blues; C&W; disco; gospel; jazz; MOR; progressive; and rock. Works with concert artists, "no nightclub locations." Current acts include Chet Atkins (country); Dave Brubeck (jazz); Hoyt Axton (country); Chuck Howard (country); Maurice Jarre (motion pictures); Bobby Voss (composer/pianist); Don McLean (MOR); Clarence Henry (jazz) and Terry Williams (country).

TALENT MANAGEMENT, 300 W. Armour, Kansas City MO 64111. (816)753-6850. President: James Foster. Management firm and booking agency. Estab. 1973. Represents individuals and groups; currently handles 80 acts. Receives 10-25% commission.

How to Contact: Arrange personal interview or submit demo tape and lead sheet. Prefers 7½ ips reel-to-reel or cassette with 5-8 songs on demo. SASE. Reports in 2 weeks.

Music: Disco; jazz; rock; soul; and top 40/pop. Works with "original groups only, no sound-alikes or impersonations." Uses night club, concert and some dance acts. Current acts include Bill Hemmans (tenor sax artist); J.R. Perales (Spanish act); and Tony Burke (vocalist).

T.D.I. DIRECTION & MANAGEMENT DIVISION, 4100 W. Flagler St., Miami FL 33134. (305)446-1900. Managers: Larry Brahms, and George Nocera. Management firm, publishing and production company. Estab. 1958. Represents artists, groups, songwriters and record producers; currently handles 6 artists and 3 songwriters.

How to Contact: Query or submit demo tape and lead sheet. Prefers cassette or disc with 3-4 songs. SASE. Reports in 1 month.

Music: Disco; soul; and top 40/pop. Works with national recording acts only. Some local band bookings as a community service. Current acts include Foxy, Celi Bee, Jimmy Bo Horne, the Ritchie Family and Laura Taylor.

TENTH HOUR PRODUCTIONS, 4470 Brownsville Rd., Pittsburgh PA 15236. (412)881-0876. President: Carl M. Grefenstette. Management agency. Estab. 1975. Deals with artists in Western Pennsylvania, Ohio and West Virginia region only. Represents artists, groups and songwriters; currently handles 10 acts. Receives 10-20% commission.

How to Contact: Query or submit demo tape only. Prefers 7½ ips reel-to-reel or cassette with 2-3 songs on demo. SASE. Reports in 3 weeks.

Music: C&W (top 40 C&W/country rock); folk (top 40); rock (top 40/country-rock/hard rock); and top 40/pop. Works with college concert bands, dance bands, bar bands and coffeehouse singles and duos. Current acts include Leslie Smith (country-rock soloist with backup band); the Flashcats ('60s soul band a la Blues Brothers); Maggie Stewart (pop, standards, etc.); and Fragile (top 40 rock).

THE TENTMAKERS CORP., 6367 W. 6th St., Los Angeles CA 90048. Publishing Coordinator: Ron Woodmansee. Management firm. Estab. 1974.

How to Contact: Query. Prefers 7½ ips reel-to-reel or cassette with 2-6 songs on demo. Reports in 1 month.
Music: Jazz; progressive; soul; and top 40/pop.

STEVE THOMAS MANAGEMENT, INC., 1901 E. N. Hamilton St., Box 11283, Richmond VA 23230. (804)355-2178. President: Steve Thomas. Management agency. Estab. 1971. Represents artists and groups; currently handles 2 acts. Receives 10-15% commission.
How to Contact: Submit demo tape only. Prefers cassette with 2-5 songs on demo. Does not return unsolicited material. Reports only if interested.
Music: Disco; rock; soul; and top 40/pop. Works primarily with dance and concert bands. Current acts include Power Play (disco band) and Sandcastle (concert/dance band).

TOBY ORGANIZATION, INC., 8899 Beverly Blvd., Los Angeles CA 90048. (213)274-7381. President: David Joseph. Management agency. Estab. 1975. Represents artists, groups and songwriters; currently handles 2 groups. Receives 15-20% commission.
How to Contact: Submit demo tape and biographical and directional materials. Prefers 7½ ips reel-to-reel or cassette with 2-4 songs on demo. SASE. Reports in 1 month. "We would appreciate a brief description of the artist's musical direction, where he wants to go, what his aims are. Also his accomplishments."
Music: Disco; MOR (pop-oriented); progressive (pop-oriented); rock (all kinds); and top 40/pop. Works with rock 'n roll groups and singer/songwriter artists. Current acts include Angel (hard rock group with theatrical show) and Tom Sullivan (MOR singer/songwriter/pianist).

ROSS TODD & ASSOCIATES, 2181 Victory Pkwy., Cincinnati OH 45206. Talent Director: John Todd. Concert promotion firm. Estab. 1970. "Artist (if act qualifies) is paid through stage exposure with big name acts."
How to Contact: Submit demo tape or submit demo tape and lead sheet. Prefers cassette with 3-8 songs on demo. Does not return unsolicited material. Reports in 1 week. "Depends on music. Sometimes we never respond."
Music: Blues; folk; jazz; progressive; rock; soul; and top 40/pop. "We are looking for the kind of band that feels it has reached a level of professionalism to be considered as a good back-up opening show for an established name band or group. Individual artists will also be given equal consideration."

TOPDRAW ARTIST MANAGEMENT, Box 2787 Station A, Champaign IL 61820. President: Jeff Ross. Management firm, production and publishing company. Estab. 1979. Represents artists, groups and songwriters; currently handles 4 groups and 3 writers. Receives 15-25% commission.
How to Contact: Query or submit demo tape. Prefers cassette with 3-6 songs on demo. SASE. Reports in 3 weeks.
Music: Disco; progressive; rock (all rock); soul; and top 40/pop. Works with anything from bar bands to concert performers. Current acts include Screams (rock); Ingrid Berry (rock); and Jett (hard rock).

TRIANGLE TALENT, INC., 9701 Taylorsville Rd., Box 99035, Louisville KY 40299. (502)267-5466. President: David H. Snowden. Booking agency. Estab. 1959. Represents artists and groups; currently handles 110 acts. Receives 10-20% commission.
How to Contact: Query or submit demo tape. Prefers cassette with 2-4 songs on demo. SASE. Reports in 2 weeks.
Music: Bluegrass; disco; rock (both heavy and funk); top 40/pop; and country. Current acts include Free Fall (rock/concert); Mid-night Star (jazz, disco/concert); Pure Pleasure (disco/top 40); Epics (show/concert); and Debi Bass (country, show/concert).

TWO RIVER PRODUCTIONS, New Brotherhood Bldg., Suite 769, Kansas City KS 66109. (913)321-4945. Owner: Gene Hill. Booking agency. Estab. 1974. Deals with artists in region. Represents individuals and groups; currently handles 35 acts. Receives 20% commission.
How to Contact: Query by phone, then submit demo tape. Include bio, photos and references. Prefers cassette with 8-10 songs on demo. SASE. Reports in 1 week.
Music: Bluegrass; blues; C&W; disco; folk; jazz (very little); MOR; polka; progressive; rock (all); soul; and top 40/pop. Works primarily with top 40/pop night club acts. Current acts include Hollywood Road (top 40/pop/disco); and K C Sound Co. (top 40/pop/disco).

HARRISON TYNER INTERNATIONAL, INC., 38 Music Square E., #115, Nashville TN

37203. (615)244-4224. President: Harrison Tyner. Management agency, publishing company and production company. Estab. 1975. Represents entertainers and songwriters; currently handles 2 acts. Receives 10-20% commission.
How to Contact: Query. Prefers 7½ or 15 ips reel-to-reel or cassette with 1-4 songs on demo. SASE. Reports in 1 month.
Music: C&W; MOR; and top 40/pop. Works primarily with male/female individual singers. Current acts include Shaun Nielsen (former backup singer for Elvis Presley) and Daniel.

UMBRELLA ARTISTS MANAGEMENT, INC., Box 6507, 2181 Victory Pkwy., Cincinnati OH 45206. (513)861-1500. President: Stan Hertzman. Management agency. Estab. 1972. Represents artists, groups and songwriters; currently handles 6 acts. Receives 10-20% commission.
How to Contact: Submit demo tape only. Prefers 7½-15 ips reel-to-reel with 1-6 songs on demo. SASE. Reports in 2-4 weeks.
Music: Progressive; rock; and top 40/pop. Works with contemporary/progressive pop/rock artists/writers. Current acts include Adrian Belew (guitarist, writer, vocalist with Frank Zappa and David Bowie); Susan Darby (vocalist); Blaze (rock group); Mike Reid (pianist/vocalist/songwriter); Danny Morgan (guitarist/vocalist/songwriter); and Carefree Day (rock group).

VALEX TALENT AGENCY, 105 E. Clinton St., Ithaca NY 14850. (607)273-3931. Publishing Vice President: Rick Gravelding. Booking Vice President: Tom Brennan. Management firm, booking agency and publishing house (Flying Horse Music). Estab. 1959. Deals with artists in northeast US only. Represents artists, groups and songwriters; currently handles 20 acts. Receives 15-25% commission.
How to Contact: Submit demo tape and lead sheet. Prefers 7½ ips reel-to-reel or cassette with 3-6 songs on demo. SASE. Reports in 1 month. "Songwriters please send material in care of Rick Gravelding, Flying Horse Music; also send cassettes or 7½ ips tapes to same."
Music: Disco; rock (hard or country); and top 40/pop. Works with recording groups, dance and bar bands. Current act include Charlie Starr (single, guitar and vocals); Bobby Comstock (rock); and Jamo (rock).

GARY VAN ZEELAND TALENT, INC., 1750 Freedom Rd., Little Chute WI 54140. (414)788-5222. Manager: Pete Sullivan. Booking agency. Estab. 1964. Represents groups; currently handles 85 acts. Receives 15% commission from road groups.
How to Contact: Query by mail or phone. Prefers cassette with 8-10 songs on demo. Include photo, songlist and references. Does not return unsolicited material. Reports in 1 week.
Music: Rock (country or regular); top 40/pop; and dance. Works primarily with lounge acts, and bar and hotel bands. Current acts include Original Family Affair; and Moxie (top 40 show and dance groups).

VASSAR'S MUSIC, Box 208, Hermitage TN 37076. (615)758-8181. Owner: Millie Clements. Management agency and music publisher. Estab. 1971. Represents individuals and groups; currently handles 2 acts. Receives negotiable commission.
How to Contact: Submit demo tape and lead sheet. Prefers cassette. SASE. Reports in 1 month.
Music: Blues; disco; jazz; progressive; rock (country); and soul. Works primarily with concert acts. Current acts include the Vassar Clements Band (progressive pop rock group); and Dave Perkins (blues soul artist).

VOKES BOOKING AGENCY, Box 12, New Kensington PA 15068. (412)335-2775. President: Howard Vokes. Booking agency. Estab. 1959. Represents individuals, groups and songwriters; currently handles 25 acts. Receives 10-20% commission.
How to Contact: Query or submit demo tape and lead sheet. Prefers 7½ ips reel-to-reel, cassette or 8-track with 3-6 songs on demo. SASE. Reports in 2 weeks.
Music: Bluegrass; C&W; and gospel. "We work with bluegrass and hard country bands who generally play bars, hotels and clubs. However, we also book in ole-time artists as singles. We want nothing to do with hard rock or country rock." Current acts include Bluefield Boys (bluegrass); Country Boys (C&W).

JIM WAGNER, INC., DBA American Management, 17337 Ventura Blvd., Suite 220, Encino CA 91316. (213)981-6500. President: Jim Wagner. Booking agency. Represents individuals and groups; currently handles 7 acts. Receives 15% commission.

How to Contact: Query. Prefers 7½ ips reel-to-reel with 1-3 songs on demo. SASE. Reports as soon as possible.
Music: C&W and progressive. Works primarily with C&W artists and groups. Current acts include Freddie Hart and the Heartbeats (C&W artist); Eddie Rabbitt and Band (C&W group); Tommy Overstreet and the Nashville Express (C&W).

WILLIAM F. WAGNER AGENCY, 13437 Ventura Blvd., Suite 223, Sherman Oaks CA 91423. (213)995-4277. Owner: Bill Wagner. Management agency and record producer. Estab. 1957. Represents artists and groups; currently handles 6 acts. Receives 15% commission. "For recording production of artists other than my own clients I receive $100/hour, live studio time; $50/hour overdub, editing and mix-down time."
How to Contact: Query, telephone for personal interview or submit demo tape and lead sheet. Prefers 7½ or 3¾ ips reel-to-reel (2- or 4-track) or cassette with 10-15 minutes on tape. SASE. Reports in 2 weeks.
Music: Blues; C&W; disco; jazz; MOR; progressive; rock (all kinds); soul; and top 40/pop. Works with singers, songwriter-singers, instrumentalists and 2- to 7-piece groups. Current acts include Bryan Fox (composer/singer/instrumentalist); Becky Saunders (contemporary/pop/MOR/rock vocalist); JoAnne Kurman (country/pop vocalist); Los Dominics (7-piece Mexican show group); and Pete Christlieb (jazz tenor).

NORBY WALTERS ASSOCIATES, 1290 Avenue of the Americas, New York NY 10015. (212)245-3939. President: Norby Walters. Management firm and booking agency. Estab. 1968. Represents individuals and groups; currently handles 50 acts. Receives 10-20% commission.
How to Contact: Submit demo tape and lead sheet. Prefers cassette with 1-3 songs on demo. Does not return unsolicited material. Reports in 2 weeks.
Music: Disco; MOR; soul; and top 40/pop. Current acts include Gloria Gaynor (top 40/pop/disco); Peaches & Herb (top 40/pop/disco); and Marvin Gaye (top 40/pop).

IRWIN WEINER MANAGEMENT CORP., 370 Lexington Ave., New York NY 10017. (212)689-0445. A&R Director: Ken Weiner. Management agency. Estab. 1977. Represents individuals, groups and songwriters. Currently handles 3 acts. Receives 20-25% commission.
How to Contact: Query; arrange personal interview; or submit demo tape. Prefers 7½ ips reel-to-reel or cassette with 3-7 songs on demo. "We prefer that the artist can top what is currently on the charts. If they cannot, it is a waste of time." SASE. Reports in 1 week.
Music: Disco; rock; soul; and top 40/pop. "We will work with any king of artists as long as they have the makings of becoming superstars." Current acts include Major Harris (R&B/RCA Records); Blue Magic (R&B/Atco Records); Mitch Weiss (rock 'n roll); and Julius Erving/Dr. J. (disco/R&B, Atlantic Records).

JERRY WEINREB/SHELLY PRODUCTIONS, 30-24 Broadway, Fairlawn NJ 07410. (201)791-1033. Management agency. Estab. 1966.
How to Contact: Query or submit demo tape and lead sheet. Prefers cassette with 1-2 songs on demo. "No hard rock. Name, address and telephone number must appear very clearly. Particular submission should be geared to listeners from age 22 and up." Does not return unsolicited material. Reports in 1 month.
Music: Blues; disco; easy listening; MOR; and top 40/pop.

WHIMPIA MANAGEMENT, 77 Milltown Rd., East Brunswick NJ 08816. (201)254-3990. Owner: William Franzblau. Management agency. Estab. 1977. Deals with artists in East Coast region only. Represents artists, groups and songwriters; currently handles 4 acts. Receives 12-20% commision.
How to Contact: Arrange personal interview or submit demo tape only. Prefers reel-to-reel or cassette with 3-8 songs on demo. SASE. Reports in 1 week.
Music: Blues; disco; jazz; rock (country rock); and top 40/pop. Works with concert and bar bands. Current acts include Kinderhook (concert act); Cowtown (bar band); and Cloverhill (bar band).

WINTERSWAN, Division of Great Plains Associates, 107 E. 8th St., Lawrence KS 66044. (913)841-4444. Presidents: Mark Swanson, Scott Winters. Management firm. Estab. 1976. Represents groups; currently handles 1 act. Receives 10-20% commission.
How to Contact: Arrange personal interview or submit demo tape. Prefers cassette with 3-10 songs on demo. SASE. Reports in 3 weeks.
Music: Progressive (C&W or country rock) and rock (straight). Works primarily with .

dance/concert bands, for small college circuit and dance halls. Current acts include Pott Country Pork 'n Bean Band (country rock).

PAUL WOLFE, Box 262, Abe Lincoln Station, Carteret NJ 07008. (201)541-9422. President: Paul Wolfe. Vice President: Gary Hills. Management firm, booking agency and record producer. Estab. 1965. Represents individuals, groups, songwriters and show and oldie acts from the US, Canada, Japan, England, France, Sweden, Belgium and Holland; currently handles 39 acts. Receives 10-15% commission; "the artist picks up his money directly — we receive deposits only with signed contracts."
How to Contact: Query, submit demo tape or submit demo tape and lead sheet. Prefers 7½ ips reel-to-reel, cassette or 8-track cartridge with 8-15 songs on demo. "Send material with demo, photographs and short bio on yourself to get a better idea of the sender." SASE. Reports in 1 month.
Music: Children's; church/religious; C&W; disco; folk; MOR; polka; progressive; rock (country or hard); and top 40/pop. Works primarily with dance bands, show groups and singles. Current acts include Sonny Ray and the Delrays; Herman's Hermits; the Jackie Wilson Tribute Show; and the History of Gold Show "all produced by this office for touring and traveling dates."
Tips: "We welcome new songwriters as well as new groups; we want to develop tomorrow's hit artist as well as our agency's future."

MICHAEL WOOD ASSOCIATES, 2705 N. Sibley Ave., Metairie LA 70003. Contact: Michael Wood, Arthur Edwards. Management firm, booking agency and production company. Estab. 1973. Represents individuals, groups and songwriters. Receives 10-20% commission.
How to Contact: Query or submit demo tape and lead sheet. Prefers cassette with 3-4 songs on demo. "Include a bio and info sheet with what you want out of the business and a tape with an itinerary where you may be seen." SASE. Reports in 1 month.
Music: Blues; C&W; disco; gospel; jazz; MOR; progressive; rock; soul; and top 40/pop. Works primarily with "show attractions and jazz legends; those that cater to the more affluent 30-60 clientele. We deliver varied convention entertainment. We are looking for artists of major label caliber." Current acts include Tom Elias and Fancy Music (cabaret show act); Cotton Club Orchestra (jazz legend); Mahogony Hall Jazz Band (jazz legend); Donna Thompson (comic/singer); and the French Quarter Fillies (musical revue).

YBARRA MUSIC, Box 665, Lemon Grove CA 92045. (714)462-6538. Owner: D. Braun. A&R Director: R. William. Booking agency, music publisher and record company. Estab. 1952. Deals with artists from Southern California. Represents groups; currently handles 3 acts. Receives 5-20% commission.
How to Contact: Query. Prefers cassette. Does not return unsolicited material. Reports in 1 month.
Music: Blues; classical (chamber, woodwind or strings); folk; and jazz (swing, dixieland, progressive or big band). Works primarily with dance-oriented dixieland, traditional jazz and swing acts. Currently represents the Dick Braun Big Band; and Dixieland Band (dance and show bands).

D.R. YELVINGTON, 8500 Nairn, Apt. 825, Houston TX 77074. (713)771-1880. Owner: D.R. Yelvington. Booking agency. Estab. 1973. Represents individuals and groups; currently handles 6 acts.
How to Contact: Query or submit demo tape and lead sheet. Prefers 7½ ips reel-to-reel or cassette with 3-6 songs on demo, or disc. Does not return unsolicited material. Reports in 2 months.
Music: Church/religious and gospel. Works primarily with gospel groups and quartets. Current acts include the Ballards of Lubbock (gospel group); the Hazel Family of Lubbock (gospel group); and the Wills Family of Fort Worth (gospel group).

Organizations and Clubs

A major benefit of membership in a club or professional organization is access to specialized information and publications. Organizations often serve as information clearinghouses, forums for idea exchange among members, and sources of market information. Some organizations also sponsor workshops, conferences and seminars; some make grants to songwriters; some sponsor contests.

Association with professional groups sometimes helps build your professional image. What's more, an organization can serve as a liaison between you and some of the people you deal with, and can sometimes act as your representative in certain kinds of disputes.

Listed in thes section are the services and activities each club or association offers to members and the prerequisites, if any, an applicant must have to join.

THE ACADEMY OF COUNTRY MUSIC, Box 508, 1777 N. Vine St., Suite 200, Hollywood CA 90028. (213)462-2351. Executive Secretary: Fran Boyd. Estab. 1964. For "professional persons connected with the country music industry. We have a separate membership for fans. For professional membership the person must be affiliated with the country music industry in some manner." Offers newsletter and showcases. "Purpose is to promote country music."

THE ALTERNATIVE CHORUS SONGWRITERS SHOWCASE, 943 N. Palm Ave., West Hollywood CA 90069. (213)655-7780. Co-Directors: Len H. Chandler Jr., John Braheny. Executive Director: Denise Battaglia. Executive Assistants: Pam Martin, David Snodey. Estab. 1971. The Alternative Chorus Songwriters Showcase, a nonprofit service organization for songwriters, auditions more than 150 songwriters/month, both live and by tape. Less than 8% of the songs auditioned are presented in a showcase, making it a focus for record industry people looking for new songs and writer/artists. 5-7 professional and amateur writers are showcased each week. "Writers must participate in the performances of their own material. This unique service is free and is sponsored by Broadcast Music, Inc. (BMI). ACSS also provides counseling, conducts lectures and interviews top music industry professionals at the showcase." Also produces an annual Songwriter Expo every August.

AMERICAN FEDERATION OF MUSICIANS, 1500 Broadway, New York NY 10036. (212)869-1330. Estab. 1896. For musicians. Members are professional musicians in all phases of the entertainment business. Applicants must be interested in working as a professional musician and pay proper initiation fee. "Purpose is the bargaining representative for professional musicians."

AMERICAN GUILD OF AUTHORS & COMPOSERS, 40 W. 57th St., New York NY 10019. (212)757-8833; or, 6430 Sunset Blvd., Hollywood CA 90028. (213)462-1108. Membership Relations: Robert B. Sour. Estab. 1931. For songwriters. Offers newsletter and workshops. Purpose: "AGAC is a songwriter's protective association. It has the best contract that exists between writer and publisher. It collects the writers' royalties from publishers and from time to time audits the books of publishers."

AMERICAN MECHANICAL RIGHTS ASSOCIATION, 250 W. 57th St., New York NY 10019. (212)246-4077. Executive Director: Mrs. R.W. Miller. Estab. 1963. Members include songwriters and music publishers from the US, Canada and 18 European countries. Applicants must have released a record, or have a record released in the US. Purpose is to collect mechanical, synchronization, and background royalties.

AMERICAN MUSIC CENTER, INC., 250 W. 57th St., Room 626, New York NY 10019. (212)247-3121. Executive Director: Margaret Jory. Estab. 1940. For musicians and composers. Members are "composers of serious American classical music, as well as critics, publishers and performers." Offers newsletter, workshops, library and reference services. Purpose is "to increase knowledge about and interest in performances of serious American contemporary music."

AMERICAN SOCIETY OF COMPOSERS, AUTHORS AND PUBLISHERS, 1 Lincoln Plaza, New York NY 10023. (212)595-3050. Membership Representatives: Paul Giamopulos, Paul Wadkovsky, Lisa Schmidt. Estab. 1914. Members are songwriters, composers and music publishers. Applicants must "have at least one song copyrighted for associate membership; have at least one song published, commercially recorded, or performed in media licensed by the society for full membership." Purpose: "ASCAP is a nonprofit, membership-owned, performing rights licensing organization that licenses its members' nondramatic musical compositions for public performance and distributes the fees collected from such licensing to its members based on a scientific random sample survey of performances."
Tips: "The society sponsors a West Coast writer's workshop open to members as well as nonmembers, and makes grants to composers that are available to nonmembers. Contact the public relations or membership departments of the New York office or the following branch offices: 6430 Sunset Blvd., Los Angeles 90028; 2 Music Square W., Nashville 37203; 60 Old Compton St., London, England."

AMERICAN SOCIETY OF MUSIC ARRANGERS, Box 11, Hollywood CA 90028. Secretary/Treasurer: Fred Woessner. Estab. 1938. For composer-arrangers and orchestrators. Members are anyone in the music profession (playing musicians, students, songwriters, etc.). Offers newsletter. "Purpose is to insure the rights and income of men who were the architects of musical performance, but were unfortunately deprived of deserved income and recognition; secured the very working conditions, page-rates, health and welfare and pensions."

BLACK MUSIC ASSOCIATION, 1500 Locust St., Philadelphia PA 19102. (215)545-8600. Manager: Brian King. Performing Arts Coordinator: Marcia DuVall. Estab. May 1978. For songwriters, musicians and anyone interested in black music. Members are individuals, companies and organizations involved in the music industry. Offers lectures, library, newsletter, performance opportunities and workshops. "Purpose is the dedication to the advancement, enrichment, encouragement and recognition of black music."

BROADCAST MUSIC, INC., 40 W. 57th St., New York NY 10019. (212)586-2000; 6255 Sunset Blvd, Suite 1527, Hollywood CA 90028; and 10 Music Square E., Nashville TN 37203. President: Edward M. Cramer. Senior Vice President: Theodore Zavin. Vice President, Public Relations: Russell Sanjek. Vice President, California: Ron Anton. Vice President, Nashville: Francis Preston. Performance rights organization. Write for further information.

CANADIAN BUREAU FOR THE ADVANCEMENT OF MUSIC, Exhibition Place, Toronto, Ontario, Canada M6K 3C3. (416)366-7551. Coordinator: Nancy Owen. Estab. 1922. For music educators. Members are teachers, retailers, technicians and anyone in the music industry. Offers music instruction in elementary schools, teacher training, newsletter, workshops and lectures and participationin competitive festivals. Purpose: to supplement music education in Canada, creating larger market for music industry, employing musicians and enlightening and broadening the minds of our youth."

CANADIAN SONGWRITERS ASSOCIATION, 1659 Bayview Ave., Suite 102, Toronto, Ontario, Canada M4G 3C1. (416)485-1158. President: John Watt. Estab. 1978. For songwriters. Offers competitions, instruction, lectures, newsletter, workshops, magazine and handbook. Purpose is to educate, assist and represent songwriters in government and industry.

CENTRAL OPERA SERVICE, Metropolitan Opera, Lincoln Center, New York NY 10023. (212)799-3467. Membership Secretary: Jeanne Kemp. Administrative Director: Maria F. Rich. Estab. 1954. For musicians, librettists, opera producers and performers and composers. Members are individuals and companies involved with or interested in opera/musical theater (producers, performers, supporters, patrons, educators, students, composers, librettists, conductors and directors) all age groups; nationally in the US and Canada and abroad. Offers information on competitions, newsletter and national and regional conferences of professionals. "The Central Opera Service (COS) is the national information agency on all aspects of opera."

COLUMBUS SONGWRITERS ASSOCIATION, 3312 Petzinger Rd., Columbus OH 43227. (614)239-0280. President: Rich Kimmle. Estab. 1977. For songwriters and musicians. Fee: $25/year. Offers competitions, field trips, instruction, newsletter, performance opportunities, social outings and workshops. Purpose is to guide and educate songwriters. Holds monthly showcases.

COMPOSERS AND LYRICISTS GUILD OF AMERICA, INC., 10999 Riverside Dr., #100, North Hollywood CA 91602. (213)985-4102. Estab. 1953. For songwriters and composers. Members are songwriters and composers employed in motion pictures and television.

COUNTRY MUSIC ASSOCATION, INC., 7 Music Circle N., Nashville TN 37203. (615)244-2840. Membership Director: Tobly Cannon. Estab. 1958. Membership falls within following categories: advertising agency; artist manager/agent; artist/musicial; composer; disc jockey; international; publication; publisher; radio/TV; record company; record merchandiser; talent buyer/promoter; and affiliated. Members must earn a portion of their income from the country music industry. Offers newsletter and lists of industry contacts. Purpose is to promote country music.

COUNTRY MUSIC FOUNDATION OF COLORADO, Box 19435, Denver CO 80219. (303)936-7762. President: Gladys Hart. Estab. 1965. Serves songwriters and musicians, promoters, publishers and record companies. "The membership roster comes from the country music industry in general, with special interest in the annual Colorado Country Music Festival." Offers lectures, newsletter, performance opportunities and an annual convention. Purpose is "to promote country music in all facets of the industry. The association provides new artists with information on the basic fundamentals essential for career advancement."

DELTA OMICRON INTERNATIONAL MUSIC FRATERNITY, Executive Office, 1352 Redwood Court, Columbus OH 43229. (614)888-2640. President: Mrs. Brad Wideman. Estab. 1909. For musicians and any others interested in music. "Members are women in music, primarily composed of collegiate women majoring or minoring in music in college but we have a number of alumni chapters and clubs as well as professional members and patrons. Applicants must meet the grade point average set in the particular college/university. If a professional musician, must be established as a practicing musician. If a National Honorary Member must be recognized nationally; if a National Patron must be a prominent man in the field of musical arts." Offers competitions, library, newsletter, performance opportunities, workshops, fraternity magazine and triennial conference as well as scholarships and grants. "Purpose is to further the cause of music in general by recognizing outstanding contributions to music by corporations, organizations and individuals."

FLORIDA COUNTRY MUSIC FOUNDATION & HALL OF FAME, 2409 Winona Ave., Indian Oaks, Leesburg FL 32748. (904)787-1051. Administrator: 'Mama' Jo Hunt. Estab. 1972. For songwriters, musicians and anyone who likes country music. "Members are people in music and anyone who would like to join our group." Offers instruction, newsletter, performance opportunities, social outings and workshops. Purpose is to help new artists put on shows where they can be heard and have records sent to radio programs. New artists can send 25 pictures or more and 50 singles or albums for promotion purposes. Individual memberships are $15/year; organization memberships are $75/year.

GOSPEL MUSIC ASSOCIATION, 38 Music Square W., Nashville TN 37203. (615)242-0303. Executive Director: Don Butler. Estab. 1964. For songwriters, broadcasters, musicians, merchandisers, promoters, performance licensing agencies, church staff musicians, talent agencies, record companies and publishers. Offers lectures, newsletter, workshops and awards programs.

INTERNATIONAL FAN CLUB ORGANIZATION, Box 177, Wild Horse CO 80862. (303)962-3543. Co-Presidents: Loudilla Johnson, Loretta Johnson and Kay Johnson. Estab. 1965. For songwriters, musicians and performers and their fan club presidents. Members are fan club presidents and/or artists/songwriters etc. Applicants must be involved in the field of country music. An artist must have a fan club—"we assist them is setting up the fan club although we do not personally manage each individual operation for them." Offers competitions, instruction, newsletter, performance opportunities, social outings, workshops, business meetings, overseas tours and showcases. Purpose is to promote/publicize country music in an effort to spread good will, understanding and enjoyment of it around the world. "We hold an annual overseas showcase (London), plus dinner/show/business meetings/showcases in Nashville, annually in conjuction with Fan Fair. We believe fan clubs are a vital part of any entertainer's life."

MEMPHIS SONGWRITERS ASSOCIATION, Box 63075, 800 Madison, Memphis TN 63075. President: Juanita Tullos. Correspondence Secretary: Frances Ferloni. Estab. 1973. For songwriters, musicians and artists; "we have people from all walks of life, including amateur and professional songwriters, publishing company executives and recording company people." Offers competitions, lectures, newsletter, performance opportunities, social outings and contact lists and guides. Purpose is to "assist the songwriter in contact information and to guide and direct the songwriter in the basic steps of songwriting." Fees: $12/year.
Tips: "We have an annual competition in which we have awards for the best original songs members have written. We solicit tapes for this once a year and 12 songs are chosen from this screening to be presented before a panel of judges."

MUSCLE SHOALS MUSIC ASSOCIATION, Box 2009, Muscle Shoals AL 35660. (205)381-1442. Executive Director: F.E. Buddy Draper. Estab. 1975. For songwriters, musicians, engineers, artists, producers, studio owners and "others interested in music and recording." Members are "from all over the world. Age limits run from 14 to 82 years old. We have over 250 active members with our board of directors meeting monthly. There are no limitations on membership if applications are approved by the board of directors." Offers competitions, newsletter, performance opportunities, social outings, workshops and seminars. "We have an annual songwriter's showcase for songwriters who can perform at the association. We have a monthly songwriter's workshop, and our newsletter is monthly." Purpose is to "assist our membership in obtaining employment; hold workshops; present at least four concerts yearly using our own members; and to hold an annual seminar with top record executives and independent producers giving lectures and serving on panels." Fee: $25/year. "Our year runs from January 1 to December 31. Applications are accepted any time but we do not prorate dues, that is, $25 is due regardless of the date joined."

MUSICIANS CONTACT SERVICE, 6605 Sunset Blvd., Hollywood CA 90028. (213)467-2191. Estab. 1969. For songwriters, musicians, agents, managers, production companies, record labels and recording studios. Average age of members is 25 (any age acceptable); any and all styles of music are acceptable. Offers performance opportunities. "We are a placement/referral service for musical performance where groups can reach musicians and vice versa."

MUSICIANS CONTACT SERVICE, 1731 Euclid St., Anaheim CA 92802. (714)776-8240. See Musicians Contact Service, Hollywood Office, for details.

NASHVILLE SONGWRITERS ASSOCIATION, INTERNATIONAL, 25 Music Square W., Nashville TN 37203. (615)254-8903. Executive Director: Maggie Cavender. Estab. 1967. For songwriters. Applicants may apply for 1 of 2 memberships; "active membership is having had at least one song published with an affiliate of BMI, ASCAP or SESAC. An associate membership is for the yet-to-be-published writer and others interested in the songwriter." Offers newsletter, counseling, seminars, symposium, workshop, showcases and awards. "Purpose is to gain recognition for the songwriter, to serve any purpose toward this recognition, and to pursue this on a worldwide basis."

NATIONAL ACADEMY OF POPULAR MUSIC, 1 Times Square, New York NY 10036. (212)221-1252. Curator: Oscar Brand. Manager/Archivist: Frankie MacCormick. Estab. 1968. Serves songwriters, musicians and visitors to their museum. Membership are songwriters and those interested in songwriting. Applicants must belong to ASCAP, BMI or SESAC. Offers library and newsletter. Purpose: "To honor and recognize the creators of American popular songs, to call attention to the important role of popular music in American life and history, and to maintain a library and archive of music and music-related material. Membership year: July 1-June 30.

NATIONAL MUSIC COUNCIL, 250 W. 57th St., New York NY 10019. (212)265-8132. Executive Secretary: Doris O'Connell. Estab. 1940. "The council is an umbrella organization chartered by Congress composed of representatives of over 60 music associations of national scope and activity. Its purpose is to provide a forum for the free discussion of our country's national music affairs and problems; coordinate action and provide for the interchange of information among its members; and to speak with one voice for music whenever an authoritative expression of opinion is desirable." Offers the *Bulletin*, a semi-annual magazine, $5/year. Full membership meetings are held in January and June of each year.

NATIONAL MUSIC PUBLISHERS' ASSOCIATION, INC., 110 E. 59th St., New York NY 10022. (212)751-1930. President: Leonard Feist. Estab. 1917. Trade Association for music publishers. Offers newsletter, workshops, special reports and information.

NEW ORLEANS JAZZ CLUB OF CALIFORNIA, Box 1225, Kerrville TX 78028. (512)896-2285. President: Bill Bacin. Estab. 1963. For songwriters, musicians and jazz fans. Members support the preservation and development of jazz music and musicians, primarily the traditional and mainstream styles. Offers instruction, library, newsletter, performance opportunities and referral services.

PERFORMING RIGHTS ORGANIZATION OF CANADA, LTD., 41 Valleybrook Dr., Don Mills, Ontario, Canada M3B 2S6. (416)445-8700. Writer/Public Relations: Charlie Gall. Publicity Manager: Nancy Gyokeres. Estab. 1940. For Canadian songwriters and publishers. Offers competitions, magazine, workshops, advice and direction. Purpose is to collect performance royalties and distribute them to songwriters and publishers.

SESAC, INC., 10 Columbus Circle, New York NY 10019. (212)586-3450. Director, Creative Services: Vincent Candilora. Estab. 1931.

SONGWRITERS RESOURCES AND SERVICES, 6381 Hollywood Blvd., Suite 503, Hollywood CA 90028. (213)463-7178. Collective staff includes Lois Arkin, Suzzane Buirgy, Kathy Gronau, Pat Luboff, Gelsa Paladino, Doug Thiele. Estab. 1974. A nonprofit membership organization dedicated to the protection and education of songwriters. Membership is $30/year. Offers song protection service, Helen King Festival of New Music, forums, music business orientation workshops, bimonthly newsletter available to anyone; most other services restricted to members and include workshops on lyric writing, harmony and composition, songwriting, song evaluation, performance and others as the need and interest develop; counseling, hotline, library, *Open Ears* (bimonthly listing of publishers and producers, type of material they're looking for, and how and who to present it to), collaborator's and artist's directories, lead sheet service and a group legal plan.

SOUTHEASTERN COMPOSER'S LEAGUE, Box 5261, Mississippi State University MS 39762; Vice President: Fred Geissler. University of Virginia, Charlottesville VA 22903; President: Frank Stewart. Estab. 1952. For composers. Members are "usually composers of concert music. They are between 18-85 years old." Applicants must be "composers of serious concert music and reside in Alabama, Arkansas, Delaware, the District of Columbia, Florida, Georgia, Kentucky, Louisiana, Maryland, Mississippi, North Carolina, South Carolina, Tennessee, Virginia or West Virginia." Offers competitions, newsletter, performance opportunities and a semiannual catalog of members' works.

Publications of Interest

Reading the "trades" (i.e., trade magazines) informs songwriters about songwriting and the music industry in general. Reading them allows you to remain competitive by monitoring what's selling, who's buying it, and who's producing it. Reading the trades also helps you to keep abreast of the appearance of new firms, the disappearance of old ones, and switches in personnel.

This list is intended to be informative, and makes no value judgment on individual publications. Inclusion in this list does not constitute endorsement, and the omission of a publication simply means that its representatives didn't take time to complete our questionnaire.

Where possible, we allow spokespersons from each magazine to describe the publication's focus.

BILLBOARD, (The International Music/Record/Tape Newsweekly), Billboard Publications, Inc., 9000 Sunset Blvd., 12th Floor, Los Angeles CA 90069. (213)273-7040. Assistant Circulation Manager: Diana McCarroll. Promotion Director: Joshua C. Simons. Weeky magazine; 108 pages. Estab. 1894. "*Billboard* documents the most recent developments in the music business, every week." Includes record charts, industry information, and "the thousands of weekly events" that tells what is happening in the music business.

BLUEGRASS UNLIMITED, Bluegrass Unlimited, Inc., Box 111, Broad Run VA 22014. (703)361-8992. Editor: Peter V. Kuykendall. Monthly magazine; 56 pages. Estab. 1966. "For those interested in the traditional branch of country music: bluegrass. We also feature other forms of traditional country music such as old-time, but our primary interest is in bluegrass. Includes feature articles, festival listings, tablature, songs, personal appearances, club listings, artist indexes and more."

CADENCE MAGAZINE, Rt. 1, Box 345, Redwood NY 13679. (315)287-2852. Subscription/Distribution Manager: Susan Miller. Monthly magazine; 80 pages. Estab. 1975. "We cover all jazz and blues or related materials sent here. We are the only publication to cover much of the material. . . . We are also planning in the future a series of recordings featuring new, promising artists in jazz and blues. Interested parties should send tapes/demo discs to the attention of the editor."

THE CANADIAN COMPOSER/LE COMPOSITEUR CANADIEN, Creative Arts Company for Composers, Authors, and Publishers Association of Canada, 1240 Bay St., Suite 401, Toronto, Ontario, Canada M5R 2A7. Subscription Dept. Editor: Richard Flohil. Published 10 times/year; 48 pages. Estab. 1965. "*The Canadian Composer* is a bilingual magazine for the members of CAPAC. Its articles are about members of the organization."

CASHBOX MAGAZINE, Cashbox Publishing Co., Inc., 6363 Sunset Blvd., Suite 930, Hollywood CA 90028. (213)464-8241. Circulation Manager: Theresa Tortosa. Subscription address: 119 W. 57th St., New York NY 10019. Weekly magazine; 75 pages. Estab. 1942. "*Cashbox* is an international music trade weekly. We provide record charts, news and information on executives, companies and artists that are making news, as well as an all-inclusive radio section. We also provide a new faces section for new artists."

CENTRAL OPERA SERVICE BULLETIN, Metropolitan Opera, Lincoln Center, New York NY 10023. (212)799-3467. Editor: Maria F. Rich. Membership Secretary: Jeanne Kemp. Quarterly magazine; 45 pages. Estab. 1957. "Includes news of new music/theater pieces, premieres, new performing arts centers, production methods, news from opera and music/theater producing organizations, listings of US and Canadian performances, government and private support to nonprofit performing arts organizations, and awards and appointments in the field."

CLARK'S COUNTRY MUSIC NEWS, 2039 Cedarville Rd., Goshen OH 45122. President: Grace Clark. Publisher: Bob Clark. Editor: G.M. Clark. Monthly magazine. "Our publication is dedicated to the promotion of country music. Although we carry arcticles on all major country artists, songwriters, etc., we always welcome information about newcomers to the industry."

CODA, THE JAZZ MAGAZINE, Coda Publications, Box 87, Station J, Toronto, Ontario, Canada M4J 4X8. (416)368-3149. Business Manager: Pan Allen. Bimonthly magazine; 36 pages. Estab. 1958. "We cover interviews, reviews and news on jazz and blues music of interest to those who are into the artistic and creative—as opposed to the commercial—aspects of the music. We have become the mose respected jazz periodical in English and have worldwide circulation to individuals and institutions."

COUNTRY SONG ROUNDUP, Charlton Publications, Inc., Charlton Bldg., Derby CT 06418.

DISCOWORLD MAGAZINE, Transamerica Corp., 352 Park Ave. S., New York NY 10010. (212)686-1636. Administrative Assistant: Jennifer San Marco. Editor: Susan Friedman. Bimonthly magazine; 64 pages. Estab. 1976. "We are a music magazine focusing primarily on disco groups, films, books, and fashion geared toward the disco lifestyle. A small rock 'n roll section has been added."

THE ELECTRIC CHELYS, (formerly *Chelys*), Rt. 2, Exeter NH 03833. (603)772-3523. Editor/Publisher: Walter Spalding. Associate Editor: Dolber Spalding. Irregular publication; 60 pages. Estab. 1976. "A journal for the plucked string. Deals with classical guitar, flamenco, lute, harpsichord, and related plucked instruments. Prints original music as well as facsimiles. Accepts original compositions and articles for publication. Payment in copies of magazine."

GUITAR AND LUTE MAGAZINE, Galliard Press, Ltd., 1229 Waimanu St., Honolulu HI 96814. Editor: Henry Adams. Quarterly magazine; 44 pages. Estab. 1974. "We cover the classic guitar, lute, and related plucked instruments. It has a varied format which is international in scope, including interviews and articles on the major performers, pedagogues, composers, and instrument builders in this field of music from around the world. Eash issue also contains news items on master classes, competitions, music festivals, etc., along with record, book and music reviews. We also include lute tablature and premiere publications of music as a regular feature."

HIGH FIDELITY/BACKBEAT MAGAZINE, ABC Leisure Magazines, Inc., The Publishing House, Great Barrington MA 01230. Subscriptions: Howard Franklin, 1 Sound Ave., Marion OH 43302. Editor: Susan Elliott. Monthly magazine; 24 pages. Estab. 1977. *High Fidelity/Backbeat* is geared to the popular music aficionado, be he a professional musician, songwriter, or well-informed listener. Coverage includes interviews with on-the-charts musicians, music business trends and practices, recording gear and techniques, sheet music reviews book reviews and jazz/pop/rock record reviews with emphasis on new artists."

HIT PARADER, Charlton Publications, Inc., Charlton Bldg., Derby CT 06418.

KEYBOARD WORLD, Keyboard World, Inc., Box 4399, Downey CA 90241. Contact: Circulation Dept. Associate Publisher: David Rivas. Monthly magazine; 48 pages. Estab. 1972. "*Keyboard World* is of interest to the keyboard hobbyist. Its editorial matter deals with instruction, personality interviews, new products, organ sheet music and record reviews."

LEE MACE'S OZARK OPRY ENTERTAINMENT NEWS, Ozark Opry, Inc., Box 242, Osage Beach MO 65065. (314)348-2270. Editor: Joyce Mace. President: Lee Mace. Tabloid published in spring, summer and fall; 8-12 pages. Estab. 1979. "Free to customers, audience, radio stations, music stores and all places of business. Designed to educate and promote tourism in Missouri and the 12-state area around it, as to what Ozark Opry is doing to contribute to the local and national entertainment industry."

MIDWEST ENTERTAINMENT REVIEW, Box 204, Bondurant IA 50035. (515)967-4170. Editor: Janet Weaver. President: Harold Luick. Monthly tabloid; 4-8 pages. Estab. 1972. "Free to radio stations, music stores and musical places of business. Designed to educate the Iowa area and the five-state area around it to what is happening at the local level of entertainment. It is promotional by association."

MUSIC CITY ENTERTAINER, 62 Music Square W., Nashville TN 37203. (615)256-1693. Contact: Advertising and Subscription Dept. Promotional Director: Connie L. Wright.

Monthly tabloid; 24 pages. Estab. 1971. "Our paper is published to inform the public and music industry of new artists—top stars—and of all people involved in the music industry. We have stories and a record chart which appears on the back page which always includes records and songs by new artists, giving the artists a chance to be read nationally."

THE MUSIC CONNECTION, 6381 Hollywood Blvd., Suite 323, Hollywood CA 90028. (213)462-5772. Contact: Subscription Dept. Biweekly magazine; 24 pages. Estab. 1977. "*The Music Connection* is a local musicians' trade magazine. Departments include a gig guide connecting musicians with agents, producers, publishers and club owners; a free classified section; music personal ads; and articles on songwriting, publishing and the music business."

MUSIC CITY NEWS, Box 22975, 1302 Division St., Nashville TN 37202.

MUSIC JOURNAL, Elemo Publishing, Box 1592, Southampton NY 11968. (516)283-2360. Monthly magazine; 60 pages. Estab. 1943. "Covers the entire music field (classical, jazz, contemporary, history-musicology, aesthetics, education, etc.) for the devotee, student and professional." Our coverage also extends to musical instrument manufacturer's, and the testing of new musical instruments, that is aimed at the musical instrument dealers nationwide.

MUSIC MAKERS, The Sunday School Board of the Southern Baptist Convention, 127 9th Ave., N., Nashville TN 37234. (615)251-2000. Contact: Church Music Dept. Music Editor: Terry Kirkland. Quarterly magazine; 36 pages. Estab. 1960. Publishes "music for use by 1st, 2nd and 3rd graders in choir at church. Includes spiritual concept and musical concept songs, plus simple rounds and partner songs."

MUSICIAN, PLAYER AND LISTENER, Amordian Press, Inc., Box 701, Gloucester MA 01930. (617)281-3110. President: Gordon P. Baird. Executive Editor: Sam Holdsworth. Magazine published 8 times/year, every six weeks; 84 pages. Estab. 1976. "The editorial thrust is directed at the generation of late '60s rockers who have grown into more mature forms of rock, jazz and jazz/rock. This is a book for those who are serious about their music, both as a player and as a listener."

MUSICIAN'S DIGEST (formerly *Musician's Guide*), Sound Advice Inc., 11 Harvard St., Worcester MA 01609. (617)752-6494. Publisher: Jerry Maisel. Contact: Subscription Dept. Monthly magazine; 80 pages. "We are an educational and informative publication for the contemporary musician and anyone in a music related field. Features include how-to articles, songwriting and publishing articles, interviews and technical articles."

NATIONAL MUSIC COUNCIL BULLETIN, 250 W. 57th St., New York NY 10019. (212)265-8132. Contact: Subscription Dept. Semiannual magazine; 44 pages. Estab. 1940. Reports activities of national music organizations, international music news, contests and competitons, government action in the field of music and music education."

NOTES: QUARTERLY JOURNAL OF THE MUSIC LIBRARY ASSOCIATION, Music Library Association, 2017 Walnut St., Philadelphia PA 19103. (215)569-3948. Editor: William M. McClellan. Quarterly magazine; 250 pages. Estab. 1934. "We cover areas of music bibliography and discography, music library problems, technical programs, histories of music librarianship and library-related articles concerning musicology, music publishing and music printing."

PAN PIPES OF SIGMA ALPHA IOTA, Sigma Alpha Iota, National Music Fraternity for Women, 2820 Webber St., Sarasota FL 33579. National Executive Offices: 4119 Rollins Ave., Des Moines, IA 50312. Editor: Margaret Maxwell. Magazine published 4 times/year (November, January, March and May); 36 pages. Estab. 1907. "We cover articles with the emphasis on the American composer. The January issue is devoted to American Music and the American composers, with a section devoted to the latest publications of their music."

PICKIN', North American Publishing Co., 401 N. Broad St., Philadelphia PA 19108. Managing Editor: Marilyn Kochman. Monthly magazine; 88 pages. Estab. 1974.

POPULAR MUSIC AND SOCIETY, Bowling Green State University, Department of Sociology, Bowling Green OH 43403. Editor: R. Serge Denisoff. Assistant Editor: Barbara Asmus. Quarterly magazine; 90 pages. Estab. 1971. "We are a scholarly journal covering all subjects of the recording industry."

RECORD WORLD, 1700 Broadway, New York NY 10019. Contact: Subscription Dept. Contains industry news, record charts, etc.

SHEET MUSIC MAGAZINE, 60 Golden Bridge Rd., Katonah NY 10536.

SONGWRITER MAGAZINE, Len Latimer Organization, Inc., Box 3510, 6430 Sunset, Suite 716, Hollywood CA 90028. (213)464-7664. Contact: Subscription Dept. Editor: Len Latimer. Monthly magazine; 56 pages. Estab. 1975. "A trade/craft magazine for professional and amateur songwriters with emphasis on MOR/pop, country and rock songwriting. Interviews with top songwriters and music business executives, how-to features and industry news."

TRUSTY TIPS FROM THE COLONEL, Trusty International, Rt. 1, Box 100, Nebo KY 42441. (502)249-3194. President: Elsie Childers. Monthly 1-page newsletter. Estab. 1974. "Producers and artists who need material contact us and we fill an 8½x11 sheet full of names and addresses of people needing songs for recording sessions or shows."

VARIETY, Variety, Inc., 154 W. 46th St., New York NY 10036. (212)582-2700. Contact: Subscription Dept. Weekly magazine; 88 pages. Estab. 1905. "Total entertainment; we cover music publishing and recording in all areas including television, stage, film, etc."

WASHINGTON INTERNATIONAL ARTS LETTER, Allied Business Consultants, Inc., 325 Pennsylvania Ave., Washington DC 20003. (202)488-0800. Business Manager: T. Snyder. Publisher: Daniel Millsaps. Magazine published 10 times/year; 8 pages. Estab. 1962. "We cover financial information for music and musicians, composers, etc. Grants, aid in all arts forms."

Workshops

Workshops are valuable sources of tips, instruction and evaluation, covering every aspect of the art from lyric writing to music theory.

The following workshop listings describe programs offered, costs, available facilities, program length and average class size. Inclusion of a workshop in this list doesn't necessarily constitute and endorsement, so checking into the background of workshop leaders and the workshops themselves before signing up is important. Such a check isn't necessarily intended to establish a workshop's reputation, but will help you find a workshop that will serve you best.

In workshops, you learn by doing, and by accepting constructive criticism. An evaluation workshop is especially helpful if you find self-evaluation difficult. Objective evaluation workshops, as one workshop official puts it, "make it harder to fool yourself; they make it harder to be egotistical."

ASCAP SONGWRITERS' WORKSHOP WEST, c/o ASCAP, 6430 Sunset Blvd., Hollywood CA 90028. (213)466-7681. Western Regional Executive Director: John Mahan. Workshop Director: Annette Tucker. Offers programs for songwriters: "ASCAP offers a tuition-free, 10-week workshop series during which songs are performed and evaluated by the workshop members as well as its director. Song casting and placing are discussed. The various song markets are analyzed. On the tenth week, a major publisher is invited to hear what the group considers to be the best of each member's work." Year-round. Class size: "There are 15 songwriters in each workshop. Two workshops run concurrently." Length: 3 hours. "Workshop classes take place in a large private home. A grand piano and stereo reel-to-reel and cassette tape playback system are among the facilities. ASCAP pays the tuition fee." Applicants are selected by the workshop director based on a "subjective analysis of material submitted on cassette or reel-to-reel by prospective members." Write or phone ASCAP for information.

CHRISTIAN WRITERS INSTITUTE, Gundersen Dr. and Schmale Rd., Wheaton IL 60187. (312)690-8567. Assistant Director: Helen Kidd. Offers programs for songwriters and musicians in writing lyrics and music as part of the annual writers conference. "These are new workshops so there is plenty of room for expansion and improvement." Annual. Class size: up to 200. Each workshop lasts 1½ hours. Cost of institute: $140 for 4 days (includes room, 9 meals, all supplies, and 20 workshops). Held on the campus of Wheaton College. Send for application.

DICK GROVE MUSIC WORKSHOPS, 12754 Ventura Blvd., Studio City CA 91604. (213)985-0905. Vice President: William Wolfe. Offers programs for songwriters in lyric writing, composition, harmony, theory, and rhythmic dictation. "Songwriters workshop is a class that combines lecture and roundtable critique to develop a more precise approach to songwriting. Many classes have advanced levels of study." Offers programs for musicians "ranging from beginning sight-reading to advanced record mixing. All classes are taught by professional musicians. Workshops are offered for guitarists; bassists; drummers; keyboardists; vocalists; and brass, reed and string players. Other classes include record production, arranging, conducting, ear-training, improvisation, film scoring, music preparation and sight-singing." Four 10-week terms/calendar year. "Enrollment is 800/term; average class size is 15. Most classes are $60, covering five 2-hour sessions. Some classes require texts or materials that are not included in the tuition fee. Record mixing classes are $200." Complete classroom facilities. "We also offer year long, full-time programs for arrangers/composers and players. Applicants must be "interviewed prior to enrolling for placement. Certain classes require auditions." Request current catalog by mail or telephone.

HAYSTACK SUMMER MUSIC WORKSHOPS, Portland State University, Cannon Beach OR. Write or call: Dona G. Beattie, Director, Box 1491, Portland OR 97207. Estab. 1969. Annual. University credit program in Songwriting, Guitar, Choral, Band, and Orff. 1979 faculty includes Bob Gibson, Ray Tate, Mike Dunbar, Frank Pooler, Frank Bencriscutto, Judy Thomas, Kate Grieshaber, and Ann Palmason. All workshops last one week. Advance registration desirable.

HINDS JUNIOR COLLEGE PIANO CAMP, Hinds Junior College, Raymond MS 39154. (601)857-5261, ext. 271. Chairman: James Leslie Reeves. Offers programs for student musicians (grades 7-12) in piano theory, musical style, piano ensemble and music appreciation. Also offers half-hour private lessons, two hours practice and recreation class. Summers only. 60 students/workshop. Length: 1 week. Cost of workshop: $80 (includes registration fee, room, meals, tuition, instruction, music and materials). Facilities include practice and recital rooms, listening equipment, media center, piano lab, and air-conditioned dormitory and music building. Send for application.

THE JACKSON SYMPHONY ORCHESTRA STRING CAMP, Hinds Junior College, Raymond MS 39154. (601)857-5261, ext. 271. Coordinator: Mikey Davis. Chairman: James L. Reeves. Offers programs for musicians in theory, music appreciation, ensemble and orchestra for ages 9-17. Summers only. 45-60 students/workshop. Length: 4 days. Cost of workshop: $55 (includes registration fee, room, meals, tuition, instruction, music and material); or $22.75 (room and meals not included). Facilities include studios, practice and recital rooms, media center, recreation area, and air-conditioned dormitory and music building. Send for application.

MANITOBA HOLIDAY FESTIVAL OF THE ARTS, INC., Box 147, Neepawa, Manitoba, Canada R0J 1H0. (204)476-3232. Administrator: Marlene Siatecki. Offers programs for musicians in various subjects; "programs vary from year to year. 1979 program concentrates on brass, string and woodwind, with individual and group instruction by the Canadian Educational Ensembles—14 highly qualified instructors. 75 musicians/workshop. Vocal music and music appreciation are also taught, as well as pottery, fibre arts, photography, theater, painting and drawing; children's program also includes dance and sports." Length: 2 weeks (summer only). Cost: $60 registration fee for adults (age 18 and over); $60 for youth (age 13-18), and $40 for children (age 6-12). Meals and lounging area available at the Neepawa Area Collegiate, Monday through Friday. Day care available for children 2-5 years. Send for brochure.

MIDWEST WRITERS' CONFERENCE, 515 25th St. NW, Canton OH 44709. (216)489-0800, ext. 475. Director: John W. Oliver Jr. Offers programs for songwriters. "The songwriting workshop is an important part of the Midwest Writers' Conference. It is led by a major editor, songwriter or publisher. The workshop includes both lyrics and the writing of music. It is, of course, writing-based rather than performance-based." Annual. Class size averages 25-40. 2 workshops, 50 minutes each; one generally focuses on lyrics, the other on music. Cost: $25. Held in the Barn Campus Center, Malone College. Send for application.
Tips: "We are now the largest writers' conference in the Midwest and hope to do all we can to encourage helpful exchanges between various sorts of writers. We are one of the first writers' conferences to pioneer in a songwriting workshop."

SONGWRITER SEMINARS AND WORKSHOPS, 119 W. 57th St., New York NY 10019. (212)265-1853. President: Ted Lehrman. Vice President: Libby Bush. Offers programs for songwriters: intermediate pop songwriting; advanced workshop; writer/performer workshop; and at-home songwriter workshop. Offers programs for musicians in basic musicianship and pop music theory. Year-round with cycles beginning in September, December, March and June. Approximately 15 in each songwriter workshop, 7 in each writer/performer workshop and 5 in each musician workshop. Each cycle lasts 11 weeks, except for the June cycle which is an 8-week cycle. Cost of workshops: $135, Pop Songwriting—Preparing for the Marketplace; $135, Advanced Songwriter Seminar and Workshop—Ready for the Marketplace; $125, Writer/Performer Workshop—Ready for a Record Label; and $10/lyric, $12.50/song when material is submitted to the at-home songwriter workshop. Top 40 single stressed. Collaboration opportunities abailable. No housing provided. Interviews held for songwriters and songwriter/performers to determine which workshop would be most helpful. Call for free brochure and/or set up interview.

SONGWRITING WORKSHOP AND THE BUSINESS OF MUSIC, Rustron Music Productions, 21200 Westmoreland Ave., White Plains NY 10606. (914)946-1689. Course Instructor: Rusty Gordon. Offers programs for songwriters "in the music industry and how it works. Lecture material is very specific and complete, covering all areas of the subject. Includes instruction in the techniques of the craft and the mechanics needed to write commercially marketable songs. We teach from both the lyrical and musical points of view. We specify universality, concept uniqueness and mood development for clear-cut media marketing." Year-round. 10 students/class. 2-hour evening classes meet once/week for 7 weeks. "The entire course including workbook/folder and all additional printed material is $75. We have a payment plan requiring $15 paid at the first class and $10 paid at each successive class. Group discount available. We have no boarding facilities. Classes are held at our main office. Applicants must be at least 16 years old. This is a college-level course. In addition, we have a new public class with unlimited enrollment at the Rauchambeau School, Fisher Ave., White Plains, New York 10606. Write for starting dates. This course will be taught year-round. Minimal fees will be set by the school. Correspondence course available; for specific details and general course information write or call 6 a.m. to 11 p.m., Monday through Thursday."

SRS WORKSHOPS, 6381 Hollywood Blvd., .503, Hollywood CA 90028. (213)463-7178. Staff Members: Lois Arkin, Suzanne Buirgy, Kathy Gronau, Gelsa Paladino, Doug Thiele. Offers programs for songwriters: performers workshop, song evaluation workshop, lyric writing, legalities of the music business, harmony and theory, guitar, collaborator's directory, leadsheet service, pamphlets, and Festival of New Music. Offers programs for musicians: guitar, harmony and theory, artist's directory, showcase information, registration service, resource books and bimonthly newsletter. Offers programs year-round. Attendance: up to 25/workshop. Length: 2-4 hours/workshop. "Some of our workshops are free to members. Others usually are $20 for 8-10 week sessions. Membership is $30." Send for application. "SRS is a nonprofit membership organization dedicated to the protection and education of songwriters. We also provide an 'Open Ears' column in our newsletter telling members which publishers, producers and artists are looking for material."

THREE WEEKS AT INDIAN HILL, Boston University, Continuing Education, 704 Commonwealth Ave., Boston MA 02215. (617)353-4128. Coordinator, Continuing Education: Rebecca Alssid. Sponsor: Boston University. Estab. 1978. Offers programs for musicians: "two weeks of the program will be dedicated to painting and mime. The third week will be in picking and fiddling, a week-long instrumental course in old-time country music of the southern mountains." Class size: 5. Length: 1 week. Cost of program: $275/week, includes tuition, dormitory room and board (linens, breakfast and dinner are provided).

WALNUT VALLEY NATIONAL FLAT-PICKING CHAMPIONSHIP, FOLK, ARTS & CRAFTS FAIR, Box 245, Winfield KS 67156. (316)221-3250. Contact: President, Walnut Valley Association, Inc. Secretary: Alene Miller. Offers programs for listeners and musicians in fiddle, banjo, mandolin, autoharp, hammered dulcimer, mountain dulcimer, guitar, and old-time country music. "Workshops are led by top entertainers." Annual. Workshops are a part of a 3-day music festival, and last about 90 minutes apiece. Tuition included in cost of festival ($8/day or $20/weekend). Held in the Winfield, Kansas Fairgrounds, which has a partially covered grand-stand and room for 10,000 cars and campers on the grounds. Dates: June 1-3, Sept. 14-16. "Motel rooms available are limited due to the event being held in a small town." Send for information.
Tips: "Any interested person may receive the *Walnut Valley Occasional* newspaper by sending name and address and requesting to be on our mailing list."

Glossary

A&R director. Record company employee who deals with new artists, songs and masters coordinating the best material with a particular artist.

Acetate dub. A demonstration record that is individually cut, often referred to as a disc.

Advance. Money paid to the songwriter or recording artist before regular royalty payments begin. Sometimes called "upfront" money, advances are deducted from future royalties.

AFM. American Federation of Musicians. A union for musicians, arrangers and other individuals.

AFTRA. American Federation of Television and Radio Artists. A union for singers, actors and others involved in TV or radio.

AGAC. American Guild of Authors and Composers.

Airplay. To be broadcast on radio.

AOR. Album-oriented rock.

Arrangement. Tailoring or adapting a composition for performance by other instruments, voices or performers.

Artist. An individual or group that performs songs.

ASCAP. American Society of Composers, Authors and Publishurs; a performing rights organization.

A-side. Side one of a single the record company will promote as having the best chance of becoming a hit.

Assignment. To transfer your rights to a song or songs to a publisher in exchange for his services.

Audiovisual. Materials such as filmstrips, motion pictures and videotapes which use audio backup for visual material.

Bed. A musical background of varying length and tempo used under the announcer's voice in commercials. Any prerecorded music used as background material.

Biannual. Twice a year.

Bimonthly. Every two months.

Biweekly. Every two weeks.

BMI. Broadcast Music, Inc.; a performing rights organization.

Booking agent. Person who solicits work and schedules performances for a professional entertainer.

Catalog. The collected songs of one writer, or all songs handled by one publisher.

Chart. The written arrangement of a song.

Charts. The weekly trade magazines' lists of the bestselling records in the pop, soul and country music fields.

Collaborator. Person who works with another in a creative situation; can be either a melodist or lyricist.

CMA. Country Music Association; organization that promotes and supports the growth of country music.

Commercial. Song written for the mass market with emphasis on the material's salability and potential profit. Also, any recorded advertisement.

Composer. Person who writes the music to a song. Also known as a melodist.

Copyright. Legal protection given authors and composers for an original work.

Cover record. A new version of a previously recorded song.

Crossover. A song that becomes popular in two or more music field, e.g., a song that is a hit in both the rock and country markets.

Cut. Any finished recording; a selection from an LP; or to record.

C&W. Country and western.

Demo. A rough recording used to demonstrate the hit potential of a song to industry personnel. A demo is usually a tape, but can mean an acetate disc.

Disc. A record.

Distributor. Person or firm that is the sole marketing agent that sells or delivers a record company's product in a particular area.

Engineer. A specially trained individual who operates all studio recording equipment and aids the producer in deciding how a song should be recorded.

Evergreen. Any song that remains popular year after year.

Folio. A softcover collection of songs prepared for sale.

Harry Fox Agency. A collection organization that handles mechanical reproduction and film synchronization income, operated by the National Music Publishers Association.

Hit. Any song achieving top 40 status by selling a large number of copies and receiving airplay.

Hook. A memorable phrase or melody line in a song which is repeated—the unique or "catchy" part.

IPS. Inches per second; a speed designation for reel-to-reel tape.

Jingle. Usually a short verse set to music designed as a commercial message.

LP. Designation for long-playing record synonomous with album and played at 33-1/3 rpm.

Lead sheet. Written version of a song containing the melody, chord symbols and the lyric which is used with a demo tape to promote the song before it is published.

Leader. A strip of white plastic or tape used at the beginning and end of a reel for easy threading, and between songs for ease in selection.

Lyrics. The words of a song.

Lyric sheet. A typed copy of a song's lyrics.

Lyricist. Person who writes the words to a song.

Manager. Person who guides an artist in all artistic stages of his career and advises in all industry dealings. In some cases, the manager secures engagements for the artist.

Market. A demographic division of the record-buying public into specific areas where one type of record is bought, i.e., C&W, R&B, etc.

Master. A completely edited and mixed tape, the finished record product. The master tape is used in the pressing of a record.

Mechanical right. A specific right granted by the US copyright law that guarantees the copyright holder the right to profit from the reproduction of his song.

Mechanical royalty. Money earned from the reproduction of a song, usually from records and tapes.

Melodist. Person who writes the melody to a song. Also known as a composer.

Mix. To blend a multi-track recording into the desired balance of sound.

MOR. Middle of the road. A song considered "easy listening" designed to satisfy the musical tastes of a number of people.

Music publisher. An individual company that performs the following functions: evaluates songs for commercial potential, then tries to have an artist record them; exploits the copyright by finding other artists to record the song or finds other uses, such as TV or film, for the song; collects income in the US and foreign countries from mechanical, performance and synchronization usage, and from the sale of sheet music; and protects the copyright from infringement.

Needle-drop. Use of a prerecorded cut from a stock music house in an audiovisual soundtrack.

Performing rights. A specific right granted by US copyright law that protects a composition from being publicly performed without the owner's permission.

Performing rights organization. An organization that collects income from the public performance of songs written by its members and then proportionally distributes this income to the individual copyright holder based on the number of performances of each song.

Pitch. To attempt to sell a song by audition; the sales talk.

Playlist. List of songs compiled by a radio station program director, usually top 40, that the station will broadcast.

Plug. A favorable mention, broadcast or performance of a song. Also means to pitch a song.

Points. The percentage record companies pay producers and artists for records sold based on the retail price.

Press. To manufacture a record from the master tape. Also, any media coverage an artist may receive.

Product. The record or tape to be sold. Also, a reference to an individual artist or group as a commodity to be sold.

Production company. Company that specializes in producing jingle packages for advertising agencies. May also refer to companies that specialize in audiovisual programs.

Professional manager. Member of a music publisher's staff who screens submitted material and tries to get the company's catalog of songs recorded.

Producer. Person who controls every aspect of recording a song from selecting material to producing the completed master.

Program director. Radio station employee who screens records and develops a playlist of songs that station will broadcast.

Public domain. Any composition with an expired or lapsed copyright, or with a copyright notice that is invalid.

Purchase license. Fee paid for music used from a stock music library.

Query. A letter of inquiry to a potential song buyers soliciting his interest.

R&B. Rhythm and blues.

Rate. The percentage of royalty as specified by contract.

Release. Any record issued by a record company.

Royalty. Percentage of money earned from the sale of records or use of a song.

RPM. Revolutions per minute; a speed designation for records.

SASE. Abbreviation for self-addressed stamped envelope. Most companies require SASE if demo tapes and lead sheets are to be returned.

Semiannual. Twice a year.

SESAC. An organization that collects income from mechanical and performing rights, and synchronization licensing usage.

Session. A scheduled time period in the studio for recording.

Shop. To pitch songs to a number of companies or publishers.

Showcase. Place where new acts perform or new material is presented on a trial basis.

Single. 45 rpm record with songs (usually from an LP) on both sides. The A-side is expected to be a hit.

Song shark. Person who deals with songwriters deceptively for his own profit.

Soundtrack. The audio, including music and narration, of a film, videotape or audiovisual program.

Split publishing. To divide publishing rights between two or more publishers.

Staff writer. A salaried songwriter who writes exclusively for one publishing firm.

Standard. A song popular year after year; an evergreen.

Statutory royalty rate. The minimum payment for mechanical rights guaranteed by law that a record company must pay the songwriter and his publisher for each record or tape sold. The rate is 2-¾ ¢ per song, or ½ ¢ per minute of playing time, whichever is greater.

Stiff. The first recording of a song that commercially fails.

Studio. An area specifically equipped for recording.

Subpublishing. Certain rights granted by a US publisher to a foreign publisher in exchange for promoting the US catalog in his territory.

Synchronization. Technique of timing the musical soundtrack to the action or mood taking place on film or videotape.

Synchronization rights. Rights granted by the copyright holder allowing his composition to be used in timed-relation to the action in a motion picture or videotape.

Top 40. Originally, a weekly trade-chart listing the top 40 hits in the country. Also a radio station with a format consisting of top 40 hits; or a category of popular music.

Track. Portions of a recording tape (e.g., 24-track tape) that can be individually recorded in the studio, then mixed into a finished master.

Trades. Publications that cover the music industry.

Work. To pitch or shop a song.

Subject Index

Musical classifications are an important consideration when submitting your work to any firm. Send only the type of material that a firm specifically requests.

The following subject classifications are for the music publisher and record company sections of *Songwriter's Market*. Simply find the name of the firm to which you would like to submit your material. At a glance, you can quickly determine if the firm prefers C&W, rock or some other form of music. Tailoring your submissions to the company's needs will save you time and give your material proper consideration.

Music Publishers

Name of Company and Page Number	Bluegrass, C&W	Children's	Coral, Church/religious, Gospel	Classical	Blues, Disco, R&B, Soul	Easy listening, MOR	Folk	Jazz	Progressive, Rock	Top 40/Pop
A Dish-A-Tunes, Ltd. 39					•					
Able Music, Inc. 39	•		•		•	•	•		•	•
Above Music Publications 40	•		•		•	•			•	•
Accretive Copyright 40	•		•		•	•				•

Name of Company and Page Number	Bluegrass, C&W	Children's	Coral, Church/religious, Gospel	Classical	Blues, Disco, R&B, Soul	Easy listening, MOR	Folk	Jazz	Progressive, Rock	Top 40/Pop
Accumulated Copyrights 40	●		●		●	●		●		●
Ace Deuce Trey Music 40					●					
Acoustic Music, Inc. 40	●		●			●	●			
Acuff Rose, Inc. 40	●									
Adventure Music Co. 41	●				●	●			●	
All Of A Sudden Music, Inc. 41					●	●				●
Al's Written Music Publishers 41	●				●	●		●	●	●
Amalgamated Tulip Corp. 42	●					●			●	
Anacrusis Music 42	●				●	●			●	●
Angela Dawn Music 42			●							
Annie Over Music 42	●					●				
April/Blackwood Music (CA) 43	●				●	●	●	●	●	●
April/Blackwood Music (NY) 43	●	●	●	●	●	●	●	●	●	●
Archer Music 43		●	●							
Arzee Music 43	●					●	●			●
ATV Music (TN) 43	●		●		●	●				●
Aviation Music/JEF Records, Ltd. 44	●				●				●	●
Axent, Ltd. 44	●	●	●	●	●	●	●	●	●	●
Baby Powder Music 44					●	●			●	●
Bainbridge Music 44					●	●	●	●	●	●
Bal and Bal Music Publishing Co. 44	●	●	●						●	●
Baradat Music 45	●				●			●	●	●
Barren River Music 45	●		●			●			●	●
Bartistic Music 45						●				●
Baruth Music 45					●		●		●	●
John Bava Music 45	●		●							
Beacon Hill Music 46			●							
The Beau-Jim Agency Inc. 46	●				●	●			●	●
Bell Holding Music 46	●				●	●	●	●		
John T. Benson Publishing Co. 46			●			●				
Hal Bernard Enterprises, Inc. 46					●				●	●
John Berthelot & Associates 47	●				●	●		●		●
Beth-Ann Music Co. 47	●		●			●	●		●	●

Name of Company and Page Number	Bluegrass, C&W	Children's	Coral, Church/religious, Gospel	Classical	Blues, Disco, R&B, Soul	Easy listening, MOR	Folk	Jazz	Progressive, Rock	Top 40/Pop
Beverly Hills Music Publishing 48	•	•	•	•	•	•	•	•	•	•
Big Cigar Music Co. 48					•	•			•	•
Big Heart Music 48	•				•	•			•	•
Big Mike Music 48					•					
Big Music 48									•	
Big Seven Music Corp. 49	•		•		•	•	•	•	•	•
Big State Music 49	•					•				
Billy Bob Publishing 49	•					•				•
Blue Cup Music 49	•					•				
Blue Mace Music 49					•				•	•
Bluff City Corp. 50	•				•				•	•
Bo Gal Music 50	•		•		•	•	•			•
Bobby's Beat Music 50	•					•				
Bondi Music 50					•				•	•
Border Star Music 50	•				•				•	
Bottom Line Music Inc. 51					•				•	•
Boxcar Music 51	•					•	•		•	•
Boxer Music 51	•					•			•	•
Tommy Boyce & Melvin Powers Music Enterprises 51	•					•				
Briarpatch Music/Deb Dave Music Inc. 51	•					•			•	
Brim Music 52	•		•			•				
Broadman Press 52			•							
Bruboon Publishing 52			•		•	•	•			•
Brujo Music 52	•				•	•			•	•
Albert E. Brumley & Sons 52	•		•							
Bug Music 53					•					•
Bush/Lehrman Productions 53	•			•	•	•			•	•
Buttermilk Sky Associates 53			•		•	•		•	•	•
B-W Music 53	•		•				•			
Cabriolet Music 53	•			•	•					
Cactus Music Co. 54	•					•		•		•
Cafe Americana 54					•	•			•	•
Caligula, Inc. 54							•		•	•

Name of Company and Page Number	Bluegrass, C&W	Children's	Coral, Church/religious, Gospel	Classical	Blues, Disco, R&B, Soul	Easy listening, MOR	Folk	Jazz	Progressive, Rock	Top 40/Pop
The Cameron Organisation, Inc. 54					•				•	•
Cam-U.S.A., Inc. 54	•				•				•	•
Candlestick Publishing Co. 54					•				•	•
Can't Stop Music 55					•	•			•	•
Cantus Publishing Co. 55				•	•				•	•
Capaquarius Publishing & Artist Mgt., Inc. 55	•		•		•					
Captain Kidd Music 55	•					•	•		•	•
Carwin Publishing Co. 55	•		•							
Casablanca Publishing 55					•	•			•	•
Don Casale Music 56	•				•	•			•	•
Catch Fire Music Enterprises 56	•				•	•			•	•
Cedarwood Publishing Co., Inc. 56	•		•		•				•	•
Cetra Music 56	•	•			•	•	•	•		•
Chapie Music 56	•	•	•	•	•	•	•	•	•	•
Chappell Music (CA) 56	•				•	•			•	•
Chappell Music (NY) 57					•	•			•	•
Char-Belle Music 57	•		•		•				•	•
Chascot Music Publishing 57			•		•					
Chevoria Music Co. 57	•				•	•			•	•
Cherry Lane Music Co. 57						•	•			•
Chevis Publishing Corp. 58					•	•			•	•
Choral Press 58		•	•							
Chris Music Publishing 58	•		•		•	•				
Ciano Publishing 58					•	•			•	•
Clab Music 59	•									
Claridge Music Inc. 59					•				•	•
Clark Music Publishing 59	•		•		•	•			•	•
Cloud Burst Music Publishing 59	•					•				•
Coat of Arms Publishing 59	•					•				
Bruce Cohn Music 60	•				•	•			•	•
Coleman, Kestin & Smith, LTD. 60	•		•		•	•	•	•		•
Colgems/EMI Music Inc. 60					•				•	•
Column One Music 60	•					•			•	•

Name of Company and Page Number	Bluegrass, C&W	Children's	Coral, Church/religious, Gospel	Classical	Blues, Disco, R&B, Soul	Easy listening, MOR	Folk	Jazz	Progressive, Rock	Top 40/Pop
Commercial Studios Inc. 60		•			•	•		•	•	•
Compo Music Publishing 60	•		•			•				•
Con Brio Music 61	•					•				•
Jerry Connell Publishing 61	•		•		•	•	•		•	•
Core Music Publishing 61									•	•
Cotillion Music Inc 61					•				•	
Country Classics Music Publishing Co. 61	•		•			•				•
Country Song Factory 62	•	•	•		•	•	•			
Country Star Music 62	•		•						•	•
Crimson Dynasty 62	•				•					
Criterion Music Corp. 62					•	•			•	•
Critique Music Publishing Co. 62	•				•	•			•	•
Crooked Creek Music 63	•				•	•				•
Crow-Smith Productions 63	•				•				•	
Cuta Rug Music 63	•								•	
Cuzz Publishing Co., Inc. 63	•		•							
Danboro Publishing Co. 63	•					•			•	•
Davida Record & Publishing Co. (CA) 63	•				•	•		•		•
Davida Record & Publishing Co. (MI) 63			•							
Dawnbreaker Music Co. 64	•	•	•	•	•	•	•	•	•	•
Dawn of Creation Publishing Co. 64		•	•	•		•				•
Deep Note Music 64	•				•				•	•
Deer Creek Publishing 64	•		•				•			
Delightful Music, Ltd. 65					•	•			•	
Demand Music 65	•		•						•	•
Derby Music 65	•		•		•	•		•	•	•
Devaney Music Publishing 65	•		•			•				•
Diamond In The Rough Music 65					•					
Diamondback Music 65									•	
Dipro Music Publishing Co. 66		•							•	•
B. L. Dixon Publishing 66					•	•				
Doc Dick Enterprises 66					•					•
Dog River Music 66	•	•	•		•				•	•

Name of Company and Page Number	Bluegrass, C&W	Children's	Coral, Church/religious, Gospel	Classical	Blues, Disco, R&B, Soul	Easy listening, MOR	Folk	Jazz	Progressive, Rock	Top 40/Pop
Donna Music Publishing Co. 67	●		●		●	●			●	●
Dooms Music Publishing Co. 67	●		●			●				
Double Diamond Music 67					●	●		●	●	●
Dovetail Publishing Co. 67	●								●	
Dragon Fly Music 67					●				●	●
Duane Music, Inc. 68	●				●	●			●	●
E.L.J. Record Co. 68					●	●				●
E & M Publishing Co. 68	●		●		●	●			●	
Early Bird Music 68	●					●				●
Earthscream Music Publishing Co. 68					●				●	●
Eastex Music 69	●									●
Eat Your Heart Out Music 69									●	●
Eden Music Corp. 69	●				●				●	●
El Chicano Music 69	●				●	●		●	●	●
Elation Music 70			●		●	●		●	●	●
Elbejay Enterprises 70	●				●					●
Elvitrue Recording Music Publishing Co. 70		●	●		●	●				
Emandell Tunes 70			●			●				
English Mountain Publishing Co. 70	●		●		●	●	●			●
Envolve Music Group 71	●		●	●		●	●	●	●	
Epp's Music Co. 71	●	●	●		●	●			●	●
Eptember Enterprises 71					●	●		●		●
Erection Publishing Co. 71	●		●		●	●			●	●
Fame Publishing Co., Inc. 71					●					●
Famous Music Publishing Companies (CA) 72					●	●			●	●
Farout Music 72					●				●	●
Farr Music, Inc. 72	●				●	●				●
Fast Fingers Music 72					●				●	
Favor Music 72	●		●		●	●		●	●	●
Fender Bender Music 73	●				●	●			●	●
Firmus Publishing 73					●	●				●
First Artists Music Co. 73	●				●	●	●		●	●
Fist-O-Funk, Ltd. 73				●	●			●		●

Name of Company and Page Number	Bluegrass, C&W	Children's	Choral, Church/religious, Gospel	Classical	Blues, Disco, R&B, Soul	Easy listening, MOR	Folk	Jazz	Progressive, Rock	Top 40/Pop
Frank Gubala Music 80					•	•				•
Gule Record 80	•		•		•				•	•
E. J. Gurren Music Group 80	•				•	•				•
Halwill Music 81					•	•	•	•	•	•
Happy Day Music Co. 81			•							
Harlem Music 81					•	•	•	•	•	•
Harrick Music, Inc. 81					•				•	•
The Harris Machine 81					•	•		•	•	•
Hartford Music Co. 81	•		•							
John Harvey Publishing Co. 82	•	•				•	•			
Hattress Music Publishing 82			•		•					•
Have A Heart Music 82	•					•			•	•
Heartstone Music Publishing Co. 82			•							
Heavy Jamin' Music 82	•		•		•	•	•	•	•	•
Heavy Music 83	•		•		•	•			•	•
Helping Hand Music 83	•					•			•	•
Hero Music Publishing 84					•				•	•
Hip Hill Music Publishing 84	•		•		•	•	•	•	•	•
The Hit Machine Music Co. 84					•	•			•	
Hitsburgh Music Co. 84	•					•				
Hornsby Music Co. 84			•		•					
Hot Gold Music Publishing Co. 85					•				•	•
House Of David 85	•		•		•	•			•	•
House Of Hi Ho 85	•		•		•	•		•	•	•
Ruben Hughes Music Co. 85	•		•		•					
Hustlers, Inc. 85	•								•	
Iquana Music, Inc. 86					•	•		•	•	•
Insanity's Music 86	•					•			•	•
Instant Replay Music Co. 86					•			•		
Intermede Musique 86						•			•	
Interplanetary Music 87					•					•
Interworld Music Group 87	•	•	•		•	•	•		•	•
Iron Blossom Music Group 87	•									

Name of Company and Page Number	Bluegrass, C&W	Children's	Coral, Church/religious, Gospel	Classical	Blues, Disco, R&B, Soul	Easy listening, MOR	Folk	Jazz	Progressive, Rock	Top 40/Pop
Ironside Publishing 87	•	•	•		•	•			•	•
Irving/Almo Music of Canada, Ltd. 87						•	•		•	•
Island Music, Inc. 87					•	•			•	•
Isonode Publishing 87	•		•			•			•	•
Dick James Music, Inc. 88	•				•	•			•	•
James S. Enterprises 88	•				•	•			•	•
Janell Music Publishing 88	•		•		•	•			•	•
Janvier Music, Inc. 88					•	•	•		•	•
Jason Dee Music 89	•				•	•				•
Jeld Music 89	•						•			•
Jibaro Music Co., Inc. 89					•	•		•		
JLT Christian Agape Music Co. 89			•							
Jo Cher Music Co. 89	•		•			•			•	•
Jobete Music Co., Inc. 90	•				•	•		•	•	•
Joli Music, Inc. 90	•				•	•		•	•	•
Jomewa Music 90						•	•			
Jon Music 90	•				•				•	
Jop Music Co. 90	•		•			•				
K-Tel Music, Ltd. 91	•	•	•		•	•	•		•	•
Kack Klick, Inc. 91						•			•	•
Bob Karcy Music 91					•	•			•	•
Karla Music Co. 91					•	•		•	•	•
Katch Nazar Music 91	•				•			•	•	
Joe Keene Music Co. 92	•					•			•	
Gene Kennedy Enterprises, Inc. 92	•		•			•				•
Kentucky Colonel Music 92	•						•			
Kicking Mule Publishing, Inc. 92	•				•		•			
King of Music Publishing 92		•			•				•	•
Kinghouse Music Publications 93	•						•			
Don Kirshner Music 93	•	•	•	•	•	•	•	•	•	•
Jimmy Kish Music Publishing 93	•		•							
Kiss Me Music 93	•				•	•			•	•
Kleanza Music 93	•					•				

Name of Company and Page Number	Bluegrass, C&W	Children's	Coral, Church/religious, Gospel	Classical	Blues, Disco, R&B, Soul	Easy listening, MOR	Folk	Jazz	Progressive, Rock	Top 40/Pop
Lackey Publishing Co. 94	•		•		•	•	•		•	•
Ladd Music Co. 94	•	•			•	•			•	•
Lambert & Potter Music Co. 94					•	•			•	•
Landers Roberts Music 94	•				•	•		•	•	•
Christy Lane Music 94	•					•			•	•
Lapelle Music Publishing 95	•		•							
Larball Publishing 96	•				•	•			•	•
Lardon Music 96		•								
Late Music 96		•			•		•	•	•	•
Don Lee Music 96	•		•			•	•			•
Rob Lee Music 97	•				•	•		•	•	•
Paul Leka Music 97	•					•			•	•
Lemhi Music Publishing 97	•					•				
Lillenas Publishing Co. 97			•							
Sonny Limbo International 97	•				•	•			•	•
Lincoln Road Music Co. 97	•				•	•			•	•
Linesider Productions 97									•	
Little Debbie Music 98					•		•		•	•
Little Fugitive Music 98	•				•					•
Little Gem Music, Inc. 98	•		•			•				
Little Joe Music Co. 98	•		•				•			
Little Otis Music 98					•	•		•	•	•
Live-Wire Music Publishers 99	•					•	•			
Lochwood Publishing Co. 99	•				•					
Lone Grove Music, Inc. 99	•	•			•	•			•	•
Lone Lake Songs, Inc. 99	•				•	•	•		•	•
Lorijoy Music, Inc. 99					•					
Love Street Publishing 99									•	•
Lowery Music Co., Inc. 100	•				•	•			•	•
Lucky Man Music 100	•						•			
Lucky Penny Music 100	•					•				•
Lucky Star Music 100					•					
Lufaye Publishing Co. 100	•									

Name of Company and Page Number	Bluegrass, C&W	Children's	Coral, Church/religious, Gospel	Classical	Blues, Disco, R&B, Soul	Easy listening, MOR	Folk	Jazz	Progressive, Rock	Top 40/Pop
Monster Music 107	•					•			•	•
Moo Moo Music 107	•		•	•	•	•	•	•	•	•
Moon June Music 107	•				•	•			•	•
Moorpark Music 107	•		•	•	•	•	•	•	•	•
Morning Music, Ltd. 107	•	•	•	•	•	•	•	•	•	•
Morning Music (USA), Inc. 108	•	•	•	•	•	•	•	•	•	•
Morris Music, Inc. 108					•	•			•	•
Musedco 108	•	•			•	•	•			•
Music Craftshop 108	•					•				
Music Designers 108	•	•			•	•	•		•	•
Music For Percussion, Inc. 109				•					•	
Musicways, Inc. 109	•				•	•			•	•
Muzacan Publishing Co. 109									•	•
My Son's Publishing 109			•		•					
Natural Groove Music 110	•		•		•			•	•	•
Nautical Music Co. 110	•				•	•			•	
Joseph Nicoletti Music 110					•	•			•	•
Nilkam Music/Kimsha Music 110					•	•			•	•
Nise Productions, Inc. 110		•	•		•		•			
Nu-Gen Publishing Co. 111	•			•		•		•		•
Nyamm Neowd Music Inc. 111			•		•	•		•	•	•
O.A.S. Music Group 111	•				•	•				•
Oak Springs Music 111	•				•	•	•		•	
Oakridge Music Recording Service 111	•		•		•					
Oceans Blue Music, Ltd. 112					•	•				•
Mary Frances Odle Recording & Publishing Co. 112	•		•		•	•			•	
Old Sparta Music 112					•	•			•	•
Omnibus 112					•	•			•	•
One For The Road Music Co. 112	•				•	•			•	•
Orchid Publishing 113	•		•							•
OSV Music Publishing 113			•							
Other Music 114	•	•		•	•		•	•	•	•
Ray Overholt Music 114			•							

Name of Company and Page Number	Bluegrass, C&W	Children's	Coral, Church/religious, Gospel	Classical	Blues, Disco, R&B, Soul	Easy listening, MOR	Folk	Jazz	Progressive, Rock	Top 40/Pop
Lee Maces Ozark Opry Music Publishing 114	●		●		●					
P.F.S. Music Co. 114	●	●	●		●	●	●		●	●
Package Good Music 114					●	●			●	●
Palamar Music Publishers 115	●		●			●				
Panther Music 115	●				●			●	●	●
Don Park Music, Inc. 115	●	●	●		●		●	●	●	
Pasa Alta Music 115			●		●	●	●	●	●	●
Paydirt Music 116	●		●							●
Peak Publishing Co. 116	●	●	●	●	●	●	●	●	●	●
Peer-Southern Organization (CA) 116	●				●	●			●	●
Peer-Southern Organization (TN) 116	●								●	●
Peer-Southern Organization (Canada) 116	●	●	●	●	●	●	●	●	●	●
Pellegrino Music Co., Inc. 116			●							
Peregrin Songs 117	●				●		●		●	
Perryal Music Co. 117			●	●	●	●		●	●	●
Pet-Mac Publishing 117	●				●	●		●	●	●
Philippopolis Music 117				●				●		
Pi Gem Music, Inc./Chess Music, Inc. 117	●				●	●			●	●
Pick-A-Hit Music 117	●									
Pinato Music 118	●				●	●		●	●	●
Pinellas Music 118									●	●
Positive Production 118						●			●	
Power-Play Publishing 118	●		●		●	●	●		●	●
Johnny Powers Music Productions, Inc. 119	●				●	●			●	●
Jimmy Price Music 119	●		●							
Ray Price Music 119	●		●			●	●		●	
Pringle Music 119	●									
Pritchett Publications 119			●		●	●				●
Prophecy Publishing, Inc. 120	●		●	●	●	●	●	●	●	●
Publicare Music, Ltd. 120	●				●	●			●	●
Purple Haze Music 120	●				●	●			●	●
QCA Music, Inc. 120			●		●			●	●	
Quality Music Publishing 121	●		●		●	●			●	●

Name of Company and Page Number	Bluegrass, C&W	Children's	Coral, Church/religious, Gospel	Classical	Blues, Disco, R&B, Soul	Easy listening, MOR	Folk	Jazz	Progressive, Rock	Top 40/Pop
Rae-Cox & Cooke Music Corp. 121			•		•				•	
H & G Randall Publishing Co. 121						•			•	•
Jim Ranne Music Co. 121	•		•		•				•	
Ray's 122					•	•				
RCS Publishing Co. 122	•				•				•	•
Ren Maur Music Corp. 122					•	•			•	•
William Rezey Music Co. 122					•				•	•
Rhythm Valley Music 123	•		•							
Rhythms Productions 123		•								
Rick's Music, Inc. 123					•	•			•	•
Charlie Roach Music 123	•		•		•				•	
Roadshow Music Group 123			•		•					•
Freddie Roberts Music 123	•		•		•	•	•		•	•
Rocket Publishing 124					•				•	
Rockford Music Co. 124					•					•
Rocky Bell Music 124	•									
Rogan Publishing Co. 124	•				•					•
Rohm Music 124									•	•
Rotiga Music Co. 125					•	•		•	•	•
Rowilco 125	•				•	•			•	•
Royal Flair Publishing 125	•									
Royal Star Publishing Co. 125	•		•		•				•	•
RSO Music Publishing Group (CA) 125					•	•	•		•	•
RSO Music Publishing Group (NY) 125					•	•	•		•	•
Run H Music, Inc. 125								•	•	
Rustic Records 126	•					•				
Rustron Music Publishers 126	•				•	•	•		•	•
S.M.C.L. Productions, Inc. 126					•	•				•
Saka Music Co. 126	•	•	•	•	•	•	•	•	•	•
Salt Lake Publishing 126	•	•	•							
Saul Avenue Publishing Co. 127	•		•		•		•			
Sawgrass Music Publishing, Inc. 127	•					•				
Scone Music 127			•			•		•		

Name of Company and Page Number	Bluegrass, C&W	Children's	Choral, Church/religious, Gospel	Classical	Blues, Disco, R&B, Soul	Easy listening, MOR	Folk	Jazz	Progressive, Rock	Top 40/Pop
Screen Gems/EMI Music, Inc. (CA) 128	●	●	●		●	●	●	●	●	●
Screen Gems/EMI Music, Inc. (NY) 128	●	●	●	●	●	●	●	●	●	●
Scully Music Co. 128					●				●	●
Robin Sean Music Publishing 128	●				●	●			●	●
Sellers Music, Inc. 128					●					●
Sesame Street Music 129		●								
Seventh Note Music 129	●				●	●				●
Seyah Music 129	●		●		●					●
Shada Music, Inc. 129						●			●	●
Shawnee Press, Inc. 130		●	●	●		●	●			
Shelton Associates 130					●	●			●	●
Sherlyn Publishing Co. 130	●				●				●	●
Short Pump Publishing 130					●			●	●	●
Show Biz Music Group 131	●		●		●	●	●			●
Silhouette Music 131			●							
Silicon Music Publishing 131	●					●			●	
Silver Blue Music, Ltd. 131					●	●			●	●
Silverline Music, Inc. 131	●									●
Sing Me Music, Inc. 131	●		●		●	●	●			●
Singing River Publishing Co. 132	●				●	●	●			●
Shelby Singleton Music Inc. 132	●		●		●	●	●	●	●	●
Sivatt Music Publishing Co. 132	●		●			●	●			
Six Strings Music 132					●	●			●	●
Mack Smith Music 132	●								●	●
Earle Smith Music 133	●				●	●				●
Snapfinger Music 133	●		●		●	●			●	●
Snoopy Music 133	●				●	●			●	●
Snowberry Music 133	●				●	●			●	●
Solar Wind Music 133				●	●	●	●	●	●	●
Song Tailors Music Co. 134	●				●	●	●	●	●	●
Songs of Calvary 134			●							
Sound of America Publishing Co. 134	●		●		●	●	●	●	●	●
Sound of Nolan Music 134					●	●			●	●

Name of Company and Page Number	Bluegrass, C&W	Children's	Coral, Church/religious, Gospel	Classical	Blues, Disco, R&B, Soul	Easy listening, MOR	Folk	Jazz	Progressive, Rock	Top 40/Pop
Southern Writers Group USA 134	•				•	•	•		•	•
Larry Spier, Inc. 135	•				•	•	•	•	•	•
Terry Stafford Music 135	•									•
Stafree Publishing Co. 135					•					•
Startime Music 136	•								•	
Starfox Publishing 136	•				•	•			•	•
Stateside Music 136					•					
Steady Arm Music 136	•				•	•	•		•	•
Steel River Music 137	•		•			•				
Stone Diamond Music Corp. 137					•	•		•	•	•
Stone Post Music 137									•	
Stone Row Music 137				•				•	•	•
Jeb Stuart Music Co. 137	•		•		•			•	•	•
Stuckey Publishing 137	•									
Sudden Rush Music 137					•	•			•	•
Sufi Pipkin Music 138	•				•	•			•	•
Sugar Bear Music 138					•					•
Sugar n' Soul Music, Inc. 138	•				•	•	•		•	•
Sulzer Music 138	•					•	•			•
Su-Ma Publishing Co., Inc. 138	•	•			•					
Suncountry Song Co. 138	•				•				•	•
Sundaze Music 138	•				•	•			•	•
Sunshine Country 139	•	•								
Sure-Fire Music Co., Inc 139	•					•	•			
Sweet Polly Music 139	•					•			•	•
Sunny Lane Music, Inc. 139	•	•				•				•
Sweet Swamp Music 140	•				•	•	•		•	•
T. P. Music Publishing 140					•	•				•
Tal Music 140	•	•			•	•		•	•	•
Tall Corn Publishing Co. 140	•	•				•		•	•	•
Telespin Music, Inc. 141						•				
Teoc Music 141	•				•		•	•		
Terrace Music Group 141	•									•

Name of Company and Page Number	Bluegrass, C&W	Children's	Coral, Church/religious, Gospel	Classical	Blues, Disco, R&B, Soul	Easy listening, MOR	Folk	Jazz	Progressive, Rock	Top 40/Pop
Tessies Tunes 141	•					•				
Textor Music 141			•							
Think Big Music 141					•	•			•	•
Third Story Music, Inc. 141					•				•	•
Three Kings Music 142	•		•			•				
3300 Publishing 142	•	•	•		•	•	•	•	•	•
Tidewater Music 142	•		•			•				
Timeless Entertainment 142					•			•	•	•
Tom Thumb Publishing Co. 142	•	•							•	
Tompaul Music 143	•		•			•	•		•	•
Top Drawer Music 143	•					•				•
Topsail Music 143	•	•			•	•	•		•	•
Tradition Music Co. 143							•			
Traitors Music 143	•								•	
Transatlantic Music 144	•				•	•			•	•
Tree Publishing Co., Inc. 144	•				•	•			•	•
Triple H Music 144	•					•			•	•
Triune Music, Inc. 145		•	•	•						
Trucker Man Music 145			•		•					•
True Music, Inc. 145	•		•		•	•	•		•	•
Trusty Publications 145	•		•		•	•	•			•
Tuff Enuff Music Publishing 145	•				•				•	•
Tumac Music & Shandy Gaff Music 145	•				•	•			•	•
TWC Music 146	•		•				•			
20th Century Fox Music Publishing 146	•				•	•			•	•
Twin Lions Music Publishing 146	•	•	•							
Tyrenic Music Co 147		•	•	•	•	•		•		•
Uncle Jack Music Co. 147	•		•		•	•				•
Under Mt. Publishing 147	•		•							
United Artists Music Publishing Group, Inc. 147	•				•	•	•	•	•	•
United Artists Music Publishing 147					•	•			•	•
Ursula Music 148	•				•	•	•		•	•
Utopia Music, Inc. 148	•		•						•	

Name of Company and Page Number	Bluegrass, C&W	Children's	Coral, Church/religious, Gospel	Classical	Blues, Disco, R&B, Soul	Easy listening, MOR	Folk	Jazz	Progressive, Rock	Top 40/Pop
Valgroup Music (USA) Co. 148						●			●	●
Valleybrook Music 148	●					●	●		●	●
Vector Music 148	●					●			●	
Vicksburg Music 149			●		●				●	●
Vokes Music Publishing 150	●		●							
Warner Bros., Inc. 150	●				●	●		●	●	●
Waste Away Music 150	●				●	●	●	●	●	●
Wasu Music 150						●			●	
Weatherly Music 150	●				●			●	●	●
Welbeck 151	●		●		●	●	●		●	●
Bobe Wes Music 151	●		●		●				●	●
Wesjac Music 151			●							
Western Head Music 151	●				●			●	●	
Wheezer Music 151	●					●			●	●
White Way Music Co. 151	●		●		●	●	●		●	●
Wild Music 151	●		●		●	●	●		●	●
Wilhos Music Publishing 152					●					●
Window Music Publishing Co., Inc. 152	●		●			●			●	●
Woodrich Publishing 153	●	●	●		●	●	●	●	●	●
Word Music 153		●	●							
Yatahey Music 153	●		●							
Ybarra Music 153						●		●		
Yo Yo Music 153	●					●			●	●
Youngwood Music Publishing 154	●					●			●	●

Record Companies

Name of Company and Page Number	Bluegrass, C&W	Children's	Coral, Church/religious, Gospel	Classical	Blues, Disco, R&B, Soul	Easy listening, MOR	Folk	Jazz	Progressive, Rock	Top 40/Pop
A & M Records, Inc. 158	•				•	•	•	•	•	•
A & M Records 158					•			•	•	•
Alarm Records 158	•				•					•
Alear Records 159	•		•				•		•	
Alegre Records, Inc. 159					•			•		
Almanac Records 159					•					
Alva Records 159	•				•	•				•
Amelgamated Tulip Corp. 159									•	•
Amalgamated Communications Industries 159	•					•			•	•
American Music Corp. 160	•						•			
American Recording Co. 160	•	•	•	•	•	•	•	•	•	•
Amherst Records 160					•	•	•	•	•	•
Amiron Music/Aztec Productions 160	•		•		•	•	•		•	•
Ansap Records, Inc. 160					•				•	•
Chuck Anthony Music, Inc. 161					•					•
Antique-Catfish Records		•	•		•	•	•		•	
Aquila Records 161		•			•	•				•
Arby Records 161	•		•		•	•	•		•	
Argus Record Productions 161		•	•		•				•	•
Ariola Records 161					•	•			•	•
Arista Records Inc. (CA) 161					•	•	•	•	•	•
Arista Records, Inc. (NY) 162	•				•	•		•	•	•
Artemis Records, Ltd. 162				•	•	•	•	•	•	•
Arzee Music Co. 162	•				•		•		•	
Associated Recording Companies 162					•	•				•
Atlantic Recording Corp. 162	•				•	•	•	•	•	•
Axent Records 162	•		•				•			•
Axent & Doug Mays Productions 163	•		•		•				•	•
Len Bailey Productions 163					•	•		•		•
Bal Records 163	•	•	•		•				•	•
Beau-Jim Records, Inc. 163	•				•	•			•	•
Beaverwood Recording Studio		•	•	•	•	•	•	•	•	•

Name of Company and Page Number	Bluegrass, C&W	Children's	Coral, Church/religious, Gospel	Classical	Blues, Disco, R&B, Soul	Easy listening, MOR	Folk	Jazz	Progressive, Rock	Top 40/Pop
Big Mike Music 164					●					
Big Sound Records, Inc. 164						●			●	●
Black Bear Records 164			●			●			●	●
Blackland Music Co. 164			●			●			●	●
Eubie Blake Music 164					●			●		
Blue Ash Records 165	●				●	●		●	●	●
Bolnik Music 165	●				●	●			●	●
Boot Records, Ltd. 165	●			●	●	●	●		●	●
Bouquet Records 165	●		●							●
Boyce & Powers Music 165	●					●				
Boyd Records 165	●				●				●	
Buckskin Records 166							●		●	●
Buddah Records 166					●			●	●	●
Capitol Records Inc. 166	●			●	●	●		●	●	●
Casablanca Record & Film Works 166					●	●				●
Castle Records 166	●				●	●		●	●	●
CBS Records 167	●				●	●		●	●	●
Celestial Records Releasing Corp. 167	●		●		●	●		●		
Chapman Records 167	●		●	●	●	●	●		●	●
Charade Records 167	●				●			●	●	●
Charta Records 167	●				●	●				●
Christy Records 168	●		●			●				
Chrysalis Records 168					●	●		●	●	●
Cin/Kay Record Co. 168	●		●							
Clark's Country Records 168	●		●						●	
Clay Pigeon Records 168						●			●	●
Cloud Burst Records 168	●					●				●
Club of Spade Records 169	●						●			
Coat of Arms 169	●					●				●
Commercial Record Corp. 169	●			●		●				●
Compo Record and Publishing Co. 170	●		●			●				●
Comstock Records	●									
Con Brio Records 170	●					●				●

Name of Company and Page Number	Bluegrass, C&W	Children's	Coral, Church/religious, Gospel	Classical	Blues, Disco, R&B, Soul	Easy listening, MOR	Folk	Jazz	Progressive, Rock	Top 40/Pop
Cord Records 170	•		•		•					
Counterpart Creative Studios 170	•	•	•	•	•	•	•	•	•	•
Country Artists Records 171	•				•	•			•	•
Country Kitchen Records	•					•	•		•	•
Country Road 171	•		•						•	
Country Showcase Records and Publishers 171	•									•
Country Star, Inc. 171	•		•			•			•	•
Creative Sound, Inc. 172			•							
Crescendo Record Co. 172						•				
Curtiss Records 172	•		•		•		•	•	•	•
Curtom Records 172					•	•			•	•
Dance-A-Thon Records	•				•	•			•	•
Dawn of Creation Records		•	•	•		•				•
Dawn Productions 172	•				•	•	•		•	•
Deddy Records 173	•									
Delta Sound Records 173	•								•	•
Derbytown Records 173	•		•							
Direction Records, Inc. 173	•				•	•	•		•	•
Dominion Bluegrass Recordings 173	•									
Domino Records 174					•	•				
Domino Records, Ltd. 174	•				•				•	•
Dynamic Artists Records 174					•				•	•
E.L.J. Record Co. 174					•	•				•
Earwax Records 174	•								•	
Educator Records, Inc. 174		•			•					
El Chicano Music 175	•				•	•		•	•	•
Elektra/Asylum/Nonesuch Records 175				•	•	•			•	•
Ember Records, Inc. 175					•					•
EMI-America/United Artists 175	•				•	•	•	•	•	•
Endangered Species Records 175									•	
Fanfare Records 175									•	•
Farr Records 176	•				•	•				•
Fire Lite Record Co. 176	•					•	•			

Name of Company and Page Number	Bluegrass, C&W	Children's	Coral, Church/religious, Gospel	Classical	Blues, Disco, R&B, Soul	Easy listening, MOR	Folk	Jazz	Progressive, Rock	Top 40/Pop
First American Records					●	●	●	●	●	●
Fist-O-Funk, Ltd. 176				●	●					●
Fleurette Records 176	●				●	●				●
Franne Records 177	●		●		●	●		●	●	●
Free Flight Records 177					●	●		●	●	●
Freeway Records, Inc. 177									●	●
Fretone Records, Inc. 177					●					●
Friendship Store Music Records 178						●	●			●
Full Sail Records 178	●	●			●				●	●
G.R.T. Record Group 178	●		●		●	●			●	●
Galaball 178					●	●		●	●	●
Garlin Sound Productions 178	●					●		●		
Ghost Records 178					●	●			●	●
Global Record Co. 179	●		●			●				
Gold Mind Records 179					●	●			●	●
Goldmount Music, Inc. 179	●	●	●		●	●	●	●	●	●
Goldust Record Co. 179	●					●			●	●
Gospel Records 180			●							
Great Southern Record Co., Inc. 180	●				●	●		●		●
Grouse Music 180	●					●	●		●	
Guld Record 180	●		●	●					●	●
Gusto Records 180	●		●	●	●	●	●		●	●
H&L Records Corp. 180					●			●	●	●
Hank's Music Enterprises, Inc. 180	●					●			●	
Happy Day Records, Inc. 181					●	●		●	●	●
Harlequin Records 181						●		●		
Heart Records 181	●					●			●	●
Heavy Sound Productions 181					●	●			●	●
The Herald Association, Inc. 181			●							
Hickory Records 181	●									
Hillside Records 182	●					●			●	●
Holly Records 182	●		●		●		●			●
Horizon Records 182					●	●		●	●	●

Name of Company and Page Number	Bluegrass, C&W	Children's	Coral, Church/religious, Gospel	Classical	Blues, Disco, R&B, Soul	Easy listening, MOR	Folk	Jazz	Progressive, Rock	Top 40/Pop
Little David Records, Inc. 188					•	•	•		•	•
Little Gem Music Inc. 188	•					•				
Littletown Records 188	•				•	•			•	•
London Records 188						•				
Long Neck Records 188	•	•	•		•	•			•	•
Love/Peace/Service Records, Inc. 188						•				•
Loy Priquan, Ltd. 188						•				•
Lucifer Records, Inc. 189					•	•			•	
Lucky Man Music 189	•					•	•			
Luna Records Co. 189		•								
M.R.C. Records 189	•		•		•	•			•	•
McKinnon Pictures/Records Co. 189	•		•		•	•		•	•	•
Mainline Records 189				•						
Majega Records 190	•	•	•			•			•	•
Maranta Music Enterprises 190					•			•	•	
Marina Records 190				•						•
Marmik 190	•	•	•		•	•				
Mazingo's, Inc. 191	•	•	•	•	•	•		•	•	•
MCA Records, Inc. 191	•				•	•		•		•
MDK Communications Ltd. 192					•	•			•	•
Mellow Man Records 192					•	•		•	•	•
Merritt & Norman Music	•				•		•	•		
Michal Recording Enterprises 192				•						
Mighty Records 192			•	•						
Mir-A-Don Records 192			•	•						
Mirror Records 193						•			•	
Mitchell Recording & Music Publishing Co., Inc. 193			•		•	•			•	•
Modern Sound Productions 193	•		•		•	•	•		•	
Molly Records 193					•	•		•	•	•
Mother Bertha Music, Inc. 193	•	•	•	•	•	•	•		•	•
Mother Cleo Productions 194	•				•	•			•	•
Motown Records Corp. 194					•			•	•	•
MSI Recording Studios 194					•	•			•	•

Name of Company and Page Number	Bluegrass, C&W	Children's	Coral, Church/religious, Gospel	Classical	Blues, Disco, R&B, Soul	Easy listening, MOR	Folk	Jazz	Progressive, Rock	Top 40/Pop
Mushroom Records 194					•			•	•	•
Music Adventures Records, Inc. 195					•	•			•	•
Music Resources International Corp. 195					•				•	•
Mystic Recording Studios 195	•		•		•	•				•
Nashville International Music Corp. 195	•		•			•			•	•
Natural Groove Records, Inc. 195	•	•	•	•	•	•	•	•	•	•
New World Records 196					•					•
Nic-Lyn Music Co. 196					•				•	•
N-M-I Production Corp. 196			•		•	•		•		•
The North Country Faire Record Co. 196					•	•				•
NRS Records and Tapes, Inc. 196	•		•		•	•			•	•
Oakridge Music Recording Service 196	•		•							
Odle Records 197	•	•	•		•	•	•		•	
Old Hat Records 197	•	•	•				•		•	•
Omnisound, Inc. 197		•	•	•			•			•
Opal Records 197	•	•	•						•	
Orbit Records 197	•				•				•	
Ovation Records 198	•									•
Lee Mace's Ozark Opry Records, Inc. 198	•		•		•					
Parasound, Inc. 198						•			•	•
Don Park Music, Inc. 198	•	•			•		•	•		
Passport Records, Inc. 198							•	•	•	•
Frank Paul Enterprises 199	•	•	•	•	•	•	•		•	•
Pedigree Records 199	•				•	•			•	•
Peer-Southern Organization 199	•				•	•			•	•
Pellegrino Music Co., Inc. 199			•							
Perryal Productions, Inc. 199			•	•	•	•			•	•
Pharoah Records 200	•				•				•	
Phonogram, Inc. 200					•	•		•	•	•
Phonogram/Mercury Records, Inc. 200	•				•	•		•	•	•
Phonogram/Mercury Records 200					•	•		•	•	•
Plantation Records 200	•				•	•	•	•	•	•
Pleiades Music 200	•	•		•	•			•	•	•

Name of Company and Page Number	Bluegrass, C&W	Children's	Coral, Church/religious, Gospel	Classical	Blues, Disco, R&B, Soul	Easy listening, MOR	Folk	Jazz	Progressive, Rock	Top 40/Pop
Polydor Records Inc. 201					•	•	•	•	•	•
Polydor Records 201					•	•	•	•	•	•
Portrait Records 201					•	•	•		•	•
Praise Records 201	•	•	•				•			
Prelude Records 201					•					
Private Stock Records, Ltd. 201					•	•			•	•
QCA Records, Inc. 201	•		•		•			•		
Rae-Cox & Cooke Music Corp. 202			•		•			•		•
Ram Records 202	•		•		•	•	•	•	•	•
Randall Records 202						•				•
Ray's Sounds 203					•	•				
RCA Records (CA) 203				•	•			•	•	•
RCA Records (TN) 203	•									•
RCI Records/Sound Studios, Inc. 203	•		•		•	•	•	•		
Red Ball Record Co. 203	•		•		•					
Redeemer Record Co. 204			•							
Ren-Maur Music Corp. 204					•	•		•	•	•
Request Records 204	•	•	•	•	•	•	•	•	•	•
Revonah Records 204			•				•			
Richtown/Gospel Truth Records 205	•	•	•	•	•	•	•	•	•	•
Robbins Records 205	•		•			•	•			•
Rota Records 205					•	•			•	•
Roulette Records Inc. 205	•		•		•	•	•	•	•	•
Royal T Music 205	•	•	•			•	•		•	•
Royalty Records of Canada, Ltd. 206	•					•			•	•
RSO Records, Inc. 206		•			•	•	•	•	•	•
Sagittar Records 206	•					•				
St. Lou-E Blu Records 206					•	•				•
Sandcastle Records 206	•					•	•	•	•	•
San-Sue Recording Studio 206	•		•			•				
Savoy Records 207			•							
Scott Records 207			•			•		•		
Seidel-Lehman Productions 207	•								•	•

Name of Company and Page Number	Bluegrass, C&W	Children's	Coral, Church/religious, Gospel	Classical	Blues, Disco, R&B, Soul	Easy listening, MOR	Folk	Jazz	Progressive Rock	Top 40/Pop
Talisman Records, Inc. Canada 213					•	•	•		•	•
Talisman Records, Inc. Canada 213					•	•	•		•	•
Tappan Zee Records 213				•	•			•	•	
Telemark Dance Records 214					•	•				
Tell International Record Co. 214	•				•	•	•	•	•	
Terock Records 214	•				•	•	•	•	•	•
Thanks Records 214	•				•	•				•
TK Records 214	•				•				•	•
Tortoise International Records 214					•	•			•	•
Trafic Records 215					•	•	•		•	•
Art Treff Publishing Co. 215		•		•	•		•	•	•	•
Trend Records 215	•		•		•	•			•	
Triangle Records, Inc. 215		•	•	•						
Trucker Man Records 215			•		•					•
Trusty Records 215	•		•		•	•	•			•
Tumac Music 216	•				•	•				•
Tyre Records 216		•	•	•	•	•		•		•
Umbrella Productions Ltd. 216					•				•	•
Velvet Productions 216			•		•				•	•
Video Record Albums of America 216	•		•		•	•				•
Vokes Music Publishing & Record Co. 216	•		•							
W.A.M. Music Corp. Ltd. 217					•	•			•	•
Waltner Enterprises 217	•					•				•
Warner Bros. Records, Inc. 217	•	•	•		•	•	•	•	•	•
Wave Records 217	•					•			•	•
Waylon Records 217	•					•			•	•
Wesjac Record Enterprises 217			•							
Westwood Records 218	•		•		•				•	
Wheelsville Records, Inc. 218			•		•					•
White Eagle Publishing 218	•								•	•
White Rock Records, Inc. 218	•	•			•	•			•	•
Wildfire Records 218	•				•	•			•	•
Wildwood Entertainment 218		•			•		•	•	•	•

Index

N

Z